GLORY SEASON

GLORY SEASON

David Brin

BANTAM BOOKS
NEW YORK • TORONTO • LONDON • SYDNEY • AUCKLAND

ISBN 0-553-07645-0

Published simultaneously in the United States and Canada

Bantam Books are published by Bantam Books, a division of Bantam
Doubleday Dell Publishing Group, Inc. Its trademark, consisting of the
words "Bantam Books" and the portrayal of a rooster, is Registered in
U.S. Patent and Trademark Office and in other countries. Marca
Registrada. Bantam Books, 1540 Broadway, New York, New York
10036.

PRINTED IN THE UNITED STATES OF AMERICA

To Cheryl Ann
who rescued Maia from Flatland
and me from loneliness

We would have every path laid open to women. . . . Were this done . . . we would see crystallizations more pure and of more various beauty. We believe the divine energy would pervade nature to a degree unknown in the history of former ages, and that no discordant collision, but a ravishing harmony of the spheres, would ensue.

—Margaret Fuller

GLORY SEASON

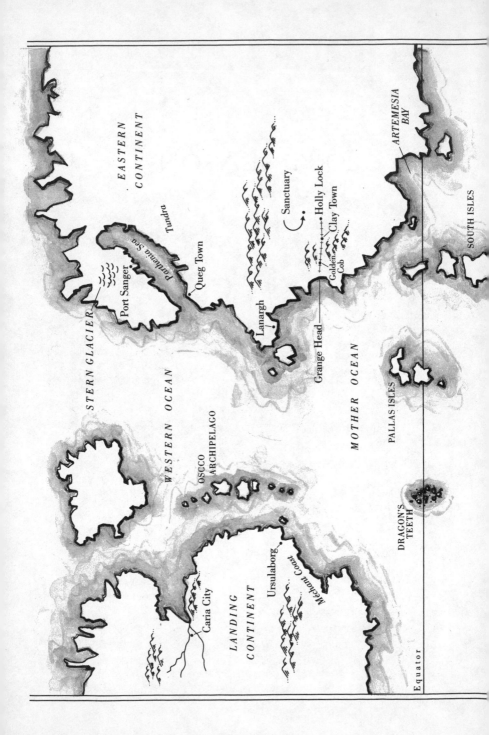

T wenty-six months before her second birthday, Maia learned the true difference between winter and summer.

It wasn't simply the weather, or the way hot-season lightning storms used to crackle amid tall ships anchored in the harbor. Nor even the eye-tingling stab of Wengel—so distinct from other stars.

The real difference was much more personal.

"I can't play with you no more," her half sister, Sylvina, taunted one day. " 'Cause you had a *father!*"

"Did n-not!" Maia stammered, rocked by the slur, knowing that the word was vaguely nasty. Sylvie's rebuff stung, as if a bitter glacier wind blew through the crèche.

"Did so! Had a father, dirty var!"

"Well . . . then you're a var, too!"

The other girl laughed harshly. "Ha! I'm pure Lamai, just like my sisters, mothers an' grandmas. But you're a *summer* kid. That makes you *U-neek*. Var!"

Dismayed, too choked to speak, Maia could only watch Sylvina toss her tawny locks and flounce away, joining a cluster of children varied in age but interchangeable in appearance. Some unspoken ritual of separation had taken place, dividing the room. In the better half, over near the glowing hearth, each girl was a miniature, perfect rendition of a Lamai mother. The same pale hair and strong jaw. The same trademark stance with chin defiantly upraised.

Here on this side, the two boys were being tutored in their corner as usual, unaware of any changes that would scarcely affect them, anyway. That left eight little girls like Maia, scattered near the icy panes. Some were light or dark, taller or thinner. One had freckles, another, curly hair. What they had in common were their differences.

Maia wondered, Was this what it meant to have a *father*? Everyone knew summer kids were rarer than winterlings, a fact that once made her proud, till it dawned on her that being "special" wasn't so lucky, after all.

She dimly recalled summertime's storms, the smell of static electricity and the drumbeat of heavy rain on Port Sanger's corbeled roofs. Whenever the clouds parted, shimmering sky-curtains used to dance like gauzy giants across distant tundra slopes, far beyond the locked city gates. Now, winter constellations replaced summer's gaudy show, glittering over a placid, frost-decked sea. Maia already knew these seasonal changes had to do with movements of Stratos round its sun. But she still hadn't figured out what that had to do with kids being born different, or the same.

Wait a minute!

Struck by a thought, Maia hurried to the cupboard where playthings were stacked. She grabbed a chipped hand mirror in both hands, and carried it to where another dark-haired girl her own age sat with several toy soldiers, arranging their swords and brushing their long hair. Maia held out the mirror, comparing her face to that of the other child.

"I look just like you!" she announced. Turning, she called to Sylvina. "I *can't* be a var! See? *Leie* looks like me!"

Triumph melted as the others laughed, not just the light-haired crowd, but all over the crèche. Maia frowned at Leie. "B-but you *are* like me. Look!"

Oblivious to chants of "Var! Var!" which made Maia's ears burn, Leie ignored the mirror and yanked Maia's arm, causing her to land hard nearby. Leie put one of the toy soldiers in Maia's lap, then leaned over and whispered. "Don't act so dumb! You an' me had the *same* father. We'll go on his boat, someday. We'll sail, an' see a whale, an' ride its tail. That's what summer kids do when *they* grow up."

With that surprising revelation, Leie returned contentedly to brushing a wooden warrior's flaxen hair.

Maia let the second doll lay in her open hand, the mirror in the other, pondering what she'd learned. Despite Leie's air of assurance, her story sounded easily as dumb as anything Maia herself had said. Yet, there was something appealing about the other girl's attitude . . . her way of making bad news sound good.

It seemed reason enough to become friends. Even better than the fact that they looked as alike as two stars in the sky.

Part One

Never understate the voyage we're embarked on, or what we knowingly forsake. Admit from the start, my sisters, that these partners cleaved to us by nature had their uses, their moments. Male strength and intensity have, on occasion, accomplished things both noble and fine.

Yet, even at best, wasn't that strength mostly spent defending us, and our children, against others of their kind? Are their better moments worth the cost?

Mother Nature works by a logic, a harsh code, that served when we were beasts, but no more. Now we grasp her tools, her art, down to its warp and weft. And with skill comes a call for change. Women—some women—are demanding a better way.

Thus we comrades sought this world, far beyond the hampering moderation of Hominid Phylum. It is the challenge of this founding generation to improve the blueprint of humanity.

—from the Landing Day Address, by Lysos

1

Sharply angled sunlight splashed across the table by Maia's bed, illuminating a meter-long braid of lustrous brown hair. Freshly cut. Draped across the rickety nightstand and tied off at both ends with blue ribbons.

Stellar-shell blue, color of departure. And next to the braid, a pair of gleaming scissors stood like a dancer balancing on toe, one point stabbed into the rough tabletop. Blinking past sleep muzziness, Maia stared at these objects—illumined by a trapezoid of slanting dawn light —struggling to separate them from fey emblems of her recent dream.

At once, their meaning struck.

"*Lysos*," Maia gasped, throwing off the covers. "Leie really did it!"

Sudden shivers drew a second realization. Her sister had also left the window open! Zephyrs off Stern Glacier blew the tiny room's dun curtains, driving dust balls across the plank floor to fetch against her bulging duffel. Rushing to slam the shutters, Maia glimpsed ruddy sunrise coloring the slate roofs of Port Sanger's castlelike clan houses. The breeze carried warbling gull cries and scents of distant icebergs, but appreciating mornings was one vice she had never shared with her earlyrising twin.

"Ugh." Maia put a hand to her head. "Was it really *my* idea to work last night?"

It had seemed logical at the time. "*We'll want the latest news before heading out,"* Maia had urged, signing them both for one last stint waiting tables in the clan guesthouse. *"We might overhear something useful, and an extra coin or two won't hurt."*

The men of the timber ship, Gallant Tern, had been full of gossip all right, and sweet Lamatian wine. But the sailors had no eye for two adolescent summerlings—two *variant* brats—when there were plump winter Lamais about, all attractively identical, well-dressed and well-mannered. Spoiling and flattering the officers, the young Lamais had snapped their fingers till past midnight, sending Maia and Leie to fetch more pitchers of heady ale.

The open window must have been Leie's way of getting even.

Oh, well, Maia thought defensively. *She's had her share of bad ideas, too.* What mattered was that they had a plan, the two of them, worked out year after patient year in this attic room. All their lives, they had known this day would come. *No telling how many dreary jobs we'll have to put our backs to, before we find our niche.*

Just as Maia was thinking about slipping back between the covers, the North Tower bell clanged, rattling this shabby corner of the sprawling Lamai compound. In higher-class precincts, winter folk would not stir for another hour, but summer kids got used to rising in bitter cold—such was the irony of their name. Maia sighed, and began slipping into her new traveling clothes. Black tights of stretchy web-cloth, a white blouse and halter, plus boots and a jacket of strong, oiled leather. The outfit was more than many clans provided their departing var-daughters, as the mothers diligently pointed out. Maia tried hard to feel fortunate.

While dressing, she pondered the severed braid. It was longer than an outstretched arm, glossy, yet lacking those rich highlights each full-blooded Lamai wore as a birthright. It looked so out of place, Maia felt a brief chill, as if she were regarding Leie's detached hand, or head. She caught herself making a hand-sign to avert ill luck, and laughed nervously at the bad habit. Country superstitions would betray her as a bumpkin in the big cities of Landing Continent.

Leie hadn't even laced her braid very well, given the occasion. At this moment, in other rooms nearby, Mirri, Kirstin, and the other summer fivers would be fixing their tresses for today's Parting Ceremony. The twins had argued over whether to attend, but now Leie had typically and impulsively acted on her own. *Leie probably thinks this gives her seniority as an adult, even though Granny Modine says I was first out of our birth-momma's womb.*

Fully dressed, Maia turned to encompass the attic room where they had grown up through five long Stratoin years—fifteen by the old calendar—summer children spinning dreams of winter glory, whispering a scheme so long forming, neither recalled who had thought it first. Now

. . . *today* . . . the ship Grim Bird would take them away toward far western lands where opportunities were said to lay just waiting for bright youths like them.

That was also the direction their father-ship had last been seen, some years ago. "It can't hurt to keep our eyes open," Leie had proposed, though Maia had wondered, skeptical, *If we ever did meet our gene-father, what would there be to talk about?*

Tepid water still flowed from the corner tap, which Maia took as a friendly omen. *Breakfast is included, too*, she thought while washing her face. *If I make it to kitchen before the winter smugs arrive.*

Facing the tiny table mirror—a piece of clan property she would miss terribly—Maia wove the over-and-between braid pattern of Lamatia Family, obstinately doing a neater job than Leie had. Top and bottom ends she tied off with blue ribbons, purchased out of her pocket. At one point, her own brown eyes looked back at her, faintly shaded by distinctly un-Lamai brows, gifts of her unknown male parent. Regarding those dark irises, Maia was taken aback to find what she wanted least to see—a moist glitter of fear. A constriction. Awareness of a wide world, awaiting her beyond this familiar bay. A world both enticing and yet notoriously pitiless to solitary young vars short on either wit or luck. Crossing her arms over her breast, Maia fought a quaver of protest.

How can I leave this room? How can they make me go?

Abrupt panic closed in like encasing ice, locking her limbs, her breath. Only Maia's racing heart seemed capable of movement, rocking her chest, accelerating helplessly . . . until she broke the spell with one serrated thought:

What if Leie comes back and finds me like this?

A fate worse than anything the mere *world* had to offer! Maia laughed tremulously, shattering the rigor, and lifted a hand to wipe her eyes. *Anyway, it's not like I'll be completely alone out there. Lysos help me, I'll always have Leie.*

At last she contemplated the gleaming scissors, embedded in the tabletop. Leie had left them as a challenge. Would Maia kneel meekly before the clan matriarchs, be given sonorous advice, a Kiss of Blessing, and a formal shearing? Or would she take leave boldly, without asking or accepting a hypocritical farewell?

What gave her pause, ironically, was a consideration of pure practicality.

With the braid off, there'll be no breakfast in the kitchen.

She had to use both hands, rocking the shears to win them free of the pitted wood. Maia turned the twin blades in a shaft of dawn light streaming through the shutters.

She laughed aloud and decided.

. . .

Even winter kids were seldom perfectly identical. Rare summer doubles like Maia and Leie could be told apart by a discerning eye. For one thing, they were *mirror* twins. Where Maia had a tiny mole on her right cheek, Leie's was on the left. Their hair parted on opposite sides, and while Maia was right-handed, her sibling claimed left-handedness was a sure sign of destined greatness. Still, the town priestess had scanned them. They had the same genes.

Early on, an idea had occurred to them—to try using this fact to their advantage.

There were limits to their scheme. They could hardly put it over on a savant, or among the lordly merchant houses of Landing Continent, where rich clans still used the data-wizardry of the Old Network. So Maia and Leie had decided to stay at sea awhile, with the sailors and drifter-folk, until they found some rustic town where local mothers were gullible, and male visitors more taciturn than the gossipy, bearded cretins who sailed the Parthenia Sea.

Lysos make it so. Maia tugged an earlobe for luck and resumed hauling her gear down the twisty back stairs of Lamatia's Summer Crèche, worn smooth by the passage of generations. At each slit window, a chill breeze stroked the newly bare nape of her neck, eliciting a creepy feeling that she was being followed. The duffel was heavy, and Maia nursed a dark suspicion that her sister might have slipped in something extra while her back was turned. If they had kept their braids for another hour, the mothers might have assigned a lugar to carry their effects to the docks. But Leie said it made you soft, counting on lugars, and on that she was probably right. There would be no docile giants to ease their work at sea.

The Summer Courtyard belied its name, permanently shadowed by the towers where winterlings dwelled behind banks of glass windows with silk curtains. The dim quad was deserted save a single bent figure, pushing a broom under dour, stone effigies of early Lamai clan mothers, all carved with uniform expressions of purse-lipped disdain. Maia paused to watch Coot Bennett sweep autumn demi-leaves, his gray beard waving in quiet tempo. Not legally a man, but a "retiree," Bennett had been taken in when his sailing guild could no longer care for him—a tradition long abandoned by other matriarchies, but proudly maintained by Lamatia.

On first taking residence, a touch of fire had remained in Bennett's eyes, his cracking voice. All physical virility was certifiably gone, but well-remembered, for he used to pinch bottoms now and then, rousing girlish shrieks of delighted outrage, and glaring reproval from the matrons. While formally a tutor for the handful of male children, he became a favorite of all summer kids for his thrilling, embroidered tales of the wild, open sea. That year, Bennett took a special shine to Maia, encouraging her interest in constellations, and the mannish art of navigation.

Not that they ever actually *talked*, the way two women might, about life and feelings and matters of substance. Still, Maia fondly recalled a strange friendship that even Leie never understood. Alas, too soon, the fire had left Bennett's old eyes. He stopped telling coherent stories, lapsing into gloomy silence while whittling ornate flutes he no longer bothered to play.

The old man stooped over his broom as Maia bent to catch his rheumy eye. Her impression, perhaps freighted with her own imaginings, was of an *active* void. Of anxious, studied evasion of the world. Did this happen naturally to males no longer able to work ships? Or had the Lamai mothers somehow done it to him, both erasing a nuisance and guaranteeing he really was "retired"? It made her curious about the fabled sanctuaries, which few women entered, where most men finally went to die.

Two seasons ago, Maia had tried drawing Bennett out of his decline, leading him by hand up narrow spiral steps to the small dome holding the clan's reflecting telescope. Sight of the gleaming instrument, where months earlier they had spent hours together scanning the heavens, seemed to give the old man pleasure. His gnarled hands caressed its brass flank with sensuous affection.

That was when she had shown him the Outsider Ship, then so new to the sky of Stratos. Everyone was talking about it, even on the tightly censored tele programs. Surely Bennett must have heard of the messenger, the "peripatetic," who had come so far across space to end the long separation between Stratos and the Human Phylum?

Apparently, he hadn't. Bewildered, Bennett seemed at first to think it one of the winking navigation satellites, which helped captains find their way at sea. Eventually, her explanation sank in—that the sharp glimmer was, in fact, a starship.

"Jelly can!" he had blurted suddenly. *"Bee-can Jelly can!"*

"Beacon? You mean a lighthouse?" She had pointed to the spire marking Port Sanger's harbor, its torch blazing across the bay. But the old man shook his head, distraught. *"Former!* . . . *Jelly can former!"* More phrases of slurred, nonsensical man-dialect followed. Clearly, something had happened that was yanking mental strings. Strings once linked to fervent thoughts, but long since fallen to loose threads. To Maia's horror, the coot began striking the side of his head, over and over, tears streaming down his ragged cheeks. *"Can't 'member* . . . *Can't!"* He moaned. *"Former* . . . *gone.* . . . *can't* . . ."

The fit had continued while, distraught, she maneuvered him downstairs to his little cot and then sat watching him thrash, muttering rhythmically about "guarding" something . . . and dragons in the sky. At the time, Maia could think of but one "dragon," a fierce figure carved over the altar in the city temple, which had frightened her when she was little, even though the matrons called it an *allegorical* beast, representing the mother spirit of the planet.

Since that episode on the roof, Maia had not tried communicating with Bennett again . . . and felt ashamed of it. "Is anyone there?" she now asked softly, peering into his haunted eyes. "Anyone at all?"

Nothing fathomable emerged, so she bent closer to kiss his scratchy cheek, wondering if the confused affection she now felt was as close as she would ever come to a relationship with a man. For most summer women, lifelong chastity was but one more emblem of a contest few could win.

Bennett resumed sweeping. Maia warmed her hands with steamy breath, and turned to go just as a ringing bell cracked the silence. Clamoring children spilled into the courtyard from narrow corridors on all sides. From toddlers to older threes and fours, they all wore bright Lamatia tartans, their hair woven in clan style. Yet, all such bids at tasteful uniformity failed. Unlike normal kids, each summer brat remained a blaring show of individuality, painfully aware of her uniqueness.

Except the boys, one in four, hurrying like their sisters to class, but with a swagger that said, *I know where I'm going.* Lamatia's sons often became officers, even shipmasters.

And eventually coots, Maia recalled as old Bennett blankly kept sweeping around the ruckus. Women and men had that much in common . . . everyone grew old. In her wisdom, Lysos had long ago decreed that life's rhythm must still include an end.

Running children stopped and goggled at Maia. She stared back, poker-faced. Dressed in leather, with her hair cropped, she must look like one of last night's revelers, gone astray from the tavern. Slim as she was, perhaps they took her for a man!

Suddenly several kids laughed out loud. Jemanine and Loiz threw their arms around her. And sweet little Albert, whom she used to tutor till he knew the constellations better than Port Sanger's twisty lanes. Others clustered, calling her name. Their embraces meant more to Maia than any benediction from the mothers . . . although next time she met any of them, out in the world, it might be as competitors.

The clanging resumed. A tall lugar with white fur and a droopy snout lurched into the courtyard waving a brass bell, clearly perturbed by this break in routine. The children ignored the neckless creature, peppering Maia with questions about her braid, her planned voyage, and why she'd chosen to snub the Parting Ceremony. Maia felt a kind of thrill, being what the mothers called a "bad example."

Then, into the courtyard flowed a figure smaller but more fearsome than the upset lugar—Savant Mother Claire, carrying a tang prod and glaring fiercely at these *worthless var brats who should be at their desks.* . . . The children took heel, with a few of the boldest daring to wave one last farewell to Maia before vanishing. The distressed lugar kept swinging the bell until the wincing matron put a stop to the clangor with a sharply driven elbow.

Mother Claire turned and gave Maia a calculating regard. Even in old age, she embodied the Lamai type. Furrow-browed and tight-lipped, yet severely beautiful, she had always, as far back as Maia remembered, cast a gaze of withering disdain. But this time, instead of the expected outrage at Maia's shorn locks, the headmistress's appraisal ended with an astonishing smile!

"Good." Claire nodded. "First chance, you claimed your own heritage. Well done."

"I . . ." Maia shook her head. ". . . don't understand."

The old contempt was still there—an egalitarian scorn for anything and everybody non-Lamai. "You hot-time brats are a pain," Claire said. "Sometimes I wish the founders of Stratos had been more radical, and chosen to do without your kind."

Maia gasped. Claire's remark was almost *Perkinite* in its heresy. If Maia herself had ever said anything remotely slighting the first mothers, it would have meant a strapping.

"But Lysos was wise," the old teacher went on with a sigh. "You summerlings are our wild seeds. Our windblown heritage. If you want my blessing take it, var-child. Sink roots somewhere and flower, if you can."

Maia felt her nostrils flare. "You kick us out, giving us nothing. . . ."

Claire laughed. "We give plenty. A practical education and no illusions that the world owes you favors! Would you prefer we coddled you? Set you up in a go-nowhere job, like some clans do for their vars? Or drilled you for a civil-service test one in a hundred pass? Oh, you're bright enough to have had a chance, Maia, but then what? Move to Caria City and push papers the rest of your life? Scrimp on salary to buy an apartment and someday start a microclan of *one?*

"Pah. You may not be all Lamai, but you're half! Find and win a real niche for yourself. If it's a good one, write and tell us what you've got. Maybe the clan will buy into the action."

Maia found the strength to voice what she had wanted to say for years. "You hypocritical cat—"

"That's it!" Mother Claire cut her off, still grinning. "Keep listening to your sister. *Leie* knows it's tooth and claw out there. Go on now. Go and fight the world."

With that, the infuriating woman simply turned away, leading the placid lugar past the nodding, bleary-eyed old coot, following her charges toward the classroom where sounds of recitation rose to fill the cool, dry air.

To Maia, the courtyard, so long such a broad part of her world, suddenly felt close, claustrophobic. The statues of old-time Lamais seemed more stony-chill and stark than ever. *Thanks, Momma Claire,* she thought, pondering those parting words. *I'll do just that.*

And our first rule, if Leie and I ever start our own clan, will be—no statues!

Maia found Leie munching a stolen apple, leaning against the merchants' gate, looking beyond the thick walls of Lamatia Hold to where cobblestone streets threaded downhill past the noble clanholds of Port Sanger. In the distance, a cloud of hovering, iridescent zoor-floaters used rising air currents to drift above the harbor masts, on the lookout for scraps from the fishing fleet. The creatures lent rare, festive colors to the morning, like the gaudy kite-balloons children would fly on Mid-Winter's Day.

Maia stared at her twin's ragged haircut and rough attire. "Lysos, I hope I don't look like that!"

"Your prayer is answered," Leie answered with a blithe shrug. "You got no hope of looking this good. Catch."

Maia grabbed a second apple out of the air. Of course Leie had swiped two. On matters of health, her sister was devoted to her welfare. Their plan wouldn't work without two of them.

"Look." Leie gestured with her chin toward the slope-sided clanhold chapel, where a group of five-year summer girls had gathered on the portico. Rosin and Kirstin munched sweet cakes nervously, careful not to get crumbs on their borrowed gowns. Their braids were all primly tied with blue ribbons, ready to be clipped in ceremony by the clan archivist. In cynical conjecture, Leie bet that the pragmatic mothers traded all that glossy hair to burrower colonies to use as nest material, in exchange for a few pints of zec-honey.

Each of those young women bore a family resemblance, having effectively shared the same mother as Maia and Leie. Still, the half sisters had grown up knowing, even better than the twins did, what it meant to be unique.

They must be even more scared than I am, Maia thought sympathetically.

Within the 'dim recesses of the chapel, she made out several senior Lamai and the priestess who had come up from the city temple to officiate. Maia envisioned wax candles being lit, setting aflicker the deep-incised lettering that rimmed the stone sanctum with quotations from the Founders' Book and, along one entire wall, the enigmatic Riddle of Lysos. Closing her eyes, she could picture every carven meter, feel the rough texture of the pillars, almost smell the incense.

Maia didn't regret her choice, following Leie's example and spurning all the hypocrisy. And yet . . .

"Suck-ups," Leie snapped, dismissing their peers with a disdaining snort. "Want to watch them graduate?"

After a pause, Maia answered with a headshake. She thought of a stanza by the poet Wayfarer . . .

> *Summer brings the sun,*
> *to spread across the land.*
> *But winter abides long,*
> *for those who understand.*

"No. Let's just get out of here."

Lamai clan mothers had their hands in shipping and high finance, as well as management of the city-state. Of the seventeen major, and ninety minor, matriarchies in Port Sanger, Lamatia was among the most prominent.

You wouldn't imagine it, walking the market districts. There were some russet-haired Lamais about, proud and uniformly buxom in their finely woven kilts, striding ahead of hulking lugars in livery, laden with packages. Still, among the bustling stalls and warehouses, members of the patrician caste seemed as scarce as summer folk, or even the occasional man.

There were plenty of stocky, pale-skinned Ortyns in sight, especially wherever goods were being loaded or unloaded. Identical except in the scars of individual happenstance, the pug-nosed Ortyns seldom spoke. Among themselves words seemed unnecessary. Few of that clan became savants, to be sure, but their physical strength and skill as teamsters—handling the temperamental sash-horses—made them formidable in their niche. "Why keep and feed lugars," went a local saying, "when you can hire Ortyns to move it for you."

A gang of those stocky clones had Musician's Way snarled, their dray obstructing traffic as six identical women wrestled with a block and tackle slung from the rafter of an upper-story workshop. Like many buildings in this part of town, this one leaned over the street, each floor jutting a little farther on corbeled supports. In some neighborhoods, edifices met above the narrow road, forming arches that blocked the sky.

A crowd had gathered, entranced by the creaking load high above —an upright harp-spinet, constructed of fine wood inlay by the Pasarg clan of musical craftswomen for export to one of the faraway cities of the west. Perhaps it would ride the Grim Bird along with Maia and Leie . . . if the workers got it safely to ground first. A gaggle of the sallow-faced, long-fingered Pasargs had gathered below, trilling nervously whenever the sash-horses stamped, setting the cargo swaying overhead. If it crashed, a season's profits might be ruined.

To other onlookers, the tense moment highlighted a drab autumn morning. Hawkers converged, selling roasted nuts and scent-sticks to the gathering crowd. Slender money rods were swapped in bundles or broken to make change.

"Winter's comin', so get yerself a'ready!" shouted an ovop seller with her basket of bitter contraceptive herbs. "Men are finally coolin' off, but can you trust *yerself* with glory frost due?"

Other tradeswomen carried reed cages containing live birds and Stratoin hiss lizards, some of them trained to warble popular tunes. One young Charnoss clone tried to steer a herd of gangly llamas past the high wheels of the jiggling wagon, and got tangled with a political worker wearing a sandwich board advertising the virtues of a candidate in the upcoming council elections.

Leie bought a candied tart and joined those gasping and cheering as the delicately carved spinet narrowly escaped clipping a nearby wall. But Maia found it more interesting to watch the Ortyn team on the back of the wagon, working together to free the jammed winch. It was a rare electrical device, operating on battery power. She had never seen Ortyns use one before, and thought it likely they had mishandled it in some way. None of the clans in Port Sanger specialized in the repair of such things, so it came as no surprise when, without a word or any other apparent sign, the Ortyns gave up trying to make it work. One member of the team grabbed the release catch while the others, as in a choreographed dance, turned and raised callused hands to seize the rope. There were no cries or shouts of cadence; each Ortyn seemed to know her sisters' state of readiness as the latch let go. Muscles bunched across

broad backs. Smoothly, the cargo settled downward, kissing the wagon
bed with deceptive gentleness. There were cheers and a few disappointed boos as money sticks changed hands, settling wagers. Maia and
her twin hoisted their duffels once more, Leie finishing her tart while
Maia turned pensive.

*The Ortyns almost read each others' minds. How are Leie and I
supposed to fake something like that?*

When they were younger, she and her sister sometimes used to
finish each other's sentences, or knew when and where the other was in
pain. But at best it had been a tentative link, nothing like the bond
among clones, whose mothers, aunts, and grandmothers shared both
genes and common upbringing, stretching back generations. Moreover,
the twins had lately seemed to diverge, rather than coalesce. Of the two,
Maia felt her sister had more of the hard practicality needed to succeed
in this world.

"Ortyns an' Jorusses an' Kroebers an' bleedin' Sloskies . . ." Leie
muttered. "I'm so sick of this rutty place. I'd kiss a dragon on the mouth,
not to have to look at the same faces till I julp."

Maia, too, felt an urge to move on. Yet, she wondered, how did a
stranger get to know who was whom in a foreign town? Here, one learned
about each caste almost from birth. Such as the willowy, kink-haired
Sheldons, dark-skinned women a full head taller than the blocky Ortyns.
Their usual niche was trapping fur-beasts in the tundra marshes, but
Sheldons in their mid-thirties often also wore badges of Port Sanger's
corps of Guards, overseeing the city's defense.

Long-fingered Poeskies were likewise well-suited to their tasks—
deftly harvesting fragile stain glands from cracked stellar snails. They
were so good at the dye trade, cadet branches had set up in other towns
along the Parthenia Sea, wherever fisherfolk caught the funnel-shaped
shells.

Near cousins to that clan, Groeskies used their clever hands as
premier mechanics. They were a young matriarchy, a summer-stock offshoot that had taken root but a few generations ago. Though still numbering but two score, the pudgy, nimble "Grossies" were already a clan to
be reckoned with. Every one of them was clone-descended from a single,
half-Poeskie summerling who had seized a niche by luck and talent,
thereby winning a posterity. It was a dream all var-kids shared—to dig
in, prosper, and establish a new line. Once in a thousand times, it happened.

Passing a Groeskie workshop, the twins looked on as ball bearings
were slipped into axles by robust, contented redheads, each an inheritor
of that clever forbear who won a place in Port Sanger's tough social

pyramid. Maia felt Leie nudge her elbow. Her sister grinned. "Don't forget, we've got an edge."

Maia nodded. "Yeah." Under her breath, she added, "I hope."

Below the market district, under the sign of a rearing tricorn, stood a shop selling sweets imported from faraway Vorthos. Chocolate was one vice the twins knew they must warn their daughter-heirs about, if ever they had any. The shopkeeper, a doe-eyed Mizora, stood hopefully, though she knew they weren't buyers. The Mizora were in decline, reduced to selling once-rich holdings in order to host sailors in the manner of their foremothers. They still coiffed their hair in a style suited to a great clan, though most were now small merchants, less good at it than upstart Usisi or Oeshi. The Mizora shopkeeper sadly watched Maia and Leie turn away, continuing their stroll down a street of smaller clanholds.

Many establishments bore emblems and badges featuring extinct beasts such as firedrakes and tricorns—Stratoin creatures that long ago failed to adapt to the coming of Earth life. Lysos and the Founders had urged preservation of native forms, yet even now, centuries later, tele screens occasionally broadcast melancholy ceremonies from the Great Temple in faroff Caria City, enrolling another species on the list to be formally mourned each Farsun Day.

Maia wondered if guilt caused so many clans to choose as symbols native beasts that were no more. Or was it a way of saying, *"See? We continue. We wear emblems of the defeated past, and thrive."*

In a few generations, Mizora might be as common as tricorns.

Lysos never promised an end to change, only to slow it down to a bearable pace.

Rounding a corner, the twins nearly plowed into a tall Sheldon, hurrying downhill from the upper-class neighborhood. Her guard uniform was damp, open at the collar. "Excuse me," the dark-skinned officer muttered, dodging by the two sisters. A few paces onward, however, she suddenly stopped, whirling to peer at them.

"*There* you are. I almost didn't recognize you!"

"Bright mornin', Cap'n Jounine." Leie greeted with a mocking half-salute. "You were looking for us?"

Jounine's keen Sheldon features were softened by years of town life. The captain wiped her brow with a satin kerchief. "I was late catching you at Lamatia clanhold. Do you know you missed your leave-taking ceremony? Of course you know. Was that on purpose?"

Maia and Leie shared brief smiles. No slipping anything by Captain Jounine.

"Never mind." The Sheldon waved a hand. "I just wanted to ask if you'd reconsidered—"

"Signing up for the Guard?" Leie interrupted. "You've got to be—"

"I'm sure we're flattered by the offer, Captain," Maia cut in. "But we have tickets—"

"You'll not find anything out there"—Jounine waved toward the sea —"that's more secure and steady—"

"And boring . . ." Leie muttered.

"—than a contract with the city of your birth. It's a smart move, I tell you!"

Maia knew the arguments. Steady meals and a bed, plus slow advancement in hopes of saving enough for one child. A winter child—on a soldier's salary? Mother Claire's derision about "founding a microclan of one" seemed apropos. Some *smart moves* were little more than nicely padded traps.

"A myriad thanks for the offer," Leie said, with wasted sarcasm. "If we're ever desperate enough to come back to this frigid—"

"Yes, thanks," Maia interrupted, taking her sister's arm. "And Lysos keep you, Captain."

"Well . . . at least stay away from the Pallas Isles, you two! There are reports of reavers . . ."

As soon as they turned a corner, Maia and Leie dropped their duffels and broke out laughing. Sheldons were an impressive clan in most ways, but they took things *so* seriously! Maia felt sure she would miss them.

"It's odd, though," she said after a minute, when they resumed walking. "Jounine really did look more anxious than usual."

"Hmph. Not our problem if she can't meet recruitment quotas. Let her buy lugars."

"You know lugars can't fight people."

"Then hire summer stock down at the docks. Plenty of riffraff vars always hanging around. Dumb idea expanding the Guard anyway. Bunch of parasites, just like priestesses."

"Mm," Maia commented. "I guess." But the look in the soldier's eye had been like that of the Mizora sweets-merchant. There had been disappointment. A touch of bewilderment.

And more than a little fear.

A month ago wardens had stood watch at the getta gate, separating Port Sanger proper from the harbor.

Maia recalled how the care-mothers used to take Lamatia's crèche kids from the high precincts down steep, cobbled streets to ceremonies at the civic temple, passing near the getta gate along the way. Early one summer, she had bolted from the tidy queue of varlings, running toward the high barrier, hoping to glimpse the great freighters in drydock. Her brief dash had ended with a sound spanking. Afterward, between sobs, she distantly heard one matron explain that the wharves weren't safe for kids that time of year. There were "rutting men" down there.

Later, when the aurorae were replaced in northern skies by autumn's placid constellations, those same gates were flung back for children to scamper through at will, running along the docks where bearded males unloaded mysterious cargoes, or played spellbinding games with clockwork disks. Maia recalled wondering at the time—were *these* men different from the "rutting" kind? It must be so. Always ready with a smile or story, these seemed as gentle and harmless as the furry lugars they somewhat resembled.

"Harmless as a man, when stars glitter clear." So went a nursery rhyme, which finished,

But wary be you, woman, when Wengel Star is near.

Traversing the gate for the last time, Maia and Leie passed through a variegated throng. Unlike the uphill precincts, here males made up a substantial minority, contributing a rich mix of scents to the air, from the aromas of spice and exotic cargoes to their own piquant musk. It was the ideal and provocative locale for a Perkinite agitator to have set up shop, addressing the crowd from an upturned shipping crate as two clone-mates pushed handbills at passersby. Maia did not recognize the face type, so the trio of gaunt-cheeked women had to be missionaries, recently arrived.

"Sisters!" the speaker cried out. "You of lesser clans and houses! Together you outnumber the combined might of the Seventeen who control Port Sanger. If you join forces. If you join with *us*, you could break the lock great houses have on the town assembly, and yes, on the region, and even in Caria City itself! Together we can smash the conspiracy of silence and force a long-overdue revelation of the truth—"

"*What* truth?" demanded an onlooker.

The Perkinite glanced to where a young sailor lounged against the fence with several of his colleagues, amused by the discomfiture his question provoked. True to her ideology, the agitator tried to ignore a mere male. So, for fun, Leie chimed in. "Yeah! What truth is that, Perkie?"

Several onlookers laughed at Leie's jibe, and Maia could not hide a smile. Perkinites took themselves and their cause so seriously, and hated the diminutive of their name. The speaker glared at Leie, but then caught sight of Maia standing by her side. To the twins' delight, she instantly drew the wrong conclusion and held out her hands to them earnestly, imploringly.

"The truth that small clans like yours and mine are routinely shoved aside, not just here but everywhere, especially in Caria City,

where the great houses are even now selling our very planet to the Outsiders and their masculinist Phylum . . ."

Maia's ears perked at mention of the alien ship. Alas, it soon grew
clear that the speaker wasn't offering news, only a tirade. The harangue
quickly sank into platitudes and clichés Maia and her sister had heard
countless times over the years. About the flood of cheap var labor ruining
so many smaller clans. About laxity enforcing the Codes of Lysos and the
regulation of "dangerous males." Such hackneyed accusations joined
this year's fashionable paranoid theme—playing to popular unease that
the space visitors might be precursors to an invasion worse even than the
long-ago horror of the Enemy.

There had been brief pleasure in being mistaken for a "clan," just
because Maia and Leie looked alike, but that quickly faded. Autumn
meant elections were coming, and fringe groups kept trying to chivvy a
minority seat or two in the face of *en masse* bloc-voting by holds like
Lamatia. Perkinism appealed to small matriarchies who felt obstructed
by established lines. The movement got little support from vars, who had
no power and even less inclination to vote.

As for men, they had no illusions should Perkinism take hold in a
big way on Stratos. If that ever seemed close to happening again, Maia
might witness something unique in her lifetime, the sight of *males* lining
up at polling booths, exercising a right enshrined in law, but practiced
about as often as glory frost fell in summer.

Though Leie was still chuckling over the Perkinites' political tract,
Maia nudged her sister. "Come on. There are better things to do with our
last morning in town."

The rising sun had sublimed away a shore-hugging fog by the time the
twins reached the harbor proper. Midmorning heat had also carried off
most of the gaudy zoor-floaters that Maia had glimpsed earlier. A few of
the luminous creatures were still visible as bright, ovoid flowers, or garish gasbags, drifting in a ragged chain across the eastern sky.

One laggard remained over the docks, resembling a filmy, bloated
jellyfish with dangling, iridescent feelers a mere twenty meters long. A
baby, then. It clutched the main mast of a sleek freighter, caressing the
cloth-draped yards, groping for treats laid on the upper spars by nimble
sailors. The agile seamen laughed, dodging the waving, sticky suckers,
then dashed in to stroke the knotty backs of the beast's tentacles, or tie
on bright ribbons or paper notes. Once a year or so, someone actually
recovered a ragged message that had been carried in such a fashion, all
the way across the Mother Ocean.

There were also stories of young cabin boys who actually tried hitching rides upon a zoor, floating off to Lysos-knew-where, perhaps inspired by legends of days long ago, when zep'lins and airplanes swarmed the sky, and men were allowed to fly.

As if proving that it was a day of fate and synchrony, Leie nudged Maia and pointed in the opposite direction, southwest, beyond the golden dome of the city temple. Maia blinked at a silvery shape that glinted briefly as it settled groundward, and recognized the weekly dirigible, delivering mail and packages too dear to entrust to sea transport, along with rare passengers whose clans had to be nearly as rich as the planet goddess in order to afford the fare. Both Maia and Leie sighed, for once sharing exactly the same thought. It would take a miracle for either of them ever to journey like that, amid the clouds. Perhaps their clone descendants might, if luck's fickle winds blew that way. The thought offered some slight consolation.

Perhaps it also explained why boys sometimes gave up everything just to ride a zoor. Males, by their very natures, could not bear clones. They could not copy themselves. At best, they achieved the lesser immortality of fatherhood. Whatever they most desired had to be accomplished in one lifetime, or not at all.

The twins resumed their stroll. Down here near the wharves, where fishing boats gave off a humid, pungent miasma, they began seeing a lot more summer folk like themselves. Women of diverse shapes, colors, sizes, often bearing a family resemblance to some well-known clan—a Sheldon's hair or a Wylee's distinctive jaw—sharing half or a quarter of their genes with a renowned mother-line, just as the twins carried in their faces much that was Lamai.

Alas, half resemblance counted for little. Dressed in monocolor kilts or leather breeches, each summer person went about life as a solitary unit, unique in all the world. Most held their heads high despite that. Summer folk worked the piers, scraped the drydocked sailing ships, and performed most of the grunt labor supporting seaborne trade, often with a cheerfulness that was inspirational to behold.

Before Lysos, on Phylum worlds, vars like us were normal and clones rare. Everyone had a father . . . sometimes one you even grew up knowing.

Maia used to ponder images of a teeming planet, filled with wild, unpredictable variety. The Lamai mothers called it "an unwholesome fixation," yet such thoughts came more frequently since news of the Outsider Ship began filtering down, through rumors and then terse, censored reports on the tele.

Do people still live in old-fashioned chaos, on other worlds? She wondered. As if life would ever offer any opportunity to find out.

With storm season over and the getta fence wide open, the harbor was a lively, colorful precinct. A season's pent-up commerce was getting under way. People bustled among the loading docks and slate-roofed warehouses, the chapels and recurtained Houses of Ease. And ship chandleries—a favorite haunt while the twins were growing up, crammed with every tool or oddment a crew might need at sea. From an early age, Maia and her sister had been drawn by the bright brasswork and smell of polishing oil, browsing for hours to the exasperation of the shopkeepers. For her part, Leie had been fascinated by mechanical devices, while Maia focused on charts and sextants and slender telescopes with their clicking, finely beveled housings. And timepieces, some so old they carried a outer ring dividing the Stratoin calendar into a little more than three "Standard Earth Years." Not even hazing by fiver boys—itinerant midshipmen who often knew less about shooting a latitude than spitting into the wind—ever kept the twins away for long.

Peering into the biggest chandlery, Maia caught the eye of the manager, a bluff-faced Felic. The clone noticed Maia's haircut and duffel, and her habitual grimace slowly lightened into a smile. She made a brief hand gesture wishing Maia good luck and safe passage.

And good riddance, I'll bet. Recalling what nuisances she and her sister had been, Maia returned an exaggerated bow, which the shopkeeper dismissed with laughter and a wave.

Maia turned around to find Leie over by a nearby pier, conversing with a dockworker whose high cheekbones were reminiscent of Western Continent. "Naw, naw," the woman said as Maia approached, not pausing in her rapid knotting of the sail she was mending. "So far ain't heard nary judgment by the Council in Caria. Nary t'all."

"Judgment about what?" Maia asked.

"The Outsiders," Leie explained. "Those Perkie missionaries got me wondering if there's been news. This var works on a boat with full access." Leie pointed toward a nearby fishing craft, sporting a steerable antenna. It wasn't farfetched that someone spinning dials with a rig like that might pick up a tidbit or two.

"As if th' owners invite *me* to tea an' tele!" The sailmaker spat through a gap in her teeth toward the scummy water glistening with floating fish scales.

"But have you overheard anything? Say, on an unofficial channel? Do they still claim only *one* Outsider has landed?"

Maia sighed. Caria City was remote and its savants only broadcast sparse accounts. Worse, the Lamai mothers often forbade summer kids to watch tele at all, lest their volatile minds find programs "disturbing." Naturally, this only piqued the twins' curiosity. But Leie was taking inquisitiveness too far, grilling simple laborers. Apparently the sail-maker agreed. "Why ask me, you silly hots? Why should I listen to lies hissing outta the owners' box?"

"But you're from Landing Continent. . . ."

"My province was ninety *gi* from Caria! Ain't seen it in ten year, nor will again, never. Now go way!"

When they were out of earshot, Maia chided, "Leie, you've got to go easy on that stuff. You can't make a pest of yourself—"

"Like *you* did, when we were four? Who tried stowing away on that schooner, just to find out how the captain got a fix on a rolling horizon? I recall we *both* got punished for that one!"

Reluctantly, Maia smiled. She hadn't always been the more cautious sister. One long Stratos year ago, it had been Leie who always took careful gauge before acting, and Maia who kept coming up with schemes that got them in trouble. *We're alike, all right. We just keep getting out of phase. And maybe that's good. Someone has to take turns being the sensible one.*

"This is different," she replied, trying to keep to the point. "It's real life now."

Leie shrugged. "Want to talk about *life*? Look at those cretins, over there." She nodded toward a paved area on the quay, laid out in a geometric grid, where a number of seamen stood idly, pondering an array of small black or white disks. "They call their game Life, and take it damn seriously. Does that make it real, too?"

Maia refused to acknowledge the pun. Whenever ships were in port, clusters of men could be found here, playing the ancient game with a passion matched only during auroral months by their seasonal interest in sex. The men, deckhands off some freighter, wore rough, sleeveless shirts and metal ringlets on their biceps denoting rank. A few of the onlookers glanced up as the sisters passed by. Two of the younger ones smiled.

If it had still been summertime, Maia would have demurely looked away and even Leie would have shown caution. But as the aurorae faded and Wengel Star waned, so too ebbed the hot blood in males. They became calmer creatures, more companionable. Autumn was the best season for shipping out, then. Maia and Leie could spend up to twenty standard months at sea before being forced ashore by next year's rut. By then, they had better have found a niche, something they were good at, and started their nest egg.

Leie boldly met the sailors' amiable, lazy leers, hands on hips and eye to eye, as if daring them to back up their bluster. One towheaded youth seemed to consider it. But of course, if he had any libido to spare this time of year, he wouldn't go wasting it on a pair of dirt-poor virgins! The young men laughed, and so did Leie.

"Come on," she told Maia as the men turned back to regard their game pieces. Leie readjusted her duffel. "It's nearing tide. Let's get aboard and shake this town off our feet."

"What do you mean, you're not sailing? For how long?"

Maia couldn't believe this. The old fart of a purser chewed a toothpick as he rocked back on his stool by the gangplank. Unshaven in rumbled fatigues, he nudged the nearby barreltop where their refund lay . . . plus a little more thrown in for "compensation."

"Dunno, li'l liss. Prob'ly a month. Mebbe two."

"A month!" Leie's voice cracked. "You spew of wormy bottom muck! The weather's fair. You've got cargo and paying passengers. What do you mean—"

"Got a better offer." The purser shrugged. "One o' the big clans bought our cargo, just t'get us to stay. Seems they likes our boys. Wants 'em sticking round awhile, I reckon."

Maia felt a sinking realization in the pit of her stomach. "I guess some mothers want to start winter breeding early, this year," she said, trying to make sense of this catastrophe. "It's risky, but if they catch the men with heat still in them—"

"Which house!" Leie interrupted, in no mood for rational appraisal. She kicked the barrel, causing the money sticks to rattle. The grizzled sailor, massing twice Leie's fifty kilos, placidly scratched his beard.

"Lesse now. Was it the Tildens? Or was it Lam—"

"Lamatia?" Leie cried, this time flinging her arms so wildly the purser scrambled to his feet. "Now, lissie. No cause t'get excited . . ." Maia grabbed Leie's arm as she seemed about to throw the sailor's stool at him. "It makes sense!" Leie screamed. "That's why they opened the guesthouse weeks early, and had us pouring wine for those lunks all night!"

Maia sometimes envied her sister's refuge in tantrums. Her own reaction, a numb retreat to logic, seemed less satisfying than Leie's way of breaking everything in sight. "Leie," she urged hoarsely. "It can't be Lamatia. They only deal with high-class guilds, not the sort of trash we can afford passage with." It was satisfying to catch the purser wincing at her remark. "Anyway, we're better off dealing with honest men. There are other ships."

Her sister whirled. "Yeah? Remember how we studied? Buying books and even net time, researching every port this tub was going to?

We had a plan for every stop . . . people to see. Questions. Prospects. Now it's all wasted!"

How could it be wasted? Maia wondered woodenly. *All those hours studying, memorizing the Oscco Isles and Western Sea. . . .*

Maia realized neither of them was reacting well to sudden despair.

"Let's go," she told her sister, scooping up the money and trying for both their sakes to keep worry out of her voice. "We'll find another ship, Leie. A better one, you'll see."

That proved easier said than done. There were many sails in Port Sanger, from hand-carved, hard-edged windwings, to stormjammers, to clippers with flapping sheets of woven squid-silk. At the diplomatic docks, just below the harbor fort, there was even one rare, sleek cruiser whose banks of gleaming solar panels basked in the angled sunshine. Maia and Leie did not bother with such rich craft, whose crews would have spurned their paltry coinsticks as fishing lures. They did try their luck with well-turned freighters flying banners of the Cloud Whale League, or the Blue Heron Society, voyager guilds whose gray-bearded commodores sometimes called at Lamatia Hall to interview bright boys for lives at sea.

According to children's fables, once upon a time boys like Albert simply joined the guilds of their fathers. Even summer *girls* used to grow up knowing which daddy-ship would take them someday, free of charge, to wherever opportunities shone brightest for young vars.

> Clone-child you must stay within,
> Home-hive to protect, renew.
> Var-child you must strive and win,
> Half-mom and half-man, it's true.
>
> Let the heartwinds blow away,
> Winter's frost, or summer's bright.
> Name the special things that stay,
> Fixed, to guide you through the night.
>
> Stratos Mother, Founders' Gifts,
> Your own skill and eager hands.
> One more boon, the lucky lifts,
> Father ticket to far lands.

One old teacher, Savant Judeth—a Lamai with unusual sympathy for her summerling charges—once testified that truth underlaid the old tales. "In those days, each sailing society kept close contact with one house in Port Sanger, carrying clan cargoes and finding welcome in clan hostels, summer and winter both. When var girls turned five, their fathers—or their fathers' compeers—used to carry them off as treasures in their own right, helping them get settled in lands far away."

To Maia it had sounded like romantic drivel, much too sappy to be true. But Leie had asked, "Why'd it stop being so?"

Momentarily wistful, Savant Judeth looked anything but typical for a stern-browed Lamai.

"Wish I knew, seedling. It may have to do with the rise in summer births. There seemed a lot when I was young. Now it's up to one in four. So many vars." The old woman shook her head. "And rivalry among the clans and guilds has grown fierce; there's even outright fighting . . ." Judeth had sighed. "All I can say is, we used to know which men would lodge here, to spark clones during cooltime and sire sons during the brief hot. Oh, and beget you summer girls, as well. But those days are gone."

Hesitantly, Leie had asked if Judeth knew their father.

"Clevin? Oh, yes. I can even see him in your faces. Navigator on the Sea Lion he was. A good egg, as men go. Your womb mother, Lysos keep her, would favor none other. You got to know men in those days. Pleasant it was, in a strange way."

And hard to imagine. Whether as noisy creatures who sheltered in the getta during summer, slaking their rut in houses of ease, or as taciturn guests during the cool seasons, lounging like cats while the Lamai sisters coaxed them with wine and plays and games of Chess or Life, either way, they were soon off again. Their names vanished, even if they left their seed. Yet, for one entire year after hearing Savant Judeth's tale, Maia used to search among the masts for the Sea Lion's banner, imagining the expression on her father's sunburnt face when he laid eyes upon the two of them.

Then she learned, Pinniped Guild no longer sailed the Parthenia Sea. The var daughters its men had sired, five long cycles ago, were on their own.

None of the better ships in harbor had berths for them. Most were already overloaded with uniques—hard-eyed var women who glared down at the twins or laughed at their plaintive entreaties. Captains and pursers kept shaking their heads, or asking for more money than the sisters could afford.

And there was something else. Something Maia couldn't pin down. Nobody said anything aloud, but the mood in the harbor seemed . . . jumpy.

Maia tried to dismiss it as a reflection of her own nerves.

Working their way along the docks, the twins found nothing suitable departing in under a fortnight. Finally, exhausted, they arrived on the left bank of the river Stopes, where tugs and hemp barges tied up at sagging wharves owned by local clans that had fallen on ill fortune or simply did not care anymore. Dejected, Leie voted for going back to town and booking a room. Surely this string of bad luck was an omen. In ten days, maybe twenty, things could change.

Maia wouldn't hear of it. Where Leie fluxed from wrath to smoldering despair, Maia tended toward a doggedness that settled into pure obstinacy. Twenty days in a hotel? When they could be on their way to some exotic land? Somewhere they might have a chance to use their secret plan?

It was in a grimy hostelry of the lowly Bizmish Clan that they met the captains of a pair of colliers heading south on the morrow tide.

The world of men, too, had its hierarchies. The sort who were smart-eyed and successful, and made good sires, were wooed by wealthy matriarchies. Poorer mother-lines entertained a lower order. Stooped, sallow-skinned Bizmai, still gritty from the mines they worked nearby, shuttled about the guesthouse, toting jars of flat beer that Maia wouldn't touch, but the coarse seamen relished. The twins met the two captains in the stifling, dank common room, where carbon particles set Maia's nictitating membranes blinking furiously until they moved outside to the "veranda" overlooking a marsh. There, swarms of irritating zizzerbugs dove suicidally around the flickering tallow candles until their wings ignited, turning them into brief, flaming embers that dropped to the sooty tabletop.

"Sure will miss this place, betcha," Captain Ran said, smacking his lips, laying his beer mug down hard. "These's friendly ladies, here. Come hot season, uptown biddies won't give workin' stiffs like us a fin or fizz, let 'lone a good roll. But here we got our fill."

Maia well believed it. Of the Bizmai in sight who were of childbearing age, half were heavy with summer pregnancies. Her nostrils flared in distaste. What would a poor clan like this do with all those uniques? Could they feed and clothe and educate them? *Would* they, when summer offspring seldom returned wealth to a household? Most of those babies would likely be disposed of in some ugly way, perhaps left on the tundra . . . "in the hands of Lysos." There were laws against it, but what law carried greater weight than the good of the clan?

Perhaps the Bizmai would be spared the trouble. Many summer pregnancies failed by themselves, spontaneously ending early due to defects in the genes. Or so Savant Judeth had explained it. *"All clones come as tried and tested designs,"* she had put it. *"While every summerling is a fresh experiment. And countless experiments fail."*

Nevertheless, the var birthrate kept climbing. "Experiments" like Maia and Leie were filling the lower streets in every town.

"That's one reason we're on a short haul, this run . . ." said the other officer. Captain Pegyul was thinner, grayer, and apparently somewhat smarter than his peer. ". . . carryin' anthracite to Queg Town, Lanargh, Grange Head, an' Gremlin Town. We may not be one o' those big-time, fruity guilds, but we got honor. The Bizmai want us stoppin' back again midwinter? We'll do that for 'em, after they been so kind durin' hot!"

That must be why the mining clan was so accommodating to these lizards. Men tended to get sentimental toward women carrying their summer kids—offspring with half their genes. In half a year, though, would these idiots even notice that few of those babes were still around?

"Gremlin Town will do fine," Leie said, draining her stein and motioning for a refill. The destination was south instead of west, but they had talked it over. A detour could be corrected later, after they had worked awhile at sea and on land. This way, they'd arrive at the Oscco Archipelago seasoned, no longer naïve.

The thinner of the two masters rubbed his stubbled jaw. "Uh huh. So long's you both'll do what yer told."

"We'll work hard. Don't worry about that, sir."

"An' yer mother clan taught you all the right stuff? Like, say, stick-fightin'?"

Maia was sure Leie also picked up the sailor's sly effort at nonchalance. As if he were asking about sewing, or smithing, or any other practical art.

"We've had it all, sir. You won't regret bringing us aboard, whichever of you takes us."

The two seamen looked at each other. The shorter one leaned forward. "Uh, it's both of us you'll be goin' with."

Leie blinked. "What do you mean?"

"It's like this," the tall one explained. "You two is twins. That's nice, but it can make trouble. We got clan women booking passage from town to town, all along the way. They may see you two, scrubbin' decks, doin' scut work, an' get the wrong idea . . ."

Maia and Leie looked at each other. Their private scheme involved taking *advantage* of that natural reaction—the assumption that two identicals were likely to be clones. Now the irony sank in, that their boon could also be a drawback.

"I dunno about splitting up," Leie said, shaking her head. "We could change our looks. I could dye my hair—"

Maia cut in. "Your vessels convoy together all the way down the coast, right?" The captains nodded. Maia turned to Leie. "Then we wouldn't be separated for long. This way we'll get recommendations from two shipmasters, instead of just one."

"But—"

"I won't like it either, but look at it this way. We double our experience for the same price. Each of us learns things the other doesn't. Besides, we'll have to go apart at other times. This will be good practice."

The startled expression in her sister's eyes told Maia a lot about their relationship. There was a soft pleasure in surprising Leie, something that happened all too seldom. *She never expected me to be the one accepting a separation so easily.*

Indeed, Maia found she looked forward to the prospect of time by herself, away from her twin's driving personality. *This should be healthy for both of us.*

Hiding her brief discomfiture behind an upraised beer stein, Leie finally nodded and said, "I don't guess it matters—"

At that instant, a flash whitened their faces, casting shadows from the direction of town. A sparking, spiraling rocket trailed upward from the harbor fortress, arcing into the sky and then exploding, lighting the docks and clanholds with stark, crawling patterns of white and dark. Silhouettes revolved around pedestrians stunned motionless by the abrupt glare, while a low growling sound rapidly climbed in pitch and intensity to become an ululation, filling the night.

Maia, her sister, and the two captains stood up. It was the seldom-heard wail of Port Sanger's siren . . . calling out the militia . . . alerting its citizens to stand to the defense.

W hat should be our desiderata, in designing a new human race? What existence do we wish for our descendants on this world?

Long, happy lives?

Fair enough. Yet, despite our technical wonders, that simple boon may prove hard to deliver. Long ago, Darwin and Malthus pointed out life's basic paradox—that all species carry inbuilt drives to try to over-breed. To fill even Eden with so many offspring that it ceases to be paradise, anymore.

Nature, in her wisdom, controlled this opportunistic streak with checks and balances. Predators, parasites, and random luck routinely culled the excess. To the survivors, each new generation, went the prize —a chance to play another round.

Then humans came. Born critics, we wiped out the carnivores who preyed on us, and battled disease. With rising moral fervor, societies pledged to suppress cut-throat competition, guaranteeing to all a "right to live and prosper."

In retrospect, we know awful mistakes were made with the best intentions on poor Mother Terra. Without natural checks, our ancestors' population boom overwhelmed her. But is the only alternative to bring back rule by tooth and claw? Could we, even if we tried?

Intelligence is loose in the galaxy. Power is in our hands, for better or worse. We can modify Nature's rules, if we dare, but we cannot ignore her lessons.

—from The Apologia, *by Lysos*

2

An acrid scent of smoke. A fuming, cinder mist rising from smoldering planks. Distress flags flapping from the singed mizzen of a crippled ship, staggering toward asylum. The impressions were more vivid for occurring at night, with the larger moon, Durga, laying wan glimmers across the scummy waters of Port Sanger's bayside harbor.

Under glaring searchlights from the high-walled fortress, a dry-goods freighter, Prosper, wallowed arduously toward safe haven, assisted by its attacker. Half the town was there to watch, including militia from all of the great clanholds, their daughters of fighting age decked in leather armor and carrying polished trepp bills. Matronly officers wore cuirasses of shiny metal, shouting to squads of identical offspring and nieces. The Lamatia contingent arrived, quick-marching downhill in helmets crowned with gaeo bird feathers. Maia recognized most of the full-clone winterlings, her half sisters, despite their being alike in nearly every way. The Lamai companies briskly spread along the roof of the family warehouse before dispatching a detachment to help defend the town itself.

It was quite a show. Maia and her sister watched in fascination from a perch on the jetty wall. Not since they had been three years old had there been an alert like this. Nor were the commanders of the clan companies pleased to learn that a jumpy watchwoman had set off this commotion by pressing the wrong alert button, unleashing rockets into the placid autumn night where a few hoots from the siren would have been proper. An embarrassed Captain Jounine spent half an hour apologizing to disgruntled matrons, some of whom seemed all the more irascible for being squeezed into armor meant for younger, lither versions of themselves.

Meanwhile, rowboats threw lines to help draw the limping, smoldering Prosper toward refuge. Maia saw buckets of seawater still being drawn to extinguish embers from the fire that had nearly sent the ship down. Its sails were torn and singed. Dozens of scorched ropes festooned the rigging, dangling from unwelcome grappling hooks.

It must have been some fight, she figured, while it lasted.

Leie peered at the smaller vessel that had the Prosper in tow, its tiny auxiliary engine chuffing at the strain. "The reaver's called Misfortune," she told Maia, reading blocky letters on the bow. "Probably picked the name to strike terror into their victims' hearts." She laughed. "Bet they change it after this."

Maia had never been as quick as her sister to switch from adrenaline to pure spectator state. Only a short time ago, the city had been girding for attack. It would take time to adjust to the fact that all this panic was over a simple, bungled case of quasilegal piracy.

"The reavers don't look too happy," Maia observed, pointing to a crowd of tough-looking women wearing red bandannas, gathered on Misfortune's foredeck. Their chief argued with a guardia officer in a rocking motor launch. A similar scene took place near the prow of the Prosper, where affluent-looking women in smoke-fouled finery pointed and complained in loud voices. Farther aft on both vessels, male officers and crew tended the tricky business of guiding their ships to port. Not a man spoke until the vessels tied at neighboring jetties, at which time Prosper's master toured the maimed vessel. From his knotted jaw and taut neck muscles, the glowering man seemed capable of biting nails in two. Soon he was joined by Misfortune's skipper, who, after a moment's tense hesitation, offered his hand in silent commiseration.

A rumor network circulated among dockside bystanders, passing on what others, closer in, had learned. Leie dropped off the jetty in order to listen, while Maia stayed put, preferring what she could decipher with her own eyes. *There must have been an accident during the fight,* she surmised, tracing how fire had spread from a charred area amidships. Perhaps a lantern got smashed while the reavers battled the owners for their cargo. At that point, the male crews would have called a truce and put both sides to work saving the ship. It looked like a near thing, even so.

Reavers were uncommon in the Parthenia Sea, so near the stronghold of Port Sanger's powerful clans. But that wasn't the only curious thing about this episode.

Seems a stupid idea, hiring a schooner to go reaving this early in autumn, Maia thought. With storm season just ending, there were plenty of tempting cargoes around. But it was also a time when males still flowed with summer rut hormones, which might kick in under tense circumstances. Watching the edgy sailors, their fists clenched in rage, Maia wondered what might drive the young vars in a reaver gang to take such a risk.

One of the men kicked a bulkhead in anger, splintering the wood with a resounding crack.

Once, on a visit to a Sheldon ranch, Maia had witnessed two stallions fight over a sash-horse herd. That struggle without quarter had been unnerving, the lesson obvious. Perkinite scandal sheets spread scare-stories about "incidents," when masculine tempers flared and instincts left over from animal times on Old Earth came to fore. *"Wary be you women,"* went a stanza of the rhyme oft quoted by Perkinites. *"For a man who fights may kill . . ."*

To which Maia added privately, *Especially, when their precious ships are in danger.* This misadventure might easily have tipped over into something far worse.

Militia officers led the band of reavers, and *Prosper*'s passengers, toward the fort where a lengthy adjudication process would begin. Maia caught one shrill cry from the pirate leader: ". . . they set the fire on purpose 'cause we were winning!"

The owners' spokeswoman, a clone from the rich Vunerri trading clan, vehemently denied the charge. If proven, she risked losing more than the cargo and fines to repair Prosper. There might even be a boycott of her family's goods by *all* the sailing guilds. At such times, the normal hierarchy on Stratos was known to reverse, and mighty matrons from great holds went pleading leniency from lowly men.

But never from a var. It would take a true revolution to reverse the social ladder that far. For summer-born women ever to sit in judgment over clones.

Maia watched the procession march past her vantage point, some of the figures limping, holding bloody gashes from the fight that led to this debacle. Medical orderlies carried stretchers at the rear. One of the burdens lay completely covered.

Perkies may be right about women having less murderous tempers, Maia contemplated. *We seldom try to kill.* It was one reason Lysos and the Founders had come here—to create a gentler world. *But I guess that makes small difference to the poor wretch under that blanket.*

Leie returned, breathless to relate all she had learned from the throng. Maia listened and made all the right astonished sounds. Some names and details she hadn't pieced together by observing . . . and some she felt sure were garbled by the rumor chain.

Did details matter, though? What stuck in her mind, as they left with the dispersing crowd, had been the expression on Captain Jounine's face as the guardia commander escorted her bickering charges over a drawbridge into the fortress.

These aren't the peaceful times she grew up in. These are tougher days.

Maia glanced at her twin as they walked toward the far pier where the colliers Zeus and Wotan lay loaded and ready for the morning current. Despite her accustomed bravado, Leie suddenly looked every bit as young and inexperienced as Maia felt.

These are our days, Maia pondered soberly. *We'd better be ready for them.*

The moons' pull had modest effect on the huge seas of Stratos. Still, tradition favored setting sail with Durga tide. After last night's excitement, the predawn departure was less poignant than Maia had expected. All these years she'd pictured looking back at Port Sanger's rugged buildings of pink stone—castlelike clanholds studding the hillsides like eagles' nests—and feeling a cascade of heady emotions, watching the land of her childhood recede from sight, perhaps forever.

There was no time for dwelling on milestones, however. Gruff-voiced chiefs and bosuns shouted orders as she and several other awkward landlubbers rushed to help haul lanyards and lash straining sheets. Supplementing the permanent crew were more than a dozen vars like herself, "second-class passengers" who must work to supplement their fares. Despite Lamatia's stern curriculum for its summerlings, a stiff regimen of toil and exercise, Maia soon found herself hard-pressed to keep up.

At least the biting chill eased as the sun climbed. Off came the leather garments, and soon she was working in just loincloth and halter. The sluggish, heavy air left her coated with a perspiration sheen, but Maia preferred wiping sweat to having it freeze on her.

By the time she finally had a spare moment to look back, the headlands of Port Sanger's bay were disappearing behind a fog bank. The ancient fortress on the southern bluff, at present covered in a spindly shroud of repair scaffolding, was soon masked by brumous haze and lost to view. On the other bank, the spire of the sanctuary-lighthouse remained a mysterious gray obelisk for a while longer. Then it too faded behind low clouds, leaving an endless expanse of ice-flecked sea surrounding her contracted world of wood planks, fiber cords, and coal dust.

For what felt like hours, Maia ran wherever sailors pointed, loosening, hauling, and tying down sections of coarse rope on command. Her palms were soon raw and her shoulders sore, but she began learning a thing or two, such as not trying to brake a lanyard by simply holding on. Fighting a writhing cable by brute force could send you flying into a bulkhead or even overboard. Watching others, Maia learned to wrap a length of hawser around some nearby post in a reverse loop, and let the rope's own tension lock it in place.

That left the converse problem of *releasing* the damned thing, whenever the mates wanted slack for some reason. After Maia was nearly slashed across the face on two occasions, a sailor took time to show her how it was done.

"Y'do it like these, an' than these," a wiry male, no taller than she was, explained without obvious impatience. Maia awkwardly tried to imitate what in experienced hands seemed such a fluid motion. "Ye'll get it," he assured her, then hurried off, shouting to prevent another landlubber from getting her leg caught in a loop of cord and being dragged over the side.

Well, I was hoping for an education. Maia now understood why a noticeable minority of the men she'd seen in her life lacked a finger or two. If you weren't careful, a surge of wind could yank a rope while your hand was busy looping a pin, tightening with abrupt, savage force, sending a part of you spurting away. With that nauseating realization, Maia forced herself to slow down and think before making any sudden moves. The shouts of the bosuns were terrifying, but no more than that awful mental image.

Nothing was made easier by the film of carbon dust coating nearly every surface. The cargo of Bizmai anthracite sent black puffs through poorly sealed cargo hatches each time the Wotan shifted in the wind. Luckily, Maia didn't have to climb the grimy sheets, which crewmen scaled with such uncanny diligence, like apes born to dwell in treelike heights amid the wind.

Whenever duties sent her to the port side, she tried stealing glimpses of their sister vessel, the Zeus, keeping pace two hundred meters to the east. Once, Maia caught sight of a trim shape she felt must be Leie, but she dared not wave. That distant figure appeared plenty busy, running awkwardly about the other collier's deck.

At last they cleared the tricky coastal waters and the convoy's course was set. A north wind rose, filling the squat sails and, as a bonus, spinning the electric generator on the fantail, giving rise to a shrill whine. When the mates seemed satisfied that all was well in hand, they shouted fore and aft, calling a break.

Maia slumped amidships as her throbbing arms and legs complained. *Get used to it,* she told them. *Adventure is ninety percent pain and boredom.* The saying supposedly went on, "and ten percent stark, flaming terror." But she hoped to give that part a miss.

A crusty ladle appeared in front of her, proffered by a stick-thin old man with a sloshing bucket. Maia suddenly realized how ravenously thirsty she was. She put her mouth to the cup, slurping gratefully . . . and instantly gagged.

Seawater!

Maia felt eyes turn toward her as she coughed in embarrassment, trying to cover the reaction. She managed to clamp down and drink some more, recalling that she was just another vagrant summerling now, no longer the daughter of a rich, uptown clan with its own artesian well. In poorer sections of town, vars and even low-caste clones drew their drinking water from the sea and grew up knowing little else.

"Bless Stratos Mother, for her mild oceans," went a sardonic adage, not part of any liturgy. *And bless Lysos, for kidneys that can take it.* Thirst overcame the bland, salty taste and she finished the ladle without further trouble. The old man then surprised her with a gap-toothed grin, tousling her ragged-cut hair.

Maia stiffened defensively . . . then self-consciously relaxed. It took more than the passing heat of hard labor to trigger male rut. Anyway, a man would have to be hard up to waste time on a virgin like her.

Actually, the coot reminded her a little of old Bennett, back when that aged male's eyes still danced with interest in life. Hesitantly, she smiled back. The sailor laughed and moved on to water others in need.

A whistle blew, ending the work break, but at least now commands came at a slower pace. Instead of the former frenzy of reefing and unfurling sails, coaxing the sluggish vessel past frothy shoals toward open water, their new chores consisted of stowing and battening down. Now that she had a chance to look around, Maia was struck by how much *less* mysteriously alien the men of the crew appeared than she'd expected. Moving about their tasks, they seemed as businesslike and efficient as any clan craftswoman in her workshop or mill. Their laughter was rich and infectious as they bantered in a dialect she could follow, if she concentrated . . . although the drift of most of their jests escaped her.

Despite their dronelike behavior ashore, ranging from boisterous to slothful, depending on the season, Maia had always known men must lead lives of toil and danger at sea. Even the crew of this grimy lug must apply both intelligence and concentration—among the best womanly traits—as well as their renowned physical strength in order to survive. She was filled with questions about the tasks she saw performed with such industry, but that would have to await the right opportunity.

Besides, she found even more interesting the *women* on board. After all, men were another race—less predictable than lugars, though better swimmers and conversationalists. But whether summer- or winter-born, women were her kind.

At the elevated aft end of the ship, distinguished by their better clothes, stood or lounged the first-class passengers, who did not have to work. Few summerlings could afford full fare, even on ships like this one, so only clones leaned on the balcony, not far from the captain and his officers. Those winter folk came from poorer clans. She spotted a pair of Ortyns, three Bizmai, and several unfamiliar types, who must have come from towns further north before changing ships in Port Sanger.

The working passengers, on the other hand, were all vars like herself—uniques whose faces were as varied as clouds in the sky. They were an odd lot, mostly older than she was and tougher looking. For some, this must be one more leg of countless many as they worked their way around the seas of Stratos, always looking for some special place where a niche awaited.

Maia felt more sure than ever that she and Leie were correct to travel separately. These women might have resented twins, just as Captain Pegyul said. As it was, Maia felt conspicuous enough when the noon meal was served.

"Here you go, li'l virgie," said a gnarly, middle-aged woman with gray-streaked hair, as she poured stew from a kettle into a battered bowl. "Want a napkin too, sweetie?" She shared a grin with her companions. Of course the var was having Maia on. There were some greasy rags about, but the back of a wrist seemed the favored alternative.

"No, thank you," Maia answered, almost inaudibly. That only brought more hilarity, but what else could she say? Maia felt her face redden, and wished she was more like her Lamai mothers and half sisters, whose visages never betrayed emotion, save by careful calculation. As the women passed around a jug of wine, Maia took her plate of mysterious curry to a nearby corner and tried not to betray how self-conscious she felt.

No one's watching you, she tried convincing herself. *Of if they are, what of it? No one has any cause to go out of their way to dislike you.*

Then she overheard someone mutter, not too softly, ". . . bad enough breathin' this damn coal dust all th' way to Gremlin Town. Do I also gotta stand th' stink of a *Lamai brat* aboard?" Maia glanced up to catch a glower from a tough-looking var in her mid-eights or nines. The woman's fair hair and sharp-jawed features reminded Maia of the

Chuchyin clan, a rival of Lamatia based up-coast from Port Sanger. Was she a Chuchyin half or quarter sister, using an old grudge between their maternal houses as an excuse to start a private one of her own?

"Stay downwind from me, Lamai virgie," the var grunted when she caught Maia's gaze, and snorted in satisfaction when Maia looked away.

Bleeders! How far must I to go to escape Lamatia? Maia had none of the advantages of being her mother's child, only an inheritance of resentment toward a clan widely known for tenacious self-interest.

So intent was she on her plate that she jerked when someone nudged her arm. Blinking, Maia turned to meet a pair of pale green eyes, partly shaded under a dark blue bandanna. A small, deeply tanned, black-haired woman, wearing shorts and a quilted halter, held out the wine jug with a faint smile. As Maia reached for it, the var said in a low voice, "Relax. They do it to every fiver."

Maia gave a quick nod of thanks. She lifted the jug to her mouth . . .

. . . and doubled over, coughing. The stuff was awful! It stung her throat and she could not stop wheezing as she passed the bottle to the next var. This only brought more laughter, but now with a difference. It came tinged with an indulgent, rough-but-affectionate tone. *Each of them was five once, and they know it*, Maia realized. *I'll get through this too.*

Relaxing just a bit, she started listening to the conversation. The women compared notes on places each had been, and speculated what opportunities might lie to the south, with storm season over and commerce opening up again. Derisory comments about Port Sanger featured prominently. The image of a whole town called to arms because some clumsy reavers spilled a lantern had them in stitches. Maia couldn't help also grinning at the farcical picture. *It didn't seem funny to that dead woman,* a part of her recalled soberly. But then, hadn't somebody written that one essence of humor is the tragedy *you* managed to escape?

From hints here and there, Maia surmised that some of these vars had worn the red bandanna themselves. *Say you gather a pack of down-and-out summerlings, resentful at society's bottom rung, and sign a sisterly compact. Together, you hire a fast schooner . . . men willing to pilot their precious ship alongside some freighter, giving your band of comrades a narrow moment to dare all, win or lose.*

Savant Judeth had explained why it was grudgingly allowed.

"It would've happened anyway, sooner or later," the Lamai teacher once said. "By laying down rules, Lysos kept piracy from getting out of hand. Call it welfare for the desperate and lucky. A safety valve.

"And if reavers get too uppity?" There had been confident menace in Judeth's smile. "We have ways of dealing with that, too."

Maia never intended to find out what the great clans did, when provoked too far. At the same time, she pondered the sanitized legends told about the very first Lamai . . . the young var who, long ago, turned a small nest egg into a commercial empire for her clone descendants. Stories were vague about where the first mother got her stake. Perhaps a red bandanna lay somewhere in a bottom drawer of the clan's dustiest archive.

As expected, most of the vars aboard were working off passage while seeking permanent employment ashore. But a few actually seemed to consider themselves regular members of the Wotan's crew. Maia found it strange enough that women were able to interact with the planet's other sapient race to reproduce. Could women and men actually live and work together for long periods without driving each other crazy? While using a stiff brush to scrub the lunch dishes, she watched some of these "female sailors." *What do they talk to men about?* she wondered.

Talk they did, in a singsong dialect of the sea. Maia saw that the petite woman who had spoken kindly to her was one of these professional seawomen. In her gloved left hand, the brunette held a treppbill, a practice model bearing a cushioned Y-shaped yoke at one end and a padded hook at the other. From the way she joked with a pair of male comrades, it appeared she was offering a challenge which, grinning, they accepted.

One seaman opened a nearby storage locker, revealing a great stack of thin, tilelike objects, white on one side, black on the other. He removed one square wafer and turned it over, checking eight paddles set along its edges and corners. Maia recognized an old-fashioned, wind-up game piece, which sailors used in large numbers to pursue a favorite pastime known as Life. Since infancy, she had watched countless contests in dockside arenas. The paddles sensed the status of neighboring tiles during a game, so that each piece would "know" whether to show its white or its black face at a given time. By the nature of the game, a single token by itself was useless, so what was the man doing, inserting a key and winding up just one clockwork tile?

If programmed normally, the simple device would smoothly flip a row of louvered panels exposing its white surface unless certain conditions were met. Three of its paddles must sense neighboring objects within a certain time interval. Two, four, or even eight touches wouldn't do. Exactly three paddles must be triggered for it to remain still.

The burly sailor approached the small woman, laying the game token on the deck in front of her, black side up. With one foot resting lightly on its upper surface he kept it from activating until, gripping her treppbill in both hands, she nodded, signaling *ready*.

The sailor hopped back and the tile started clicking. At the count of eight, the woman suddenly lanced out, tapping the piece at three spots in rapid succession. A beat passed and the disk remained still. Then the eight-beat countdown repeated, only *faster*. She duplicated her feat, choosing a different trio of paddles, making it seem as easy as swatting zizzers. But the piece had been programmed to increase its tempo. Soon the tip of her treppbill moved in a blur and the clock-ticking was a staccato ratchet. Sweat popped out on the small woman's brow as her wooden pole danced quicker and quicker . . .

Abruptly, the disk louvers flashed with a loud *clack!* turning the upper surface white. "Agh!" she cried out. "Twenty-eight!" a sailor shouted, and the woman laughed in chagrin as her comrades teased her for falling far short of her record.

"Too much booze an' lazin' about on shore!" they chided.

"*You* should talk!" she retorted, "jutzin' with them Bizzie hoors!"

One of the men started rewinding the game piece for another try, but Wotan's second mate chose that moment to descend from the quarterdeck and call the small brunette over for a talk. They spoke for a few minutes, then the officer turned to go. The woman sailor fished a whistle out of her halter and blew a shrill blast that got the attention of all hands.

"Second-class passengers aft," she called in an even tone, motioning for Maia and the other vars to stand in a row by the starboard gunwales.

"My name is Naroin," the petite sailor told the assembled group. "Rank is bosun, same as Sailor Jum and Sailor Rett, so don't forget it. I'm also master-at-arms on this tub."

Maia had no trouble believing the statement. The woman's legs bore scars of combat, her nose had been broken at least twice, and her muscles, if not manlike, were imposing.

"I'm sure you all saw last night that the rumors we been hearin' are true. There's reaver activity farther north than ever this year, an' it's startin' earlier. We could be a target anytime."

Maia found that a stretched conclusion to reach from one isolated incident, and apparently so did the other vars. But Naroin took her responsibilities seriously. She told them so, laying the padded bill across her back.

"Captain's given orders. We should be ready, in case o' trouble. We're not goin' to be anybody's sealfish steak. If a gang o' jumped-up unniks tries hopping this ship—"

"Why would anyone want it!" a var muttered, eliciting chuckles. It was the sharp-jawed woman who had cursed earlier about "Lamai brats."

"What kind of atyp bleeders'd hop us for a load o' *coal?*" the half-Chuchyin went on.

"You'd be surprised. The market's up. B'sides, even a coerced split of profits could ruin the owners—"

Naroin's explanation was interrupted by an offensive blat, imitating a fart. When the bosun glanced sharply, the Chuchyin var nonchalantly yawned. Naroin frowned. "Captains' orders needn't be explained to likes of you. A crew that doesn't drill together—"

"Who needs drill?" The tall var cracked her knuckles, nudging her friends, apparently a tight-knit group of tested traveling companions. "Why fret about lugar-lovin' reavers? If they come, we'll send them packin' for their daddies."

Maia felt her cheeks redden, and hoped no one noticed. The master-at-arms simply smiled. "All right, grab a bill an' show me how you'll fight, *if* the time comes."

A snort. The Chuchyin variant spat on the deck. "I'll just watch, if it's all the same."

Naroin's forearms revealed bowstring tendons. "Listen, summer-trash. While on board, you'll take orders, or swim back where you came from!"

The tall woman and her comrades glared back, confrontation certain in their hard faces.

A low voice interrupted from behind. "Is there a problem, Master-at-Arms?"

Naroin and the vars swiveled. Captain Pegyul stood at the edge of the quarterdeck, scratching a four-day growth of beard. Banal of appearance back at the Bizmai tavern, he now cut an impressive figure, stripped down to his blue undershirt, something males never did in port. Three brass armrings, insignia of rank, circuited an arm like Maia's thigh. Two other crewmen, taller and even broader in the shoulders, stood bare-chested behind him at the head of the stairs. Despite the redolent tension, Maia found herself fascinated by those torsos. For once, she could credit certain farfetched stories . . . that sometimes, in the heat of summer, a particularly large and crazy male might purposely torment a lugar into one of those rare but awesome furies the beasts were capable of, just to wrestle the creature one-on-one, and occasionally win!

"No, sir. There's no problem," Naroin answered calmly. "I was just explaining that all second-class passengers will train to defend the ship's cargo."

The captain nodded. "You have your crewmates' backing, Master-at-Arms," he said mildly, and walked away.

The shiver down Maia's back wasn't from the north wind. Generally speaking, men were supposedly as harmless, four-fifths of the year, as lugars were all the time. But they were sentient beings, capable of *deciding* to get angry, even in winter. The two big seamen remained, observing. Maia sensed in their eyes a wariness toward any threat to their ship, their world.

The Chuchyin made a show of examining her fingernails, but Maia saw perspiration on her brow. "Guess I could spar a bit," the tall var muttered. "For practice." Still feigning nonchalance, she stepped over to the weapons rack. Instead of taking up the other padded training bill, she grabbed a trepp meant for combat, made of hard Yarri wood with minimal wrapping round the hook and prong.

From the rigging, two of the women crew gasped, but Naroin only backed onto the broad, flat door covering the aft hold, scuffing a film of coal dust with her bare feet. The tall var followed, leaving tracks with her sandals. She did not bow. Nor did the short sailor as they began circling.

Maia glanced toward the two shirtless seamen, who now sat watching, all wrath gone from their docile eyes. Once more, she felt a half-excited, half-nauseated curiosity about sex. Her ignorance was normal. Few clans let summer daughters enter their Halls of Joy, where the dance of negotiation, approach, refusal, and acceptance between sailor and mother-to-be reached its varied consummations, depending on the season. Among the ambitions she shared with Leie was to build a hall of their own, where she might yet learn what delights were possible—unlikely as it seemed—in mingling her body with one such as those, so hirsute and huge. Just trying to imagine made her head hurt in strange ways.

The two women finished their preliminary swings, waving and thrusting their bills. Naroin seemed in no hurry to take the offensive, perhaps because of her padded, ill-balanced weapon. The Chuchyin var spun her chosen trepp in one hand with panache. Suddenly she leapt forward to sweep at her opponent's well-scarred legs—

—and abruptly found those legs wrapped around her throat! Naroin hadn't awaited the traditional exchange of feints and parries, but instead rammed her awkward bill onto the deck, using it as a pole to vault over her foe's slashing weapon, landing with one leg across each of the other woman's shoulders. The var staggered, dropped her trepp, and tried to claw at the master-at-arms, but found her hands seized with wiry strength. Her knees buckled and her face started to color between the woman sailor's tightening thighs.

Maia breathed at last as Naroin jumped back, letting her opponent collapse to the sooty hatch. The dark-haired sailor grabbed the Yarri-wood weapon dropped by her foe and used its Y-shaped yoke to pin the var's neck to the cargo door. Naroin was barely breathing hard.

"Now what'd you expect, comin' at me that way? Bare wood against padding? No courtesy, then choppin' a cripple blow? Try that against reavers and they'll do more'n take our cargo or sell you for a season's labor. They'll sea-dump you an' any other wench who cheats. And our men won't lift a finger, hear? *Eia!*"

The female crew shouted in refrain. "Eia!" Naroin tossed the bill aside. Wheezing, the half-Chuchyin crawled off the makeshift arena, covered with black smears. A glance at the quarterdeck showed that the men had departed, but assorted clones watched from first class, wearing amused expressions.

"Next?" Naroin asked, looking down the file of vars, no longer appearing quite so small.

I know what Leie would do now, Maia thought. *She'd wait for others to wear Naroin down, pick out some weakness, then go at it with all panels charged.*

But Maia wasn't her sister. Back in school she might watch a dozen bouts without recalling who had won, let alone who parried when for points. While her churning guts wanted to find some dim shadow, her rational mind said, *Just get it over with.* Anyway, if Naroin was trying to encourage proper womanly combat virtues, Maia could offer a good contrast to the Chuchyin, and surprise those who called her "virgie."

Fighting a queasy tremor, she stepped forward, silently drew the other padded training bill from the rack and faced the arena. She ignored the staring clones and vars, ritually scuffed the dust thrice, and bowed. Bearing her own cushioned weapon, Naroin beamed beneficence toward Maia's courtesy. Both of them extended their bills, hook end forward, for that first, formal tap . . .

Someone splashed water in her face. Maia coughed and sputtered. It stung not only of salt but of coal. A blur slowly resolved into a face . . . an old man's . . . the one who earlier had tousled her hair, she dimly recalled.

"Here, now. Y'all hokay? Nothin' broke, i'zer?"

He spoke a thick mannish dialect. But Maia got the drift. "I . . . don't think so . . ." She started to rise, but a sharp pain lanced through her left leg, below the knee. A bloody cut went halfway around the calf. Maia hissed.

"Mm. Ah see yet. S'not so bid. Here's sum salve that'll seer a beet."

Maia felt a whimper rise in her gorge and stifled it as he applied medicine from an earthenware jar. The agony departed in waves like an outgoing tide. Her throbbing pulse settled. When she next looked, the bleeding had stopped.

"That's . . . good stuff," she sighed.

"Our guild maybe small 'n' poorly, bit we got smart tube-boys beck in sanctuary."

"Mm, I'll bet." Between shipping seasons, some men dealt with extra time on their hands by fiddling in laboratories, either as guests in clanholds or at their own craggy hermitages. Few of the bearded tinkerers had much formal education, and most of their inventions were at best one-season marvels. A fraction reached the attention of the savants of Caria, to eventually be published or banned. This salve, though—Maia vowed to get a sample and find out if anyoné yet had the marketing rights.

She rose up on her elbows and looked around. Two pairs of second-class passengers were out on the hatch cover, sparring under shouted direction from the master-at-arms. Several others lay sprawled like she was, nursing bruises. Meanwhile, two female crew members sat by the forward cowling, one blowing a flute while the other sang in a low, sad alto voice.

The old man tsked. "Really pushin' this yar. Fool'sh, runnin' fems too ragged t'work. Not roit, boy my lights."

"I s'pose," Maia murmured noncommittally. She rose to sitting position and then, grabbing a nearby rail, managed to hobble onto one leg. She was still woozy, and yet felt vaguely relieved. Real pain was seldom as bad as the expectation.

Funny, hadn't Mother Claire once said that about *childbirth*? Maia shivered.

One of the practicing vars shouted and landed on the hatch with a loud thump. The women playing music switched to an ancient, plaintive melody that Maia recognized—about a wanderer, yearning for a home, a beloved, all of the hearth-joys that came so easily to some, but not others.

Resting against the gunnels, Maia gazed across the seascape and found the *Zeus* keeping pace a bit behind, plowing through choppy waves with billowed sails. So far, this voyage had been at least as much a learning experience as her sister promised.

I do hope Leie's finding her trip just as interesting, came Maia's biting thought.

Two weeks later, on hitting their first landing in Queg Town, the twins finally set eyes on each other after their longest separation, and their reactions were identical. Each looked the other up and down . . . and simultaneously broke up laughing.

On the lower part of Leie's right leg, in a spot perfectly mirroring her own left, Maia saw a strip of new, pink scar tissue, healing neatly under the benign influence of sun, air, hard work, and saltwater.

P roblem number one—lacking natural controls, our human descendants will tend to overbreed until Stratos can no longer support their numbers. Shall we then have come all this way to repeat the catastrophe of Earth?

One lesson we've learned—any effort to limit population cannot rest on persuasion alone. Times change. Passions change, and even the highest flown moralizing eventually palls in the face of natural instinct.

We could do it genetically, limiting each woman to just two births. But variants who break the programming will outbreed all others, soon putting us back where we started. Anyway, our descendants may at times *need* rapid reproduction. We mustn't limit them to a narrow way of life.

Our chief hope lies in finding ways of permanently tying self-interest to the common good.

The same holds for our other problem, which provoked this coalition to drop half-measures, leaving the Phylum's bland compromisers behind. The problem which drove us to this faraway world, seeking a lasting solution.

The problem of sex.

—*from* The Apologia, *by Lysos*

3

L anargh, their second port of call, was not counted among the chief cities of the world. Not in a league with those rimming the coast of Landing Continent. Still, the metropolis was big enough to give the twins pause after weeks evading icebergs on the high seas.

In Queg Town, the owners had found few buyers for Port Sanger coal. So the Zeus and Wotan wallowed with waves lapping high along their dented flanks. Whenever lookouts spotted floating isles of ice, auxiliary motors strained to alter course and miss the terrible white growlers. The wind was a fickle ally. Bosuns shouted and all hands heaved at balky sails. One jagged berg passed chillingly near *Wotan*'s starboard withers—leaving Maia dry-mouthed and grateful they were convoying. In case of a mischance, only the Zeus was close enough to save them.

When they next neared shore, the former monotony of tundra had been replaced by stands of fog-shrouded conifers, giant redwoods whose ancestors had come to Stratos along with Maia's, tortuously, from Old Earth. The terran trees liked the misty coast, encouraged by forestry clans in their slow, silent struggle with native scrub. Sinuous trails showed where harvesters had recently dragged cut logs, to be herded in great rafts to market.

Maia's breath came short and quick as the Wotan finally rounded Point Defiance, where a famed stone dragon lay shadows of its broad wings over the harbor strait, symbolizing the protective love of Stratos

Mother. Carved long ago, it honored the repulse, at great cost, of a landing force sent down by the Enemy foeship, during dark, ancient days when women and men together fought to save the colony, their lives, and posterity. Maia knew little about that bygone era—history wasn't deemed a practical curriculum—but the statue was a stirring sight nonetheless.

Lanargh's famous five hills then appeared, one after another, lined with pale stone tiers, clanholds, and gardens, stretching for kilometers along the bay and into green-flanked mountainsides. The twins had always pictured Port Sanger as large and cosmopolitan, since its trade dominated much of the Parthenia Sea. But here, at the pivot of a vast ocean, Maia saw why Lanargh was properly called "Gateway to the East."

After tying at the quay assigned them by the harbor mistress, the crew watched the captain set off with the Bizmai cargo-owners to meet potential clients. Then liberty was called and the hands themselves spilled ashore, shouting with pleasure. Maia found Leie waiting at the foot of the wharf. "Beat ya again!" Maia's twin laughed, eking out another minor victory, knowing Maia didn't give a damn.

"Come on," Maia answered, grinning. "Let's get a look at this place."

More than five hundred matriarchal clans dwelled in the city, filling broad piazzas and clamoring market avenues with contingents of finely dressed, elaborately coiffed, magnificently uniformed clones, their burdens carried on well-oiled carts or the backs of patient lugars in liveried tunics. There were sumptuous scents of strange fruits and spices, and creatures the twins had only read about, such as red howler monkeys and flapping *mere*-dragons, which rode upon their owners' shoulders, hissing at passersby and snatching grapes from unwary vendors.

The sisters roamed plazas and narrow shopping streets, eating sweets from a pâtissière's stall, laughing at the antics of a small clan of agile jugglers, dodging the harangues of political candidates, and pondering the strangeness of such a wide, marvelous world. Never before had Maia seen so many faces she didn't recognize. Though Port Sanger held a population of several thousand, there had never been more than a hundred distinct visages to know while growing up.

For the first time, they tasted what life might be like if their secret scheme succeeded. Although they were humbly dressed, some vars they encountered stepped aside for them in automatic deference, as if they were winter-born. "I knew it!" Leie whispered. "Twins are rare enough that people simply jump to the wrong conclusion. Our plan can work!"

Maia appreciated Leie's enthusiasm. Yet, she knew success would count on filling in countless details. They shouldn't spend their free moments playing games, she insisted, but combing the port for useful information.

Unfortunately, the town was a babble of strange tongues. Whenever clone-sisters met on the street, they often spoke an incomprehensible rasp of family code, handed down by hive mothers and embellished by their daughters for generations. This frustrated Leie at first. Back in easy-going Port Sanger, common speech had been the norm.

Then Leie grew enthusiastic. "We'll need a secret jarg too, when we start our own clan."

Maia neglected to remind her sister that as little girls they *had* experimented with codes, cryptograms, and private jargon, until Leie grew bored and quit. Privately, Maia had never stopped making anagrams or finding patterns in letter blocks scattered on the crèche floor. It might even have been what first triggered her interest in constellations, for to her the sparkling stellar patterns always seemed to hint at the Creator's private code, one that was open to all who learned to see.

Strolling the grand plaza in front of Lanargh's city temple, the twins watched a group of kneeling sailors receive blessing from an orthodox priestess wrapped in burgundy-striped robes. Raising her arms, the clergywoman called for intercession from the planet spirit, its rocks and air, its winds and waters, so that the men might reach safe haven at their journey's end. The singsong benison finished with a favorite passage about the sanctity of comradeship amid shared danger. Yet, the holy woman's quavering delivery showed that clerics, too, had a "language" all their own, especially when quoting the mysterious Fourth Book of Scriptures.

"Soto their ships ontime ofneed kaul uponthat whichishidden . . ."

No wonder Book Four was popularly known as the Riddle of Lysos. It even had its own eighteen-letter alphabet, which used to bring Maia pleasurable diversion during long weekly services in the Lamatia chapel, silently puzzling over cryptic passages incised on the stone walls.

Leie glanced at the clock set in the Temple's face and sighed. "Oops, sorry. Gotta get back to work now."

Maia blinked. "What? On first day?"

"Ain't it var's luck? Mop an' pail duty. Our chief wants ol' *Zeus* to get more customers than Wotan, even though it all goes to the same owners and guild." She grimaced. "Are your bosuns as awful as ours?"

Maia wouldn't have used that word. "Hard," maybe, and quick to catch when you were inattentive. But she was learning a lot from Naroin and the others, and growing stronger by the day. Anyway, Leie was clearly fibbing. Maia bet her sister was on punishment detail, probably for mouthing off when she should have kept quiet.

Despite that, Maia grunted sympathetically. "Unloading coal for a living. Huh. I guess the mothers'd be proud of us for starting at the bottom."

"Not for long, though!" Leie answered. "Someday we'll sail back into Port Sanger with enough coin sticks to buy the place!" She laughed, and her cheerfulness forced Maia to smile.

It felt different walking through town alone, and not simply because no one stepped aside for her anymore. Maia had enjoyed pointing things out to Leie, sharing the sights. It had been comforting knowing another person in this sea of strangers was an ally.

On the other hand, the town seemed more *vivid* this way. Sound and smell and vision felt sharper as she grew more aware of the downside of city life. Sweating var laborers, dragging loads on creaking carts. Beggars, some crippled, shaking tithe cups bearing wax temple seals. Sly-looking women who leaned against the corners of buildings, eyeing her speculatively, perhaps wondering how well her purse was tied on. . . .

It was right for us to take separate ships, Maia thought, feeling both wary and alive. *We needed this. I needed it.*

There were placards she had never seen before, denoting clans she didn't know, offering goods she had never heard of. Some shop floors were shared by a dozen midget enterprises, each with a pretentious, hand-painted heraldic device, run by single women pooling together for the rent, each hoping to begin the slow rise to success. At the other extreme, the city hospital seemed both modern and colorless, the white-jacketed professionals within having no need to advertise their family affiliations.

A blatting sound, a horn and crashing cymbals, caused the street crowd to divide for a new disturbance. Onlookers laughed as a short parade wound its way downhill. The male membership of a secret society, dressed in flamboyant outfits and carrying mystery totems, wove across the cobblestones to applause and good-natured catcalls from the throng. Some of the men seemed sheepish, lugging ornate model ships and wooden zep'lins on their shoulders to the beat of thumping drums, while others held their chins out, as if daring anyone to make fun of their earnest ritual. Only a few spectators seemed unfriendly, such as when one cluster of frowning women pointedly refused to step aside, forcing the procession to wind around them.

Perkinites, Maia thought, moving on. *Why don't they leave the poor men alone and pick on someone their own size?*

Lanargh offered a wider range of services than she had ever imagined, from palmists and professed witches all the way to esteemed phrenologists, equipped with calipers, cranial tapes, and ornate charts. Maia considered having a reading done, till she saw the prices and decided nothing could be done about the shape of her head, anyway.

Glancing through one expensive glass window, Maia watched three high-browed redheads consult with customers over leather-bound folders. Perusing gilt posters, Maia gleaned that this was a local branch of a farflung family enterprise, one offering commercial message services. On a separate chart, the redheads advertized a local sideline—designing private languages for up-and-coming houses.

"Now there's a niche," Maia murmured admiringly. Success on Stratos often lay in finding some product or service no one else had mastered. This was one she might have enjoyed exploring herself. She sighed. "Too bad it already seems pretty well filled."

"They're all filled, sister. Don't you know? It's one of the foretold signs."

Maia spun around to face a young woman about her own age and height, wearing a cowled robe with the embroidered stripes of some religious order. The priestess, or dedicant, clutched a sheaf of yellow pamphlets, peering at Maia through thick spectacles.

"Um . . . signs of what, sister?" Maia asked, overcoming surprise.

A friendly, if fervent, smile. "That we are entering a Time of Changes. Surely you've noticed, a bright fiver like yourself, that things are on edge? Clan matrons have long complained about the climbing summer birthrate, but do they act to stop it? A force within Stratos Herself wills that it be so, despite all inconvenient consequences."

Maia overcame her accustomed reaction to being accosted by a clergywoman—an impulse to seek the nearest exit. "Mm . . . inconvenient?"

"To the great houses. To the bureaucracy in Caria. And especially to those selfsame hordes of summerlings, for whom there's no place on this planet. No place save one."

Aha! Maia thought. *Is this a recruitment drive?* The priesthood was even less selective than the Port Sanger city guard. By taking vows, any var might guarantee a full meal bowl for the rest of her days. If it also meant forsaking childbearing, or ever establishing a clan of one's own, how many summerlings achieved that anyway? Abjuring sex someday, with a sweaty man, was no decision-stopper. All Stratos was your lover when you took the robe, and all Stratoins your children.

Still, why go recruiting? In Lanargh, a stone thrown in any direction would pass over some priestess or deacon. More were choosing that route to safety every day.

"Meanin' no disrespect," Maia said, backing away. "I don't think the Temple is my place."

The priestess seemed undismayed. "My child, that's obvious from the look of you."

"But . . . then what . . . ?" Maia suddenly found her hand filled with a printed broadsheet. She glanced down at the first few lines.

The Outsiders—
Danger or Challenge?

Sisters in Stratos! It should be obvious by now that the sages and councilwomen of Caria are concealing the truth about the spaceship in our skies, said to contain emissaries from the Hominid Phylum, which our ancestors left so long ago. Why have they told the public so little? The savants and officials make excuses, talking about "linguistic drift" and careful "quarantine procedures," but it is growing apparent to even the lowliest that our great ones, sitting on lofty seats within the Council, Temple and University, are in their deepest hearts cowards. . . .

It was hard to follow the run-on screed, but a tone of antagonism to authority was stridently clear. Maia looked again at the dedicant, seeing that the stripes of her robe were broken with colored threads. "You're a heretic," she breathed.

"Smart lass. Not many where you're from?"

Maia found herself smiling faintly. "We're a bit out of the way. We had Perkinites—"

"*Everyone* has Perkinites. Specially since the Outsider Ship gave 'em an excuse to spread boogie-man stories. You know the ones. . . . Now that Stratos is rediscovered, the Phylum will send fleets of ships full of drooling, hairy, unmodified males, worse than the Enemy of old."

"Well"—Maia grinned at the image—"that may exaggerate what they say."

"And your local Perkies may be milder than ours, O virgin from the frozen north!" The heretic laughed sardonically. "At any rate, even the temple hierarchy's in a lather over alien humans barging in, possibly changing Stratos forever. It never seems to occur to the silly smugs that it might be *the other way around*. That this may be the moment Lysos was planning for, from the very start!"

Maia was confused. "You don't see the starship as a threat?"

"Not my order, the Sisters of Venture. In early days, restored contact might've been harmful. But now our way of life is proven. Sure, we have problems, injustices, but have you read about the way things were back on the Old Worlds, before our founders' exodus?"

Maia nodded. It was favored fare in books and on the tele.

"Animal chaos!" The woman waxed passionate. "Picture how violent and uncertain life was, especially for women and children. Now realize, *it's probably still going on out there!* That is, on whatever worlds haven't been destroyed, by the Enemy, or by aggression among male humans."

"But the Outsider proves some colonies still—"

"Exactly! There may be dozens of surviving, battered worlds, crying out for what *we* can offer—salvation."

Maia had backed away until a gritty wall jabbed her spine. Yet she felt torn between flight and fascination. "You think we should welcome contact . . . and send *missionaries?*"

The dedicant, who had been hunching forward in pursuit, now stood straighter and smiled. "I was right about you being a sharpie. Which brings up my original comment about there being a reason for everything, including the surge in summer births, even though niches seem so few." She raised one finger. "Few here on Stratos! But not out *there.*" The finger jabbed skyward. "Destiny calls, and only timid fools in Caria stand in the way!"

Maia saw fervor in the young woman's eyes, a belief transcending logic and all obstacles. *Suppose you find yourself insignificant in the world, dwarfed by the mighty. How to feel important after all? All you need is a convenient conspiracy. One that's keeping you from taking your rightful place as a leader toward the light.*

Only there are so many lights. . . .

Maia withheld judgment on the Venturist's actual idea, which had a grand sound, and might even be worth discussing. "I'll give it a read," she promised, holding up the pamphlet. "But . . ."

Her voice trailed off. The priestess was staring past her shoulder. In a distracted tone, the young dedicant said, "Very good. But now I must go. To the stars, sister."

"Eia, sister," Maia replied conventionally to the unusual farewell, watching the striped robe vanish into the crowd. She turned to see what had spooked the heretic, and soon caught sight of four sturdy women pushing through the throng, nonchalantly swinging walking sticks they didn't seem to need . . . not for walking, at least.

Temple wardens, Maia realized. There were priestesses and then there were priestesses. Although heresy was officially no crime, the temple hierarchy had ways of making it less comfortable than following classical dogma. Of the fringe groups, only Perkinism was strong enough that no one dared rough up its adherents.

Oh, I guess there are still niches, Maia thought, watching the stern women move along, causing even members of the city watch to step aside. *Vars with muscle can always find employment in this world.*

Which suddenly reminded her, she was due back at the Wotan before dusk. Kitchen duty. And there'd be patarkal hell to pay if she was late!

Maia stuffed the heretical tract into a pocket, to show Leie later. Giving the Temple warders a wide berth, she found her bearings and hurried through the market crowd toward the unmistakable aroma of the docks.

"Work now, gawk later!" Bosun Naroin snapped, late on their fourth day in port.

Maia's attention had wandered toward a distracting sight at the foot of the wharf. Drawing back quickly, she nodded—"Yessir"—and concentrated on resetting the conveyor belt, making sure that buckets hauling coal out of the ship's hold did not jitter or spill. Sometimes it took muscle to lever the balky contraption into line. Even after all seemed in perfect order, Maia watched the buckets warily for a while to be sure. Finally, she lifted her head above the portside rail once more.

What had drawn her gaze before was the arrival of a car, cruising with a methane-driven purr down the bayside embankment, toward the pier where Wotan was moored.

A car, she thought. For personal transport and nothing else. There had been two in all of Port Sanger—used on ceremonial occasions or to carry visiting dignitaries. Other motor vehicles had been nearly as rare, since most products entered and left her hometown by sea. In cosmopolitan Lanargh, one might glimpse a motor-lorry down any street, each employing a driver, several loaders, and a guardian who walked in front bearing a red flag, making sure no children fell beneath the rumbling wheels. They were impressive machines, even if their growling, chuffing rumble frightened Maia a little.

For several days, one battered, ugly high-bed had been coming to the pier to fill its hopper with coal from the Parthenia Sea. The unloading crew grew to hate the sight of the thing. *But hey, it's a job,* Maia thought as the truck's bin filled with Port Sanger anthracite, bound for a family-run petrochemical plant for conversion to molten plastic, then used by certain other Lanargh clans for making fine injection-moldings.

Her gaze drifted once more to the foot of the wharf. The car had parked, but no one had yet emerged. Curious.

She turned back to make sure the returning, empty buckets weren't clipping Wotan's cargo hatch. If the conveyor jammed, the sweating team below would blame her. "Hold!" Maia cried when the clearance narrowed thinner than she liked. Naroin echoed with a shout. While the saw-toothed buckets rumbled to a halt, Maia kicked free a pair of chocks and set a pry bar under the conveyor's frame, straining to jigger the massive apparatus several times until the new arrangement seemed right. Finally, she bent to pound the chocks back into place, then called, "Ready away!" Naroin threw a lever and precious electricity poured from the ship's accumulators, setting the scarred machinery into motion with a rumble of grinding gears.

It was hard work, but Maia felt grateful to be out on deck. Her stints below, shoveling coal into the ever-hungry buckets, had been like sentences to hell. Floating grit stuck to your perspiration, running down your arms and sides in sooty rivulets. It got into everything, including your mouth and underwear. Finally, like the others, she had stripped completely.

Nor could she complain, for this crew was luckier than most. Half the ships in port used *human-powered* winches to unload, or doubled-over stevedores, groaning as they dumped gunnysacks onto horse-drawn wagons. Even those freighters equipped with electric or steam-driven gear used it sparingly, relying mostly on muscle power.

"Savin' wear and tear on the machinery," Naroin had explained. "Some seasons, var labor's cheaper'n replacement parts." This year, it seemed especially so.

Not that summer women worked alone. Clones supervised unloading delicate merchandise, and men appeared whenever their specialized skills were needed. Still, the sailors mostly spent time caring for their precious ships, and no one expected different. What men and vars had in common was that both had fathers—though seldom knew their names. Both were lowlife in the eyes of haughty clones. Beyond that, all resemblance dimmed.

Everything seemed to be running smoothly, so Maia returned to the portside rail, fleeing the dust. Rubbing the back of her neck, she turned and saw that someone had left the motorcar at the base of the pier, and was walking this way. A man, dressed in foppish lace and wearing a wide-brim hat, sauntered toward the Zeus and Wotan, dodging the black plume wafting from the truck bed. Whistling, the male paused to inspect the paint flaking from the Wotan's aft. He buffed his shoes, then squinted at the sky. *So that's what a person looks like when they're trying not to look suspicious,* Maia observed with amusement. This character was no sailor, nor did he look like the type to be kept waiting.

Sure enough, three crewmen appeared, one from her own ship and two from Leie's, hurrying down the gangways with exaggerated noncha-

lance. The stranger, with a courteous flourish, led the sailors behind the
girth of the motortruck, where bucket after bucket of black hydrocarbons
showered into an already-creaking loading bin.

Now what are they doing back there? Maia wondered as they remained hidden from sight. *As if it's any of my business.*

An echoing cry from the ship's hold sent her scurrying to adjust the
conveyor again, prying away at the apparatus so that the buckets flowed
smoothly to reach the coal hillocks below. No sooner had she finished
jiggering the inboard end than a shout from the woman lorry driver told
Maia that the *other* boom needed one last shift to fill the cargo bed
properly. Kicking away the forward chocks, Maia looked forward to diving with a whoop over the side just as soon as the loading run was over.
Even the scummy dockside water seemed fantastically inviting at this
point.

The final chock stayed stuck. With a sigh, she crawled underneath
the conveyer to pound it with the heel of her hand, already bruised and
sore. "Come on, you stupid, atyp chunk!" she cursed the tightly wedged
block. Her hand throbbed. "Move! You lugar-made piece of homlog—"

A sharp, nipping pain in an alarming quarter caused Maia to jump,
slamming her head against a bucket, which responded with a low,
throaty gong.

"Ow! What the tark'l hell—?"

Emerging, rubbing her head with one hand and left buttock with the
other, Maia blinked in confusion at three sailors who stood grinning, just
beyond arm's reach. She recognized the off-duty crewmen who had
seemed so ineptly casual with the stylish male from town. Two smirked,
while the third let out a high-pitched giggle.

"Did . . ." Maia almost couldn't bring herself to ask. "Did one of
you *pinch* me?"

The nearest, tall and rangy with several days' beard, laughed again.
"An there's more where'n that come from, if yer want it."

Maia tilted her head, quite sure she'd misheard. "Why would I want
more pain than I've already got?"

The giggler, who was short but barrel-chested, tittered again. "Only
hurts at first, sweets . . . then ye ferget all that!"

"Ferget ever'thing but feeling good!" the first one added, to Maia's
growing confusion and irritation. The third man, of average height, with a
dark complexion, nudged his companions. "Come on. You can whiff she's
just a virgie. Let's go clean up an' head for Bell House."

There was an eager wildness in the small one's eyes. "How 'bout it,
li'l var? We'll fetch yer sister off'n our ship. Dress you both fancy. It'll
look like some pretty little clan, holdin' a frost party for us. Like that
idea? Your own little Hall o' Happiness, right on board!"

He was so close, Maia caught a strange, off-sweet odor, and glimpsed a powdery stain at one corner of his mouth. More importantly, she now recognized, in stance and manner, several signs taught to girls at an early age. His eyes stroked her body closer than the clinging dust. Breathing heavily, his grin exposed teeth glistening with saliva.

There was no mistaking these omens of male rut.

But it wasn't summer anymore! All the myriad cues that set off aurora season in males were months gone. Oh, surely some men retained libido through autumn, but to make blatant advances . . . on a *var*? One covered head to toe in grime, yet? One without a hint of fecundity-scents from past births?

It was incredible. Maia hadn't a clue how to react.

"Button an' jet," a stern voice cut in.

The lanky sailor kept leering, but the other two stepped back for Wotan's master-at-arms. "Uh, bosun"—the darker man nodded—"We're off duty, so we were just—"

"Just leaving, so my work party can go off-duty too, was that it?" Naroin asked, fists on hips, forming the words sweetly, but with an edge that cut.

"Uh huh. Come on, Eth. Eth!" The dark sailor grabbed the one ogling Maia, breaking his unnerving stare and dragging him off. Only then did Maia start controlling her own adrenaline surge. Her mouth felt dry from more than coal dust. The pounding in her chest slowly abated.

"What," she inquired of Naroin, "was *that* all about?"

The master-at-arms watched the three sailors walk away, their footsteps neither uneven nor intoxicated. Rather, there was a prowling, even *graceful* menace to the way they departed. Naroin glanced at Maia.

"Don't ask me."

Without another word, she got down and crawled under the conveyor to pound at the recalcitrant chock, giving Maia a few moments more to recover. It was a kindness, yet something had not escaped Maia's notice. Naroin's answer implied ignorance. That was what the phrase usually meant. *"Don't ask me."*

But the tone hadn't conveyed ignorance. No, it had been an order, pure and simple.

Maia's curiosity flared.

Leie waxed enthusiastic as the sisters strolled the market quarter before dusk, munching fish pies, listening to the cacophonous street-jabber, speculating what deals, intrigues, and treachery must be going on all around them. "This detour could be the best thing to happen to us!" Leie announced. "When we finally do reach the archipelago, we'll know much more about commercial prospects. I was thinking . . . maybe next summer we should get work in one of these plastics factories. . . ."

Maia let her twin rattle on, feeling pensive, restive. This afternoon's incident had left her sensitized. The heretic's crumpled pamphlet lay unforgotten in her pocket, a reminder that the fervid activity on all sides might not be "normal," even for a big-city port.

Now that Maia looked for them, she saw signs everywhere of an economy under strain. Near the city hall, bulletin boards showed basic labor, even skilled crafts, going for record low wages. Long-term contracts were nonexistent, and the sole civil-service post on offer was in the city guard. *Just like back home,* Maia thought. *Only more so.*

Then there were the men, more than she had ever seen before. And not just playing endless Game of Life tournaments on quayside grids, or whittling to pass the time between voyages, but moving briskly, intently, quite some distance inland. Look down any crowded street and you'd catch sight of two or three, standing out amid the crowds of women. Again, all the shipping *might* explain it. Except why were such a high percentage of them so young?

In nature, just being male was enough to lower an animal's life expectancy, and it was no different among humans on Stratos. Storms and shifting reefs, icebergs and equipment failures, sent ships down every year. Few men lived to become retirees. Still, there seemed so *many* young ones on the streets. It made her nervous.

While most sailors were well-behaved, strolling, shopping, or drinking quietly at taverns set aside for their kind, each day had its whispered tales of incidents like one overheard last night—concerning a bloody corpse found in an alley, the killer fleeing wild-eyed, pursued by city guardswomen armed with stun tridents.

After the episode next to the conveyor belt, Maia found herself overreacting to those lazy smiles of halfhearted flirtation young men normally cast this time of year, more as a courtesy than any kind of offer. When one gangly youth winked at her, Maia scowled back, eliciting a look of hurt dismay that instantly made her feel embarrassed, contrite.

Should all males be feared, because a few go crazy?

It wasn't only men causing problems, after all. The three races— winter folk, men, and vars—mingled peaceably for the most part. But the twins had seen incidents of rowdy summerlings—wildly varied in shape and color, but united in poverty—harassing small groups of identicals from some local clan. Frustration boiling over in rebellious hostility.

Are these really signs? The heretic spoke of a "time of changes," a term familiar from teledramas and lurid storybooks. Stability, the great gift of Lysos and the Founders, was never guaranteed to any particular generation. Even scripture said a perfect society must flex, from time to time.

Is it just Lanargh, or is this happening all over Stratos? Maia felt more determined than ever to try catching the tele-news tonight.

She reacted with a startled jump to a nudge in the ribs, and quickly saw that they had wandered onto the chief city square. Strollers, who had spent midday under shaded loggias, were emerging to enjoy the late sun's slanting rays. Leie pointed across the broad piazza toward a row of elegant, multistoried houses. "Over there, leaning against that column. Ain't that your bosun, trying to look invisible?"

Maia picked out the trim figure of Naroin, resting one shoulder on a pillar, acting as if she had only to watch the world go by. *What's she up to? That var never relaxed a day in her life.*

As if reading her thoughts—which she still did all too often—Leie nudged Maia a second time. "I bet your bosun's spying on that lot over there."

"Hm. . . . Maybe." Naroin appeared well-positioned to discreetly observe a mixed gathering of lavishly dressed males and females sitting at an open-air café. The men didn't look like sailors, while the women had a massaged, billowy appearance Maia associated with pleasure clans, specializing in relieving the tensions of others in houses of ease. Several such houses lined the square, positioned to serve clients coming from the harbor in summer, and uptown in winter. Above each entrance, gaily painted signs depicted a leaping rabbit, a snowflake, a grinning bull clutching a bell between its jaws. Servants labored on the house overlooking the café, changing the decorations from warm, aurora shades to those of frost.

In autumn, the two clienteles of such places overlapped like incoming and ebbing waves, which explained the mixed group at the veranda café. Maia wondered what the men and women found to talk about.

Was Naroin's surveillance also out of curiosity?

Unlikely. Especially when Maia noticed among the loungers a man in a floppy hat. "So that's the guy?" Leie asked. "I don't know what he did to Lem and Eth, but those boys sure got in trouble. Think your bosun's gonna pick a fight? The fop's got twice her mass."

Whatever the reason or season, Maia wouldn't bet against the petite sailor. *"Don't ask me,"* the Naroin had said. Or, *Keep your nose out of this.*

Despite the power of her own inquisitiveness, almost hormonally intense, Maia decided to quash it. At her station in life, wisdom dictated keeping a low profile.

And yet . . .

An abrupt clattering broke out to their left. The bell tower overlooking the piazza emitted a loud *thunk*, and beaten copper doors, green with verdigris, rattled open. Soon the famous clock figures of Lanargh would emerge to start their stately dance—five minutes of choreographed automation, finishing with the tolling of Three-Quarters Day. Crowds began moving up to watch the sublime, hundred-year-old gift from Gollancz Sanctuary perform its evening ritual, timed to satellite pulses from Caria University, halfway around the world.

Maia hadn't realized it was so late. The program she wanted to watch would be on soon. "Come on," she urged. "Or we'll miss the news."

Leie shook her head. "There's lots of time. I want to see the first part again. We'll go after that, I promise."

Maia sighed, knowing by instinct when Leie's tenacity could be fought, and when it was futile. Fortunately, they had a good view as the clock-tower doors finished opening with a reverberating clang. Then, first out its portal, emerged the bronze figure of the He-Ape, knuckle-walking above the onlookers, carrying a twitching four-legged animal under one arm and a sharpened stone in its mouth. The ape turned three times to a ratcheting beat, appearing to scrutinize those below. Then the figure rose up on its hind legs, miraculously unfolding into the erect figure of a man, now carrying loops of chain. The stone in his mouth had transformed into the stylized phallic protuberance of The Bomb.

Leie's eyes gleamed with appreciation, the intricate play of bronze plates seemed so smooth and natural. It was a renowned rendition of one of the most famous allegorical tales on Stratos—a metaphor for one side of evolution.

Another door parted. The figure of a She-Ape emerged, carrying her traditional bundle of fruit. *Same as last time, and the time before,* Maia thought. *It's cute, but monotonous.*

She took a moment to glance back toward the café . . . and started in surprise. Only moments had passed, but now empty bottles lay where the lounging customers had sat. Naroin, too, had vanished.

Oh, well. She shook her head. *None of my business. Besides, it's time to head uptown.*

Maia tugged her sister's arm. Leie tried to shrug her off, entranced by the swiveling dance of metal figures. But now Maia insisted. "We've seen this part twice already! I don't want to miss the broadcast again."

Leie sighed dramatically, and Maia thought, *I wish for once she wouldn't milk it, every time I want something, making it a "favor" to be repaid.*

"All right," Leie agreed with an exaggerated shrug. "Let's go watch the news."

Behind them, across the cobbled plaza, the giant figure of Mother Lysos emerged through her own door above the other automatons, holding a bioscope in the crook of one arm. Looking down benignly, she took the scroll of law in her other hand, and used it to strike a mighty blow, severing forever the chains binding Woman to the will of Man.

Sure enough, a long queue had formed four streets uphill, outside the wooden amphitheater. Maia groaned in frustration.

"Guess we'll have to wait our turn," Leie said. "Oh well."

That was her twin, all right. Hot-tempered toward the faults of others. Fatalistically philosophical about her own. Maia fumed quietly, craning to see any sign of movement ahead. A guardia marshal stood by the ticket booth, both to keep order and to make sure no under-five summerlings from town crèches sneaked in without notes from their clan mothers. Women by the door could be seen leaning inside, listening to snatches of amplified speech, then popping out to report to their friends. Murmurs of progressively degraded news riffled back to the sisters. As during the night of the reavers, Leie listened avidly and joined in this bucket brigade, even when the snippets were so obviously debased as to be worthless.

"You were right," Leie reported. "There was a piece about the Outsiders." She gestured vaguely skyward. "No pictures yet of the one that landed."

Maia exhaled disappointment. She had never before thought much about the Grand Council's stinginess with news. Power and wisdom went together, the clan mothers taught. Now though, Maia wondered if the heretic was right. The savants, councillors, and high priestesses seemed unwilling to say much, as if fearing the reaction of the masses.

From a clone's point of view, I guess every person who's not one of your full sisters is an unpredictable dilemma. It's just the same for us vars, only we're used to it. Maia found it a curiously comforting insight—that there was one way in which the winter-born went through life more afraid than summerlings. *Uncertainty must be their biggest dread.*

The middle moon, Athena, hung above the western horizon, a slender crescent with the plain of Mare Virginitatis brightening rapidly as the sun quenched behind a bank of sea clouds. It was a clear evening above Lanargh, with a chill in the air. The first stars were coming out.

There were separate lines for first-class and second-class viewing. The latter queue moved in stuttered fits toward the ticket booth, staffed by several pug-nosed women wearing spectacles and expressions of bemused skepticism. *You'd think with demand this high, they'd build more theaters, no matter how much sets cost out here. Could all this public interest have taken them by surprise?*

By the time standing room was available, and the twins squeezed into the back of the sweaty room, the program had finished with the headlines and main features, and was into a nightly segment called "Commentary." The young interviewer on the big wall screen looked familiar, naturally, since the same show appeared back home in Port Sanger. Her guest was an older woman, from attire clearly a savant from the university.

". . . despite all assurances we have received, what guarantee do we have that our Outsider friends are harmless, as they claim? We Stratoins recall with horror the last time danger arrived from space—"

The interviewer cut in. *"But, Savant Sydonia, when the Enemy came, it was in a giant vessel, big as an asteroid! We can all see—those of us living in towns with astronomy clubs—that the Visitor Ship is far too small to carry armies."*

Maia felt a thrill of luck. They were discussing the aliens, after all. On the screen, the wise-looking savant nodded her head of noble gray hair. Camera beams highlighted wisdom lines around her eyes, though Maia suspected some of them might be makeup.

"There are dangers beyond outright invasion. Serious potentialities for harm to our society. Remember, consciousness isn't everything! Sometimes the race has more wisdom than its individual members."

The young interviewer frowned. *"I don't quite follow."*

"There are signs—portents, if you will. For example, one might mention the increase, during the last several seasons, of—"

A sudden, jerky shift. Maia would have missed it, had she blinked. Studio editing. Something excised from the interview before transmission.

"—making it impossible to completely dismiss the prospect of harm coming from restored contact with the Phylum . . . much as we deplore some of the wilder fear campaigns being waged by certain radical groups . . ."

Blips like that were common on shows 'cast by Caria City. So common, Maia might not have given it much thought, if she hadn't been so intensely interested in the answer. Now, she wondered. *The heretic has a point. Vars grow up not expecting to be told much. We get used to it. But aren't we citizens, too? Doesn't this affect us all?*

Just having such thoughts made Maia feel bold and rebellious.

". . . so we must all strive together to reinforce the underpinnings of this good world left us by Lysos and the Founders. One that tests our daughters, but leaves them strong. Even the interstellar Visitor proclaims

wonder over all we've achieved, especially our remarkable social stability, as hominidal colonies go."

Maia took note. The savant seemed to be confirming the common rumor, that just one alien had actually landed on the surface of Stratos.

"It is important, therefore, to keep all other aspects in perspective, and remember what is fundamental. These accomplishments—this world and proud culture of ours—are worth defending with all the dedication we can muster from our souls."

It was a stirring speech, uttered with passion and eloquence. Maia saw many of the heads between her and the screen nod in solemn agreement. Of course, those up front would be clones from lesser families, or rich vars. Anyone who could afford front seats already had a vested interest in the social order. Yet, many others seemed as moved by the savant's words. Even Leie, when Maia turned to glance at her sister.

Of course Leie, the perpetual optimist, assumed it was just a matter of time before the two of them established their own clan. They would someday be revered grandmothers of a great nation. Any system that let quality rise in such a way might be stern, but could it be called unjust?

Could it? Maia long ago gave up arguing the topic. She never won contests of opinion with her twin.

". . . so we are asking all citizens, from clanhold to sanctuary, to keep on the lookout. If anyone notices anything peculiar, it is her—or his —duty to report it at once—"

The change in the thread of Savant Sydonia's words caught her by surprise. Maia whispered. "What's she onto now? I missed—"

Leie hushed her curtly.

". . . to inform the local guardia office in any large town. Or go to any major clanhold and tell the senior mothers what you have seen. There are rewards, up to a Level Three stipend, for information serving the interest of Stratos in these times of stress and danger."

The young interviewer smiled ingratiatingly. *"Thank you, Savant Sydonia, of Clan Youngblood and the Caria University. Now we turn to this month's summary of tech judgments. Reporting from Patents Hall, here is Eilene Yarbro. . . ."*

Leie dragged Maia outside by the wrist.

"Did you hear?" she asked excitedly, once they were some distance away, beside one of Lanargh's countless canals. "A Class Three stipend . . . just for tattling!"

"I heard, Leie. And yes, it's enough to start a hold, in some inexpensive town. But did you notice how vague they were? You don't find that strange? Almost like they're desperate to learn something, but julping at the thought of anybody finding out what they're looking for!"

"Mm," Leie grunted. "You have a point. But hey, you know what?" Her eyes gleamed. "That must mean they're underplaying what they're actually willing to pay. A stipend for information . . . and how much more for keeping quiet afterward? A whole lot, I'll bet!"

Yeah, lots more. Like a garrote in the dark. There were legends of ancient parthenogenetic clans whose daughters brought status and wealth to the hive by hiring out as stealthy assassins. Not all scary stories told to little summerlings were baseless.

But Maia didn't mention this. After all, Leie lived for possibilities, and her enthusiasm tugged at something similar within Maia—a zest for living that she might otherwise have been too reserved, too withdrawn to tap. She differed so from her sibling, even though they were as alike genetically as any pair of clones. It had made Maia more willing than most vars to accept the notion of individuality among winter folk.

"We've got to keep our eyes open!" Leie said, turning a great circle with her arms, and finally staring up at the starry vault overhead.

Constellations had emerged while they were inside, painting the heavens with sweeping, diamond brilliance. The radiance of the galactic wheel. At expected intervals, Maia caught sight of rhythmically pulsing pinpoints that weren't stars or planets, but rotating satellites vital to navigators at sea. She saw no sign of the Visitor Ship, but there was the black obscurity of the Claw, which bad little girls were told was the open, grabbing hand of the Boogey Man, reaching for children who failed their duty. Now Maia knew it as a dusty nebula, nearby in stellar terms, obscuring direct line of sight to Earth and the rest of the Human Phylum. That must have been comforting to the Founders, providing added shelter against interference by the old ways.

All that was over, now. Something had emerged from the Claw, and Maia doubted even great savants knew yet whether it meant menace or promise. The dark shape made her shiver, childhood superstitions clashing with her proud, if limited, scientific knowledge.

"If only we knew what the savants are looking for," said Leie wistfully. "I'd shave my head to find out!"

Practically speaking, if the grand matrons of Caria sought something, it was doubtful two poor virgins on a frontier coast would stumble across it. "It's a big world," Maia sighed in reply.

Naturally, Leie took a different spin on her sister's words.

"It sure is. Big, wide open, and just waiting for us to *take* it by the throat!"

*W*hy does sex exist?

For three billion years, life on Earth did well enough without it. A reproducing organism simply divided, thus arranging for its posterity to be carried on by two almost-perfect copies.

That "almost" was crucial. In nature, true perfection is a blind alley, leading to extinction. Slight variations, acted on by selection, let even single-cell species adapt to a changing world. Still, despite eons of biochemical innovation, progress was slow. Life remained meek and simple till just half a billion years ago, when it made a breakthrough.

Bacteria were already swapping genetic information, in a crude fashion. Now the system of exchange got organized, increasing patterned variability ten thousand-fold. Sex was born, and soon came many-celled organisms—fish, trees, dinosaurs, humans. Sex did all that.

Yet, because nature accomplished something in a certain way, must we follow suit when we design our new humanity? Modern gene-craft can outpace sex another thousand-fold. Within overall mammalian limitations, we can paint with colors never known to poor, blind biology.

We can learn from Mother Nature's mistakes, and do a better job.

—*from* Methods and Means, *by Lysos*

4

There was little rain. Nevertheless, the squall swiftly turned into a vicious gale.

The freighter Wotan wallowed through deep, rolling seas, sliding half-sideways down serrated slopes, abeam to a wind that seized its masts like lever arms, so that the poorly balanced ship heeled dangerously with each stiffening gust, its helm not responding.

Screaming, the mate berated his captain for taking on too little ballast in Lanargh. Earlier, he had cursed because they were too laden to flee the surprise tempest. Ignoring the first officer's shrill imprecations, the master sent sailors aloft to break the wind's grip on the masts. Shivering in icy spray, barefoot crewmen took to the swaying sheets, clenching hatchets in their teeth, edging crablike along slippery spars to hack at rigging, torn canvas—anything the vicious storm might clutch and use to heel them over to their doom.

Dimly, through waves of churning nausea, Maia peered after the brave seamen, unable to credit such skill or fortitude. Needles of saltwater stung her eyes as she squeezed the gunnels, watching sailors take horrific risks high above, wielding axes one-handed, shouting as they struggled in common to save the lives of everyone aboard. Nor were there only men up there. Higher-pitched cries told of female crew who had also climbed into the gale, riding masts that whipped like tortured snakes.

Vars like her. How could human beings do such things? Maia felt queasy at the thought. Plus shame at being too landlubber-inept to lend a hand.

"Ware below!" a voice bellowed. Something fell out of the chaos overhead, a ropy tangle that clanged off the gunnels, then slithered toward the dark, hungry waters. Blearily, Maia stared after the mass of blocks and rigging, which might have taken her along had it struck just a bit farther aft. But try as she might, she could not spy a safer place on deck than right here between the masts, gripping the railing for dear life.

One thing for sure, she wasn't about to join other passengers cowering below. Out here one must face the storm unsheltered, staring at soaring mounds and abyssal gullies of heaving ocean. But across that terrifying vista, that maelstrom, she had last sighted the Zeus. Her twin rode that other frail matchbox of wood and cloth and flesh, and if Maia was too ill and clumsy to help Wotan's struggling crew, at least she could keep watch, and call if she saw anything.

Mostly what she saw was watery nature, a conspiracy of foamy sea and sodden air, trying its best to kill them. The green hillocks, taller and steeper than the clanholds of Port Sanger, arrived in a rhythm well-timed to deepen the ship's pendulous roll. On passing the next crest, *Wotan* heeled far to starboard, hanging precipitously, about to spill over a terrifying slant. The entire vessel shivered.

Just then, a fresh gusset struck the other side, yanking mightily at the groaning masts, levering the freighter's great bulk over its keel. Loudly protesting, the infirm ship listed and plummeted downslope. Gravity rotated, becoming a *sideways* force, pressing Maia against the rails. One leg slipped between, dangling into space. In horror, she saw the gray-green sea reach with foam-flecked gauntlets . . .

Time slowed. For a suspended moment, Maia thought she heard the waters call her name.

Then, as if bemused by her helplessness, the ocean-beast slowed . . . paused . . . halted just meters away. Eyeless, it looked at her. Like an unhurried predator staring straight through her soul.

Next time . . . Or the time after . . .

The trough bottomed out. Maia's heart pounded as the freighter's list began slowly to roll the other way again, drawing back the hungry waters. Gravity's fickle tug rotated toward the deck, once more.

Suddenly, from underneath came a sharp, splintering crash. A horrible, fell vibration, like wooden ribs snapping. New, panicky cries pealed.

". . . Eai! The cargo's shifted! . . ."

An image came to mind, unasked for. . . . Tons of coal moving in black, liquid waves from one side of the hold to the other, assailing the inner hull as the sea hammered from without. *Wotan sobbed,* Maia thought, listening to the horrific sound. Dark figures ran past, prying at the cargo hatch with steel bars, sending the door flying off like a leaf caught in the wind. Not waiting for help, the dim forms dove inside, presumably to try shifting the load with their bare hands.

Maia glanced overboard as the sea rolled back again, nearly cresting at the gunnels this time, before receding even more reluctantly than before. Just a few more such oscillations, and Wotan was surely doomed. The cries of those aloft rose in pitch and urgency, along with sounds of frantic chopping. Someone screamed. An ax glittered in the rainswept beam of an emergency lantern, tumbling to the raging sea. Belowdecks echoed the wails of those facing a different hopeless task.

By utter force of will, Maia overrode her nausea, as wild as the storm. Her hands uncurled from the vibrating rail and pushed off. "I'm . . . coming . . ." she managed to croak, for no one to hear. Knowing she lacked any skill to aid those struggling aloft, Maia stumbled upslope across the slippery deck, toward the yawning darkness of the hatch.

Inside the hold, all hell had broken loose, as well as several partitions meant to guard the contents against shifting. One barrier had given way in the worst possible place, near the bow, where all that mass suddenly piling starboard added to their list and worsened the rudder's lumberous response. Dim electric bulbs, running on reserve batteries, swung wildly and cast dervish shadows as Maia grimly traversed a creaky catwalk straddling huge bins half-filled with chunky coal. Black dust rose like spindrift, clogging her throat and causing her nictitating membranes to close over her eyes, just when she needed more light, not less!

Stumbling down a crumbly talus, Maia came upon an infernal scene, where shattered boards let tons of coal pile rightward in great sloping mounds. Other vars had already joined the men below, toiling to tame the rebel cargo, tossing it morsel by morsel over groaning walls into yet unbroken compartments. Someone handed Maia a shovel and she dug in, adding what she could to the pitiful effort. Through the suffocating haze, she saw that a trio of clones were also hard at work—first-class passengers whose clan must have taught its daughters that dirty hands were less objectionable than dying.

A good thing to remember for our daughters' curriculum, pondered a remote part of her, exiled to a far corner along with potions that kept gibbering in stark terror. There wasn't time for dread *or* detachment as Maia bent to her task with a will.

More helpers arrived carrying buckets. An officer began shouting and pointing, organizing a human chain—women in the middle, passing plastic pails, while men shoveled and filled at one end, heaving coal over a partition at the other. Maia's job was to keep one shoveler provided with fresh buckets, then send each laden pail on its way. Although desperation lent her strength, and danger hormones surmounted her nausea, she had trouble keeping up with the frantic pace. The male sailor's wedge-shaped torso heaved like some great beast, emitting heat so palpable she dimly feared it might ignite the flying coal, sending everyone to patarkal hades in one giant fireball.

The rhythm accelerated. Agony spread from her hands, up her fatigued arms, and across her back. Everyone else was older, stronger, more experienced, but that hardly mattered, with all lives at stake together. Only teamwork counted. When Maia fumbled a bucket, it felt like the world coming to an end.

Concentrate, dammit!

It didn't end, not yet. No one chided, and she did not cry, because there was no time. Another pail took the fallen one's place and she bore down, striving to work faster.

Bucket by bucket, they chewed away at the drift. But despite all their efforts, the tilt seemed only to increase. The black mountain climbed higher up the starboard bulkhead. Worse, the bin they had been loading, on the port side, began to creak and groan, its straining planks bowing outward. No telling how long that partition would hold against a growing gravitational discord. Every pailful they tossed just added to the load.

Suddenly, a startling, earsplitting crash pounded the deck overhead. Something heavy must have come loose from the rigging, at last. Through the ringing in her skull, Maia heard sounds of distant cheering. Almost at once, she felt the freighter slip out of the wind's frustrated clutches. With a palpable moan, Wotan's tiller finally answered its helmsman's weary pull and the ship broke free, turning to run before the storm.

In the hold, a var near Maia let out a long sigh as the awful list began to settle. One of the clones laughed, tossing her shovel aside. Maia blinked as someone patted her on the back. She smiled and started to let go of the bucket in her hands—

" 'Ware!" Someone screamed, pointing at the mountain of coal to the right. Their efforts had paid off, all right. Too quickly. As the starboard tilt gave way, momentum swung the ship past vertical in a counterclockwise roll. The sloping mass trembled, then started to collapse.

"Out! Out!" An officer cried redundantly, as screaming crew and passengers leaped for ladders, climbed the wooden bins, or merely ran. All except those nearest the avalanche, for whom it was already too late. Maia saw a stupefied look cross the face of the huge sailor next to her, as the black wave rumbled toward them. He had time to blink, then his startled yell was muffled as Maia brought her bucket down upon his shoulders, covering his head.

The momentum of her leap carried her upward, so the anthracite tsunami did not catch her at once. The poor sailor's bulk shielded Maia for an instant, then she was swimming through a hail of sharp stones, frantically clawing uphill. Grabbing for anything, her hand struck the haft of a shovel and seized it spasmodically. As her legs and abdomen were pinned, Maia just managed to raise the tool, using the steel blade to shield her face.

A noise like all eternity ending brought with it sudden darkness.

Panic seized her, an intense, animal force that jerked and heaved convulsively against burial and suffocation. Terrifying blindness and crushing weight enveloped her. She wanted to maul the enemy that pressed her from all sides. She wanted to scream.

The fit passed.

It passed because nothing moved, no matter how she strained. Not a thing. Maia's body returned to conscious control simply because panic proved utterly futile. Consciousness was the only part of her that could even pretend mobility.

With her first coherent thought, finding herself blanketed by tons of stony carbon, Maia realized that there were indeed worse things than acrophobia or seasickness. And there was yet one item heading the catalogue of surprises.

I'm not dead.

Not yet. In darkness and battered agony, straddling a fine zone between fainting and hysteria, Maia clung to that fact and worked at it. The press of warm, rusty steel against her face was one clue. The shovel blade hadn't kept the avalanche from burying her, but it had protected a small space, a pocket filled with stale air, rather than coal. So perhaps she'd suffocate, rather than drown. The distinction seemed tenuous, yet the tangy smell of metal was preferable to having her nostrils full of horrible dust.

Time passed. Seconds? Fractions of seconds? Certainly not minutes. There couldn't be that much air.

The ship had stopped rocking, thank Stratos, or the shifting cargo would have quickly ground her to paste. Even with the coal bed lying still, nearly every square inch of her body felt crushed and scraped by jagged rocks. With nothing to do but inventory agonies, Maia found it possible to distinguish subtle differences in texture. Each chunk pressing her body had a sadistic personality so individual she might give it a name . . . this one, Needle; that one under her left breast, Pincher; and so on.

As fractions stretched into whole seconds and more, she grew aware of one, unique point of contact—a tight, throbbing constriction that felt smooth but rhythmically adamant. With shock, she realized someone was holding onto her leg! Hope coursed through Maia that she had been tossed upside down, leaving a foot exposed, and those pulsating squeezes meant help was coming!

Then she realized. *It's the big sailor!*

His hand must have connected with her foot at the last moment, while she swam the carbon tide. Now, whether conscious or dying, the man maintained this thin thread of human contact through their common tomb.

How ironic. Yet it seemed no more bizarre than anything else right now. It was company.

Maia felt sorry for Leie, when the news came. *She'll imagine the end was more horrible than it is. It could be worse. I can't think how right now, but I'm sure it could be worse.*

As she pondered that, the pulsing grip around her ankle tightened abruptly, spasmodically, clenching so hard that Maia moaned in fierce new pain. She felt the sailor's terrible convulsions, and his reflexive strength yanked her downward, stabbing her in a hundred places, making her gasp in anguish. Then the fierce grip began subsiding in a chain of diminishing tremors.

The throbbing constrictions stopped. Maia imagined she heard a distant rattle.

See? she told herself, as hot tears swept her eyes in total darkness. *I told you. I told you it could be worse.*

Quietly, she prepared for her own turn. The scientio-deist liturgy of her upbringing rose in her mind—catechistic lines Lamatia Hold dutifully taught its summer children in weekly chapel services, about the formless, maternal spirit of the world, at once loving, accepting, and strict.

> *For what hope hath a single, living "me,"*
> *A mind, brief, yet self-important? Clinging*
> *After life like a possession? Some thing she can keep?*

She knew prayers for comfort, prayers for humility. But then, Maia wondered, if the soul field really does continue after organic life has ceased, what difference would a few words, mumbled in the dark mean to Stratos Mother? Or even the strange, all-seeing thunder god said to be worshiped privately by men? Surely neither of them would hold it against her if she saved her breath to live a few seconds longer?

Perceptory overload gradually shut down part of her agony. The claustrophobic pressure surrounding Maia, at first a horrid mass of biting claws, now had a numbing effect, as if satisfied to slowly crush all remaining sensation. The only impression increasing with time was of *sound*. Thumps and distant, dragging clatters.

Heartbeats passed, one by one. She counted them, at first to pass the time. Then incredulously, because they showed no imminent sign of stopping. Experimenting, Maia opened her mouth slightly, exposing her tongue and inner lips to sense what her battered, dust-covered face could not—a faint thread of cool air that seemed to stream down the shovel blade from somewhere near her hairline!

Yet, there had to be at least a meter of coal overhead. Probably much more!

There was no easy answer to this puzzle, and she tried not to think too hard. Even when Maia made out footsteps crunching overhead, and the hurried scrape of tools, she paid scant heed, clinging to the blanket of numb acceptance. Hope, if it raised her metabolism, was the last thing she needed right now.

Maybe it would be better if I slept awhile.

So Maia drifted in and out of anoxic slumber, vibrations along the shovel blade telling her how slow the progress of the rescuers remained. *As if it matters.*

Without warning, the tool shifted, and the blade that had succored her suddenly threatened to gouge her neck, causing Maia to squirm in terror. All at once, the black swaddling of coal became more tight, constricting, suffocating, than ever. Hysteria, so long held at bay by resigned numbness, sent tremors of resurgent fury coursing through her pinned arms and legs. Maia desperately fought a rising in her gorge.

Then, unexpected and unbidden, *light* struck her eyes with abrupt, painful brilliance, outbalancing even clawing panic, driving out all thoughts with its sheer, blinding beauty. Uncovered, her ears filled with noise—rattles, rasps, and hoarse shouts. Maia took long, shuddering gasps as blurry shapes congealed into silhouettes and finally soot-streaked faces, starkly outlined by swaying bulbs. On their knees, sailors and passengers used bare hands to clear more coal away from her head. Someone with a rag and bucket cleaned her eyes, nose, and mouth, then gave her water.

Finally, Maia was able to choke out words. "Don't . . . b-bother . . . w-w-me." She shook her head, cutting fresh scrapes along her neck. "Ma . . . man . . . down . . . right."

It came out barely a gargle, but they acted as if they understood, commencing to dig furiously where Maia indicated with her chin. Meanwhile, others more gradually liberated the rest of her. When she was almost free, an overturned yellow bucket came into view below, and the work went even faster.

At that point, Maia could have saved them effort. The hand still clutching her ankle was growing cold. Yet she could not bring herself to say it. There was always a chance. . . .

She had never known his name. He was not even a member of her race. Still, tears flowed when she saw his purple face and bulging eyes. Hands pried his fingers off her leg, and with that break of contact she knew with tragic certainty and unwonted loss that they would never again share communication, this side of death.

Seabirds cried possessive calls of territoriality, warning others of their kind to keep away from private nesting niches, chiseled in the steep bluffs overlooking Grange Head harbor. Jealous of their neighbors, the birds virtually ignored a small group of bipeds who swung along the cliffs, hanging from slender ropes, taking turns harvesting molted feathers in great bags and alternately chipping still more roosts for this year's crop of mating pairs. From a distance, or even from the birds' close vantage point, no one could distinguish among the sunburned, narrow-boned, black-haired women performing these strange tasks. They all looked identical.

Idly, without much interest, Maia watched the harvester family labor along those vertiginous heights, working their feather farm. It was a niche, all right. Not one she'd ever be tempted to fill. Yet, something equally at the fringe was probably her destiny now. All the fond hopes and ambitious schemes of childhood lay broken, and her heart was numb.

With a heavy sigh she looked at the figures she had scratched on her slate. The calculations needed no further massaging. Gingerly, because each movement still caused her pain, she flipped the tablet over and slid it across the chart table.

"I'm done, Captain Pegyul."

The tall sallow-faced sailor looked up from his own figures and stared at her a moment. He scratched behind his battered green cap. "Well, give me another minute, then, will yer?"

Sitting on a railing nearby, Naroin the bosun puffed her pipe and gave Maia a headshake. *Don't show up officers.* That would be her advice.

What do I care? Maia responded with a shrug. With the navigator and second mate lost in the storm, and the first mate in bed with a concussion, there had been only one person aboard able to help Wotan's master pilot this tub. Struggling to turn a hobby into a useful skill, Maia had quickly learned why tradition demanded more than one eye at a sextant, to cross-check each measurement. The custom proved valid during the last two dreadful weeks, retracing their way back on course. Each of them had made mistakes often enough to cause disaster, if the other hadn't been there to notice.

But here we are. That's what matters, I guess.

She was willing to humor the captain's wish for this final exercise, comparing notes on technique here in a safe harbor, one whose official position was known down to the centimeter. It helped pass the time while her wounds healed, and while going through the motions of looking out to sea, hoping to spot a sail she knew would never come.

The captain threw down his stylus and uncovered a chart, peering at the coordinates of Grange Head harbor. "Gak. Yer right. M'dawn sighting was off 'cause of the red satellite in th' Plough. It's the five-pulser, not the three. Thet's why m'longitude was wrong."

Maia tried to be gallant, for Naroin's sake. "It's an easy mistake in twilight, Captain. The Outsiders put up the new strobe this summer, as a favor to the Caria Navigation Authority, after the old five-second light burned out."

"Mmph. So you said. A new strobe-sat. Fancy thet. Musta been published. Our sanctuary tele's been fritzin', but thet's no excuse. Oughta stay up t' date, dammit.

"We'd hed it easy for so long, though," he sighed. "Queer for a summer storm t'come so late, this yer."

You can say that again, Maia thought. Aftereffects of the gale had lain strewn across still-choppy waters the following day, when the winds finally calmed enough for searching. Planks and other floating debris fished out of the sea showed that theirs hadn't been the only drama during the night. The capping moment came as they cruised back and forth, desperately seeking, when a broken clinker board was hauled in and turned over, showing parts of the letters Z-E-U-

The passengers and crew had stared in numb silence. Nor had the next few days encouraged hope. Lingering silence on the radio turned worry to despair. Assisting the crew to get their wounded ship to port had offered blessed distraction from Maia's pain and gnawing anxiety.

I've got to get ashore. Maybe the feel of solid ground will help.

"Thanks for everything you taught me, Captain." Maia said woodenly. "But now I see they've finished loading the barge. I shouldn't keep them waiting."

She bent gingerly to take the strap of her duffel, but Pegyul seized it and swung it over his shoulder. "Yer sure I can't get ye t'stay?"

She shook her head. "As you said, there's a chance my sister's still alive out there. Maybe they'll limp into port, or she might've been rescued by some other ship. Anyway, this was our destination when the storm hit. Here's where she'll come, if she can."

The man looked dubious. He, too, had taken losses when the *Zeus* vanished. "Yer welcome with us. Ye'd have a home till spring, an' each three-quarter year efter."

In its way it was a generous offer. Other women, such as Naroin, had taken that path, living and working in the periphery of the strange world of men. But Maia shook her head. "I've got to be here, in case Leie shows."

She saw him accept her choice with a sigh, and Maia wondered how this could be the same person she had dismissed so two-dimensionally, back in Port Sanger. Flaws were still apparent, but now they comprised part of a surprisingly complex blend for so simple a creature as a man. After handing her bag down to the pilot of the waiting barge, topped off with a consignment of dark coal, Captain Pegyul drew from one of his pockets a compact brass tool.

"It's m'second-best sextant," he explained, showing her how the three sighting arms unfolded. There were two leather straps for attaching it to the owner's arm. "Portable job. Been meanin' t'fix the main reflector, ret here. See? Sort o' hair loom, it is. Even had a redout for the Old Net, see here?"

Maia marveled at the miniaturized workmanship. The old readout dials would never light again, of course. They marked it as a relic of another age, battered and no match for the finely hand-wrought devices produced in modern sanctuary workshops. Still, the sextant was an object of both reverence and utility.

"It is very beautiful," she said. When he refolded it, Maia saw that the watchcase cover bore an engraving of an airship—a flamboyant, fanciful design that obviously could never fly.

"It's yers."

Maia looked up in surprise. "I . . . couldn't."

He shrugged, trying to make matter-of-fact what she could tell was an emotion-laden gesture. "I heard how ye tried to save Micah with the bucket. Fast thinkin'. Mighta worked . . . if luck was diff'rent."

"I didn't really—"

"He was me own boy, Micah. Great, hulkin', cheerful lad. Too much Ortyn in him, though, if y'know what I mean. Never would of learned to use a sextant right, anyway."

Pegyul took Maia's smaller hand in his huge callused one and put the brass instrument firmly in her palm, closing her fingers around the cool, smooth disk. "God keep ye," he finished with a quaver in his voice.

Maia answered numbly. "And Lysos guide you. Eia."

He nodded with a faint jerk, and turned away.

Fully loaded, the coal barge slowly crossed the glassy bay. Grange Head didn't look like much, Maia thought glumly. There was little industry besides transhipping produce for countless farming holds strewn across the inland plains, accessing the sea here by narrow-gauge solar railway. Sunlight wasn't enough to lift fully laden trains over the steep coastal hills, so a small generating plant offered a steady market for Port Sanger coal. The solitary pier lacked draft to let old Wotan dock, so its cargo came ashore boatload by boatload.

Naroin smoked her pipe, quietly regarding Maia. "Been meanin' to tell you," she said at last. "That was some trick you pulled durin' the avalanche."

Maia sighed, wishing it had occurred to her to lie about the damned bucket, instead of semiconsciously babbling the whole story to her rescuers. Her impulsive act hadn't been thought-out enough to be called generous, let alone heroic. Sheer instinct, that was all. Anyway, the futile gesture hadn't saved the poor fellow.

However, Naroin wasn't referring to that part of the episode, it turned out. "Usin' the shovel the way you did," she said. "That was quick thinking. The blade gave you a little cave to breathe in. And raisin' the handle signaled us where to dig. But tell me this, did you *know* we make those hafts out o' hollow bamboo? Did you figure air might pass through?"

Maia wondered where Naroin kept herself summers, so she could avoid ever being trapped in the same town. "Luck, bosun. You're out of season if you see more in it. Just dumb luck."

The master-at-arms shrugged. "Expected you'd say that." To Maia's relief, the older woman let it drop there, allowing Maia to ride the rest of the way in silence. When the barge bumped along the town dock, with its row of hand-built wooden cranes, the bosun stood up and shouted. "All right, scum, let's get at it. Maybe we can clear this hole in the coast before the tide!"

Maia waited till the barge was tied securely, and the others had scrambled ashore, before stepping carefully across the gangplank with her duffel. The rock-steady pier made her feel momentarily queasy, as if the roll of a ship were more natural than a surface anchored to rock. Pressing her lips in order to not show her pain, Maia set off for town without a backward glance. Counting her bonus, she could afford to rest and heal for a while before looking for work. Still, the coming weeks would be a time of trial, staring out to sea, clutching the magnifier on her little sextant in forlorn hope each time a sail rounded those jagged bluffs, fighting to keep depression from enveloping her like a shroud.

"So long, Lamai brat!" someone shouted at her back—presumably the sharp-faced var who had been so hostile, that first day at sea. This time the insult was without bite, and probably meant with offhand respect. Maia lacked the will to reply, even with the obligatory, amiably obscene gesture. She just didn't have the heart.

"In ancient days, in olden tribes, men obliged their wives and daughters to worship a stern-browed male god. A vengeful deity of lightning and well-ordered rules, whose way it was to shout and thunder at great length, then lapse into fits of maudlin, all-forgiving sentimentality. It was a god like men themselves—a lord of extremes. Wrangling priests interpreted their Creator's endless, complex ordinances. Abstract disputes led to persecution and war.

"Women could have told them," Lysos supposedly continued. *"If men had only stopped their bickering and asked our opinion. Creation itself might have been a bold stroke of genius, a laying down of laws. But the regular, day to day tending of the world is a messy business, more like the inspired chaos of a kitchen than the sterile precision of a chartroom, or study."*

Intermittent breezes ruffled the page she was reading. Leaning on the crumbling stone wall of a temple orchard, looking past the sloping tile roofs of Grange Head, Maia lifted her gaze to watch low clouds briefly occult a brightly speckled, placid sea, its green shoals aflicker with silver schools of fish and the flapping shadows of hovering swoopbirds. The variegated colors were lush, voluptuous. Mixing with scents carried by the moist, heavy wind, they made a stew for the senses, spiced with fecund exudates of life.

The beauty was heavy-handed, adamantly consoling. She got the point—that life goes on.

With a sigh, Maia picked up the slim volume again.

"A living planet is a much more complex metaphor for deity than just a bigger Father, with a bigger fist," the passage went on. *"If an omniscient, all-powerful Dad ignores your prayers, it's taken personally. Hear only silence long enough, and you start wondering about His power. His fairness. His very existence.*

"But if a World-Mother doesn't reply, Her excuse is simple. She never claimed conceited omnipotence. She has countless others clinging to Her apron strings, including myriad species unable to speak for themselves. To

Her elder offspring She says—go raid the fridge. Go play outside. Go get a job.

"*Or better yet, lend me a hand! I have no time for idle whining.*"

Maia closed the slim volume with a sigh. She had spent a good part of the afternoon pondering this excerpt, purported to have been written by the Great Founder herself. The passage was not part of formal scripture. Yet, even while working in the temple garden, Maia kept thinking about it. Priestess-Mother Kalor had lent her the book when more traditional readings failed to help ease her heart-pain. Against all expectation it had helped. The tone, more open and casual than liturgy, was poignantly humorous in parts. For the first time, Maia found she could picture Lysos as a person she might have liked to know. After weeks of depression, Maia managed her first, tentative smile.

Her injuries had been worse than anyone thought, on stepping from the *Wotan*'s barge some weeks ago. Or perhaps the will to heal was lacking. When the manager of the small, dingy hotel found her in bed one morning, sweating and feverish, the clone had sent for sisters from the local temple, to come fetch Maia for tending.

"*So sorry, younger sister,*" the acolytes replied each morning. "*There is no sign of the Zeus. No woman resembling you has made landfall.*" The temple mother even paid out of her own pocket to make Net calls to Lanargh and other ports. The ship Leie had been aboard was listed missing. Its guild had filed for insurance and was in official mourning.

Maia had thanked Mother Kalor for her kindness, then went to her cell and threw herself, sobbing, onto the narrow cot. She had wailed and clenched her fists, pounding the mattress till all sense left her fingers. She slept most of each day, tossed and turned each night, and lost interest in food.

I wanted to die, she recalled.

Mother Kalor had seemed unconcerned. "*This is normal. It will pass. We vars tend to cleave more closely, when we bind to someone. It makes mourning harder than any clone can understand.*

"*Unless the clone has lost* all *of her family at once, that is. Then such devastation you or I could not imagine.*"

But Maia *could* imagine. In a sense she had lost a family, a clan. All her life, Leie had been there. Sometimes infuriating or stifling, that presence had also been her companionship, her ally, her mirrored reflection. The separation on departure morn had been Maia's idea, a way to develop independent skills, but the ultimate goal had always been a common one. The dream shared.

She had cursed herself. *It's my fault.* If they had stayed together, they would be united now, living or dead.

The priestess said all the expected things, about how survivors should not blame themselves. That Leie would have wanted Maia to prosper. That life must persevere. Maia appreciated the effort. At the same time, she felt resentment toward this woman for interfering in her misery. This var who had chosen to become a "mother" the safe and convenient way.

At last, partly in exhaustion, Maia started to let go. Youth and good food sped physical healing. Theological contemplations played a small part, as well. *I used to wonder how it is that men still have a thunder god. An all-seeing deity who watches every action, cares about all thoughts.*

Old Coot Bennett had spoken of his faith, which he thought fully consistent with devotion to Stratos Mother. *Apparently it's passed down within the male sanctuaries, and couldn't be eradicated now, even if the savants and councillors and priestesses tried.*

But how did it get started? There were no men among the Founders, when the first dome habitats bloomed on Landing Continent. Multiple lab-designed generations came and went before the Great Changes were complete. *Our ancestors knew nothing but what the Founders chose to tell them.*

So how did those first Stratoin men learn about God?

It was more than an intellectual exercise. *If Leie's gone, perhaps her soul field has joined with the planet's, and is part of the rainbow I see out there.* The image was poetic and beautiful. Yet there was also something tempting about Old Bennett's notion of afterlife in a place called heaven, where a more personal continuation, including memories and a sense of self, was assured. According to Bennett, the dead could also hear you when you prayed.

Leie? She projected slowly, solemnly. *Can you hear me? If you do, could you give a sign? What's it like on the other side?*

There might have been a reply in the play of light upon the water, or in the distant cries of gulls. If so, it was too subtle for Maia to grasp. So, she took wry comfort imagining how her twin might respond to such an impertinent request.

"Hey, I just got here, dummy. Besides, telling you would spoil the fun."

With a sigh, Maia turned around and took a pair of pruning shears from the pocket of her borrowed smock. While healing, she had paid for room and board by helping tend the orchard of native Stratoin trees each temple was obliged to keep as part of a duty toward the planet. It was gentle work, and seemed to carry its own lesson.

"You and me, we're both endangered, aren't we?" she told one short, spindly shrub she had been caring for, before abstraction took her away. Eons of evolution had equipped the jacar tree's umbrella leaves with chemical defenses to keep native herbivores at bay. Those toxins had proved useless at deterring creatures of Earthly stock, from rabbits to deer to birds. All found the jacar delicious, and only rarely did it take to cultivation. This garden's five specimens were listed in a catalog maintained in faraway Caria.

"Maybe we both belong in a place like this," Maia added, taking a final snip and stepping back to regard a finished job. Then she turned to regard the orchard, the flower beds, the stucco-walled temple of refuge. *Having second thoughts?* she asked herself. *A little late for that, now that you've said you're leaving.*

On her way back to the gardener's shed, she walked past the tumbled walls of an older building. An earlier temple, one of the sisters had explained, suggesting Maia ask Mother Kalor if she wanted to know more. First Maia had explored the ruins by herself, and been struck to find an eroded bas-relief, still faintly visible under clinging fingers of ivy. The easiest figure to recognize was a fierce, protecting dragon, a favorite symbol for the planetary spirit-deity, its wings outstretched above a scene of tumult. Jets of flame seemed to spear from its open jaws toward a hovering wheel-shape, defaced almost to nothing. Looking nearer, Maia had found that the "fire" consisted of thin lines originating from the dragon's *teeth*.

Digging underneath the metaphorical beast, she had discovered, half-buried in the loam, a fierce battle of demons—one group bearing *horns* on their heads and the other *beards*—locked in hand-to-hand struggle so savage that, even muted by age, the sculpture made Maia shiver.

Later on, she had learned that it was an ancient work, from a time soon after the Enemy came and nearly smashed hominid culture on Stratos. And no, Mother Kalor explained when asked, those demon horns were allegorical. The real foe had none.

On closely inspecting the crumbly, sandstone faces, they had found that only half of the defending figures were bearded. Nevertheless, Maia asked, "Were they heretics?"

"Those who built this temple? I hardly think so. There are Perkinites and others inland, of course. But to my knowledge, Grange Head has always been orthodox."

Mother Kalor offered free use of the temple archives, and Maia was tempted. Had she been here for any other reason, she might have let curiosity lead her. But there seemed little point, nor energy to spare amid the tedium of grief and recovery. Anyway, Maia had made herself a vow—to be practical from now on, and live from day to day.

Upon reaching the shed, she removed her smock and handed the pruning shears back to the chief gardener, who sat at a table tending seedlings. The elderly nun's beneficent smile showed what peace could be attained down this life path. The gentle path called the Refuge of Lysos.

The priestess-mother hadn't seemed hurt by Maia's refusal of novice's robes. She took it as a tribute to the temple's ministrations that Maia was ready to set forth once more. "Your place is in the thick of things," Kalor had said. "I'm sure fate and the world have a role for you."

The kindness and gentleness she had received here lifted Maia's heart. *I'll always remember this place.* It was like folding a memento, to put away in an attic. She might take the memory out to look at, from time to time, but never to wear again.

In other days she had felt one special reaction, on encountering some new idea, or person, or thing. She had always savored telling her twin about it. That fine anticipation had been far richer than simply remembering for its own sake. But from now on, whatever good things Maia found in the world, she must learn to esteem them all by herself. That naked fact continued to form a void deep within, despite a gradual deadening of her pain. Though lessening with time, the faint sense of loss would remain with her for as long as she lived, and she would call it childhood.

C onsider the nightmares of children. Or your own fears, walking down some darkened lane. Do you invent ghosts? Beasts of prey? Or do most dire phantoms take the form of *men*, lurking in shadows with vile intent? For adults and infants, women and men, fear usually comes in male raiment.

Oh, often so does rescue. Our faction never claimed all men were brutes. To the contrary, history tells of marvelous human beings who happened to be male. But consider how much time and energy those good men spent just countering the bad ones. Cancel out both sides and what is left? More trouble than the good is worth.

That was the rationale behind early parthenogenesis experiments on Herlandia—attempting to cull masculinity from the human process entirely. Attempts that failed. The need for a male component seems deeply woven through the chemistry of mammalian reproduction. Even our most advanced techniques cannot safely overcome it.

Herlandia was a disappointment, but we learn from setbacks. If we must include men in our new world, let us design things so they will get in the way as little as possible.

—*from* Forging Destiny, *by Lysos*

5

T he voice, reading aloud, was among the most soothing Maia had
ever heard.

" '. . . And so, now that you've left the coastal mountains far behind, the grassy plains of Long Valley roll by your window like purple-
crested crinolines, starched for show. A vast sea of low, unmoving waves.
From your hurtling chariot, your gaze reaches across the prairie ocean,
seeking anything to break the undulating monotony, making what it can
of any post or protuberance that might imaginatively be called topography.

" 'And you seek not in vain! For, far beyond this glorious expanse
of blandness, you glimpse sequestered columns of wind-sculpted stone,
green-crested rock monoliths, giving the eye something faraway to cling
to. These are the distant Needle Towers, testaments to the power and
persistence of natural erosion which carved them long before the arrival
of humans on Stratos. . . .' "

Already half-stupefied by the thrumming magnetic rails and the
dusty sameness of the prairie, Maia listened to the other occupant of the
baggage car orate from a volume with finely chased leather bindings.
Though the air was parched, her companion never seemed to run dry.

" 'According to recent reports, the elders who rule Long Valley have
ordained that male sanctuaries be built · on several far-off Needles,
breaking a tradition of seasonal banishment which started with the first
Perkinite settlements. . . .' "

The hitchhiker called her book a "travel guide." Its apparent aim? To describe what the reader was seeing, while she was seeing it. But Tizbe Beller spent more time with her nose between the pages, making excited pronouncements, than actually looking through the grimy window at a succession of dreary farms and ranches. *Does someone actually make a living writing such things?* Maia wondered. Her companion proclaimed this one a masterpiece of its genre. Clearly, Tizbe came from a different background than Lamatia Clan, which gave its summer kids little exposure to the fine arts.

"'. . . Currently, all men of virile years are banished from the valley each hot quarter, and kept away until the end of rut season. . . .' "

Maia's fellow traveler lay atop a pile of coarse gunnysacks, her blonde hair tied in a simple bun. Tizbe's clothing, ragged-looking from a distance, proved on closer inspection to be soft and well-made, clashing with the girl's claim of utter poverty. As Maia's assistant, she was supposed to pay for her passage by helping sling freight all the way to Holly Lock. So far, Maia was unimpressed.

Don't be hasty to judge, she thought. *Mother Kalor wouldn't approve.*

Before departing Grange Head, Maia had given the orthodox priestess a letter to deliver to any young woman passing through who resembled her. After all, Church doctrine held that miracles were possible, even in a world guided by chance and molecular affinities.

"Must you go inland, child?" Mother Kalor had asked. *"Long Valley is Perkinite country. They're a lock-kneed, fanatical bunch of smugs, and don't much care for men or vars."*

"Maybe so," Maia had replied. *"But they hire vars for all sorts of jobs."*

"Jobs they won't do themselves."

"I can't turn down steady work," Maia had answered, ending all argument. One thing for certain, if Leie ever did show up, she'd dish out hell if Maia hadn't been busy during their separation, using the time profitably.

What luck that a railroad clan was just then looking for someone with a knack for figures. The work didn't involve differential calculus, only simple accounting, but Maia had been pleased to find some part of her education useful. Leie, too, would have been a cinch, with her love of machines. If only . . .

Fortunately, Tizbe broke Maia's gloomy thought-spiral.

"Listen to this!" The young hitchhiker lifted a finger and changed to a deep, somewhat pompous tone. " 'Of special interest to travelers is the system of freight and passenger carriage used in Long Valley, ideally suited to a pioneering subculture. The solar railway, operated jointly by the Musseli, Fontana, and Braket clans, should get you to your destination without excessive delays.' " Tizbe laughed. "That Fontana train was four hours late yesterday! And this Musseli clunker isn't doing much better."

Maia felt compelled to return a wry smile. Yet, Tizbe's contempt seemed unfair. Musseli Clan ran their trains on time during the cool seasons, when men of Rail Runner Guild helped drive the engines. Most males were banished each summer, though, and the long-limbed, flattish-faced Musseli were left short-staffed. They might have hired female engineers just as good as men—itinerant vars, or even a hive-clan of specialists. That would put the enterprise solely in the hands of women year-round, like everything else in Long Valley. But the region's leaders were caught between their ideology of radical separationism on the one hand and biological needs on the other. In order to produce clone-daughters, they must have men around from autumn to spring, to perform the vital "sparking" function. Keeping ample numbers of men occupied between brief sparkings meant giving them work. Here on the high plains, locomotives served the same secondary function as ships along the coast: to keep a small supply of men available, in compact, mobile, easy-to-manage groups.

Hence the dilemma. If the notoriously touchy male engineers took offense over the hiring of summer replacements, they might not return at all next year. Which would be catastrophic, like leaving the orchards unpollinated. So, each summer, the rail clans just made do.

Now, with its young men home from coastal sanctuaries, Rail Runner Guild was coming back to strength. Soon schedules would be met again. But Maia didn't bother trying to explain any of this. Tizbe seemed smugly certain she and her book had all the answers.

" 'The three rail-clans operate competing freight lines, each in partnership with a male guild, with shared ownership of capital approved by an act of the Planetary Council in the year. . . .' "

A surprisingly close working relationship between the sexes, Maia pondered. Yet, hadn't Lamatia Hold once welcomed the same ships and sailors, year after year? Those flying the Pinniped banner? Preserving for them rights of all kinds, ranging from commerce to procreation? Who was she to say what was normal, and what aberration?

Perhaps the heretic in Lanargh is right. These may all be signs of changing times.

The solar-electric locomotive sped along, faster than the swiftest horse or sailing ship. At each stop, out swarmed Rail Runner maintenance boys, toting tools and lubricants, and Musseli girls armed with clipboards and crate hooks, hurrying to service the machines and expedite cargo under the scrutiny of older supervisors. Maia had noticed that many of the orange-clad males bore faces strikingly similar to the female clones in maroon overalls.

Imagine, sisters continuing to know their own brothers, and mothers their sons, long after life has turned them into men. Maia could think of several drawbacks and advantages to such a close relationship. She recalled sweet little Albert, whom she had tutored for a life at sea, and thought how nice it might have been to see how he grew up. The stray thought reminded her of those childish dreams of someday finding her own father. As if happenstance of sperm and egg meant anything in a big, hard world.

A world capable of snapping stronger bonds than those.

Stop it. Maia shook her head vigorously. *Let go of the pain. Leie would.*

After reading silently for a while, Tizbe looked up from her gunnysack chaise. "Oh, this part's lovely, Maia. It says, 'Long Valley retains many quaint features of a frontier region. From your stateroom, be sure to observe the rustic little towns, each with its monotone grain silo and banks of solar cells . . .' "

There was that word *quaint* again. It seemed to refer patronizingly to anything simple or backward, from the viewpoint of a city-bred tourist. *I wonder if Tizbe finds me quaint, too.*

" '. . . between the towns and zones of cultivation, note stretches of native kuourn grass, set aside under ecological rules even stricter than decreed by Caria City. . . .' "

They had seen many such oases—great lakes of waving stalks with purple flowers. The Perkinite cult governing this valley worshiped a Stratos Mother whose wrath toward planet abuse was matched only by her distrust of the male gender. Yet, Maia felt sure much of the plains was off-limits for another reason—to prevent competition.

When Long Valley first opened for settlement, young vars must have swarmed in from all over Stratos, forming partnerships to tame the land. Affiliations that became powerful, interclan alliances when successful women settled down to raise daughters and cash crops. That, in turn, meant pitching in to build a railroad, to export surplus and import supplies, comforts.

And men. Despite their slogans, the Perkinite utopia soon began to resemble the rest of Stratos. You can't fight biology. Only push at the rules, here and there.

"Oh! Here's a good part, Maia. Did you know there are more than forty-seven local species of zahu? It's used for all sorts of things. Like—"

A shrill whistle thankfully interrupted Tizbe's next eager recount-

ing. It was the ten-minute warning before their next stop. Maia glanced
at the wall chart. "Clay Town comin' up."

"So soon?" asked the hitcher. Maia threw open her ledger, running
a fingertip along today's bills of lading. "Can't you hear the whistle blowing? Come on, you read numbers, I'll fetch boxes."

She kept her finger by the starting place until Tizbe sauntered over.
Then Maia hurried to the single aisle running the length of the car,
between tall racks of shelving. "What's the first number?" she called.

There followed a long pause. "Um. Is it 4176?"

Maia winced. That had been the final entry at their last stop, only
an hour ago. "Next one! Start where it says Clay Town on the left."

"Oh! You mean 5396?"

"Right!" Grabbing a block and tackle that hung from an overhead
rail, Maia scanned the shelves. She found the correct box, hooked its
leather strap, pulled the chain taut, and swung the package out, hauling
it along the track to where she could lower it gently by the door. "Next."

"That would be . . . mm, let's see . . . 6178?"

Maia sighed and went looking. Fortunately, the awkward Musseli
sorting system wasn't too hard to puzzle out, although it might have been
meant to confuse as much as to clarify. "Next?"

"Already? I lost my place. . . . Ah! Is it 9254?"

Strictly speaking, it should have been Maia at the ledger and her
assistant doing the hauling. But Tizbe had whined about having to do
work "suited for lugars and men." She couldn't get the gliding winch to
work. She picked up a sliver. Maia had a theory about this creature.
Tizbe must be a var-child from some big-city clan, so rich and decadent
they pampered even their summerlings, kissing them on the brow and
sending them off unequipped to survive past their first year. Perhaps
Tizbe expected to live off appearance and charm alone.

I wonder why she looks familiar, though.

Despite, or maybe because of, Tizbe's assistance, the pile by the
door wasn't quite finished by the time the second whistle blew. The
locomotive's flywheel audibly changed tone as the train began braking.
Maia hurried the pace. Her hands had callused from hard work, yet the
rough chain bit her fingers whenever the car jostled. The last, heavy
package almost got away, but she managed to lower it down with just an
echoing thump.

Short of breath, Maia rolled open the sliding door as rows of towering kilns and brick ovens grew like termite mounds around the train,
enveloping it in an aroma of glazed, baked earth. "Welcome to Clay
Town, hub of Argil County," Tizbe sang with false enthusiasm. For a
while, everything was red or dun-colored. Stacks and crates of ceramics
swam past in a blur.

Abruptly, the aromatic kiln district gave way to residences, row after row of petite houses. Here in Long Valley, important matriarchies built their citadels near their fields or pastures, leaving towns to small homesteads, sometimes derisively called microholds. From the decelerating train, Maia watched a woman stroll by, holding the hand of a little girl who was obviously her clone-daughter. Half the population of the valley apparently lived this way—single women, winter-born but living varlike existences, with jobs that barely paid the bills and let them raise one winter child, exactly the way their mothers had, and grandmothers, and so on. One identical next-self to inherit and carry on. A thin but continuing chain.

It seemed a simpler, less presumptuous sort of immortality than the binge-or-bust cycles of great houses. *You could do worse,* Maia thought. In fact, there seemed something terribly sweet and intimate about the solitary mother, walking alone with her child. Ever since her own grand dreams shattered, Maia had begun thinking in more modest terms. The Musseli were beneficent toward their employees, treating several score singleton women almost like full members of their commune. Perhaps, if she worked hard at this job, Maia might win a long-term contract. Then, after saving up to build a house. . . .

Even after all that, there remained the problem of men. Or a man. You had to start off with a winter birth. It was rare to be able to conceive any other time of year, till you'd had a clone. But getting pregnant in winter wasn't as simple as going into the street and calling, "Hey, you!"

Well, don't think of that now. Take care of things one step at a time.

The train slowed into the Clay Town railyard with a hiss and squeal. Passengers began alighting. From two cars back came bumping sounds as men and lugars wasted no time hauling heavy farm machinery off a flatbed car. Nearer at hand, Maia saw the local Musseli freightmistress approach, clipboard in hand, striding ahead of a towering lugar laden with packages. *Smile,* Maia told herself. *Try not to act like you're only five.*

"Is this all of it?" the woman snapped, pointing to the pile by the door.

"Yes, madam. That's all."

As Maia handed over the bills of lading, Tizbe sidled alongside, muttering "Excuse me" in a low voice. The young blonde squeezed past carrying her travel bag. "Think I'll go have a look around," she drawled casually.

Maia called after her. "It's only a forty-minute stop! Don't get los—" She cut off as Tizbe turned a corner and vanished from sight.

"*If* it's convenient for you, right now?"

Maia jerked back to face the freightmistress. Her face flushed. "Sorry, madam. I'm ready when you are." Bending over the ledger, while carefully cross-checking the packages, Maia chided herself for worrying about a stupid hitchhiker.

She's just another silly var. None of my concern. Maia, you've got to try thinking more like Leie.

Leie certainly wouldn't have bothered. Leie would have said "good riddance."

But with the freightmistress grudgingly satisfied, and ten minutes to go before departure, Maia went looking for her errant assistant. She had reached the far end of the platform, with no sign yet of the irritating blonde, when a whistle blew some distance beyond the kiln district—another train approaching the station.

A young man could be seen holding a lever that would magnetically transfer the oncoming locomotive to one of three sets of rails. Several young women stood nearby, giggling, perched on a wooden walkway in front of a tall house with red curtains. As she neared, Maia saw two of them open their blouses and lean over the youth, shaking their well-proportioned torsos. His color, already flushed, grew redder by the minute. Maia wondered why.

"Not now!" He muttered at the women. "Go back inside an' wait a minute!"

The young man was trying to concentrate on the approaching train, still half a kilometer away, its flywheels squealing as it began to brake. The young women seemed to relish the effect they were having. One pointed in glee, causing the others to laugh uproariously. The youth's taut trousers barely concealed a stiffening bulge. He looked up, saw Maia watching, and turned away with an embarrassed moan. This only brought more gales of hilarity from the local women.

"Hey, Garn," one shouted. "You sure yer holdin' the right stick?"

"Go 'way!" he shouted hoarsely, trying to look over his shoulder at the approaching train. Across the poor fellow's brow emerged a line of perspiration.

"Aw come on," another topless var crooned, jiggling at him. "Want another taste?" She proffered a clear bottle. Instead of liquid, it brimmed with a fine, bluish, iridescent powder. One corner of the boy's mouth bore a similar stain.

"What's goin' on here!"

Everyone turned toward the nearby red-curtained house. At the doorway stood a burly older man and—Tizbe!

But not the Tizbe she knew. Maia blinked. Her instant impression was that the var hitchhiker had, in just twenty minutes, changed her clothes, dyed her hair, and gained ten years!

Lysos, Maia thought, realizing how she'd been had. *Leie and I planned to travel about, pretending we were clones. I never expected to see the trick pulled in reverse!*

"These frills distractin' you, Garn?" the big man asked, wiping his lips with the back of one hand. Shaking his head vigorously, the youth replied. "N-no, Jacko, they just—"

"Lennie, Rose, get your iced-up perfs inside!" cursed the woman who looked like Tizbe. "No one's supposed to *see* that stuff, let alone get free samples!"

"Aw, Mirri, we were just testin'—" one girl whined, dodging a slap. The bottle was snatched out of her hand and she ran for the house.

So, Maia confirmed. *Tizbe's no var. And her type gets meaner with age.*

With a cold eye, the older woman turned and glared at Maia. "Who the vrilly hell are you?"

Maia blinked. "Ah . . . nobody."

"Then take off, Nobody. You haven't seen—"

"Garn!" the big man shouted. The youth below, confused by both commotion and his hormones, had forgotten the oncoming train and begun leaning on the lever, perhaps to spare his painful tumescence. There came a deep, electric hum and click. In dismay, he pushed the lever the other way, and shoved too far. Two loud, grinding clicks. He yanked back. . . .

A shrill toot filled the air as an alarmed engineer threw his emergency brakes, watching helplessly as momentum carried the oncoming locomotive along slick, invisible magnetic fields onto a track already occupied by another train.

The boy dove under the platform. Everyone else ran.

Maia knew now why her assistant baggage handler had looked familiar.

Past the crowd that gathered to gawk at the damage, Maia saw once more the woman she had mistaken for the hitchhiker, conversing intently with the real Tizbe. One or both had dyed her hair, but side by side it was obvious. They wore older and younger versions of the same face.

And now Maia recalled where she'd seen that visage before. Several sisters of their clan had been lounging at a café on the main square in Lanargh, outside another house equipped with plush curtains. Looking a second time, Maia saw the same emblem above the building overlooking the tracks—a grinning bull, grasping in its jaws a ringing bell.

Most towns possessed houses of ease—enterprises catering to human cravings, especially those of deep winter and high summer. "Escape valves," Savant Judeth had called them. "Bordellos," said Savant Claire, with finality that forbade even asking what the latter word meant.

The reality seemed rather ordinary and businesslike. Such houses provided one outlet for seamen who lacked invitations to clanholds when aurorae made their blood run hot. And in deep winter, when men were more interested in game boards than physical recreations, even normally cool Lamai sisters sometimes felt need of "a comfort." Especially when glory fell from heaven, they would head downtown, to visit one of those elegant palaces catering to richer hives.

Naturally, such profitable establishments were run by specialized clans, although frequent use was made of hired var labor. Maia and Leie had never thought themselves pretty or vapid enough for such a career. Still, they used to speculate what went on inside such places.

Both Tizbe and "Mirri" looked her way, causing Maia to turn quickly, feeling a chill of apprehension. *What are such high-class smugs doing out here in the sticks?*

It was pure luck of Lysos that no one had been seriously hurt in the wreck, considering how the two trains met in a tangle of sheet metal and spraying lubricants. Medics from the town clinic were still treating scratches and lacerations as the engineer of the second train shouted, pointing at his locomotive, then at the boy, Garn, who looked downcast and miserable.

Garn's older colleague yelled back, clenching his hands menacingly. In a sudden outburst, Jacko reached out and pushed the aggrieved engineer, who stumbled two paces, blinking in surprise. That only seemed to catalyze Jacko. Although physically no larger, he loomed over the retreating engineer, who now raised both hands placatingly.

Jacko punched him in the face.

Onlookers gasped as the engineer fell down. Whimpering, he tried crawling backward, holding a bloody nose. With dismay he saw Jacko follow, bearing down, clearly intent on more mayhem. Reading the engineer's bewilderment, Maia sensed the fallen man was furiously trying to *remember* something he had known in the past, but lately forgotten—like how to form a fist.

Abruptly, the woman Maia had mistaken for Tizbe was at Jacko's side, tugging his arm. It looked impossible, like trying to restrain a berserk sash-horse. Panting hard, Jacko appeared not to notice until Mirri reached up and took his ear, twisting it to get his attention. He winced, paused, started to turn. Gradually, her crooning words penetrated, until he finally nodded jerkily, allowing her to pull his elbow, drawing him about and leading him through the hushed crowd toward the red-curtained house.

Of course. That's another of their jobs. Despite all the laws and codes and sanctuaries, despite the well-tended hospitality halls of the great clans, there were always troubles in coastal towns during high summer, when aurorae danced and bright Wengel Star called out the old beast in males. Rutting men with nowhere to go, brawling and making enough noise to shame storm-season tempests. Pleasure clans knew sophisticated lore for handling such situations. The house mistress seemed quite skilled, luckily for the poor engineer.

Only it's not summer! Maia thought, struggling with confusion. *This shouldn't have happened.*

Through the dispersing throng, Maia glanced past the wreck at Tizbe—the real one this time—who looked right back at her, eyes filled with a glint of dark speculation.

H umans aren't like certain fish or plants, for whom sex is but one option. Something in sperm is vital to form the crucial placenta, which nurtures babies in the womb. Reproduction entirely without males —parthenogenesis—appears to be impossible for mammals. The best we can do is emulate a process used by some creatures on Earth, called amazonogenesis. Mating with a male is still needed, to spark conception, but the offspring are clones, genetically identical to their mother.

"Fine," said the early separationists of Herlandia. "We'll design males to serve this purpose, and no other!"

Remember the Herlandia drones? Tiny, useless things, their creation cannot be called cruel, since they were programmed for unending bliss, stroked like pampered lap dogs, always eager at beck and call, to do their duty.

They were abominations! To take powerful, graceful beings such as men—so full of curiosity and zest for life—and turn them into phlegmatic freaks, this was abhorrent. Naturally it failed. Even without direct genetic involvement, pallid fathers will sire a pallid race.

Besides, shall we eliminate variability entirely? What if circumstances change? We may need the gene-churning magic of normal sexuality, from time to time.

The Enemy's arrival at Herlandia brought that experiment to an abrupt, well-deserved end. Naturally, the womenfolk of that colony world defended their brave new civilization with no end of ingenuity and courage. But when they most needed that special wrath which makes warriors, they found that they had purposely jettisoned one of its primal fonts. Lap dogs aren't much help when monsters prowl the sky.

That, my sisters, is another reason we should not entirely abandon the male side.

Our descendants may encounter times when it has its uses.

6

There were no recitations from the travel guide when the journey recommenced. Tizbe read her book in silence, or stared through the dusty window at the monotonous countryside. Maia found the silence unnerving. Her thoughts roiled from all she had seen, and more she suspected lay unseen. Until now, she had attributed many queer incidents to "other ports, other lands." Now she knew with a sinking feeling. *Something's happening. And I don't think I'm going to like it.*

Back home, one thing always used to make her more aggressive than Leie—curiosity. Even punishment seldom dissuaded Maia from pursuing inquiries that were "none of a summerling's business." She had sworn to suppress the trait, especially since the storm. *I'm practical now. A lone var has to be.* But there was no real option of turning away, this time. Like a loose tooth, the agony of leaving this mystery alone would drive her crazy.

Whenever she felt certain the other woman wasn't looking, Maia sneaked glances at Tizbe's carpet-sided valise, which almost certainly held more than just clothing.

Dammit. Can I afford more trouble?

The young blonde yawned, put her book aside, and stretched across the gunnysacks, giving Maia a good look at the dark roots of her dyed hair. After Clay Town, she knew this was no spoiled summerling, wandering in idle search of a cushy niche, but a full daughter-member of a hive with connections stretching far beyond Maia's own limited experience. Tizbe wasn't just "looking around." She was on duty, working for her family business.

Picture a rich, powerful clan. Its chief livelihood is pleasure houses. A complex, profitable enterprise, demanding much more than strong hands and a pretty face.

Although they ran no house in Port Sanger, she had seen the type on occasion, walking proudly in fine traveling robes or riding lugar-borne litters, tending business at the best holds, and even dropping by for visits with the Lamai mothers.

Special, door-to-door massage service? Maia wondered. But that was too simplistic. Few of those visits had been in high summer or winter. Lamais were a self-controlled lot, who never thought of sex at other times of year.

Couriers, then? A door-to-door *message* service? Their main business would be a perfect cover for a profitable sideline, delivering communiqués between allied clans, for example. But what sort of message would be worth the fees they'd charge?

Pretty damn dangerous ones, Maia figured. *Or,* she added, looking at the valise. *Dangerous goods.*

That bottle of blue-green powder, glistening and sloshing like liquid . . . It was something you gave men, apparently. Something linked to one youth's inconvenient erection, another man's unseasonal rage. Maia recalled the earlier incident aboard the Wotan, when those sailors seemed aroused by her nakedness, despite it being autumn and she a mere summerling, a virgin, and filthy besides. *That* time the mysterious courier had been male, but after weeks at sea and on the rails, she now knew groups of women and men were capable of cooperating in complex endeavors.

Including crime?

The blonde woman lay sprawled with one arm over her eyes, snoring softly. Maia stood up with a sigh. *I know I'm gonna regret this.*

She took one hesitant step. Another. A floorboard creaked, making her flinch. She peered near her feet. Through the dust, nail heads showed where the joists were. Maia resumed her creep more carefully, until finally she crouched next to the sleeping woman.

The suitcase was woven from coarse fabric, with designs of abstract, interlocking geometric forms. A soft hum told of some metal part vibrating in harmony with the magnetic-pulse impeller of the locomotive. Examining the lock mechanism, she saw that the simple keyhole was cosmetic camouflage. Three small buttons protruded along one side. Maia blew a silent sigh, recognizing expensive technology. There would be a code for pressing them in a certain order, or an alarm might go off.

Maia backed away cautiously, and returned with a thin, stiff length of wire, normally used to bind heavy articles of baggage. Checking once more that her "assistant" still slept, she began working one end of the wire between the heavy fabric's warp and weft. With a final shove, it pierced through and met softer resistance, presumably Tizbe's clothes. Pushing farther revealed nothing. Maia drew the wire out again, and repeated the procedure a few centimeters away, with the same result.

I could be wrong . . . about a lot of things. Maia squatted on her haunches, pondering. Prudence urged that she forget about it.

Curiosity and obstinacy were stronger. She shifted her weight, maneuvering to get at the satchel from another angle . . .

A floorboard groaned, like a dying animal. Maia's breath caught. *It can't have been as loud as that! It's just because I'm nervous.* Eyeing Tizbe, Maia wondered what she'd say if the clone wakened to find her here. The hitchhiker smacked her lips and changed position slightly, then settled down again, snoring a little louder. Dry-mouthed, Maia positioned her tool at a new location and worked it once more between the fibers. It resisted, penetrated, and then halted with an abrupt, faint tinkling sound.

Aha!

She repeated the experiment several more times, delving a rough map of the satchel's interior. For a var on the road, Tizbe seemed to be carrying few personal effects and a lot of heavy glass bottles.

Gingerly, Maia backed away until she was safely at her desk again. She tossed aside the wire, chewing her lower lip. *So, now you know Tizbe's a courier, carrying something mysterious. You still can't prove anything illegal's going on.* All the sneaking around, the whispers at dockside, rich clones pretending to be poor vars, those might point to crime. *Or they might have legitimate reasons for secrecy, business reasons.*

A second aspect worried Maia more. *The chaos in Lanargh may have been partly caused by this. The accident in Clay Town sure was. Could anything that makes so much trouble be legal?*

In theory, the law was where all three social orders met as equals. In practice, it took time to learn the marsh of planetary, regional, and local codes, as well as precedents and traditions passed down from the Founding, and even Old Earth. Large clans often deputized one or more full daughters to study law, argue cases, and cast block votes during elections. What young var could afford to give more than a passing glance through dusty legal tomes, even when they were available? The system might seem intentionally designed to exclude the lower classes, except why bother, since clones far outnumbered summerlings, anyway?

Maia shook her head. She needed advice, wisdom, but how to get

it? Long Valley didn't even have an organized Guardia. What need, with
reavers and other coastal troubles far away, and men banished during rut
time?

There was one place Maia could go. Where a young var like her was
supposed to take troubles beyond her grasp.

She decided she had better try something else, first.

The train's last stop for the day was Holly Lock. This time, Tizbe didn't
even pretend to help as Maia hauled packages, struggled with the cum-
bersome Musseli accounting system, then faced the scrutiny of a hair-
splitting freightmistress. With an airy "g'bye-see-you-round!" the blonde
traveler was gone. By the time Maia finished, she was telling herself
good riddance. Let those cryptic bottles be someone else's problem.

Holly Lock was little more than a cluster of warehouses, grain ele-
vators, and cattle chutes on one side of the tracks, and a warren of small
houses for singleton vars and microclans on the other. There was nothing
resembling even the modest "town center" of Port Sanger, where a few
civil servants performed their functions, ignored by the population at
large. Hefting her bag, Maia paused in front of the station office, where
an older, slightly-less-unfriendly-looking Musseli chatted with a burly
woman whose suntan was the color of rich copper. As Maia stood indeci-
sively in the doorway, the stationmaster looked up with a raised eyebrow.
"Yes?"

On impulse, Maia decided. "Excuse me for intruding, madame,
but . . ." She swallowed. "Can you tell me where I'd find a savant in
town? One who has net access? I need to buy a consultation."

The two older women looked at each other. The stationmaster
snickered. "A savant, you say? A sav-ant. I think mebbe I heard o' such
things. Is they anythin' like smart bees?" Her sarcastic rendition of man-
speech made Maia blush.

The woman with the weathered skin had eyes that crinkled when
she smiled. "Now, Tess. She's an earnest little varling. Lysos, can you
figure what a consult's gonna cost her, not gettin' clan rates? Must need
it pretty bad." She turned to Maia. "Got no licensed savants in this part
o' the valley, little virgie. But tell you what. I'm swinging past Jopland
Hold on my way back to the mine. Could give you a lift."

"Um. Do they have—"

"An uplink, sure. Richest mothers in these parts. Got full console
an' everything. But maybe you won't have to use it. What you're really
needing, I figure, is some good motherly advice. Could save you the cost
of a consult."

Motherly advice was what she had been taught to seek, if ever in trouble out in the world. Ideally, the mothers of the largest, best-respected local clan were available not just to their own daughters, but anyone, even man or var, who was righteous and in need. In fact, Maia didn't have much appetite for a band of elderly clones, accustomed to holding feudal court out in the sticks, pouring platitudes and assigning her verses from the Book of the Founders.

But she says they have a console.

"All right," she said, and turned to the stationmaster. "I'm afraid that means—"

"Don't tell me. You may not make it back in time to catch the 6:02. Oh, shoot." The Musseli yawned to show how upset she was. "I guess there's always another var waitin' in the pool. Come back and we'll put you in queue for another run, sometime."

Great. Lost seniority and maybe a week waiting around for another train. This is already costing me plenty.

Maia had a gnawing feeling it was going to add up to a lot more, before she was done.

W e are programmed to find sex pleasurable for one simple reason—because animals who mate have offspring. Those who do not mate have none. Traits that result in successful reproduction get reinforced and passed on. Evolution is that simple.

It is therefore useless to bemoan as evil the fact that men tend toward aggression. Among our ancestors, aggression often helped males have more offspring than their competitors. "Good" or "evil" had little to do with it.

That is, until we reached consciousness, at which point, good and evil became pertinent indeed! Behaviors which might be excusable in dumb beasts can seem perverted, criminal, when performed by thinking beings. Just because a trait is "natural" does not oblige us to keep it.

While Herlandia's radicals went too far, we can surely do better than those timorous compromisers back on New Terra or Florentina, making timid, minuscule changes by consensus only. For instance, without eliminating male feistiness entirely, we can channel it to certain narrow seasons, as in rutting animals like deer and elk. Other inconvenient or dangerous traits can be quarantined, isolated, so our daughters need no longer face them year-round, day in, day out.

Boldness and insight are needed for this endeavor, as well as compassion for the inevitable struggles our descendants shall have to endure.

7

The sun was low when Maia finished helping the big woman load her buckboard. On their way out of town, they paused at the transients' hostel, where Maia ran inside to store her duffel. Not that it held much of value. Just clothes and a few mementos, including a book of ephemerides Leie had given her as a birthday present. There was also a small, blackened lump of stone. A gift from Old Coot Bennett—before the light left his rheumy eyes—which he had sworn was a true meteorite. Maia didn't want to leave her possessions, but it made no sense to haul them to Jopland Hold and back for just one night. Stuffing a few items into her jacket pockets, she took a receipt from the Musseli attendant and hurried to catch her ride.

Heavily laden, the horse-drawn wagon moved slowly along the narrow dirt road north of town, jostling over ruts and bumps left untended since the storms of summer. Floating dust tickled the membranes under Maia's eyelids, causing them to flutter intermittently, dimming vision. "Valley council keeps puttin' off fixin' these paths," the wagon's owner complained. "The biddies say there's no money, but always seem to find it b'fore harvest time! Farmers run everything here, virgie. Remember that, an' you'll get by."

Perkinite farmers, Maia added silently. The sect appealed to smaller clans, not long risen above the status of lowly vars. Even the wealthiest clans in Long Valley were modest by coastal standards, unless they were cadet branches of more-extended hives elsewhere.

Maia's benefactor came from such a branch. She was a *Lerner*. Maia knew the family, whose scattered offshoots had wedged holdings throughout Eastern Continent, wherever there were ore deposits too meager to attract big mining concerns, and communities with needs a small-time forging operation could fill. Hard experience had taught Lerner Clan the limits of their talents. Whenever one of their operations grew large enough to draw competition, they would always sell out and move on.

It's a niche, though, Maia supposed. Few vars established a name-line of their own, let alone one so numerous. She was in no position to judge.

Calma Lerner seemed friendly enough. A woman with man-sized hands nearly as hard as the gritty, reddish ingots Maia had helped load, brought on today's train from far-off Grange Head. The alloys would be mixed with local iron, using household recipes passed down from mother to daughter for generations, to make unpretentious Lerner Steel.

Back in Port Sanger, the local Lerners did not endure the prairie sun, and so were much paler. Yet, there was a sense of familiarity, as if she and Calma ought to be gossiping about acquaintances they had in common. Of course they had none. The familiarity went one way. Nor would Calma likely recall Maia if they met again. People tended not to bother memorizing, or even much noticing, a face with just one owner.

Still, as tawny countryside rolled slowly by, the older woman began showing some of her clan's well-known affability, letting herself be drawn out about life on this great, flat, alluvial plain. Calma and her family worked the earth out north of Holly Lock, where faulting had brought to surface a rare fold of bedrock containing a promising mix of elements. Back when settlement at this end of the valley was still new, three young cadets from an established Lerner hold had arrived from the coast to work those narrow seams and set up smithies. Across four generations there had been hard times and some years of prosperity. There were now six adults in the midget offshoot clan, and four clone daughters of various ages. That did not count one summerling boy, plus a dozen or so transient var employees.

When she discovered that Maia's education included a tape course in chemistry, Calma began warming to her, growing effusive about the challenges and delights of metallurgy on the frontier—shaping and transforming the raw stuff of the planet to satisfy human needs. "You can't imagine the satisfaction," she said, waving broad arms toward the horizon, where the setting sun seemed to set fire to a sea of grain. "There's great opportunities out here for a youngster with the right hardworkin' attitude. Yes. Fine opportunities indeed."

Out of courtesy, and because she had taken a liking to her companion, Maia refrained from laughing aloud. Some dead ends weren't hard to spot, and poor Calma was describing a real loser. "I'll think about it," Maia replied carefully, concealing amusement.

With a sudden pang, she realized she had been filing away the Lerner clone's words. Storing them with the habitual intention of repeating them later . . . for Leie. She couldn't help it. Patterns of a lifetime die hard. Sometimes harder than frail human beings.

"You'd think they already had enough wine for a funeral," she recalled complaining to her twin one winter when they were four, as they labored at a ratcheted crank, operating pulleys to descend into a pit of stone. *"Are they gonna have us goin' up and down all night?"*

"Could be," Leie had replied breathlessly, her voice echoing down the narrow dumbwaiter shaft. Clicking softly, the winch marked each centimeter of descent like the beating of a clock. *"There was glory frost on the sills this morning an' you know that puts 'em in a party mood. I'm bettin' the Lamais have more in mind than a ceremony to mulch three grandmas."*

Maia recalled wincing at the sarcastic image. Although Lamais were cool toward their var-daughters, they tended to mellow with age, even going as far as showing real affection late in life. Two of the departed grannies had almost been nice. Besides, it was wrong to speak ill of the dead. *They say Stratos reuses all the atoms we give back to her, and each piece of us goes on to help new life.*

Abstract solace had seemed pallid that day, after Maia's first direct contact with death. The cramped elevator car had felt stifling, rocking unpleasantly as they turned the crank. Their lanterns set the stone walls glittering where moisture leaked from the poorly caulked kitchens above, and echoes of their heavy breathing had fluttered like trapped souls against the walls of the pit. When the wooden box hit bottom, they stepped out with relief. In one direction, sealed bins contained enough grains and emergency supplies to withstand a siege. Tier upon tier of shelving held kegs and glittering rows of wax-dipped bottles.

Carrying a hand-scrawled list, Leie sauntered toward the wine racks to fetch the vintages they had been sent for. Knowing her sister wouldn't mind a brief desertion, Maia had walked down another narrow aisle, using her lantern to play light across a stone portal enclosing a door made lavishly of reinforced steel.

The surrounding rock was a maze of deep cuts and grooves. Some incisions were twisty, others straight and wide enough to slip a blade inside. A few knobs would depress a little if you pushed, emitting enticing clicks, hinting at some hidden mechanism.

The one time she had asked a Lamai about the door, Maia had received a slap that left her ears ringing. Leie used to fantasize about what mysterious riches lay beyond, while Maia was seized by the puzzle itself. Smuggling paper and pencil to trace the outlines, she would spend hours contemplating combinations and secret codes. It had to be a tough one, since the Lamai blithely sent unsupervised varlings to the cellar, on errands.

On that day, after finishing loading bottles aboard the dumbwaiter, Leie had come alongside to put an arm around Maia's shoulder. *"Don't let the vrilly jigsaw get you down. Maybe we can sneak a hydraulic jack down here, one smuggy piece at a time. Bam! No more mystery!"*

"It's not that," Maia had answered, shaking her head despondently. *"I was just thinking about those old women, those grandmas. We knew 'em. They were always around while we were little, like the sun an' air. Now they're just lying in the chapel, all stiff and . . ."* She shivered. The funeral had been their first to attend, as four-year-olds. *"And all those others in the first row, lookin' like they knew it was gonna be their turn soon."*

Full-blood Lamais normally lived a ripe twenty-eight or twenty-nine Stratoin years. When one of them went, however, a whole "class" tended to follow within weeks. No one expected this to be the last funeral of the season, or of the month.

"I know," Leie replied in a voice gone unusually reflective. *"It scared me, too."*

Maia had rested her head against her sister's, comforted by knowing someone understood the questions troubling her soul.

On their way back up the dank elevator shaft, Leie had tried to lighten the mood by relating some gossip picked up that morning from another town varling. It seemed several younger sisters of Saxton Clan had started a ruckus near the harbor, harassing sailors until, in desperation, the men called the Guardia and—

A covey of spiny-fringed pou birds erupted across the road, causing the sash-horses to neigh and prance while Calma Lerner pulled the reins, speaking to soothe the frightened beasts. The birds vanished into a cane brake, pursued by a clutch of pale foxes.

Maia blinked, holding her breath for several seconds. The flood of memory had briefly seemed more vivid than the dusty present. Perhaps the rocking wooden bench seat reminded her of the creaking dumbwaiter. Or some other subconscious cue, a smell, or glitter in the twilight, had triggered the unsought fit of retrospection.

Funny. Now that her train of thought was broken, Maia couldn't recall what choice bit of hearsay Leie had shared with her that day, while the two of them hung suspended between cellar and scullery. Only that she had guffawed, covering her mouth to keep her squeals from echoing throughout the house. Her sides had hurt for hours afterward, both from laughter and the effort of suppressing it, and Leie had joined in, giggling, barely able to hold the crank still. A wine bottle tipped over, cracking and dribbling red liquid across the wooden floor. The crimson pool had spread and found its way through wooden slats to audibly splatter, after a brief delay, into the tomblike cellar far below.

Why don't you leave me alone? Maia thought plaintively, shaking her head and fighting tears. Memory wasn't what she wanted or needed, right now. Poignancy was a bitter tang in her mouth and eyes.

Yet it was a mixed thing. While renewed mourning hurt, the sweetness of that recollected laughter seemed to suffuse a deeper part of her, permeating the wound with a sad pleasure, a tryst solace. Against her will, Maia found herself wearing a faint smile.

Maybe all we get is moments, she thought, and decided not to resist quite so hard if another happy memory came to mind.

Calma Lerner hadn't spoken in some time, perhaps sensing her passenger's absorption. So Maia gave a start when the woman abruptly announced, "Your stop's comin' up. Jopland Hold. Over past that orchard."

While Maia's thoughts had turned inward and the afternoon faded, a dark expanse of fruit trees had appeared just beyond a gurgling watercourse. She peered at the plantation, whose disciplined array of slender trunks made ever-changing row-and-lattice patterns. As the wagon clattered across a plank bridge, the cultivated forest seemed to explode around Maia in an ecstasy of planned geometry, a crystalline study in living wood. The rapidly dimming light only enhanced each viewing angle, trading ease of distance for an impression of infinity.

Soon Maia noticed that the trees came arrayed with an illumination all their own. Dim flickerings along the myriad branches made her blink in surprise. At first they looked like decorations, but then she realized they must be glow beetles, setting the orchard's columns and intersections glittering with earnest, insectoid mating displays. Shimmering wavelets coursed down the serried avenues. One could trace those ripples, Maia observed, much as one might briefly track the parallel harmonies of a four-part fugue . . . only by letting go.

It must be a sight later on, she thought, wishing she could stay and swim forever in this pocket galaxy, a swarm of miniature stars.

The road emerged from the forest, leaving the rippling lattice behind. Up ahead, the more-stolid light of a lesser moon fell on a cluster of handsome farm buildings, including a two-story house made of adobe or reinforced sod. Antennas aimed toward the sparse array of satellites still functioning in high orbit.

"Jopland Home," Calma Lerner repeated. "Since it's late, they'll put you up in a barn, I figure. Code of hospitality. But if you get on their wrong side, don't worry. Just follow my wheel ruts northwest three kilos, bank right at the big willow, go two more klicks an' follow your nose. People say they can smell Lerner Hold long before they get to it. Never noticed, myself."

"Thanks." Maia nodded. "Oh, is that easy to do? I mean, getting on their wrong side."

Calma shrugged. "Everyone around here comes to Jopland for judgments, sooner or later. You learn to be careful *how* you say things. That's all."

The wagon pulled by a tall gate in the slotted fence without slowing. Maia swung out and walked alongside for a few meters. "Thanks for the warning, and the lift."

"Nothin' to it. Good luck with your *con-sult-ation!*" The big woman laughed with an airy wave. Soon the wagon was gone from sight, trailing a low cloud of dust.

Several large carriages filled the drive in front of the main house. A young woman, probably a var servant, curried more horses at a watering trough. *This must be the social hub of the county,* Maia thought, knocking at the front door. A towering lugar soon answered, dressed in a green-and-yellow-striped vest that had seen better days. The white-furred creature tilted its grizzled head, and an inquiring mew escaped its muzzle.

"A citizen seeks wisdom," Maia pronounced clearly, slowly. "I ask guidance from the mothers of Jopland Hold."

The lugar stared at her for several seconds, then made a low, rumbling sound at the back of its throat. It turned, vaguely motioning for Maia to follow.

While the outside walls were adobe, the interior of the mansion was richly lined with veneered hardwood, foreign to these upland plains. Wall sconces gave off pale electric illumination, highlighting a garish emblem over the main stairway—a plow encircled with sheaves of wheat. *At least there are no statues,* Maia thought.

The lugar spread two heavy, sliding doors and ushered her into a brighter room, presumably the main hall. A drifting haze stung Maia's eyes. *Men,* she saw in surprise. There were about a dozen of them, sprawled on somewhat worn sofas and cushions puffing long-stemmed pipes while four young servants hurried from the kitchen carrying steins of brown ale. The male nearest the door was reading quietly under a lamp. Further away, two of them faced a flickering telescreen, watching some faraway sporting competition. Several in the far corner could be seen poring over a miniature Game of Life set, only a meter on a side, its gridlike surface covered with tiny black, white, or purple squares that clicked and throbbed under the players' concentrated gaze, sweeping mysterious, ever-changing patterns across the board. The rest of the men sat quietly, immersed in their own thoughts. Few had even bothered changing out of their work clothes—red, orange, or black one-piece uniforms of the three railroad guilds. Maia guessed every male within forty miles must be in this room tonight. *The clans are starting winter wooing early, just like back home,* she thought.

Twice in that first sweep of the room, Maia had seen men yawn. No doubt most had put in a long day's work before coming out this way. Still, they didn't appear to be showing fatigue, but ennui.

Looks like I came at a bad time.

No adult women were visible, yet. Except in summer, men generally preferred evenings that started quietly, without pressure. So the chosen Joplands were probably in back somewhere, changing from ranch gear into garments the mail-order catalogs promised would stoke that dormant spark of male desire. Maia glanced at the four serving girls stepping carefully around their guests, trying to be unobtrusive. Two of them, though of different ages, wore identical features—olive of complexion, small-built, but with well-toned muscles. Their proudest adornment was their silky black hair, which they kept long despite the valley's ever-wafting dust.

Those must be winter daughters, Maia decided, estimating their ages at four and five. The other two girls, older and not as well dressed, were definitely not identical and probably var employees.

Several men glanced up when Maia entered. Most quickly lost interest and went back to what they had been doing, but one young fellow, clean-shaven and tidier than the others, took more than a moment in his perusal, and even smiled faintly when she met his eyes. He shifted in his chair, and Maia felt a fluttering panic that he was about to come over and speak to her! What could she possibly say if he did?

At that moment, a brush of air told Maia of doors opening behind her. The young man looked past her, sighed, and sank down again. With an odd mix of relief and disappointment, Maia turned to see what had caused such a reaction.

"Who are *you*, and what are you doing here?"

The imperious tone seemed not at all anomalous coming from the short, dowdy figure confronting Maia, arms crossed. Apparently Joplands went to flesh with age, although the woman's shoulders implied considerable strength, even late in life. The lovely skin tone of the youngsters had gone to leather, but the silken black hair was unchanged. That was another thing about being a var. Unlike normal folk, you had no clear idea what you'd look like when you got older. Maia wasn't sure she didn't prefer it that way.

"A citizen comes beseeching aid," she said, bowing courteously before the elder Jopland. "I've seen your uplink, O Mother, and must ask aid in consulting the sages of Caria."

She hadn't meant to speak loudly, but her words carried. Suddenly, the room's relative quiet fell to utter hush. A glimmer of interest seemed to rise beneath the hooded eyelids of the nearby men, much to the irritation of the Jopland matriarch.

"Oh, *must* you, variant-daughter? You figure on saying something the savants might be interested in?"

"I do, Mother. And I see your system is operational." She gestured toward the ancient tele. From the look on the old woman's face, Maia had just given her one more reason to hate the machine, but it was a valued accessory for attracting men to soirées like this one. "By the ancient codes," Maia concluded, "I ask help arranging my call."

A deeply pursed frown. The elder obviously hated having codes quoted to her by a statusless stripling. "Hmph. You have lousy timing." There was a pause. "We aren't obliged to pay your charges. I expect you can cover them?"

When Maia reached for her purse, the crone hissed. "Not here, witling! Have you no shame?" Maia blinked in confusion. Was there some local Perkinite custom against handling money in front of men? "Forgive me, Mother." She bowed again.

"Mm. This way, then. And you!" The old woman snapped her fingers at one of the var serving girls. "That gentleman's glass is empty!" With a sniff, she turned and led Maia down a narrow hallway.

The corridor took them by a room where, in passing, Maia glimpsed several young women making preparations. Jopland fems were handsome creatures in their prime, Maia conceded, between ages six and twelve. Especially if you liked strong jaws and boldly outlined brows. But then, there was no accounting for the tastes of men, who grew increasingly finicky as Wengel Star receded and the aurorae died.

The young Joplands shared mirrors with one pair and a trio of clones from other families—the first type tall, with frizzy hair, and the other broad of shoulder and hip, with breasts ample enough to feed quadruplets. Apparently, Jopland shared the expense of hosting with a couple of allied clans. By the looks of banked enthusiasm Maia had witnessed in the Main Hall, they probably had to throw several such evenings to get just a few winter pregnancies.

Given the size of the house, Maia had expected to see more fecund

Joplands, till she realized. *There's talk of a population drop in the valley, just when it's rising elsewhere.*

Of course. The boom along the coast comes mostly from "excess" summer births. But these smugs are Perkinites. Men are kept away in summer, just to avoid that kind of pregnancy! That explained why she had seen no var-daughters, women half-resembling their Jopland mothers.

Maia wanted to linger, curious how these frontier women managed something even rich, attractive, seaside Lamatia found tricky at times. "*This* way," the elder Jopland hissed, interrupting her perusal.

"Uh, sorry, ma'am." Bending her head, Maia hurried after her reluctant hostess.

The communications chamber was spare, barely a cabinet. The standard console lay on a rickety table, bundles of cable exiting through a hole in the wall. Only the chairs looked comfortable, for mothers to use during long-range business calls, but those were pulled away and a bare stool set in front of the table instead. With a gnarled finger, the aged Jopland touched a switch causing the small screen to come alight with a pearly glow.

"Guest call. Accounting on completion," she told the machine, then turned to Maia. "If you can't cover the charges, you'll work it off. One month per hundred. Agreed?"

Maia felt a flare of anger. The offer was outrageous. *The rudest Port Sanger summerling has better breeding than you, "mother."* But then, breeding and style weren't what it took to win and hold a niche out here on the prairie. Once again, Maia recalled—a var's place wasn't to judge.

"Agreed," she bit out. The Jopland smiled.

This had better not cost a lot! Working for clones like these would be patarkal hell.

Maia sat down facing the standard-model console. Somewhere she had heard that it was one of just nine photonic devices still massproduced in ancient factories on Landing Continent. Others included the all-purpose motors used on the solar railway, and the Game of Life set she had glimpsed minutes before, in the main hall. Maia had never actually used a console in earnest. She tried recalling Savant Judeth's cursory lessons back at Lamatia. *Let's see . . . it's on voice mode, so if I phrase my request—*

Maia suddenly realized she hadn't heard the door close. Turning, she saw the Jopland matriarch leaning against the jamb, arms crossed.

"I ask the courtesy-right of privacy," Maia said, hating the other woman for making it necessary. The crone smirked. "Clock's already ticking, virgie. Have fun." With a click, the door closed behind her.

Damn! Now Maia saw the chronometer display in the upper left corner of the screen, whirling rapidly. It showed charges of eleven credits already! Nervously, she spoke toward the machine. "Uh, I need to talk to someone . . . a savant? Or someone in the guardia?"

This was going badly. "Oh yes! In Caria City!"

The screen, which had so far remained obtusely blank, at last resolved into a pattern of boxes. *A logical array,* she recalled from lessons. Along the top it said:

Query Address Zone — City of Caria
generic reference-type sought
Imprecise partial cues — "savant" and/or "guardia"
Suggested clarification — SUBJECT MATTER? _____

Maia perceived it would be a mistake to try parsing her question in the proper formal way. What she saved in processing costs would be more than lost in connection time. Perhaps, if she just *talked* at it, the machine would extract what it needed.

"I'm not sure. I've seen strange things, in Lanargh and in Clay Town. Men acting like it was summer, but it's not, you know? I think they must've eaten or sniffed something. Something people want kept secret. Some kind of blue powder? In glass bottles? . . ."

The screen flickered several times, with boxes rearranging themselves across the screen, each containing one or more of her spoken words. An array of interlinking arrows kept shifting connections between the boxes as she spoke. Maia had to concentrate to keep the dazzling puzzle from transfixing her. ". . . there was a girl from one of the pleasure clans, I think they use an emblem with a bull and a ringing bell. She's carrying the bottles like some sort of courier—"

Suddenly the boxes seemed to collapse, as if her thoughts had abruptly resolved in neat cubes, coalescing into a configuration of pristine clarity, a logically consistent whole. The picture lasted just an instant, too brief to read consciously. Maia felt a pang of loss when it vanished.

The pattern was replaced by a human face—a woman wearing her slightly wavy brown hair in a simple fall down one side, kept in place by an elegant gold barrette. In handsome middle age, the woman regarded Maia for a long moment, then spoke with a voice of authority.

"You have reached Planetary Equilibrium Security. State name and nascence affiliation."

Maia had never heard of the organization before. Nervously, she identified herself. For official purposes a var used the last name of her maternal clan, though it felt strange mouthing the words—"Maia per Lamai."

"All right, please go back over your story. From the beginning this time, if you please?"

Maia was gnawingly aware that charges had eaten half her meager savings. "It all began when my sister and I took our first var-voyage jobs on the colliers Wotan and Zeus. When we hit Lanargh I saw a man in fancy clothes who wasn't a sailor come down to the docks and meet three of our sailors who then acted real strange, pinching me and saying summery stuff even though it was autumn and I was filthy and, well, they couldn't have smelled any, well, you know, I'm just a . . ."

"A virgin. I understand," the official said. "Go on."

"In fact, my sister and I . . ." Maia swallowed hard, forcing herself to concentrate on bare facts. The Lysos-damned clock seemed to be speeding up! "We saw men acting that way all over town! Then in Grange Head I got this job working on the railroad and I saw the same thing happen in front of a house in Holly Lock that's run by the same pleasure clan and Tizbe—"

"Hold . . . hold it!" The woman in the screen shook her head in puzzlement. "Why are you talking so fast?"

In agony, Maia watched the counter take up her last savings. Now she was doomed to a month working for the Joplands. "I . . . can't afford to talk to you anymore. I didn't know it would be so expensive. I'm sorry."

Downcast, she reached for the cutoff switch.

"Stop! What are you *doing*?" The woman held up a hand. "Just . . . hold it a second."

She turned to her left, leaning out of Maia's field of view. Maia looked up at the corner of the screen where the counter spun on for a moment and then . . . stopped! She stared. An instant later, the digits rippled, turning into a row of zeros!

"Is that better?" the woman asked, reappearing. "Can you talk easier now?"

"I . . . didn't know you could do that."

"Your mothers never mentioned reversing charges on important calls to the authorities?"

Maia shook her head. "I guess . . . they must've thought it'd make us spendthrift, or lazy."

The policewoman let out a snort. "Well, now you know. So. Are we calmer? Yes? Let's backtrack, then, to where you say you first saw this bottle of blue powder."

In the end, Maia realized she hadn't a whole lot to offer.

Her fantasies had ranged from disaster—her story proving to be trivial or stupid—all the way to miraculous. *Could this be what that savant on the tele in Lanargh had been talking about, when she offered big rewards for "information"?* She had wondered.

The truth seemed to lie somewhere in between. The official, who called herself Research Agent Foster, promised Maia a small but worthwhile fee to come to Grange Head in fourteen days, and tell her story in detail to a magistrate who was scheduled to pass through about then. Her expenses would also be covered, so long as they were modest. Agent Foster did not volunteer any explanations for the events Maia had seen, but from her demeanor of attentive but unbothered interest, Maia got the impression this was one of many leads in a case already long under way.

They seem awfully calm about it, Maia thought. Especially if someone was meddling with the sexual cycle of the seasons. It had already caused one accident, and who knew what chaos might ensue if it got out of hand?

The agent gave her a number to use if she ever had to call again, then signed off, leaving on the screen something else Maia hadn't heard of before, a requisition on Jopland Clan for one night's guest lodgings and a meal, at Colony expense.

When she went to the door, Maia found the matriarch standing there, wearing a broad smile. "Did you finish your consultation, daughter?" she asked eagerly.

"Yes. I'm finished now."

"Good. I'll have one of the servants show you a pallet in the barn. In the morn we'll discuss how you'll work off your debt."

For the first time in weeks Maia felt a sense of relish, of anticipation. Leie would have loved this.

"Your pardon, Revered Mother, but the barn won't do. In the morning, after a good breakfast, I'll be happy to discuss your, um, lending me transportation back to town."

The Jopland elder blanched, then flushed crimson in a reversal that was surprising, given her dark complexion. She pushed Maia aside and hurriedly read the screen, gargling in rage. "How did you do this! I warn you, if this is some city trick—"

"Lysos, I don't think so. You're welcome to call Planetary Equilibrium Security, if you want to verify it."

Maia did not even know what the words meant, but they had dramatic effect. The old woman swayed as if she had been struck. Only after visible effort did she manage to speak in a harsh whisper. "I'll take you to your room."

Out in the hallway, Maia heard distant sounds of music and laughter. Apparently, a decent party had gotten under way, after all. As a var, she was used to not being invited to such affairs, and was unsurprised when the crone led her in the other direction. It was a bit disturbing, though, when they descended steps into the farmyard. Two dogs came to growl briefly at Maia before sidling away at a sharp command from her host.

"It's not the barn I'm taking you to, don't worry. But we're goin' around the house. I don't want you disturbing our guests."

Through front-facing windows, Maia heard hearty male laughter. Farther along, they passed before several dimly lit rooms from which came breathy, hoarse sounds unmistakable as anything but passion. *Well,* she thought, feeling her ears grow warm, *the Joplands ought to be happy. Seems they're getting their money's worth tonight.* Odds-on, at least one winter clone would be ignited by the labor of these hardworking men.

At the far end of the southern wing stood several small apartments, each with its own door and plank porch. There were no keys or locks. The matriarch pushed into the last one and stood on tiptoe in order to tighten a bare bulb. Only wan illumination spilled forth, explaining why there was no switch. That bulb would never get too hot to touch. Over in one corner, a pair of folded blankets lay atop a packed-straw mattress. Maia shrugged. She had slept worse.

"Cockcrow for breakfast, or none," her reluctant host said, departing without another word. Maia closed the door, then set to laying out the bedclothes. Finding a pitcher of water on a rickety table, she washed her face, took a long drink from the spout, and reached up to turn out the light.

Elsewhere in the rambling farm complex, people were vigorously occupied making strong, atonal harmonies. *The music of joy,* poets sometimes called it. To Maia it sounded much more serious.

Of course, there were different rhythms for each time of year. In summer it was men who eagerly sought, while skeptical women sometimes let themselves be convinced. These were patterns Maia had known all her life. Nature's way.

Well, the way chosen for us by Lysos and the Founders, Maia pondered, listening in the dark. *It's hard to imagine any other.*

Maia had thought about sex—two willing partners coming together, whether by wooing or after being wooingly pursued. It seemed an act partly sublime, but also filled with all the frenetic, damp, clasping after life that came from certain knowledge of it slipping away. A fusion aimed at immortality, some called it.

As a young virgin, Maia would not feel that hormonal rush of desire, if at all, until winter's deepest nadir. Still, for as much as a year before departing Port Sanger she had begun experiencing sensations she felt must surely be related. A faint longing, a void. She vaguely suspected sex might have a role in filling it. A partial role.

Sighs and murmured cries. The sounds were fascinating, yet again Maia wondered if there wasn't something more to it than a mere rubbing, release, and a mixing of fluids. A union that enhanced and magnified what each party brought separately.

Or am I just naive? It was a private suspicion she had never dared share, even with Leie. *"You want to keep a smelly, scratchy man as a pet?"* her twin might have taunted. Even now, Maia had no idea what it was she really desired, as if her desires had any relevance to the world.

It took an hour or two. Then matters settled down, allowing the prairie wind to win by default, rustling the tall cane fields beyond the house and yard. Still, Maia couldn't sleep. Her feelings were achurn from all that had occurred today. Finally, with a sigh, she threw off the thin blankets, went to the door, and stepped out to inhale the night.

The scents were heavier than she was used to, growing up in the icy north. Yet one musty-pleasant aroma she identified quickly. It accompanied a low, humming rumble, emanating from the open-sided lugar barracks, where those shaggy, obsessively gentle creatures huddled at night, whatever the temperature. Their piquant scent, she had once read, was one of countless features programmed by the founders, who gave the beasts great physical strength to serve womankind, breaking one link of dependency that used to bind females to males.

Certainly the aroma was less pungent than the sweat tang given off by sailors back on Wotan, whenever hard labor brought on that glistening, other-species sheen. Did men also perspire so while making love? The thought added to Maia's heavy ambivalence of attraction-revulsion.

Walking under the stars, she greeted with a smile her friends Eagle and Hammer. The familiar constellations winked at her. On impulse, Maia snapped two leather catches, opening the brass sextant at her wrist. Unfolding the alignment arms, she took angle sightings on the horizon, on Ophir, the polestar, and the planet Amaterasu. Now, if only she had a decent chronometer . . .

Dogs barked at some neighboring clanstead. Something winged and swift fluttered a few meters overhead. Wind rustled the trees by the river, where glow beetles were still busy at their mating display, more persistently amorous than humans, casting glittering, ecstatic wavefronts to eerie rhythms. Whole swatches of forest came alight, then winked off in unison. *I wonder if there's a pattern,* Maia thought, fascinated by the spectacle of countless individual insects, each reacting only to its nearest neighbors, combining in a life-show of tantalizing intricacy, like the constellations that had always drawn her, or a labyrinthine puzzle. . . .

As she reached the corner of the house, an ebb in the breeze caused the quiet to deepen, abruptly revealing a low murmur of voices.

". . . you don't know what she said to the Pessies?"

"That's what scares me! I got no clue what she was at them about. But they reversed charges, so it must've been more'n a nuisance call. We already heard from cousins on the coast about a police agent nosing around. This stinks. You people promised discretion, complete discretion!"

The fire bugs were forgotten. Maia slipped into shadows and peered toward the rear veranda. She could make out the second speaker. It was the mother Jopland, or one roughly the same age. The other person lay hidden, but when she laughed, Maia felt a shock of recognition.

"I doubt she was calling about our little secret. I know the wench, and I'll bet tit-squirrels to lugars that she's no agent. Couldn't figure her way out of a gunnysack, that one."

Thank you, Tizbe, Maia thought with a chill. All of a sudden things seemed to make sense. No wonder the Joplands had a successful wooing party, after such a dismal start! While she had been talking to authorities in Caria, Tizbe must have arrived carrying bottles brimming with distilled summer. What wouldn't the Joplands pay to have their slow population decline turned around in a simple, efficient way? All the more so for devout Perkinites, who didn't even *like* men.

They were planning to give up their summer-banishment rule. The valley councils were going to build sanctuaries, like along the coast. But with Tizbe's powder there'd be no need to compromise their radical doctrine.

Maia had wondered if there was a practical side to the drug. Now she had her answer.

I was bothered by incidents in Lanargh, and the train collision in Clay Town. But those happened because people were fooling around with the stuff, because it's new. If it's used carefully, though, to help make winter sparking easier, where's the harm? I didn't hear any of the men tonight crying out in misery.

Naturally, the Perkinites' long-range goal was unattainable. Perkies were crazy to dream of making men as rare as jacar trees, drug or no drug. Meanwhile, though, if they found a short-term method for having their way in this valley, so what? Even conservative clans like Lamatia tried to stimulate their male guests during winter, with drink and light shows designed to mimic summer's aurorae. Was this powder fundamentally different?

Maia was tempted to walk up and join the conversation, just to catch the look on Tizbe Beller's face. Perhaps, after getting over her surprise, Tizbe would be willing to explain, woman to woman, why they were going to such lengths, or why Caria City should give a damn.

The temptation vanished when Maia's former assistant spoke again. "Don't worry about our little var informer. I'll see to things. It'll all be taken care of long before she ever makes it back to Grange Head."

A sinking sensation yawned in Maia's gut. She backed around the corner of the house as it began dawning on her just how much trouble she was in.

Bleeders! I don't know anybody. Leie's gone. And I'm in it now, right up to my neck!

One great mystery is why sexual reproduction became dominant for higher life-forms. Optimization theory says it should be otherwise.

Take a fish or lizard, ideally suited to her environment, with just the right internal chemistry, agility, camouflage—whatever it takes to be healthy, fecund, and successful in her world. Despite all this, she cannot pass on her perfect characteristics. After sex, her offspring will be jumbles, getting only half of their program from her and half their re-sorted genes somewhere else.

Sex inevitably ruins perfection. Parthenogenesis would seem to work better—at least theoretically. In simple, static environments, well-adapted lizards who produce duplicate daughters are known to have advantages over those using sex.

Yet, few complex animals are known to perform self-cloning. And those species exist in ancient, stable deserts, always in close company with a related sexual species.

Sex has flourished because environments are seldom static. Climate, competition, parasites—all make for shifting conditions. What was ideal in one generation may be fatal the next. With variability, your offspring get a fighting chance. Even in desperate times, one or more of them may have what it takes to meet new challenges and thrive.

Each style has its advantages, then. Cloning offers stability and preservation of excellence. Sex gives adaptability to changing times. In nature it is usually one or the other. Only lowly creatures such as aphids have the option of switching back and forth.

Until now, that is. With the tools of creation in our hands, shall we not give our descendants choice? Options? The best of both worlds?

Let us equip them to select their own path between predictability and opportunity. Let them be prepared to deal with both sameness and surprise.

8

C alma had been right. You could zero in on Lerner Hold by sense
of smell alone.

That was fortunate. Maia could tell north by the positions of the
stars, seen through a gathering overcast. But compass directions are useless when you have no map or knowledge of the territory. Only Iris, the
smallest moon, lit Maia's path as she followed a rutted trail over wavelike prairie knolls until one branch turned and dropped abruptly into a
maze of water-cut ravines. A tangy, metallic odor seemed to come from
that direction, so with a pounding heart she took the turn.

Plunging into the canyon, Maia had to feel her way at first, her
fingers tracing a thick layer of living topsoil that soon gave way to hard
laminations of clay. Maia found herself descending a series of hellish
rents in the ground, as if the skin of Stratos lay raked open by gigantic
claws.

Her pupils adapted, splitting slitwise to let in a maximum of light.
Succeeding beds of clay and limestone alternately shone or glittered or
simply drank whatever moonbeams reached this deep into the canyon. It
all depended, Maia supposed, on what mix of tiny sea creatures had
fallen to the ocean bottom during whatever long-ago sedimentary ages
laid these beds. Soon even the sinuous bands gave way to hard native
rock, twisted and tortured by continental movements that had taken
place before protohumans walked on faraway Earth. Interchanging patterns of light and dark stone reminded her of those towering "castle"

pillars she had seen in the distance from the railway—rocky remnants of once proud mountains that used to stand here, but had since been all but ground away by rainstorms and rivers and time.

Time was one thing Maia didn't figure she had a wealth of. Did Tizbe intend to wait till morning to spring a trap on her? Or would the young Beller come during the night to the room Maia had been given, accompanied by a dozen well-muscled Jopland fems? After overhearing those sinister words in the farmyard, Maia had chosen not to stay and find out.

Escaping Jopland Hold was easy enough. Stepping quietly to avoid alerting the dogs, she had crept down to the nearby stream that ran beside the orchard, and then sloshed a kilometer or so through icy water with her shoes tied together, hanging from her neck, until the mansion was well out of sight. Next she had to spend several minutes rubbing sensation back into her half-frozen feet before lacing up again. Shivering, Maia then spent an hour trampling a path across successive wheat fields until at last finding the road.

So far, so good. Thinking through her predicament was much harder. After weeks of depressed numbness, the abrupt effect of all this adrenaline was both dizzying and exhilarating. She couldn't help comparing her situation to those adventure reels Lamatia let summerlings watch during the high seasons, when the mothers were too busy to be bothered. Or illicit books Leie used to borrow off young vars from more lenient holds. In such tales, the heroine, usually a beautiful, winter-born sixer from an up-and-coming clan, found herself thrown against the dread schemes of some decadent house whose wealth and power was maintained by subversion rather than honest competition. Usually there was a token man, or a shipload of decent, clear-eyed sailors, in danger of being gulled by the evil hive. The ending was always the same. After being saved by the heroine's insight and courage, the men promised to visit the small virtuous clan each winter for as long as the heroine's mothers and sisters wanted them.

Virtue prevailing over venality. It seemed exciting and romantic on page or screen. But in real life, Maia had no mothers *or* sisters to turn to. She was a lone summerling fiver without a friend in the world. Clearly, Tizbe and her Jopland clients could do whatever they pleased to her.

That's if they catch me, Maia thought, biting her lip to stop a quiver. Clenching her fists also helped. Defiance was a heady anodyne against fear.

Uh oh.

Coming to a dead stop, she swallowed hard. The trail had been meandering along a lip halfway down the canyon wall, but on turning a corner she found it suddenly plunging straight for a precipice. A rickety suspension bridge lay ahead, half of it in shadows and half reflecting painful moonlight to her dark-adapted eyes.

I must've taken a wrong turn. Calma could never have taken her wagon across that!

Tracing its spidery outline, Maia saw that the bridge hung over a gulch strewn with heaping mounds of ash and slag, trailing from a row of towering beehive structures on the opposite ridge. Here and there, Maia glimpsed red flickers from coal fires that were banked for the night, but never allowed to go out.

Iron foundries, she recognized with some relief. So this was Lerner Hold after all. Calma must have taken a slower freight route across the canyon floor. This was the more direct way.

Setting foot on the creaky, swaying bridge would have been frightening even by daylight. But what choice had she? *I was never very good at this,* she thought, remembering camping trips with other summerlings on the steppe near Port Sanger. She and Leie had loved the expeditions, putting up cheerfully with biting bugs and bitter cold. But neither of them had much love for crossing streams on teetering logs or skittish stones.

The bridge was definitely worse. Stepping forward cautiously, Maia took hold of the guide rope, which stretched across the ravine at waist level. She worked her way from handhold to handhold and plank to groaning plank, fearing at any moment to hear a shout of pursuit behind her, or the snap of some cable giving way. Eerie silence added further discomfort, driving home her loneliness.

Finally, on reaching the other side, she leaned against one of the anchor pillars and let out a ragged sigh. From the promontory, Maia surveyed the trail down which she had come. There was no sign of any full-scale search party, whose lights would be visible for kilometers. *You're probably making more of this than it deserves,* she thought. *To them you're just a stupid var who stuck her nose where it didn't belong. Lay low for a while and they'll forget all about you.*

It made sense. But then, maybe she *was* too stupid to know how much trouble she was in. Standing there, Maia felt the wind grow colder. Her fingers were numb, almost paralyzed, even when she blew on them. Shivering, she rubbed her hands and began peering among the furnaces and cliffside warehouses for the mansion where this branch of Lerner Clan dwelled and raised its daughters.

The house was a disappointment when she found it. She had envisioned the industrial Lerners constructing an imposing structure of steel arches, lined with stone or glass. What she came upon was a one-story warren, made of sod bricks, that rambled over half an acre. Just a few windows faced a front courtyard strewn with scrap and reclaimed junk of every description.

The windows were dark. If not for the soft hissing of the idle furnaces—and the odors—Maia might have thought the place deserted.

There was another sound, she realized. A faint one. Maia turned. She stepped carefully through the scrapyard until, rounding a corner of the house, she came in sight of a jumble of low structures, even more ramshackle than the "mansion." Each had a small chimney from which trailed thin columns of smoke. *Housing for the employees,* she guessed.

One of these dwellings, set apart from the rest, seemed different. Dim light from the narrow curtained window illuminated a raked gravel path . . . and a small bed of neatly tended flowers. Approaching, Maia made out soft strains of music coming from within. She also smelled the aromas of cooking.

By the time she reached the door, Maia was shivering too much from the cold to be shy about lifting her hand and knocking.

Since taking jobs with the foundry only a month before, Thalla and Kiel had transformed the little cabin at the far end of the workers' compound. "You'll give up that foolishness soon enough," the other employees had said. But the two young women faithfully set aside an hour each day, even after long, grueling shifts at the furnaces, to tend their garden and put their frayed house in order.

It had been tall, broad-shouldered Thalla who opened the door that night, clucking in concern and drawing Maia inside, putting her with a blanket and steaming teacup by the smoldering peat fire. Kiel, with her almost-pure black complexion and startlingly pale eyes, was the one who went to the Lerner clan mothers the next morning, and returned shortly with word that Maia could stay.

Naturally, she would have to work. "You'll start in the scrap pile," Kiel announced the morning after Maia's flight from Jopland Hold. "Then you're to spend a week learning how to shovel and ladle with the rest of us. Calma Lerner says if you're still around after that, she'll talk to you about an after-hours 'prenticeship in the alloys lab."

The black woman laughed scornfully. "A 'prenticeship. Now that's a good one!"

Laboring for a clan of smiths wasn't the life path Maia would have chosen. But barring some brilliant strategy to get to Grange Head without crossing paths with Tizbe's gang, or the Joplands, it would have to do. Anyway, it was honorable work.

"What's wrong with an apprenticeship," she asked the older girl. "I thought—"

"You thought it was a way up the ladder, right." Kiel waved a scarred, callused hand in dismissal. "Maybe in a fancy city, where you can hire a clone from some lawyer hive to go over your contract for you. But here? I guess you don't know what 'after hours' means at Lerner Hold, do you?"

Maia shook her head.

"It means you get no wages for 'prentice time, no room-and-board points. In fact, *you* pay for the privilege of workin' extra in their lab. They charge you, for lessons!"

"No quicker way into debtor's trap," Thalla agreed. "Except gambling."

Debtor's Trap was something Thalla and Kiel talked about all the time, as if they feared falling into bad habits if they ever let the subject drop. Only constant attention and thriftiness would let them prevail. Along with weeding the garden and sweeping the floor, the two young women ritually counted their credit sticks each night.

"It's possible to come out ahead, even after food an' lodgings are deducted," Thalla said on the second evening, while helping Maia gingerly dab where hot cinders had scorched her skin. Heavy leather aprons and goggles had spared her body a worse singeing, but wearing all that armor made more exhausting the work of dragging heavy ladles brimming with molten, sunlike heat. It was labor even harder than working on ships, calling for the strength of a man, the patience of a lugar, and the disciplined diligence of a winter-born clone. Yet, only vars were employed in the furnaces. Only vars in need of work would put up with the miniature, artificial hell.

"Isn't it required by law?" Maia asked, dipping her washcloth sparingly in a shallow basin of rationed water. "I thought employers had to pay enough so you could save."

Thalla shrugged. "Sure it's the law, handed down since the time of Lysos . . ."

Maia half-raised her hand at mention of the First Mother's name, but stopped short of drawing the circle sign. Somehow, she didn't figure Kiel and Thalla were religious.

"It's close to the edge, though," the stocky woman went on. "Buy a few luxuries from the company store. Lose a few credits gambling . . . you see how it goes. Get into debt an' there's no escape till Amnesty Day, in late spring! And *then* where do you go? Me, I don't plan stayin' here past my seventh birthday. Got things to do, y'know."

Maia refrained from pointing out that despite their dedication,

Thalla and Kiel spent money on more than bare necessities. They had a little radio, and paid Lerner Hold for electricity to run it, sometimes late into the night. They bought flower and vegetable seedlings for the garden.

But then, maybe those *were* necessities. As she fell into the routine of labor at the mill, Maia came to see how such trimmings of civilization, slim as they were, made a key difference between holding your heading and losing your way, drifting into the endless half-life that seemed the fate of other var employees. Oh, the vars worked hard. Off hours, they laughed and sang and threw considerable energy into their games of chance. But they weren't going anywhere. Proof lay in the next vale, upwind and out of sight of the factory, where the crèche and playgrounds lay. Children, both winter- and summer-born, were housed and schooled there. Every single one had been born of a Lerner mother. No var's womb had ripened here for as long as anyone recalled.

Maia, too, began counting her credits each night. Some went toward secondhand work clothes, a bar of soap, and other needs. When the weekly electricity bill came, Maia paid one-third. That left very little. Against all expectation, Maia found herself feeling homesick for the sea.

The policewoman promised me a stipend for showing up at Grange Head, she pondered wistfully. Even a modest reward for testifying would match what she cleared through hard labor here. *Almost a week has passed. You could find out if it's safe to make a break.*

Her housemates quickly guessed that Maia was in flight from serious trouble. Though they did not press, and she withheld details, Maia took a chance and told the two women it was the mothers of Jopland Clan who were after her. That seemed to raise her standing with Kiel and Thalla. Kiel volunteered to check things out next Greersday, when the supply wagon went to town. If it wasn't too heavily laden, off-duty var employees could hitch a ride, for a small fee. Kiel had shopping to do, anyway. "I'll look around for you, virgie, and see if the coast is clear."

"I wish you'd tell us what you did to those biddies," the dark woman said on her return, dropping her groceries on the rickety table and turning to Maia, wide-eyed. "You've sure gotten those Perkies riled. At train time I saw two Joplanders hanging around the station, about as subtle as a plow, pretending to be waiting for someone while they checked every var who came or went. Saw another pair on horseback, patrolling the road. They're still lookin' for you, vestal girl."

Maia sighed. So much for a quick getaway. *Make a note. Next time you take on those more powerful than you, pick a place with more than one back door.* Holly Lock was about as far into the middle of nowhere as she could have found, and the railroad was the only fast way out of the valley. Even stealing a horse would do no good. The hue and cry would track her down long before she got near the coastal mountains, let alone Grange Head.

"Guess you made a smart choice after all," Thalla suggested. "Headin' further inland instead of tryin' for shore. Last place they'll look is stinky Lerner Hold."

Apparently. Or maybe Maia's pursuers didn't feel any need to check every hut and farmstead. All they had to do was watch all exits, and wait.

"Were they asking questions? Putting out my description?" she asked Kiel, who shrugged.

"Now, what var would tattle another var to a Perkinite? They know better than to ask."

That sounded a bit facile to Maia. Antagonism between clones and summerlings was pretty intense in Long Valley. But she didn't have much faith in var solidarity. More likely the other Lerner workers would sell her in a trice, for a big enough reward. Fortunately, only Thalla and Kiel seemed to much notice her existence. The renowned Jopland trait of stinginess was her chief hope. Plus the fact that Lerners themselves weren't Perkinites, and had a tradition of staying at arm's length from local politics.

We'll see if I'm still hot in a week or so. If they lose interest, I could try walking out in stages, traveling by night and doing hobo labor for meals along the way . . .

Maia felt deeply the loss of her bag, left with the stationkeepers in Holly Lock. The duffel contained her last mementos of Leie. Thinking about losing them made her feel even more lonely and sad.

At least she had two new friends. They were no substitute for Leie, but the sisterly warmth shown by Thalla and Kiel was the biggest reason Maia felt reluctant to go. The work was hard and the little cottage wasn't much more than a hut, but it felt closer to "home" than anywhere she'd been since departing her attic room in Port Sanger, ages ago.

Days passed. The rhythm of the furnaces, the stench of local brown lignite, the rumbling of the metal rollers . . . even the heat ceased bothering her quite as much. The day set for her appointment at Grange Head came and went, but Maia didn't figure the magistrate missed her much. She had told the officer in Caria all she knew. She had done her duty.

Besides, listening to Kiel and Thalla talk each night, Maia began to wonder. What *did* she owe to a power structure that offered so little to vars like her, while other women flourished simply because of a twist of birth timing? Her roommates didn't seem to think it was heretical to ask questions about the way things worked. It was a frequent topic of conversation.

Sometimes at night they tuned their radio to a strange station, twisting dials to catch tinny voices reflected off high, magnetic layers. *"No one can count on justice from corrupt officials in Caria City, who are bought an' sold by the great hive-clans of Landing Continent. It's up to the oppressed classes themselves to take a bold hand and change things. . . ."*

Maia suspected the station was illegal. The words were angry, even rebellious, but more surprising to Maia was her own reaction. She wasn't shocked at all. She turned to Kiel and asked if "oppressed classes" referred to summerlings like them.

"Sure does, virgie. Nowadays, with every niche sewn up by one clan or another, what chance do poor vars like us have to get something of our own started? Only way things will change is if we get together and change them ourselves."

The voice on the radio echoed these sentiments. *". . . The tools used for suppression are many. We have seen a tradition of apathy promulgated, so that the nonclone turnout in elections on Eastern Continent hardly reached seven percent last year, despite intense efforts by the Radical Party and the Society of Scattered Seeds . . ."*

That was how Savant Claire used to refer to the var-children Lamatia Hold cast forth each autumn. *Scattered seeds.* In theory, summerlings were supposed to search for and eventually find that special occupation they were born to be good at, then take root and flourish. Yet so many wound up in dead ends, either taking vows and sheltering in the church, or laboring like the Lerner employees, for room, board, and enough coinsticks to buy a few cheap pleasures.

Maia thought about all she had witnessed since leaving Port Sanger. "Some say there've been a lot more summer births, lately. That's why there are so many of us."

"Blood-spotting propaganda crap!" Thalla cursed. "They always complain there's too many vars for open niches. But it's just an excuse for poor pay. Even if you get a job, there's no tenure. And usually it's work no better than fit for a man."

That answered Maia's next question, whether males were also included under the classification of "oppressed classes." Kiel had a point, though. Sure, the Lerners were good at what they did. In the furnaces and forges they always seemed to know where the next problem would arise, and watching a Lerner work metal was like seeing an artist in action. Still, did that give them the right to monopolize this kind of enterprise, wherever small-time foundries made economic sense?

"Perkinites are the worst," Thalla muttered. "They'd rather have no summerlings at all. Would reopen the old gene labs if they could. Fix things so there'd just be winter brats. Nothing but clones, all the time."

Maia shook her head. "They may get their way without reopening the labs."

"What do you mean?" Both young women asked. Looking up quickly, Maia realized she had almost let the secret slip.

What secret? she pondered. *The agent never exactly told me not to speak. Besides, Thalla and Kiel are my kind, not like some faraway clone of a policewoman.*

"Um," she began, lowering her voice. "You know that trouble I got in at Jopland Hold?"

"The mess you didn't want to talk about?" Thalla leaned forward eagerly. "I been putting one an' three together and have got a theory. My guess is you tried crashing that party they held a couple weeks back, sneaking in to get yourself a man without payin'!" Thalla guffawed until Kiel pushed her arm and shushed her. "Go on, Maia. Tell us if you feel ready."

Maia took a deep breath. "Well, it seems at least some of the Perkinites have found a way to get what they want. . . ."

She went on to tell the whole story, feeling a growing satisfaction as her companions' eyes widened with each revelation. They had categorized her as some sweet, helpless young thing to be given sisterly protection, not an adventuress who had already been through more excitement and danger than most saw in a lifetime. When she finished, the other two turned to look at each other. "Do you think we should—" Thalla began.

Kiel shook her head curtly. "Maybe. We'll talk about it tomorrow. Right now it's late. Past a fiver's bedtime, no matter what a born pirate she's turned out to be." Kiel gave Maia's ragged haircut a friendly tousle, one that conveyed newfound respect in an offhand way. "Let's all kick in," she concluded, and reached over to turn off the radio.

When the light was out and all three of them had settled into their cots, Maia lay still for a long time, thinking.

Me? A born pirate?

Yet, why not? With her tender muscles starting to throb less and tauten more each passing day, Maia was toughening more than she had ever thought possible. And now, listening to rebel radio stations? Sharing police business with homeless, radical vars?

What next? she wondered. *If only Leie could see me now.*

Suddenly, all her newfound toughness was no bulwark against resurgent grief. Maia had to bear down in order not to sniffle aloud. *Damn,* she thought. *Damn it all to patarkal hell.* The kindness of her house-

mates only made her more vulnerable, it seemed, by easing the numbness she had wrapped herself in since leaving the temple at Grange
Head. *Maybe I'd be better off alone, after all.*

From neighboring cottages could be heard the rattle of dice and
hoarse laughter, even a snatch of bawdy song. But it was quiet in their
hut until Thalla began snoring, low and rhythmically. A while later, Maia
heard Kiel get up. Although Maia kept her eyes closed, she felt eerily
certain the older woman was watching her. Then there came the creaking
of the front door as Kiel slipped outside. Half-asleep, Maia presumed the
dark girl had gone to visit the outhouse, but by morning she had still not
returned.

Thalla didn't seem worried. "Business in town," she explained tersely.
"Greersday wagon'll be full of wrought iron, so no passengers, but we got
a couple of investments to look after, the two of us. Places we put our
money so's it won't evaporate out here. That happens, y'know. Coinsticks
just vanish. I wouldn't leave mine under my pillow, if I was you."

Maia blinked, wondering how Thalla knew. Had she looked? Suppressing an urge to rush back to the cot and check her tiny stash, Maia
also took note how deftly the older var had managed to change the subject. *None of my business, I suppose,* she thought with a sniff.

Work continued at the same steady, numbing pace. On her eigh-
teenth day at Lerner Hold, Maia and most of the other workers were
assigned to haul barrowloads of preprocessed iron ore from a mine two
miles away, staffed entirely by a clan of albino women whose natural
pallor had become tinted by rusty oxides, permeating their skin.

The next day, a caravan of huge dray-llamas arrived, carrying charcoal for refining the ore. Tall gaunt-eyed women tended the beasts, but
took no part in unloading which, apparently, was beneath their dignity.
Maia joined the team of vars lugging bag after heavy bag of sooty black
chunks to a shed by the furnaces, while an elderly Lerner paid off the
teamsters in new-forged metal. Within a few hours, the caravan was
heading back up country. Their journey would take them past three distant, stony pillars that gave the northeast horizon its character, and onward toward barely visible peaks where yet another clan filled a small
but thriving niche—cutting trees and cooking them into ebony-colored,
log-shaped, carbon briquettes. It was a simpleminded rustic economy.
One that functioned, though, with no space left for newcomers.

Afterward, while sponging away layers of grime, Maia patiently en-
dured another of Calma Lerner's daily visits. The clanswoman "dropped
by" each evening, just before supper, with an obstinacy Maia was starting to respect. She would not take no for an answer.

"Look, I can tell you have an educated background for a summer child. Come from a classy line of mothers, I reckon. Ought to do something with your life, you really should."

I plan to, Maia answered in her thoughts. *I'm planning to run, not walk, out of this valley just as soon as it's safe, and never again set foot near a piece of coal, ever!*

But Calma was likable enough, and Maia had no wish to offend. "I'm just saving up to move on," she explained.

The Lerner shook her head. "I thought you came here 'cause of what we talked about that day in the wagon. You know, studyin' metallurgy? If that wasn't it, why're you here?"

This line of inquiry Maia didn't want to encourage. So far there had been no sign of Tizbe or the Joplands looking for her here. They must have figured she'd head west, toward the sea. But inquiries by Calma, or even loose gossip, could change that.

"Um. Look, maybe I'll think about that apprenticeship. I'm just not sure about the arrangements, that's all."

Calma's expression transformed and Maia could almost read the older woman's thoughts.

Aha! The little one is just staking a bargaining position, hoping for a better deal. Maybe I can drop the lesson fee a bit. In exchange for what? A term contract?

"Well," the older woman said aloud. "We can talk about it whenever you're ready." Which Maia immediately translated as meaning *Let her slave at the forge another week. By then she'll accept if we give a point or two.*

In fact, Calma's face was so easy to read, Maia felt she understood how such a talented family never amounted to much in the world of commerce. *They might go far in partnership with a businesslike clan.* But some families just couldn't work closely with groups other than themselves. Especially over generations, which was how long many interclan alliances lasted.

Although Maia filed this insight away for future reference, she no longer contemplated sharing such tidbits. Leie's loss still felt like a cavity within her, but the ache dulled with each passing day. Through it all, she had begun to see the outlines of her future, unwarped by the inflated dreams of childhood.

If she was clever and hardheaded, she might manage to be like Kiel and Thalla, slowly saving and searching, not for some fabled niche, or anything so grandiose as establishing her own clan, but to find a tiny chink in the wall of Stratoin society. A place to live comfortably, with a little security. *You could do worse. You've seen people who have done much worse.*

To pass the second and third evenings Kiel was away, Thalla enlightened Maia on strange customs practiced in the seaports of the Southern Isles. The stocky young woman seemed equally amazed when Maia described mundanities of Port Sanger life she herself had long taken for granted. Then they listened to the radio awhile—to a station playing music, not political commentary—until sleep time came.

Maybe when Kiel returns, she'll say the coast is clear, Maia thought as she drifted off. She felt no ties to Lerner Hold, but would she be able to tear herself away from her new friends? For the sake of this comradeship, she felt tempted to stay.

Work, and recovery from work, took up nearly all of the next day, from dawn to dusk. Mealtime was a fragrant lentil stew with onions and spices, a supper Maia felt sure Thalla had prepared in expectation of Kiel's return. But the dark woman did not show. Thalla only laughed when Maia worried aloud. "Oh, we got plans, we do. Sometimes she's away a week or more. Lerners got to put up with it 'cause nobody's better'n Kiel at cold-rollin' flat sheet. Don't you worry, virgie. She'll be back presently."

All right, I won't worry. It was surprisingly easy to do. In a few short weeks, Maia had learned the knack of letting go and living from day to day. Not even the priestess at the temple had been able to teach her that. Physical exhaustion, she admitted, was a good instructor.

That evening, Maia took their small oil lantern into the ebbing twilight to visit the toilet before going to bed. For privacy, it had become her habit to wait until all the other vars finished. Along the way to the outhouse, she liked to watch the stars, which were beginning to show winter constellations to good advantage. Stratos was slowing in its long outward ellipse, although the true opening of cool season still lay some weeks ahead.

Turning a corner in the warren of laborers' bungalows, Maia saw someone leaning against the tilted door of the outhouse, facing the other way. *Oh, well,* she thought. *Everyone has to take turns.*

She approached and set the lantern down. "They been in there long?" she asked the woman waiting ahead of her, who shook her head.

"No one's inside."

"But then, why are you . . ."

Maia stopped. Something was wrong. That voice.

"Why am I waiting?" The woman turned around. "Why, for you of course, my meddlesome young friend."

Maia gaped. "Tizbe!"

The pleasure-clan winterling smiled and gave an offhand salute. "None other than your loyal assistant baggage handler, in person. Thought it was time you and I had a talk, *boss.*"

Despite her racing heart, Maia felt proud not to show a quaver in her voice. "Talk away," she said, spreading her hands. "Choose a subject. Anything you like."

Tizbe shook her head. "Not here. I have a place in mind."

"All right. Where—"

Maia stopped suddenly, sensing movement. She whirled just in time to glimpse several identical black-clad women bearing down upon her, holding fuming cloths.

Joplands, Maia recognized the instant before they seized her. She felt their brief surprise at her strength. But the farm women were stronger still. Struggling, Maia managed to dodge the damp rags long enough to catch sight of one more figure, standing a short distance away.

Calma Lerner watched with tight lips pressed together as Maia was taken to the ground and her mouth and nose covered. Black fabric cut off vision. A cloying, sweet aroma choked her, invading her brain and smothering all thoughts.

She roused through a cloudy, anesthetic haze to see stars jouncing about like busy glow beetles high in the sky, and dimly recalled that stars weren't supposed to do that. Only vaguely in her delirium did it occur to Maia that this might be a matter of perception. It was hard to focus while lying supine, tied to the bottom of a rattling, horse-drawn wagon.

Through the night, Maia drifted in and out of drugged slumber, punctuated by intervals when someone would lift her head to dribble water down a cloth into her parched mouth. She sucked like a newborn baby, as if that primal reflex were the only one left her. Dreams confronted Maia with memories drawn randomly from storage, twisted, and made vivid with embellishments by her unrestrained subconscious.

She had been a little over three Stratoin years old . . . nine or ten by the old calendar. It was Mid-Winter's Day and Lamatia's summerlings had been fed and told to go to their rooms, to stay there till the gong rang for evening meal. But the twins had been making plans. At noontime, Maia and Leie knew all full-Lamai folk would be in the great hall to take part in the Ceremony of Initiation. For weeks, the six-year-old class of Lamais had been excitedly wagering which of them would receive ripening, and which would have to await another winter, maybe two. Among clones, with little to distinguish between them, whoever managed to conceive during her first mature solstice had an advantage over her peers, rising in status as her generation matured, perhaps eventually taking a leading role in running the clan.

Maia and Leie were as one in not wanting to miss this, despite rules putting the rites off-limits to mere half daughters. They had spent many furtive hours discovering the route to use—which entailed first slipping out their bedroom window, then around a dormer and down a rain gutter, along a wall lined with decorative, crenelated fortifications, through a loose window into an attic, and down a rope ladder that they had prehung inside a sealed-off, abandoned chimney . . .

In Maia's dream, each phase of the adventure loomed as vivid and immediate as it had to her younger self. The possibility of falling to her death was terrifying, but less awful than the thought of getting caught. Capture and punishment were, in turn, negligible deterrents next to the ghastly possibility that she and Leie might not get to *see*.

Reaching their final vantage point was the most dangerous part. It meant worming their way along the steep, sloping dome of the great hall itself, whose arching ribs of reinforced concrete held in place huge mottled lenses of colored glass. Crawling the lip so that no shadows would cast into the hall, Maia and her sister finally gathered the courage to poke their heads over a section of tinted window, to catch their first glimpse of the ceremony under way below.

The interior was a swirling confusion of brightness and shadow. The glassy roof poured winter daylight into the chamber, transformed into a brilliance reminiscent of summer nights. Colored panels cast clever imitations of aurorae against the walls below, while others glinted and flashed as gaudily as Wengel Star, when the sun's small, bitterly bright companion shone high in the summer sky. A roaring fire in one corner of the room gave off heat the twins could feel outside. The flames were colored with additives guaranteed to simulate the spectrum of the northern lights.

It was a spectacle worth every pain taken to get there. Neither Leie nor Maia would have had the courage to come alone.

Still, it took a while to stifle the tremulous certainty that someone was going to look their way. The kids spent more time nudging each other and giggling than stealing quick glances through the burnished lenses. Finally they realized that nobody below was interested in the ceiling at a time like this.

Dancers wove rippling patterns as they undulated before the central dais, waving filmy fabrics that also mimicked ionic displays. The troupe had been hired from Oosterwyck Clan, famed for their beauty and sensuality. Their success rate was well-advertised and only rich clans could afford their services at this time of year.

Censers emitted spirals of smoke, whose aroma was supposed to simulate the pheromones that best aroused males. Behind a veiled curtain, silhouettes told of the assembled mothers and full sisters of Lamatia Hold, watching discreetly offstage so as not to put off their guests.

Maia nudged Leie and pointed. "Over there!" She whispered unnecessarily. Since the music only reached them as a faint murmur, it was doubtful anything they said would be heard below. Leie turned to peer in the direction she had indicated. "Yeah, it's the Penguin Guild captain, and those two young sailors. Exactly the ones I predicted. Pay up!"

"I never betted! Everybody knew Penguin Guild owes Lamatia for that big loan the mothers gave 'em last year."

Leie ignored the rejoinder. "Come on, let's get a better look," she urged, pulling Maia's arm, causing her to teeter precariously on the steeply tilted wall of the dome. "Hey, watch it!"

But Leie had already slithered to where a great piece of convex glass bulged from the arching roof. Maia heard her sister take in a sudden gasp, then titter nervously.

"What is it?" Maia exclaimed, sliding over.

Leie held up a hand. "No. Don't look yet! Get a good hold an' set your feet good. Got it? Don't look yet."

"I'm not looking!" Maia whined.

"Good, now close your eyes. Move a little closer and I'll move your head to see best. Don't open till I say so!"

It was one of those rituals that seemed so natural when you were three. Maia felt her sister's hand take her braid and maneuver her until she brushed cool glass with the tip of her nose. "Okay, you can look now," Leie said, suppressing a giggle.

Maia cracked one eye, and at first saw only a blur. The glass had several thin layers, separated by air pockets. She pulled back a bit and an image fell into focus. At least it *seemed* focused, remarkably magnified from this great height. Still, what she saw appeared more a jumble of fleshy colors—peppered with short black fur that was patchy in most places, but thick where one small pink appendage joined the intersection of two large ones. The latter, she realized, must be somebody's legs. The small one in between . . .

"Oh!" she cried, rocking back until she had to flail for balance. Leie grabbed her, laughing at her surprise. Almost instantly Maia was back against the glass, trying again to bring the scene back into focus. "No, let me in now. It's my turn!" Leie importuned. But Maia held fast and her twin grudgingly moved on to find another place, which she quickly declared to be "even better." Maia was too intent to notice.

So that's what a man looks like without clothes, she thought. The magnifying effects of the glass were confusing, and she found it hard to get any sense of proportion, let alone relate what she was seeing to those sterile diagrams she had studied in school. *Where do they keep it while they're walking around? I'd of thought it'd get in the way, hanging like that.*

Maia was too embarrassed by her next thoughts to voice them even subvocally. Fascination won a hard-fought battle over revulsion and she peered eagerly, hoping to see when the thing changed. *Does it really get bigger than that?*

A hand entered her field of view, and reached past the limp appendage to scratch a hairy thigh. Maia drew back so her field of view encompassed the arm and torso and head of the reclining man, resting on silk pillows as he watched the dancers. He turned to say something to another man, lounging to his right, who laughed, then straightened and leaned forward with a more sober expression on his face, as if trying to pay close attention to the show. By their elbows lay piles of food and drink. The first man picked up a wineglass, draining it. He did not seem to notice the enticingly clad woman who moved to his side to refill it, nor others waiting nearby, prepared to move in with privacy curtains, at need.

"C'mere and see the sixers!" Leie called urgently. With some reluctance, Maia tore herself away, leaving her perch to sidle near her sibling. "Over by the north wall," Leie suggested.

This pinkish pane was flawed by ripples, and the magnification wasn't as good as back at the clear lens. It took a while to find the right viewing position, but Maia at last perceived a covey of girls waiting off to one side, dressed in pale, filmy gowns. They were made up to look less virginal—and no doubt doused liberally to fool the male sense of smell. Naturally, men were more attracted to older women who had already birthed once or twice. But this ceremony was for sixers alone. It was their special day and the mothers had spared no expense.

Maia did not have to count. There were thirteen of them, she knew. An entire class of Lamai winterlings, all primly, delectably identical, but each one hoping she would be the one reached for, when and if the moment came.

They'd be lucky if two or three made it this year. You didn't expect much from sixers. At that age, whether you were a lowly var or haughty cloneling, your body only produced the right chemistry for reproduction during the height of winter. Even at seven, your fecund season wasn't broad. Most women, even when they had the full backing of their clan, never got a ripening until they were eight or more. By then their season was wide enough to overlap some of the summer passion left in males during autumn, or starting to bud in springtime.

Lamatia wasn't counting on much out of today's solstice ceremony, but it was important anyway. A rite of passage for newly adult members of the clan. An omen for the coming year.

Now, as Maia watched, Lamai sixers began joining the Oosterwycks in the dance, slipping in one by one with their meticulously practiced steps. Somehow—probably by design—the smoother movements of the dusky professionals seemed to cause attention to flow toward the lighter-haired neophytes. The sixers had studied their moves with typical Lamai care. The dance was choreographed to give each one equal time, sweeping in controlled stages ever closer to their audience, yet Maia saw how eagerly each tried in little ways to upstage her sisters. Somehow, it only served to make them look more alike.

Leaning back to take a wide view of the proceedings, it struck Maia how the men below were in a situation they would possibly have killed for, only half a year ago, when all city gates were locked and guardia patrols kept a fierce eye on those few males allowed passes from nearby sanctuaries. In summer, men howled to get in.

Now, with womenfolk at their peak of receptivity, the male sailors lay there looking as if they'd rather have a good book, or something diverting on the tele. Perched on the edge of the dome, watching things she had only heard vaguely described before, Maia felt a sense of wonder mixed with jarring insight.

Irony. It was a word she had learned just recently. She liked the sound it made, as well as its slippery unwillingness to be pinned down or defined. One learned its meaning by example. This was a fine example of irony.

I wonder why Lysos made it this way . . . so nobody ever gets exactly what she or he wants, except when she or he doesn't want it?

"Maia, psst!" Leie waved from the clear, convex section. "Come look!"

"Has one of them gotten big?" Maia asked breathlessly as she hurried over, almost losing her footing along the way. She quivered with an eerily enticing mixture of repugnance and excitement as she put her head next to her twin's.

What swam into focus was not the mysterious appendage, after all. It was the bearded face of a man Maia recognized—the handsome, virile captain of the freighter *Empress* whose hearty laugh and thundering voice were such a delight to hear whenever the mothers had him and his officers to dinner. Half of Lamatia's summerling boys wanted to ship out with him; half the summer girls fantasized he was their father.

But the sixers below weren't seeking *fathers* for their children. Not this time of year. The same physical act was more valuable in winter than in summer, because fathering had nothing to do with it.

What the sixers sought was *sparking*, insemination as catalyst to start a placenta forming. Triggering a clonal ripening within. And

this captain was said to have sparked seven, sometimes eight or
more winterlings some years, all by himself! Like in the nursery
rhyme . . .

> Summer Daddy,
>> sperm comes easy.
> Eager Daddy,
>> makes a var.
>
> Winter Sparker,
>> sperm comes precious.
> Wonder Sparker,
>> one goes far!

The captain's eyes narrowed as he followed the movements of the dancers, now gyrating around him, almost in arm's reach. His oiled, powerfully muscled body reminded Maia not so much of a lugar's as that of a
perfect race horse, rippling with more power than any human ought ever
need. His face, hirsute yet full of that strange masculine intelligence,
seemed to concentrate on a thought, tracking it intensely. As one Lamai
sixer whirled close, he squinted, working his jaw in what appeared to be
the start of a smile, a dawning eagerness. He lifted his hand . . .

And used it to cover his mouth, trying gallantly but in vain to stifle
a gaping yawn.

It was dawn before the muddle of dreams and warped recollections gave
way to a foggy sense of reality. Dawn of which day, Maia could not tell,
since her body ached as if she had been wrestling fierce enemies night
after endless night. Only in stages did she come to realize her hands
were bound in black cloth, and so were her legs. She was in the back of
a jouncing buckboard, triced up like a piece of cargo.

Blearily, Maia managed to wrestle her torso up against what felt
like several sacks of grain, so the level of her eyes came even with the
sideboards of the wagon. Above her loomed the backs of two women
driving the team. From behind, they didn't look much like Joplands.
They said nothing, and did not look back at her.

Turning her head was painful, but it brought some of the countryside into view—a high, rolling steppe covered with sparse grass, apparently too dry for farming. Red- and orange-tinted cirrus clouds laced a
rich blue sky, still lustrous with latent night. There was a faint cawing of
some large bird, perhaps a raven or native mawu.

*I remember now. They were waiting for me at the toilet. They
grabbed me. That awful smell . . .* It still filled her nostrils, as the fad-

ing tendrils of her dreams reluctantly vacated recesses of her foggy brain. Thought came sluggishly, like heavy syrup from a jar.

A wagon. They're taking me someplace. North, from the looks of things.

That much was simple enough from the angle of the rising sun. To see more meant struggling to a sitting position, which took several increments in order to keep from fainting. When at last she craned around to see what lay ahead, the wagon took a turn in the road, bringing a tower of monumental proportions into abrupt view. It spired into the sky, columnar and prismoidal, light and dark bands alternating along its height. Without being able to bring all faculties to bear, Maia guessed it must be over two hundred meters high and a third of that across.

The spire was scarred in places. Scaffolding told of recent excavations that had gouged the natural obelisk, leaving piles of rocky debris around its base. A series of arched window-openings followed one pale band of stone, girdling the periphery halfway up. A second row of smaller perforations paralleled the first, a few meters below.

Near the base of the stone monolith, a broad, steep ramp came into view, leading upward toward a gaping portal.

Maia's captors were taking her straight toward it.

W e were lucky to find a habitable world in such an odd binary-star system, of a type seldom visited. Its orbital peculiarities, as well as size and dense atmosphere, should keep our colony hidden for a long time.

Those same features mean genetic tinkering will be required, before the first settlers step outside these domes. While making ambitious changes in such fundamentals as sex, we shall also have to modify humans to live and breathe in the air of Stratos. As on other colony worlds, carbon dioxide tolerance and visual-spectrum sensitivities must be adjusted. Moreover, shortly before departing the Phylum, we acquired recent designs for improved kidneys, livers, and sensoria, and shall certainly incorporate them.

This planet's slow, complex orbit presents special challenges, such as ultraviolet excess whenever the dwarf companion, Waenglen's Star, is near. We may find this seasonal variation useful, providing environmental cues for our planned two-phase reproductive cycle. But first we must make sure the humans and other animals we plant here will be rugged enough to thrive.

—from the Landing Day Address, by Lysos

9

An extensive cavity had been drilled into the mountain monolith, creating a network of rooms and corridors. Perhaps the workwomen had taken advantage of preexisting caves or fissures. By the time they finished with their machines and explosives, however, the warren of tunnels and storage chambers owed little to nature. The man sanctuary had been near completion when all further work was abruptly canceled, leaving an empty shell, inhabited only by echoes.

Maia's glimpse of the outside was brief and harried as her captors drove their wagon up a long earthen ramp leading to a massive wooden portal. One of them leaped off to knock on the door, sending deep, resonant booms reverberating within. The other clambered back to untie Maia's ankles. Peering through a drugged daze, Maia saw the ramp was surrounded by dusty rock tailings, dumped from openings that girdled the stone tower halfway up. The upper row consisted of airy galleries, broad enough to let in summer breezes when the sanctuary was meant to have its largest population. The lower circumference of windows were mere slits in comparison.

None of this had come cheaply. It was one hell of an investment to write off.

That was among her few lucid, observational thoughts while being dragged off the wagon and through the gate at a pace almost too brisk for her wobbly feet to manage. Maia stumbled behind the two massive, harsh-faced fems, who had left her arms bound in front to use as a kind of leash. They did not speak, but nodded to a third representative of their kind, who locked the outer door and accompanied them inside. Maia did not know the name of their clan.

It was hard to give more than a cursory look around, as her captors pulled her up endless flights of stairs, along deserted, empty corridors, then through a central hall equipped with wooden dining trestles and a massive fireplace. Farther down one of the main tunnels—lit by strings of dimly powered glow bulbs—they passed an indoor arena capable of seating several hundred spectators, overlooking a vast grid of intersecting lines.

Maia obtained only glimpses, as more passageways went by in a blur, followed by more tiring stairs, until at last they reached a heavy wooden door set in the stone wall with iron hinges and a stout padlock. Still blinking through a fog of unreality, Maia felt a peculiar sense of misplaced pride on recognizing that the hardware, and even the iron key the guard pulled from her vest, were all products of the forges at Lerner Hold.

"Look," she said to the women with a mouth as dry as sand. "Can't you tell me—"

"Yell jest have t'wait," one of the stolid clones answered gruffly, pulling back the door as Maia's other custodian sent her whirling into the dark room. Maia couldn't even spread her arms for balance. A few meters inside, she tripped and fell amid what felt like scattered bundles of rough, scratchy fabric.

"Atyps! Bleeders!" she screamed from the floor, her voice breaking. Maia's curse was punctuated by the door slamming shut, and a clank as the bolt was thrown. It was a desolating sound that hurt her ears and savaged her already bruised soul.

Silence and darkness settled all around. She tried to rise, but a wave of nausea made that impractical, so she lay still for several minutes with her head down, breathing deeply. At last, the dizziness and drugged stupor seemed to ease a bit. When she tried sitting up, waves of pain swarmed her aching arms and along her sides. Maia felt a sob rise in her throat and suppressed it savagely. *I won't give them any satisfaction!*

Weeks ago, the physical sensations coursing her body would have left her a quivering, fetal ball. Now she found inner resources to fight back just as fiercely, overcoming pain's tyranny by force of will. It would be another matter dealing with the pit of hopeless depression yawning before her. *Later,* she thought, putting off that rendezvous with despair. One thing at a time.

As her eyes adapted, Maia began to make out details of her prison. A single spear of daylight penetrated through a high, narrow opening in the stone wall opposite the door. Other walls were lined with wooden crates, and burlap-covered bundles lay strewn across the floor. The ones Maia had landed on seemed to contain bedding or curtain material . . . fortunately, since they had cushioned her fall.

A storage chamber, she thought. The builders must have already begun stocking supplies for the intended sanctuary, when the project was called off. Were they now trying to recoup some of their investment by turning the place into a brig? Maia hadn't seen signs of other occupants. What a joke if all this were set aside just for her! A big, expensive jail for one unimportant varling who knew too much.

Maia pushed to her knees, swayed, and managed awkwardly to stand. Not allowing herself a pause that might break her momentum, she at once began casting about for some way to extricate herself from her bonds.

Fine crystalline dust wafted from freshly cut stone, sparkling in the narrow window's angled shaft of sunlight. A whitish gray patina covered every surface, including broom tracks where the floor had last been swept. Looking up, Maia saw that a rail ran down the center of the barrel-vaulted ceiling, reminding her of the cargo crane she had used in the Musseli Line baggage car. Only here the winch had not been installed.

She searched among the stencil-lettered boxes. CLOTHING—MALE, one crate displayed along its side. Another contained DISHES and two announced WRITING MATERIALS. She had never thought of men as being particularly literate, but there were many crates of the latter.

Maia tried to think. Broken dishes might be useful to cut the layers of fabric wrapped around her forearms. Unfortunately, all the boxes were nailed firmly shut. She could feel her little portable sextant, still strapped to her left arm. One of its appendages might be sharp enough, but its bulge was out of reach beneath the same cloth fetters.

Sitting on a crate, Maia bent to examine the bindings more closely. She blinked, then sighed in disgust. "Oh! Of all the patarkal . . ."

Just under her wrists, where she had been least likely to notice, the fabric was simply *laced* together, finishing in a simple slipknot.

"Bleeders and rutters!" Maia muttered as she lifted her arms and twisted to grab the loose ends with her teeth. After some tugging, the knot gave way, and soon she was picking the laces free one by one. Relapses of dizziness kept interrupting, forcing her to pause and breathe deeply. By the time she finished, Maia had reevaluated her first impression—the bindings weren't so dumb after all. No doubt the jailers had meant for her to free herself eventually, but this wasn't something she could have managed earlier, with guards nearby.

At last she flung the cloths aside with a curse. Her hands tingled painfully as full circulation returned. Rubbing them, Maia stretched, waving her arms and walking to get the kinks out.

Near the door, she found a small table she hadn't noticed before, on which stood a pitcher of water and a dented cup. Forcing her trembling hands to master the movements, she poured and drank ravenously. When the pitcher was half-empty, she put the cup down and wiped her mouth with the back of her wrist.

I don't suppose there's anything to eat?

There was no food, but underneath the table she found a large ceramic pot with a lid. Glazed depictions of sailing ships battled high seas along its side. She removed the cover and squatted on the cold porcelain to relieve yet another of her body's cataloged complaints.

As immediate concerns were satisfied, more afflictions came to the fore, awaiting attention. Despair, her old nemesis, seemed to rise up and politely ask, *"Now?"*

Maia shook her head firmly. *I've got to keep busy. Not think for a while.*

She set to work struggling to push heavy boxes together and then levering one on top of another. Strenuous labor set off renewed waves of dizziness, which she waited out before recommencing. Finally, a makeshift pyramid lay beneath the high window. Clambering onto the ultimate pile of folded carpets, she was at last able to bring her eyes level with the narrow slit, to peer out upon a vast expanse of prairie that began right below her at the foot of a steep, vertical drop. The hole looked pretty narrow to worm through, but even if she managed, it would take a warehouse full of rugs and curtains, tied together, to make a rope long enough to reach the valley floor. This room might not have been designed as a prison, but it would do.

To think I used to dream of seeing the inside of a man sanctuary, Maia thought sardonically, and climbed down.

She tried prying at a couple of crates, but nothing persuaded them to open. Maia did manage to get some of the rugs unrolled to make a bed of sorts—more like a nest—over in one corner. Her stomach growled. She drank and used the chamber pot again. Beyond that, there seemed nothing left to do.

"Now," the voice of despair said with assertion, unwilling to brook further delay, and Maia buried her face in her hands.

Why me? she wondered. Loneliness, her arch enemy, never seemed content. Its return visits were each more brutal than the last, ever since that awful storm tore the ships *Wotan* and *Zeus* apart from one another, and she from her twin. Maia had thought that tragedy her nadir. What more could the world possibly do to her?

Apparently, a whole lot more.

Maia lay down with a length of soft blue curtain material wrapped around her shoulders, and waited for her keepers to come with food . . . or word of her fate. *Thalla and Kiel will worry about me,* she thought, trying to raise an image of friendship for whatever tenuous comfort it offered. She had sunk too low to fantasize that anyone might actually search for her. The solace she sought was simply to imagine somebody on Stratos cared enough to notice she was gone.

The dour-faced guardians returned soon after Maia fell into an exhausted, fitful slumber. Their noise roused her, and she rubbed her eyes as one of them dropped a clattering tray onto the rickety table. Maia could not tell if it was the same pair that had freighted her from Lerner Hold, or if those two had rotated duties with others exactly like them. Stepping back to the door, the sisters watched her with eyes as round and brown and innocent as a doe's.

They had brought food, but little news. When she asked between ravenous spoonings of nondescript stew what was to become of her, their monosyllable answers conveyed that they neither knew nor cared. About the only information Maia was able to pry loose was their family name— Guel—after which they fell into taciturn silence.

What talent or ability had enabled the original ancestress of such broody, beetle-browed women to establish a parthenogenetic clan? What niche did they fill? Surely none requiring affability or great intelligence. Yet, for all Maia knew, the trio she had seen were part of a specialized hive with thousands of individual members, all descended from an original Guel mother who had proved herself excellent at . . .

She wondered. At driving prisoners crazy with sheer sullenness? Perhaps Guel Clan operated jails for local towns and counties across three continents! Maia could hardly disprove it from past experience, this being her first time in prison.

Watching them carry off the dishes, shuffling awkwardly and muttering to each other as they fumbled with the key, Maia contemplated an alternate theory—that these were the sole clone offspring of one farm laborer whose strength and curt obtuseness were qualities some local clan of employers had found useful. Useful enough to subsidize producing more of the same.

Now that hunger was abated, Maia recalled other discomforts. "Hey!" she cried, hurrying to the door and pounding until a querulous voice answered from the opposite side. Maia shouted through the jamb, asking her keepers for soap and a washcloth. And oh yes! Some of the dried takawq leaves all but the rich in this valley used as toilet paper.

There came a low grunt in response, followed by the sound of heavy, receding footsteps.

Come to think of it, unless the idea was to torture her with minor annoyances, this lack of amenities indicated her jailers were indeed amateurs. Just a trio of bullies hired locally for a special assignment. Recalling some of the radical declarations she'd heard over Thalla's radio, Maia made herself a promise. She would not show her keepers any of the habitual respect a unique was supposed to offer those fortunate enough to be born even low-caste clones.

They can't keep me here forever, can they? she wondered plaintively.

Try as she might, Maia could not think of a single reason why they couldn't.

There were other, hurtful questions, such as why Calma Lerner had turned her in to the Joplands. *How much did they pay? Not very much, I bet.* Her heart felt heavy thinking about the betrayal. Although there had been no fealty between them, she had been so sure Calma liked her.

Like has nothing to do with it, when rich clans are involved.

Clearly this was about the drug that made males rut out of season. The clan mothers of this valley had an agenda for its use, and weren't about to brook interference. *Perkinites dream of a nice, predictable world, where everyone grows up knowing who and what she is. Every girl a cherished member of her clan, knowing her future. No muss or fuss from gene mixing. No vars and as few men, as seldom, as possible.*

According to Savant Judeth, the aristocracies of ancient Earth used to justify suppressing those below them on the basis of "innate differences," an assumption that almost never survived scrutiny, once opportunity came to children of rich and poor alike. But there would be no need for oppression or false assumptions in a Perkinite world. Each family and type would find its own level and niche based on talents well-proven by time. Each clan would do what it did best, what it *liked* doing best, in a changeless atmosphere of reliable and mutual respect. Perkinite preachers spoke of a utopic end to all violence, uncertainty, chaos. A stratified world, but a fair one.

Men and vars, even as minorities, irritated this serene equation.

Back in Port Sanger, Perkinism was a mere fringe heresy. Each summer, the clans would invite chosen sailors to come up from the Lighthouse Sanctuary, partly in order to have some var and boy children, but mostly for good, neighborly relations. It kept the shipping guilds happy, and helped make men feel duty-bound to try their best, half a year later. Besides, even in summer, it was sometimes *nice* to have men around, so long as they behaved.

But opinions varied on that. The Long Valley Perkies just wanted to see men when clones had to be sparked.

But the summer ban robs men of what they look forward to all the other seasons. No wonder they lack enthusiasm in winter.

Men had another reason to feel cheated in the Perkinite equation— of the sons they needed to replenish their guilds. It didn't take genius to see the trap the radical separationists had fallen into. *With a low birthrate, the labor shortage draws outsider fems like me, seeking work but also disrupting the peace with our strange faces and voices, our unpredictability.*

It was a cycle the Perkinites couldn't win, as shown by the decision to build this sanctuary, where men might live inland year-round. The thin edge of the wedge. Change would gain momentum as more vars were born, and Perkinite mothers learned to like, or even love them a little. The Orthodox church would gain members. Things would grow more like elsewhere on Stratos.

Then came the Bellers' shiny blue powder—offering the Perkies a way out. *All they'll need is a few dozen doped-up males. Work 'em from clanhold to clanhold like drone bees, till they collapse. They may die smiling, but it's still cruel and stupid.*

Maia shuddered to think what kind of male would put up with more than a week or two in such a role. The kind who'd father low-quality variants, if you took one to bed during summer.

But the Perkinites weren't looking for "fathers" at all! In winter, any sperm would do. *It might work,* Maia saw. No need to keep the railroad men around, with their stiff, easily provoked pride. No summerlings to mess your tidy predictabilities. Producing clones at will, the valley's population could fill to exact specifications, set by the richest clans. Even var laborers could be replaced at society's lowest rung. Simply choose a few with the strongest backs and weakest minds, and make *them* clone mothers. A tailor-made working class.

It wasn't what the Founders had in mind, long ago. The priestesses of Caria wouldn't approve. Guilds of men and *ad hoc* societies of vars would fight it . . . especially radicals like Thalla and Kiel. Clearly, the Perkinites wanted time to establish a *fait accompli* before facing this inevitable opposition from a position of strength.

Earlier, Maia had nursed hopes that Tizbe's backers might let her go with a stern lecture and admonishment to keep silent. That possibility seemed less likely, the more she pondered all the implications.

She tracked time by the progress of a narrow trapezoid of light, cast through the window onto the opposite wall. Her jailers returned with an evening meal just as the oblong shape climbed halfway toward the ceiling and took a rosy tint. They brought the takawq leaves but had forgotten the other items. Listening to her repeated request, they responded with sullen nods and departed, leaving Maia to deal with her loneliness and the oncoming night.

Enforced inactivity brought forth all the aches and strains that had come from weeks laboring in furnaces at Lerner Hold—not to mention the aftermath of being drugged, tied, and bounced around the back of a wagon. Maia's muscles had gradually stiffened during the course of the day, and her tendons throbbed. Stretching helped, but with the coming of darkness she quickly fell into a doze that alternated between comatose slumber and shallow restlessness, exacerbated by her never-absent fears.

In the middle of the night she dreamed the water tap in the corner of her bedroom was dripping. She wanted to bury her head under her pillow to cut off the sound. She wanted Leie, whose cot lay closer to the faucet, to get up and turn it off! It stopped just as she floundered toward wakefulness.

Had she dreamed it? "Leie . . . ?" she began, about to tell her twin about the absurd, awful nightmare of imprisonment.

In a rush, Maia recalled. She threw her arm over her eyes and moaned, wishing with all her might to go back into the dream, as irritating as it had seemed. To be back in her aggravating little attic room, with her aggravating sister safely in bed nearby. She groaned, "Oh . . . Lysos," and prayed desperately that it were so.

When her keepers came with breakfast, they brought a small bundle wrapped in cord. Before sitting down to eat, Maia opened it and found all the items she had asked for, including a new shirt and set of breeches sewn from scratchy but clean homespun. By the sheepish expressions on the warders' faces, she guessed they were supposed to have provided the basics from the start, and had just let it slip what they used for minds. Perhaps they had even gotten a dressing-down from their bosses. So much for the notion that they were hereditary, professional jailers.

She felt more alert today. By lunchtime, Maia had explored every meter of her prison. There were no secret passageways she could find, though most castles in fairy tales seemed replete. Of course, palaces of fable tended to be far older than this shiny new fortress on the high steppe.

New in one sense, ancient in others, as revealed by looking at the walls. The stone, which from miles away looked like layers of some grand confection, was up close a complex agglomerate of many textures and embedded crystals. A few looked vaguely familiar from ancient, blurry, color plates Savant Mother Claire had passed around, too faded to be used any longer in the upper school, but good enough to teach sum-merlings a dollop of geology. Unfortunately, the only minerals Maia could recognize were biotite, for its gray flecks, and dark, glossy horn-blende. Too bad these were granitic rocks, not sedimentary. It might have been diverting to scan the walls for fossils of ancient life-forms that had thrived on Stratos long before the planet's ecosystem was forced to compromise with waves of modified Terran invaders.

Maia exercised for a while, washed up, tried again futilely to pry open some of the crates, and made a decision not to wait for her keepers to warm toward her. It was time to take initiative.

"From now on," she told one of them over lunch. "Your name shall be Grim. And *yours*," she said, pointing at the other, "will be *Blim*."

They looked at her with expressions of surprise and dismay that pleased her no end. "Of course, I may choose better names for you, if you're good."

They were grumbling unhappily when they took the dishes away. Later, over dinner, she switched names on them, confusing them further still. *Why not?* Maia pondered. It was only fair to share the discomfort.

Sunset, day number two, she thought, using a nail she found to scrape a second mark on the inside of the wooden door. The sun's spot on the wall climbed higher, dimmed, and went out. Shadows of crates and stacked bundles grew progressively more eerie and intimidating as dusk fell. Last night, she had been too stupefied to notice, but with the arrival of full darkness, the shapes around her seemed to take on fright-ening gremlin forms. Outlines of unsympathetic monsters.

Don't be a baby. Maia chided herself for reacting like a bedwetting two-year-old. With a pounding heart, she forced herself to stand and approach the most fearsome of the silhouettes, the teetering pyramid of boxes and carpets she herself had stacked below the little window. *See?* she thought, touching the scratchy side of a crate. *You can't let this drive you crazy*.

Nervously, she fondled her sole possession, the little sextant. A glitter of stars could be seen through the stone opening, tempting her. But to climb up there in the dark . . . ?

Maia screwed up her courage. *Piss on the world, or it'll piss on you.* That was how Naroin, her old bosun, would have put it. She had to do this.

Moving carefully from foothold to handhold, Maia climbed the arti-ficial hill, sometimes stopping to hold on tightly as a creak or abrupt teetering set her pulse racing. The ascent took several times as long as it would have in daylight, but Maia persevered until at last she was able to peer through the slit opening. A breeze chilled her face, bringing scents of wild grass and rain. Between patches of glowering cloud, Maia could just make out the familiar contours of the constellation Sappho glittering above the dark prairie.

Okay. We go back down now? her body seemed to ask.

Trembling, Maia forced herself to stay long enough to take a sighting, although the horizon was vague and she could not read the dial of the sextant. *I'll do better tomorrow night,* she promised herself. Gratefully, but with a sense of having won a victory over her fears, she carefully clambered down again.

As she lay upon her makeshift bed, exhausted but stronger in spirit, the clicking sound resumed. The one from last night, which she had associated with a dripping faucet. It was real, apparently, not a figment of her dreams. Another irritant among many.

Maia shrugged aside the distant noise and the looming figures her imagination manufactured out of shadows. *Oh, shut up,* she told them all, and rolled over to go to sleep.

"I'm going to lose my mind without something to do!" she shouted at her jailers the next morning. When they blinked at her in confusion, she demanded. "Haven't they got books here? Anything to *read?*"

The jailers stared, as if uncertain what she was talking about. *They're probably illiterate,* she realized. *Besides, even if the sanctuary architects designed in a library, shelves and all, it still would have been up to the men themselves to bring books and disks and tapes.*

So she was surprised when Blim (or was it Grim?) returned after a while and laid four dog-eared paper-paged books on the table. In the stocky woman's eyes Maia saw a flicker of entreaty. *Don't be hard on us, and we won't be hard on you.* Maia picked up the volumes, probably abandoned here by the construction workers. She nodded thanks and played no name games with her warders when they carried off her tray.

Rationing herself to a book a day, she decided to start with the one bearing the most lurid cover. It depicted a young woman, armed with bow and arrows, leading a band of compatriots and a few protected men through the vine-encrusted ruins of a demolished city. Maia recognized the genre—var-trash—printed on cheap stock to sell for the delectation of poor summerlings like herself. A fair number of nonclone women loved reading fantasies about civilization's collapse, when all of society's well-ordered niches would be overturned and a young woman might win her way to founder status by quick thinking and simple heroics alone.

In this book, the premise was a sudden, unexplained shift in the planet's orbit. Not only did this cause melting of the great ice sheets of Stratos, toppling all the stolid clans and opening the way for newer, hardier types, but in a stroke the inconvenient behavior patterns of men were solved, since now, by a miracle of the author's pen, the aurorae appeared in winter!

It really was trash, but wonderfully diverting trash. By the end of the story, the young protagonist and her friends had everything nicely settled. Each of them seemed destined to have lots of lovely, look-alike daughters, and live happily ever after. *Thalla and Kiel would love this,* Maia thought when she put the novel aside. It must have been left by some var on the construction crew. No winter-born clanling would enjoy the scenario, even in fantasy.

She scraped another mark on the door. That evening Maia climbed the pyramid with more confidence. Through the narrow window, she watched the steady west wind push sluggish, red-tinted clouds toward distant mountains, where steeply angled sunlight also caught a double row of tiny luminescent globes—a small swarm of migrating zoor-floaters, she realized. Their airy sense of freedom made her heart ache, but she watched until dusk grew too dim to see the colorful living zep'lins any longer.

By then the constellations had come out. Her hand was steady as she peered closely through her portable sextant, noting when specific stars touched the western horizon. Recalling the date, this gave her a fairly good way to keep track of time without a clock—as if there were any need. *Maybe next I can figure a latitude,* she thought. That, at least, would partly pin down where her prison lay.

Knowing the time told her one thing. The clicking resumed that night, almost exactly at midnight. It went on for about half an hour, then stopped. For some time afterward, Maia lay in the darkness with her eyes open, wondering.

"What do you think, Leie?" she whispered, asking her sister.

She imagined Leie's response. *"Oh, Maia. You see patterns in every smuggy thing. Go to sleep."*

Good advice. Soon she was dreaming of aurorae flickering like gauzy curtains above the white glaciers of home. Meteors fell, pelting the ice to a staccato rhythm, which transformed into the cadence of a gently falling rain.

The second book was a Perkinite tract, which showed that the work crew must have been mixed—and rather tense.

". . . it is therefore obvious that the seat of the human soul can lie only in the mitochondria, which are the true life-motivators within each living cell. Now, of course, even men have mitochondria, which they inherit from their mothers. But sperm-heads are too small to contain any, so no summer baby, whether female or male, gets any of its essential soul-stuff from the male 'parent.' Only motherhood is therefore truly a creative act.

"Now we have already seen that continuity and growth of the soul takes place via the miracle of cloning, which enhances the soul-essence with each regeneration and renewal of the clonal self. This gradual amplification is only possible with repetition. Just one lifespan leaves a woman's soul barely formed, unenlightened, which is one reason why equal voting rights for vars makes no sense, biologically.

"For a man, of course, there is not even a beginning of soulness. Fatherhood is an anachronism, then. The true role of the soul-less male can only be to serve and spark . . ."

The line of reasoning was too convoluted for Maia to follow closely, but the book's author seemed to be saying that male humans were better defined as domestic animals, useful, but dangerous to let run around loose. The only mistake made long ago, on the Perkinites' beloved, lamented Herlandia, had been not going far enough.

This was heresy, of course, defying several of the Great Promises sworn by Lysos and the Founders, when they made men small in number, but preserved their rights as citizens and human beings. In theory, any man might aspire to heights of individual power and status, equal to even a senior mother of a high clan. Maia knew of no examples, but it was supposed to be possible.

The writer of this tract wanted no shared citizenship with lower life-forms.

Another Great Promise had ordained that heretics must be suffered to speak, lest rigor grasp women's minds. *Even loony stuff like this?* Maia wondered. To try understanding another point of view, Maia kept reading. But when she came to a part that proposed breeding males to be docilely milked on special farms, like contented cows, she reached her limit. Maia threw the book across the room and went into a flurry of exercise, doing pushups and situps until pounding sounds of pulse and breath drowned out all remnants of the author's hateful voice.

Dinner came and went. Darkness fell. This time, she tried to be ready just before midnight, lying on her back with eyes closed. When the clicking started, she listened carefully for the first ten seconds, and tried to note if there was a pattern. It followed a rhythm, all right, made of repeated snapping sounds interspersed with pauses one, two, or more beats in duration.

click click, beat, click, beat, beat, click click click . . .

Maybe she was letting her imagination run away with her. It sounded like no code she had ever heard. There were no obvious spaces that might go between words, for example. Was there any reason for the clicking to happen at the same time each night?

It might just be a faulty timepiece in one of the great halls, or something equally mundane. *I wonder how the sound carries through the walls.*

Sleep came without any resolution. She dreamed of brasswork clocks, ticking with the smooth, just rhythms of natural law.

The third book was even riper than the prior two—a romance about life in the old Homino-Stellar Phylum, before Lysos and the Founders set forth across the galaxy to forge a new destiny. Such accounts, dealing with an archaic, obsolete way of life, ought to be fascinating and instructive. But Maia had read widely in the genre as a four-year-old, and been disappointed.

Like so many others, this tale was set on Florentina, the only Phylum world familiar to most schoolgirls, since that was where the Founders' expedition began. The story even featured a cameo appearance by Perseph, a chief aide to Lysos. But for the most part, the exodus was seen in glimpses, being planned offstage. Meanwhile, the poor heroine, a sort-of everywoman of Florentina, suffered the trials of living in a patriarchal society, where men were so numerous and primitive that life could only have been a kind of hell.

"I did not mean to encourage him!" Rabaka cried, covering the left side of her face so that her husband would not see the bruises. "I only smiled because—"

"You SMILED at a strange man?" he roared at her. "Have you lost your mind? We men will seize any gesture, any imaginable cue as a sign of willingness! No wonder he followed you, and pushed you into the alley to have his way."

"But I fought. . . . He did not succeed—"

"No matter. Now I shall have to kill him!"

"No, please . . ."

"Are you DEFENDING him, then?" Rath demanded, his eyes filling with flame. "Perhaps you would prefer him? Perhaps you feel trapped with me in this small house, bound together by our vows for eternity?"

"No, Rath," Rabaka pleaded. "I just don't want you to risk—"

But it was already too late to stem his rush of anger. Rath was already reaching for the punishment strap that hung upon the wall. . . .

Maia could only take it half a chapter at a time. The writing was execrable, but that wasn't what made her stomach queasy. The incessant violence repulsed her. *What kind of masochist reads this kind of stuff?* she wondered.

If the point was to show how different another society could be, the book was successful, in a gut-churning way. On Stratos, it was virtually unheard-of for a man to lift his hand against a woman. The Founders had laid an aversion at the chromosome level, which was reinforced from one generation to the next. Summer matings were a man's only chance to pass on his genes, and clan mothers had long memories when the time came to send out invitations during aurora season.

On Florentina, though, there had been a different arrangement. *Marriage.* One man. One woman. Stuck together forever. Apparently, women even *preferred* quasi-slavery to a single life, because vast numbers of other men patrolled outside, in ceaseless rut, always eager to pounce. The brutal consequences depicted on page after page of the historical novel left Maia nauseated by the time she finished.

Of course she had no way of knowing how accurate the depiction was, of Old Order life on a Phylum world. Maia suspected just a little authorial exaggeration. There might have been specific cases like the one described, but if things were this bad for all women, all the time, they surely would have poisoned their husbands and sons long before gene-molding came along with alternate solutions.

Still, it was enough to give a girl religion again. *Bless the wisdom of Lysos*, Maia thought, drawing a circle over her breast.

Again that evening she exercised hard, running in place, doing pushups and step workouts, on and off crates. At dusk, she went back to the window and found that she could just manage to squeeze into the long, narrow passage. Thoughts of escape blossomed, until she reached the far end where it was possible to look straight down at the valley floor . . . a hundred meters below.

I might be able to come up with a plan. Find a way to get some of these crates open. Maybe start weaving a rope from yarn taken from the carpets? There were possibilities, each of them dangerous. It would take some mulling over. Anyway, she obviously had plenty of time.

There were no majestic zoor-floaters to watch as night fell, though several birds fluttered past, pausing on their way to roost long enough to taunt her, squawking at this silly, flightless human, crammed within her cleft of stone.

Maia felt too agitated to try using the sextant. She climbed back down, fell asleep early, and had strange dreams most of the night. Dreams of escape. Dreams of running. Dreams of ambivalence. Of wanting/not wanting the company of someone for the rest of her life. Leie? Clone-daughters? A *man*? Images of a fictional but still vivid Florentina World confused her with combined revulsion and fascination.

Later, when she clawed her way, moaning, out of a dream about being buried alive, Maia awakened to find herself tangled in the rough, heavy drapes she used for blankets, forced to struggle just to extricate herself. *I don't like this place,* she thought, when at last she was breathing freely again. She sagged back. *I wonder how you go about unweaving a carpet.*

The narrow window showed a sliver of the constellation Anvil, so the night was more than half over. *Missed the clicking, this time,* one part of her commented. The rest didn't give a damn. When sleep reclaimed her, there were no more nightmares.

She had saved for last what seemed the best book of the four. It was printed on good paper and came with the imprint of a Horn City publishing company. "A literary classic," proclaimed the flashing microadvert on its binding, when turned to the light. On the copyright page, Maia read that the novel was over a hundred years old. She had never heard of it, but that came as no surprise. Lamatia Hold was fanatic in preferring to teach its var-daughters practical skills over the arts.

Certainly the writing was better than any of the other books. Unlike the historical fantasy, or the var-trash romance, it was set in the Stratos of everyday life. The story opened with a young woman on a voyage, accompanied by a fellow cloneling her own age. They were carrying commercial contracts from town to town, arranging deals, making money for their faraway hold and clan. The writer delightfully conveyed many hassles of life on the road, dealing with bureaucrats and senior mothers who, as broad and amusing caricatures, brought to Maia's lips her first faint smile in a long time. Below these picaresque encounters, the author laid a current of underlying tension. Things were not as they seemed with the two protagonists. Maia discovered their secret early in chapter three.

The pair weren't clonelings at all. Their "clan" was a fiction. They were just a couple of vars. Twins . . .

Maia blinked, startled to the quick. *But . . . that was our idea! It's what Leie and I planned to do.*

She stared at the page, outrage turning swiftly to embarrassment. *How many people must have read this book by now?* Flipping to the title page, she saw that paper printings alone were in the hundreds of thousands. And that left out versions on disk, or floating access . . .

We would've been laughingstocks, the first place we tried it, Maia realized with horrified chagrin. In retrospect, she saw with abrupt clarity how the idea *must* have occurred to others, countless times, even before this novel was written. Probably lots of var twins fantasized about it. *At least some of the Lamai mothers should have known, and been able to warn us!*

Maia paused. *Wait a minute!* She flipped pages and looked again at the names of the protagonists. . . . *Reie and Naia?* No wonder they had sounded familiar. She shook her head in numb disbelief. *We . . . were NAMED after characters in this Lysos-damned storybook?*

Maia saw purple, thinking about the petty joke Mother Claire and the others had pulled on the two of them. At least Leie had been spared ever knowing what fools they'd been.

She hurled the book across the room and flung herself onto her dusty bed, crying out of loneliness and a sense of utter abandonment.

For two days she was listless, spending most of her time sleeping. The late night clicking was no longer of interest. Not much of anything was.

Still, after a while boredom began penetrating even the self-pitying bleakness Maia had crafted for herself. When she could stand it no longer, she asked her jailers once more for something to help pass the time. They looked at each other, and responded that they were sorry, but there were no more books.

Maia sighed and went back to picking at her meal. Her warders watched morosely, clearly affected by her mood. She did not care.

At first, Maia used to fantasize about rescue by some authority, like the Planetary Equilibrium officer she had spoken to, or the priestess of the temple at Grange Head, or even a squadron of Lamai militia, wearing bright-plumed helmets. But she nursed no illusions about her importance in the grand scheme of things. Nor did any word arrive from Tizbe. Maia now saw that there was no need for the drug messenger or anyone else to come visit or interrogate her.

Hope had no place in her developing picture of the world. *Even the Lerners are so high above you, they have to bend over to spit.*

She remembered Calma, standing in the moonlight while Tizbe and the Joplands took her prisoner. Until that moment, Maia had thought of her as an individual, a decent person—a little awkward and transparent, but sweet in her way. *Now I know better . . . a clone is a clone. Thalla and Kiel were right. The whole system stinks!*

It was sacrilege, and Maia didn't care. She missed her friends. Even if she had only known them for a few weeks, they had shared with her the curse of uniqueness, and would understand the feelings of betrayal and desolation that swept over her now.

Desperate for some way out of her funk, Maia reread the escapist, var-trash novel, and found it more satisfying the second time. Perhaps because she identified more with the implied wish, to see everything come crashing down. But then it was finished. A third reading would be pointless. None of the other books was worth even a second look.

Lethargically, she spent the afternoon atop her makeshift pyramid, staring across the desert plain. It was a sea of grass you could get lost on, if you didn't know what you were doing. Here and there she thought she could trace outlines of regular features, like the footprints of vanished buildings. But no one had ever lived on this arid plateau, as far as she knew.

The next morning, along with her breakfast, Maia's jailers brought something new. It was a large shiny box with a handle, like one of those hard suitcases rich travelers sometimes carried. "Got lots o' these stacked in 'nother room," one of them told her. "Hear it's a way to pass th' time. Y'might try it." The woman shrugged, as if such a long speech had used up her allotment of words for the day.

After they left, Maia took the case over to where there was a good patch of light, and released the simple catch. The box unfolded once, then the two halves unfolded again. More clever hingings invited more unlayering until she had in front of her a wide, flat surface of pale material covered with finely etched vertical and horizontal lines.

Life, she realized. Maia had never before seen a board quite like this, obviously an expensive model, too good to take to sea. It must be the kind men used while trapped in sanctuary, to help distract themselves during hot-season quarantine.

They brought me a patarkal game of bleeding Life!

It was too rich. Maia guffawed with a touch of hysterical release. She laughed and laughed, until at last she wiped tears from her eyes and sighed, feeling much better.

Then, for lack of anything better to do, she felt along the front panel for the power switch and turned the machine on.

W hy, in nature, is the male-female ratio nearly always one to one? If wombs are costly while sperm is cheap, why are there so many sperm producers?

It is a matter of biological economics. If a species produces fewer females than males, daughters will be more fruitful than sons. Any variant individual who picks up the trait of having more female offspring will have advantages, and will spread the mutant trait through the gene pool until the ratio evens out again.

The same logic will hold in reverse, if we planners try to simply program-in a birth ratio sparse in males. Early generations would reap the benefits of peace and serenity, but selection forces will reward son-production, favoring its occurrence with rising frequency, eventually annulling the program and landing us right back where we started. Within mere centuries, this planet will be like any other, aswarm with men and their accompanying noise and strife.

There is a way to free our descendants from this bio-economic cul-de-sac. Give them the option of self-cloning. Reproductive success will then reward women who manage to have offspring *both* sexually and especially non-sexually. In time, a desire to have like-self daughters will saturate the gene pool. It will be stable and self-reinforcing.

The option of stimulated self-cloning lets us at last design a world with the problem of too many males permanently solved.

10

Maia already knew the basic rules. Lamatia Clan wanted all its daughters, winter and summer alike, to know about the "peculiar male obsession with games." Such familiarity could be useful any season, in maintaining good relations with some mannish guild.

Games came in a wide range. Many, like Poker, Dare, and Distaff, were as popular among females as males. And although Chess was traditionally more well-liked by men, four generations of planetary supreme grandmasters had come from the small, intellectual lineage of Terrille clones. Which might help explain why ever more male aficionados had switched to the Game of Life, during the last century or so.

Technically, any Life match was over before it began. Two men—or teams of men—faced off at opposite ends of a board consisting of anywhere from two score to several hundred intersecting horizontal and vertical lines. During the crucial preparation phase, each side took turns strategically laying rows of game pieces in the squares between the lines —choosing to place them either white or black side up—until the board was full. Simple rules were programmed into the pieces, or sometimes into the board itself, depending on how rich the players were and what kind of set they could afford.

As a little girl, Maia used to watch in fascination as sailors from docked freighters spent hours winding up old-fashioned watch-spring game pieces, or collecting the solar-powered variety after soaking on rooftops by the piers. Each team might spend up to ten minutes between

turns huddled, arguing strategy until the referee called time and they
had to lay down another row on their side of the playing field. After
which they would watch, arms crossed, contemptuously sneering as their
opponents fussed and laid a layer of their own, on the other side. The
teams would continue alternating, laying new rows of white or black
pieces, until the halfway boundary was reached, and all empty squares
were filled. Then everyone stepped back. After proclaiming an ancient
invocation, the referee would then stretch out his staff toward the timing
square.

Most women found all of the arguments and arm waving leading up
to this point profoundly tedious. Yet, whenever a major match was finally
about to get under way, people would start arriving—from poor var laborers to haughty clanfolk descending from castles on the hill—all
gathering to stand and watch, awaiting the tap of the referee's
stick. . . .

When, suddenly, the quiescent pieces wakened!

Maia especially loved the times when players used the spring-
wound disks, which, on sensing the condition of their neighbors, would
respond by buzzing and flipping their louvers with each beat of the game
clock—white giving over to black, black becoming white, or mysteriously remaining motionless with the same face up until the next round.

The process was controlled by preset rules. In the classic version of
Life, these were absurdly simple. A square with a black piece was defined as "alive." White side up meant "unliving." Its state during an
upcoming round would depend on its *neighbors'* status the round *before.*
A white piece would "come alive," turning black next turn, if exactly
three of its eight neighboring squares (including corners) were black *this*
turn. If a site was already black, it could remain so next round if it
currently had two or three living neighbors. Any more or less, and it
would switch back to white again.

Someone once told Maia that this simulated living ecosystems.
"Among plant and animal species, whenever population density climbs
too high in a neighborhood, there often follows a collapse. Everything
dies. Similarly, death also reigns if things get too sparse." Ecology
thrives on moderation, or so the game seemed to say.

To Maia, that just sounded like rationalization. The game got its
name, she was sure, from the *patterns* that surged across the board just
as soon as the referee gave his starting rap. From that moment, each
individual game piece remained on the same spot, but its abrupt changes
of state contributed to waves of black and white that crisscrossed the
playing area with great speed and hypnotic complexity. Even Perkinite
missionaries, standing on their portable pedestals, would lapse in their

denigrations of all things male long enough to stare and sigh at the entrancing, rippling waves.

Certain initial patterns appeared to animate on their own. A compact "glider" would, if left alone, cruise from one end of the board to the other, changing shape in a four-stage pattern that repeated over and over as it inched along. Another grouping might throb in place, or send out branching limbs that budded, like flowers sending forth seeds that sprouted in their turn.

Sometimes pattern was the sole objective. There were form-generating contests, with prizes going to the most intricate final design, or to the purest image obtained after twenty, fifty, or a hundred beats. Variants using more complex rules and multicolored pieces produced even more sophisticated displays.

More often, though, the game was played as a battle between two teams. Their objective: to lay down starting conditions such that when play commenced, the sweep of shapes would carry their way, wiping clear their opponents' territory, so that the last oases of "life" would be on their side of the board.

The contests could appear brutal at times, just like nature. Besides gliders and other benign forms, there were "eaters," which consumed other patterns, then rebounded off the edge to sweep back across the playing field as voracious as ever. More sophisticated designs passed harmlessly off most patterns, but devoured any *other* eater they came across!

Ship crews and guilds hoarded techniques, tricks, and rules of thumb for generations, yet the strategy of laying down initial rows before the game was still more art than science. Frequently both teams wound up staring in surprise at what they'd wrought . . . patterns surging back and forth for a good part of an hour in ways unexpected by either side. Draws were frequent. During summers, occasional fistfights erupted over accusations of cheating, though Maia was at a loss how one could cheat in Life.

She had to admit there was something aesthetic about the game's essential simplicity and the intricate, endless variety of forms it produced. As a child she had found it alluring, in an eerie sort of way, and had even tried asking questions. It took some time getting over the taunting and humiliation that had brought on, more from her own peers than from men. Anyway, by age four she found herself reaching the same conclusion as so many other women on Stratos.

So what?

Yes, the patterns were interesting up to a point, beyond which the passion males poured into the game became symbolic of the gulf separating the sexes. Other pastimes, like card games, at least involved people looking at or talking to each other, for instance. It was hard to comprehend treating little bits—*things*—as if they were really alive.

Yet here she was, in prison, without anyone else to look at *or* talk to, with all the books read and nothing to do but stare at the unfolded game board. Maia pondered. *I've already tried a thing or two girls don't usually do—like studying navigation.*

That was merely unusual, though. Not unheard-of. This game was another matter. If there were women on Stratos who had ever achieved expert status at Life, they were almost certainly labeled terminally strange.

Well, better strange than batty, she decided. Anger and loneliness waited on the wings, like unwelcome aunts, ready to drop in at the slightest invitation, provoking useless, unproductive tears. *I'll go crazy without something to keep my mind busy.*

The board felt smooth. There were no physical pieces. Instead, each tiny white square would turn ebony at the command of an electro-optic controller buried in the machine itself. She recalled the old-time clatter and clack with fondness. This system felt chill and remote.

Let's see if I can figure it out.

A couple of small lights winked on the display. She had no idea what PROG MEM or PREV.GAME.SAV meant. Those could be explored later, when she had mastered the simplest level. As soon as she turned on the machine, half of the squares along the four edges of the game board had gone black, so that an alternating checker sequence snaked around the perimeter. She recalled that this was one of several ways of dealing with the edge problem, or what to do when moving Life patterns reached the limits of the playing field.

Ideally, in the perfect case, there wouldn't be an edge at all, just an endless expanse to give the patterns room to grow and interact. That was why big tournament games featured immense boards, and took days, even weeks, to set up. Maia recalled how, one day at Lamatia Hold, Çoot Bennett had told her a secret. Sophisticated electronic versions of Life, such as the one in front of her, could actually keep track of patterns even after they had "left the stage," pretending that the artificial entities continued existence even several board-lengths away, in some sort of imaginary space! At first, Maia had been convinced he was having her on. Then she felt thrilled, wondering if any other woman knew about this.

Later she realized—of course the Caria savants knew, since they controlled the factories that made the game sets. They just didn't *care.* For a machine to go on pretending that imaginary objects existed in some fictitious realm the player couldn't even see was like the unreal multiplying with itself, manipulating tokens of replicas of symbols, which in turn stood for make-believe things, which were themselves emblems. . . . Some of the mathematician clans at Caria University probably studied such abstractions, but Maia doubted they ever made the man-error of mistaking them for real.

Solving the edge problem was another matter when teams were forced to use simple lines scratched on a dock or cargo hatch, playing with wind-up or sun-powered pieces. As a partial solution, men sometimes laid rows of static, unpowered black or white pieces along the rim of the playing field, to try constraining the action. Maia knew the slang term for the alternating checker border was "the mirror," although only a few life patterns would actually reflect off the fixed boundary back into the game arena. Others would simply be absorbed or destroyed.

An edge pattern also made starting the game easier, since any square in the first playing row already had either one or two "living" neighbors, just below it.

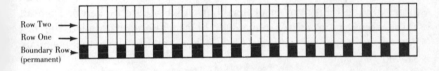

Removing the thin writing stylus from its slot on the control panel, she stroked a square on the first row, turning it black.

The solitary "living" square was born with two black neighbors on the fixed boundary row below, touching it at the corners. Now Maia gave it another black neighbor, to its left. With three black, or living, neighbors now, the first activated square should remain "alive" . . . at least through the second round.

Maia sighed. *All right. Let's see if I can make a simple ladder.*

She worked her way across the first row, turning a few squares dark, leaving some blank, and so on. Maia did not feel ready to take on more complicated starting conditions quite yet, so after touching about forty squares she called it enough. The rest of the board was left pale, untouched.

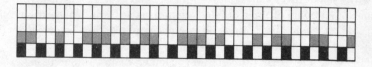

Knowing the rules, Maia could guess what might happen to a particular square next round, by carefully counting the number of black neighbors it had *now*. It didn't take much effort to project the fates of up to a dozen squares, one or two rounds into the future. Then she lost track. To find out what would happen after that, she must set the game in motion.

Peering at the control panel, she found a button embossed with a figure of a cowled man holding a long staff. *The symbol for a referee,* Maia decided, and pressed the button. A low note pulsed slowly, the traditional countdown. At the eighth beat the game commenced, and change abruptly rippled along the active row. Wherever a square had precisely the right number of neighbors, that square flickered. Then all those squares turned, or remained, black. Those that failed the test turned, or remained, white. The checker pattern along the boundary stayed the same.

Now there were some black squares on the *second* active row, as well as the first. A few spots on the formerly all-white expanse had met the conditions for coming alive.

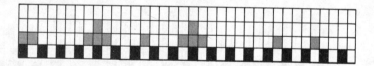

With the next timing pulse, more squares died than were born, and it was only with the fourth round that any positions came alive on the third row. Maia saw with mild chagrin that she had chosen a losing sequence for her initial condition. *Ah, well.* She waited till the last, gasping cluster of dark points expired, and immediately tried again with a new pattern along the first row.

This time pretty much the same thing happened, except near the far left, where an entity took shape—a small group of cells that winked on and off in a repeating pattern, over and over. *Oh, yes,* Maia remembered. *That's a "microbe."*

While its individual parts flickered with different rhythms, each unit choosing a different tempo to flip from dark to pale or back again, the isolated configuration as a whole kept renewing itself. After twenty beats, the rest of the board lay empty, but this small patch remained stable, repetitiously persistent. Maia felt a flush of pleasure at having reinvented one of the simplest Life-forms on just her second go. She wiped the board and tried again, creating microbes all across the bottom edge. If left alone, they would whirl and gyre in place until the batteries ran out.

That was the extent of her beginner's luck. Maia spent much of the next hour experimenting without finding another self-sustaining form. It was frustrating, since she recalled that some of the classics were absurdly simple.

A metallic clanking behind her announced the guards' arrival with lunch. Maia got up, spreading her arms and stretching a crick in her back. Only when she went over to sit down at the table, and felt the stout women staring at her, did it come to her attention that she was *humming,* and must have been doing so for some time.

Huh! Maia thought. But then, it wasn't surprising to be glad something had drawn her from her troubles for a while. *We'll see if this diversion lasts as long as those books did.* To which she added, *Just don't count on my being too distracted to notice, my fat Guel keepers, if you ever relax your guard, or stop coming in pairs. Someday you'll slip up. I'm watching.*

After the bland meal, she purposely avoided the game board and went instead to her "gymnasium," contrived out of rugs and boxes. Running in place, stretching, doing situps and pullups, Maia drove herself until a warm, pleasant ache spread from her shoulders to her toes. Then she removed her clothes and used water from the pitcher to take a sponge bath. Fortunately there was a small drain in the floor to carry away the effluent.

While drying herself, she looked over her body. After months of hard labor, it was only natural she should find muscles where none had shown before. Nor did she mind the fine scars that laced her hands and forearms—all earned by honest labor. What did surprise her was a pronounced development of her breasts. Since her last inspection, they had gone from petite to appreciable—or ample enough to be a bit sore from being jounced, the last hour or so. Of course, it was common knowledge that Lamai mothers passed on a dominant gene for this. They seldom left their var-daughters unendowed. Still, predictable or not, it was an event. One Maia had not expected to celebrate in jail.

She had, in fact, always envisioned someday sharing it with Leie.

Shaking her head, she refused to be drawn into bleakness. For distraction, Maia walked back to the carpet and sat down in front of the electronic Life simulator.

If only there were a manual, or some teaching program to go with this damn game, she pondered. Maia had glimpsed men at dockside carrying around heavy reference books, which they pored over between matches. There would also be treatises on the subject, written by female anthropologists, filed at Caria University and big-city libraries. None of which helped her here.

Those two little lights attracted her notice again. PROG MEM, one label read. Some sort of memory? *For storing preplanned programs, I suppose.*

The other button said PREV.GAM.STOR.

"Previous game storage?" She had presumed this board was new, having been shipped in for men who would now never arrive. But the light winked, so maybe there *was* an earlier game stored in memory.

Guess I could replay it and pick up a pointer or two, she thought, then noticed nearby a tiny window with a string of code letters displayed. **VARIANT RULE: RVRSBL CA 897W**, it said mysteriously. Maia made a guess. Sometimes men changed the rules of the game, as if Life itself weren't complicated enough. It might take *five* living neighbors for a black square to stay alive. Or the program made squares to the left more influential than those on the right. The possibilities were endless, which helped the whole thing seem all the more pointless to most women.

Oh, this is idiotic. I'll never learn anything from this. Maia paused, then impulsively pressed the button to see what the memory cache contained. Immediately the game board swirled into action. First the checkered boundary contracted inward from all sides till it enclosed a much smaller number of squares. She counted fifty-nine across and fifty-nine lengthwise. Surrounding the restricted game area was a border much more complex than the simple mirror pattern of before. The board flickered another time, and all at once the zone within the new boundary filled with chaos. A splotchy scattering of black dots covered the first nine rows, like choca-bits strewn across a birthday cake.

Lysos! This was completely over Maia's head. The WIPE button beckoned . . . but curiosity stayed her hand. After all, this represented a lot of labor by the game's previous owner. If nothing else, the patterns might be pretty to watch.

Sighing, she touched the referee symbol. The clock ticked down, eight, seven, six, five, four . . .

The dots began to dance. Wherever an open space had the right number of neighbors, next round there was a black, or living square at that location. Others that had been black, but failed the programmed criteria, turned white the following round. With each clock throb, the patterns changed in whirling waves, some fragmenting or scattering upon touching the boundary, while others reflected back, adding to the maelstrom within. Ephemeral shapes appeared and vanished like bubbles passing through the plane of the board. Maia could only breathe a sigh as waves crashed against stable entities, transforming them. She saw gliders and noted their simple, crushed-triangular form. In one corner appeared a "glider gun," which spat out little flapping arrows at regular intervals, sending them whizzing across the board. There were spectacular collisions.

It was enthralling to watch. Maia wondered if this would turn out to be one of those programs that became self-sustaining, with the whole board in a state of perpetual flux for as long as the machine was left on, each moment's array unlike any that had come before.

Then, the pace began to slacken. Rapidly zipping entities started merging into complex but stationary units, arrayed in five deep columns across the board. Each of these underwent further evolution, slowing the rate of change still further as they converged on what she guessed must be a preplanned, final form.

She could see it happening. Each step grew out of the one preceding it. Still, it took her by surprise when the patterns coalesced into individual letters.

Words.

HELP! PRISONER –
39° F8 16′ N, 67° F8 54′ E

The letters flickered, as if seen through turbid water, their component dots still blindly switching on and off, obeying set rules, unaware of anything more than two rows or columns away. Only collectively did they carry meaning, and that began dissolving as stern, mathematical laws tore fleeting cogency into swirls of returning chaos. Some driving force was spent. Blank patches spread, devouring the brief patterns.

In seconds it was over. Maia stared at the pale game board—now empty, featureless—trying to convince herself she'd seen it: *meaning*, startling and unforeseen.

M any species use environmental cues to trigger reproduction at certain times of year, leaving the rest peaceful and quiet. Humans have lost this ancient linkage with the calendar, resulting in our incessant obsession with, and subjugation to, sex.

The time has come to restore wisdom to our rhythm of life, reestablishing serenity and predictability to the cycle of our years. Stratos seems ideal for this purpose, with its distinctive, planet-wide seasons. The birth ratio we foresee—of clones to old-style, sexually-derived offspring—need not be programmed-in. It will arise naturally out of two uneven periods of potential impregnation, separated by long stretches of relative calm.

There are plenty of environmental effects we can utilize as cues, to trigger desire at appropriate times. Take the incredible, world-wide aurorae of high summer, during the planet's closest approach past tiny, fierce Waenglen's Star. If male chimpanzees are visually aroused by a mere flash of pink female swelling seen at long range through a forest, how difficult can it be for us to program a similar color-response in our males, triggered by these startling blue sky displays? Similarly, winter's special frost will signal changes in our women descendants, preparing them for amazonogenic cloning.

There will be side-effects we cannot now predict, but the possibility of error should not deter us. We are only replacing one rather arbitrary set of stimuli and impulses with another. The new rules will, in fact, be more flexible and varied than the monotone lusts of old.

One thing will remain constant. No matter what changes we make, the drama of birth and life will remain a matter of choice, of mind. We are not animals, after all. The environment may suggest. It may provoke. But in the end, our descendants will be thinking beings.

It is by their thoughts and sentiments and strong wills that their way of life will be decided.

11

Around midnight, the star-filled patterns of the winter sky rose over the high mountains crowning the eastern horizon, casting glittering reflections across glaciers tucked in alpine dales. Summertime's celestial rush was over, tapering to a planetary glide as Stratos climbed its elliptic track toward the longest season. More than two Earth years would pass before the great plummet into spring. Till then, the Pelican of Euphrosyne, Epona, and the Dancing Dolphin would be regular occupants of night's high throne.

Maia often used to wonder what it might be like to live on Florentina, or even Old Earth. Very strange, she imagined, and not just due to the primitive breeding patterns still followed there. She had read that on most habitable worlds, seasons were due to axial tilt, rather than orbital position. And winter was a time of *bad* weather.

Here, under the thick atmosphere of Stratos, summer's necessary but brief disruptions passed quickly and were soon forgotten, while winter brought a long time of placid predictability. Rainclouds arrived in periodic, sweeping fronts, showering their moist loads across the continents, then replenishing over humid seas. For protracted intervals between storms, the sun nourished gently bowing, light-hungry crops, outshining its companion, Wengel Star, so overpoweringly that the white dwarf was no more than a faint glitter in the daytime sky, too dim to provoke even a sailor on leave. At night, no aurorae blared, only sprinkled constellations, twinkling like mad above the restless jet stream.

It will be Autumn-End Day soon, Maia thought, watching the constellation Thalia climb slowly toward zenith. *They'll be putting up decorations in Port Sanger. All the pleasure houses will close till midwinter, and men from the sanctuaries will stroll through wide-open gates, making paper airplanes of their old visitor passes. They'll get sweets and cider, and children will ride their shoulders, pulling their beards, making them laugh.*

Although rutting time had been effectively over before she and Leie departed on their ill-starred voyage, Autumn-End Day would mark the true start of winter's extended time of peace, lasting for nearly half of the long, uneven track of seasons, during which males were as harmless as lugars and the biggest problem was getting them to look up from their books, or whittling, or game boards. Half of the City Watch would disband till springtime. What need for patrols, with the streets as safe as houses?

Maia had known she would probably never again celebrate Autumn-End in Port Sanger. But she hadn't figured on spending a festival day in prison. Would she still be here at Farsun Time, as well? Somehow, she doubted her jailers would throw a gala then, either—offering hot punch and luck tokens to passersby. (*What* passersby?) Nor were any of the Guel guards likely to dress up as the Frost Lady, carrying her magic ladder, waving a wand of plenty, and giving treats and noisemakers to good little girls.

No, dammit! By Farsun Day, I'm going to be far away from here! She quashed a wave of homesickness.

Maia shook away distracting thoughts and lifted her miniature sextant, concentrating on the immediate problem. She could not be sure of the exact time, let alone the date. Without an accurate clock, it was impossible to fix her east-west position accurately, even if the instrument was in perfect working order. Longitude was going to be fuzzy.

But you don't need the exact time to figure *latitude.* You just have to know the sky.

I wish I had my book of ephemerides, she thought, wondering if the stationmistress at Holly Lock had thrown out her duffel yet, along with her meager possessions. The slim volume carried the positions of major sighting stars to all the accuracy she'd ever need. Without it, memory would have to do.

Maia rested her elbows on the sill of the narrow opening in the wall, and took another reference on Taranis, a compact stellar cluster where it was said the Enemy long ago laid waste to two planets before coming here to meet defeat on Stratos. Twisting a dial moved the image in her cross-hairs till it kissed the south horizon's prairie-sharp edge in the sextant's tiny mirror. She lowered the device in order to peer at the dial, and jotted another figure in her notebook.

At least there had been a ready solution to the problem of writing implements. Near the base of her makeshift observing pyramid, awkwardly covered by piled-up rugs, lay the broken ruin of a storage box. Maia had struggled for over an hour, soon after sunset, to heave the crate all the way up here by the window. Then, just half a second after she pushed it off, the box lost all that altitude, hitting the stone floor edge-on.

The crash made a horrible racket, bringing guards to the door with muttered inquiries. But she had managed to appease the Guels, shouting that she'd only fallen while exercising. "I'm all right, though. Thank you for being concerned!"

After a long pause, the Guels finally went away, grumbling. Maia dared not count on their incuriosity surviving a repetition. Fortunately, the crash had loosened several slats, spilling paper and writing utensils onto the floor. By then, the stars were out. For the next hour, she applied her rusty navigation skills to fixing the location of this high-plains prison.

Maia lifted the notebook into Durga's wan light and added up the final result. *Longitude is close to the one in the message,* she thought. *And latitude's nearly identical!*

At first, contemplating the communiqué that had appeared so astonishingly on the Game of Life board, she concluded it must be a bad joke. Someone at the factory must have inserted the plea—the way, as kids, she and Leie used to carefully pry open petu nuts and replace the meat with slips of paper saying, "Help! Squirrels are holding us in a petu tree!"

Now she knew better. The message had not been coded before shipment. Whoever logged the memorandum had done so in a location very close to here. Within tens of kilometers. Yet she had seen no sign of any towns or habitations near this stone monolith. It was doubtful the countryside could support any.

In effect, that could only mean the writer dwelt in this same tower, perhaps just meters away. Maia felt a bit guilty that another person's predicament could bring such joy. *I'm not happy you're in jail,* she thought of her fellow prisoner. *But Lysos! It's good not to be alone anymore!*

They must be in similar situations—locked in storage chambers not designed as jail cells, but effective nonetheless. Yet, the other prisoner had proved resourceful. Finding herself in a storeroom filled with male-oriented recreation devices, she had managed to see in them a way to send the equivalent of messages in bottles.

Maia pondered the other inmate's ingenious plan. These electronic game sets were costly, and the matriarchs of Long Valley weren't spend-thrifts. Sooner or later, they would order the games and other amenities shipped off for resale . . . perhaps to some sanctuary on the coast, or a seafarers' guild . . . eventually falling into the hands of someone able to read the programmed message. Any sailor would then know at once where a person was being held against her will.

There were assumptions, of course. The Perkinite clan mothers might not act to cut their losses in the unfinished sanctuaries until abso-lutely sure the new drugs were working. That might take some time. Nor was that all, Maia thought cynically. *Even if the games do get shipped, and assuming the messages aren't erased or read by wrong parties along the way. . . . Even if someone believes the plea, and reports it, then what?*

It wasn't as though the planetary authorities had swarms of mighty aircraft, or armies to send round the world at a moment's notice, just to correct far-off injustices. What forces Caria City had, it hoarded for emergencies. More likely, some lone investigator or magistrate would be sent the long way—by sea, then by train and horseback, taking the best part of a year to arrive, if ever.

Assuming we're still here by then.

Maia wasn't sure she could hold out that long. The other prisoner had a lot more patience.

Still, it's a better plan than anything I came up with. Imagine figur-ing out how to do all this with a Game of Life set! Lacking a lifetime of practice, who could have created a message like that from scratch?

A man? Maia snorted disdainfully. Someone with a savant's skills, surely.

I wish I could meet her. Talk to her. Maybe there's a way.

Maia guessed it must be close to midnight. She was about to poke her head out the window again, to check the progress of the stars, when suddenly she heard it start. The nightly clicking.

Hastily, she angled her notebook into the moonlight and started making marks. A slash for every click, a dash for each beat that a pause lasted. After about twenty seconds, she stopped and read over the initial portion.

"Click, click, pause, click," she recited slowly. "Click, click, pause, pause . . . yes. I'm sure it's the same as the other night!"

Maia crammed the notebook in her belt and scrambled down the pyramid of boxes so quickly the unsteady construct teetered. Near bot-tom, her toe caught a fold of carpet, and she sprawled onto her hands and knees. Ignoring her scrapes, Maia came to her feet running.

"Where is it?" she whispered, concentrating. Peering through the darkness, she followed her ears to the east wall. Crouching, tracing her hand along the cool stone, she had to creep to her right, pushing bundles and boxes aside. Reaching past a pile of stiff cushions, her fingers met what felt like a small metal plate, set low near the floor. The clicking sounded very close now!

Feeling the outlines of the plate, Maia's hand brushed a tiny button in its center, which abruptly lit the area with stabbing blue electricity. With a reflexive yelp, she flew backward, landing hard. For six or eight heartbeats, Maia sat numb on the cold floor, sucking tingling fingertips before finally recovering enough to scramble up again, throwing cushions in all directions, clearing space until she saw that smaller sparks accompanied each audible click, momentarily illuminating the plate in the wall.

Funny how I never noticed that before. Probably because I was looking for secret passages and trapdoors! Just goes to show, you never learn anything useful from fantasy novels.

Until today, she hadn't imagined there might be ways to receive messages in this cell, or that those irritating clicks might really contain a code. But what else could they be? Would anything purely random, like a short circuit, repeat similar patterns two nights in succession?

Still trembling, she pulled out her notebook and pencil and returned to copying down intermittent flashes in front of her. Even with dark-adapted eyes, Maia could hardly see the marks she made. *We'll worry about that by daylight,* she told herself when the clicking stopped, about five minutes later. *Luck is definitely taking a tack my way.*

She knew there was little evidence to support such a broad conclusion. But hope was a heady brew, now that she had tasted some. Slipping the notebook under a pile of bedding, Maia wrapped herself in her makeshift blankets and tried to settle her mind for sleep.

It wasn't easy. Her thoughts collided with fantasies and improbable scenarios of rescue, such as the policewoman from Caria, arriving in a grand zep'lin, waving seal-encrusted writs. Other images were less cheering. Memories of Leie beckoned Maia back toward despondency. Drifting sporadically toward full consciousness, she wondered if the clickings were really a message. If so, was it aimed at her, specifically?

Idiot, she thought while passing through layers of half-slumber. *How could anybody know you were here?*

Eventually, Maia dreamed of Lysos.

The Founder was dressed in a flowing gown, and sat with piles of molecules to one side, adding one at a time to a string, like pearls on a necklace, or wooden balls on an abacus. The molecular chains *clacked* each time another joined the queue. Laying DNA codons in an endless chain, Lysos hummed sweetly as she worked.

. . .

It took two more nights to copy the entire message and confirm she had it right, an exercise in patience unlike any Maia had known since she and Leie worked to solve the secret gate in Lamatia's wine cellar. Taking the time was necessary, though. Only on the third day did Maia feel ready to load the entire code string onto the Game of Life board.

She began by making sure the board was set up with the same special rules as before, when it had played that "message in a bottle." The little window said **RVRSBL CA 897W**. Maia hoped the program would make sense of the clicks in the night. As before, the game area contracted to a square just fifty-nine units on a side, surrounded by a complex border.

Okay, let's get started. Maia commenced laboriously turning each transcribed click into a black square, and leaving a space blank where there had been a second's worth of pause. On finishing one row of fifty-nine, she continued marking the next level, wrapping the presumed message back and forth like a snake climbing a brick wall. After what felt like hours, she finished fitting the entire sequence into the assigned space. The match couldn't be a coincidence! The resulting jumble of dots offered no meaning perceptible to the eye.

Exhausted, she was relieved to hear the rattle of keys at the door. Maia covered the game board, though it probably made no difference if the Guels saw. Her muscles and joints hurt from spending so much time bent over the machine. *This had better be worth it,* she thought while silently eating under her keepers' dull gaze.

If I was off by even one space, it could ruin the whole thing. What'll I do if it doesn't work?

The answer was obvious. *I'll just try again. What else is there to do?*

The guards took away her tray and slid the bolt. Breathlessly, Maia got back to the game board and double-checked her transcription. She crossed her arms and tugged both earlobes for luck, then pressed the start button.

Swirling cyclones of pulsing Life forms instantly told her she was right. The nightly clickings *had* been meant for this! They were a recipe. A complex set of starting conditions for this weird game. Despite the variant rules, most of the patterns were once again recognizable. Two glider guns fired fluttering wedge shapes across a terrain strewn with microbes and eaters, beacons and dandelions. Scores of other shapes merged and separated. An "ecology" expanded to fill the entire fifty-nine-by-fifty-nine array. Maia poised over the board, pencil in hand, but the patterns were so enthralling, she was almost caught short when the chaotic forms coalesced suddenly into rows of rippling letters.

CY, TELL GRVS IMAT
49° 16′ 67° 54′
NO DEAL W/ ODO!
LV IF NEC

Once more, the message began dissolving almost as soon as it took form. Maia hurriedly scribbled it down before it vanished, along with all other "living" remnants on the board. Soon the board lay pale and empty before her. She stared at the copied version of the four-line missive, reading it over and over again.

Clearly, it hadn't been meant for her, after all. Several of her favorite fantasies evaporated. No matter. There was more than enough here to keep her speculating about the sender's intent. *Could "CY" stand for a friend or clanmate of the other prisoner? Is "GRVS" a group or clan powerful enough to come and set her free?* Maia's imagination would come up with the wildest notions if she let it, so she firmly stayed down to earth. The other prisoner might be a business rival of the local Perkinites, perhaps kept here by the Joplands and their allies to coerce a better deal.

The last, self-sacrificial phrase in the message, demanding to be abandoned, if necessary, bespoke somber stuff. Or was she wrong assuming that it meant "Leave if necessary"?

Could it have to do with the drug that makes men rut in winter?

Possibly the other prisoner was no more virtuous than Tizbe or the Joplands, merely a competitor. That hardly mattered at this point. Right now Maia couldn't be choosy about her allies.

The strangest thing about this eavesdropped message, as opposed to the one Maia had read earlier, was that it seemed directed not at some random person who might later pick it up, as she had picked up the game board, but at a specific individual. Using resold games to send notes "in a bottle" could have been but a side venture. A backup plan. These nightly clicking episodes seemed aimed at something more immediate, as if the prisoner intended her messages to get through much sooner and more directly.

Maia recalled the metal plate in the wall. Sparks in the night.

The place must be wired for telephone, or some low-level commlink, Maia speculated. Having never been in a sanctuary before, she had no reason to be surprised by this, yet she was. *Maybe men demand it in the design before they'll move in. I wonder what they need it for?*

Whatever the cable's original purpose, the other prisoner was clearly using it for something . . . sending electrical pulses. But to where? As far as Maia could figure, the wires weren't attached to anything.

A possibility struck her. *Is the other prisoner using the wire as . . . an antenna? Trying to send a radio message?* Maia knew in abstract that you generated radio waves by pushing electrons rapidly back and forth down a wire. But household comm sets and the ones used aboard ships —countless generations removed from their ancient origins—were grown in solid blocks out of vats, and sold in units smaller than the palm of your hand. Probably only a scattering of individuals in universities understood how they were made anymore.

She must be a savant. They're holding a savant prisoner here!

Maia recalled the evening in Lanargh, when she and Leie had watched the news broadcast, and heard the mysterious offer of a "reward for information." Maybe it was about this!

I've got to get in touch with her. But how?

She decided. *First I'll have to write a message.*

There was no question of doing it the way the savant had, by coding starting conditions the Game of Life rules would turn into written words after a thousand complex gyrations. And with a little contemplation, Maia realized she didn't have to. After all, the trick of sending a message in a bottle, or a message by radio, involved coding it so that, hopefully, only the right recipient would decipher it. But Maia wasn't trying to communicate with anyone beyond these sanctuary walls. She could send regular block letters!

With the stylus, she blackened squares on the game board until it read

FELLOW PRISONER!
HEARD CLICKS IN WIRE
MY NAME IS MAIA

Regarding what she'd written, she reconsidered. The first line was obvious. As for the second, perhaps the savant didn't know she was making noise elsewhere in the citadel, each time she transmitted, but it would be apparent once Maia's reply got through.

There was another reason to simplify. She must translate her message into rows of dots and dashes, unraveling the words like peeling layers off a cake. Three lines of letters took twenty-one rows of game squares to produce, each fifty-nine squares wide, she calculated a total of 1,239 intersections that had to be labeled black or white with an on or off pulse. Over a thousand! True, the other prisoner had sent even more, but not with such long pauses as Maia's approach called for. Extend a pause for five beats or more and the recipient will surely lose count.

Finally, she settled on a much simpler first effort.

I'M MAIA I'M MAIA I'M MAIA

It was still 413 pulses long, after the rows were unwrapped into a linear chain. That seemed manageable, though, especially since it would be rhythmical.

Now how to send it.

She had considered pounding on the walls, or perhaps the drain-pipe. But those sounds probably wouldn't carry far. If they did, it would alert the guards.

I'll have to do it the same way, she concluded. *Through the wire.*

There was just one possible source for the electricity required, and one mistake would cut off her only contact with the outside world. Maia didn't hesitate. Gingerly, she turned the Life set over and pried open the cover to the battery case.

She decided to wait until this evening's midnight transmission was over. Huddled under unwrapped curtains, she watched the savant's message create a staccato of sparks against the wall, verifying that it was the same as before. The series of clicking arcs stopped at the usual time, leaving her to peer through dim moonlight, cast by the slit window. Expecting this, Maia had practiced her moves earlier. Still, it took several awkward tries to grasp loose wires extracted from the back of the game set and bring them to the plate in the wall.

Before her lay the message she planned to send. Maia had used big, blocky squares and spaces, intended to be read even by dim light.

Well, here goes, she thought.

Touching one wire to the nub on the wall had no effect. But placing one against the nub and the other on the plate caused a spark that startled her briefly. Setting her teeth, Maia leaned forward to better see the paper sheets, and started tapping—creating a spark for each black square and resting a beat for each white one.

She had no idea whether this was doing anything but draining the batteries. Theoretically, she should be able to restore them by putting the game board in the window, to absorb sunlight. But in fact, she might be ruining them for nothing.

It was hard keeping track of her place, staring closely at row after row of hand-blackened squares. Despite the cold, she soon had to blink away beads of sweat, and at one point saw that she had skipped an entire line! There was nothing to be done about it. One error like that ought to leave the message readable, but she could not afford to let it happen again.

Finally reaching the end of the last row, Maia sighed in relief and sat back, stretching her arms. A break in time would let the other party know a termination had been reached. But the savant probably had been taken by surprise. So after a short breather, Maia bent forward to repeat the entire exercise.

Is anything getting through? she wondered. *I've forgotten what little I knew about voltages and such. Maybe I needed to make a resistor, or a capacitor. Maybe I'm just pouring electricity into the ground, without creating sparks anywhere else.*

Click, click, pause, pause, pause, *click* . . . She tried to concentrate, keeping a steady rhythm as the savant had. This was especially important counting the long pauses making up margins on both sides of her simple message. Talking aloud seemed to help. Inside she kept hearing the message she was trying to send, as if part of her was broadcasting by force of will.

I'm Maia . . . I'm Maia . . . I'm Maia . . .

This second time was much harder. Her fingers felt on the verge of cramping, her neck ached from leaning forward, and her eyes stung from sweat-salt. Still she kept at it stubbornly. Comfort held no attraction. What mattered was the slim chance of talking to someone.

Please hear me . . . I'm Maia . . . oh, please . . .

By the time she finished the second transmission, her hands were too numb even to let go of the insulated wires, so she just sat there, staring at the blank stone wall, listening to the tension in her spine slowly unwind. There would be no third attempt. Even if she and the batteries had the stamina, it would be too risky. The guards might be accustomed to one set of clicks in the night, like a friendly cricket. But too big a change in routine just wouldn't do.

A sudden spark made her jump. It took a moment to realize she hadn't caused it by misplacing the wires. No, it came from the wall! More sparks followed. Maia scrambled for her pencil and pad.

Each tiny arc illuminated her accompanying slashmark. Darkness she noted with a dash. It was easier work than sending, though her eyes now hurt worse than ever. With rising excitement, Maia realized this was no repetition, but an entirely new message. She had gotten through!

Then, as abruptly as before, it ended, and she was left in silence, staring at several sheets of mysterious code.

Frustration made her already tense muscles quiver. Even if she carried the game board up to the window, there would not be enough light to reassemble it properly. Not until morning.

I can't wait till morning. I can't! Maia fought down a strangling wave of impatience. *You can do whatever you have to do,* she answered herself, and forced her taut body to relax, one muscle at a time. Finally, she was breathing evenly again.

Well, at least I can tidy this up, she thought, looking at her scrawled transcription. Standing, Maia took a few moments to stretch, then carefully climbed her pyramid of boxes toward the slit.

Durga was no longer in sight. A lesser moon, Aglaia, shone barely bright enough for her to work. Gradually, line by line on a fresh page, she drew each "click" as a black square. Each pause translated into a blank one. At the end of the first row of fifty-nine, she moved up to the next and began snaking backward again. This way, if she succeeded in repairing the game device tomorrow, she'd be able to load the starting conditions right away, and quickly set the game in motion to read the message.

It was hard work. After this she might even be able to sleep.

So intent was she on copying squares in long rows that she failed to notice the difference in the pattern for some time. Finally it occurred to her. Unlike before, the "clicks" seemed to come already clustered in tight groups. Blinking, Maia pulled back, and saw—

. . . ʜɪ ᴍᴀɪᴀ. ᴛ˙ᴍᴏʀᴏ. − ʀᴇɴɴᴀ . . .

Of course. She answered the way I sent, without coding! I can read it tonight!

Maia quickened her pace. Two rows later, the message could be read.

. . . HI MAIA. T'MORO. − RENNA . . .

The wind picked up, riffling her papers, sending them tumbling down the makeshift platform like a flurry of discarded leaves. All but the single sheet she clutched in both fists, soon smeared by hot, grateful tears.

S ome of our expedition's more radical members claim that I am not angry enough to lead this effort. That I do not hate or fear males enough to design a world where their role is minimized. To these accusations I reply—what hope has any endeavor which is based on hate and fear? I admit, I proudly avow, to having liked and admired certain men during my life. What of it? Although our sons and grandsons will be few, the world we create should have a place for them as well.

Other critics declaim that what really interests me is the challenge of self-cloning, and expanding the range of options for human reproduction. They say that if males were physically able to bear copies of themselves without machines, I would have given them the power, too.

That is possibly true. But then, what is a man whom you have equipped with a womb? A womb-man would necessarily take on other traits of woman, and cease being identifiable as male at all. That is not an appealing or practical innovation.

In the end, all of our clever gene designs, and corresponding plans for cultural conditioning, will come to nought if we are smug or rigid. The heritage we give our children, and the myths we leave to sustain them, must work with the tug and press of life, or they will fail. Adaptability has to be enshrined alongside stability, or the ghost of Darwin will surely come back to haunt us, whispering in our ears the penalty of conceit.

We wish our descendants happiness. But over time one criterion alone will judge our efforts.

Survival.

1 2

Over the following days, Maia and her new friend learned to communicate despite the thick walls separating them. From the first, Maia felt stupid and slow, especially when Renna went back to sending coded, compacted messages designed to be deciphered by the Game of Life board. Maia could not blame her, since the method was more efficient, enabling a full screen to be sent in just a few minutes. Yet it made Maia's responses seem so clumsy in comparison. One line of text was all she could manage after a day's work, and sending it left her exhausted, frustrated.

> . . . DON'T . . FRET . . MAIA . . .
> . . . I'LL TEACH ANOTHER CODE . . .
> . . . FOR SIMPLE LETTERS . . . WORDS . . .

Gratefully, Maia copied down the system Renna transmitted, one called Morse. She had heard of it, she was sure. Some clans based their commercial ciphers on variants of very ancient systems. *Another item that should have been in the Lamatia curriculum*, she thought grimly.

$$O = +++, \quad P = -++-, \quad Q = ++-+$$

The code seemed simple enough, with each plus sign standing for a long stroke and each dash for a short one. It greatly speeded Maia's next effort, though she remained awkward, and kept making mistakes.

IF YOU KNOW MORSE WHY USE LIFE CODING
ISN'T IT HARDER

To this question, Renna answered,

HARDER. SUBTLER. WATCH

And to Maia's astonishment, the game board proceeded to shake her friend's letters into coruscating patterns, like a fireworks show on Founders Day.

Maia found even more amazing the next message Renna sent. Though compacted, it was long, taking up thirty-one rows by the time Maia finished laying down a snaking chain of black and white squares. Pressing the launch button set off a wild, hungry "ecology" of mutually devouring pseudo-entities that finally resolved, after many gyrations, into what looked like a *picture* . . . a crude sketch of plains and distant mountains, seen through a narrow window. It was recognizably a scene looking out from this very stone tower—not the view from Maia's window, but similar.

The other prisoner followed this with

LIFE IS UNIVERSAL COMPUTER
CAN DO MORE THAN MORSE
& HARDER TO EAVESDROP

Maia was impressed. Nevertheless she answered

I DID. Y NOT OTHERS?

Renna's reply seemed sheepish.

NOT AS CLEVER AS I THOUGHT

The game board next rippled to show a slim face with close-cropped hair, eyes rolled upward in embarrassment, shoulders in the act of shrugging. The caricature made Maia giggle in delight.

Thankfully, she hadn't damaged the Life set during that first experiment. Over the following days, Renna taught her how to connect the machine directly to the wall circuit, so she could send messages directly, instead of laboriously and dangerously touching wires by hand. Renna still made transmissions at high power every midnight, attempting to use crudely generated radio waves to contact friends somewhere out there, beyond the walls. The rest of the time, they communicated using low currents, to avoid arousing the guards.

Renna was so friendly and welcoming, reinforcing Maia's sense of a warm, maternal presence. Maia soon felt drawn into telling her story. It all came spilling out. The departure from Lamatia. Leie's loss. Her encounters with Tizbe and involvement in matters far murkier than any young var should have to deal with, newly fledged from her birth clan. Laying it out so starkly brought home to Maia how unfair it was. She'd done nothing to deserve this chain of catastrophes. All her life, mothers and matriarchs had said virtue and hard work were rewarded. Was *this* the prize?

Maia apologized for stumbling through the story, especially when emotion overcame her at the sending key. **THIS IS HARD FOR ME**, she transmitted, trying to keep her hand from trembling. Renna's reply offered reassurance and understanding, along with some confusion.

**AT 16 YOU
OUGHT TO BE HAPPY
SUCH A ROTTEN SHAME**

Sympathy, after so long, brought a lump to Maia's throat. So many older people forgot there had been a time when they, too, were inexperienced and powerless. She was grateful for the compassion, the shared empathy.

Conversing with her fellow prisoner was an adventure of awkward moments followed by cordial insights. Of double meanings and hilarious misunderstandings, like when they disagreed which moon hung in plain view, in the southern sky. Or when Renna kept misspelling the names of cities, or quotations from the Book of the Founders. Obviously, she was doing this on purpose, to draw Maia out of her funk. And it was working. Challenged to catch her fellow prisoner at intentional inconsistencies, Maia found herself paying closer attention. Her spirits lifted.

Soon she realized something astonishing. Even though they had never met in person, she was starting to feel a special kind of hearth-affection toward this new friend.

It wasn't so difficult when you were winter-born. Hearth feelings were predictable after many generations.

For instance, three-year-old Lamais almost always passed through a phase when they would tag after a chosen clone-sister just one class ahead of them, doing whatever that older sibling asked and pining at the slightest curt word. Later, at age four, each winter Lamai took her own turn being the adored one, spending the better part of a season taking out on a younger sister the heartbreaks she had received the year before.

During her fifth-year winter, a Lamatia Clan full-daughter started looking beyond the walls, often becoming obsessed with a slightly older cloneling from a neighboring hold, usually a Trevor, or a Wheatley. That phase passed quickly, and besides, Trevors and Wheatleys were family allies. Later on, though, came a rough period when Lamai sixers seemed inevitably bound, despite all their mothers' warnings, to fixate on a woman from the tall, stately Yort-Wong merchant clan . . . which was awkward, since the Yort-Wongs had been feuding off and on with Lamatia for generations.

Knowing in advance what to expect didn't keep Lamai sixers from railing and weeping during their autumn of discontent. Fortunately, there was the upcoming Ceremony of Passage to distract them. Yet, when all was said and done, how could the brief attentions of a man ease those pangs of unrequited obsession? Even those lucky sixers chosen for sparking emerged from their unhappy Yort-Wong episode changed, hardened. Thereafter, Lamai women wore emotional invulnerability as armor. They dealt with clients, cooperated with allies, made complex commercial-sexual arrangements with seamen. But for pleasure they hired professionals.

For companionship, they had each other.

It had been different from the very start for Maia and Leie. Being vars, they could not even roughly predict their own life cycles. Anyway, hearth feelings ranged so, from almost rutlike physical passion all the way to the most utterly chaste yearnings just to be near your chosen one. Popular songs and romantic stories emphasized the latter as more noble and refined, though all but a few heretics agreed there was nothing wrong with touching, if both hearts were true. The physical side of hearthness, between two members of the female species, was pictured as gentle, solicitous, hardly like *sex* at all.

Maia's own experience remained theoretical, and in this area Leie was no bolder. The twins had certainly felt intimations of warmth toward others—classmates, kids they befriended in town, some of their teachers—but nothing precocious or profound. Since turning five, there had simply been no time.

Now Maia felt something stronger, and knew well what name to use, if she dared admit it to herself. In Renna she had found a soul who knew kindness, who would not judge a girl unworthy, just because she was a lowly var. It hardly mattered that she hadn't rested eyes on the object of her fixation. Maia created a picture in her mind, of a savant or high civil servant from one of the faraway sophisticated cities on Landing Continent, which would explain Renna's stiff, somewhat aristocratic way of speaking in text. No doubt she came from a noble clan, but when Maia asked, all Renna said was

MY FAMILY MADE CLOCKS, BUT I
HAVEN'T SEEN THEM IN A WHILE
SEEM TO HAVE LOST TRACK OF TIME

Maia found it hard always to tell when Renna was joking or teasing, although clearly she never meant it in a mean way. Renna wasn't much more forthcoming about how she came to be a prisoner in this place.

THE BELLERS TOOK ADVANTAGE
OF A LONELY TRAVELER

Bellers! The family Tizbe belonged to! The pleasure clan that did a profitable side business carrying goods and performing confidential services. So Maia and Renna had a common enemy! When she said as much, Renna agreed with what seemed reluctant sadness. Maia tried asking about "CY" and "GRVS," who must be Renna's clanmates or allies, but her fellow prisoner responded there were some things Maia was better off not knowing.

That did not prevent them from talking frequently about escape. First they must work out their relative positions in the stone tower. Crawling into the stone casement, Maia craned her head around and saw a continuous row of slit windows like this one, presumably illuminating other storerooms, girdling the citadel's circumference five meters below the grand gallery of columned patios she had glimpsed on arrival, that first day. Comparing the positions of certain landmarks, they ascertained that Renna's window lay just around the bend, facing due east while Maia's looked southeastward. Turning in the opposite direction, Maia could just make out the gate-ramp of the unfinished sanctuary, forlorn and covered with prairie dust.

Maia was full of ideas. She told Renna of her experiments unraveling carpets, learning how to weave a rope. While approving her enthusiasm, Renna reminded Maia that the drop was much too far to trust a bundle of twine, amateurly wrapped by hand.

Looking at her handicraft, she was forced to admit Renna was probably right. Still, Maia continued spending part of each day unwinding lengths of tough fiber and retying them into a finger-width strand, trying to imitate by memory the weaving patterns used by sailors aboard the *Wotan*. *It's something to keep busy*, she thought. While Renna kept up her midnight attempts to radio for help, Maia wanted to contribute something, even as futile as winding string.

She was careful to hide all signs—of both ropemaking and talking to Renna—from her jailers. During meals, Maia told them how fascinated she was with the Game of Life, and how grateful to have been introduced to its world of intricacy. Their eyes glazed as she expected. All the Guels wanted was the comfort of routine. She happily let them have it.

So it came as a surprise when she heard the rattle of keys in the middle of one afternoon, hours before dinnertime. Maia barely managed to throw a rug over her work and stand up before the door swung open. On entering, the two Guel guards appeared tense, agitated. Maia saw why when a familiar figure stepped between them.

Tizbe Beller! The former baggage-car assistant looked around the storeroom, hands folded behind her. An expression of faintly amused disgust crossed her young face as she perused the sweat-stained towel hanging by the cracked washbasin, and the covered chamber pot just beyond. Her nose wrinkled, as if meeting odors a coarse var could not be expected to notice.

Maia made herself stand tall. *Go ahead and sneer, Tizbe. I've kept myself fit and civilized in here. Let's change places and see you do better!*

Her defiance must have shown. Although Tizbe's amusement continued unabated, her expression did change. "Well, captivity doesn't seem to have hurt you, Maia. Not where it counts. You're positively blossoming."

"Go to Earth, Tizbe. Take your Jopland and Lerner friends with you."

The cloneling feigned a moue of shock. "Such language! Keep this up, and you'll be too rough for polite society."

Maia laughed curtly. "You can shove your polite—"

But Tizbe got the better of her again, simply by stifling a yawn and waving a hand vaguely in front of her. "Oh, not now, if you don't mind. It's been a hard ride and I have to leave bright and early. We'll see though. Before that, I might have a chance to drop in again and say goodbye."

Then, to Maia's shock, she turned to go. "But . . . aren't you here to—"

Tizbe looked back from the door. "To question you? Torture you? Ah, that would be just the thing for one of those trashy novels I'm told you've been reading. Villains are supposed to gloat and rub their hands together, and talk to their poor victims a lot.

"Sorry to disappoint you. I really would try to fit the role if I had the time. Honestly, though, do you have any information I could possibly want? What material benefit would I gain by questioning one more Venturist spy?"

Maia stared at her. "One more what?"

Tizbe reached into one of her sleeves and drew forth a tattered, folded sheet of heavy paper. After a moment, Maia recognized the leaflet she had accepted in Lanargh, from the hand of that earnest young heretic wearing eyeglasses. So, her captors had gone to Holly Lock and sifted through her things. She did not even bother acting offended.

"Venturist . . . you think I'm one of them, because of *that*?"

Tizbe shrugged. "It did seem unlikely for a spy to carry around blatant evidence. Throw in your comm call from Jopland, though, and it's reason enough to take precautions. You've turned official eyes this way sooner than expected, for which you'll pay." She smiled. "Still, we have things well in hand. If it weren't for more urgent matters, I'd not bother coming all this way.

"As it is, I felt behooved to check on you, Maia. Glad to see you not all wrapped in self-pity, as I expected. Maybe, when everything's settled, we'll have a talk about your future. There may be a place for a var like you—"

Maia cut in. "With your gang of criminals? You . . ." She searched for phrases she had heard over Thalla's radio, at Lerner Hold. "Inheretist exploiters!"

Tizbe shook her head, grinning. "Showing our radical colors at last? Well, solitude and contemplation can change minds. I'll have some books sent to you. They'll show the sense in what we're doing. How it's good for Stratos and all womankind."

"Thanks," Maia replied sharply. "Don't bother including *The Perkinite Way*. I've read it."

"Oh yes?" Tizbe's eyebrows lifted. "And?"

Maia hoped her smile conveyed indulgent pity.

"I think Lysos would have liked to study sickies like you under a microscope, to see what she did wrong."

For the first time, the other woman's reaction wasn't another tailored mask. Tizbe glowered. "Enjoy your stay, var-child."

The guards followed her out, trying not to meet Maia's eyes as they closed the door, then fastened it with a hard, metallic clank of Lerner steel.

Tizbe didn't give a damn about me. I'm just an irritant, to be stored away and forgotten.

It was just one more blow to Maia's pride, confirming what she already knew about her insignificance in the world.

So it wasn't me that brought her all the way out here, but something "urgent."

Maia realized with sudden certainty—*It's Renna!*

The possibility of danger to her friend terrified Maia. She rushed to the wall, where the game board was already plugged in, but then made herself stop. The distance between their cells was not great. Tizbe could be at Renna's door by the time Maia tapped a warning, and if Tizbe heard the clicking, it would let on that the prisoners had a way of communicating. Maia imagined what life might be like, if she found herself cut off yet again. The gaping sense of threat and emptiness felt like when she had first come to realize that Leie was gone.

Sitting in front of the game board only enhanced Maia's feeling of impotence. She got up and climbed her pyramid of boxes to crawl into the window, where she poked her head beyond the rocky lip to peer toward the front gate. There Maia glimpsed several figures tending a string of tethered horses. The Beller's escorts, presumably.

She clambered down again. To avoid pacing uselessly, Maia sat down and resumed plaiting her rope, keeping her pencil handy nearby and anxiously hoping for the clicking sounds that would tell her Renna was all right. The long, hard quiet stretched on and on, until a rasp of keys caused her to throw a rug over her work once more. She stood up as the guards entered and put her dinner on the rickety table. Maia ate silently, hurriedly, as eager for her jailers to leave as they were to be gone.

When they left, she hated the return of solitude.

What if Tizbe has already taken Renna away?

Several times, Maia interrupted her work to go to the window. The third time she looked, the horses and escorts were gone. A panicky chill arrested when she saw no traffic on the road. As twilight settled and temperatures dropped, they must have all gone inside, where the empty halls offered plenty of room for women and mounts.

Maia climbed down and resumed worrying, while her fingers plaited fibers together. *Tizbe said they'd be leaving tomorrow, but she never said whether or not they—*

The first clicks from the wall plate sent her heart leaping.

Renna! She's safe!

Maia threw her weaving aside and picked up her notebook. Soon it was clear that Renna wasn't sending any ornately planned Game of Life scenario, but a rushed series of simple Morse dots and dashes. The message ended. Concentrating, Maia had to guess at meanings for several of the letters and words. Finally, she cried out. "No!"

MAIA. DONT ANSWR. THEY R TAKNG ME AWAY. WILL REMBR U ALWYS. GOD KEEP U SAFE. RENNA.

·   ·   ·

It can get bitterly cold on the high plains, especially on early winter evenings, to one lying perched up high along a precipice, exposed to the wind.

There was barely room to stretch prone in the window niche, whose gritty, chill surface rubbed Maia's shoulders on both sides. Using a plank from the broken box as a sort of fishing rod, Maia still had to lean out so the rope hung properly, to keep its burden from scraping against the rough cliff face. The leverage helped as she rocked the plank gently left to right, back and forth, pumping gradually until the rope began to swing like a pendulum.

It took concentration not to let her shivering interfere. Nor was the shaking due entirely to the cold. By moonlight, the ground looked awfully far away. Even if she had a rope long enough—one made by master craftswomen, not hand-twined by an inexperienced fiver—she would never have been able to get herself to climb down all that distance.

Yet, look what you're trying to do, instead!

After getting Renna's message, there had passed over Maia a wave of utter panic. It wasn't just envisioning months, perhaps years, stretching ahead in loneliness. The loss of this new friend, when she had still not gotten over Leie, felt like a physical blow. Her first impulse was to curl up under piles of curtain material and let depression take her. There was a sick, sweet-sour attraction to melancholy, as an alternative to action.

Maia had been tempted for all of thirty seconds. Then she got to work, searching for some way to solve her problem, reevaluating every possibility, even those she had previously discarded.

The door and walls? They would take explosives to breach. She turned over in her mind ways of calling the guards and overpowering them, but that fantasy was also absurd, especially with them at their wariest, and Tizbe's escorts to back them up.

That left the window. She could just barely manage to squeeze through, but to what purpose? The ground was impossibly far. Turning left, she could make out more storerooms, visible as slit-windows stretching away on both sides. They seemed almost as out of reach as the prairie floor. Besides, why trade one prison cell for another?

Looking about desperately, she had finally twisted around to look upward, and saw the pillared loggia overhead, part of a grand patio girdling the sanctuary, five or six meters higher.

If only somebody would drop a rope down, she had fantasized ironically.

Desperation led to inspiration.

Could I send one up?

It would be a gamble at best. Even if it was possible to swing a rope and bob the way she had in mind, she'd still need something to act as a grappling hook. Yet, it mustn't interfere as she oscillated the rope back and forth along the wall, giving it momentum to rise and—if all went well—catch on the railing overhead.

She refused to think about the last drawback—trusting her weight to the makeshift contraption. *Cross that bridge when we come to it*, Maia thought.

Back inside, she had started by ripping apart her supply of notebooks for the springlike clips that bound loose pages inside. *Maybe I can rig some of these to pop open when they hit. . . .*

It was difficult to put into practice. First she had to tear the clips out and then use a wooden plank to lever them into the shape she wanted. Tying several together at the end of her rope, she practiced on the sill of the window until she felt sure the improvised hook would catch, two times out of three. The short section of cable used in the trial held her weight, though trusting her life to the improvised gimmickry seemed lunatic, or desperate, or both.

Maia wrapped a single loop of thread around the clips to bind them into a compact bundle, to keep the cluster from clattering and rattling as she swung it back and forth. Ideally, it would come apart on impact with the balcony, and not at some inopportune moment before. Finally, she had crawled back into the window carrying some curtain material for padding, and a plank with a notch in one end, to use as a fishing pole. Once settled in, she commenced laying out rope.

It was hard to even see the cable's end when it was hanging straight down. Once she set the pendulum in motion, however, she could make out the makeshift grapnel whenever it passed before a small patch of snow on the ground. Soon it rose high enough to occult a low white cloud bank, veiling one of the moons to the east.

Back and forth . . . rocking back and forth. Despite her arrangements to let the plank take most of the weight, Maia's arms were tiring by the time the swinging rope rose high enough to point horizontal, level with the row of storeroom windows. Her heart caught each time the bundle of clips tapped or snagged against some protuberance, forcing her to lean even farther to avoid catching it on the backswing.

"Come on, you can hold better than that!" she remembered Leie used to say, back when they were both four and a half, and would sneak out at night to paint mothers blue. After the third time a statue in the Summer Courtyard had been defaced, the clan matriarchs had locked all doors leading to the yard, and sprinkled marker dust around the monuments, to trace anyone who stepped in it.

That did not stop the incidents.

"I'm doin' as best I can!" she had hissed back at Leie on the night of that final foray, gripping one end of a rope made of bedsheets, the other wrapped around her sister's feet. Lowering Leie from the roof, with paintbrush and bucket in hand, had been easier on prior occasions because there were crenelated battlements Maia could use for leverage. But that last time it had been just her own, preadolescent muscles, battling the insistent pull of gravity.

Now, over a year later, as she struggled to control a distant weight that jerked and fought like a fish caught at the end of her line, Maia moaned, "I'm . . . doin' . . . as best I . . . can!" Her breath whistled as she held on, letting out and taking up slack, trying to force momentum into a pendulum that seemed reluctant to rise much past horizontal and kept yanking at her burning shoulders on each downward swing.

Under questioning the next day, Leie had insisted she was acting alone. She refused to implicate Maia, even though it was clear she could not have done it without help. Everyone knew Maia had been the one with the rope. Everyone knew she had been the one unable to hold on when a tile broke, loosening her grip, causing Leie to go crashing in a clatter of paint and tracer dust and chipped plaster.

After taking her punishment stoically, Leie never brought up the subject, not even in private. It was enough that everybody knew.

Grimly, Maia held on. *Renna,* she thought, gritting her teeth and ignoring the pain. *I'm coming. . . .*

The grapnel had now reached the stone balustrade in its highest rise. Frustratingly, it would not go over the protruding lip, though it touched audibly several times. Maia tried twisting the plank so that the rope would come closer to the wall at the top of each swing, but the curve of the citadel defied her.

Obviously the idea was workable. Some combination of twists and proddings would make it. If she took her time and practiced several evenings in a row . . .

"No!" she whispered. "It's got to be tonight!"

Two more times, the grapnel just clipped the balcony, making a soft, scraping sound. In agony, Maia realized she had only a couple more attempts before she would have to give up.

Another touch. Then a clean miss.

That's it, she realized, defeated. *Got to rest. Maybe try again in a few hours.*

Resignedly, with numbness spreading across her shoulders, she began easing off on the rhythmic pumping action, letting the pendulum motion start to die down. On the next swing, the bundle did not quite reach the level of the balustrade. The one after that, its peak was lower still.

The next cycle, the grapnel paused once more . . . just high enough and long enough for someone to quickly reach over the balcony and *grab* it, in a one-handed catch.

The surprise was total. Throbbing with fatigue, shivering from the cold, for a moment Maia could do nothing else but lay in the stone opening and stare along the rough face of the citadel, looking upward toward an unexpected dark silhouette, leaning outward, holding onto her rope, eclipsing a portion of winter's constellations.

Maia's first thought was that Tizbe or the guards must have heard something, come to investigate, and caught her in the act. Soon they would arrive to take away her tools, boxes, even the curtains she had unraveled to make rope, leaving her worse off than before. Then she realized the figure on the loggia was not calling out, as a guard might. Rather, it began making furtive hand motions. Maia could make no sense of them in the dark, but understood one thing. The person gesturing at her was as concerned for silence as she was.

Renna? Hope flashed, followed by confusion. Her friend's cell lay some distance beyond and lower down. Unless her fellow inmate had also come up with an inspired, last-minute plan . . .

The shadowy figure began moving westward along the balustrade, handing Maia's rope around pillars along the way. On reaching a spot directly overhead, the silhouette made hand gestures indicating Maia should wait, then vanished for a few moments. When it returned, something started snaking downward along Maia's hand-woven cable toward her.

Ah, Maia realized. *She didn't like the looks of my workmanship. Well, fine. I'll use her store-bought one instead. See if I care.*

In fact, Maia was relieved. She paused to consider going back inside her cell to get . . . what? There were only four books and the Game of Life set, none of which she cared much about. Except for the sextant, strapped to her wrist, she was free of the tyranny of possessions.

After tying the new rope under her shoulders, Maia inched outward until most of her weight hung from the taut cable. At that point it occurred to her that this could be a trap. Tizbe might be toying with her, while arranging for her death-fall to appear part of an escape attempt.

The thought passed as Maia realized, *What choice do I have?*

She braced her feet against the wall, legs straight, and prepared to start climbing, stepping upward while pulling hand over hand. Then, to her surprise, the rope tautened rapidly and she found herself being hauled straight up, directly and swiftly. *There must be a whole gang of them up there,* Maia thought. *Or a block and tackle.*

As the balcony drew near, she composed her face so as not to show the slightest chagrin if it turned out to be Tizbe and the guards, after all. *I'll fight,* she vowed. *I'll break free and take them on a chase they'll never forget.*

Arms reached down to haul her over the side . . . and Maia's composure broke when she saw who had helped her.

"Kiel! Thalla!"

Her former cottage-mates at Lerner Hold beamed while freeing her of the rope. Kiel's dark features split with a broad, white grin. "Surprised?" she said in a whisper. "You didn't think we'd leave you to rot in this Perkinite hole, did you?"

Maia shook her head, overwhelmed that she had been remembered after all. "How did you know where I—"

She cut off, upon seeing that they weren't alone. Standing behind the two var women, coiling rope over one shoulder, stood . . . a man! Beardless and slim for one of his kind, he smiled at her with an intimacy she found rather forward and disconcerting.

A man's participation helped explain how just three of them could lift her so quickly, while it raised other questions even more perplexing . . . like what one of his race was doing so far upland, involving himself in disputes among women.

Thalla chuckled lowly, patting Maia's shoulder. "Let's just say we've been searching some time. We'll explain later. Now it's time to scoot." She turned to lead the way. But Maia shook her head, planting her feet and pointing the other direction.

"Not yet! There's someone else we've got to rescue. Another prisoner!"

Thalla and Kiel looked at each other, then at the man. "I thought there were just two," Thalla said.

"There were," the man answered. "Maia—"

"No! Come on, I know where she is. Renna—"

"Maia. I'm here."

She had turned and already taken several steps down the dark corridor when the words cut her short. Maia swiveled, peering past Thalla and Kiel, who stood grinning in amusement. The man moved toward her, on his face a gentle look of irony. He lifted his gaze and shrugged in a gesture and expression she abruptly recognized. Her jaw dropped.

"I should have said something," he told her in a voice that came across queerly accented. "It slipped my mind that men are the gendered class, here. That you'd naturally assume I was female unless told otherwise. Sorry to have shocked you. . . ."

Maia blinked. In her astonishment, she could barely speak. "You're . . . a man."

Renna nodded. "That's how I've always seen myself. Though here on—"

Kiel hissed. "Come on! Explain later!"

Maia would not move. "What are you talking about?" She demanded. "How could you have—"

Renna reached out and took one of Maia's hands. "Truth is, by your standards I'm probably not even human at all. You may have heard of me. In Caria City they call me the Visitor. Or the Outsider."

A cloud moved out of the way—or a moon chose that moment to suddenly cast pale light upon his face, showing its odd proportions. Not so extreme you would have stopped and stared, on seeing him at a dockside café. Still, when you looked for it, the effect was striking—a lengthiness of jaw and a breadth of brow that seemed somehow unworldly. Nostrils shaped to take in different air. A stance learned walking on a different world. Maia shivered.

"Now or never!" Thalla urged, taking both of them in tow while Kiel skulked ahead, scouting for danger in the shadows. Maia stumbled at first, but soon they picked up the pace and were running past ghostly, empty halls, united by a need to leave this place of stillborn silences. *That's right,* Maia realized. *Explanations can wait.* For the moment, she let a rising exhilaration drive out all other feelings. All that mattered now was the taste of freedom!

Later. Later would be soon enough to worry this puzzle—that her first adult love had turned out to be an alien from the stars.

Part Two

T he founders of this colony chose an excellent site to conceal their utopia. Partly hidden by dust nebulae, orbiting a strange multiple-star system where most explorers would not bother looking for habitable worlds . . . Stratos must have seemed ideal to isolate their descendants from the strife and ferment raging elsewhere in the galaxy.

Yet, the Enemy eventually found them. And now, so have I. . . .

. . .

It is a testament to their fierce independence that they never tried calling for help when the foe-ship came. The people of Stratos simply fought the Enemy, and won. The colonists have reason to be proud. Without direct aid from the Human Phylum, they countered a surprise attack and annihilated the invaders. Their victory has become the stuff of legends, altering their social structure even while seeming to validate it.

They claim this ratifies their secession, obviating any need for alliance with distant cousins.

So far, in conversations from ship to ground, I've refrained from citing our records, which mention that very same foe-ship, describing it as a broken ruin, fleeing the Battle of Taranis to lick its wounds or die. Stratos has never sampled the full terror stalking the stars. Even in ignorance, it has benefited from protection by the Phylum. No part lives but in reliance on the others.

This will not be an easy concept to impart, I fear. Some of these Herlandist radicals seem to find my arrival more traumatic than that of the Enemy, so long ago. An affront to be ignored if possible.

What do their leaders fear from renewed contact with distant kin?

Negotiations for my long-delayed landing are done at last. They assure me of facilities adequate to launch my aeroshell back into orbit when the visit is completed, so there's no need to go auto-mine an asteroid and build an ungainly, all-purpose craft. Tomorrow I descend to start discussions in person.

I have never been so nervous before a mission. This sub-species has much to offer. Their bold experiment may enrich humanity. Too bad, as chance had it, they were rediscovered by a male peripatetic.

The omens might have been better were I a woman.

13

M aia was soon disoriented in the stealthy dash through dark corridors and down unlit stairs. Kiel, who led the way, kept rushing ahead and then causing a bump and jostle each time she stopped abruptly to use a small penlight, consulting a hand-drawn map.

"Where did you get that?" Maia whispered at one point, pointing at the vellum diagram.

"A friend worked on the digging crew. Now be quiet."

Maia took no offense. A few gruff words were nothing compared to what else Kiel and Thalla had done. Maia's heart was full to bursting that her friends had come all this way, at untold risks, to rescue her.

And Renna, she reminded herself. As they hurried through the gloomy halls, she tried not to look at the person she had just seen for the first time, whom she had beforehand thought she knew so well. A creature from outer space. Perhaps sensing her discomfort, Renna hung a few paces behind. Maia felt irritated with him, and with herself, that her feelings were so obvious. "Is he telling the truth?" she whispered to Thalla, as Kiel consulted her map again near a meeting of two vast, unlit dormitory chambers. "About being . . . you know?"

Thalla shrugged. "Never know with males. Always goin' on about their travels. Maybe this one's been farther than most."

Maia wanted to believe Thalla's nonchalance. "You must have suspected something when you picked up the radio message."

"What radio message?" Thalla asked. As Kiel motioned them forward again, Maia found her confusion redoubling. She pursued whispered questions as they walked.

"If you didn't get a message, how did you find us?"

"Wasn't easy, virgie. Day after they took you, we tried following the trail. Seemed to be takin' you east, but then a big gang of sisters from Keally Clan rode up and drove us off. By the time we circled round, the tracks were cold. Turns out they pulled a switch over by Flake Rock, so it wasn't east, after all."

Maia shook her head. She had been unconscious or delirious during most of the ride out from Lerner Hold, so she had no idea how long it had taken.

Thalla grinned. The tall woman's pale face was barely visible in the reflection of Kiel's swaying beam off stone walls. "Finally, we got wind o' this Beller creature, comin' upland with an escort. Kiel had a hunch they might be headin' for this abandoned site. We got some friends together an' managed to tag along out o' sight. An' here we are."

Thalla made it sound so simple. In fact, it must have involved a lot of sacrifice, not to mention risk. "Then you didn't come just for . . . him?" Maia jerked her head backward, toward the one taking up the rear. Thalla grimaced.

"Ain't a man a man? It'll drive the perkies crazy he's gone, though. Reason enough to take him, at least till the coast. There he can join his own kind."

In the dark, Maia could not read Thalla's features. The woman's tone was tense and perhaps she wasn't telling the whole truth. But the message was sufficient. "You came for me, after all."

Thalla reached over as they walked, giving Maia's shoulder a squeeze. "What are var-buddies for? Us against a Lysos-less world, virgie."

It was like a line from that adventure book Maia had read, about stalwart summer women forging a new world out of the ruins of a brittle, broken yesterday. Suddenly, Kiel interrupted with a sharp hiss. Their guide covered her light and motioned for quiet. Silently, almost on tiptoe, they joined her near an intersection, where their dim corridor crossed another one, more brightly lit. Kiel cautiously leaned out to peer left, then right. Her breath cut short.

"What is it?" the man asked, catching up from behind, his voice carrying startlingly. Thalla's hand made a chopping sign and he said no more. Standing still, they could hear faint sounds—a clinking, a low rattle, voices rising briefly, then fading to a low murmur. Kiel moved her hands to pantomime that there were people in sight, some distance down the cross corridor.

What now? Maia worried, a tightness in her throat. Clearly Kiel's map was incomplete. Would it offer an alternate route? Was there enough time?

To Maia's surprise, Kiel did not motion for them to turn around. Instead, she took a deep breath, visibly braced herself, and stepped boldly into the light!

Maia knew it was only her dark-adapted eyes overreacting. Still, when Kiel entered the wan illumination of the hallway, it was as if she had briefly gone aflame. How could anyone *not* notice such a shining presence?

But no one did. The older var glided smoothly across the exposed area without a sound, reentering darkness in safety on the other side. There was no change in the mutter of conversation. Thalla took the next turn, trying to imitate Kiel's liquid, silent stride. Sudden reflection off her pale skin seemed even more glaringly impossible to ignore, lasting two ponderously long seconds. Then she, too, was across.

Maia glanced at the man, Renna, who smiled and touched her elbow, urging her to go ahead. It was a friendly gesture, an expression of confidence, and Maia briefly hated him for it. She could just make out the two women, dim figures across the bright intersection, also waiting for her. To Maia, her own heartbeat sounded loud enough to echo off the rocky walls. She got a grip on herself, flaring her nostrils, and stepped forward.

Time seemed to telescope, fractional seconds stretching into subjective hours. Maia's distant feet moved on their own, freeing her to glance right toward a searing image of bracketed flamelight . . . of broken furniture burning in a chiseled fireplace, while silhouetted figures drank from goblets, leaning over to watch the arcing fall of dice onto a wooden table. Their cries made Maia's skin crawl.

The scene was so dazzling, she became disoriented and veered off course to collide with a sharp corner of the intersection. Thalla had to yank her the rest of the way into blessed darkness. Maia rubbed where her forehead had struck stone, blinking to reaccustom her eyes to obscurity.

She looked up quickly. "Renna?" she whispered, casting about.

"I'm here, Maia," came a soft reply.

She turned to her left. The man stood with Kiel a little farther down the dim hallway. Maia hadn't heard or sensed him cross. Embarrassed by her outburst, she looked away. This person was not at all like the sage, older woman she had envisioned. Though there had been no lies, she nonetheless felt betrayed, if by nothing else, then by her all-too-human tendency to make assumptions.

Unless it has to do with the ships or sparking, you just suppose a person is female till you learn otherwise. I guess that's not very nice.

Still . . . he should have told me!

Now she and Thalla took up the rear while Renna and Kiel forged ahead. For the first time, Maia noticed that the man was carrying a small blue pouch at his belt and something much larger strapped across his back. A slim case of burnished metal.

A Game of Life set, she realized. *Oh, he's a man, all right!*

I was such an idiot, picturing some noble savant who'd figured out how to send such clever messages out of pure resourcefulness. I don't suppose those tricks were difficult for a man who's spent his whole life playing the game.

It was obvious enough, now. But trapped in her cell with only clicks in the night for company, she had been looking more through wishes than reason. How strange, to feel a sense of *mourning* for a friend who stood just a few meters away, alive, healthy, and, for the moment, free. Yet the Renna Maia had imagined was dead, as surely as Leie. This *new* Renna was an unwelcome replacement.

Unfair? Maia knew it.

LIFE'S unfair. So? Find Lysos and sue her.

Minutes later, Kiel led them to a narrow door where she knocked twice. The wooden portal swung open, revealing a stocky blonde woman holding a crowbar like a weapon. The door showed signs of damage, its lock-hasp pried away, a broken padlock on the floor.

"Got 'em?" the gate guardian asked. She was tall, rangy, fair-haired, and tough-looking. Kiel only nodded. "Come on," Thalla said, leading the way down another short flight of stairs. Maia smelled the night even before a chill wind touched her skin. It had a freshness she had never felt from the open window of her cell. Then they were outside, under the stars.

From the postern gate they stepped onto a broad stone porch, just one meter above the level of the plain. Kiel strode to the edge, brought her fingers to her mouth, and whistled the call of a gannen bird. From the darkness came a trilling reply, like an echo, followed by the sound of hoofbeats. The tall blonde pushed the door back into place as four women came riding up, each holding the reins of one or two spare mounts.

Unleashing bundles tied to the back of one animal, Thalla thrust into Maia's hands a rough wool coat, which she gratefully slipped on. She was still buttoning when Kiel took her arm and motioned toward the edge of the platform, where a sash-horse had been brought alongside. Moonlight glistened along the beast's striped flanks as it snorted, blew and stamped. Maia couldn't help cringing a bit. Her riding experience had been confined to tame beasts guided by skilled Trevor wranglers, hired for springtime outings so Lamai summerlings could check one more item off their mothers' "life-preparation" syllabus as quickly and cheaply as possible.

"He won't bite, virgie," the woman holding the bridle said, laughing.

Pride overcame apprehension, and Maia managed to grab the saddle horn without trembling. Slipping her left foot into the stirrup, she swung astride. The horse danced, testing her weight. She reached over to accept the reins, feeling elated when the creature did not bolt the next instant. Relieved, Maia bent to pat its neck.

"What the hell is *that?*"

They were gruff words of protest. Maia turned to see the man, Renna, pointing at the beast in front of him. Kiel came alongside and touched his arm, as if to ease his fears.

"It's a horse. We use them here for riding and—"

Renna cocked his head. "I know what a horse is. I meant, what's that thing on its back?"

"On its back? Why . . . that's a saddle, where you ride."

Perplexed, he shook his head. "That blocky thing's a saddle? Why is it different than the others?"

All the women, even Maia, burst out laughing. She couldn't help it. The question was so incongruous, so unexpected. Maybe he *was* from outer space, after all! Renna's look of confused consternation only made her giggle more, covering her mouth with her free hand.

Kiel, too, tried to conceal mirth. "Naturally, it's a *side*saddle. I know you'd prefer a wagon or palanquin, but we just haven't got . . ." The woman stopped in midsentence and stared. "What are you doing?"

Renna had jumped off the porch and was reaching underneath the mount selected for him. "Just . . . making a slight . . . adjustment," he grunted. "There."

To Maia's astonishment, the bulky, cushioned saddle slid sideways and tumbled to the ground. Then, even more surprisingly, the man took the horse's mane in his hands and, in a single bound, leaped aboard straddle-wise, like a woman! The others reacted with audible gasps. Maia winced at an involuntary twinge in her loins.

"How can you—" Thalla started to ask, dry-mouthed.

"Stirrups would be nice," he interrupted. "But we can take turns riding bareback till we rig something up. Now, let's get the hell out of here."

Kiel blinked. "Are you sure you know what you're—"

In answer, Renna flicked the reins and set his mount cantering, then trotting toward the place where the sun had set hours ago. The direction of the sea. As they stared after him, he let out a cry of such exultation that Maia felt a thrill. The man had given voice to what wanted out of her own lungs. Amazement gave way to pure joy as she, too, dug in her heels. Her mount complied willingly, hastening on the same bearing, kicking dust toward the memory of her imprisonment.

The escape party didn't take the direct route to safety, toward the outlet of Long Valley. The Perkinites would surely look there first. Kiel and the others had a plan. After that initial exuberant trot, the caravan settled into a brisk but deliberate walk, roughly south by southwest.

About an hour after departure, there came a faint sound in the distance behind them. A low clanging. Turning around, Maia saw the thin, moonlit, rocky spire where she had been jailed, by now diminished with distance and beginning to sink into the horizon. High along its dark flank, several bright pinpoints told of windows coming alight.

"Bloody moonset!" Kiel cursed, clucking to her mount and setting a quicker pace. "I was hoping we'd have till morning. Let's make tracks."

Kiel didn't speak figuratively, Maia soon realized. The band kept purposely to open ground, where speed was good but the horses' hooves also left easily-followed impressions. "It's part of our plan, so's to make the Perkies lazy," Thalla explained as they rode along. "We have a trick in mind. Don't worry."

"I'm not." Maia replied. She was too happy to be concerned. After running the horses for a while, they halted, and the tall, rough-looking blonde rose high in her stirrups to aim a spyglass rearward. "No sign of anyone breathin' down our necks," she said, collapsing the tube again. The pace slowed then, to keep their mounts from tiring.

Prompted by a brief query from Thalla, asking how she had been treated in prison, Maia found herself spilling whole run-on paragraphs about her arrival at the stony citadel, about the terrible cooking of the Guel jailers, how awful it had been to spend Autumn End Day in a place like that, and how she never hoped to see the insides of a man sanctuary again. She knew she was jabbering, but if Thalla and the others seemed amused, she didn't care. Anyone would jabber after such a sudden reversal of fortunes, from despair to excitement, with the fresh air of freedom filling her lungs like an intoxicant.

There followed another period of quick trotting and more brisk walking. Soon a lesser moon—Aglaia—rose to join Durga in the sky, and someone started humming a sailor's chantey in greeting. Another woman pitched in with words, singing a rich, mellow contralto. Maia eagerly joined the chorus.

> *"Oh blow, ye winds of the western sea,*
> *And blow ye winds, heigh-ho!*
> *Give poor shipmen clemency,*
> *And blow, ye winds, heigh ho!"*

After listening a few rounds, Renna added his deeper tenor to the refrain, which sounded appropriate for a sailing ballad. He caught Maia's eye at one point, winking, and she found herself smiling back shyly, not terribly displeased.

More songs followed. It soon grew clear to Maia that there was a division among the women. Kiel and Thalla and one other—a short brunette named Kau—were city-bred, sophisticated, with Kiel clearly the intellectual leader. At one point, all three of them joined in a rousing anthem whose verses were decidedly political.

> *"Oh, daughters of the storm assemble,*
> *What seems set in stone can still be changed!*
> *Who will care whom you resemble,*
> *When the order of life is rearranged?"*

Maia recalled the melody from those nights sharing a cottage at Lerner Hold, listening to the clandestine radio station. The lyrics conveyed an angry, forceful resolve to upset the present order, making a determined break with the past. The other four women knew this song, and lent support to the chorus. But there was a sense of restraint, as if they disagreed in some parts, while thinking the verses too soft in others. When their turn came again, the others once more chose songs Maia knew from school and crèche. Traditional ballads of adventure. Songs of magic lamps and secret treasures. Of warm hearths left behind. Of revealed talents, and wishes coming true. The melodies were more comforting, even if the singers weren't. From their accents and features, she guessed the two shorter, stockier ones must be from the Southern Isles, legendary home of reavers and sharp traders, while the other two, including the rangy blonde, spoke with the sharp twang typical of this part of Eastern Continent. Maia learned the blonde was named Baltha, and seemed to be the leader of the four.

All told, it seemed a tough, confident bunch of vars. They had no apparent fear, even if by some chance Tizbe Beller and her guards caught up with them.

The singing died down before their next break to adjust tack and trade mounts. After resuming, for a while everyone was quiet, allowing the metronome rhythm of the horses' hooves to make low, percussive music of an earthier nature. No longer distracted, Maia took greater note of the cold. Her fingers were especially sensitive, and she wound up keeping her hands in the pockets of the thick coat, holding the reins through layers of cloth.

Renna trotted ahead to ride next to Kiel, causing some muttering among the other women. Baltha was openly disapproving.

"No business a man ridin' like that," she said, watching from behind as Renna jounced along, legs straddling his mount. "It's kinda obscene."

"Seems he knows what he's doing," Thalla said. "Gives me chills watchin', though. Even now that he's got a normal saddle. Can't figure how he doesn't cripple himself."

Baltha spat on the ground. "Some things men just oughtn't be let to do."

"Right," one of the stocky southerners added. "Horses were made for women. Obvious from how we're built an' men aren't. Lysos meant it that way."

Maia shook her head, unsure what to think. Later, when happenstance appeared to bring her alongside Renna's mount, the man turned to her and said in a low voice, "Actually, these animals aren't much different than ones I knew on Earth. A bit stockier, and this weird striping. I think the skull's bigger, but it's hard to recall."

Maia blinked in surprise. "You're . . . from Earth? The real . . . ?"

He nodded, a wistful expression on his face. "Long ago and far away. I know, you thought maybe Florentina, or some other nearby system. No such luck, I'm afraid.

"What I meant, though, is that your friends back there are wrong. Half the worlds in the Human Phylum have horse variants, some much stranger than these. Women ride more often than men, it's true. But this is the first time I've heard it said males aren't built for it!" He laughed. "Now that you mention it, I guess it does seem strange we don't hurt ourselves."

"You heard all that?" Maia asked. At the time, she'd thought he was too far ahead.

He tapped one of his ears. "Thicker atmosphere than my birthworld, by far. Carries sound better. I can hear whispers quite some distance, though it also means I get splitting headaches when people shout. You won't tell, will you?"

He winked for the second time that night, and Maia's sense of alienation evaporated. In an instant he was just another harmless, friendly sailor, on winter leave after a long voyage. His confidential disclosure was natural, an expression of trust based on the fact that they had known each other and shared secrets before.

Maia looked up at the starry vault. "Point to Earth," she asked.

Rising in his stirrups, Renna searched the sky. At last he settled back down. "Sorry. If we're still awake near morning, I should be able to find the Triffid. Sol is near its left eye-stalk. Of course, most of the nearer stars of the Phylum are hidden behind the God's Brow nebula—what you call the Claw—just east of the Triffid."

"You know a lot about our sky, for someone who's been here less than a year."

Renna let out a sigh. His expression grew heavier. "You have long years, on Stratos."

Maia sensed it might be better for the moment to refrain from further questions. Renna's face, which had appeared youthful on first sight, now seemed troubled and weary. *He's older than he looks*, she realized. *How old would you have to be, to travel as far as he has? Even if they have freezers on starships, and move close to the speed of light.*

She couldn't put all the blame for her ignorance on Lamatia's selective education. Such subjects had always seemed far removed from matters she had expected to concern her. Not for the first time, Maia wondered, *Why did we virtually abandon space? Did Lysos plan it that way? Maybe to help make sure no one found us again?*

If so, it must have only made for a worse shock to the savants and councillors and priestesses in Caria, when the Visitor Ship entered orbit, last winter. They must have been thrown into utter chaos.

This has to be what that old bird was talking about, on the tele in Lanargh! Maia realized. *Renna must have already been kidnapped then. They were putting out feelers, trying to find him without disturbing the public.*

Maia knew what Leie's thought would be, at this point. The reward!

It must be what Thalla and Kiel and the others are after. Of course Thalla had been lying, back in the sanctuary corridors. They hadn't come for her, after all. Or at least not her alone. Their main objective must have been Renna all along, which explained the sidesaddle. Why else bring such a thing all this way, unless to fetch a man?

Not that she blamed them. Maia was accustomed to being unimportant. That they had bothered to spring her, as well, was enough to win her gratitude. And Thalla's attempt to lie about it had been sweet.

The open plain ended abruptly when they arrived at broken ravine country similar to the type Maia remembered, where Lerner Clan dug their ores and spilled slag from their foundry. She guessed this was much farther north and east, but the contours were similar—tortured eroded canyons crossing the prairie like scars of some ancient fight. Carefully, the party dropped into the first set of narrow washes, descending past nesting sites where burrower colonies made vain, threatening noises to drive the humans and horses away. The chirruping sounds grew triumphant as their efforts seemed to work, and the threat passed.

Baltha took over navigating the increasingly twisty maze where, at some points, only the topmost sixty degrees or so of sky were visible, making for slow going even after two oil lanterns were lit.

A halt was called by a shallow, gurgling stream and everyone dismounted, some gingerly. None more so than the man, who hissed and rubbed his legs, walking out stiffness. Baltha's colleagues nodded knowingly. In fact, though, only embarrassment kept Maia from hobbling about just like him. Instead, she stretched surreptitiously, behind her horse. Nearby, the leaders gathered round a lantern.

"This must be the place," Kiel said, jabbing a map sketched onto lambskin, so much tougher than paper. Baltha shook her head. "Another stream, a klick or so on. I'll tell ya when."

"You're sure? We wouldn't want to miss—"

"Won't," the tall blonde said, curtly. "Now let's mount. Wastin' time."

Maia saw Thalla and Kiel look at each other dubiously after Baltha left. "Comes off knowin' the place like her own back-hand." Thalla muttered. "Now how would that be? Only Perkinites grow up 'round here."

Kiel made a cautioning sign to her friend. "One thing for sure. That's no damn Perkinite."

Thalla shrugged as Kiel rolled up the map. "There's worse," she said under her breath. When the two of them walked past Maia, Thalla gave her a tousle on the top of her head. The gesture would have seemed patronizing if there hadn't been something like genuine affection in it.

With the elation of escape starting to fade into physical fatigue, Maia realized, *There's more going on here than I thought. I'd better start paying closer attention.*

Half an hour later, they reached another stream under looming canyon walls. This time, Baltha signaled for everyone to guide their mounts into the shallow watercourse before she spoke.

"We split up here. Riss, Herri, Blene, an' Kau will go on toward Demeterville, making tracks and confusing the trail. Maia, you'll go too. The rest'll wade upstream about two klicks before heading west, then south. We'll meet sou'west of Clay Town on the seventh, if Lysos guides us."

Maia stared at the strangers she had been told to accompany, and felt a frisson course her spine. "No," she said emphatically. "I want to go with Kiel and Thalla."

Baltha glowered. "You'll go where you're told."

Panic welled and Maia's chest was tight. It felt like a repetition of her separation from Leie, when they parted in Lanargh for the last time, on separate ships. A certainty overwhelmed her that once out of sight, she would never see her friends again.

"I won't! Not after all that!" She jerked one hand in the direction of the prison tower that so recently held her in its grip. Maia turned to her friends for support, but they wouldn't meet her eyes. "The upstream party ought to be small as possible . . ." Kiel tried to explain. But Maia learned more from the woman's uneasy demeanor. *This was arranged in advance,* she realized. *They don't want me along while they escape with their precious alien!* A heavy resignation swarmed into Maia's heart, overwhelming even her burning resentment.

"Maia comes with us."

It was Renna. Maneuvering his horse next to hers, he went on. "Your plan counts on our pursuers following an easy trail to the larger party, while we others make our getaway. That's fine for me. Thanks. But not so good for Maia when they catch up."

"The girl's just a larva," Baltha retorted. "They don't care about her. Probably aren't even looking for her."

Renna shook his head. "You want to risk her freedom on a bet like that? Forget it. I won't let her be taken back to that place."

Through surging emotion, Maia saw a silent interplay among the women. They had thought of Renna as a commodity, but now he was asserting himself. Men might rank low on the Stratos social ladder, nevertheless they stood higher than most vars. Moreover, most of *these* vars must have served on ships, at one time or another. It surely influenced matters that Renna had a well-cultivated "captain's voice."

Kiel shrugged. Thalla turned and grinned at Maia. "Okay by me. Glad to have you with us, virgie."

Baltha cursed lowly, accepting the swing of consensus, but not gracefully. The rangy blonde brought her mount over near her friends, who were taking the other route, and leaned over to clasp forearms with them. In a similar manner, Thalla and Kiel embraced Kau. The parties separated then, Baltha carefully swiveling her mount down the center of the current. Taking the rear, Maia and Renna called farewell to their benefactors, who had already begun climbing a thin trail up the next canyon wall. One of them—Maia couldn't make out who—lifted a hand to wave back, then the four women disappeared around a bend.

"Thank you," Maia said to Renna softly, as their mounts sloshed slowly along. Her voice still felt thick from that moment of surprise and upset.

"Hey," the man said with a smile. "We castaways have to hang together, right? Anyway, you seem like a tough pal to have along, if trouble's ahead."

Of course he was jesting with her. But only partly, she realized with some surprise. He really did seem glad, even relieved, that she was coming with him.

Traveling single file, they fell into silence, letting the horses pick a careful path along the uneven streambed. Fortunately, they were out of the wind. But the surrounding winter-chilled rocks seemed to suck heat right out of the air. Maia put her hands under her armpits, squeezing the coat tight, exhaling breath that turned into visible fog.

Anyway, it was reassuring knowing that each minute put more distance behind them. The escape plan was a risky one, counting on panic and excessive haste on the part of their pursuers. True professionals— like the Sheldon clan of hunters back in Port Sanger—wouldn't be fooled by so simple a trick. Maia hadn't heard of tracking skill being much famed among Long Valley's farmers, but it was still an assumption.

Even if they slipped their immediate pursuers, they remained surrounded by enemies. Few places on Stratos were politically more homogeneous than this upland colony of extremists, with allied Perkinite clans stretching all the way to Grange Head. Once aroused by the news, there would be posses and mobs swarming after them from all directions.

Maia thought she could now see the big picture . . . how desperate the Perkinites must be. Much more was involved than their radical plan to use a drug to promote winter sparking. The hive matriarchies of Long Valley had become involved in a far more brazen scheme: kidnapping the Interstellar Visitor—Renna—right out of the hands of the council in Caria City. It was a risky endeavor. But how better to reduce, maybe eliminate, the chance of restored contact with the Hominid Phylum?

Nothing would make extreme Perkinites crazier than having the sky open up. Spaceships calling regularly from those old worlds of "animal rut and sexual tyranny." Worlds where fully half of the inhabitants are men.
Half.

Despite having read those lurid novels, it was hard to picture. What, in the name of Lysos, did a world need with so many extra males? Even if they were quiet and well-behaved most of the time, which she doubted, there were only so many tasks a man could be trusted with! What was there for them to *do*?

Contact would change Stratos forever, polluting it with alien ideas, alien ways. Despite her hatred of those who had imprisoned her, Maia wondered if they might not have a point.

She found herself reacting tensely again, when Renna maneuvered his mount alongside. But all he had for her was a smile and a question about the name of a species of shrub that clung tenaciously to the canyon walls. Maia answered, guessing it related to a type found at the Orthodox temple in Grange Head. She couldn't tell him whether it was a purely native life-form or descended from bioengineered Earth varieties, released by the Founders.

"I'm trying to get an idea how introduced forms were designed to fit in, and how much adaptation took place afterward. You have some pretty sophisticated ecologists at the university, but figures are hardly a substitute for getting out and seeing for yourself."

Although they were hard to make out in the dim starlight, his features seemed revived from the earlier moodiness. Maia found herself wondering if his eyes would shine strange colors by day, or if his skin, which she had only seen in lantern or moonlight, would turn out to be some weird, exotic shade.

Perhaps it was a mistake to interpret an alien's facial expressions by past experience, but Renna seemed excited to be here, away from cities and savants and, especially, his prison cell, finally exploring the surface of Stratos itself. It was contagious.

"All told, it seems your Founders were pretty good designers, making clever changes in the humans, plants, and animals they set down here, before fitting them into the ecosystem. They made some mistakes of course. That's hardly unusual. . . ."

It felt blasphemous, hearing an outsider say such things. Perkinites and other heretics were known to criticize some of the *choices* made by Lysos and the other Founders, but never before had Maia heard anyone speak this way about their *competence*.

". . . Time has erased most of the errors, by extinction or adaptation. It's been long enough for things to settle down, at least among the lower life-forms."

"Well, after all, it's been hundreds of years," Maia responded.

Renna tilted his head. "Is that how long you think humans have lived on Stratos?"

Maia frowned. "Um . . . sure. I mean, I don't remember an exact figure. Does it matter?"

He looked at her in a way she found odd. "I suppose not. Still, that fits with the way your calendars . . ." Renna shook his head. "Never mind. Say, is that the sextant you told me about? The one you used to correct my latitude figures?"

Maia glanced at her wrist and the little instrument wrapped in its leather case. Renna was being kind again. Her improvements to his coordinates, back in jail, had been minimal. "Would you like to see it?" she asked, unstrapping the sextant and holding it toward him.

He handled it carefully, first using his fingertips to trace the engraved zep'lin design on the brass cover, then unfolding and delicately experimenting with the sighting arms. "Very nice tool," he commented. "Handmade, you say? I'd love to see the workshop."

Maia shivered at the thought. She had seen enough of male sanctuaries.

"Is this the dial you use for adjusting azimuth?" he asked.

"Azimuth? Oh, you mean star-height. Of course, you need a good horizon . . ."

Soon they were immersed in talk about the art of navigation, picking their way through a maze of terms inherited from altogether different traditions—his using complex machines to cross unimaginable emptiness, and hers from a heritage of countless lives spent refining rules learnt the hard way, battling the elements on Stratos's capricious seas. Renna spoke respectfully of techniques that she knew had to seem primitive, in view of how far he had come—from those very lights Maia used as guideposts in the sky.

Sometimes, when a moon cleared the canyon walls to shine directly on his face, Maia was struck by a subtle difference which seemed suddenly enhanced. The long shadow of his cheekbone, or the way, in dim light, his pupils seemed to open wider than normal for Stratoin eyes. Would she have even noticed if she didn't already know who, or what, he was?

They cut short the discussion when Baltha called a break. Their guide indicated a path to take their tired mounts onto a stony beach, where the party dismounted and spent some time rubbing and drying the horses' feet and ankles, restoring circulation to parts numbed by cold water. It was hard labor, and Renna soon stripped off his coat. Maia could feel heat radiating from his body as he worked nearby. She remembered the sailors on the *Wotan*, whose powerful torsos always seemed so spendthrift of energy, wasting half of what they ate and drank in sweat and radiation. As cold as she was, especially in her fingers and toes, Renna's nearby presence was rather pleasant. She felt tempted to draw closer, strictly to share the warmth he squandered so freely. Even the inevitable male odor wasn't so bad.

Renna stood up, a puzzled expression on his face. Scanning the sky, his eyes narrowed and his brows came together in a furrow. Only as Maia rose to come alongside did she begin to notice something as well, a soft sound from overhead, like the distant buzzing of a swarm of bees.

"There!" he shouted, pointing to the west, just above the rim of the canyon.

Maia tried to sight along his arm. "Where? I can't . . . Oh!"

She had seldom seen flying machines, even by daylight. Port Sanger's small airfield was hidden beyond hills, with flight paths chosen not to disturb city dwellers. Not counting the weekly mail dirigible, true aircraft came only a few times a year. But what else could those lights be? Maia counted two . . . three pairs of winking pinpoints passing overhead as the delayed rumbling peaked and then followed the glitters eastward.

"Cy must've heard!" Renna shouted, as the canyon cut off sight of the moving stars. "She got through to Groves. They've come for us!"

For you, don't you mean? Maia thought. Still, she was glad, intensely glad. This certainly verified Renna's importance, for Caria to have sent such a force so far, impinging on the sovereignty of Long Valley Commonwealth, and even risking a fight.

Baltha, Thalla, and Kiel refused to even consider turning back.

"But it's a rescue party! Surely they've come with enough force to—"

"That's good," Kiel agreed. "It'll distract the bitches. Keep them off our trail. Maybe they'll be so busy scrapping and arguing, we'll have smooth sailing to the coast."

Maia saw what was going on. Kiel and her friends had invested a lot in rescuing Renna. Apparently, they weren't about to hand him over to a platoon of policewomen, who could claim they would have had him free tonight anyway. Far better from Kiel's point of view to deliver him personally to a magistrate at Grange Head, where their success would be indisputable and the reward guaranteed.

Maia saw Renna consider. Would the women try to stop him if he turned around by himself? A male's strength might not compensate much for the world-wise ferocity of Baltha, who looked like a born fighter and was never far from her effective-looking crowbar. The match was doubly dubious in winter, when male tempers ebbed toward nadir. Renna's odds would improve with Maia by his side, but she wasn't sure she could bring herself to fight Thalla and Kiel.

Anyway, suppose he did turn around. Tizbe wouldn't have waited long to set out on their trail. Even if the prison-citadel was taken by Carian forces, Renna and Maia were likely to stumble into the Beller and her guards on the open prairie. They'd only be captured and taken to another hole, probably far worse than the one they had just left.

We really haven't got much choice, Maia realized.

Still, in that moment her loyalties crystallized. She moved to stand next to Renna, ready to support whatever he decided. There was a long pause while the drone of engines faded gradually to a whisper, and then nothing. At last, the man shrugged.

"All right, let's ride."

C y complained about having to use archaic codes to guide my shuttle down the ancient landing beam. I was too nervous to be sympathetic. "Who had to learn an entirely new language?" I groused, while white flame licked the viewing ports and a heavy atmosphere tried to crush my cocoon like a grape in a vice. "It's supposedly a dialect based on Florentinan, but they have parts of speech nobody's seen be-fore—feminine, masculine, neuter, *and* clonal . . . with redundancy cases, declensions, and drift-stop participles . . ."

I was jabbering to stave off raw terror. Even that diversion vanished when Cy asked me to shut up, letting her concentrate on getting me down in one piece. That left nothing to do except listen to the shrieking-hot wind against the hull plates, centimeters from my ear. Normal landings are bad. But I had never heard sounds like these. Stratoins breathe air thick enough to swim in.

It being summer when the Council finally voted permission to land, aurorae followed me down—curtains of electricity tapped into magnetic coils streaming off the red sun's dwarf companion. I was headed for low latitudes, but even so, ribbons of ionic lightning caused sparks to crackle along a console, uncomfortably near my arm.

Ballistic crisis passed. Soon the lander was cutting tunnels through vast water-vapor clouds, then turning in a braking swoop over a quilt of dark forests and bright meadows. Finally, a riverside gleam led to clear signs of habitation and industry. For most of a Terran year, I had looked on this terrain from space, half-dead from the ennui of waiting. Now I pressed the window, drinking in the loveliness of Stratos . . . the somber luster of native vegetation and more luminous greens of Earth-derived life, the shimmer of her multicolored lakes, the atmospheric refraction which gives every horizon a subtle, concave bend. Hills rose to surround me. With a final stall that set my stomach spinning, Cy set the shuttle rolling across twenty hectares of pavement, split here and there by shoots of intruding grass. By the time the shuttle cooled enough to let down a narrow ramp, a welcoming party was already waiting.

I imagine their embroidered gowns would have fetched magnates' prices on Pleasence, or even Earth. Of the five middle-aged women, none smiled. They kept their distance as I descended, and when we exchanged bows. No one offered to shake hands.

I've had warmer receptions . . . and far worse. Two of the women identified themselves as members of the reigning council. A third wore clerical robes and raised her arms to make what sounded like a cautious blessing. The remaining pair were university dons I'd already spoken with by videx. Savant Iolanthe, who seemed cautiously guarded, with sharply evaluating gray eyes, and Savant Melonni, who had seemed friendly during the long negotiations, but now kept well back, regarding me like a specimen of some rare and rather dubious species. One with a reputation for biting.

During the months spent peering in frustration from orbit, I've seen how most settlements rely on wind and solar and animal power for transport—fully in line with what I know of Lysian-Herlandist ideology. Industrialized regions make some use of combustion-powered land craft, however, and I was shown to a comfortable car equipped with a hydrogen-oxygen engine. To my amazement, nearly everything else, from chassis to furnishings, was crafted out of finely carved wood! I later surmised that this doesn't just reflect the planet's comparative poverty in metals. It is a statement of some sort.

I sat alone in one compartment, isolated from the others by a pane of glass. Which was just as well. My intestines complained noisily from prelanding treatments and, despite having spent several megaseconds acclimatizing to a simulated Stratos atmosphere, my lungs labored audibly in the heavy air. An assault of strange odors kept me busy stifling sneezes, and the carbon dioxide partial pressure triggered recurrent yawns. I must have been a sight to behold.

Yet, none of that seemed to matter in my elation to be down at last! This seems such a sophisticated, dignified world and folk, especially in comparison to what I met on Digby, or on godforsaken Heaven. I'm certain we can reach an understanding.

As our vehicle reached the edge of the landing field, escorts fell in ahead and behind . . . squadrons of finely-arrayed *cavalry*, making a splendid show in glittering cuirasses and helmets. The impression of uniformity and discipline was enhanced when I saw that the unit consisted entirely of tall women from a single family of Stratoin clones, identical down to each shiny button and lock of hair. The soldiers looked formidable. My first close view of clan specialization in action.

On leaving the landing area, we passed the other part of the spaceport, the launching facility, with its ramps and booster rails for sending cargoes skyward, which must eventually carry my own shuttle, when the time comes to depart.

I saw no sign of activity. Through an intercom, one of the scholars explained that the facility was fully functional. "Carefully preserved for occasional use," she said with a blithe wave of one hand.

I could not imagine what the word "occasional" meant to these people. But the word left me uneasy.

14

O cean surrounded her, threatening to engulf her. She clung to a splintered, oily timber, bobbing and jerking as contrary waves fought to possess it. Rain fell in blinding sheets, angled by gale-driven winds. In the distance, she watched a sailing vessel glide away, slicing through towering swells, ignoring her calls, her pleas to turn back.

On the deck of the departing ship, a girl stared in her direction, blindly, unseeing.

The girl had her own face. . . .

Dread welled up. Maia wanted to escape. But dreams had a way of trapping her by making her forget there was a "real" world to flee to. It took a whisper of true sound intruding on the dreamscape, to provide something to follow upward, outward, toward consciousness.

She wondered muzzily how she came to be lying here, wrapped in a scratchy woolen blanket, stretched upon gritty ground. Stone canyon walls felt like her jail cell, cold and enclosing, and the low clouds hung overhead like a dour ceiling. She propped up on one elbow, rubbing her eyes, looking at the leftover embers of a tiny campfire, then at the tethered horses, browsing shrubs down to bare twigs over by the stream. Two curled forms lay close enough to offer warmth on one side. From glimpses of unkempt hair poking from the blanket rolls, she recognized Thalla and Kiel and relaxed a bit, recalling she was among friends. Maia smiled, thinking once more about what they had done, rescuing her from

the pit where Tizbe Beller and the Joplands and Lerners had consigned
her.

Turning to her other side, Maia saw two empty blankets that had
been thrown back, their occupants gone. The nearest bedroll was still
slightly warm to touch. That person's departure must have been what
vexed her sleep, pulling her from disturbing dreams and memories of
Leie.

Oh, yes. Renna. The Outsider had been a welcome heat source in
the chill before dawn, when they had collapsed in exhaustion from their
hard ride. Sight of his blue pouch and Game of Life set reassured her
that he wasn't gone for good.

The big blonde, Baltha, had been sleeping just beyond. Maia lay
back, staring at the sky. Why would both of them get up at the same
time? Did it matter? It wouldn't be hard to slip back into slumber . . .
and hopefully dream better dreams. . . .

A faint clatter—pebbles rolling down a slope—banished sleep and
crystallized intent as she sat up. Slipping on her shoes, Maia crawled
away from Thalla's still form before standing and walking toward the
source of the sound, somewhere upstream, where the surrounding bluffs
had crumbled to give way to sloping ground. A flash of movement caught
her eye, rounding the nearest hillock. She headed in that direction and
was soon clambering over boulders, washed ice-smooth by successive
summer floods.

The widening canyon offered less shelter from the cold. Maia exhaled fog and her fingertips grew numb from grabbing handholds lined
with frost. A vaguely familiar scent made her nostrils flare, drawing her
back to winters in Lamatia Hold, when Leie used to throw open the
shutters on wintry mornings, thumping her chest, and inhaling the frigid
air while Maia complained and burrowed in the covers. The unbeckoned
memory brought a faint, sad smile as she climbed.

Maia stopped, listened. There was a scrape, a stone rattling downslope somewhere ahead and to her right. The way looked tricky. She
paused, feeling torn between curiosity and a growing awareness of her
replete bladder. Now that she was fully awake, it did seem a bit pointless, following people who were obviously out doing what she herself
ought to find a place and do. *Let's just take care of business, eh?* She
began casting about for a convenient niche out of the wind.

The first spot she tried already had an occupant. Or occupants. A
hissing squeal made Maia jump back in fright as a living *rainbow*
flapped at her. She hurriedly retreated from the crevice where a mother
zim-skimmer was tending its young—a cluster of tiny gasbags that inflated and deflated rapidly, wheezing in imitation of their belligerent

dam. Smaller cousins of zoor-floaters, the skimmers had much worse temperaments, and poison quills that fended off Earth-descended birds seeking their tender flesh. The spines caused fierce allergic rashes, if a human was unlucky enough to brush one. Maia backed away, eyeing the deceptively diaphanous forms. Once safely out of sight, she turned and hurried along the half trail.

That was when, rounding a corner, she caught sight of someone just ahead.

Baltha.

The tall woman squatted, peering over a set of boulders at something downslope, out of Maia's view. On the ground beside the var lay a small camp spade and a lidded wooden box, small enough to cover with one hand. While Baltha stared ahead intently, she idly reached out to brush a nearby rock, then brought her fingers to her face, sniffing.

Maia blinked. *Of course.* She scanned the ledges closest to her and saw, amid thin patches of normal white snow, streaks that shone with a diamondlike glitter. *Glory frost. It's winter, all right.* The march of seasons had more effect on high, stratospheric winds than on the massive bulk of sea and land and air below. Varieties of turbulence unknown on other worlds recycled water vapor through ionic fluxes until an adenated ice formed. Occasionally, the crystals made their way to ground in soft, predawn hazes, as unique a sign of winter as Wengel Star's flamboyant aurorae were to summer. Maia stretched toward the nearest sprinkling of glory frost. Static charge drew the shiny pseudogems to her fingertips, which tingled despite their morning numbness. Purple and golden highlights sparkled under innumerable facets as she turned them in the light. A visible vapor of sublimation rose from the points of contact.

In winters past, whenever glory had appeared on their sill, Maia and Leie used to giggle and try inhaling or tasting the fine, luminescent snow. The first time, she, not her sister, had been the bold one. "They say it's just for grownups," Leie had said nervously, parroting the mothers' lessons. Of course that only made it more enticing.

The effects were disappointing. Other than a faint fizzing sensation that tickled the nose, the twins never felt anything abnormal or provocative.

But I'm older now, Maia reflected, watching her body heat turn fine powder into steam. There was something faintly different about the aroma, this time. At least, she could swear . . .

A sound sent her ducking for cover. It was a low whistling. A man —Renna, of course—could be heard tramping some distance away. Soon he came into sight, emerging from one of the countless side tributaries that would feed the river during the rainy season. He, too, carried a camp shovel and a bundle of takawq leaves, making the purpose of his errand obvious.

Why did he go so far from camp, then? Maia wondered. *Is he that shy?*

And why is Baltha spying on him?

Maybe the tall var feared the Outsider would run away, trying to contact the Caria City forces that flew over last night. If so, Baltha must be relieved to see Renna pass by, whistling odd melodies on his way back to camp. *Don't worry, your reward is safe,* Maia thought, preparing to duck out of sight. She had a perfect right to be here, but no good would come of antagonizing the older woman, or being caught spying, herself.

But to Maia's surprise, the blonde did not turn to follow Renna downhill. Rather, as soon as he was gone, Baltha picked up her box and shovel and slipped over the shielding rocks to clamber down the other side, hurrying in the direction from which the man had just come. Possessed by curiosity, Maia crept forward to use the same outcrop that had served as Baltha's eyrie.

The rugged woman strode east about twenty meters to a niche just above the high-water line. There she used the camp spade to dig at a mound of freshly disturbed soil and begin filling the small box. *What in atyp chaos is she doing?* Maia wondered.

"Hey, everybody!" The shout, coming from downstream, caused Maia to leap half out of her skin. "Baltha! Maia! Breakfast!"

It was only Thalla, calling cheerily from the campsite. Another Lysos-cursed morning person. Maia backed out of sight before Baltha could look around. Remembering to give the mother zimmer a wide berth, she started scrambling back down the eroded slope.

The meal consisted of cheese and biscuits, stone-warmed on rocks taken from the fire. By now it was late morning, and since it was probably safe to travel by daylight in these deep canyons, all five travelers were back in the saddle before the sun rose much above the cavern's southeast rim. They made good time, despite having to stop every half hour to warm the horses' feet.

About an hour after noon, Maia realized something ill-smelling and foul-colored had entered the stream. "What is it?" she asked, wrinkling her nose.

Thalla laughed. "She wonders what the bad smell is! How soon we forget pain when we're young!"

Kiel, too, shook her head, grinning. Maia inhaled again, and suddenly recalled. "Lerners! Of course. They dump their slag into a side canyon, and we must be passing—"

"Just downstream. Helps navigation, don't it? See, we're doin' all right without your fancy stars to guide us."

Maia felt overwhelming resurgent resentment toward her former employers. "Damn them!" She swore. "Lysos curse the Lerners! I hope their whole place burns down!"

Renna, who had been riding to her right, frowned at her outburst. "Maia, listen to yourself. You can't mean—"

"I don't care!" She shook her head, afroth with pent-up anger. "Calma Lerner handed me over to Tizbe's gang like I was a slab of pig iron on sale. I hope she rots!"

Thalla and Kiel looked at each other uncomfortably. Maia felt a delicious, if vile, thrill at having shocked them. Renna pressed his lips and kept silent. But Baltha responded more openly, reigning up and laughing sardonically. "From your mouth to Stratos Mother's ear, virgie!" She reached into one of her saddlebags and drew forth a slender, leather-bound tube, her telescope. "Here you go."

Puzzled, Maia overcame sudden reluctance in reaching for the instrument. She lifted it to peer where Baltha pointed. "Go on, up at that slope, yonder to the west an' a bit north. Along the ridgeline. That's right. See it?"

While she learned to compensate for the horse's gentle breathing, the telescope showed little but jumbled images, shifting blurs. Finally, Maia caught a flash of color and steadied on a jittering swatch of bright fabric, snapping in the wind, yanking at a tall, swaying pole. She scanned and other flags came into view on each side.

"Prayer banners," she identified at last. On most of Stratos they were used for holidays and ceremonies, but in Perkinite areas, she knew, they were also flown to signify new births—

—and deaths.

"There's yer Calma Lerner up there, virgie. Rotting, just like you asked. Along with half her sisters. Gonna be short on steel in the valley, next year or two, I figure."

Maia swallowed. "But . . . how?" She turned to Kiel and Thalla, who looked down at their traces. "What happened?" she demanded.

Thalla shrugged. "Just a flu bug, Maia. Was a rash of sneezing in town, a week or two before, no big deal. When it reached the hold, one of the var workers got laid up a few days, but . . ."

"But then, a whole bunch of Lerners went and popped off. Just like that!" Baltha exclaimed, snapping her fingers with relish.

Maia felt dreadful—a hollowness in her belly and thickness in her throat—even as she fought to show no reaction at all. She knew her expression must seem stony, cold. Out of the corner of her eye, she saw Renna briefly shiver.

I can't blame him. I'm terrible.

She recalled how, as a child, she used to be frightened by macabre stories the younger Lamai mothers loved telling summer brats on warm evenings, up on the parapets. Often, the moral of the gruesome tales seemed to be "Careful what you wish for. Sometime you might get it." Rationally, Maia knew her outburst of anger had not caused death to strike the metallurgist clan. Yet, it was dismaying, the vengeful streak she'd shown. Moments ago, if she could have done anything to cast misfortune on her enemies, she would have shown no pity. Was that morally the same as if she'd killed the Lerners herself?

It's not unheard-of for sickness to wipe out half a clan, she thought, trying to make sense of it all. There was a saying, "When one clone sneezes, her sisters go for handkerchiefs." It drew on a fact of life Leie and Maia had learned well as twins—that susceptibility to illness was often in the genes. In this case, it hadn't helped that Lerner Hold was far from what medical care existed in Long Valley. With all of them presumably laid up at the same time, who would care for the Lerners? Just var employees, who weren't brimming with affection for their contract-holders.

What a way to go . . . all at once, broken by the thing you're most proud of, your uniformity.

The group resumed riding silently, immersed in their own thoughts. A while later, when Maia turned to Renna in hope of distraction, the man from space just stared ahead as his mount slogged along, his eyebrows furrowed in what seemed a solid line of dark contemplation.

They slipped out of the maze of canyons after nightfall, climbing a narrow trail south and west of the dark, silent Lerner furnaces. Despite the lower temperatures out on the plain, emerging into the open came as a relief. Starlight spread across the prairie sky, and one of the smaller moons, good-luck Iris, shone cheerily, lifting their spirits.

Thalla and Kiel jumped from their mounts on spotting a large patch of glory frost, protected by the northern shadow of a boulder. They rolled in the stuff, pushing it in each other's faces, laughing. When they remounted, Maia saw a light in their eyes, and wasn't sure she liked it. She approved even less when each of them started jockeying to ride near Renna, occasionally brushing his knee, engaging him in conversation and making interested sounds at whatever he said in reply.

Alone with her thoughts, Maia did not even look up to measure the constellations' progress. She had the impression it would be many days yet before they would catch sight of the coastal range and begin seeking a pass to the sea. Assuming, of course, they weren't spotted by Perkinites along the way.

And then? Even if we make it to Grange Head? Then what?

Freedom had its own penalties. In prison, Maia had known what to expect from one day to the next. Going back to being a poor young var, searching for a niche in an unwelcoming world, was more frightening than jail in some ways. Maia was only now coming to realize how she had been crippled by being a twin. Rather than the advantage she had imagined it to be, that accident of biology had let her live in fantasies, assuming there would always be someone to put her back against. Other summer girls left home knowing the truth, that no plan, no friendship, no talent, would ever by itself make your dreams come true. For the rest, you needed luck.

After having ridden most of the day and half the night, they made camp once more in the shelter of a gully. Kiel managed to start a fire with sticks gathered near the bone-dry watercourse. Except for cups of hot tea, they ate supper cold from the dwindling larder in their saddlebags.

As the others made ready for bed, Renna gathered several small items from his blue pouch. One was a slender brush of a kind Maia had never seen before. He also picked up a camp spade, a canteen, and takawq leaves before turning to leave. Baltha seemed uninterested, and Maia wondered, was it because there was no place he could escape to in this vast plain? Or had Baltha already gotten what she wanted from him? Maia had intended to pull Renna aside and tell him about the southerner's strange actions, the morning before, but it had slipped her mind. Now, her feelings toward him were ambivalent again, especially with Thalla and Kiel still acting decidedly wintry.

"Don't get lost out there!" Thalla called to Renna. "Want me to come along and hold your hand?"

"That may not be what needs holding," Kiel commented, and the other vars laughed. All except Maia. She was bothered by Renna's reaction to the kidding. He blushed, and was obviously embarrassed. He also seemed to enjoy the attention.

"Here," Kiel said, tossing her penlight. "Don't confuse it with anything else!"

Maia winced at the crude humor, but the others thought it terribly funny. Renna peered at the cylindrical wooden case with the switch and lens at one end. He shook his head. "I don't think I'll have any trouble telling the difference." The three older women laughed again.

Doesn't he realize he's encouraging them? Maia thought irritably.

With no aurorae or other summer cues to launch male rut, none of this was likely to go anywhere, and right now the mood was light. But if he feigned interest just to tease the women, it could lead to trouble.

As Renna passed by her, carrying the camp shovel awkwardly in front of him, Maia blinked in surprise and fought not to stare. For the briefest instant, until he vanished from the light, she thought she'd caught sight of a distension, a bulge which, thank Lysos, none of the others appeared to have noticed!

The fire faded and the big moon, Durga, rose. Thalla snored beside Kiel, and Baltha stretched out next to the horses. Maia was drifting off with her eyes closed, envisioning the tall spires of Port Sanger above the glassy waters of the bay, when a thump yanked her awake again. She looked left, where a blocky object had fallen onto Renna's blanket. The man sat down next to it and began pulling off his shoes. "Found something interesting out there," he whispered.

She raised herself to one arm, touching the crumbled block. "What is it?"

"Oh, just a brick. I found a wall . . . and old basement. Not the first I've seen. We've been passing them all day."

Maia watched as he pulled off his shirt. Unshaven and unwashed for several days, he exuded maleness like nothing she had seen or smelled since those sailors aboard the Wotan, and that, after all, had been at sea. Were a man to show up at any civilized town in such condition, he would be arrested for causing a public nuisance. That would go doubly in summer, and fourfold in high winter! Being an alien, perhaps Renna didn't know the rules of modesty boys were taught at an early age, rules that held especially when glory had fallen. Attractiveness, at the wrong times, can be a kind of annoyance.

"I never saw any walls," she answered absently. "You mean people lived near here?"

"Mm. From the weathering, I'd say about five hundred years ago."

Maia gaped. "But I thought—"

"You thought this valley was settled for only a century or so, I know. And the planet just a few hundred years before that." Renna lay back against the saddle he was using for a pillow, and sighed. Apparently untroubled by the cold, he picked up the decomposing brick and turned it over. The muscles of his arms and chest knotted and shifted. Now that she was used to it, his male aroma did not seem as pungent as that of the Wotan sailors. Or was winter affecting her, as well?

"Um," she said, trying to keep up her end of the conversation. "You mean I'm wrong about that?"

He smiled with an affectionate light in his eyes, and Maia felt a mild thrill. "Not your fault. The savants purposely muddy the histories made available outside Caria City. Not by lying, exactly, but giving wrong impressions, and implying that precise dates don't matter.

"It's true that Long Valley was pioneered a century ago, by fore-mothers of the Perkinite clans living here today. Almost no one had lived here for a long time, but several hundred years before that, this plain used to support a large population. I figure waves of settlement and recession must have crossed this area at least five or six times . . ."

Maia waved a hand in front of her face. "Wait. Wait a minute!" Her voice rose above a whisper, and she paused to bring it down again. "What're you saying? That humans have been on Stratos for . . . a thousand years?"

Renna still smiled, but his brow furrowed as it did whenever he had something serious to say. "Maia, from what I've been able to determine by talking to your savants, Lysos and her collaborators planted hominid life on this world more than *three* thousand years ago. That's compatible with their date of departure from Florentina, though much would depend on the mode of transport they used."

Maia could only blink, as if the man had come right out and told her that womankind was descended from rock-salamanders.

"They intended their design to last," he went on, looking at the sky. "And I've got to hand it to them. They did one hell of an impressive job." With that, Renna put aside the ancient brick and opened his blanket to slip inside. "Goodsleep, Maia."

She answered, "Goodsleep," automatically, and lay back with her eyes closed, but it took a while for her thoughts to settle down. When at last she did drift off, Maia dreamed of puzzle shapes, carved in ancient stone. Blocks and elongated incised forms that shifted and moved over each other like twined snakes coiling across a wall of mysteries.

Maia had wondered if the escape would change rhythm, now that they were in the open. Would the group hole up by day, keeping out of sight until nightfall? After hectic, almost-continuous flight, she wouldn't mind the rest.

That, apparently, was not the plan. The sun was still low when Baltha shook her awake. "Come on, virgie. Get your tea and biscuits. We're off in a sneeze and a shake."

Thalla was already tending the rekindled fire while Kiel prepared the mounts. Standing and rubbing her eyes, Maia searched for Renna, finding him at last downstream, sitting in a semicircle of objects. When Maia drew near, she recognized the brick from last night, and several bent aluminum fixtures—a hinge and what must have been a large screw —plus several more lumps impossible to identify. The man had the

Game of Life set on his lap. After examining one of his samples for a while, he would use a stylus to write an array of dots on the broad tablet, then press a button to make the pattern vanish. Into memory, she presumed.

"Hi!" he greeted cheerfully as she walked up, carrying two cups of tea. "One of those for me?"

"Yeah. Here. What're you doing?"

Renna shrugged. "My job. Found a way to use this game set as a kind of notepad, to store observations. Awkward, but anything's better than nothing at all."

"Your job," she mused. "I never got to ask. What *is* your job?"

"I'm called a peripatetic, Maia. That means I go from one hominid world to another, negotiating the Great Compact. It sounds grand. But really, that's just to keep me busy. My real job is . . . well, to keep moving and stay alive."

Maia thought she understood a little of what he had said. "Sounds a lot like my job. Moving. Staying alive."

The man who had been her fellow prisoner laughed appreciatively. "When you put it that way, I guess it's the same for everybody. The only game in town."

Maia recalled the night before, the way shifting winds would bring his aroma as she slept fitfully, waking once to find that she was using his chest as a pillow, and he asleep with one arm over her shoulders. This morning, he seemed a different person. Somehow he had found a way to clean up. His stubble had been scraped away in places, transforming it into the beginnings of a neat beard. Right now she could smell herself more than him.

Moving to place herself downwind, she asked, "Then you aren't here to invade us?"

She had meant it as a joke, to make fun of the rumors spread by fearmongers ever since his ship appeared in the sky, one long year ago. But Renna smiled thinly, answering, "In a manner of speaking, that's exactly what I'm here for . . . to prepare you for an invasion."

Maia swallowed. It wasn't the answer she'd expected. "But you—"

She didn't finish. Thalla called, leading a pair of horses, "Off your bottoms, you two! Daylight riding's hard and fast, so let's get at it!"

"Yes, ma'am!" Renna replied with a friendly, only-slightly-mocking salute. He left his archaeological samples where they lay and stood up, folding the game board. Maia hurried to tie her bedroll to her saddlebag, and glanced back to see Renna bending over to check the cinch buckle of his mount. *I wonder what he meant by that remark. Could the Enemy be coming back? Did he come across the stars to warn us?*

While Maia was looking at the man, Kiel crossed between them and

smoothly, blithely, reached out to *pinch* him as she passed by! "Hey!"
Renna shouted, straightening and rubbing his bottom, but clearly more
surprised than offended. Indeed, his rueful smile betrayed a hint of enjoyment, causing Kiel to chuckle.

Lysos, what a shameless tease, Maia grumbled to herself, irritation
pushing aside her earlier train of thought. Miffed without quite knowing
why, she ignored the man's glances after that and rode ahead with Baltha
for most of that afternoon. Her annoyance only grew as Renna took small
detours several times with Kiel and Thalla, showing them ruins he spotted and explaining which structure might have been a house and which a
craftworks. The two women were embarrassingly effusive in their show of
interest.

Baltha snorted. "Silly rads," she muttered. "Making a fuss like that,
trying to talk to a man, even when it won't get 'em anywhere. As if those
two could handle a sparking if they got one now."

"You don't think they're trying to—"

"Naw. Just flirting, prob'ly. Pretty damn pointless. You know the
saying—

> *"Niche and a House, first of all, matter,*
> *Then sibs and allies, who speak the same patter,*
> *Only then, last of all, a man to flatter.*

"Still makes plenty sense to me," she finished.

"Mm," Maia answered noncommittally. "What's a . . . rad?"

Baltha glanced at her, sidelong. "Pretty innocent, ain't you, virgie?
Do you know anything at all?"

Maia felt her face flush. *I know what you've got hidden in your
saddlebag,* she thought of saying, but refrained.

"Rad stands for 'radical'—which means a bunch of overeducated
young city varlings with dimwitted ideas about changing the world.
Think they're all smarter than Lysos. Idiots."

Maia recalled now, listening to the tinny radio in the cottage at
Lerner Hold. The clandestine station used the word to represent women
calling for a rethinking of Stratoin society, from the ground up. In many
ways, rads were polar opposites to Perkinites, pushing for empowerment
of the var underclass through restructuring all of the rules, political and
biological.

"You're talking about my friends," Maia told Baltha, in what she
hoped was a severe tone.

Baltha returned a sarcastic moue. "Am I? Now there's a thought.
Yer *friends.* Thanks for setting me straight." She laughed, making Maia
feel foolish without knowing why. She turned straight ahead, ignoring the
other woman, and for several minutes they rode in silence. Eventually,

though, curiosity overcame her resentment. Maia turned and spoke a question in carefully neutral tones. "So, from what you say, I figure you don't want to change the world?"

"Not a whole lot. Just shake it up a little. Knock down some deadwood to make room in the forest, so t'speak. Let in enough light for a new tree or two."

"With you being a founding root, I suppose."

"Why not? Don't I look like a foundin' mother to you? Can't you jus' picture this mug on a big painting, hangin' over th' fireplace of some fancy hall, someday?" She held her head high, chin outthrust.

Trouble was, Maia *could* picture it. The founding mothers of a lot of clans must have been just as piratically tough and ruthless as this rugged var. "Fine. Let's say you knock down a clearing and set your own seed there. Say your family tree grows into a giant in the forest, with hundreds of clone twigs spreading in all directions. What'll be your clan policy toward some *new* sapling, that tries to set root nearby someday?"

"Policy? That'll be simple." Baltha laughed. "Spread our branches an' cut off th' light!"

"Don't others also deserve a place in the sun?"

Baltha squinted at Maia, as if amazed by such naïveté. "Let 'em fight for it, like I'm fight'n right now. It's the only fair way. Lysos was wise." The last was intoned solemnly, and Baltha drew the circle sign over her breast. Maia recognized a look of true religion in the other woman's eyes. A version and interpretation that conveniently justified what had already been decided.

Lasting silence settled after that. They rode on and the afternoon waned. Baltha consulted her compass, correcting their southwestward path several times. At intervals, she would rise in the stirrups and play her telescope across the horizon, searching for signs of pursuit, but only twisted shrubs with gnarled limbs broke the monotony, reminding Maia of legendary women, frozen in place after encountering the Medusa-man.

When the party of fugitives stopped, it was only to stretch the kinks out of their legs and to eat standing up. There were no more jokes about Renna's wincing accommodation to his saddle. By now they were all hobbling. Dusk fell and Maia expected a call to set camp, but apparently the plan was to keep riding. *No one tells me anything,* she thought with a sigh. At least Renna looked as tired and ignorant as she felt.

Two hours after nightfall, with tiny, silvery Aglaia just rising in the constellation Ladle, Baltha called a sudden halt, motioning for silence. She peered ahead into the darkness, then cupped her hands around her mouth and trilled a soft birdcall.

Seconds passed.

A reply hooted from the gloom, then a pause, and another hoot. A spark flashed, followed by a lantern's gleam, barely revealing a bulky form, like a rounded hillock, several hundred meters ahead. As they rode forward, shadows coalesced and separated. The object appeared to be squared off at one end, bulbous at the other. Hissing softly, it stood where a pair of straight lines crossed from the far left horizon on an arrow-straight journey to the right. The blurry form resolved, and Maia abruptly recognized a small maintenance engine for the solar railway, sitting on a spur track, surrounded by tethered horses and murmuring women.

There were cries of joyful reunion as Baltha galloped to greet her friends. Thalla and Kiel embraced Kau. Renna dismounted and held Maia's gelding while she descended, heavy with fatigue. Leading their tired beasts around the dark engine they handed the reins to a stocky woman wearing Musseli Clan livery. Another Musseli gave Renna a folded bundle that proved to be a uniform of one of the male rail-runner guilds.

So, the Musseli weren't in cahoots with the Perkinite farmer clans. It figured, given their close relationships with guildsmen, some of whom were their own brothers and sons. *Too bad I never got a chance to see what life is like in a clan like that. It must be curious, knowing some men so well.*

Apparently, the cabal were going to try getting Renna out the fast way, in one quick dash by rail. Without cars to weigh it down, the engine might reach Grange Head by midday tomorrow—assuming no roadblocks or search parties cut their path. Thalla, Kiel, and the others might be collecting their reward money by dinnertime. Maia figured they'd even provide a good meal and night's lodging to their virgin mascot, before sending her on her way.

Renna grinned happily, and gave Maia's shoulder a squeeze, but inwardly she felt herself already putting distance between them, protecting herself from another inevitable, painful goodbye.

Peripatetic's Log:

Stratos Mission:

Arrival + 40.177 Ms

C aria, the capital, surrounds and adorns a plateau overlooking where three rivers join the sea. Inhabitants call her "City of Gold," for the yellow roof tiles of clanholds covering the famed thirteen hills. But I have seen from high orbit a sight more worthy of the name. At dawn, Caria's walls of crystalline stone catch inclined sunlight, reemitting into space an off-spectrum luminance portrayed on Cy's panels as an amber halo. It's a marvel, even to one who has seen float-whales graze on clouds of frothy creill, above and between the metrotowers of Zaminin.

Often, over the last year, I have wished for someone to share such visions with.

Travelers enter Caria through a broad, granite portal, topped by a stately frieze—Athena Polias, ancient protectress of urban dwellers, bearing the sage visage of this colony's chief founder. Alas, the sculptor failed to catch that sardonic smile I've come to know from studying shipboard files on Lysos, when she was a mere philosoph-professor on Florentina, speaking abstractly about things she would later put into practice.

As our procession arrived from the spaceport, all seemed peaceful and orderly, yet I felt sure those majestic city walls weren't built just for decoration. They quite effectively demark outside from inside. They defend.

Traffic flowed beneath Athena's outstretched caduceus—its twined snakes representing coiled DNA. To avoid attracting notice, our cavalry escort peeled off at that point while my guides and I went on by car. My landing isn't secret, but has been downplayed. As on most deliberately pastoral worlds, competing news media are banned as unwholesome. The council's carefully censored broadcasts somehow portray renewed contact with the Phylum as a minor event, yet one also tinged with dire threat.

Radio eavesdropping could never tell me what the average woman-on-the-street thinks. I wonder if I'll get a chance to find out.

Envisioning life on a planet of clones, I couldn't help picturing phalanx after phalanx of uniform faces . . . swarms of identical, blank-eyed bipeds moving in silent, coordinated lockstep. A caricature of humans-as-ants, or humans-as-bees.

I should have known better. Bustling crowds thronged the portals, sidewalks, and bridges of Caria, arguing, gawking, haggling, and laughing as on any hominid world. Only now and then did I make out an evident pair, or trio, or quintet of clones, and even within such groups the sisters varied by age and dress. Statistically, most of the women I glimpsed must have been members of some parthenogenetic clan. Still, people are not bees, and no human city will ever be a hive. My blurred first impression showed a jumble of types, tall and short, broad and thin, all colors . . . hardly a stereotype of homogeneity.

Except for the near absence of males, that is. I saw some young boys playing, and a scattering of old fellows wearing the green armbands of "retirees." But, it being summer, mature men were scarcer than albinos at high noon, and twice as conspicuous. When I caught sight of one, he seemed out of place, self-conscious of his height, stepping aside to make way for surging clusters of bustling womankind. I sensed that, like me, he was here as a guest, and knew it.

This city was not built by, or for, our kind.

The classical lines of Caria's public buildings hearken to ancient Earth, with broad stairways and sculpted fountains where travelers refresh themselves and water their beasts. The clear preference for foot and hoof over wheeled traffic reminds me of civic planning on Dido, where motorcars and lorries are funneled to their destinations out of sight, leaving the main avenues to more placid rhythms. Following one hidden guideway, our handmade auto swept by the squat apartment blocks and bustling markets of a crowded quarter Iolanthe called "Vartown," then cruised upslope behind more elegant, castlelike structures with gardens and polished turrets, each flying the heraldic banner of some noble lineage.

My escorts paused briefly at the inner palisade which guards the acropolis. There, I got my first close look at lugars, white-furred creatures descended from Vegan Ur-Apes, hauling stone blocks under the guidance of a patient woman handler. Lysos supposedly designed lugars to overcome one argument for having sons—the occasional need for raw physical strength. Another solution, robots, would have required a perpetual industrial base, dangerous to the founders' program. So, typically, they came up with something self-sustaining, instead.

Watching the lugars heft huge slabs, I couldn't help feeling puny in comparison—which may have been another part of the plan.

I am not here to judge Stratoins for choosing a pastoral solution to the human equation. All paths have their costs. My order requires that a peripatetic appreciate all he or she sees, on any Phylum world. "Appreciate" in the formal sense of the word. The rules don't say I must approve.

Caria's builders used the central plateau's natural contours to lay out temples and theaters, courts, schools, and athletic arenas—all described in proud detail by my ardent guides. Wooded lanes accompanied the central boulevard past imposing compounds—the Equilibrium Authority, and the stately University—until at last we drew near a pair of marble citadels with high, columned porticos. The twin hearts of Caria. The Great Library on the left, and to the right, the main Temple dedicated to Stratos Mother.

. . . And Lysos is her prophet . . .

The drive had achieved its clear purpose. Their capital is a showpiece worthy of any world. I was impressed, and must be very sure to show it.

1 5

The Musseli engineer packed her passengers away from the controls, near the body-warm stacks of power cells that made the locomotive go. Maia's nose twitched at a familiar scent of coal dust, rising from the reserve fuel bin, yet she felt too excited to let it perturb her. Freedom was a stronger redolence, affecting her like intoxication. Her heart sped as she leaned past the battery casing, prying open a narrow, dusty window to let rushing air play across her face.

The prairie raced by, illuminated by pearly, suffused light from newly risen Durga. There were gullies and ravines, fenceposts and ragged battalions of haystacks, and occasional pocket forests where the porous terrain stored enough rainwater to sustain native trees. Maia had come to hate these high plains, yet now, with escape at last credible, the land seemed to whisper its own side of the story, reaching out to persuade her with stark beauty.

Summer storms have their way with me. Wind and blazing sun desiccate my sodden soil. In winter, ice splits the scattered pebbles down to dust. The poor loam leaks and seeps. I bleed.

And what the wind and sun and ice leave, humans break with steel plows, or bake into bricks, or turn into golden grain which they ship across the sea.

Where are my prancing lingaroos? The grazing pantotheres, or nimble coil-boks, who used to roam my plain in numbers vast? They could not compete with cattle and mice. Or, if they could, humans intervened, im-

proving strains they chose to use. New hooves mark my trails, while the old vanish into zoos.

No matter. Let invaders displace native creatures, who displaced others before them. Let my soil turn to rock, to sand, to soil once again. What difference do changes make, sifted by the sieve of time?

I wait, I abide, with the patience of stone.

Renna, and then Kiel, urged Maia to stretch out where a half-dozen other women lay together like swaddled cordwood, all facing the same way for lack of room to turn. Not that discomfort kept any of them awake. In Thalla's words, these weren't pampered clonelings, to be irked by a mattress-covered pea. Their synchronized *r-r-ronn* of breathing soon drowned the gentle whine of the electric motors.

"No, thanks," Maia told her friends. "I couldn't sleep. Not now. Not yet."

Kiel only nodded, settling into a niche near the brake box to doze sitting up. Renna, too, reached his limit. After badgering the poor, confused engineer with questions for just half an hour, he uncharacteristically let that suffice, and collapsed onto the blankets that had been thrown for his benefit over the widest space—a deck plate covering the thrumming engine gearbox. Its lullaby soon had him snoring with the best of them.

Maia unbuckled her sextant and sighted a few familiar stars. Although fatigue and the car's vibration made it a rough fix, she was able to verify they were heading in the right direction. That didn't entirely preclude the possibility of treachery—*Am I growing cynical with age?* she pondered dryly—but it felt reassuring to know that each passing second brought them closer to the sea. Maia quashed her misgivings. *Kiel and the others know more than I do, and they seem confident enough.*

Maia wasn't the only insomniac keeping the engineer silent company. Baltha stood watch by the portside window, caressing her crowbar like a short-style trepp bill, as if eager to have just one whack at an enemy before making good their escape. Once, the rugged woman exchanged a long, enigmatic look with Maia. For the most part, each kept territorially to her own pane of cool glass, Baltha peering ahead and sniffing for danger, while Maia pretended to do her part, keeping lookout on the starboard side.

Not that bare eyes would do much good in the dark. *At this speed, we'd barely see a thing before we hit it.*

Moon-glint reflections off the arrow-straight rails diffracted hypnotically past her heavy, drooping eyelids. Maia let them close—*just for a minute or two.* There was no arresting of images, however. She continued picturing the locomotive, rushing across a chimeric rendition of the steppe, at first just like the moonlit plain outside, then increasingly the landscape of a dream. The gentle, frozen, prairie undulations began to move, to roll like ocean waves lapping either side of the steel-steady rails.

Fey certainty struck Maia. Something lay ahead, just out of sight. Premonition manifested as a vivid, prescient image, of this hurtling engine bound unalterably toward collision with a towering pile of rocks, recently lain across the tracks by a grinning Tizbe Beller.

"Run if you like," her former tormentor crooned menacingly, like a storybook witch. *"Did you honestly think you could escape the power of great clans, if they really want to stop you?"*

Maia moaned, unable to move or waken. The phantom barricade loomed, graphic and frightening. Then, moments before impact, the stones making up the wall transformed. In a stretched instant, they metamorphosed into glistening *eggs*, which cracked open, releasing giant, pale birds. The birds spread vast wings and bound free of their dissolving shards, exhaling fire, sailing unconstrained to join their brethren, the glittering stars.

In her dream, Maia felt no relief to have them go. Rather, waves of desolate loneliness hit her, like a pang.

How come? she wondered. A reproving plaint from childhood. *How come they get to fly . . . while I must stay behind?*

Morning broke while Maia slept, curled in a blanket that steamed when struck by the newly risen sun. Renna gently shook her shoulder, and put a hot cup of tcha between her hands. Squinting at his open, unguarded face, Maia smiled gratefully.

"I think we're going to make it!" the man commented with a tense confidence Maia found endearing. She would have been hurt if he said it to humor her. But rather, it felt as if *she* were the adult, charmed and indulgently warmed by his naïve optimism. Maia had no idea how old Renna was, but she doubted the man would ever outgrow his sunny, mad enthusiasm for new things.

Breakfast consisted of millet meal and brown sugar, mixed with hot water from the engine's auxiliary boiler. The fugitive train did not stop, or even slow, while they ate. Grasslands dotted with grazing herds swept by. Now and then, an unknowing cowhand lifted her arm to wave at the passing locomotive.

Between checks on her instruments, the Musseli driver told Maia and the others what she had heard yesterday, before coming to the rendezvous. There had indeed been fighting at the prison-sanctuary, the same night Maia and Renna saw aircraft cross the sky. Planetary Authority agents, using surprise to redress their small numbers, landed on the stony tower, seizing the erstwhile jail. *Too late to do us much good,* Maia thought sardonically. *Except by distracting the Perkies. That could improve our chances a bit.*

The next day, local militias had been called up throughout Long Valley. Matriarchs of the senior farming clans vowed "to defend local sovereignty and our sacred rights against meddling by federal authorities . . ." Accusations flew in both directions while neither side mentioned anything at all about the Visitor from the stars. In practical terms, there could still be plenty of trouble for the fugitive band, and no likelihood of more help from Caria City forces until they reached the sea.

To make matters worse, the population of the valley grew denser as they neared the coastal range. The locomotive streaked past hamlets and sleepy farming towns, then larger commercial centers and clusters of light manufacturing. Several times they had to slow to gingerly maneuver by heavy-laden hopper cars filled with wheat or yellow corn.

More often, the path seemed to open up like magic before them. At towns, they were nearly always waved on by stationmistresses who, Maia realized, must be part of the conspiracy. Bit by bit, the scope of this enterprise seemed to grow.

Are all the railroad clans involved? They're not Perkies, but I'd have thought they'd at best stay neutral. It's got to be pretty damn serious for a hard-nosed bunch like the Musseli to risk customer relations for a cause.

Maia pondered how, once again, she was probably missing the big picture. *I used to think this was all about that drug which makes men summery in winter. But that's just one part of it . . . not as important as Renna, for instance.*

Could it be that he's just one piece, too? Not a pawn like me, but no king, either. I could get killed without anyone ever taking the time to explain why.

Small surprise there. One advantage of a Lamatian education was that she and her sister hadn't been raised to expect fairness from the world. *"Roll with the blow!"* Savant Claire had shouted, hitting Maia over and over with a padded stick during what was supposed to have been varling "combat practice," a torture session that stretched on and on, until Maia finally learned to fall with the impact, not against it.

How I still hate you, Claire, Maia thought, remembering. *But I'm starting to see your point.*

The exodus across the plains had a syncopated cadence—long intervals of boredom punctuated by anxious, heart-stopping minutes passing through each town. Nevertheless, all seemed to be going well until just before noon. Then, at a town called Golden Cob, they were met by an unpleasant sight—a lowered customs gate, barring their path. In lieu of the Musseli station master, a squad of tall redheads waited on the platform, all armed and dressed in militia leathers, comparing the engine's markings with numbers on a clipboard. Maia and the vars ducked out of sight, but despite the engineer's complaints, the guardswomen insisted on inspecting the loco. *En masse,* they grabbed the ladder frames and proceeded to climb aboard from both sides.

There followed a stretched moment as two groups of women stared at each other in jittery silence. One guard spotted Renna, opened her mouth to shout . . . .

A shrill ululation pealed from above. The lead redhead looked up— too late to duck the dull end of Baltha's crowbar, which caught her along the jaw. From the metal roof, where the lanky southern var had lain, Baltha threw herself upon the close-pressed mass of militia.

Instantly, a free-for-all burst in the close cabin confines. Women screamed and charged. There was no room for fancy action with trepp bills, so both sides forsook polished staves for flailing fists and makeshift cudgels.

At first, Maia and Renna stood frozen at the rear. For all her adventures, Maia's first battle rocked her back. Her stomach flipped and she heard her heart pounding over the din. Glancing up, she saw Renna's alien eyes widen impossibly. Sweat prickled and veins stood out. It wasn't *fear* she read, but trouble of another sort.

The melee surged toward them. One redhead slugged Thalla's friend, Kau, knocking the petite var down. When the militiawoman raised her foot to follow through, Renna cried out, "No!" He took a step, fists clenched. Suddenly it was Maia's turn to yell.

"Get back!" she screamed, diving between Renna and the guard, managing to fling them in opposite directions. A fist rebounded off her right temple, setting both ears ringing. Another blow struck between two ribs, and she retaliated, hitting something soft with an elbow. Ignoring lancing pain, thrashing in the tight press of struggling women, Maia succeeded at last in dragging the fallen Kau out of the fray.

"Take care of her," she shouted to Renna. "And don't fight! A man mustn't!"

While he absorbed that, Maia turned and dove back into the brawl. It was a torrid, grunting struggle, devoid of ritual or courtesy or elegance. Fortunately, it was easy to tell friend from foe, even in the stifling dimness. For one thing, the enemy had bathed today, and smelled much better than her comrades. It was a resentful comparison that lent her the strength to wrestle women much larger and stronger than herself.

Terrifying while in doubt, the battle grew exhilarating when she realized her side was winning. Maia helped pin one thrashing redhead so Thalla could truss her with loops of preknotted cord. Getting up, Maia saw Baltha holding two clonelings in necklocks, banging their heads together. No assistance needed there, so she hurried past to help a southern var who was preventing one last militiawoman from diving out the door.

With an opening clear, Kiel leapt like a dark blur from the slowly crawling train, and ran ahead to raise the customs gate just in time. Hands reached down to haul her in as the driver poured on amps.

At the outskirts of town, the victorious refugees slowed down long enough to dump the squad of bruised and bound redheads beside the tracks. Then the Musseli opened her throttle again. The engine whined, accelerating westward at high speed.

Maia and the others were too keyed up to relax, talking loudly and pacing until their hearts began to settle. The sole exception was Renna, whose demeanor remained icy-deliberate while performing first aid on various cuts, bruises, and one broken wrist. He was a soothing presence, so long as there was work to do. When that was done, however, he began shivering and broke into a sweat. Maia watched his fists clench as he walked stiffly to the open door by the engineer and rinsed his head in the rushing breeze.

"What's wrong?" Maia asked, coming alongside, watching his tendons tauten like bowstrings.

"I . . ." He shook his head. "I'd rather not say."

But Maia thought she understood. On other worlds, men used to do most of the fighting. Bloody, terrible fighting, by accounts. For all she knew, it was still like that, out there. During the battle, Maia had briefly read his eyes. Something had been evoked that he did not much like.

"I guess Lysos knew what she was talking about, sometimes," Maia said in a low voice.

Renna shot her a look under furrowed brows. Then, slowly, there spread across his face a smile. An ironic smile that this time conveyed respect, along with affection.

"Yeah," he answered. "I guess maybe now and then she did."

Fortunately, that was the last substantial town before the coastal range. Their engine had to decelerate to climb the steepening grade. But then, so would any pursuit sent after the commotion at Golden Cob. Watching Kiel and Baltha pore over a map, Maia saw they were more worried about what lay ahead. Looking over their shoulders, Maia guessed the Perkinites had one more chance to stop them, near a village named

Overlook, where a narrow defile seemed perfect for a hastily organized roadblock.

Too perfect, she later discovered. An ambush had, indeed, been ordered. Nearby clans dispatched squads in response to warnings from Golden Cob, and began throwing up barricades. Yet, by the time the locomotive reached Overlook, the danger was passed. Local vars had surprised the gathering militia with mob force, driving them away before the train arrived.

The counterstroke turned out not to be as spontaneous as it looked, Maia learned. Several of the mob leaders crammed in among the escapees, joining the final leg of the exodus as soon as the last barriers were cleared away. Maia soon realized they were friends of Thalla and Kiel.

I get it. Kiel and her pals can read a map as well as Perkies can. If one place is perfect for an ambush, it can also be just right for ambushing the ambushers. Maia learned that the newcomers had recently taken jobs in the village, just in case of an eventuality like this.

How could a bunch of vars be so well organized? Such long-range thinking was supposedly limited to clone families, with generations of experience and a view of life that stretched beyond the individual's.

Never mind, she told herself. *What matters is, it worked!*

With shouted cheers, the refugees at last waved goodbye to Long Valley. The locomotive was more crowded than ever during the final stretch over the pass, but no one minded. First sight of the blue ocean triggered an outbreak of singing that lasted all the way down to Grange Head.

Two more of Kiel's friends were waiting in town, so that a fair contingent bid thankful farewell to the engineer, then trooped together from the railyard to the Founders' Gospel Inn, a hostel overlooking the harbor. The new women wore garb of sailing hands—small surprise in a trading port. No doubt most of Kiel's bunch, and Baltha's, had worked their way over on freighters like those moored in the bay.

Maybe someone'll put in a word . . . get me a job on one of the ships.

Thinking seriously about the future wasn't something she had done in a long time. One compensation of helplessness, of living like a leaf, blown by winds far stronger than yourself. Soon, the downside of freedom would present itself—the curse of decision-making.

Kiel installed the elated adventurers on the hotel veranda, arranged for rooms, and set off with Baltha "to do business." Presumably that meant dickering with the local magistrate, and probably making comm calls to officials halfway round the world. The rest of the party was to stick together, watching out for any last-minute move by the Long Valley clans. They weren't out of Perkinite reach, yet. Safety still lay in numbers.

Which suited Maia fine. For the first time, it really seemed likely she wasn't going back to prison. Her worries had started evaporating on first sight of the beautiful sea. Even the drab stucco and brick warehouses of the trading port seemed more gay than the last time she had been here, an innocent fiver, immersed in mourning and despair.

With its view overlooking the harbor, but some distance from dockside fish smells, the hotel was far superior to the cheap transients' lodge where she had lain wracked with fever, months ago. When Maia learned she would have her own small room, with a real mattress, she hurried to look it over, finding herself barely able to conceive of such luxury. You could even walk alongside the bed and spread your arms without touching a wall!

The impression of spaciousness was enhanced by her lack of worldly possessions. *I'd hang something on the clothes-hooks, if I owned anything but what I'm wearing.*

Back on the veranda, her compatriots had settled in with bottles of beer, watching the shadows lengthen. A few had chipped in for a newspaper, a luxury since in most towns the press was run by subscription only, for the richest clans. The rads sourly disparaged the *Grange Head Clipper*, which featured mostly commodities prices, along with bickering among candidates in upcoming elections, to be held in a month, on Farsun Day.

"Perkies runnin' against Ortho-doxies," sniffed Kau. "Some choice! An' look, barely any mention of planetwide issues. Nothin' to tempt a var or man to think about votin'. And not a hint about any missin' Visitor from space!" She and Thalla spoke longingly of the two-page weekly put out by their own organization, back in Ursulaborg. "Now *there's* a newspaper!" Kau commented.

Maia paid scant attention. Freedom was too fresh and pristine to complicate with politics. Everyone knew such matters were worked out long in advance, by ancient mothers living in golden castles, in Caria City. Instead, she scanned the hills rimming the bay. Perched above all other structures, the Orthodox temple of Stratos Mother was a white sanctuary, shimmering in the afternoon sunshine. Maia recalled the refuge with gratitude, and made a note to visit the reverend mother. Partly to pay respects, and partly . . . to ask if any messages had come for her.

There wouldn't be any, of course. Despite all that had taken place, all she had done to insulate her grief, Maia knew what would happen when the priestess shook her head and compassionately spread her hands. Maia would experience all over again her sister's loss, the sense of hopelessness, that yawning pit, threatening to swallow her whole.

That visit could wait another day or two. For now it would do to lean back with the others on the hotel's long porch, have a glass of tepid beer, share a tall tale or two, and keep her mind diverted with simple things.

All I really want from life right now is a hot shower and a soft place to sleep for days.

By consensus and natural gallantry, everyone agreed that Renna should take his turn with the bath first. The man started to protest, then chuckled, and said something mysterious about what one does when in a place called "Rome." Two women accompanied him to stand watch outside the bathroom door, guarding his privacy.

After Renna left, several vars began pounding the table in earnest, shouting gaily for more ale. Except for Thalla, Maia hardly knew any of them. Kiel's friend, Kau, passed the time polishing a wooden truncheon with a barely legal edge and point, wincing on occasion when she gingerly touched Renna's bandage over her right ear. One of Baltha's companions, a woman with a strong South Isles accent, kept pacing, looking toward the mountains and then out to sea again, muttering impatiently.

Maia found herself unable to stop scratching. The mere idea of a bath had infected her mind, causing her to notice itches that, till now, she had pushed to the background.

Fortunately Renna didn't take long, for a man. He emerged wearing a smallish hotel robe, transformed with a trimmed beard, combed hair that curled as it dried in the breeze, and a rosy tone to his fresh-scrubbed skin. He bowed to the approving whistles of the southlanders, and accepted from Kau a stein of the local, watery brew. "It's a wonder what a scrub can do for a boy," he commented. Toweling his hair one-handed, he took a long swallow. "So, who's next? Maia?"

She started to protest. She was lowest in status. But the others agreed by acclamation. "After all, it's been as long for you as it was for him!" Thalla said kindly. "That Perkie jail must've been awful."

"You're sure . . . ?"

"Of course we're sure. Don't worry about th' hot water, sweets. Soon, we'll be able to afford a lakeful. Shower good an' sit in the tub long as you like."

"Yeah, we'll be busy, anyway," Kau added, sitting next to Renna.

"Busy getting drunk as dic-pigs, you mean," Maia jested, and felt warmed when they all laughed in a comradely way. Renna winked. "Go on, Maia. I'll make sure everyone behaves."

That brought more hooting. Maia gave in with a smile of gratitude. Before hurrying toward the luring smell of steam and soap, she unstrapped the little sextant from her wrist and handed it to Renna

"Maybe you can stop the sun filter from wobbling. Give you something to do with your hands." Thalla sputtered in her beer and several others guffawed. "Shouldn't be too hard for a hotshot star traveler to do," Maia finished.

"You kidding?" he protested. "I barely make it to the can and back without a computer!"

"Would he be here with us, if he didn't have a knack for getting lost?" Thalla agreed, shouting after Maia, then added, louder still, "Innkeeper! More ale!"

The bathroom lay up a double flight of plank stairs. Closing the door behind her, Maia could still hear the women below, joking and laughing, and Renna's deeper voice joining in occasionally. Mostly, his contributions sounded like questions, though Maia could not make out words. Often, his queries brought on gales of laughter, which he seemed to take in good grace.

It felt strange undressing in the richly tiled bathroom, equipped with amenities she had to remind herself how to use. Maia kicked her soiled garments into a corner and went first to the shower, adjusting the knobs until hot water from the rooftop heater flowed steadily. *They probably use good ol' Port Sanger coal,* she thought incongruously. Stepping under the stream, she proceeded to lather her body. The soap was harsh and doubtless homemade, but less expensive than importing the real thing from some specialist clan, far away. Nevertheless, it felt luxurious. Turning off the water between rinsings, Maia proceeded to scrape off layer after layer of grime, until her skin squeaked when rubbed. Then she started on her hair, scrubbing her scalp and working out tangles.

Don't know why I bother, she wondered. *It's in such a state, I'll probably have to hack it all off anyway.*

Rinsing carefully one last time, Maia turned off the tap and tiptoed over to the broad wooden tub, by a small window overlooking the wharfs of Grange Head. She flipped back the hinged cover, exposing the steaming surface. To her relief, the water was pristine. There were stories about male sailors who forgot—or had never been taught—the proper procedure, and who actually used the *bath* for cleaning themselves, leaving the tub coated with soap and scum for the next person. With men, one just never knew what to expect, and as an alien, Renna might have been doubly confused.

Then again, perhaps there was only one civilized way. However barbaric their unmodified sexual patterns, cultured people on other worlds probably bathed the same way as on Stratos.

Alas, there would be no time to ask about that, or countless other quandaries, before escorted aircraft came from the west to whisk Renna away. At odd moments during their escape, she had pictured going with him all the way to Caria and seeing the city's wonders. But in more lucid reflection Maia knew—she might as well ask to be taken along when he departed for the stars.

I wonder if he'll remember me when he's hobnobbing with savants and council members . . . or flying between planets long after I'm food for worms. It was a tough, wry contemplation, appropriate for the type of hard, worldly person she decided to become—ready for anything, shocked by nothing. And, especially, vulnerable to nobody.

The shower had been tepid, but the bath was so hot that it stung her innumerable cuts and scratches. Maia slipped lower by stages, until water sloshed over the sides into a waiting drain.

Heaven! Heat seemed to melt every part that was tense or callused, uncoiling muscles that had been taut without her noting. Troubles and worries she still had, but they went limp for the time being, along with her body. The sensuousness of lying completely motionless matched any active pleasure she knew.

Languidly, Maia lifted one arm to look at it from all sides, let it drop, and did the same thing with the other, regarding where recent months had left their marks. Next she examined each leg. A small scar on this shin, a healing scratch on that ankle, a couple of tender spots saddle-rubbed during that long ride on horseback . . . and one small battle wound that she made a mental note to keep clean over the days ahead, lest it get infected. Even here, in "civilization," medical care was catch-as-catch-can, and she hardly had the resources to pay.

There was a knock, and the door started swinging. Thalla stuck her head in. "Everythin' all right?" the stocky woman asked.

"Oh! Fine, great . . . I'll get out." With a sigh, Maia reached for the rim.

"Don't be silly. You just got in!" Thalla chided. "I just heard the innkeeper's got a washload goin'. We're tossing in our grungies. Want yours done, too?" She nodded toward the filthy garments in the corner.

Maia winced at the thought of ever wearing them again, but they were all she had. "Yeah, please. Kind of you."

Thalla swept up the clothes. "Don't mention it. Enjoy your bath. An' have all the luck in the world."

She closed the door and Maia sank back into the tub, relishing how the heat swarmed in again. It had been disappointing, thinking it was over so soon. Now she felt happier than if she had been left undisturbed! Not that everything melted in the hot water. The sound of the locomotive, its electric thrum along the rails, was still in her head. Nor, try as she might, could Maia push aside all her worries.

Staying ashore was out of the question. Tizbe and the Joplands would surely catch up with her. The sea was her only option. With what Maia had learned about navigation—and the Game of Life—perhaps some captain could be persuaded to give her a trial billet on crew, not just as passenger, second class. Ideally a slot to last through late spring, when rut season forced women ashore. By that time, she ought to have saved a credit or two.

In all justice, she should get a small portion of the reward Kiel and Baltha were collecting. Maia trusted Renna to stick up for her, though from the size of the getaway cabal, her share still wasn't likely to be large.

There was also the matter of her appointment with the PES investigator, now long overdue because of circumstances beyond her control. Was it too late to make good her promise? Would testimony before a local magistrate suffice? Part of her determination was personal. *Tizbe Beller locked me up to keep me from talking. So that's exactly what I'll do!* Of all the sensations warming her—freedom, cleanliness, the physical luxury of the bath—she dwelled for a few minutes on revenge. *The Bellers and Joplands will be sorry they ever made me their enemy,* she vowed grandly.

It wasn't a sound that tickled Maia's attention. Rather, she grew gradually, uncomfortably aware of a certain *lack* of sound. Frowning, it began to dawn on her that it had been a while since she'd heard the murmur of conversation on the porch below. Or the pacing of the var on watch, or the clinking of bottles, or Renna's persistent, naïve questions.

Suddenly, the bath no longer felt luxurious, but confining. *I'm probably turning into a prune, anyway,* she thought. Her relaxed muscles had to be coaxed into lifting her weight out of the tub. While toweling herself, Maia could not suppress a rising sense of foreboding. Something was wrong.

Maia lowered the cover of the bathtub and climbed on top to reach the solitary window, wiping the foggy pane and pressing close to peer down, onto the veranda. Rows of empty bottles lay along the balcony railing, but where the women had been sitting, no one remained in sight.

Probably Kiel and Baltha came back with news, she thought. But nobody was visible near the main entrance, either. *Did they go in to eat?* she wondered.

Maia shoved upward against the window until it slid along wooden tracks, sash weights rattling on both sides. Fresh, chill air streamed in, sowing goose bumps as moisture evaporated from her skin. She stuck her head out and called, "Hey! Where is everybody?"

A few locals were in view near a warehouse, loading a horse-drawn wagon. When she stretched a little farther and turned left, she saw a crowd down at the embankment, far below, moving toward one of the piers. Maia's heart surged when she recognized Thalla's stocky form and Baltha's shock of blonde hair.

No. They wouldn't do that to me!

But there was Renna. Taller than Baltha, walking awkwardly with his arms around two of the women, rocking from side to side.

"Lysos!" Maia cried, hopping back onto the tiles. Her clothes were gone—no doubt to help strand her here. With a curse, she now recalled Thalla's parting words, which *had* seemed odd for someone you expected to see again!

Clutching a towel, Maia dashed from the room and swept downstairs, only to be blocked momentarily by the innkeeper, holding a cloth bag and a paper envelope.

"Oh, it's you, miss. Your friends told me to give you—"

Her words cut off as Maia pushed her aside and streaked out the front door, leaping down the steps onto the gravel road. Shopkeepers stared and a trio of three-year-old clones giggled, but Maia dug in, kicking pebbles as she ran, ignoring the bite of cold sea air. Turning fast at the embankment, she skidded and sprawled hard onto hands and knees, but was up again in an instant, not bothering to check for bleeding or to pick up the spilled towel. Maia ran naked past loading cranes and moored ships, to amazed looks from sailors and townswomen alike.

Two longboats had already set out from the pier, oarswomen pulling with steady, even strokes. When Maia reached the end of the wharf, she screamed at Kiel, who sat near the helmsman in the second boat.

"Liar! Damn you! You can't just—" Stamping, she sought the words to express her fury. Kiel's jaw dropped in surprise, while several of the vars Maia had fought next to now laughed at the sight of her standing there, unclothed and quaking with anger.

The dark woman cupped her hands and called back. "We can't take you along, Maia. You're too young and it's dangerous! The letter explains—"

"Julp on your damn letter!" Maia screamed in anger and disappointment. "What does *Renna* have to say about . . ."

Then she saw what she had not noticed before. The man from space had a glazed, unhappy look on his face, and was not focusing on anything or anybody in particular. "You're kidnapping him!" she cried, hoarsely.

"No, Maia. It's not what you—"

Kiel's voice cut off as Maia dove headfirst into the frigid water and came up sputtering. She inhaled a painful, salty rasp, then set out after the boat, swimming with all her might.

C loning, as an alternate mode of reproduction, was used long before the emigration from Florentina World. An egg cell, carefully prepared with a donor's genetic material, is implanted within a chemically stimulated volunteer, or the artificial womb recently perfected on New Terra. Either way, the delicate, expensive process is generally reserved for a world's most creative, or revered, or wealthy individuals, depending on local custom. I know of no planet where clones make up a significant fraction of the population . . . except Stratos.

Here, they comprise over eighty percent! On Stratos, parthenogenetic reproduction is as easy or hard, as cheap or dear, as having babies the normal way. Results of this one innovation pervade the whole culture. In my travels, I have never witnessed such a bold experiment in redirecting human destiny.

This was the essence of my address before the Reigning Council in Caria. (See appended transcript.) There was an element of diplomatic flattery, since I left all my troubled questions for another occasion. Time and observation will surely reveal cracks in this feminist nirvana, but that by itself is no indictment. When has any human culture been perfect? Perfection is another way of spelling death.

Some in the audience seemed eager for my proxy recognition of their founders' accomplishments. Others smiled, as if indulgently amused that a mere man might speak to a topic beyond his natural ken. Many simply stared blankly, unable to decide.

Then there was the quiet, polite rancor I could not miss on the faces of a large minority. Their hostility reminded me that Lysos, for all her scientific genius, had also been leader of a militant, revolutionary band. Centuries later, there remains a deep undercurrent of ideological fervor here on Stratos.

The season of the year is no help. Can it be coincidence that consent-to-land was finally granted during midsummer, when suspicion of males runs highest? Were opponents of contact hoping I'd misbehave, and so sabotage my mission?

Perhaps they count on assistance from Wengel Star. Or from hot season's shimmering aurorae. If so, the Perkinists will be disappointed. I am unaffected by glowing cues in their summer sky.

Still, I must take care. The men of this world are used to being few, surrounded by womankind, while I was shaped in a different society, and have just spent two lonely years of my own subjective span in cramped isolation between the stars.

1 6

ncised figures on a granite wall . . . geometric forms . . . nested, twining-rope patterns . . . a puzzle, carved in ancient rock . . .

"We can't stay down here much longer. I told you! Your code's no better'n a Lamai's spit!"

Focus on an image . . . of a child's hand . . . reaching upward toward a star-shaped knot of stone . . .

"Shut up, Leie. Lemme think. Was it this one? Um—I can't 'member."

. . . yes, this one. The star-shaped knob. She must touch the stone. Twist it a quarter turn. A quarter turn to the right.

It was hard to do, though. Something was making her sluggish. A force of will was needed just to make her arm extend, and motion felt like pushing through a jar of bec honey. The dank air of the cellar felt humid, smothering. The stone outcrop receded, even as she stretched out for it.

. . . a star-shaped stone . . . key to the sequence of opening.

The image wavered. Her own hand warped, growing indistinct behind swells of dizzying distortion. The surrounding, twining-rope carvings began to slither, twisting and writhing like awakening snakes.

"Too late," Leie's voice warbled from somewhere out of sight, mixing sadness with recrimination. A grinding sound told of the walls closing in, converging to crush them, to immure them in granite, leaving no escape.

"You're always so damn late . . ."

What hurt most was a vague sense of betrayal. Not by her sister, but the patterns. She had felt so certain of them. The figures on the wall. She had put her faith in them, and now they wouldn't play.

Blurry patterns. Fickle, blurry forms, carved in living, moving stone. . . .

". . . is . . . she . . . doin' . . . any . . . better?"

It was a woman's distant tenor that surged and faded so . . . as if each word came floating out of a mist, packaged in its own quavering bubble.

The reply, when it came, was much deeper, like a sea god intoning from the depths.

". . . think . . . so. . . . doctor said . . . hour ago . . . ought to . . . soon."

At first, the voices were welcome intrusions, stirring and dissipating the clinging terror-strands of a bad dream. Soon, however, the words became irritants, luring her with hints of meaning, only to jerk away all sense, teasing her, thwarting an easy slide to quiet sleep.

The tenor returned, wavering less with each passing moment.

"Good thing . . . or those . . . heads would be . . . same as . . . ing murderers."

A pause. The sea god intoned, "I . . . never forgive myself."

". . . had nothin' . . . with it! Damn fools, tryin' to . . . her behind, like some kid. Could've told 'em she . . . stand for it. . . . Spunky little var."

At least they were friendly voices, she realized. Soothing. Unthreatening. It was good knowing she was being cared for. No need to worry yet over things like how, or why. Natural wisdom counseled her to leave it for now. Let well enough alone.

Wisdom. No match for the troublemaker Curiosity.

Where am I? she wondered despite herself. *Who are these people?*

From that moment, each word arrived defined. Freighted with meaning, context.

"So you've told me," the deeper voice resumed. "We had some chance to exchange life stories in prison, but she never mentioned the details you told me. Poor girl. I had no idea what she's been through."

The man's voice . . . was Renna's. A small knot of worry unraveled. *I haven't lost him yet.*

"Yeah, well, if I'd kept my ears an' eyes open, I'd have connected her with those rumors goin' around, an' gone ashore to check for myself instead of sittin' on the ship like a dorit."

The higher voice was also familiar, tugging at Maia's recollection from what seemed ages ago, in a different life.

"And how about me? Swallowing a Mickey Finn, and letting those women carry me off like a partridge on a pole?"

"Swallowing a Mick . . . ? Ah, you mean a Summer Soother."

Maia's breath caught in surprise. *Naroin! What is she doing here? Where is here?*

"Yeah. Pretty dumb, all right. I thought spacemen were supposed to be smartguys."

Renna chuckled ruefully. "Smart? Not especially. Not by the enhanced standards of some places I've visited. The main trait they seem to want in peripatetics is patience. We— Say, did you hear that? I think she's stirring."

Maia felt a small cool hand along the side of her face.

"Hello, Maia? Can you hear me, younger? It's me, your old master-at-arms from the *Wotan*. Eia! Up an' at 'em."

The hand was calloused, not smooth. Yet it felt good just having someone touch her again. Someone who meant her well. Maia almost feigned sleep, to prolong it.

"I . . ." Her first word came out more a croak than decipherable speech. "C-can't . . . open my eyes . . ." The lids felt locked shut by crusty dryness. A damp cloth passed gently over her brow, moistening them. When it pulled away, the world entered as brightness. Maia blinked and could not stop. Without conscious will, her leaden hands lifted to rub her eyes clumsily.

Two familiar faces swam into focus, framed against wood paneling and a ship's porthole.

"Where . . ." Maia licked her lips and found her mouth too dry to salivate. "Where bound?"

Both Naroin and Renna smiled, expressing relief.

"You gave us a scare," Renna answered. "But you're all right, now. We're heading due west across the Mother Ocean, so our destination seems likely to be Landing Continent. One of the big port cities, I figure. Better for their plans than where they found us, out in the boondocks."

"They?" Bleariness kept intruding, causing the pale man and dark-haired woman to split into four overlapping figures. "You mean Kiel? And Thalla and Baltha?"

Naroin shook her head. "Baltha's just a hired stick, like me. We aren't part of the Big Scheme. Those other two are the paymasters. Seems a secret league of Rads has got plans for your starman, here."

"No end to excitement on wonderful Stratos," Renna added sardonically.

"Maybe . . . you could write a travel guide book," Maia suggested, concentrating to control her dizziness. Renna laughed, especially when Naroin looked at them both quizzically and asked what in Lysos's name a "travel guide" was.

"What are you doing here?" Maia asked the woman sailor. "This can't be Wotan."

That much was obvious. Every surface wasn't coated with a film of black, anthracite dust. Naroin grimaced. "Nah. Wotan banged into a lighter in Artemesia Bay. Captain Pegyul an' I had words over it, so I took my wages an' papers an' got another berth. Just my luck to land one haulin' the weirdest atyp contraband I ever saw—no offense, Starman."

"None taken." Renna appeared unbothered. "Think we'll have any chance to jump ship along the way?"

"Wouldn't bet on it, Shoulders. That's one crowd o' dogged vars escortin' you. B'sides, I'm not sure I wouldn't let things ride, if I was you. There's a lot worse lookin' for your handsy alien tors than's got you right now, if you follow. Even worse than crazy Perkie farmers."

Renna wore a guarded expression. "What do you mean?"

"Don't you know?" Naroin shrugged and changed the subject. "I'll go tell the customers our drowned wharf mouse has come around. Just you two remember the first rule o' summerling survival." She tapped the side of her head. "Small mouth. Big ears."

Naroin gave Maia a parting wink and left, sliding the cabin door shut along its rails. Renna watched her go, shaking his head slowly, then turned back to Maia. "Want some water?"

She nodded. "Please."

He cradled her head while holding a brown earthenware cup to her mouth. Renna's hands felt so much larger than Naroin's, if not noticeably stronger. He laid Maia's head back on the folded blanket she had been given for a pillow.

Or rather, lent. *I don't own a thing in the world,* Maia thought, recalling the betrayal of Thalla and Kiel, that naked sprint through the streets of Grange Head, and her plummet into the icy bay. *And my best, maybe only, friend on Stratos is a stranger who knows even less than I do.*

The thought would have made her laugh bitterly, if she had energy to spare. Maia fought a losing battle just to keep her eyes open.

"That's all right," Renna commented. "Sleep. I'll stay right here."

She shook her head. "How long . . ."

"You were out most of three days. Had to drain half a liter of water out of you, when they dragged you aboard."

So much for those swimming lessons the mothers paid for, she thought. Laps in the Port Sanger municipal pool had prepared her for real-life trials about as well as the rest of Lamatia's much-vaunted summerling education.

"You've been here all the time?" Maia questioned Renna through an enveloping languor. He dismissed it with an offhand wave. "Had to go to the can once or twice, and . . . oh! I held onto something for you. Thought you might want it when you woke."

Maia could barely focus on the glitter of brass as he slipped a small object, cool and rounded, between her hand and the coverlet. *My sextant!* she realized happily. It was just a silly, half-broken tool, of little utility. Yet it meant so much to have something familiar. Something allied to memories. Something that was hers. Tears welled in her eyes.

"Hey, hey," Renna soothed. "Just rest now. I'll be here."

Maia wanted to protest that no one had to keep watch over her, but she lacked the will to speak. Part of her felt it was untrue.

Renna gently placed his hand over the one holding the sextant. His touch was warm, his calluses more evenly spread than Naroin's coarse ridges. They must have come from more subtle labors, or perhaps even deliberate exercise, though, as she drifted off, Maia found herself wondering why anyone would ever lift a finger she or he didn't have to. Better, it seemed, simply to lie in bed forever.

"What are you going to do, make me lie in bed *forever*?" Maia pounded the covers with both fists, causing the doctor to pull away the stethoscope. "Now, don't get all worked up. I just said you should take it easy awhile. You're young an' strong, though. Get up whenever you like."

"Eia!" Maia shouted, throwing the covers aside and bounding onto the wooden deck. Too quickly. She felt a rush of dizziness, but refused to let it show. "Anybody have some clothes to lend me? I'll work off the debt first thing."

"You don't owe anybody," Kiel said from the foot of the bed. "We'll make up what was in the package we left for you, at the hotel. Clothes and some money. It's yours, free and clear."

"I don't want your charity," Maia snapped.

Standing across the small cabin, by the door, Thalla frowned unhappily. "Now don't be mad, Maia. We only—"

"Who's mad?" Maia interrupted, clenching a fist. "I understand why you did it. You've got big-time, political uses for Renna, and figured I'd just get in the way. Even though I'm a var like you."

Thalla and Kiel looked pained, and relieved that Renna had stepped outside during the examination. "We're engaged in dangerous business," Kiel tried to explain.

"Too dangerous for me, but okay for Renna?"

"It's probably a lot safer for the alien to come with us, than simply handing him over to the PES in Grange Head. There are . . . *factions* in Caria City. Factions that don't have sweet plans for our Outsider."

Maia found that believable. "And you rads *don't* have plans, I take it?"

"Of course we do. We want to make a better world. But the peripatetic's goals aren't incompatible with our—"

The physician closed his bag with a loud snap. His authoritative glare must have been learned at Health Scholarium. "S'cuse me for interruptin', ladies, but did you say something about gettin' this poor girl some clothes?"

Medicine was one rare track of higher education in which gender hardly mattered. Some excellent practitioners were men, who seldom let the innate mood swings of their sex interfere with professionalism. Thalla nodded quickly, at once the attentive and compliant var. "Yes, Doctor. I'll get 'em now."

At the door she turned back. "Meanwhile, don't you run around naked on deck, Maia! Not a good habit in the big cities we're headed to!" She giggled at her own wit and departed. Maia briefly glimpsed Renna pacing outside. He looked relieved when Thalla gave thumbs-up while closing the door.

"The youngster is undernourished," the physician went on telling Kiel, while regarding Maia over the rims of his glasses. Maia crossed her arms and lifted her chin while he clucked disapprovingly over her thinness. "I'll tell Cook double rations for a week. You make sure she eats every bite."

"Yes, Doctor." Kiel nodded obediently, waiting till he left before mimicking his stern look with knitted eyebrows and pursed, smacking lips. Under other circumstances, Maia might have found the lampoon hilarious. Now she succeeded in remaining grim, sending the dark var what she hoped was a fierce glower.

Kiel answered with a shrug. "All right. Crawl back under the covers. I'll answer your questions."

Maia chose to take the maternalistic tone as patronizing. She remained standing and held up one finger. "First, what are you planning to do with him?"

"Who, Renna? Why, nothing much. There are some areas of technology we want to ask about. He may not know the answers in detail, but he can give us a general idea what's possible and what isn't. The solutions may lie in his ship's computer.

"Mostly, though, we want to take him somewhere safe and comfortable, while we dicker with certain people in Caria."

"Dicker? About what?"

"About how to get him back to the State Guest House without an accident happening along the way, and from there safely to his ship. He won't really be out of danger till then."

"Danger," Maia repeated, rubbing her shoulders. "From whom?"

"From people who've convinced themselves they can forestall the inevitable. Who think contact would mean the end of the world. Who would fight it by killing the messenger."

Maia had figured as much. Still, it was chilling to hear it confirmed.

"Oh, it's not the whole government," Kiel went on. "I'd say the majority of savants, and a good many council members, realize change is coming. They argue over ways of slowing it down as much as possible . . ."

"And you don't want it slowed," Maia guessed.

Kiel nodded. "We want to speed it up! Lots of us aren't willing to wait two or three generations till the next starship comes, and then through more delays, and more. The old order's finished. Well past time to turn it on its head."

"So Renna's a bargaining chip."

Kiel frowned. "If you want to put it that way. In the short term. Over the long run, our goals are compatible. If he does have a legitimate complaint or two about our methods, can he honestly say he's not among friends? We want him to live and accomplish his mission. The rest is just details."

Against her own wishes, Maia found herself believing Kiel. *Am I being gullible? Why should I even listen, after what she tried to do?*

"You could help him call his starship, to come and get him."

Maia didn't like Kiel's indulgent smile, as if the suggestion were naïve. "The ship had but one lander. Anyway, it can only be sent back into space from the launching facility at Caria."

"Convenient." Maia sat on the edge of the bed. "So Renna's stuck down here, where he just happens to be useful against your enemies."

Kiel accepted the point with a nod. "You met some of them in Long Valley. Mighty old clans, holding place in a static social order not by competing in an open market, the way Lysian logic says they should, but by conniving together, suppressing anything that might bring change.

"Take that drug plot you uncovered. Suppose they have their way and alter the balance of reproduction on Stratos. There'd be almost no summerlings born! Nothing but clones and a few tame males, raised as drones to be milked dry each winter."

"I already figured that out," Maia grumbled uncomfortably.

Kiel's eyebrows arched. "Did you also figure out why the Perkinites didn't eliminate our visitor from the stars, just as soon as they got their hands on him? They plan to squeeze data out of him, like juice from a doped-up sailor."

"So? You want information, too."

"But with different goals. *They* want to learn how to shoot down hominid starships"—Maia gasped; Kiel went on without a pause—"and much more. They think Renna can help solve a problem that stumped even Lysos: how to spark clonal pregnancies entirely without sperm."

"But . . ." Maia stammered. "The placenta . . ."

"Yes, I know. Basic facts of life we're taught as babes. You need sperm to trigger placental development, even if all the egg's chromosomes come from the mother. It's the basis for our whole system. Meant they had to arrange things so a few 'normal,' sexually induced pregnancies occur each summer, in order to get boys to spark the following generation. Vars like you and me are mere side effects, virgie."

Maia shook her head. Kiel was oversimplifying by leagues, especially about the motivations of Lysos and her aides. Still, if the great clans ever found out how to reproduce at will, without even brief participation by males, it would make Tizbe Beller's rutting drug look like a glass of warm tea.

"Did Renna mention anything like this, when he was in Caria?"

"He did. The big dummy doesn't comprehend that there are some things people simply oughtn't to know."

Maia agreed on that point. Sometimes Renna seemed too innocent to live.

"You see what we're up against," Kiel concluded, forming a fist. Her dark complexion flushed. "Sure, we Rads are also proposing big changes, but in the opposite direction! We'd redirect life on Stratos toward more normal modes for a human species . . . toward a world right for people, not beehives from pole to pole."

"You'd take us back to when men were . . . *fifty* percent?"

Laughter broke Kiel's earnest scowl. "Oh, we're not that crazy! For now, our near-term goal is only to unfreeze the political process. Get some debate going. Put more than a few token summerling reps on the High Council. Surely that's worth supporting, whatever you think of our long-range dreams?"

"Well . . ."

"Maia, I'd love to be able to tell the others you're with us."

Kiel was trying to meet her eyes. Maia preferred looking away. She paused for a long moment, then gave a quick half-nod.

"Not yet. But I'll . . . listen to the rest."

"That's all we can ask." Kiel clapped her on the shoulder. "In time, I hope you'll find it in your heart to forgive us for stupidly underestimating you. That'll be the last time, I promise.

"And meanwhile, since you've shown yourself to be such a woman of action, who better to choose as our guest's bodyguard, eh? You'd keep a special eye on him. Prevent anyone from slipping things into his feed, as we did at Grange Head! What better way to make sure we stay honest? Does that sound acceptable to you?"

Kiel was being wry, but the offer appeared genuine. Maia answered with grudging respect. "Acceptable," she said in a low voice. It was irritating to know that Kiel could read her like a book.

Game tokens lay scattered across the cover of the cargo hold—small black and white tiles with whiskerlike sensors protruding from their sides and corners. At first, Renna had marveled how each piece was built to meticulous precision. But, after spending all morning winding one after another of the watchspring mechanisms, some of the romance went out of contemplating them. Fortunately, the efficient gadgets needed just a few twists with a winding key. Nevertheless, Renna and Maia had only finished prepping half of the sixteen hundred game pieces by the time lunch was called.

How do I keep getting talked into weird stuff like this? Maia wondered as she got up and stretched her throbbing arms. *I'll be a wreck by evening.* Still, it beat peeling vegetables, or the other "light work" tasks she'd been assigned since being let out. And the prospect of her first formal Life match had Maia intrigued, if not exactly breathless.

Maia dutifully supervised the dishing out of Renna's food, making sure it came from the common pot and that the utensils were clean. Not that anyone expected an assassination attempt way out here on the Mother Ocean. More likely, someone on the crew might try to dope him, just to stanch the endless flow of alien questions. It was always easy to find Renna on board. Just look for a disturbance in the sailors' routine. On the quarterdeck, for instance, where Captain Poulandres and his officers took on harried looks after long sessions of amiable inquiry. Or teetering precariously, high in the rigging, peering over sailors' shoulders as they worked, thoroughly upsetting the protective pair, Thalla and Kiel, who watched anxiously below.

When Renna mentioned his curiosity how the Game of Life was played at sea, Poulandres seized a chance to divert the strange passenger's attention. A challenge match would take place that very evening. Renna and Maia against the senior cabin boy and junior cook.

Hey, Maia thought at the time. *Did anyone hear me volunteer?*

Not that she really minded, even when her wrists ached from the endless, repetitive twisting. A fresh east wind filled Manitou's electric generator and stretched its billowing sails, causing the masts to creak gently under the strain. It also filled Maia's lungs with growing hope. *Maybe things are going to work out, this time.*

I'm going to see Landing Continent.

If only Leie were here, so we could see it together.

Unlike the creaky, old Wotan, this was a fast vessel, built to carry light cargoes and passengers. Its sailors were well-accoutered, befitting members of a prestigious guild. Cabin boys, newly chosen from their mother clans, ran errands with enthusiastic dash. Maia found the officers' uniformed splendor both impressive and more than a little pompous.

After her spell in Long Valley, where men had been scarcer than red lugars, it seemed strange now, living with so many around. Her experience with the Beller drug undermined Maia's confidence in winter's sure promise of male docility. *What was it like before Lysos?* she wondered. *You never knew which men were dangerous, or when.*

Surreptitiously, she watched the sailors, comparing them to Renna, the alien. Even the obvious things were startling. For instance, his eyes were of a dark brown hue seldom seen on Stratos, set anomalously far apart. And his long nose gave the impression of an ever-curious bird. Mild differences, really. *But if Renna's not from outer space,* Maia thought, *then he's from someplace equally strange.*

Other differences ran deeper. Renna was always *peering.* His visual acuity was fine; he simply hungered for more light, as if daytime on Stratos was dimmer than he was used to. This counterbalanced an uncanny sensitivity to sound. Maia knew he overheard the jokes people made about him.

No one made fun of his beard, now lustrous and curly dark. A summer beard few Stratoin men could match this time of year. But there was some teasing concerning his diet. Normal ship's fare was all right—grain and legume porridge, supplemented by fish stew. But he politely refused red meat from the ship's cooler, citing "protein allergies," and would not drink seawater under any circumstances. The cook, grumbling about "finicky land-boys," tapped a freshwater cask just for him. Kiel shrugged and paid for it.

Maia felt she was well over the hearth-pangs that had filled her lonely solitude at the prison-sanctuary. Except in his intelligence and essential goodness, Renna bore no resemblance to the person she had pictured while exchanging coded messages in the dark. It was just another loss, and no one's fault, in particular.

Still, why did she find herself occasionally washed by illogical feelings of jealousy when Renna spent time talking to Naroin, or Kiel, or other young vars? *Am I attracted to him in a . . . sexual way?* It seemed unlikely, given her youth.

Even if I were, what would jealousy have to do with it?

Maia sought within. Some thoughts seemed to make her feel all wound-up inside. Others provoked disconcerting waves of warmth, or desolation.

Then again, maybe I'm making a big deal out of nothing.

It might have helped to talk out her confusion, but Maia wasn't comfortable confiding in strangers. For that, there had always been Leie.

The sea had Leie, now. Although an endless reach of ocean surrounded her, Maia didn't like to look upon it.

After lunch, Renna excused himself to the curtained platform that extended from the poop deck over open water. He always took longer than others with his postprandial toilet, and there were wagers concerning what he did in there. Passersby reported strange sounds coming from behind the screen.

"Sounds like a lot o' scrubbin' an' spittin'," one sailor reported.

Maia made sure nobody intruded. Whatever his alien needs, Renna deserved privacy. At least he kept himself cleaner than most men!

The women on board, all vars, fell into three types Maia could discern. Half a dozen, including Naroin, were experienced winter sailors, comfortable working side by side with the more numerous male crew. Worldly and capable, they appeared more amused than interested in the political obsessions of the paying passengers.

Next were twenty-one rads, partners in the bold scheme to hustle Renna from captivity. Thalla and Kiel must have taken jobs at Lerner Forge to cover their real mission, ferreting out where the Perkinite clans held their prisoner. Maia wondered, had her ex-housemates cleverly followed the alien's trail halfway around the world? More likely, their team was one of many sent to scour the globe. Either way, the Radical cabal appeared large, resolute, and well organized.

In high spirits after their successful foray, the rads were talkative, excited, and clearly better educated than the average var. Their soft-voweled city accents hardly impressed the third group—eight rough-looking women, most of whom spoke the low, drawling dialect of the Southern Isles. As Naroin put it, Baltha and her friends were along as "hired sticks." Mercenary guards to fill out the expedition's complement. The southlanders scarcely concealed their contempt for the idealistic rads, but seemed happy to take their pay.

Renna emerged from the toilet platform, zipping his blue pouch. He stretched, inhaling deeply. "Never thought I'd get used to this air. Felt like breathing syrup. But it kind of grows on you after a while. Maybe it's the symbiont at work."

"The what?" Maia asked.

Renna blinked and was thoughtful for a moment. "Mm—something I took before landing, to help me adjust to walking around on a different planet. Did you know only three other hominid populations are known to live at such atmospheric pressures? It's because of the thick air that Stratos is habitable. Keeps the heat in. Normally, no one would look for real estate near such a small sun. Lysos made a brilliant gamble here, and won."

Almost as brilliantly as you changed the subject, Maia thought. But that was all right. It pleased her to see Renna learning to control what he revealed. At this rate, in a few seasons he might be able to play poker with a four-year-old.

"We have more pieces to wind," she reminded him. They went back to the cargo hatch where he sighed, lifting a squarish game token. "And to imagine, I called these little devils ingenious. I still don't see why they refuse to use the game board we brought from the citadel."

"It's tradition," Maia explained, gingerly turning one of the tiles, careful of the protruding antenna-feelers. "Those mass-produced game boards are powerful . . . I never knew *how* powerful till getting to play with one. But I do know they're lower in status than handmade ones. They're meant for summer, when most men are cooped up in sanctuaries. Unable to travel."

"Because of the weather?"

"And restrictions by local clans. It's a rough time for men. Especially if you're unlucky, and get no invitation to town. When it's not raining, there's the aurorae and Wengel in the sky, setting off frustrating feelings. A lot of men just close the shutters and distract themselves with crafts and tournaments. My guess is that right now a computer game board reminds them too much of a time they'd rather not think about."

Renna nodded. "I guess that makes sense. Still, it occurs to me perhaps there's another reason sailors prefer mechanicals. I get a feeling you aren't considered a real man unless you can build all your own tools, with your own hands."

Maia reached for another game piece to wind. "It has to be that way, Renna. Sailors can't afford to specialize, like women in clans do." She motioned at the complex rigging, the radar mast, the humming wind-generator. "You're never sure you'll have the right mix of skills on a voyage, so every boy expects to learn most of them, in time."

"Uh-huh. Sacrificing perfection of the particular in favor of competence in the general." Renna pondered for a moment, then shook his head. "But I'm convinced it goes deeper. Take that miniature sextant on your wrist, so much more ornate and clever than needed for the task."

Maia put down the winding key and turned her arm to regard the sextant's brass cover, with its ornate, almost mythological rendition of a huge airship. Renna motioned for her to open it. Next to the folded sighting arms and finely knurled wheels, there were sockets for electronic hookups, now plugged and apparently unused for ages. Renna reached over to touch a tiny, dark display screen. "Don't let the vestiges of high tech fool you, Maia. There's nothing that couldn't be handmade in a private works, using techniques passed on from teacher to pupil for generation after generation. It's that passing on of skill that interests me."

Maia felt for a moment as if she were listening to Renna rehearse a report he planned to give at some future time and place, describing the customs of an obscure tribe, located at the fringes of civilization. *Which is what we are, I guess.* She inhaled, suddenly acutely conscious of the weight of air in her lungs. Was it really heavy, compared to other worlds? Despite Renna's remarks, the round, red sun didn't look feeble. It was so fierce, she could only look straight at it for a few seconds without her eyes watering.

Renna went on. "I find it interesting that such elaborate skills get passed on so attentively, far beyond what officers need to teach in order to get good crew."

Maia folded the sextant away. "I hadn't thought of it that way before. We're taught that men don't have . . ." She searched for the right word. "They don't have *continuity*. The middies adopted by sailing masters are rarely their own sons, so there's no long-range stake in the boys' success. Yet, you make it sound almost like the way it is in clans. Personal teaching. Close attention over time. Passing on more than a trade."

"Mm. You know, the more I think about it, the more I'm sure it was designed this way. Sure a family of clones does it more efficiently, one generation training the next. But at base, it's just a variation on an old theme. The master-apprentice system. For most of human history, such systems were the rule. Progress came through incremental improvements on tried-and-true designs."

Maia recalled how, as children, she and Leie used to peer into the workshop of the Yeo leatherworkers, or Samesin clockmakers, watching older sisters and mothers instruct younger clones, as they themselves had been taught. It was how young Lamais learned the export-import business. You wouldn't imagine such a process to be possible among men, no two of whom ever shared the same exact talents or interests. But Renna implied there was less difference than similarity. "It's a traditional system, perfect for maintaining stability," the star voyager said, putting a wound-up game piece aside and lifting another. "There is a price. Knowledge accumulates additively, almost never geometrically."

"And sometimes not at all?" Maia asked, feeling suddenly uneasy.

"Indeed. That's a danger in craft societies. Sometimes the trend is negative."

She looked down, suddenly feeling something like shame. "We've forgotten so much."

"Mm," Renna's dark eyebrows came together. "Not so much, perhaps. I've seen your Great Library, and spoken with your savants. This isn't a dark age, Maia. What you see around you is the result of deliberate planning. Lysos and the Founders carefully considered costs and alternatives. As products of a scientific era, they were determined to prevent another one happening here."

"But—" Maia blinked. "Why would scientists want to stop science?"

His smile was warm, but something in Renna's eyes told Maia this was a topic fraught with personal pain.

"Their aim wasn't to stop science as such, but to prevent a certain kind of scientific *fever*. A cultural madness, if you will. The sort of epoch in which questioning becomes almost a devotional act. In which all of life's certainties melt, and folk compulsively doubt old ways, heedless of whatever validity those ways once had. Ego and 'personal fulfillment' take precedence over values based on community and tradition. Such times bring terrible ferment, Maia. Along with increased knowledge and power comes ecological danger, from expanding populations and misuse of technology."

No pictures formed in Maia's head to accompany his words. The content was entirely abstract, without reference to anything she knew. Yet, she felt appalled. "You make it sound . . . terrible."

His exhalation was heavy. "Oh, there are benefits. Art and culture flourish. Old repressions and superstitions shatter. New insights illuminate and become part of our permanent heritage. A renaissance is the most romantic and exciting of times, but none lasts very long. Way back, before the Phylum Diaspora, the first scientific age barely got us off the homeworld before collapsing in exhaustion. It came as close to killing as liberating us."

Maia watched Renna and felt positive he spoke from more than historical erudition. She saw an ache in his dark eyes. He was remembering, with both regret and deep longing. It was a kind of homesickness, one more final and irredeemable than her own.

Renna cleared his throat, briefly looking away.

"It was during another such age—the Florentina Revival—that your famous Lysos grew convinced that stable societies are happier ones. Deep down, most humans prefer living out their lives surrounded by comfortable certainties, guided by warm myths and metaphors, knowing that they'll understand their children, and their children will understand them. Lysos wanted to create such a world One with net contentment maximized not for a brilliant few, but over time for the maximum number."

"That's what we're taught." Maia nodded. Though once again, it was a different way of phrasing familiar things. Different and disturbing.

"What you aren't taught, and my private theory, is that Lysos only adopted sexual separatism because Perkinite secessionists were the strongest group of malcontents willing to follow her into exile. They provided the raw material Lysos used to make her stable world, isolated and protected from the ferment of the hominid realm."

Never had Maia heard the Founder spoken of like this. With respect, but of an almost-collegial sort, almost as if Renna had known Lysos personally. Anyone hearing this would have to believe one basic truth—the man was, indeed, from another star.

For a long time, Renna looked out across the sea, contemplating vistas Maia couldn't begin to picture. Then he shrugged. "I ramble too much. We started talking about how sailors are taught to scorn a man who relies on tools he doesn't understand. It's the major reason they despise me."

"You? But you crossed interstellar space! Wouldn't sailors—"

"Respect that?" Renna chuckled. "Alas, they also know my ship is the product of vast factories, built mostly by robots, and that I couldn't control the least part of it without machines almost smarter than I am, whose workings I barely comprehend. You know what that makes me? The savants have spread mocking fairy tales. Ever hear of the *Wissy-Man*?"

Maia nodded. It was a name boys called each other when they wanted to be cruel.

"That's me," Renna finished. "Helpless Wissy-Man. Dispatched by fools, slave to his tools. Rescued by vars after crossing the stars."

Renna gave a short laugh, almost a snort. It did not sound amused.

That evening's Life match was a disaster.

Sixteen hundred game pieces, fully wound, had been divided into two sets of stacks on each side of a cargo hatch grooved with forty vertical lines crossed by forty horizontal. Maia and Renna joined the other passengers for dinner, eating from chipped porcelain bowls, looking out over choppy seas. Then, with an hour of daylight remaining, they went back to await their opponents. The junior cook and a cabin boy arrived a few minutes later, the former still wiping his hands on his apron. *They don't take us very seriously*, Maia guessed. Not that she blamed them.

As the visiting team, she and Renna were invited to make the first move. Maia swallowed nervously, almost dropping the pieces she carried, but Renna grinned and whispered, "Remember, it's just a game."

She smiled back tentatively, and handed him the first tightly-wound piece. He put it in the extreme lower right corner of the board, white side up.

They had talked over strategy earlier. "We'll keep it simple," Renna had said. "I learned a few tricks while sitting around in jail. But I was mostly trying to write messages or paint pictures. I'll bet it's lots different with someone opposing you, trying to wreck what you create."

Renna had sketched on a notepad what he called a "very conservative" pattern. Maia recognized some of the primitive forms. One cluster of black tokens in the left corner would sit and "live" forever if left untouched by any other moving pattern of black dots. Their strategy would be to try to defend this oasis of life until the time limit, concentrating on defense and making only minimal forays into enemy territory with gliders, wedges, or slicers. A tie would do nicely.

While Renna laid down that first row, the boys nudged each other, pointing and laughing. Whether they already saw naïveté in the design, or were just trying to goad the neophytes, it was unnerving. Worse, from Maia's perspective, were the jibes of women spectators. Especially Baltha and the southlanders, who clearly thought this exercise profoundly male-silly. A female crew member named Inanna whispered in a comrade's ear, and they both laughed. Maia felt sure the joke was about her.

She was doing herself no good, nor was it clear what Renna was going to learn.

Then why are we doing it?

The first row was finished. At once, the cook and cabin boy began laying down forty pieces of their own. They used no notes, although Maia saw them confer once. A few seamen observed idly from the quarterdeck stairs, whittling sticks of soft wood into lacy, finely curled sculptures of sea animals.

When the boys signaled their turn finished, Renna took a long look and then shrugged. "Looks just like our first row. Maybe it's coincidence. Might as well continue with our plan."

So they laid another forty, mostly white side up, seeding enough strategically located black pieces so that when the game commenced and all the wound-up springs were released, a set of pulsing geometric patterns would embark on self-sustaining lifespans, setting forth to take part in the game's brief ecology.

At least, we hope so.

It went on that way for some time as the sun set beyond the billowing, straining jib. Each side took turns laying forty disks, then watching and trying to guess what the other team was up to. There came one interruption when the wind shifted and the chief bosun called all hands to the rigging. Dashing to their tasks, sailors hauled lanyards and turned cranks in a whirl of straining muscles. The tack maneuver was accomplished with brisk efficiency, and all was calm again before Maia finished forty breaths. Naroin leaped down from the sheets, landing in a crouch. She grinned at Maia and gave thumbs-up before sauntering back to a spot along the port rail favored by the female crew members, who smoked pipes and gossiped quietly as game preparations resumed.

"Those devils," Renna said after eight rows had been laid. Maia looked where he pointed, and momentarily saw what he meant. Apparently, their opponents had copied the same static "oasis" formation to sit in their most protected corner. *In fact,* she realized. *They're mimicking us right along!* Only slight variations could be seen along the left-hand side. *What's the purpose of that? Are they making fun of us?*

Differences began to creep in after the tenth row. Suddenly, the cook and cabin boy began laying down a completely different pattern. Maia recognized a glider gun, which was designed to fire gliders across the board. She also saw what could only be a cyclone—a configuration with the attribute of sucking to its doom any moving life pattern that came nearby. She pointed out the incipient design to Renna, who concentrated, and finally nodded.

"You're right. That'd put our guardian in danger, wouldn't it? Maybe we should move him to one side. To the right, do you think?"

"That would interfere with our short fence," she pointed out. "We've already laid two rows for that pattern."

"Mm. Okay, we'll shift the guardian leftward, then."

Maia tried to visualize what the game board would look like when completed. Already she could see how entities now in place would evolve during the first two, three, even five or six rounds. This particular area of hatch cover would be crossed by a newly launched mother ship. That area over there would writhe in alternating black and white swirls as a mustard seed turned round and round . . . a pretty but deceptively potent form. When she tried to follow the path of projectiles from the other side, Maia came to a horrified realization—one set of gliders would carom off the mirror-edge and come back spearing obliquely toward the very corner they had worked and planned so hard to protect!

Renna scratched his head when she pointed out the incipient disaster. "Looks like we're cooked," he said with a frown. Then he winced as Maia's fingernails bit his arm.

"No, look!" she said, urgently. "What if we build our own glider gun . . . over there! We could set it to fire *back* into our own territory, intercepting their—"

"What?" Renna cut in, and Maia was briefly afraid she'd overstepped, injecting her own ideas into what was essentially his design. But he nodded in growing excitement. "Ye-e-s, I think it might . . . work." He reached out and squeezed her shoulders, leaving them tingling. "That'd do it if we got the timing right. Of course, there's the problem of debris, after the gliders collide. . . ."

There was hardly enough room in the last few rows to lay down the improvised modifications. Fortunately, their opponents didn't place another cyclone near the boundary. Maia's new glider gun lay right along the border, with no room to spare. She was exhausted by the time the last piece had been set. *And I thought this was a lazy man's game. I guess spectators never know until they try a sport for themselves.*

It was long past sunset. Lanterns were lit. Thalla arrived with a pair of coats. Slipping hers on, Maia realized everyone else had already dressed for the chill of evening. She must have been putting out too much nervous energy to notice.

Captain Poulandres approached, dressed in a cowled robe and carrying a crooked staff in his role as master and referee. Behind him, all the ship's company save the helmsman, lookout, and sailmaster found perches from which to watch. They lounged casually, many wearing amused expressions. Maia saw none of the usual laying of bets.

Probably no takers for our side, whatever the odds.

Silence fell as the captain stepped forward to the edge of the game board, where the timing square was ready to send synchronized pulses to all pieces. At a set time, each of the sixteen hundred tiny units would either flip its louvers or rest quiet, depending on what its sensors told it about the state of its neighbors. The same decision would be made a few seconds later, when the next pulse arrived. And so on.

"Life is the continuation of existence," the captain intoned. Perhaps it was the cowl that lent his voice a deep, vatic tone. Or maybe it was part of being captain.

"Life is the continuation of existence," the ship's company responded, echoing his words, accompanied by a background of creaking masts and flapping sails.

"Life is the continuation of existence, yet no thing endures. We are all patterns, seeking to propagate. Patterns which bring other patterns into being, then vanish, as if we've never been."

Maia had heard the invocation so many times, recited in countless accents at dockside arenas in Port Sanger and elsewhere. She knew it by heart. Yet this was her first time standing as a contestant. Maia wondered how many other women had. No more than thousands, she felt sure. Maybe only hundreds.

Renna listened to the ancient words, clearly entranced.

". . . We cannot control our progeny. Nor rule our inventions. Nor govern far consequences, save by the foresight to act well, then let go.

"All is in the preparation, and the moment of the act.

"What follows is posterity."

The captain held out his staff, hovering above the winking timing square.

"Two teams have prepared. Let the act be done. Now . . . observe posterity."

The staff struck down. The timing square began chiming its familiar eight-count. Even though she was prepared, Maia jumped when the flat array of sixteen hundred black and white pieces seemed all at once to explode.

Not *all* at once. In fact, fewer than half flipped their louvers, changing state because of what they sensed around them. But the impression of sudden, frantic clattering set Maia's heart racing before a second wave of sound and motion suddenly crossed the board. And another.

Fortunately, she did not have to think. Any Game of Life match was already over the moment it began. From now on, they could only stand and watch the consequences unfold.

Peripatetic's Log:

Stratos Mission:

Arrival + 43.271 Ms

l found it hard overcoming prejudices, during my first visit to a
Stratoin home.

It wasn't the concept of matriarchy, which I've met in other guises
on Florentina and New Terra. Nor the custom that men are another
species, sometimes needed, often irksome, and fortunately rare. I was
prepared for all that.

My problem arises from growing up in an era obsessed with individuality.

Variety was our religion, diversity our fixation. Whatever was different or atypical won favor over the familiar. Other always came before

self. An insane epoch, say psychohistorians . . . even if its brief glory produced ideal star travelers.

In voyaging, I've encountered many stabilized societies, but none more contrary to my upbringing than Stratos. The unnerving irony of this world's fascinating uniqueness is its basis in changelessness. Generations are not rent by shifting values. Sameness is no curse, variety no automatic friend.

It's just as well we never met. Lysos and I would not have gotten along.

Nonetheless, I was delighted when Savant Iolanthe asked me to spend some days at her family's castlelike estate, in the hilly suburbs of Caria. The invitation, a rare honor for a male in summer, was surely a political statement. Her faction is the least hostile toward restored contact. Even so, I was cautioned that my visit was to be "chaste." My room would have no windows facing Wengel Star.

I told Iolanthe to expect no problems in that regard. I will avert my gaze, though not from the sky.

Nitocris Hold is an ancient place. Iolanthe's clone-line has occupied the sprawling compound of high walls, chimneys, and dormered roofs for most of six hundred years. Related lineages dwelled on the site almost back to the founding of Caria.

Our car swept through an imposing gate, cruised along a garden-rimmed drive, and halted before a finely sculpted marble entrance. We were formally greeted by a trio of graceful Nitocri who, like Iolanthe, were of stately middle age, dressed in shimmering yellow silken gowns with high collars. My bag was carried off by a younger clan-sister. More siblings bearing distinctive Nitocris features—soft eyes and narrow noses—rushed silently to move the car, seal the gate, and usher us inside.

So, for the first time, I entered the sanctum of a parthenogenetic clan, prime unit of human life on Stratos. "They aren't bees or ants," I thought silently, suppressing facile comparisons. Within, I repeated the motto of my calling—

"Let go of preconceptions."

The savant cheerfully showed me courtyards and gardens and grand halls, unperturbed by a crowd of children who whispered and giggled in our wake. The Nitocri keep no domestic employees, no hired vars to carry out unpleasant tasks beneath the dignity of wealthy clones. No Nitocris resents taking her turn at hard or dirty chores, such as scouring fire grates, or scrubbing lavatories, or laying down roof tiles. All is well-timed according to age, with each girl or woman alternating between onerous and interesting tasks. Each individual knows how long a given phase will last. After a set interval, a younger sister will be along to take over whatever you are doing, while you move on to something else.

No wonder even children and youths move gracefully, with such assurance. Each clone-daughter grows up watching elders just like her, performing their tasks with a calm efficiency derived from centuries of practice. She knows the movements unconsciously before ever being called upon to do them herself. No one hurries to take on power before her time. "My turn will come," appears to be the philosophy.

At least, that's the story they were selling me. No doubt it varies from clan to clan, and almost certainly works less than perfectly even among the Nitocri. Still, I wonder . . .

Utopians have long imagined creating an ideal society, without competition, only harmony. Human nature—and the principle of selfish genes—seemed to put the dream forever out of reach. Yet, within a Stratoin clan, where all genes are the same, what function remains for selfishness? The tyranny of biological law can relax. Good of the individual and that of the group are the same.

Nitocris House is filled with love and laughter. They seem self-sufficient and happy.

I do not think my hosts noticed when I involuntarily shivered, even though it wasn't cold.

17

There was glory on deck the next morning. Freshly fallen from high, stratospheric clouds, the delicate frost coated every surface, from spars and rails to rigging, turning the Manitou into a fairy ship of crystal dust, glowing in a profusion of pink sunrise refractions.

Maia stood atop a narrow flight of stairs leading up from the small cabin she shared with nine other women. She rubbed her eyes and stared at the sweetly painful dawnlight glitter outside. *How pretty,* she thought, watching countless pinpoints of rose-colored brilliance change, moment by moment.

She recalled occasions when Port Sanger received such a coating, causing shops and businesses to close while women hurried outside to sweep puffballs from their windowsills into vacuum jars for preservation. A sprinkle of glory disrupted daily life far more than thicker falls of normal snow, which simply entailed boots and shovels and some seasonal grumbling.

Certainly *men* preferred dense drifts of the regular kind. Even slippery ice, making the streets slick and treacherous, seemed to perturb the rough sailors nowhere near as much as a thin scattering of lacy glory. Most males fled to their ships, or beyond the city gates, until sunlight cleansed the town, and its women citizens were in a less festive mood.

That was on shore, Maia remembered. *Here, there's no place for the poor fellows to run.*

From the narrow doorway at the head of the stairs, Maia inhaled a cool, faintly cinnamon odor. This was no minor dusting, like in Long Valley. The air felt bracing, and provoked a tingling in her spine. Sensations vaguely familiar from prior winters, yet enhanced this time.

Of course, she hadn't been a grown woman before. Maia felt combined eagerness and reluctance, waiting to see if the aroma would have a deeper effect, now that she was five.

There was movement on deck, male sailors shuffling with the desultory slowness of dawn-shift workers. They were physically unaffected by the icy encrustation, yet the captain's expression seemed unhappy, irritated. He snapped at his officers and frowned, contemplating the fine, crystal dusting.

The unhappiest person in sight was the only female—the youngest of Kiel's company of Rads, a girl about Maia's age. She was using a broom to sweep glory frost into a square-mouthed bucket, which she proceeded to empty over the side before going back for another load.

Maia sensed a stirring behind her—another woman rising with the sun. She glanced back and nodded a silent good-morning as Naroin climbed the short, steep steps to squeeze alongside. "Well, look at that," the older var commented, sniffing the soft, chill breeze. "Quite a sight, eh? Too bad it's all got to go."

The petite sailor redescended, plunging momentarily into the dimness of the narrow cabin. She reached onto the bunk Maia had just vacated, and returned bearing Maia's coat. "There you go," Naroin said with a kindly tone, and pointed at the girl outside, sweeping the deck dejectedly. "Your job, too. Law of th' sea. Women stay below till the frost goes. Except virgies."

Maia blushed. "How do *you* know I'm a—"

Naroin held up a hand placatingly. "Just an expression. Half o' these vars"—she jerked her thumb at those still sleeping below—"never had a man, an' never will. Nah, it's a matter of age. Youngsters sweep up. Go on, child. Eia."

"Eia," Maia responded automatically, slipping on the coat. She trusted Naroin not to lie about something like this. Still, it seemed unfair. Her feet shuffled reluctantly as the bosun gently pushed her outside and shut the door behind her. Chill air condensed her breath in steamy plumes. Rubbing already-numb hands, Maia sighed and went to the utility locker to fetch a broom.

The other girl gave her a look that seemed to say, Where have *you* been? Maia lifted her shoulders in the same silent language.

I didn't know anything about it. Do I ever?

It was logical, when she thought about it. Glory didn't affect women as strongly as summer's aurorae did men, thank Lysos. Still, it drew those of fertile age toward ideas of sex at exactly the time of year when most men preferred a good book. What males found irksome but avoidable on land could not be escaped so easily at sea. Fivers and sixers, who were less affected by the seasons, and unattractive to males anyway, naturally got the job of sweeping up, so other women might be permitted to emerge before noon.

The chore soon lost whatever attraction lay in novelty, and Maia found the faintly pleasant tingling in her nose less fixating than advertised. Carrying bucketsful to the rail, she could not escape the sensation of being watched. Maia felt certain some of the sailors were pointing at her, sniggering.

The reason had nothing to do with the glory fall, and everything to do with last night's fiasco of a "competition." It was bad enough being a lowly young var, on a voyage not of her choosing. But the Life match had left her a laughingstock.

Sure enough, one of her opponents, the cook's assistant, was firing up his stove under the eaves of the poop deck. The boy grinned when Maia's sweeping brought her nearby. He lisped through a gap left by two missing teeth, "Ready for another game? Whenever you an' the Starman want, me an' Kari are ready."

Maia made as if she hadn't heard. The youth was clearly no intellect, yet he and the cabin boy had made quick hash of Renna's carefully-thought-out Game of Life plan. The rout became obvious within a few rounds.

With each pulse, ripples of change had swept the board. Black pieces, representing "living" locations, turned white and died, unless conditions were right to go on living. White pieces flipped over, coming alive when the number of black neighbors allowed it. Patterns took shape, wriggling and writhing like organisms of many cells.

The forty-by-forty grid was by no means the largest Maia had seen. There were rumors of boards vastly bigger, in some of the towns and ancient sanctuaries of the Méchant Coast. Yet, she and Renna had worked hard to fill their side with a starting pattern that might thrive, all to no avail. Their labors began unraveling from almost the very start.

One of their opponents' designs began firing self-contained gliders across the board, configurations that banked and flapped at an oblique angle toward the edge, where they caromed toward the oasis Renna and Maia had to preserve. Maia watched with a lump in her throat as the other glider gun on this side—her own contribution to Renna's plan— launched interceptors that skimmed past their short fence barrier just in time to—

Yes! She had felt elation as their antimissiles collided with the enemy's projectiles right on schedule, creating explosions of simulated debris.

"Eia!" she had cried in excitement.

Intent as she had been on that threat, Maia was rudely yanked back by an abrupt roar of laughter. She turned to Renna. "What is it?"

Ruefully, her partner pointed toward the synthetic figure they had counted on to hold the center of the board. Their "guardian," with its flailing arms and legs, had seemed guaranteed to ward off anything that dared approach. But now Maia saw that a bar-shaped entity had emerged from the other side of the board, approaching inexorably. At that instant, she experienced a queer sense of recognition, perhaps dredged out of childhood memory, from watching countless games at dockside in Port Sanger. In a strange instant, the new shape suddenly struck her as . . . obvious.

Of course. That shape will absorb . . .

The flickering intruder made contact with the branching patterns that were the guardian's arms, and proceeded to suck them in! To the eye, it seemed as if their opponents' creature was devouring game pieces, one by one, incorporating organs from the guardian into its growing self.

It's actually a simple shape, she recalled thinking numbly. Boys probably memorize it before they're four.

As if that weren't enough, the invader pattern began displacing the guardian's undamaged core. Beat by beat, the pseudobeast she and Renna had built was pushed backward, rending and flailing helplessly, smashing through all their fences. Helplessly, they watched the destructive retreat grind all the way to the near left corner, where their vulnerable oasis was promptly and decisively crushed. From that moment on, life quickly dissipated from their half of the game board. Laughter and amused booing had sent Maia fleeing in shame to her cabin.

It was only a game, she tried convincing herself the next morning, as she swept. *At least, that's what women think, and they're the ones who count.*

Still, memory of the humiliation lingered unpleasantly as glory frost evaporated under the rising sun. Those thin patches she and the other young var had missed soon sublimed. With visible reluctance, Captain Poulandres went to the railing and rang a small bell.

At once, the deck thronged with women passengers and crew, inhaling the last aromas and looking about with liveliness in their eyes. Maia saw one broadly built var come up behind a middle-aged sailor and pinch him, causing the man to jump with a low yelp. The husky victim whirled around, wearing a harassed expression. He responded after an instant with a wary laugh, shaking a finger in admonishment, and quickly retreated to the nearest mast. An unusual number of sailors seemed to have found duties to perform aloft, this morning.

It wasn't a universal reaction. The assistant cook seemed pleased by the attentions of women gathered round the porridge pot. And why not? Aroused fems were seldom dangerous, and it was doubtful the poor fellow got much notice during summertime. He would likely store a memory of brief flirtation to carry him through lonely months in sanctuary.

Two nearby vars, a short blonde and a slender redhead, were giggling and pointing. Maia turned to see what had them going.

Renna, she thought with a sigh. The Visitor had approached one last, half-full bucket she had neglected to dump overboard. He bent to scoop a handful of glory frost, bringing it up to sniff, delicately, curiously. Renna looked perplexed for a moment, then his head jerked back and his eyes widened. Carefully, he dusted off his hands and thrust them into his pockets.

The two rads laughed. Maia didn't like the way they were looking at him.

"I guess if one were desperate enough . . ." one said to the other.

"Oh, I don't know," came the reply. "I think he's kind of exotic-looking. Maybe, after we reach Ursulaborg."

"You got hopes! The committee's already picked those who'll get first crack. You'll wait your turn, and chew a kilo of ovop if you're lucky."

"Yuck," the second one grimaced. Yet a covetous gleam did not leave her eye as she watched the man from space depart for the quarterdeck.

Maia's thoughts whirled. Apparently, the rads had designs to keep Renna busy while they sheltered him and dickered with the Reigning Council. Her first reaction was outrage. How dare they assume he'd go along, just like that?

Then she bit back her initial wrath and tried hard to see it calmly. *I guess he's in their debt,* Maia admitted reluctantly. It would be churlish to refuse his rescuers at least an effort, even in the dead of winter. The Radical organization had no doubt promised members of the rescue party rewards if they succeeded—perhaps sponsorship of a winter sparking, with an apartment and trust fund to see a first cloneling child through primary schooling. *The leaders, Kiel and Thalla, will be first,* Maia realized. Given her education and talents, Kiel would then be in a good position to become a founding mother of a growing clan.

So politics is just part of it, Maia thought, considering the motives of her former cottage-mates. *None of my damn business,* she told herself, knowing that she cared intensely, anyway. The first rad glanced at Maia standing nearby, listening. "Of course, there's an element of choice on *his* part, too," she said. "Equal rights, y'know. And there's no accounting for alien tastes. . . ." The var turned to Maia, and winked.

Maia flushed and strode away. Leaning on the starboard rail, she stared across foam-flecked waves, unable to contain her roiling thoughts. The busybody had voiced a question Maia herself hadn't admitted: *I wonder what Renna likes in women?* Shaking her head vigorously, she made a resolute effort to divert her thoughts. Troublesome maunderings like these were at best impractical, and she had vowed to be a practical person.

Think. Soon they'll take Renna far away and you'll be alone in a big city. When he's long gone, you'll be left to live off what you know.

What assets do you have? What skills can you sell? She tried to concentrate—to bring forth a catalog of resources—but found herself facing only disconcerting blankness.

The blankness was not neutral. Born in a tense moment of angst, it spread outward from her dark thoughts and seemed to color her view of her surroundings, saturating the seascape, washing it like a canvas painted from a savage palette, in primitive and brutal shades. The air felt charged, like before a lightning storm, and a sense of fell expectation set her heart pounding.

Maia tried closing her eyes to escape the distressing epiphany, but extracted impressions only pursued her. Squeezing her eyelids shut caused more than familiar, squidgy sensations. A coruscation of light and dark speckles flickered and whirled, changing too fast to be tracked. She had known the phenomenon all her life, but now it both frightened and fascinated her. Combining in overlapping waves, the speckles seemed to offer a fey kind of meaning, drawing her away from centered vision toward something both beautiful and terrible.

Breath escaped her lungs in a sigh. Maia found the will to rub her eyes and reopen them. Purple blotches throbbed concentrically before fading away, along with that eerie, unwelcome sense of formless form. Yet, for a stretch of time there lay within Maia a vague but lingering surety. Looking outward, she no longer saw, but continued imagining a vista of everchanging patterns, stretching in infinite recursion across the cloud-flecked sky. Momentarily, the heavens seemed made of ephemeral, quickly altering, emblematic forms, overlapping and merging to weave the illusion of solidity she had been taught to call reality.

Relief mixed with awed regret as the instant passed. It could only have lasted moments. The atmosphere resumed its character of heavy, moist air. The wood rail beneath her hands felt firm.

Now I know I'm going crazy, Maia thought sardonically. As if she didn't have troubles enough already.

Breakfast was called. Tentatively, as if the deck might shift beneath her feet, Maia went to take her turn in line. She watched the cook serve two portions—one for Renna and a double scooping for herself, by order of the ship's doctor. She turned, looking for the Visitor, and found him deep in conversation with the captain, apparently oblivious to the fool he had made of himself last night. She approached from behind, and caught his attention just long enough to make sure he noticed his plate on the chart table, near his elbow. Renna smiled, and made as if to speak to her, but Maia pretended not to notice and moved away. She carried her own bowl of hot, pulpy wheatmeal forward, all the way to the bowsprit, where the ship's cutting rise and fall met alternating bursts of salty spray. That made the place uncomfortable for standing, but ideal for being left alone, tucked under the protective shelter of the forward cowling.

The porridge nourished without pretense at good taste. It didn't matter. She had mastered her thoughts now, and was able to contemplate what she might do when the ship reached port.

Ursulaborg—pearl of the Méchant Coast. Some ancient clans there are so big and powerful, they've got pyramids of lesser clans underneath them, who have client families of their own, and so on. Clones serving clones of the same women who first employed their ancestors, hundreds of years ago, with everybody knowing her place from the day she's born, and all potential personality conflicts worked out ages ago.

Maia remembered having seen a cinematic video—a comedy—when she and Leie were three. Coincidentally, the film was set in the magnificent Ursulaborg palace of one such grand multiclan. The plot involved an evil outsider's scheme to sow discord among families who had been getting along for generations. At first, the stratagem seemed to work. Suspicions and quarrels broke out, feeding on each other as women leaped to outrageously wrong conclusions. Communication shattered and the tide of misunderstandings, both incited and humorously accidental, seemed fated to cause an irreparable rift. Then, at a climactic moment, the high-strung momentum dissolved in an upswell of revelation, then reconciliation, and finally laughter.

"We were made to be partners," said one wise old matriarch, at the moral denouement. *"If we met as vars, as our first mothers had, we would become fast friends. Yet we know each other better than vars ever could. Is it possible we Blaine sisters could live without you Chens? Or you without us? Blaines, Chens, Hanleys, and Wedjets . . . ours is a greater family, immortal, as if molded by Lysos herself."*

It had been a warm, mushy ending, leaving Maia feeling terribly

glad to have Leie in her life . . . even if her sister had muttered derisively, at the movie's end, about its manic illogic and lack of character
development.

Leie would have loved to see Ursulaborg.

There was no land in sight. Nevertheless, she looked past the bowsprit to the west, blinking against spray that hid a salty bitterness of
tears.

Renna found her there. The dark-eyed man called down from the
foremast. "Ah, Maia, there you are!"

She hurriedly wiped her eyes and turned to watch him clamber into
the sheltered area. "How are you doing?" he asked cheerfully. Dropping
to sit across from her, he leaned forward to squeeze her hand.

"I've been unhappier," she answered with a shrug, somewhat befud-
dled by his warmth. It pierced the protective distance she had been
working to build between them. Maia made sure not to yank her hand
back, but withdrew it slowly. He appeared not to notice.

"Isn't it a fine day?" Renna inhaled, taking in the broad expanse of
sunny and cloud-shaded patches of sea, stretching to every horizon. "I
was up at dawn, and for a little while I thought I saw a swarm of Great
Pontoos, off to the south among the clouds. Someone said they were just
common zoor-floaters. . . . I've seen lots of those. But these looked so
beautiful, so graceful and majestic, that I figured—"

"Pontoos are very rare now."

"So I gather." He sighed. "You know, this planet would seem perfect for flying. I've seen birds and gasbag creatures of so many types. But
why so few aircraft? I know spaceflight might disrupt your stable pastoralism, but what harm would it do to have more zep'lins and wingplanes?
Would it hurt to give people a chance to move around more freely?"

Maia wondered how a man could be so talkative, so early in the
day? *He would've gotten along better with Leie.*

"They say long ago there were a lot more zep'lins," she answered.

"They also say *men* used to fly them, like seaships, but then were
banished from the sky. Do you know why?"

Maia shook her head. "Why don't you ask them?"

"I tried." Renna grimaced, looking across the ocean. "Seems to be a
touchy subject. Maybe I'll look it up when I get back to the Library, in
Caria." He turned back to her. "Listen, I think I've figured something
out. Could you tell me if I'm wrong?"

Maia sighed. Renna seemed determined to wear down her carefully
tailored apathy with sheer, overpowering enthusiasm. "Okay," she said
warily.

"Great! First, let's verify the basics." He held up one finger. "Summertime matings result in normal, genetically diverse variants, or vars. Is that word derogatory, by the way? I've heard it used insultingly, in Caria."

"I'm a var," Maia said tonelessly. "No point being insulted by a fact."

"Mm. I guess you'd say I'm a var, too."

Of course. All boys are vars. Only the name doesn't cling to them like a parasite. But she knew Renna meant well, even when dredging clumsily through matters that hurt.

"All right, then. During autumn, winter, and spring, Stratoin women have parthenogenetic clones. In fact, they often can't conceive in summer till they've already had a winter child."

"You're doing fine so far."

"Good. Now, even cloning requires the involvement of men, as *sparklers*, since sperm induces placental—"

"That's *sparkers*," Maia corrected in a low voice.

"Yeah, right. Okay, here's the part I've been having trouble with." Renna paused. "It's about how Lysos meddled with sexual attraction. You see, on most hominid worlds, sex is an eternal distraction. People dwell on it from puberty to senility, spend vast measures of time and money, and sometimes act incredibly disagreeably, all because of a gene-driven, built-in obsession."

"You make it sound awful."

"Mm. It has compensations. But, arrangements on Stratos seem intended to cut down the amount of energy centered on sex. All in keeping with good Herlandist ideology."

"Go on," she said, growing interested despite herself. *Do people on other planets really think about sex more than I do? How do they get anything done?*

Renna continued. "Stratoin men are stimulated by visual cues in the summer sky, when women are *least* aroused. Today, on the other hand, I got to witness this peculiar ice-frost you get in winter—"

"Glory."

"Yeah. A natural product of some pretty amazing stratospheric processing that I plan looking into. And it stimulates *women*?"

"So I'm told." Maia felt warm. "According to legend, Lysos took the Old Craziness out of men and women, and looked around for someplace to put it. Up in the sky seemed safe enough. But one summer Wengel Star came along. He stole some of the madness and made a flag to wave and shine and put the old rut back into men, through their eyes."

"And during high winter it sneaks back down as Glory?"

"Right, seizing women through their noses."

"Mm. Nice fable. Still, doesn't it seem queer that women and men should be so perfectly off-sync in desire?"

"Not perfectly. If it were, nobody'd get born at all."

"Oh sure, I'm oversimplifying. Men can enjoy sex in winter and women in summer. But how odd that males are aggressive suitors during one season, only to grow demure half a year later, when women seek *them* out."

Maia shrugged. "Man and woman are opposites. Maybe all we can hope for is compromise."

Renna nodded in a manner reminiscent of an absentminded but eager savant from Burbidge Clan, whom the Lamai mothers used to hire to teach varlings trigonometry. "But however carefully Lysos designed your ancestors' genes, time and evolution would erase any setup that's not *naturally* stable. Those few males who escaped the program just a little would pass on their genes more often, and so on for their offspring. The same holds for women. Over time, male and female urges would come into rough synchrony again, with lots of tension and two-way negotiating, just like on other worlds.

"But here's the brilliant part. On Stratos there's greater payoff, in strict biological terms, for a woman to have clone children than normal sons and daughters, who carry only half her genes. So the trait of women seeking winter matings would *reinforce*."

Maia blinked. "And the same logic applies to men?"

"Exactly! A Stratoin male gets no genetic benefit from sex in winter! No reason to get all worked up, since any child spawned won't be his in the most basic sense. The cycle tends to *bolster* the cues Lysos established." He shook his head. "I'd need a good computer model to see if it's as stable as it looks. There are some inherent problems, like inbreeding. Over time, each clone family acts like a single individual, flooding Stratos with . . ."

Renna's enthusiasm was infectious. Maia had never known anyone so uninhibited, so unrestrained by conventional ideas. Still, a part of her wondered. *Is he always like this? Was everybody like this, where he came from?*

"I don't know," she cut in when he paused for breath. "What you're saying makes sense . . . but what about that happy, stable world Lysos wanted? Are we happy? Happier than people on other planets?"

Renna smiled, meeting her eyes once more. "You get right to the heart of the matter, don't you, Maia? How can I answer that? Who am I to judge?" He looked up at low, white cumulus clouds, whose flat bottoms rode an invisible pressure layer not far above the Manitou's topmast. "I've been to worlds which might seem like paradise to you. All your terrible experiences, this year, would have been next to impossible on Passion or New Terra. Law, technology, and a universal maternal state would have prevented them, or instantly stepped in with remedies.

"On the other hand, those worlds have problems rarely or never seen here. Economic and social upheavals. Suicide. Sex crimes. Fashion slavery. Pseudowar, and sometimes the real thing. Solipsism plagues. Cyberdysonism and demimortalism. Ennui. . . ."

Maia looked at him, wondering if he even noticed his lapse into alien dialect. Most of the words had no meaning to her. It reinforced her impression that the universe was vast, unfathomably strange, and forever beyond her reach.

"All I can do is speak for myself." Renna continued in a low voice. He paused, looking across the sun and shadow-splashed sea, then turned back and squeezed her hand again, briefly. His face crinkled in a startling manner at the edges of the eyes, and he smiled.

"Right now *I'm* happy, Maia. To be here, alive, and breathing air from an endless sky."

Maia cheered up considerably once the talk moved on to other things. Answering Renna's questions, she tried to explain some of the mysterious activities of Manitou's sailors—climbing the rigging, unfurling sails, scraping salt crust, oiling winches, tying lanyards and untying them, performing all the endless tasks required to keep a vessel in good running trim. Renna marveled at myriad details and spoke admiringly of "lost arts, preserved and wonderfully improved."

They told more of their personal stories. Maia related some of the amusing misadventures she and Leie used to have, as young hellions in Port Sanger, and found that a poignant warmth of recollection now overcame much of the pain. In return, Renna told her briefly of his capture while visiting a House of Ease in Caria, at the behest of a venerable state councillor he had trusted.

"Was her name Odo?" she asked, and Renna blinked. "How did you know?"

Maia grinned. "Remember the message you sent from your prison cell? The one I intercepted? You spoke of not trusting someone called Odo. Am I right?"

Renna sighed. "Yeah. Let it be a lesson. Never let your gonads get ahead of clear thinking."

"I'll take your word for it," Maia said dryly. Renna nodded, then looked at her, caught her expression, and they both broke down, laughing.

They continued telling stories. His concerned fascinating, faraway worlds of the Great Phylum of Humanity, while Maia lingered over the tale of her ultimate conquest, with Leie's help, of the most secret, hidden part of Lamatia Hold, solving the riddle of a very strange combination lock. Renna seemed impressed with the feat, and claimed to feel honored when she said it was the first time she had ever told anyone about it.

"You know, with your talent for pattern recog—"

A shout interrupted from the radar shed. Two boys went scrambling up the mainmast, clinging to an upper spar while peering in the distance. One cried out and pointed. Soon, the entire ship's complement stood at the port rail, shading their eyes and staring expectantly.

"What is it?" Renna asked. Maia could only shake her head, as perplexed as he. A murmur coursed the crowd, followed by a sudden hush. Squinting against reflections, Maia finally saw an object hove into view, ahead and to the south.

She gasped. "I think . . . it's a greatflower tree!"

It had all the outward appearances of a small island. One covered by flagpoles draped with tattered banners, as if legions had fought to claim and hold a tiny patch of dry land in the middle of the sea. Only this isle drifted, floating at an angle to the steady progress of the ship. As they approached, Maia saw the flagpoles were like spindly tree trunks. The ragged pennants weren't ensigns at all, but the remnants of glowing, iridescent petals.

"I saw a clip on these, long ago," Maia explained. "The greatflower lives off tiny sea creatures. You know, the kind with just one cell? Below the surface, it spreads out filmy sheets to catch them. That's why Poulandres ordered us to move away, instead of going closer for a better look. Wouldn't be right to hurt it, just out of curiosity."

"The thing looks pretty badly damaged already," Renna commented, noting the frayed flowers. Yet he seemed as enthralled as Maia by those remaining fragments, whose blue and yellow and crimson luminance seemed independent of reflected sunlight, shimmering across the waters. "What are those? *Birds*, picking away at the plant? Is it dead?"

Indeed, flocks of winged creatures—some with filmy wingspans wider than the Manitou's spars—swarmed the floating island like midges on a dying beast, attacking the brightly hued portions. Maia replied, "I remember now. They're *helping* it. That's how the greatflower breeds. The birds carry its pollen in their wings to the next tree, and the next."

As they watched, a small detachment of dark shapes swirled off the cloud of birds and came swooping toward the Manitou. At the captain's sharp command, crewmen dove belowdecks, emerging with slingshots and wrist catapults, which they fired to drive the graceful, soaring beasts away from the straining sails. The fliers inflicted only a little damage with narrow jaws filled with jagged teeth, before losing their appetite for canvas and flying away . . . though not before one tried nipping at the bright red hair of one of the boys aloft. An event that everyone but the poor victim seemed to find hilarious.

The greatflower flowed past only a hundred meters away. Its maze of color could now be seen extending beneath the water's surface, in tendrils that floated far behind. Schools of bright fish darted among the drifting fronds, in counterpoint to the frenetic feeding of the birds. Maia snapped her fingers. "Too bad we missed seeing one in late summer, when the flowers are in full bloom. Believe it or not, the trees use them as *sails*, to keep from being blown ashore during storm season. Now I guess the currents are enough, so the sails fall apart."

She turned to Renna. "Is that an example of what you mean by . . . adaptation? It must be an original Stratoin life-form, or you'd have seen things like it before, wouldn't you?"

Renna had been staring at the colorful, floating isle with its retinue of scavengers, as it drifted behind *Manatou*'s wake. "It's too wonderful for me to have missed, in any of the sectors I've been. It's native, all right. Even Lysos wasn't clever enough to design that."

Soon another greatflower hove into view, this time with fuller petals, diffracting sunlight in ways Renna excitedly described as "holographic." In turn, Maia told him about a tribe of savage sea people who had cast their lot forever with the greatflowers, sailing them like ships, collecting nectar and plankton, netting birds and fish, and snaring an occasional, castaway sailor to spark their daughters for another generation. Living wild and unfettered, the runaway society had lasted until planetary authorities and seafaring guilds joined forces to round them up as "ecological irresponsibles."

"Is that story true?" Renna asked, both dubious and entranced at the same time.

In fact, Maia had based it on very real tales from the Southern Isles. But the connection with greatflowers was her own invention, made up on the spur of the moment. "What do *you* think?" she asked, with an arched eyebrow.

Renna shook his head. "I think you're quite recovered from your near-drowning. Better have the doctor take you off whatever he's been giving you."

The last greatflower fell astern, and both crew and passengers soon returned to the tedium of routine. To pass the time, Renna and Maia used her sextant to take sightings on the sun and horizon, comparing calculations and trying to guess the time without looking at Renna's watch. They also gossiped. Maia laughed aloud and clapped when Renna puffed his cheeks in a caricature of the chief cook, announcing in anomalously squeaky tones that lunch would be delayed because glory frost had gotten in the pudding, and he'd be cursed before he fed it to "a bunch o' randy vars, too hepped t'ken a man from a lugar!"

"That reminds me of a story," she responded, and went on to relate the tale of a sea captain who let his passengers frolic in a late-evening glory-fall, then fell asleep, ". . . only to waken hours later when the women set fire to his sails!"

Renna looked perplexed, so she explained. "See, some people think flames overhead can simulate the effects of aurorae, get it? The glory-doped women ignited the ship. . . ."

"Hoping to get the men excited, too?" He looked appalled. "But . . . would it work?"

Maia stifled a giggle. "It's a joke, silly!"

She watched him picture the ludicrous scene, and then laughed aloud. At that moment Maia felt more relaxed than she had in—who knew how long? There was even a hint of what she had experienced back in her prison cell . . . of something more than acquaintanceship. It was good having a friend.

But Renna's next question took her aback.

"So," he said. "Do you want to help me get ready for another Life match? Captain Poulandres has agreed to let us try again. This time the other side has to wind the pieces, so we can concentrate on coming up with a new strategy."

Maia blinked at him. "You're kidding, right?"

"Y'know, I never imagined the competition version involved so many tricky permutations. It's more complicated than painting pretty pictures with a reversible Life variant, as I did with my set in jail. It'll be a challenge holding our own against even junior players."

Maia could not believe his penchant for understatement. Just when she thought she was starting to understand Renna, he surprised her again. "All they want to do is laugh at us. I won't be embarrassed like that again."

Renna seemed puzzled. "It's only a game, Maia," he chided lightly.

"If you think that, then you don't know much about men on Stratos!"

Her hot response gave Renna pause. He pondered for a moment. "Well . . . all the more reason to explore the matter further, then. Are you sure you won't . . . ?" When Maia shook her head firmly, he sighed. "In that case, I'd better get to work if I'm to have a game plan ready by this evening." He stood up. "We'll talk later?"

"Mm," she replied noncommittally, finding a way to occupy her hands and eyes, folding the sighting rods of her sextant with meticulous care as he departed with a cheery goodbye. Maia felt irked and confused as his footsteps receded—as much by his obstinacy in continuing to play the stupid game as by the way he took her refusal so well.

I guess I should be grateful to have a friend at all. She sighed. *Nobody's ever going to find me indispensable, that's for sure.*

It turned out he needed her even less than she had thought. When lunch was called, Maia took Renna his plate as usual, only to find him sitting near the fantail with the electronic Life Set on his lap, surrounded by a cluster of extremely attentive young rads.

"So you see," he explained, gesturing from one corner of the board to the other. "If you want to create a simulated ecology that'll do *both* things—resist invasion from the outside *while* persisting in a self-sustaining manner—you have to make sure all elements interact in such a way that— Ah, Maia!" Renna looked up with unmistakable pleasure. "Glad you've changed your mind. I had an idea. You can tell me if I'm being an idiot."

Don't tempt me, she thought in a flash of jealous temper. Which was silly, of course. Renna appeared oblivious, too caught up in his enthusiasm for concepts to notice that these vars weren't swarming over him out of any love of abstractions.

"Brought you the chef's special," she said, trying to maintain a light tone. "Of course, if anyone *else* is hungry . . ."

The other women shot her daggers. By unspoken agreement, two of them got up to fetch, so the rest could keep Renna attended.

They're the idiots, Maia thought, noting that other clusters of women could be seen following any ship's officer who stepped off the sacrosanct quarterdeck. All this had been provoked by the morning's glory fall. She doubted any of the vars actually wanted to get pregnant here and now. Not without a niche and bankroll to raise a child securely. Maia had seen women putting pinches of ovop leaf in their cheeks, as a safeguard against conception.

Even if pleasure was the sole objective, however, their hopes were ill-fated. Great clans spent fortunes entertaining men in winter, getting them in the mood. Without incentives, most of Manitou's sailors would choose whittling and games over providing exertive services free of charge. *Well . . . I've seen exceptions,* Maia admitted. But Tizbe Beller's drug was doubtless far too dear for rads to afford, even if they had the right contacts.

"Go on," one of the young women urged Renna. It was the slim blonde Maia had overheard earlier, now leaning against Renna's shoulder to look at the game board, hoping to distract his attention back from Maia. "You were talking about ecology," the rad said in a low voice. "Explain again what that has to do with the patterns of dots."

She's acting stupid on purpose. Maia watched Renna shift uncomfortably. *And it's going to backfire on her.*

Sure enough, Renna lifted his eyes in a silent sigh, and gave Maia an apologetic glance before answering. "What I meant was that each individual organism in an ecosystem interacts primarily with its neighbors, just like in the game, though, of course, the rules are vastly more complex . . ."

Maia felt a moment of triumph. His look meant he preferred her conversation to the others' close-pressed attentions, no matter that they were older, physically more mature. Naturally, his reaction would have been different in summer, when rut turned all men into—

Wait a minute. Maia stopped short suddenly. *We talked about seasonal sexuality on Stratos. Deep-down, though, I kept assuming that it applied to him.*

Does it, though? Would summer and winter have anything to do with what Renna feels?

Maia backed away, watching as the Earthman patiently described how the array of black or white cells crudely simulated a kind of "life." Despite the simple level of his explanation, he seemed intent to look only at the game board, avoiding direct contact with his audience. For the first time, Maia noticed a sheen of perspiration on his brow.

"They got plans for him, you know."

Maia whirled. A tall, fair-haired woman had come up from behind. The rugged easterner, Baltha, picked her teeth with a wood sliver and leaned against the aft capstan. She grinned at Maia. "Your Earthman is worth a lot more to these rads than they're lettin' on, y'know."

Maia felt torn between curiosity and her dislike of the woman. "I know they need information, and advice from his ship's library. They want to know if something in it can help make Stratos more like other worlds."

Baltha raised an eyebrow. Perhaps the acknowledgment was mocking. "Information's nice. But I bet they seek help of a quicker sort."

"What do you mean?"

Baltha tossed the toothpick in an arc that carried it overboard. "Think about it, virgie. You see how they're already workin' on him. He'll be asked to earn his keep, in Ursulaborg. An' I just bet he's able."

Maia's face felt warm. "So? So he sparks a few—"

Baltha interrupted. "Sparks, hell! You just can't see, can you?

Think, girlie. He's an *alien*! Now that may mean he's too different even
to spark Strato-fems like us. Can't tell unless they try. But what about th'
other extreme? What if his seed works, all right? What if it works the
old-fashioned way, *even in winter?*"

Maia blinked as she worked out what Baltha meant. "You mean, his
sperm might not spark clones . . . but instead go all the way and make
vars?" She looked up. "No matter what time of year it is?"

Baltha nodded. "Then, what if his var-sons inherited that knack?
An' their sons? An' so on? Now wouldn't *that* throw a spanner in Lysos's
plan?" She spat over the side.

Maia shook her head. "Something sounds wrong about that—"

"You bet it's wrong!" the big var cut in again. "Meddlin' with the
design set down by our foremothers an' betters. Arrogant rad bitches."

Actually, Maia hadn't meant "wrong" in that sense. Although she
couldn't spot the flaw at that moment, she felt certain there was something cockeyed with Baltha's reasoning. It struck Maia intuitively that
the design of human life on Stratos wouldn't be so easily diverted, not
even by seed taken from a man from the stars.

"I thought you hated the way things are, as much as the rads do,"
she asked, curious about the venom in Baltha's voice. "You helped them
get Renna away from the Perkinites."

"Alliance of convenience, virgie. Sure, my mates an' me hate
Perkies. Stuck-up clans that want a lock on everything without keepin'
on earnin' it. Lysos never meant that to happen. But from there on, we
an' the rads part. Bleedin' heretics. We just want to shake things up, not
change the laws o' nature!"

Why is she telling me this? Maia wondered, seeing a gleam in
Baltha's eyes as she regarded Renna. "You have ideas about using him,
too," Maia surmised.

The blonde var turned to look at her. "Don't know what you mean."

"I saw what you collected in your little box," Maia blurted, eager to
see how Baltha would react when confronted. "Back in the canyon, while
we were escaping."

"Why, you little sneak . . ." the woman growled. Then she stopped
and a slow grin spread across her rugged features. "Well, good for you.
Spyin's one of th' true arts. Might even be your niche, sweetums, if you
ever learn to tell enemies from friends."

"I know the difference, thanks."

"Do you?"

"Like I can tell you'd use Renna for your own ends, at least as
much as the rads want to."

Baltha sighed. "Everybody uses everybody else. Take your *friends,*

Kiel an' Thalla. They used *you*, kiddo. Sold you to th' Bellers, in hopes of trackin' you to jail, an' maybe findin' their Starman wherever you were stashed."

Maia stared. "But . . . I thought Calma Lerner . . ."

"Think what you like, citizen," Baltha answered sarcastically. "I know better than tryin' to tell nothin' to a smart fiver, who's *so* sure she knows who's her good pals, an' who ain't."

The eastlander turned and sauntered away, wandering to the railing that overlooked the cargo deck, where she began a low conversation with a large blonde woman, one of the female deckhands serving aboard the Manitou. Below, on the main deck, Naroin's voice could be heard, calling a small band of women away from bothering sailors to take their turn at obligatory combat practice. Baltha grinned back at Maia, then picked up her own polished short-trepp, and slid down the gangway to join the session. Soon there came a staccato clicking of sticks, and a thump as somebody hit the ground.

Maia's thoughts roiled. She saw Thalla, about to take her turn in the practice ring, pluck a bill from the weapons rack. Glancing up, Thalla smiled at her, and in a rush, Maia was filled with an outraged sense of confirmation. *Baltha's right, damn her! Kiel and Thalla must have used me.*

A tidal surge of hurt and betrayal caused each breath to catch painfully in her throat. She had been angry with her former cottagemates for trying to leave her behind in Grange Head, but this was worse. Far worse. *I . . . can't trust anybody.*

The sense of perfidy hurt terribly. Yet, what strangely came to mind most strongly right then was the memory of cursing Calma Lerner and her doomed clan. *I'm sorry*, she thought. Even if Baltha turned out to be wrong, or lying, Maia felt ashamed of what she'd said in wrath, invoking maledictions on the hapless smithy family, whose members had never done her any real harm.

In the background, contrasting to her dark brooding, Renna's voice continued blithely, describing his strategy for the evening's match. ". . . so I was thinking, I could put a *pinwheel* at each end of the board, near the boundary . . ."

The voice was an irritation, scraping away at Maia's guilt-wallow. *Even if Baltha lied, I'll never be able to trust Thalla and Kiel again. I'm as alone now as ever I was in my prison cell.*

She closed her eyes. The rhythmic clicking of battle sticks was punctuated by Naroin's shouted instructions. Renna droned on. ". . . Naturally, they'll be struck by simulated objects coming from my opponents' side of the board. Most of those will be deflected by the pinwheel's arms. But there are certain basic shapes that worry me . . ."

Vagaries of wind caused the steersman to order a slight turn, bringing the sun around from behind a sail to shine on Maia's closed eyelids. She had to tighten them to sever innumerable stabbing, diffracted rays. In her sadness, Maia felt a return of that odd, *displaced* feeling she had experienced that morning. Sunlight enhanced those omnipresent speckles in their ceaseless dance before covered retinas . . . a dance without end, the dance that accompanied all her dreams. Void of will, her awareness drew toward their flicker and swirl, seeming to laugh at her troubles, as if all worries were ephemera.

The speckled pavane was the only lasting thing that mattered.

". . . You see how even a simple *glider*, striking at an angle, will cause my pinwheel to break up. . . ."

Unasked-for memories of those long days and nights in prison swarmed over her. Maia recalled how she had been entranced by the Life game, the patterns wonderfully mysterious as Renna's artistry unfolded in front of her. That had been a far more subtle exercise than playing a simple set match, throwing simulated figures against those devised by an opponent. But it was a cheat, since he had been able to use a form of the game that was *reversible*. The machine did all the work. No wonder he was having so much trouble dealing with the most trivial concepts of the competitive version.

She did not have to be looking at the board to envision the shapes he was describing. In her current state of consciousness, she could not *prevent* envisioning them.

The rads sitting around him must be bored out of their minds, one part of her contemplated with some satisfaction. Yet it was a small part. The rest of her had fled from unbearable unhappiness into abstraction, only to be caught in a swirl of cavorting forms.

". . . So I was thinking of placing an array of simple beacon patterns around the pinwheel, like this . . . you see? That ought to protect it from at least the first onslaught—"

"Wrong!" Maia cried out loud, opening her eyes and turning around. Renna and the women stared in surprise as she strode toward them, brusquely shooing aside one of the surprised vars to get at the game board. She took the stylus out of Renna's hand and quickly erased the array he had been building at one end of the boundary zone.

"Can't you see? Even I can. If you want to protect against gliders, you don't let your shapes just sit there, waiting to be hit. Your barrier's got to go out to *meet* them. Here, try—" She bit her lip, hesitating a moment, then drew a hurried swirl of dots on the display. Maia reached over to flick on the timing clock, and the configuration began throbbing, sending out concentric ovals of black dots that dissipated upon reaching a distance of eight squares from the center. It was reminiscent of the persistent, cyclic pattern of waves emanating from where drips from a faucet strike a pool of water. Left alone, the little array would keep sending out waves forever.

Renna looked up in surprise. "I've never seen that one before. What's it called?"

"I . . ." Maia shook her head. "I don't know. Must've seen it when I was a kid. It's obvious enough, though. Isn't it?"

"Mm. Indeed." Shaking his head, Renna took back the stylus and drew a glider gun on the other side of the board, aimed at the figure she had just drawn. He restarted the game clock, causing a series of flapping missiles to be fired straight toward with the pattern of concentric waves. They collided . . .

. . . and each one was swallowed with scarcely a ripple!

"I'll be damned." He shook his head admiringly. "But how would you defend this pattern against something larger, like was thrown against us last night?"

Maia snapped. "How should I know? Do you think I'm a boy?"

Several of the rads chuckled, uncertainly, and Maia didn't care if they were laughing with, or at her. One of the young women got up with a sniff and walked away. Maia rubbed her chin, looking at the game board. "Now that you mention it, though, I can suggest one way to fend off that bulldozer contraption the cook and cabin boy used against us."

"Yes?" Renna made room on the bench and another var reluctantly gave way as Maia sat down. "Look, I don't know the terminology," she said, with some of her accustomed uncertainty returning. "But it's obvious the thing's crossbar doohickey *reflects* certain patterns which . . ."

She drew as she spoke, with Renna occasionally interjecting a comment, or more often a question. Maia hardly noticed as the other vars drifted away, one by one. Their opinions didn't matter anymore, nor was she any longer embarrassed being seen interested in the male-silly game. Renna took her seriously, which none of her fellow womenfolk ever had. He paid close attention, contributing insights, sharing a growing pleasure in an abstract exercise.

By suppertime, they thought they had a plan.

W hat is sentience to the universe? Brief moments of insight? The self-contemplation of mayflies?

What is the point of human life, if so much of it must be spent climbing through awkward childhood and adolescence, slowly gathering the skills needed to comprehend and create . . . only to begin that long decline to extinction? Lucky the woman or man who achieves excellence for even a brief span. The light shines brightly for mere moments, then is gone.

On some worlds, drastic life extension is justified in the name of preserving rare talents. It starts with good intentions, but all too often results in a gerontocracy of habit-ridden minds in robot-tended bodies, suspiciously jealous of any thought or idea not their own.

Stratoins think they know a better way. If an individual proves herself—say in the marketplace of goods or ideas—she continues. Not with the same body or precise memories, but genetically, with inborn talents preserved, and a continuity of upbringing that only clone-parenting provides. When all factors are right, the first mother's flowering of skill carries on. Yet, each daughter is a renewal, a fresh burst of enthusiasm. Preservation needn't mean calcification.

Stratoins have struck a different arrangement with death. There are costs, but I can see the advantages.

Fortunately, summer council sessions are brief. I needn't endure more than a few hours of sullen looks from the majority, or hostile glares by extreme Isolationists. Much of my time is spent with savants at the university. What I like best, however, is observing life on Stratos, with Iolanthe Nitocris often serving as my keeper/guide.

Yesterday, to my delight, she finally obtained a pass to show me Caria's Summer Festival.

The fairgrounds lay upstream, in the morning shadow of the acropolis. Banners flutter above silken pavilions and avenues bedecked with flowered arches. Zenner trees sway to the musical murmur of the crowds, while pungent, exotic aromas loft from food stalls. Jugglers caper, thrilling all with feats of derring-do. Outside the walls of Caria, citizens seemed eager to drop the serene pace of daily life in favor of a livelier beat.

I felt conspicuous, and not just because I'm an alien. (Some in the throng surely knew, or guessed.) Most of the time, I was also the only mature male in sight. Shouting boys ran a gauntlet of knees, like children on any world, and there was a sprinkling of old men, but virile adults remain at safe distance, in their summer sanctuaries. Several times Iolanthe, as my vouch-woman, was asked to show my papers. The council seal, plus my calm demeanor, reassured the marshals I was not about to start bellowing and tearing off my clothes at any minute.

Iolanthe seemed pleased. This would score in my favor.

If only she knew how difficult I find it here, at times.

The day's procession was led by a chariot bearing the festival grand matron, whose spear and crested helm harkened to the goddess of the city gates. Behind came musicians and dancers, blowing pipes and performing fantastic, whirling leaps, as if this vast world were no heavier than a moon. Their floating gowns seemed to catch the air, and laid hooks in my heart.

Many venerable clans sent marching ensembles, to whose instrumental euphonies the crowds sang along . . . until an abrupt musical variation set onlookers laughing in delighted surprise. Tight formations of brightly burnished cavalry pranced among the bands, followed by ugar-borne palanquins carrying women dignitaries, bedecked with laurels and medals. Mothers and older siblings bent to tell wide-eyed clan daughters what honor or achievement each emblem represented.

At last, the excited audience surged into the avenue, merging with the final contingents, dissolving the parade into an impromptu Mardi Gras. No one noticed or cared when a summer shower swept by, dampening heads, clothes, and flowered canopies, but not the joyful spirit. Some in the crowd did double-takes on spotting me, but others only smiled in a friendly way, urging me to join in the dance. It was exhilarating and fun, but the dampness, the closeness . . .

I asked Iolanthe to take me away from there. Some of the younger Nitocri with us seemed disappointed, but she agreed at once. We departed the main avenue to explore the rest of the fair.

At the racetrack, horse breeders showed off their prize stock, then stripped the oiled champions of wreaths and fine bows, setting on their backs petite riders from renowned jockey clans. Eager and taut, the mounts leaped at the starting horn, accelerating to bound over the first of many obstacles, then braking to daintily skirt intricate mazes before pounding past the far straightaway in a fury of lathered desire. Winning clans welcomed their entrants with bouquets, embraces, and endearments that would have warmed any lover.

Our next stop could have been an agricultural fair on any of a dozen worlds. Many of the ribbon-bedecked plants and animals were unfamiliar to me, but not the proud looks of young girls who had spent months nurturing their charges for this day. West of Caria, Stratoin balloon-creatures of many types are fostered for their beauty, or the fragrance they exude, or the tricks some breeds can be taught to perform. All of these were on display. Nearby, women whistled to radiant-plumed birds, which dove and swooped, carrying buttons or pieces of colored cloth to contestants who chose winning numbers from a guessing board.

In the craft halls, I witnessed tournaments of pottery, woodworking, and other skills. Many coastal industrial clans had sent their brightest daughters, I was told, to participate in a close-watched competition involving the use of coal and clay and simple ores, hand-working raw materials all the way to finished tools. There were even holovid cameras to cover that event, while mere horse-races went untelevised.

By the riverside we watched water competitions, beginning with sculls and shells and rowing barges. Most were pulled by teams of bronzed, well-muscled, identical women, who needed no coxswain to guide their perfect unison. The culminating trial, however, was a regatta of trim sailing sloops, threading a hazardous course amid sandbars and shallows. To my surprise, these larger craft were crewed by teams of energetic young men. When I learned what prize they strove for, I knew why they competed with such fervor.

It was a thrilling battle of skill, raw energy, and luck. Two of the leading craft, contending violently for the wind, collided, entangling their sails, driving them together on a gravel bank. Whereupon a more cautious team swept by the judges' buoy, to raucous cheers from watchers on shore. Amused women chuckled and pointed as the lucky dozen males, preening with eyes afire, were led away by representatives of clans who had chosen to have summer offspring this year.

It reminded me of the racecourse—those leashed stallions, prancing off to stud for their proud owners. With that thought, I had to look away.

"Come. I know you'll want to see this," Iolanthe said. She and her sisters led me to a pavilion at the far end of the fairgrounds, dingier than most, made of a gray, coarse fabric meant to last many seasons. On entering, I blinked for a moment, wondering what was simultaneously strange and familiar about the people gathered at various booths and exhibits. Then I realized. Almost no one looked alike! After weeks in Caria, meeting delegations of high clans, getting used to double, triple, and quadruple visions of the same facial types, it felt disorienting to see so much diversity in one place. There were even some elderly men, come from far citadels to show their crafts and wares.

"This place is for vars," I essayed a guess.

Iolanthe nodded. "Or singleton envoys from poor, young clans. Here, anyone with something new and special to display gets her chance, hoping for that lucky break."

What point was she trying to make? That Stratoin society allows for change? That their founders had left ways for newness to enter, from time to time? Or was she subtly suggesting something else? Moving from booth to booth, I was struck by a certain deficit. A lack of smoothness or the relaxed presumption of skill that daughters of an older clan wore as easily as clothes on their backs.

The women under this tent were eager to show the products of their labor and ingenuity. Buyers from great trading houses could be seen threading the aisles, aloofly on the lookout for something worth their time and interest. Here, in a moment, a var's success could be made. Generations later, her innovation might become the basis for a clan's wealth.

Clearly that is the hope. And just as clearly, few in this vast room would see it come true. How often hope comes salted with a bitter tang.

They used to say, on Earth, that we find immortality through our children. It is a solace, although most of us know that when we die, we stop.

On Stratos, though . . . I no longer know what to think. Under that canopy, at the far end of the festival grounds, I felt something familiar that had seemed remote at Nitocris Hold, or in the marbled chambers of the acropolis.

Beneath the Var Pavilion, I remarked a familiar scent of mortality.

18

T heir opponents offered to waive the rules.

It was done quite often, Maia knew. About one Life match in five that she had witnessed featured some agreed-on variation. These ranged from using odd boundaries to altering the fundamental canons of the game—including more than two colors, or changing the way pieces responded to the status of their neighbors.

In this case, nothing complicated was involved. To save time—and perhaps rub home the helplessness of their adversaries—the junior cook and cabin boy suggested that each side lay down *four* rows at a turn, instead of just one. Since their own round came first this time, it was a generous concession, like spotting a chess opponent one rook. Maia and Renna would get to see large swaths of the other side of the board, and discuss possible changes before placing each layer of their own.

Maia watched tensely as the two youths positioned their game pieces. Seconds passed, and she felt a knot slowly unwind in her belly. *They aren't very imaginative, after all,* she thought. *Or they're being lazy.* The boys' oasis zone was already apparent, protected by a spiky variety of a standard pattern called "long fence."

Maia found it bemusing, standing here reading a game board this way. Last night, during their first match, she had experienced one or two moments of inspiration, but had been too confused and worried to enjoy the process, or let go and watch the game as a whole. That had changed with this afternoon's epiphany and during the subsequent session exploring possibilities with Renna. Now she felt strangely detached, yet eager, as if a barrier had broken, releasing something serenely beyond mere curiosity.

Almost certainly, it had been triggered by that cruel conversation with Baltha, causing her to despair at last of comradeship from woman-kind. But that didn't go all the way toward explaining her sudden passion for this game.

Face it. I'm abnormal.

It hadn't begun with this voyage, or on meeting Renna, or even studying navigation with old Bennett. At age three, she used to love going down by the piers, watching sailors scratch their beards and mull over arrays of clicking game pieces. Many women enjoyed the dance of shapes and forms, yet there had always been something implicit in the townsfolk's *indulgent* appreciation. No one came right out and said it wasn't for girls. The tenor of complaisant scorn sufficed, especially when shared by Leie. Eager to fit in, young Maia had mimicked words of affectionate contempt, suppressing, she now saw in retrospect, that early fascination.

I've always loved patterns, puzzles. Maybe it's all a mistake. I should have been a boy.

That passing, sardonic thought she did not take seriously. Maia felt profoundly female. No doubt what she'd stumbled on was simply a wild talent manifesting itself. One lacking much use in real life, alas. She knew of no lucrative niche in Stratoin society for a woman navigator who was also able to play man-games.

No niche. No golden road to matriarchy. But perhaps a life. Naroin seems to do all right, spending most of each year at sea.

It was funny, contemplating a career as a woman-sailor. There were attractions to the rough camaraderie Naroin and the other var hands shared with the seamen. On the other hand, a life of hauling ropes and yanking winches . . . ? Maia shook her head.

Spectators gathered. The boys laid down their pieces, hurrying along for a stretch, then stopping to point and argue before reaching consensus and resuming. Maia stifled a yawn, shoved her hands back into her coat pockets, and shifted her feet to keep up circulation. The midwinter evening was mild. Tiered banks of low, dark clouds served to keep in some of the day's warmth. While a range of ocher, sunset shades still tinted those along the western fringe, lanterns overlooking the cargo game area were switched on.

Up on the quarterdeck, the helmsman sniffed the air and exchanged a look with the captain, who returned a brief nod. The tiller turned a few degrees. Soon, a gentle shift in the ship's swaying accompanied an al-tered rhythm from the creaking masts. Without being told, two sailors

sauntered to a set of cranks by the starboard side, ratcheting them just
enough to tauten a sail.

Maia wondered. Was it something intrinsic to males, that made
them sensitive to cues of wind and wave? Was that why no woman officer
served on oceangoing ships? She had always assumed it was something
genetic. *But then, I thought men couldn't ride horses, till Renna did it,
and men also sailed the sky in zep'lins, long ago, before they were banned.
Maybe it's just another self-fulfilling myth.*

The point was moot. Even if a woman like her were as innately
able, five was much too old to start learning sea craft. *Just because you
know how to sight stars, that doesn't qualify you to buck a thousand-year
tradition. Besides, sailors would raise hell if a woman rose above bosun.*
There weren't many niches in Stratoin society that males could call their
own. They would not willingly open this bastion to the overpowering
female majority.

*Listen to yourself. A minute ago you were modestly willing to settle
for a quiet, comfortable life, like Naroin. Now you're grumbling 'cause
they won't put officer's rings on your arms!* Maia chuckled silently. *More
proof of bad upbringing. A Lamatia education leads to a Lamai-sized ego.*

"Right. Now it's our turn."

At Renna's word, Maia looked over to the other side of the game
board, where their opponents had finished laying down four rows. Even
from limited experience, she saw it as a completely pedestrian pattern.
Not that it mattered, given the strategy she and Renna had agreed upon.
Maia returned her partner's smile of encouragement. Then they split up,
he to start laying in the left corner, and she on the right.

Naroin had volunteered to carry prewound game pieces for Maia,
deftly passing one over each time Maia lifted her hand. Maia paused
frequently to consult the plan she and Renna had worked out. A sketch
she kept rolled up to prevent peeking by spectators in the rigging.

Got to be careful not to miss a row or column, she reminded herself.
This close, you risked losing that sense of overall structure which
seemed to leap out of a game board when viewed whole. Just one piece,
laid in the wrong place, often doomed a "living" design—as if a person's
kidneys had been attached incorrectly from the start, or your cells produced a wrong-shaped protein. Maia chewed her lip nervously as she
neared the middle, where her work would meet Renna's. On finishing,
she could only wait, worrying a cuticle as he placed his final tokens on
the board. At last, he straightened from his stoop, and stretched. Maia
stood alongside as they checked.

The two portions meshed, and by rushing through the first turn, they
had given their opponents little time to ponder. Sure enough, the two

youths frowned, obviously perplexed by the sequence she and her partner had created.

Good! I feared my idea was obvious . . . one they taught boys their first year at sea.

That didn't mean it was going to *work*, only that she and Renna had surprise going for them. The cook and cabin boy seemed rattled as they commenced laying four more rows on their side. Naroin nudged Maia. With a smile, the petite bosun pointed to the quarterdeck, where last night the ship's officers had leaned on the rail, casually watching the amateurs' humiliation. Tonight, a similar crowd had gathered, but this time their expressions were hardly idle. A cluster of ensigns and midshipmen flipped the pages of tall, gilt-edged books, alternately pointing toward the game board and arguing. To the left, three older men seemed to need no reference volumes. The ship's navigator and doctor exchanged a mere glance and smile, while Captain Poulandres puffed his pipe, resting his elbows on the finely carved banister, showing no expression save a glitter in his eye.

The boys finished their turn and appeared taken aback when Maia and Renna did not linger, analyzing what they'd done, but immediately proceeded to create four more rows of their own. Maia found it easier to envision the patterns, this time. Still, she kept glancing at the sailor who lounged by the port rail, holding a timer.

When she and her partner checked their work again, Maia looked across the cargo hatch and had the satisfaction of seeing the cook clench his fists nervously. The cabin boy seemed agitated. Commencing their turn, the boys quickly botched one of their figures, eliciting laughter from men watching overhead. The captain cleared his throat sharply, warning against audience interference. Blushing, the boys fixed the error and hurried on. They had built an elaborate array of defenses, consisting of powerful, unsubtle figures intended to block or absorb any attack. Next, they would presumably start on offense.

At last, the two youths stood back and signaled that it was Maia's and Renna's turn. Renna motioned her forward. "No!" she whispered. "I can't. You do it." But Renna just smiled and winked. "It was your idea," he said.

With a sigh, swallowing a lump in her throat, Maia took a step forward and she spoke a single word.

"Pass."

There followed a stunned silence, punctuated by the sharp sound of a junior officer slapping his palm decisively onto an open book. His neighbor nodded, but down on deck confusion reigned. "What d'yer mean?" the cook asked, looking left and right for guidance. This broke the tension as other men abruptly laughed. For the first time, Maia felt sorry for her opponent. Even she had seen games in which one side or the other skipped a row, leaving every space blank. What she was doing here, skipping four rows at once—that was the daring part.

Patiently, Poulandres explained while Naroin and other volunteers helped spread one hundred and sixty tokens, all white face up. In moments the boys were told to proceed, which they did with much nervous fumbling, piecing together a formidable array of aggressive-looking artillery patterns. When they looked up at last, Maia stepped forward again and repeated, "Pass!"

Again, volunteers quickly spread four rows of white pieces, while the audience murmured. *Even if our pattern won't function as planned, this was worth it.* On the other side, the boys went back to work, perspiring for lack of a break. For her part, Maia was starting to shiver from inactivity. Looking aft, she saw several common seamen drift over to ask questions of an ensign who, pointing at the board, made motions with his hands and whispered, trying to explain.

So what we're attempting is in the books, after all. Probably part of game lore, but rarely seen, like fool's mate in Chess. Easy to counter, providing you know what to do.

Renna and I have to hope we're playing against fools.

It didn't matter in one sense. Maia was pleased simply to have stirred their calm complacency. Maybe now they'd lend her some of those gilt-edged books, instead of patronizingly assuming they'd make no sense to her.

The other side of the board filled with a crowd of gaudy, extravagant figures, many of which Maia now saw were excessive and mutually contradictory, lacking the elegance of a classic Life match. On their own side, meanwhile, eight rows of enigmatic black and white dots terminated in a broad expanse of simple white.

I can't wait to ask the name of our pattern. Maia hungered to consult those volumes. *It's simple enough in concept, even if it turns out flawed.*

What she had realized this afternoon, in a flash of insight, was that the *boundary* was truly part of the game. By reflecting most patterns that struck it, the edge participated crucially.

So why not alter it?

Maia had first imagined simply creating a *copy* of the boundary, a little further up their side of the board, to screw up any carom shots attempted by their foes. But that wouldn't work. Inside the board, all persistent patterns had to be self-renewing. The boundary pattern wasn't a stable one. If recreated elsewhere, it quickly dissolved.

But what about creating a pattern that acted like a boundary *part of the time,* while turning transparent to most types of missiles and gliders much of the rest? One example of such a structure had popped into mind this afternoon. It would reflect simple gliders eight beats out of ten, and so long as the anchor points at both ends were left alone, it would keep renewing. Given what they had faced last night, their opponents clearly planned shooting a lot of stuff at them. Overkill, nearly all of which would now come right back in their faces! With luck, their opponents would wreak more havoc on themselves than on the resilient, simple pattern Renna and Maia had created.

From the enclosed cabin behind the helm, a sailor wearing a duty armband hurried to the captain's side and whispered in his ear. The commander frowned, knotting his caterpillar eyebrows. He gestured for the doctor to take over as referee, and crooked a finger for the navigator to follow.

Meanwhile, tired and haggard, the boys finished their terminal swath and resignedly listened to Maia declare "pass" for the final time. While the last white pieces were laid, the doctor could be seen shrugging into formal, pleated robes, topped by a peaked hood. With poised dignity, the old man sauntered downstairs amid a susurration of talk. Men followed to crowd around the board, pointing, excitedly consulting sage texts. Many, like the cook and cabin boy, just looked confused.

The referee took his traditional pose near the timing square.

Silence reigned. "Life is continuation—" he began.

A cracking sound, like a sliding door hitting its stops, interrupted the invocation. Hurried footsteps thumped across the quarterdeck. The Manitou's captain appeared, gripping the banister while a sailor came alongside and blew a brass horn—two short peals and a long note that tapered slowly into utter quiet. No one seemed to breathe.

"For some time we've been picking up a radar trace," Poulandres told his crew and passengers. "Their bearing intersects ours, and they appear fast enough to overhaul. I've tried raising them, but they will not answer.

"I can only assume we are targets of reavers. Therefore I must ask the paying passengers. Will you resist, and defend your cargo?"

Still blinking in surprise, Maia watched Kiel step forward. "Hell, yes. We'll resist."

The officer nodded. "Very well. I shall maneuver accordingly. You may consult our female crew, who will assist you under the Code of the Sea. Everyone to action stations."

The horn blew again, this time a rapid tattoo as sailors ran to the rigging and women hurried to assemble by the forecastle. Maia looked numbly at the game board. *But . . . we were about to find out. . . .*

A hand took Maia's arm. It was Thalla, guiding her to where someone had already unlocked the weapons cabinet and was passing out
trepp bills. Maia glanced back at Renna, his mouth slightly agape, staring at the commotion. *He's even more confused than I am,* she realized,
feeling sorry for her friend from the stars.

Renna started to follow, but a sailor put a hand out. *"Men don't
fight,"* Maia saw him say, repeating the lesson she had taught him during
the escape from Long Valley. The sailor led Renna off, and Maia turned
to find her place along a row of vars, gathering with weapons in hand.

"Will you follow my tactical orders?" Naroin asked Kiel and Thalla,
who represented the rad company. They nodded.

"All right, then. Inanna, Lullin, Charl, stand ready to receive
squads." Naroin assigned passengers to follow each of three experienced
female sailors to positions along the ship's gunwales. Maia was among
those in the bosun's own group, stationed toward the bow, where the rise
and fall of Manitou's cutting prow felt most pronounced. She sensed a
change in the breeze as the ship altered course, presumably to try evading confrontation.

"Better relax," Naroin told her squad. "They may be faster, but a
stern chase is a long chase. Could be daybreak 'fore they catch us." With
that, she sent two vars below for blankets. "We'll get hot soup soon," she
assured the nervous women. "Might as well stay rested. Ever'body get
down, out of th' wind."

They settled onto the deck with their bills at hand. Naroin reached
over to tap Maia on the knee. "Lucky break for someone, the horn
blowin' when it did. Judgin' by what I seen, those dappy rim shots were
the lucky ones!"

Maia shrugged. "I guess we'll never know." A clattering aft told of
game pieces being swept into their storage boxes, at captain's orders.

"They prob'ly arranged all this to keep you from humiliatin' two o'
their boys," Naroin said, causing Maia to stare back at her. But the
woman sailor grinned and Maia knew she was joking. Sea captains took
honor in the games almost as seriously as the safety of their ship and
crew.

Women made tentlike shrouds of their blankets, covering their
heads and shoulders, settling in for a long wait. True to the bosun's word,
a crewman soon arrived, carrying a kettle. Bowls clattered at his waist.
The junior cook did not look at Maia when he reached her, but the cup
sloshed when she took it from his hand, scalding her fingers. Wincing
within, she managed to show no outward reaction. At least the thick
broth was tasty and its warmth welcome, especially as gaps appeared
between the clouds and the night chilled. One woman blew a flute, un-
melodiously. There were attempts at gossip. None got very far.

"Say," Naroin offered. "I found out somethin' you might be interested in."

Maia looked up. She had been stroking the smooth wooden stave, wordlessly contemplating what might come in a few hours. "What's that?" she asked blankly.

Naroin brought up a hand to shield her mouth, and lowered her voice. "I found out what he does, spendin' that extra time behind the curtain . . . You know? After meals?"

It took a moment to grasp that Naroin was referring to Renna. "After . . . ?"

"He's cleanin' his mouth!"

Curiosity battled anger that the woman had spied on Maia's friend. "Cleaning . . . his *mouth*?"

"Yup." Naroin nodded. "You've seen that little brush of his? Well, he sticks it in seawater—even though he won't drink the stuff—then pops it in an' carries away like a deckhand tryin' to finish KP in time for a party! Scours those white gnashers good, with lots o' swishin' an' spittin'. Beats anythin' I've seen."

"Um," Maia replied, trying to come up with an explanation. "Some people would smell better if they did that, now and then."

"Good point." Naroin laughed. "But after *every* meal?"

Maia shook her head. "He *is* an alien. Maybe he's worried about . . . catching diseases?"

"But he eats our food. Kind o' hard to see what good mouth-cleanin' does, after the fact."

Maia shrugged. It might otherwise be a topic worth further speculation. But right now it seemed petty and pointless. Good intentions or no, she preferred that Naroin leave her alone. Fortunately the bosun seemed to sense this, and conversation lapsed.

Durga rose, backlighting the clouds and casting shafts of pearly radiance through gaps in the overcast, onto patches of choppy sea. Those patches, and the star-filled openings above them, corresponded like pieces of a child's puzzle and the holes they were meant to occupy. Maia glimpsed bits of constellations, and could tell the ship was fleeing southward before the wind. The bow's steady rise and fall felt like a slow, steady heartbeat, carrying them not just through dark seas, but through time. Each moment drew new patterns out of old configurations of wood, water, and flesh. Each novel, fleeting rearrangement set conditions for yet more patterns to follow.

It wasn't just an abstraction. Somewhere in the darkness, a fast, radar-equipped vessel prowled, ever closer. "Don't think about it," Naroin told the nervous women in her squad. "Try to get some sleep."

The idea was ludicrous, but Maia pretended to obey. She curled underneath her blanket as the bow rose and fell, rose and fell, reminding her of the horse's rhythmic motion while fleeing across the plains of Long Valley. Maia closed her eyes for just a minute . . .

. . . and woke to a sharp pain, jabbing her thigh. She sat up, blinking. "I . . . what . . . ?"

Women were milling around the forecastle, muttering in a dim, gray light. There was a smoky quality to the air, and a faint smell of soot. Something poked her leg again, and Maia turned to follow the impertinent curve of a deck shoe, up a scar-worn leg to a face belonging to *Baltha*. The tall easterling var had stripped to the waist, her breasts restrained with a tightly wrapped leather halter. Baltha's blonde hair was tied back with a pink ribbon that seemed anomalously gay, given the glitter of feral combativeness in her eye. She grinned at Maia, stroking her trepp bill. "This is it, virgie. Ready for some fun?"

"Get back to your post," Naroin snapped at the tall blonde. Baltha shrugged and sauntered away, rejoining her friends near where the cook tended a steaming cauldron. The rough-looking mercenaries from the Southern Isles stretched and toyed with their bills, poking one another playfully, showing no outward sign of nerves.

A cabin boy handed Maia a hot cup of tcha, which seemed to course through her, opening veins and briefly intensifying the dawn chill. There had been dreams, she recalled. Their last shreds were already dissipating, leaving only vague feelings of dire jeopardy.

Unlike the night before, there was no wind save a faint, intermittent zephyr, but a chugging vibration told that auxiliary engines were running, pushing the ship in clumsy flight. Holding her cup in one hand, Maia clutched the corners of her blanket and looked out to sea.

The first thing she noticed was an archipelago of jutting islets—resembling upended splinters of stone that had been wave-washed smooth over epochs far longer than humanity had been on Stratos. Erupting from abyssal water, the precipitous spires stretched like a sinuous chain of blunt needles, ranging from northwest to southeast. Rather than meeting a distinct horizon, they faded with distance into a soft, mysterious haze. Some of the nearer isles were large enough for their moss-encrusted flanks to converge on forest-topped ridges, from which spilled slender, spring-fed waterfalls.

"Poulandres was trying to reach those," explained the young rad, Kau, when Maia wandered near the portside rail. A scar near her ear showed where Renna had tended her wound, after the fight aboard the Musseli locomotive. "Captain hoped to slip the reavers' radar among 'em. But the wind let us down, and sunrise came too soon, alas. Now it's going to be stand and fight."

The dark-haired var gave Maia an amiable nudge. "Want to see the enemy?"

Do I have any choice? Maia reluctantly turned away from the entrancing isles to look where Kau gestured, toward a misleadingly rosy dawn. When she saw their pursuer, she gasped.

It's so close!

A grimy-looking vessel cleaved the ocean, flinging spray from its bows. Only two sails were unfurled, but oily black fumes spilled from a pair of dark smokestacks. Agitated figures could be made out, milling on deck. The Manitou's engines, generally reserved for harbor maneuvers, were no match for that power.

Kau commented. "Reavers often hide big motors inside normal-looking clippers. No getting away from this bunch, I'm afraid."

The two girls heard a sigh. Standing nearby, looking at the foe-ship, Naroin recited:

> *"How Fast they came! Holy Mother, didst thou*
> *With lips divinely smiling, ask:*
> *What new mischance arrives upon thee now?"*

There was sincere regret in the bosun's sigh, yet Maia watched the rippling of slim, taut muscles under Naroin's arms. Regret was not unstained by anticipation.

"Come on," the older woman said, nodding toward Baltha's squad. "Those southlanders have it right. Let's get ready."

Naroin gathered the foremost detachment of passengers, and started by inspecting their trepps, then passed out lengths of noosed rope which each woman hung from her belt. Soon she had them running through stretching routines. Maia threw herself into the exercises. The combination of hot tcha and exertion in minutes had her blood flowing, pounding in her ears. She smelled everything with unwonted intensity, from burning coal to the separate salt tangs of sea and perspiration. Colors came to her with an almost-painful vividness.

"Yah!" Naroin cried, swinging her bill. The women imitated. "Yah!" As they practiced, Maia sensed the pervading mood of fear evaporate. What replaced it wasn't eagerness. Only a fool could not see that pain and defeated humiliation might lay ahead. Even one or more deaths, if full battle could not be avoided. Facing professionals would be more fearsome than skirmishing with part-time clone militiawomen had been, back in Long Valley.

Still, being a var meant knowing you might spend time as a warrior. Nor were these just any vars. Those who helped Thalla and Kiel had known it would be a risky enterprise. For the first time since Grange

Head, Maia felt a sense of linkage to these rads. The one to her left grinned and clapped Maia on the back when Naroin called a break. Maia returned the smile, feeling limber, though far from happy.

"*Hailing Manitou!*" An amplified male voice caused heads to turn. Maia hurried back to the rail and choked when she saw how close the reaver was. Its bowsprit came abeam with their own ship's fantail. "*Hailing Manitou. This is the Reckless, calling for you to heave over!*"

Manitou's captain lifted a bullhorn and shouted back. "*By what right do you accost us?*"

"*By the Law of Lysos, and the Code of Ships! Will you split your cargo, sir?*"

Maia watched Poulandres turn to consult Kiel, standing by his side, who shook her head emphatically. He accepted her answer with a passive shrug and lifted the bullhorn once more.

"*My employers will fight for what is theirs. The cargo cannot be divided!*"

Maia shook her head. *I should think not.* She saw Renna, standing near the cockpit, swiveling back and forth, staring in amazement. *Does he realize they're talking about him?* She gripped her bill tightly, glad that her alien friend would be safe on the neutral territory of the quarterdeck during the coming fray.

The Reckless drew closer. It was a smaller ship than the Manitou. That, plus its powerful engines, made defense by maneuver useless. Neither captain would risk damaging his beloved ship in a collision. Not without insurance that neither reavers nor rads could afford.

A crowd of women had gathered at the approaching ship's starboard rail, clutching bills, truncheons, and loops of coiled cord. More clambered the masts, edging onto the swaying spars. All wore the infamous red bandanna. A chill coursed Maia's shoulder blades.

"*Understood, sir,*" one of the bearded men at the tiller of the reaver answered through his own megaphone. "*Will you accept trial by champion, then?*"

Again, a consultation with Kiel, followed by another headshake. Most reaver bands employed special champions, professional fighters among professionals. The rads knew their odds were better in a melee, though at inevitable cost. This wasn't about sharing a hold full of cotton, coal, or dry goods. Theirs was a cargo worth fighting for.

Captain Poulandres passed on Kiel's refusal.

"*Very good,*" the master of the other ship replied. "*Then my passengers instruct me to say, Prepare for boarding!*"

No further conversation was required. While the smaller vessel moved in, Maia saw Kiel shake hands with the captain, then leap to the cargo deck, taking up her bill and yelling to her comrades. Poulandres immediately called all male crew members aft. The seamen hurried, shouting encouragement to their female colleagues.

Maia looked beyond the lower deck, with its crowd of nervously waiting vars, and saw Renna in earnest conversation with the ship's doctor. The old man, with an expression of someone explaining the obvious to a child or fool, motioned with his hands, pointing to the men on both ships and shaking his head. *Except for women sailors, it's strictly a battle between passengers,* Maia internally voiced the doctor's explanation.

Lysos had said it first, according to texts read aloud in temple services. *"Who can banish all strife? Fools who try only turn routine avarice, aggression, into outright murder. As we act to minimize conflict, let us see that what remains is balanced and restrained by law."*

Renna met Maia's eyes. His fists were clenched and he shook his head. Maia answered with a brief, thin smile, appreciating his message but also recalling the next line of verse, chanted so often in the chapel of Lamatia Hold.

"Above all, never lightly unleash wrath in men. For it is a wild thing, not easy to contain."

Maia glanced across the narrowing gap of open sea. There were men on that side, too, watching from their sanctuary zone with dark, brooding eyes.

Perhaps it really was better this way, she realized.

Renna crossed his arms and tugged both earlobes. The Stratoin signal for good luck made Maia smile, hoping that her friend had remembered to plug his sensitive ears. This was going to be a noisy affair. She nodded back at him, then turned to face the enemy.

"Eia!" Came a roar of female voices from the other vessel. Kiel raised her bill over her head and the rads replied as one. *"Eia!"*

Suddenly, the air whistled with grappling hooks and a profusion of snaking ropes. Defenders ran to cut the tautening lines, but could not reach enough cables before the hulls met with a dull boom. More hooks flew. Shouting raiders leaped, climbing hanging strands. Naroin called to her squad, "Steady, girls . . . steady . . . Now!"

Reflexes rescued Maia from fear's rigor. Practice told her arms and legs what to do, but their force flowed not from faith, reason, courage, or any other abstraction. Her will to move came from a need not to be left behind. Not to let the others down.

Yelling at the top of her lungs, although her cries were lost amid the rising clamor, she marched forward with her trepp locked at one hip, guarding Naroin's flank as the battle joined.

.   .   .

There seemed no end to them. The reaver ship must have been packed to the bulkheads, and warriors kept on coming.

Not that the first wave had it easy. Professionals or no, they found it hard clambering from a low deck to a higher one, while those above rained down nets, cold oil, and blocks of wood. Naroin set an example, dealing out snaring blows, hooking raiders under the armpits like gaffed fish and prying them loose to fall onto their comrades. When one snarling attacker made it over the Manitou's rail, Naroin seized the woman by her hair and halter. Pivoting on her pelvis, she hurled the invader to the deck, there to be pounced on by waiting teams, trussed by the arms and legs, and carried aft. Inspired by Naroin's example, Kiel and a tall rad from Caria also made captures, while Maia and the others fought to rap knuckles, unhook hands, and generally knock senseless those swelling up from below. Maia experienced elation each time an enemy fell. When a savage trepp strike just missed her face, the whistle of wood splitting air fed a hormone-level sense of invincibility.

On another plane, she knew it was illusion. More raiders swarmed upward from the Reckless like members of an insect horde, unflinching at all efforts to deflect it. Soon Maia was busy parrying buffets from a corsair who managed to straddle the railing—a tall, rangy woman with jagged teeth and several fierce scars. There was no help, Naroin being occupied with another thrashing foe. Alone, Maia tried to ignore the sweat-sting in her eyes as she traded clattering blows with her growling opponent. In a sudden, twisting swipe, the corsair landed a glancing clout to Maia's left hand, drawing a startled, anguished cry. Maia nearly lost hold of her weapon. Her next parry came almost too late, the next later still. . . .

The end of a trepp bill appeared out of nowhere, snaking beneath Maia's arm to meet the reaver's leather-bound chest with a loud thump, throwing her off balance. A distant part of Maia actually winced in sympathy, for the blow must have hurt something awful. But her opponent just yelled an oath of defiance as her arms flung out and she fell backward, striking the hull with her upper body. Astonishingly, the woman hung onto the railing by one scarred leg, a knotted cord of striated muscle.

Another red-clothed head immediately popped over—a new arrival using her comrade as a scaling ladder. Not without a twinge, Maia brought her bill around to hook the ankle of her earlier foe, yanking the leg from its mooring. Both invaders fell . . . to the deck of the other ship, she hoped. Though, if they splashed between the creaking, banging hulls, she shouldn't care. The code of battle said as much. "Honest risk in honest struggle."

You're not getting Renna! That voiceless cry lent Maia strength. Adrenaline overwhelmed pain as she whirled her stave to assist the woman to her left, who had helped her the moment before. Now Thalla was *corps à corps* with a grim-faced reaver several centimeters taller and much heavier. Seeing no other way, Maia cut a sharp blow to the raider's thigh. The woman buckled. Taking advantage, Thalla used the yoke portion of her bill to pin her foe to the ground. An eye-flick of thanks was all she could spare.

"Virgie, watch out!"

The yell accompanied a flash overhead. Swiveling barely in time, Maia ducked a noose cast by an attacker riding one of the foe-vessel's mast spars. It was a nasty tactic that risked strangling the victim. Maia seized the dangling cord and gave a savage yank with all her might. The screaming invader fell a long time before crashing into a tangle of fellow red-bandannas.

Something changed in the roar of combat, palpably spreading from that event. The rising tide, till now fed by pressure below, seemed to lose momentum. For an instant, the rail near Maia was clear for meters in both directions. "Well done!" Naroin cried, offering Maia a grin.

There was just time for a moment's thrill before another voice—Renna's, she realized—screamed one chilling word: *"Treason!"*

The starman's cry made Maia glance back just in time to flinch as Thalla collided with her, backpedaling before a fierce assault. Maia's former cottage-mate desperately fended blows from an unexpected quarter, *behind* the defensive line. Struggling to keep her footing, Maia gasped, recognizing the assailant . . .

Baltha! The hireling's trepp bill whirled like the vanes of a wind generator, slapping and toying with Thalla's frenetic efforts to parry. Nor was Baltha alone in her betrayal. With a pang, Maia saw the entire squad of Southern Isles mercenaries had donned scarlet bandannas, falling on the defenders from behind. Several headed straight toward where Naroin and most of the other rads went on, blithely unaware, confidently dealing with more groping hands at the rail.

"Watch out!" Maia yelled. But her voice was overwhelmed by the roar of confused battle. Trapped behind Thalla, she knew there was nothing she could do for either of her comrades. Fractions of seconds seemed to stretch endlessly as she worked her way around writhing, struggling forms, trying to bring her own weapon up, watching helplessly as Naroin was struck from behind with an unsporting head shot that toppled the small woman like a poleaxed steer.

Maia yelled in rage. She found her opening and launched herself at the bosun's assailants in a fury, catching one with a belly blow that sent her to the deck, gasping. The other southerling parried Maia's strike and fought back with an expression that shifted from grimness to amusement as she recognized the young fiver who liked playing men's games.

The ironic smile faded as Maia attacked in a blur of energetic, if inexpert blows, driving the traitor away from Naroin's crumpled form, step by step, right up to the portside rail.

More red bandannas appeared. Maia managed to slash one pair of hands a glancing stroke while still pressing her attack on the turncoat. The hands fell away, to be replaced by others. This time a younger face, soot-stained, flushed with heat and adrenaline, hove into view.

Maia blocked a heavy buffet from her chief opponent's bill, and caught it in the yoke-hook of her own. Twisting with all her strength, she managed to yank her foe's trepp away.

That face . . .

To evade Maia's followup, the panicked southerling flung herself over the railing. Maia wasted no time swiveling to divert her strike at the newcomer now struggling to bring her own weapon up.

Maia froze, halting as if she had been quick-frozen. Sweat-blinded, save through a crimson-rimmed tunnel of terror and wrath, she peered at the face—a mirror to her own.

"Le . . . Le . . ." she goggled.

Recognition also lit the young reaver's eyes. "I'll be a bleedin' clanmother," she said with a wry, familiar smile. "It's my atyp twin."

Too stunned to move, Maia heard Renna's voice shouting through her muzzy shock. But Leie's presence filled every space, engulfing her brain. Glancing past Maia's shoulder, her sister said, "You better duck, honey."

Slowly, glacially, Maia tried to turn.

There was a distant crumping tumult of polished wood striking somebody's skull. She had come to know the nuances of such sounds, and pitied the poor victim.

Dimly perceived movement followed, as if viewed through an inverted telescope. Perplexed by the suddenly approaching deck, Maia wondered why her muscles weren't responding, why her senses all seemed to be shutting down. She tried speaking, but a faint gurgle was all that came out.

Too bad, she thought, just before thinking nothing at all. *I wanted to ask Leie. . . . We have so much . . . catching up to do. . . .*

Peripatetic's Log:

Stratos Mission:

Arrival + 50.304 Ms

Myth envelopes the male-female bond. Countless generations since supposedly winning conscious control over instinct, most hominids still cling to notions of romantic love and natural conception—the way of a woman with a man. Even where societies encourage experimentation and alternative lifestyles, the presumption remains that a parental pair, one male and one female, compose continuity's spindle.

On Stratos, few songs or stories celebrate what is elsewhere obsession. Males are necessary, sometimes even liked, but they are peripheral beings, somewhat quaint. Anachronistic.

Passion has its brief seasons on Stratos. Otherwise, this world does not seem to miss it.

．　．　．

Still, partnership happens, often through business or cultural alliances. Caria's leading symphony orchestra has long consisted mostly of musicians from four extraordinarily gifted groups—O'Niels provide the strings, Vondas focus on woodwinds, Posnovskys at horns, and Tiamats on percussion. (I hope to hear them if I'm still here in autumn, when the season starts.)

On occasion, clans join in even closer associations. Relationships that might be called romantic, marital. They may even share offspring.

It's simple, in practice. First, both clan A and clan B arrange to have clutches of summer offspring. If clan A has a boy child, it does the usual thing, raising him carefully and then fostering him to one of the oceangoing guilds. Except in this case, he promises to return one summer, when he's older.

Meanwhile, clan B has had summer daughters. One is chosen to receive the best education a variant girl can get. She is sponsored a niche, even a winter pregnancy, all so she'll be ready to repay the debt when the son of house A returns from sea. Any child resulting from that union is then technically the heterozygous grandchild of both clans.

It makes for interesting comparisons. If one likens clans to individuals, that makes the girl-intermediary the equivalent of an egg, and the boy a sperm. The two clans fill the role of lovers.

At times I find all of this quite boggling.

. . .

How much more can I take? I must keep my mind on the job. Yet that job is to investigate the intimate workings of this human subspecies. I cannot escape the subject of sex, from dawn to dusk. Sometimes my head feels like it's spinning.

If only the women of this world weren't so beautiful.

Damn.

19

T hat thing'd break up in the first good squall. Or even sooner, when you drop it over th' cliff. How d'you plan on steerin' the smuggy thing?"

With a bang that made Maia wince, the big sailor, Inanna, slammed down the rock she had been using for a hammer. "Bosun, you just shut up. You're no shipcrafter, an' you sure ain't givin' orders no more."

Maia watched Naroin consider this, then reply with a shrug. "It's your necks."

"Ours to risk," Inanna assented, gesturing at the other women, hard at work cutting saplings and dragging them toward an area laid out with chalk lines on the rocky bluff. "You two are free to come along. We can use good fighters. But all the arguin' and votin' are over. Either put up or take your samish asses to 'tarkal hell."

Preparing to give a hot reply, Naroin cut short when Maia grabbed her arm. "We'll think about it," Maia told Inanna, trying to pull Naroin away. The last thing anybody needed, right now, was to have a shouting match come to blows.

For a long moment, Naroin seemed rooted in stone, unmovable until she abruptly decided to let it go. "Huh!" she said, and swiveled to march up the narrow, forested trail toward the campsite. Despite being taller, Maia had to hurry to keep up. All this noise and shouting wasn't easing the headache she had nursed since awakening, days ago, with a concussion, a captive of reavers.

"They may have the wrong plan," Maia suggested, trying to calm Naroin. "But it keeps them busy. There'd be fights and craziness without something to do."

Naroin slowed to look at Maia, and then nodded. "Basic command principle. Shouldn't need you to remind me." She glanced back at where the women sailors of the Manitou labored alongside a half-dozen of Kiel's younger rads, cutting and trimming saplings with primitive tools, laying out the beginnings of a rude craft. "I just hate to see 'em try something so dumb."

Maia agreed, but what to do? It had all been decided at a meeting, three days after the reavers dumped them on this spirelike isle whose name, if any, must be lost to another age. Naroin had argued for a different scheme—the building of one or two small boats, which a few selected volunteers might sail swiftly westward in search of help. That proposal was voted down in favor of the raft. *"Everyone goes, or nobody!"* Inanna declared, carrying the day.

Left out was how they proposed to make such a big contraption seaworthy, then get it down the sheer fifty-meter drop, and away from the spuming interface of wave and rock. Only one place along the forested rim of the jagged promontory featured a way down. There a winch had lifted the prisoners and their provisions, just before the Reckless and the captured Manitou sailed off. Inanna and her friends still schemed to use the lifting machine, despite its metal casing, locks, and earlier warnings of booby traps. In the long run, however, they might have to resort to building a primitive crane of timbers and vines.

"Idiots," Naroin muttered. She thrashed at the low foliage by the trail, using a short stave she had trimmed just after landfall. It was no trepp bill, but the small, wiry seawoman seemed more comfortable with it in her hands. "They'll never make it, an' I'm not drownin' with 'em."

Maia was getting fatigued with Naroin's impatient temper. Yet, she did not want to be alone. Too many dark thoughts plagued her when solitude pressed close. "How can you be sure? I agree your plan would have been better, but—"

"Bleeders!" Naroin slashed with her staff, and leaves flew. "Even a bunch o' frosty jorts oughta see that raft's all wrong. Say they do get it down, an' the sea don't smash it right up. They'll just get plucked again, like floatin' melons. If the pirates don't grab the chance to send 'em straight to Sally Jones on the spot."

"But we haven't seen a sail since we were marooned. How would the reavers know when and where to find them unless . . ." Maia stopped. She stared at Naroin. "You don't mean . . . ?"

The bosun's lips were thin. "Won't say it."

"You don't have to. It's vile!"

Naroin shrugged. "You'd do the same, if you was them. Trouble is, there's no way to tell which one it is. Or maybe two. Didn't know any o' them var hands before I hired on, at Artemesia Bay. Can't be sure of any of 'em."

"Or even me?"

Naroin turned and regarded Maia straight on. Her inspection was long and unsettlingly sharp. After five seconds, a slow smile spread. "You keep surprisin' me, lass. But I'd bet my sweet departed berry on you, despite you bein' no var."

Maia winced. "I told you before. That was my twin."

"Mm. So I recall from th' old *Wotan* days. At least, it's what you two said then. I admit, that wasn't clone-sister sweetness I saw, when she dumped you here."

Maia managed not to flinch a second time. The reminder was like stretching new scar tissue. The memory was still intense, of Leie's soot-streaked face, peering at her through that concussion haze, murmuring in a low, urgent voice of the necessity of what she was about to do.

"I'm happy you're alive, Maia. Truly, it's a miracle. But right now you're a smuggy nuisance to have around. My associates have a thing about people who look too much alike, if you know what I mean. Even if they believed me, there'd be suspicions. My plans would be set back. I can't afford to have you screw things up, right now."

There had been a wet, sticky sensation. Something tingling slathered across Maia's face, and a burning sensation crossed her scalp. At the time, Maia had been semidelirious, frantic to speak to her unexpectedly living sister, unable to comprehend why her mouth was gagged. Only much later, when she had a chance to scrub at one of the island's tiny freshwater springs, did she figure out what Leie had done. Using coal tar and other chemicals from the Reckless engine room, Leie had darkened Maia's skin and hair, altering her appearance in a makeshift but effective way.

"This won't fool anyone for long," Leie had murmured, examining her handiwork. *"Maia, be still! As I was saying, it's a lucky break your captain chose to flee right toward our base. No one'll have a chance to look at you closely before we dump off the first group of prisoners."*

From Leie's remarks, Maia later gathered that the reaver base lay amid this very archipelago of devil-fang peaks. Apparently, the pirates planned to divide their captives, interning some on isolated isles. First to be marooned would be those least dangerous to the raiders' plans—Manitou's women crew members. While sorting through the wounded, Leie had managed to put Maia with that group.

"You'd never believe what I've been through since the storm split us

up, Maia. While you were following your bosun friend around, leading the peaceful life of a deckhand, I've seen and done things . . ." Leie had shaken her head, as if at a loss to explain. *"You wouldn't like where we're taking the rads and their space-pervert creature, so I've arranged for you to be dropped off where you'll be more comfortable. Just sit tight till I figure things out, you hear me? By summer I'll get you to some town. We'll think up a way for you to help me with my plan."*

Leie's eyes had been filled with that old enthusiasm, now enhanced by a new, fierce determination. Through a fog of injury, pain, and confusion, Maia wondered what adventures had so changed her sister.

Then the import of Leie's words sank in. Leie and the reavers were going to put her ashore, and sail off with Renna! Kiel and Thalla and the men of the Manitou, as well. That was when Maia started struggling against her bonds, grunting to tell Leie she had to speak!

"There there. It'll be all right. Now, Maia, if you don't settle down, I'm going to have to . . . Aw, hell, I should've expected this. You always were a wengel-headed pain."

Maia caught a scent of strong herbs and alcohol as Leie pushed a soaked cloth over her nose. A cloying, choking sensation spread through the nasal passages and sinuses, making her want to cough and gag. Events got even more vague after that, but still, she had a distinct image of her sister leaning forward, kissing her on the forehead.

"Nighty-night," Leie murmured. Darkness followed.

The memory of pain and betrayal still hurt Maia, darkening and confusing her natural joy to find that Leie lived. But there was another matter. Burning foremost in her mind was one fact she focused on. An innocent, helpless man was being held captive somewhere on one of those other isles, without a friend in the world.

Except me. I must get to Renna!

Through the blue funk of her thoughts, she followed Naroin along a trail overlooking the bright sea, walking in silence back to where the reavers had dumped enough food and supplies to last until the next promised shipment. Lean-tos and makeshift tents made a ragged circle, offset from the trees. A cook fire was tended by one crew-woman whose ankle had been broken in the failed battle. She looked up desultorily and nodded without a word, going back to stirring lentils in a slowly simmering pot.

Naroin returned to her own chief pastime, using sharpened pieces of chert to shave a tree limb into a primitive bow. Not a legal weapon. But then, it wasn't legal, either, for the reavers to have dumped them here. Seizing the Manitou should have been followed by "dividing the cargo," then letting its crew and passengers go.

The special nature of this "cargo" made that unlikely, especially when it was one eagerly sought by every political force on the planet. When Maia last saw Captain Poulandres, hands bound on the quarter-deck of his own ship, the red-faced man had been threatening to raise hell, building toward a full summer rage by sheer anger. The reavers ignored him. Clearly, Poulandres had no idea what trouble he was in.

"It's for huntin'," Naroin said about the bow and slim arrow shafts. No one had seen anything larger than a bush shrew on the isle, but nobody complained. Anyway, the authorities were far away.

Maia threw herself on the blanket she had spread under a rough lean-to, atop a bed of shredded grass and leaves. Of her three posses-sions, her clothes and Captain Pegyul's sextant she kept with her always. The last item, a slim book of poems, she had found on her person as a ship's boat rowed the captive sailors to internment. During the ride up the creaky winch-lift, she had managed to focus on one randomly chosen page.

> *Have I been called? What is the aim*
> *Of thy great heart? Who is to be*
> *Bought by thy passion? Sappho, name*
> *Thine enemy!*

> *For whoso flies thee now shall soon pursue;*
> *Who spurns thy gifts shall give anon;*
> *And whoso loves thee not, whate'er she do,*
> *Shall love thee yet, and soon.*

A gift from Leie, she realized. Ever the more verbal of the two, while Maia had been the one attracted to things visual—patterns and puzzles. It could be taken as a peace offering, or a promise, or just an impulsive thing, with no more meaning than a friendly pat on the head.

She flipped through a few more poems, trying to appreciate them. But the gift, however well intended, was spoiled by a lingering sick-sweet odor left by the knockout drug. In her own eyes, Leie might have had good reasons for the act. Nevertheless, it mixed in Maia's heart with Tizbe Beller's ambush, the pragmatic betrayals of Kiel and Thalla, and the awful treachery of Baltha's southerlings. The list invited despair, if contemplated, so she refused,

Instead, Maia turned to the back flyleaf of the book, made of a slick, synthetic material meant to protect the paper pages from moisture during long voyages. She had discovered another use for the wrapping sheet. By spreading it open and weighting the corners with stones, she acquired a flat surface that she'd scribed with thin, perpendicular lines.

Between these, with a stick of charcoal taken from the fire, Maia marked arrays of tiny dots, separated by many empty spaces. Wetting a rag with spit, she wiped away the old pattern and redrew a different version.

It's more than just a matter of shapes, she thought, trying to recapture insights from last night's fireside contemplation. It had all seemed so clear, then.

There's another level than just thinking about how an individual group of dots mutates, and moves across the board. There's a relationship of some sort between the number of living dots per area—the density—and whatever next-neighbor rule you're using. If you change the number of neighbors needed for survival, you also change . . .

It was a struggle. Sometimes concepts came at her, like glowing baubles winking at the boundaries of vision, of comprehension. But crippling her was lack of vocabulary. The notions she fought with needed more than the simple algebra she'd been grudgingly taught at Lamai Hold. More and more she resented how they had robbed her of this, arguably her one talent, driving her from math and other abstractions by the simple expedient of making them seem boring.

It gets even more beautiful if you let the rules include cells farther than next-neighbors, she thought, trying to concentrate. Experimenting in her head was a wild process, hard to keep up for long. Yet, she had briefly succeeded in picturing a Game of Life set in three dimensions, whose products had been lattice structures of enticing, complex splendor, not merely marching crystalline rows, but forms that curled into smoky, twisting patterns, impossible to visualize save for bare instants at a time.

Maia closed the book and sank back, laying a forearm across her eyes, drifting in a tidal flux somewhere between pure abstraction and memories of hopelessness. The nearby scraping sounds of Naroin, grinding stone against wood, reminded her of something long ago. Of Leie, grunting and levering a device against a huge, ornate door. Then, too, there had been the sounds of wood and metal rubbing rock.

"*It's my turn to try,*" Leie had said, a long year ago and far away, deep under the cellars of Lamatia Hold. "*Your subtle stuff didn't work, so now we'll try getting in my way!*"

Maia recalled the twined snake figures. Rows of mysterious symbols. A star-shaped knob of stone that *ought* to have turned, clockwise, if the puzzle made any sense at all. . . .

There was a rustle of footsteps. Real noise, not recollection. A shadow occulted the sun. Maia lifted her arm and looked up to see a trim figure blocking one quarter of the sky. "I found something up there in the ruins," said a voice, reedy and young. It might have been that of a girl, except that every now and then, it cracked, briefly shooting down a whole octave to a lower register. "You ought to come, Maia. I have never seen anything like it."

She sat up, shading her eyes. A gangling boy stood looking down at her. *"The reavers' practical joke,"* Naroin had called him, and others agreed. Young Brod was a nice enough kid. He was nearly her age, although at five, boys fresh from their mother-clans were childish, almost unformed. This one shouldn't be here at all.

Officially, Brod was a hostage, taken by the women reavers to ensure cooperation by the sailors of the ship they had hired, the Reckless. But Naroin surely had it right. The young midshipman had been left partly in jest, showing someone's warped sense of humor. "Enjoy yer next glory fall!" one raider in a red bandanna had taunted as the last winch-load lifted away, leaving the "low threat" prisoners stranded together on this lonely spire.

Maia slowly stood up, sighing because the boy had chosen her to befriend, when she would have preferred solitude. *I do need the exercise,* she told herself. Aloud, she said, "Lead on."

The youth's puppy-eager smile was sweet and winter-harmless. She felt sorry for the kid when spectral frost next coated the grass and trees, when the rough sailor women would surely take their frustrations out on him. Even if by chance he was able, that wouldn't relieve the tension. There wasn't a scrap of ovop leaf among the supplies.

"This way. Come on!" Brod said impatiently, hurrying ahead of her into the trees. Maia took a deep breath, sighed, and followed.

The sheer island prominence had once been settled. That much had been clear as soon as the last load of internees arrived atop the plateau, hearing the black winch box shut down with an electronic buzz and booby-trapped clank. Early exploration uncovered tumbled, vine-encrusted ruins, remnants of ancient walls. The fringes of extensive edifices could be seen before the summit of the ridgetop was obscured by dense forest.

Brod had taken it upon himself to continue surveying the interior, especially since Maia and Naroin lost the raft dispute. He had tried to cast his vote along with them, only to learn that a boy's opinion wasn't solicited or welcome. The women crewfolk figured they knew enough about sailing to dispense with the advice of a raw, city-bred midshipman. At the time, Maia had thought it a needless slight.

"It's some distance up this way, into the thicket," Brod told her, pushing and occasionally hacking a path with a stick. "I wanted to find the center of all this devastation. Did it happen all at once, or was this settlement abandoned slowly, to let nature do the work?"

Walking just behind him, Maia felt free to smile. When they had first met, he had introduced himself as "Brod Starkland," carelessly still appending the name of his motherclan. Naroin knew of the house, prominent in the city of Enheduanna, near Ursulaborg. Still, it was a kid's mistake to let it slip. The boy was going to have to shuck his posh, Méchant Coast accent and learn man-dialect, real quick.

On further thought, perhaps Brod had been left here with the full agreement and approval of his crewmates, to take some starch out of him, or simply to get him out of their hair. Somehow, Maia doubted he was prime pirate material. *Maybe he and I are alike in that way. Nobody particularly wants or needs us around.*

The trail continued past tall, gnarly trees and tangled roots, mixed with broken stonework. Brod spoke over his shoulder. "We're almost there, Maia. Get ready for an eye-opener."

Still smiling indulgently, Maia noted that a clearing was about to open a short distance ahead. Probably a very big ruin, filled with stones so large that trees could not grow. She had seen some like that, during the horseback flight across Long Valley. Perhaps Lamatia Hold would look that way, centuries from now. It was something to contemplate.

Just as the trees ended, Brod stepped to the right, making room for Maia. At the same time, he thrust out a protective arm. "You don't want to get too close . . ."

At that moment, Maia stopped listening. Stopped hearing much of anything. A soundless roar of vertigo swelled as she halted, staring over a sudden, sheer precipice.

Steepness, all by itself, wouldn't have stunned her. The cliffs surrounding this island-prison were as abrupt, and higher still. But they lacked the *texture* of this deep bowl in front of her, which had been gouged with violence out of the peak's very center. The surface of the cavity was glassy smooth, as if rock had flowed until abruptly freezing in place, like cooling molasses.

What happened? Was it a volcano? Might it still be active?

The material was darkly translucent, reminding her of Stern Glacier's ancient ice, back in the remote northlands. Here and there, Maia thought she could perceive blocky outlines, as if the rock just behind the fused layer was ordered by levels or strata, subdivided into partitions, catacombs, parallel geologic features from the planet's ancient past.

Such surfacial contemplations were just how her foremind kept busy while the rest jibbered. "Ah . . . ah . . ." she commented succinctly.

"Exactly what I said at first sight," Brod nodded, agreeing solemnly. "That sums it in a kedger's egg."

· · ·

Maia wasn't sure why neither she nor Brod mentioned his discovery to the others. Perhaps the unspoken consensus came from their being the two youngest, least-influential castaways, both recently jettisoned by those they were supposed to think of as "family." Anyway, it seemed doubtful any of the castaways would be able to shed light on the origins of the startling crater. The women seemed intimidated by the thicket, and avoided going any deeper than necessary to cut wood.

Naroin delved some distance during hunting forays, but the older woman gave no sign of having seen anything unusual. Either the former bosun had lousy eyesight, which seemed unlikely, or she, too, knew how to keep a good poker face.

Since last talking with Naroin, Maia had begun dwelling on dark, suspicious thoughts. Even her refuge in the chaste, ornate world of game abstractions grew unsettled. It was hard paying attention to mental patterns of shifting dots, when she kept remembering that Renna languished somewhere among those scattered isles, perhaps one visible from the southern bluffs. And then there was a long-delayed talk to be had with Leie.

One day followed another. By snaring and shooting small game to supplement the dry-tack larder, Naroin eased some of the tension that had followed the raft-building vote. That project surged and stalled, then plunged forward again with each difficulty met and overcome. Several solidly built platforms of trimmed logs now lay drying in the sunshine, their bark-strip bindings well lashed and growing tauter by the hour. Maia had begun wondering if Inanna, Lullin, and the others might know what they were doing, after all.

Charl, a stout, somewhat hirsute sailor from the far northwest, managed to use a long pole to snag the cable hanging below the locked winch mechanism. Believing the reavers' warnings of booby traps, the var delicately managed to loop the heavy cord through a crude block and tackle of her own devising. In theory, they could now lower things halfway down before having to switch to handmade vine ropes. It was a clever and impressive feat.

None of the escape team's competence at construction seemed to impress Naroin. But Maia, despite her doubts, tried to help. When asked by Inanna to prepare a rutter—a rough navigational guide—Maia tried her best. Ideally, the escapees had only to get out of the narrow archipelago of narrow islets and then head northwest. The prevailing currents weren't perfect, this season. But the winds were good, so if they kept their sail-made-of-blankets properly filled, and a good hand on the tiller, it should be possible to reach Landing Continent in less than two weeks. Maia spent one evening, assisted by Brod, reviewing for the others how to sight certain stars by night, and judge sun angle by day. The women paid close attention, knowing that Maia herself had no intention of leaving the island chain. Not while both Leie and Renna were presumably just a few leagues away.

There was one more thing Maia could do to help.

Brod found her one day, as she walked the latest of a long series of circuits of the island, dropping pieces of wood into the water at different times and watching them drift. The boy caught on quickly. "I get it! They'll have to know the local currents, especially near the cliffs, so they won't crash up against them."

"That's right," Maia answered. "The winch isn't located in the best place for launching such a fragile craft. I guess the site was chosen more for its convenient rock overhang. They'll have to pick the right moment, or wind up swimming among a lot of broken bits of wood."

It was a chilling image. Brod nodded seriously. "I should've figured that out first." There was a hard edge of resignation in his voice. "Guess you can tell I'm not much of a seaman."

"But you're an officer."

"Midshipman, big deal." He shrugged. "Test scores and family influence. I'm lousy at anything practical, from knots to fishing."

Maia imagined it must be hard for him to say. For a boy to be no good at seamanship was almost the same as being no man at all. There just weren't that many other employment opportunities for a male, even one as well educated as Brod.

They sat together on the edge of the bluff, watching and timing the movement of wood chips far below. Between measurements, Maia toyed with her sextant, taking angles between various other islands to the southwest.

"I really liked it at Starkland Hold," Brod confided at one point, then hurriedly assured her, "I'm no momma's boy. It's just that it was a happy place. The mothers and sisters were . . . are nice people. I miss 'em." He laughed, a little sharply. "Famous problem for the vars of my clan."

"I wish Lamatia had been like that."

"Don't." He looked across the sea at nowhere in particular. "From what you've said, they kept an honorable distance. There's advantages to that."

Watching his sad eyes, Maia found herself able to believe it. A tendency runs strong in human nature to feel sentiment toward the children of your womb, even if they are but half yours. Maia knew of clans in Port Sanger, too, that bonded closely to their summer kids, finding it hard to let go. In those cases, parting was helped by the natural, adolescent urge to leave a backwater port. She imagined the combination of a loving home, plus growing up in an exciting city, made it much harder to forsake and forget.

That did not ease a pang of envy. *I wouldn't have minded a taste of his problem.*

"That's not what bothers me so much, though," Brod went on. "I know I've got to get over that, and I will. At least Starkland throws reunions, now and then. Lots of clans don't. Funny what you wind up missing, though. I wish I never had to give up that library."

"The one at Starkland Hold? But there are libraries in sanctuaries, too."

He nodded. "You should see some of them. Miles of shelves, stuffed with printed volumes, hand-cut leather covers, gold lettering. Incredible. And yet, you could cram the whole library at Trentinger Beacon into just five of the datastore boxes they have at the Enheduanna College. The Old Net still creaks along there, you know."

Brod shook his head. "Starkland had a hookup. We're a librarian family. I was good at it. Mother Cil said I must've been born in the wrong season. Would've done the clan proud, if I'd been a full clone."

Maia sighed in sympathy, relating to the story. She, too, had talents inappropriate for any life path open to her. There passed several long minutes in which neither spoke. They moved on to another site, tossing a leafy branch into the spuming water and counting their pulses to time its departure.

"Can you keep a secret?" Brod said a little later. Maia turned, meeting his pale eyes.

"I suppose. But—"

"There's another reason they keep me mostly ashore . . . the captain and mates, I mean."

"Yes?"

He looked left and right, then leaned toward her.

"I . . . get seasick. Almost half the time. Never even saw any of the big fight when you were captured, 'cause I was bent over the fantail the whole time. Not encouraging for a guy s'posed to be an officer, I guess."

She stared at the lad, guessing what it had cost him to say this. Still, she could not help herself. Maia fought to hold it in, to keep a straight face, but finally had to cover her mouth, stifling a choking sound. Brod shook his head. He pursed his lips, tightening them hard, but could not keep them from spreading. He snorted. Maia rocked back and forth, holding her sides, then burst forth with peals of laughter. In a second, the youth replied in kind, guffawing with short brays between inhalations that sounded much better than sobs.

The next day, a vast squadron of zoor passed to the north, like gaily painted parasols, or flattish balloons that had escaped a party for festive giants. Morning sunlight refracted through their bulbous, translucent gasbags and dangling tendrils, casting multicolored shadows on the pale waters. The convoy stretched from horizon to horizon.

Maia watched from the precipice, along with Brod and several women, remembering the last time she had seen big floaters like these, though nowhere near this many. It had been from the narrow window of her prison cell, in Long Valley, when she had thought Leie dead, had yet to meet Renna, and seemed entirely alone in the world. By rights, she should be less desolate now. Leie was *alive*, and had vowed to come back for her. Maia worried over Renna constantly, but the reavers weren't likely to harm him, and rescue was still possible. She even had friends, after a fashion, in Naroin and Brod.

So why do I feel worse than ever?

Misery is relative, she knew. And present pain is always worse than its memory. This softer captivity didn't ease her bitterness thinking of Leie's actions, her angst for Renna, or her feelings of helplessness.

"Look!" Brod cried, pointing to the west, the source of the zoor migration. Women shaded their eyes and, one by one, gasped.

There, in the midst of the floating armada, emerging out of brightness, cruised three stately, cylindrical behemoths, gliding placidly like whales among jellyfish.

"Pontoos," Maia breathed. The cigar-shaped beasts stretched hundreds of meters, more closely resembling the fanciful zep'lin on her sextant cover than the surrounding zoor, or, for that matter, the small dirigibles used nowadays to carry mail. Their flanks shimmered with facets like iridescent fish scales, and they trailed long, slender appendages which, at intervals, dipped to the waves, snatching edible bits, or siphoning water to split, with sunlight, into hydrogen and oxygen.

Despite protective laws passed by council and church, the majestic creatures were slowly vanishing from the face of Stratos. It was rare to sight one anywhere near habitable regions. *The things I've seen,* Maia thought, noting the one, great compensation for her adventures. *If I ever had grandchildren, the things I could have told them.*

Then she recalled some of Renna's stories of other worlds and vistas, strange beyond imagining. It brought on a pang of loss and envy. Maia had never thought, before meeting the Earthling, of *coveting* the *stars.* Now she did, and knew she would never have them.

"I just remembered . . ." young Brod said contemplatively. "Something I read about zoor and such. You know, they're attracted to the smell of burning sugar? We have some we could put on the fire."

Women turned to look at him. "So?" Naroin asked. "You want to invite 'em over for supper, maybe?"

He shrugged. "Actually, I was thinking that flying out of here might be better than trying to sail that raft. Anyway, it's an idea."

There was a long stretch of silence, then women on both sides laughed aloud, or groaned, at the sheer inanity of the idea. Maia sadly agreed. Of all the boys who tried hitching rides on zoors each year, only a small number were ever seen again. Still, the notion had a vivid, fanciful charm, and she might have given it a thought if the prevailing winds blew toward safe haven . . . or even dry land. While terribly bright, Brod clearly did not have practical instincts.

His longing expression, followed by sheepish blushing, finished off one lingering doubt Maia had nursed—that Brod might just possibly be a spy, left here by the reavers to watch over the prisoners. She had grown suspicious after all that had happened, the last few months. But no one could fake that sudden shift from wistfulness to embarrassment! His open thoughts seemed more like her own than old Bennett's had ever been. Or, when you got right down to it, most of the women she had known. He was much less romantically mysterious than her hearth-friend, the Earthling stranger, but that was okay, too.

You're turning into a real man-liker, Maia pondered, patting Brod on the back and turning to go back to work. *Perkinites, who only use 'em for sex and sparking, just don't know what they're missing.*

The raft had been prepared in four parts, to be linked quickly by hand as each was lowered at high tide. The vars practiced all the necessary movements over and over again, on a clearing by the converted winch. While it would doubtless be many times harder on bobbing seas, they finally felt ready. The first window for a launch would come early the next morning.

There were reasons for haste. Provisions would run out in eight to ten days. A lighter from the reaver colony was due about then. Inanna and the others wanted to leave well before that.

And if the lighter never came? All the more reason to depart soon. Either way, they'd be hungry but not starved by the time they reached the Méchant Coast.

No one tried very hard to persuade Maia and Naroin to change their minds and come along. Someone ought to stay and put up a pretense, when and if the supply ship came, thus giving the raft crew more time to get away. "We'll send help," Inanna assured.

Maia had no intention of waiting around for the promise to be kept. Those left behind would set to work at once on Naroin's alternate plan. Maia had motives all her own. If a crude dinghy did get built, she would not sail with Naroin and Brod to Landing Continent, but ask to be dropped off along the way. It had to be possible to find out which neighboring island held Renna and the rads—the secret reaver base where Maia planned on snaring Leie, pinning her down, and getting a word in for a change.

The night before launching day, eighteen women and one boy sat up late around the fire, telling stories, joking, singing sea chanteys. The vars kidded young Brod about what a pity it was that glory had been so sparse, and was he sure he didn't want to come along, after all? Though relieved in a way, by the kindness of the weather, Brod also seemed ambivalently wistful at his narrow escape. Maia guessed with a smile that something within him had been curious and willing to take up the challenge, if it came.

Don't worry. A man as smart as you will get other chances, under better circumstances.

The mood of anticipation had everyone keyed up. Two of the younger sailors, a lithe, blonde sixer from Quinnland and an exotic-looking sevener from Hypatia, started banging spoons against their cups to a quick, celebratory rhythm, then launched a session of round-singing.

> *"C'mere C'mere . . . No! Go away!"*
> *That's what we heard the ensign say.*
> *"I know I promised to attack,*
> *But I lost the knack,*
> *Seems I just lost track,*
> *Can I come back?*
> *Is it spring, today?*
> *C'mere, c'mere, c'mere, c'mere,*
> *Oh, c'mere you . . . No, go away!"*

It was a famous drinking song, and it hardly mattered that no one had anything to drink. The singers alternately leaned toward Brod, then shied off again, to his embarrassment and the amusement of everyone else. Taking turns one by one, going around the circle, each woman added another verse, more bawdy than the last. At her turn, Maia waved off with a smile. But when the round seemed about to skip past Brod, the young man leaped instead to his feet. Singing, his voice was strong, and did not crack.

> *"C'mon up . . . No, Stay away!"*
> *The mothers of the clan do say.*

> *"We really didn't mean to goad,*
>   *Or incommode,*
> *We thought it* snowed,
> *But it* rained *today.*
> *C'mon, c'mon, c'mon, c'mon,*
> *Oh, c'mon up . . . No, Stay away!"*

Most of the sailors laughed and clapped, nodding at the fairness of his comeback. A few seemed to resent his jumping in, however. The same ones who, days back, had argued against counting the vote of a mere boy.

More songs followed. After a lighthearted beginning, Maia noticed the mood grow steadily less gay, more somber and reflective. At one point, the girl from Hypatia looked down, letting her hair fall around her face as she chanted a soft, lovely melody, *a cappella.* An old, sad song about the loss of a longtime hearth-mate who had won a niche, started a clan, and then died, leaving clone-daughters who cared nothing of their var founder's callow loves.

> *"There is her face, I hear her voice,*
> *Images and sounds of youth gone by.*
>   *She lives on, unknowing me,*
>   *Immortal, while I'm bound to die."*

The wind picked up, lifting sparks from the ebbing fire. After that song, silence reigned until two older vars, Charl and Trotula, began beating a makeshift drum, taking up a quicker beat. Their choice was a ballad Maia used to hear on Port Sanger's avenues from time to time, chanted by Perkinite missionaries. An epic of days long ago, when heretic tyrannies called "the Kingdoms" fluxed through these tropic island chains. The period wasn't covered much in school, nor even in the lurid romances Leie used to read. But each springtime the chant was sung on streetcorners, conveying both danger and tragic mystique.

> *Strength to rule, mighty and bold,*
> *Bringing back the father's way,*
>   *As in human days of old,*
> *Strength to rule, their legacy.*
>
> *By the light of Wengel's pyre,*
> *Taking fiercely, eyes aflame,*
>   *Came the bloody men of fire,*
> *Summer's empire to proclaim. . . .*

Sometime between the Great Defense and the Era of Repose—perhaps more than a thousand years ago—rebellion had raged across the Mother Ocean. Emboldened by their recent high renown, after the repulsion of terrible alien invaders, a conspiracy of males had vowed to reestablish patriarchy. Seizing sea-lanes far from Caria, they burned ships and drowned men who would not join their flag. In the towns they captured, all restraints of law and tradition vanished. Aurora season was a time, at best, of unbridled license. At worst, horror.

> . . . *Summer's empire, never chosen,*
> *By the women. Cry at fate!*
> *For a destiny unfrozen,*
> *Cry for vigilance, too late!*

When Maia had once asked a teacher about the episode, Savant Claire had smirked in distaste. "People oversimplify. Perkies never talk in public about the Kings' *allies*. They had plenty of help."

"From whom?" Maia asked, aghast.

"Women, of course. Whole groups of them. Opportunists who knew how it had to end." Claire had refused to give more detail, however, and the public library posessed but scanty entries. So curious had it made Maia, that she and Leie tried using their twin trick to feign clone status, briefly gaining entrance to a Perkinite meeting—until some locals fingered them as vars, and tossed them out.

During the lengthy ballad, Maia watched attitudes chill toward Brod. Women seated near him found excuses to get up—for another cup of stew, or to seek the latrine—and returned to sit farther away. Even the Quinnish sixer, who had flirted awkwardly with Brod for days, avoided his eyes and kept to her mates. Soon only Maia and Naroin remained nearby. Bravely, the youth showed no sign of noticing.

It was so unfair. He had had no part in crimes of long ago. All might have remained pleasant if Charl and Tortula hadn't chosen this damned song. Anyway, none of these vars could possibly be Perkinite. Maia contemplated how prejudice can be a complex thing.

> . . . *So to guard the Founders giving,*
> *And never the fate forget,*
> *Of those future, past, and living,*
> *To be saved from Man's regret.*

No one said much after that. The fire died down. One by one, tomorrow's adventurers sought their beds. On her way back from the toilet area, Maia made sure to pass Brod's shelter, separate from all the others, and wished him goodnight. Afterward, she sat down again by the coals, lingering after everyone else had turned in, watching the depleted logs brighten and fade when fanned by gusts of wind.

Some distance away, toward the forest, Naroin lifted her head. "Can't sleep, snowflake?"

Maia answered with a shrug, implicitly bidding the other woman to mind her own business. With briefly raised eyebrows, Naroin took a hint and turned away. Soon, soft snoring sounds rose from scattered shadows on all sides, lumps indiscernible except as vague outlines. The coals faded further and darkness settled in, permitting constellations to grow lustrous, where they could be seen between low clouds. The holes in the overdeck grew narrower as time passed.

Without stars to distract her, Maia watched as sporadic breezes toyed with the banked campfire. Stirred by a gust, one patch would bloom suddenly, giving off red sprays of sparks before fading again, just as abruptly. She came to see the patterns of bright and dark as quite unrandom. Depending on supplies of fuel, air, and heat, there were continual ebbing and flowing tradeoffs. One zone might grow dim because surrounding areas were lit, consuming all the oxygen, or vice versa. Maia contemplated yet another example of something resembling, in a way, ecology. Or a game. A finely textured game, with complex rules all its own.

The patterns were lovely. Another geometry trance beckoned, ready to draw her in. Tempted, this time she refused. Her attention was needed elsewhere.

Quietly, without making sudden moves, Maia took a stick and rolled one of the stronger embers into her dinner cup. She covered it with a small, chipped plate from the supplies left by the reavers, and waited. An hour passed, during which she thought about Leie, and Renna, and the ballad of the Kings . . . and most of all, about whether she was being stupid, getting all worked up over a suspicion based on nothing but pure logic, bereft of any supporting evidence at all.

Eventually, someone came to sit by her.

"Well, tomorrow's the big day."

It was a low voice, almost a whisper, to avoid waking the others. But Maia recognized it without looking up. *Thought so,* she told herself as Inanna squatted to her left.

"Wouldn't of expected you being too excited to sleep, seeing as how you're staying behind," the big sailor said in casual, friendly tones. "Will you miss the rest of us so much?"

Maia glanced at the woman, who seemed *overly* relaxed. "I always miss friends."

Inanna nodded vigorously. "Yah, we got to choose a mail drop, maybe in some coast city. One time or another, we'll all get together again, hoist brews, amaze the locals with our tale." She leaned toward Maia, conspiratorially. "Speaking of which, I got a little something, if you want a nip." She pulled out a slim flask that swished and gurgled. "The Lysodamn reavers missed this, bless 'em. Care to lift a couple? For no hard feelings?"

Maia shook her head. "I shouldn't. Alky goes to my head. I'd be no good when you need help launching."

"You'll be no good if you're up restless all night, neither." Inanna removed the cap and Maia watched her take a long pull, swallowing. The sailor wiped her mouth and held out the flask. "Ah! Good stuff, believe it. Puts hair where it belongs, an' takes it off where it don't."

With a show of reluctance, Maia reached for the flask, sniffing an aroma of strong mash. "Well . . . just one." She tipped the pewter bottle, letting a bare trickle of liquor down her throat. The ensuing fit of coughs was not faked.

"There now, don't that warm yer innards? Frost for the nose and flamejuice for the gut. No matching the combination, I always say."

Indeed, Maia felt a spreading heat from even that small amount. When Inanna insisted she have another, it was easy to show ambivalence, both attraction and reluctance at the same time. Despite her best efforts, some more got by her tongue. It felt fiery. The third time the bottle went back and forth, she did a better job blocking the liquor, but heady fumes went up her nose, making her feel dizzy.

"Thanks. It seems to . . . work," Maia said slowly, not trying to fake a slur. Rather, she spoke primly, as a tipsy woman does, who wants not to show it. "Right now, how-ever, I . . . think I had better go and lie down." With deliberate care, she picked up her plate and cup and shuffled toward her bedroll, at the campsite's periphery. Behind her, the woman said, "Sleep well and soundly, virgie." There was no mistaking a note of satisfaction in her voice.

Maia kept the appearance of a tired fiver, gladly collapsing for the night. But within, she growled, now almost certain her suspicions were true. Surreptitiously, while climbing under the blanket, she watched Inanna move from the fire ring toward her own bedroll at the far quadrant of the camp. A dimly perceived shadow, the woman did not lie down, but squatted or sat, waiting.

I never would have figured all this out before, Maia thought. *Not until Tizbe and Kiel and Baltha—and Leie—taught me how sneaky people can be. Now it's like I knew it all along, a pattern I can see unfolding.*

It had started with the debate, soon after their internment, over whether to build one big raft or a couple of small boats. Naroin had been right. In this archipelago, a dinghy with a sail and centerboard might weave in and out past shoals and islets with a good chance of getting away, even if spotted. A raft, if seen, would be easy prey.

But that assumed reaver ships were just hanging around, patrolling frequently. In fact, lookouts had seen only two distant sails in all the days since their maroonment. It would take a major coincidence for pirates to show just when the raft set forth.

Unless they were warned, somehow.

Maia found the whole situation ridiculous on the face of it.

Why would they intern a bunch of experienced sailors on an island without supervision? They'd have to know we'd try escaping. Try to get help. Alert the police.

Naroin's sullen mutterings after the crucial vote had set Maia on the path. There had to be a spy among them! Someone who would guide the inevitable escape attempt in ways that made it more vulnerable, easier to thwart. And, especially, someone well positioned to warn the pirates in time to prepare an ambush.

What's their plan? I wonder. To capture those on the raft and bring them back? The failure would surely cause morale to plummet, and hamper subsequent attempts.

But that won't guarantee against other tries. They must mean to transfer any escapees to a more secure prison, like where they took Renna and the rads.

But no. If that were the case, why not put the sailors there in the first place?

Coldly, Maia knew but one logical answer. *As ruthless as they seemed after the fight, breaking the Code of Combat and all, they couldn't go so far as deliberately killing captives. Not with so many witnesses. The men of the Reckless. Renna. Not even all of the reavers' own crew could be trusted with a secret like that.*

But to take care of things later on? Use a small ship, manned by only the most trusted. Come upon a raft, wallowing and helpless. No need even to fight. Just fling some rocks. Gone without a trace. Too bad . . .

Maia's anger seethed, evaporating all lingering traces of alky high. Lying as if asleep, she watched through slitted eyes the dark lump that was Inanna, waiting for the lump to move.

It might have been better, safer, to check out her suspicions in a subtler way, by going to bed when everyone else did, and then crawling off behind a tree to keep watch. But that could have taken half the night. Maia had no great faith in her attention span, or ability to be certain of not drifting off. What if it was hours and hours? What if she was wrong?

Better to flush the spy out early. Maia had decided to make it seem as if she intended to stay up all night long. An irksome inconvenience, perhaps causing the reaver agent to feel panicky. Speed up the spy's subjective clock. Make her act before she might have otherwise.

And it worked. Now Maia had a target to watch. Her concentration was helped no end by knowing she was right.

The dark blur didn't move, though. Time seemed to pass with geologic slowness. More seconds, minutes, crawled by. Her eyes grew scratchy from staring at barely perceivable contrasts in blackness. She took to closing them one at a time. The patch of shadow remained rock-still.

Smoke from the smoldering coals drifted toward her. Maia was forced to shut her eyelids longer, to keep them from drying out.

Panic touched her when they reopened. Sometime in the last . . . who knew how long . . . she might have strayed—even dozed! She stared, trying to detect any change on the far side of the camp, and felt a growing uncertainty. Perhaps it wasn't *that* faint blob she was supposed to be watching, after all. Maybe it was another one. She had drifted and now her target was gone. Oh, if only there were a moon, tonight!

If only I'd found whatever she plans to signal with. That had been Maia's ulterior reason for performing circuit after circuit of the island, ostensibly studying the hourly tides. She had poked her head under logs and into rocky crannies all over the perimeter. Unfortunately, whatever lay hidden had stayed that way, and now she must decide. To wait a little longer? Or try moving into the woods and begin searching for someone who might already have a growing head start?

Damn. No one could be this patient. She has to be gone by now.

Well, here goes . . .

Maia was about to push aside the blanket, but then abruptly stopped when the shadow moved! There was a faint sound, much softer than young Brod's stentorian snoring. Maia stared raptly as a blurred form unfolded vertically, then slowly began moving off. At one point, a patch of stars were occulted by something with the general outline of a stocky woman.

Now. As silently as possible, Maia threw off the blanket and rolled over. She took from beneath her bedroll the things she had prepared earlier. A stave thickly wrapped at one end with bone-dry vines. A stone knife. The cup containing a warm, barely glowing ember. Following a carefully memorized path, she hurried quietly into the forest, to a chosen station, where she stopped and listened.

Over there, to the east! Pebbles crunched and twigs broke, faintly at first, but with growing carelessness as distance fell between the spy and the campsite. Maia forced herself to pause a little longer, verifying that the woman didn't stop at intervals, listening for pursuit.

There were no lapses. Excellent. Cautious to make as little noise as possible, with eyes peeled for dry sticks on the forest floor, Maia started to follow. The trail led deeper into the woods, explaining why her surveys on the bluffs had found nothing. It had been reasonable to hope the signaling device was kept where a flasher or lantern might be seen from another island. But Inanna was clearly too cagey to leave things where they might be discovered by chance.

Maia's foot came down on something parched and crackly, whose plaint at being crushed seemed loud enough to wake Persephone, in Hades. She stopped dead still, trying to listen, but was hampered by the adrenaline pounding of her heart. After a long pause, at last Maia heard the soft sound of footsteps resume, moving off ahead of her. Something lit only by starlight briefly cut across a lattice of trees, disturbing their symmetry. She resumed the pursuit, wariness redoubled.

That was fortunate. As clouds thickened and darkness fell even deeper, it was a faint odor that stopped her short again. A change in the flow of air, of wind. Her quarry's footsteps took a sudden veer leftward, and Maia abruptly realized why.

Straight ahead, in the direction she had just been moving, a thick cluster of stars briefly emerged, casting a thousand gleaming reflections from a face of sheer concavity. The crater—far more intimidating than it had seemed by day. The glass-lined precipice yawned not meters away, like the jaws of some mighty, ancient thing, hungry for a midnight snack. Maia swallowed hard. She turned to the left and continued, watching the ground more closely than ever. Fortunately, the trail soon receded from the terrible pit. Some distance onward, there came a faint sound, like a scraping of stone against stone. Maia paused, heard it repeat. Then she waited some more.

Nothing. Silence. Just the wind and forest. Grimly, in case it was a trap, Maia extended her frozen stillness for another count of sixty. At last, she resumed her forward stalk, concentrating to keep a bearing toward that final, grating sound. A break in the cloud cover, near the horizon, showed a corner of the constellation Cyclist. She used it for reference while skirting trees and other obstacles, until finally concluding that something had to be wrong.

I must've gone too far. Or have I?

She could not see or hear anyone. The idea of an ambush was not to be dismissed.

Two more steps forward and her feet left loam. They seemed to scuff a flat, sandy surface, scored at regular intervals by fine grooves. Peering about, Maia realized she stood amid massive, blocky forms, in a clearing where not even saplings grew. She reached out to the nearest pile of weathered stone. *Worked* stone with eroded, right angles. It was one of many ruins peppering the island plateau. Few places were better suited for springing a trap.

Quietly, she felt her way along the wall till it ended. Passing to the other side, she verified that no one waited behind. Not there, at least. Maia knelt and laid her burdens on the ground. She closed one eye, to protect its dark-adaptation—a habit taught her long ago, during astronomy nights, by Old Coot Bennett—and raised the cup holding the ember. Shielding it with one hand, she blew until it glimmered in spots, then laid it down with the tinder-wrapped end of her stave on top. Maia took the chert knife in her left hand, and grabbed the stave's haft in her right. A smoldering rose.

Abruptly, the torch flared with an audible *whoosh.* Maia quickly stood, holding it above and behind her head to shine everywhere but in her eyes. Stark shadows fled the garish-bright stone walls and tree trunks. Hurrying to exploit surprise, she rushed to circumnavigate the ruins, peering in all corners while Inanna would be blinking away spots.

Nothing. Maia hurried through another circuit, this time checking places where someone might have hidden, even the lower branches. At any moment, if necessary, she was ready to use the flaming brand as a weapon.

Damn. Inanna must've been just far enough to duck out when I lit the torch. Too bad. Thought I'd finally figured out how to do something right. I guess people don't change.

Feeling deflated, disappointed, Maia sought the nearest flat area amid the ruins and sat down.

The stone jiggled beneath her.

She stood up and turned around, holding the torch toward the slab. It looked like just another chiseled chunk of wall, atop a pile of others. *Come on. You're jumping to conclusions.*

A breeze caused the flames to flicker upward.

Upward? Maia held out her hand, and felt a thin stream of air. With her foot she gave the slab a tentative shove. Stone grated stone, a familiar sound. The slab moved much too easily.

"Well I'm an atyp bleeder." Maia blinked at a sudden mental vision of the glass-rimmed crater, as it had looked by daylight. She had briefly pictured a network of regular shapes behind the slag coating, then dismissed it as an artifact of her overactive pattern-recognition system. Now though, the mental conception loomed . . . of layers that she had rationalized as sedimentary, but which imagination shaped into rooms, corridors.

"Of course."

Someone *had* dug some sort of mine or tunnel system here. Perhaps they had delved for safety, to no avail against whatever had melted that awful hole.

Bending to examine the stone, Maia sought its secret. *Tip it back? No, I see. Push to the left . . . then up!*

The slab rotated, revealing a stout makeshift hinge arrangement of slots and pins. A set of rubble stairs, quite rough in the upper portion, dropped into darkness. Carefully, Maia lifted one leg and stepped over the sill, lowering herself gingerly below the forest roots.

My torch is already half used up. Better make this quick, girl.

The steps ended about five meters down, followed by a low tunnel under primitive archworks. Maia had to duck as flames licked the ceiling, igniting cobwebs in fleeting, sparkling pyres. Finally, the coarse passage spilled into an underground room.

Dust and stone chips covered every surface, save a wooden table and chair, surrounded by scrape marks and foot tracks. In one corner lay a trash midden, the freshest layer consisting of still aromatic orange peels and chicfruit rinds. *Someone's been eating better than the rest of us,* she thought, wryly. A wooden box revealed a bag of stale sesame crackers and one orange, on its last legs. *No wonder it's so urgent to launch the raft soon. You were running out of goodies, Inanna.*

A blanket hung tacked over the sole exit. Maia tore it down. A few meters beyond, fresh stairs plunged anew. She proceeded to rip the blanket into strips, wrapping half of them around the torch, just below the burning part. One strip lit early and she dropped it, dancing away and cursing in whispers. Maia jammed the remainder under her belt, along with the knife, and set forth.

The dusty sense of age only increased as she descended, spiraling down the cylindrical shaft. These stairs were original equipment, finely carved and worn down several centimeters in the middle, by countless footsteps. Each one was shaped as the sector of a circle, resting one radial edge atop the one below it. In the middle, disklike projections from each wedge lay stacked, one above the next, all the way down, forming a round, vertical banister that she used to steady herself while dropping lower and lower, round and around.

After perhaps ten meters, Maia paused where a door and landing gave into dark rooms. Torchlight revealed arched ceilings, some collapsed, trailing off toward utter blackness. There were no sounds. Undisturbed dust showed that no one had walked these quarters in years. Feeling eerily chilled, she continued downward, passing a second landing . . . and a third . . . and yet another, until at last she sensed distinct sound rising up the shaft. Faint, as yet indistinct, its source lay below.

Oh, for a dumbwaiter, Maia recalled sardonically, contemplating climbing all this on the way back. *Even the Lysodamned Lamai wine cellar wasn't like this. Hateful place, but at least they had a winch-lift. And a string of two-watt bulbs.* It wasn't clear what she'd do if she was caught down here with the torch gone out. It should be simple, in theory, to get back. Just follow the stairs upward, then grope her way toward fresh air. In practice, it would probably be scary as hell. *I wonder what kind of lamp Inanna's got.*

Now the walls of the stairwell were cracked, as if tortured by some ancient blow or tremor. Worse, the steps themselves were splintered, chipped. Their undersides had given way, here and there, raining stone debris onto the stairs below. Some teetered in a fashion Maia found unnerving. There were gaps in places.

Maia was pretty sure, now. The huge, slag-rimmed crater wasn't volcanic, or natural at all, but an artifact of war. Some folk had once delved here, deeply, seeking protection. And someone else had come down after them, shaking the deepest levels. The scale of these ancient events frightened Maia, and right now the last thing she needed was more fear.

The sounds grew closer—distant, occasional plinkings. And a breeze. Fresh and decidedly cool.

Maia almost staggered when the stairs ran out. The tight spiral gave no warning, halting abruptly where a room opened ahead, featuring doors leading in three directions. At first she had to just walk the chamber's perimeter, trying to straighten the unconscious crouch she had assumed during the descent. Finally, Maia wet a finger to feel the breeze, watched the flickering of the dying torch, and peered for footprints.

That door.

Beyond lay a passage hewn from island rock, extending past room after dead-black room, as far as the dim pool of torchlight stretched. Maia extended the brand inside the first chamber, and found it stripped, save for one huge, polished stone bench that had a regular array of uniform holes drilled in its upper surface, as if someone had arranged it to hold dowel pegs for some strange game. Yet, Maia felt instinctively that "games" were never played in this cryptlike place. It gave her chills.

The plinking grew louder as she resumed walking. A low susurration also waxed and waned rhythmically. The torch began to sputter. It was time to decide whether to wind on more strips or let the thing go out. It took all her courage to make the logical choice.

Maia strode forward with her left hand touching the wall on that side, eyes trying to memorize the lay of the hallway before— Then it happened. The last flicker died. Plunged in sudden, total darkness, she slowed but grimly kept moving, fighting an urge to shuffle. Instead, Maia lifted her feet high to avoid making unnecessary sound.

Abruptly, her fingertips lost contact with the left wall, setting off a wave of vertigo. *Don't panic. It's just the next doorway, remember? Move ahead, keep your arm out, you'll meet the other jamb.*

It took ages . . . or a few seconds. She must have turned to overcompensate, for the next physical contact came when she banged the far side of the entrance with her elbow. It hurt, yet restored touch felt reassuring. So did getting beyond the doorway. In pure blackness, it was even easier than before to fantasize monsters. Creatures that had no need for light.

The true Stratoins, she thought, trying to tease herself out of a panicky spin. There were silly tales that older siblings told their sisters, about mythical, primal inhabitants of Stratos, driven long ago from sight by the hominid invasion. Once shy, innocent, they now dwelled belowground, far from the open sky. Bitter, vengeful . . . hungry. It was a fairy tale, of course. No evidence existed, to her knowledge, for anything like it.

But then, I never heard of hundred-meter craters gouging out the middle of mountains, either.

Another doorway swallowed Maia's hand, making her jump higher than the last time, convincing her susceptible imagination that vindictive jaws were about to close, all the way up to her shoulder. When the wall resumed, this time striking her wrist, she let out a physical sigh.

Stop it. Think about something else. Life, the game.

She tried. There was plenty to work with. The speckles that her visual cortex produced, for lack of input from the eyes, created a panorama of ephemeral dots, flickering like Renna's game board, set to high speed. It was alluring to think there might be meaning there. Some great secret or principle, found among the random, background firings taking place inside her own skull.

Then again, maybe not.

Maia grimly picked up the pace, passing another door, and another. Before long, she felt certain the sounds had grown louder, more distinct. Soon she knew her first suspicions were right. It could only be the surge and flood of tide-driven water. *I must be all the way down, near the sea.*

She caught a scent of fresh air. More important, Maia could almost swear that up ahead the awful darkness was relieved by a faint glimmer. A dim source of light. Even before she consciously made out the floor, it became easier to walk. Faint distinctions in the murky dim gave her more faith in her footing.

Soon they were more than hints. Up ahead, she saw what could only be a reflection. A wall, faintly illuminated by some soft source, out of direct view.

Maia approached cautiously. It was the face of a T-bar intersection, lit from one side. She edged along the right-hand wall, sidled to the corner, and poked around just one eye.

It was another hallway, terminating after about twenty meters in a large chamber. The source of light lay within, though not in view. As she began stalking closer, Maia saw that strange, rippling reflections wavered across the ceiling of the deep room. The plinking sounds were louder, an unmistakable dripping of liquid onto liquid. In the distance, a rolling growl of waves pounded against rock.

So that's it. Maia paused at the entrance, whose once proud double doors now sagged toward the walls, reduced to mold-covered boards bound by rusty hinges. Within, there stood another table, on which lay an oil lantern with a poorly adjusted wick. Beyond, half of the broad alcove descended to a wide pool of seawater. After ten meters, the placid surface passed under a rocky shelf, part of a low tunnel that led toward darkness and finally—judging from the muffled sounds—the open sea. A small boat lay tethered to a dock, mast down, sail furled but ready.

Maia gripped her wooden stave in both hands, ready to swing it, if necessary. She looked left and right, but no one was in view. Nor were there any other exits. The emptiness was more unnerving than any direct confrontation.

Where is she?

Maia approached the table. Next to the lantern lay a boxy case, open to reveal buttons and a small screen. She recognized a commconsole, attached to a thin cable that led into the sea-tunnel. An antenna, presumably. Or perhaps a direct fiber link to another island? That sounded extravagant. But over time, it might prove worthwhile, if this prison-trap was used frequently.

The screen was illuminated with one line of tiny print. Perhaps the message would reveal something. Maia put the stave on the table and leaned forward to read.

THERE IS A PRICE FOR NOSINESS . . .

Oh, bleeders . . .

Maia snatched her weapon as a shattering din exploded behind her. Swiveling with the dead torch in hand, she glimpsed the ancient, moldy door strike its frame and shatter as a woman-shaped fury charged. In-anna's howl shook the stone walls, making Maia flinch, cleaving air and missing the reaver, who agilely dodged the wild swing, seized Maia's shirt and belt, and used raw strength plus momentum to fling her through the air.

Maia's arc lasted long enough for her to know where she was headed. Releasing the useless stave, she inhaled deeply before bitter water snatched her in an icy fist. Shock spewed half the air back out of her lungs, a force-driven spray. Still, Maia kept from spluttering at once to the surface. By willpower, she ducked *down* and kicked, swimming as deep as she could manage and to the right. If it was possible to put in some distance without Inanna knowing, she might be able to clamber out quickly, setting the stage for an even fight—youthful desperation against experience.

An even fight? Don't you wish.

Maia felt her limit nearing. At the last second, she aimed for the sharp, black pool-edge and surfaced. Gasping, she threw her arms over the side, followed by an ankle, straining to lift. But almost at once a lancing pain struck her leg, knocking it back in. Blinking saltwater, Maia saw her foe already standing over her, foot raised for another blow.

Stoked by urgency, she focused on that object and lunged, seizing and twisting. Inanna teetered with a cry and came down hard, loudly striking the stone floor with her pelvis.

Again, Maia struggled to get out. This time she had one knee on the shelf and pushed . . .

The other woman recovered too quickly. She rolled over, knocking Maia back, throwing her into the water once more. Then Inanna's arms and fists were windmills, landing blows around the girl's head. One hand seized Maia's scalp, pushing her below the surface. Maia pulled hard to get away, to swim elsewhere, even the middle of the pool. The tunnel might offer shelter, of sorts, though beyond that lay the open sea and death.

She got some distance, then stopped with a sudden, jarring yank. Inanna had her hair!

Maia burst out, sucking air, and felt herself hauled back toward the edge. She kicked against the stone jetty, hoping to drag Inanna in with her. But the big woman held fast, pulling Maia near then, once again, resumed pressing Maia's head, forcing her under.

Bubbles escaping her mouth, Maia clutched at her belt. The blanket strips got in the way, but at last she found the sliver of stone. Working it free from folds of belt and trousers brought her almost to her limit before success rewarded her. Desperately, without much effort to aim, she flung her arm around and slashed.

A scream resonated, even underwater. The pressure gave way and Maia emerged, grabbing air with shattered sobs. Then, almost without respite, the hands returned. Maia stabbed at them, connecting another time. Suddenly, her wrist was seized in a solid grip.

"Good move, virgie," the reaver snarled through gritted teeth, biting back pain. "Now we'll do it slowly."

Still holding Maia's wrist, Inanna used her other hand to resume pushing Maia's head deeper . . . then yanked her up again to gasp a reedy wheeze. The blurred expression on the woman's face showed pure enjoyment. Then the moment's surcease ended and Maia plunged down again. Still struggling, she tried to leverage against the wall, straining with her thrashing legs. But Inanna was well braced, and weighed too much to drag by force.

Numbness from the cold enveloped Maia, swathing and softening the ache of bruises and her burning lungs. Distantly, she noticed that the water around her was turning colors, partly from encroaching unconsciousness, but also with a growing red stain. Blood ran in rivulets from Inanna's cuts, down Maia's arms and hair. Inanna would be weakened badly. Good news if the fight had much future.

But it was over. Maia felt her strength ebb away. The stone sliver fell from her limp hand. The next time Inanna hauled her head out, she barely had the power to gasp. Blearily, she saw the reaver look down upon her, a quizzical look crossing her face. Inanna started to bend forward, pushing for what Maia knew would be the final time.

Yet, Maia found herself dimly wondering. *Why is there so much blood?*

The woman kept coming forward, leaning farther than necessary just to murder Maia. Was it to gloat? To whisper parting words? A kiss goodbye? Her face loomed until, with a crash, all of her weight fell into the water atop Maia, carrying them both toward the bottom.

Astonished surprise turned into galvanized action. From somewhere, Maia found the strength to push away from her foe's fading grip. Her last image of the reaver, seared into her brain, was the shock of seeing an *arrowhead* protruding through the base of Inanna's neck.

Breaking surface, Maia emerged too weak for anything but a thin, whistling, inadequate, inward sigh. Even that faded as she sank again . . . only to feel distantly another hand close around her floating hair. It was the last she thought of anything for a while.

"I suppose I could of conked her, or done somethin' else. I had one nocked, though, ready to fly. Anyway, it seemed a good idea at th' time."

Maia couldn't figure out why Naroin was apologizing. "I am grateful for my life," she said, shivering on the chair, wrapped in what seemed a hectare of sailcloth, while the former bosun went over Inanna's body, searching for clues.

"That makes us even. You saved me from bein' a dolt. I figured on followin' the bitch, too, but lost her. Would of fell into that crater, too, if you hadn't lit the torch when you did. As it was, I had th' devil of a time, findin' those stairs after you'd gone in."

Naroin stood up. "Lugar steaks an' taters! Nothin'. Not a damn thing. She was a pro, all right." Naroin left the body and stepped over to the table, where she peered at the comm console. "Jort an' double jort!" she cursed again.

"What is it?"

Naroin shook her head. "What it *isn't* is a radio. Thing must be a cable link. Maybe to a infrared flasher, set up on the rocks, outside."

"Oh. I . . . hadn't th-thought of that poss-ssibility." There was nothing to do about the shivering except stay here, enveloped in the sail taken from the tiny skiff. No dry clothes were to be had from the dead, and Naroin was much too small to share. "So we can't call the police?"

With a sigh, Naroin sat on the edge of the table. "Snowflake, you're talkin' to 'em."

Maia blinked. "Of course."

"You know enough now to figure it out, almost any time. I figure, better tell you now than have you yell '*Eureka*' all of a sudden, outside."

"The drug . . . you investigated—"

"In Lanargh, yeah. For a while. Then I got reassigned to somethin' more important."

"Renna."

"Mm. Should've stuck with you, it seems. Never imagined a case like this, though. Seems there's all sorts that don't care what it takes to make use of your starman."

"Including your bosses?" Maia asked archly.

Naroin frowned. "There's some in Caria that're worried about invasion, or other threats to Stratos. By now I'm almost sure *he's* harmless, personally. But that don't guarantee he represents no danger—"

"That's not what I meant, and you know it," Maia cut in.

"Yeah. Sorry." Naroin looked troubled. "All I can speak for is my direct chief. She's okay. As for the politicos above her? I dunno. Wish th' Lysodamn I did." She paused in silence, then bent to peer at the console again.

"Question is, did Inanna have time to send word o' the escape attempt tomorrow? Have to assume she did. Kind of sinks any plan to take advantage of our uncovering her. With a reaver comin', there's no way to even use this little dinghy." Naroin gestured toward the boat moored nearby. "Sure, you saved a bunch o' lives, Maia. The others upstairs won't sail into a trap now. But that still leaves us stuck here to rot."

Maia pushed aside the folds of rough cloth and stood up. Rubbing her shoulders, she began pacing toward the water and back again. Through the tunnel came sounds of an outgoing tide.

"Maybe not," she said after a long, thoughtful pause. "Perhaps there is a way, after all."

I might have it all wrong. This grand experiment isn't about sex, after all. The goal of minimizing the danger and strife inherent in males . . . that was all window dressing. The real issue was cloning. Giving humans an alternative means of copying themselves. If men were able to carry their own duplicates, as women can, my guess is that Lysos would have included them, too.

Psychologists here speak of womb envy among boys and men. However successful they are in life, the best a male Stratoin can hope for is reproduction by proxy, not personal creation, and never duplication. It's a valid enough point on other worlds, but on Stratos it's beyond dispute.

. . .

Preliminary results from the cross-specific bio-assays are in, show-ing that I'm not overtly contagious with any interstellar plagues . . . at least none spreadable to Stratoins by casual contact. That's a genuine relief, given what Peripatetic Lina Wu inadvertently caused on Reichsworld. I have no wish to be the vehicle for such a tragedy.

Despite those results, some Stratoin factions still want me kept in semiquarantine, to "minimize cultural contamination." Fortunately, the council majority seems to be moving, ever so gradually, toward relax-ation. I have begun receiving a steady stream of visitors—delegations from various movements and clans and interest groups. Security Council-lor Groves isn't happy about this, but there is nothing, constitutionally, she can do.

Today it was a deputation from a society of heretics wishing to hitch a ride, when I depart! They would send missionaries into the Hominid Realm, spreading word of the "Stratos Way." Cultural contamination that is directed outward is always seen as "enlightenment."

I explained my ship's limited capacity, and they were little molli-fied by my offer to take recordings. Not that it matters. In a few years, or decades, they will get to deliver their sermons in person.

When I was sent to follow up remote robot scans of this system, I expected iceship launches to await receipt of my report. But the Floren-tina Starclade wasted no time. Cy informs me that her instruments have picked up the first iceship already. It appears the Phylum will arrive sooner than even I expected, sealing permanent reunion, making moot all of the sober arguments by councillors and savants about preserving their noble isolation.

Presently, despite their decaying instrumentalities, the savants of Stratos will know as well, and start demanding answers.

Better that I tell them first.

Before that, another matter must be dealt with . . . my worsening mental and physical health.

It is not the gravity or heavy atmosphere. Periodically, I suffer spells when my symbionts struggle, and I must rest in my quarters for a day or two, unable to venture outside. These episodes are few, fortunately. For the most part, I feel hale and strong. The worst problem facing me is psychoglandular, having nothing to do with air or earth.

As a summertime male visitor, unsponsored by any clan, my position in Caria has been ambiguous. Even those clans who approve of my mission have been wary in private. It would be too much to fancy they might treat me like those favored males they welcome each aurora time. No one wants to be the first risking accidental pregnancy with an alien whose genes might perturb the Founders' Plan.

That near-paranoiac caution had advantages. The chill attitude helped restrain my dormant drives. Even after long voyages, I have never sought the attentions of women, save those who cared for me.

With autumn's arrival, however, attitudes are softening. Social encounters grow warmer. Women look, converse, even smile my way. Some acquaintances I now tentatively call friends—Mellina of Cady Clan, for instance, or that stunning pair of savants from Pozzo Hold, Horla and Poulain, who no longer bristle, but actually seem glad of my presence. They draw near, touch my arm, and share lighthearted, even provocative, jests.

How ironic. As my isolation lessens, the discomfort grows. By the day. By the hour.

Iolanthe, Groves, and most of the others seem oblivious. While consciously aware that I function differently than their males, they seem unconsciously to assume the autumnal diminishment of Wengel Star also damps my fires. Only Councillor Odo understands. She drew me out during a walk through the university gardens. Odo thinks it a problem easily solved by visiting a house of ease, operated by one of those specialist clans who are expert at taking all precautions, even with a randy alien.

I'm afraid I turned red. But, embarrassment aside, I face quandaries. Despite the female-to-male ratio, Stratos is no adolescent's moist fantasy come true, but a complex society, filled with contradictions, dangers, subtleties I've not begun to plumb. The situation is perilous enough without adding risk factors.

I am a diplomat. Other men—envoys, priests, and emissaries through all eras—have done as I should do. Risen above instinct. Exercised professionalism, self-control.

Yet, what celibate of olden times had to endure such stimulation as I do, day in, day out? I can feel it from my raw optic nerve all the way down to my replete roots.

Come on, Renna. Isn't it just a matter of sexual cues? Some species are turned on by pheromones, or strutting displays. Male hominoids are *visually activated*—chimpanzees, by rosy, estrous colors; Stratoin men, by estival lights in the sky. Old-fashioned hu-men react to the most inconvenient incitement cues of all—incessant, perennial, omnipresent. Cues women cannot help displaying, whatever their condition, or season, or intent.

No one is to blame. Nature had her reasons, long ago. Still, I am increasingly able to understand why Lysos and her allies chose to change such troublesome rules.

For the thousandth time . . . if only a woman peripatetic had drawn this mission!

Dammit, I know I'm rambling. But I feel inflamed, engulfed by so much untouchable fecundity, flowing past me in all directions. Insomnia plagues me, nor can I concentrate at the very time I must keep my wits about me. A time when I shall need all of my skills.

Am I rationalizing? Perhaps. But for the good of the mission, I see no other choice.

Tomorrow, I will ask Odo . . . to arrange things.

20

"The bitchies are gettin' impatient," Naroin commented, peering at the tiny screen. "I caught sight o' their prow a second time, an' a glint o' binocs. They're just holdin' back till the right moment."

Maia acknowledged with a grunt. It was all she had breath for, while pulling at her oars. Powerful, intermittent currents kept trying to seize their little boat and smash it against the nearby cliff face. Along with Brod and the sailors, Charl and Tress, she frequently had to row hard just to keep the skiff in place. Occasionally, they had to lean out and use poles to stave off jagged, deadly rocks. Meanwhile, with one hand on the tiller, Naroin used Inanna's spy device to keep track of events taking place beyond the island's far side.

This wouldn't be so difficult, if only we could stand off where the water's calm, Maia thought, while fighting the merciless tide. Unfortunately, the fibers leading to Inanna's farflung microcameras were of finite length. The skiff must stay near the mouth of the underground cave, battling contrary swells, or risk losing this slim advantage. Their plan was unlikely enough—a desperate and dangerous scheme to ambush professional ambushers.

I only wish someone else had come up with a better idea.

Naroin switched channels. "Trot an' her crew are almost done. The last raft parts have been lowered to the sea. They're lashin' the provisions boxes now. Should be any minute."

Maia glanced back at the display again, catching a blurred picture of women laboring across platforms of cut logs, struggling to tie sections together and erect a makeshift mast. As predicted by Maia's research, the tides were gentle on that side, at this hour. Unfortunately, that was far from true right now at the mouth of the spy tunnel.

At last, the sea calmed down for a spell. No wall of rock seemed about to swat them. With sighs, Maia and the others rested their oars. They had passed a busy, sleepless night since the fatal encounter with Inanna, the reaver provocateur.

First had come the unpleasant duty of rousing all the other marooned sailors, and telling them that one of their comrades had been a spy. Any initial suspicions toward Maia and Naroin quieted during a torchlit tour into the island's hidden grottoes, and were finished off by showing recorded messages on Inanna's comm unit. But that was not the end to arguing. There followed interminable wrangling over Maia's plan, for which, unfortunately, no one came up with any useful alternative.

Finally, hours of frantic preparations led to this early-morning flurry of activity. The more Maia thought, the more absurd it all seemed.

Should we have waited, instead? Simply avoided springing Inanna's trap? Let the reavers go away disappointed, and then try to slip away in the skiff at night?

Except, all eighteen could not fit in the little boat. And by nightfall the pirates would be querying their spy. When Inanna failed to answer with correct codes, they would assume the worst and try other measures. Not even the little skiff would be able to slip through a determined blockade by ships equipped with radar. As for those left behind, starvation would solve the reavers' prisoner problem, more slowly, but just as fully as an armed assault.

No, it has to be now, before they expect to hear from Inanna again.

"Eia!" Naroin shouted. "Here they come! Sails spread and breaking lather." She peered closer. "Patarkal jorts!"

"What is it?" young Brod asked.

"Nothin'." Naroin shrugged. "I thought for a minute it was a *big* bugger, a two-master. But it's a ketch. That's bad enough. Fast as blazes, with a crew of twelve or more. This ain't gonna be easy as mixin' beer an' frost."

Charl spat over the side. "Tell me somethin' I don't know," the tall Méchanter growled. Tress, a younger sailor from Ursulaborg, asked nervously, "Shall we turn back?"

Naroin pursed her lips. "Wait an' see. They've turned the headland and gone out o' view of the first camera. Gonna be a while till the next one picks 'em up." She switched channels. "Lullin's crew has spotted 'em, though."

The tiny screen showed the gang of raft-builders, hurrying futilely to finish before the reaver boat could cross the strait between neighboring isles. It was patently useless, for the most recent image of the sleek pirate craft had shown it slashing the choppy water, sending wild jets of spray to port and starboard as it sprinted to attack.

"Will they board?" Tress asked.

"Wish they would. But my guess is takin' prisoners ain't today's goal."

The current kicked up again. Maia and the others resumed rowing, while Naroin turned switches until she shouted. "Got 'em! About three kilometers out. Gettin' closer fast."

Keep coming . . . Maia thought each time she glanced at the display, until a looming expanse of white sailcloth filled the tiny screen. *Keep coming closer.*

At last, the raft crew cast loose their moorings of twisted vines. Some of them began poling with long branches, while two attempted to raise a crude mast covered with stitched blankets. For all the world, it looked as if they really were trying to get away. Either Lullin, Trot and the others were good actors, or fear lent verisimilitude to their ploy.

Naroin kept counting estimates of the reaver ship's approach. The ketch was under a thousand meters from the raft. Then eight hundred, and closing.

The situation on the raft grew more desperate. One agitated figure began pushing boxes of provisions off the deck, as if to lighten the load. They bobbed along behind the raft, very little distance growing between them.

"Six hundred meters," Naroin told them.

"Shouldn't we get closer now?" Brod asked. He seemed oddly relaxed. Not exactly eager, but remarkably cool, considering his earlier confessions to Maia. In fact, Brod had insisted on coming along.

"Lysos never said males can't ever fight," he had argued passionately, last night. *"We're taught that all men are reserve militia members, liable for call-up in case of really big trouble. I'd say that describes these bandits!"*

Maia had never heard reasoning like that before. Was it true? Naroin, a policewoman, ought to know. The former bosun had blinked twice at Brod's assertion, and finally nodded. *"There are . . . precedents. Also, they won't be expecting a male. There's an element of surprise."*

In the end, despite gallant protests by some of the others, he was allowed to come along. Anyway, Brod would be safer here than on the raft.

"Be patient an' clam up," Naroin told the boy, as they fought choppy currents. "Four hundred meters. I want to see how the bitchies plan on doin' it. . . . Three hundred meters."

Brod took the rebuke mildly. Looking at him a second time, Maia saw another reason for his relative quiet. Brod's complexion seemed greenish. He was clamping down on nausea. If the youth was trying to show his guts, Maia hoped he wouldn't do so literally.

It was getting near decision time. Plan A called for battle. But if that looked hopeless, those on the skiff were to try fleeing downwind, keeping the bulk of the island between them and the raiders. Only in that way might those sacrificing themselves on the raft get revenge. But, given the enemy's possession of radar, Maia knew the unlikeliness of a clean getaway. For all its flaws, the ambush scheme still seemed the best chance they had.

"Three hundred meters," Naroin said. "Two hundred an' eight. . . . *Bleedin'* jorts!"

Her fist set the rail vibrating. This sound was followed almost instantly by a roll of pealing thunder, anomalous beneath clear skies.

"What is it?" Maia asked, turning in time to glimpse, on the viewer screen, a sudden spout of rising water that just missed the little raft, splashing its frantic crew.

"Cannon. They're usin' a cannon!" Naroin shouted. "The Lyso-dammed, lugar-faced, man-headed jorts. We never figured on this."

Guilt-panged because the plan had been her idea, Maia craned to watch, fascinated as Naroin switched camera views of the approaching reaver boat. At its prow, a flash erupted through smoke lingering from the first shot. Another tower of seawater almost swamped the wallowing raft. "They've got 'em straddled," Naroin snarled, then snapped at Maia. "What're *you* lookin' at? Mind yer oars! I'll tell what's happenin'."

Maia swiveled just as a tidal surge washed their tiny craft toward a jutting rock. "Pull!" Brod cried, rowing hard. Heaving with all their might, they managed to stop short of the jagged, menacing spire. Then, as quickly as it came, the bulging sea-crest ran back out again, dragging them along. "Naroin! Turn!" Maia cried. But the preoccupied bosun was cursing at what she saw in the screen, taking notice only when a mesh of fiber cables suddenly stitched across the water, stretched to their utter limit, and abruptly snatched the electronic display out of her hands. The spy device flew some distance, then met the waves and sank from sight.

The policewoman stood up and shouted colorfully, setting the boat rocking, then quickly and forcibly calmed herself as more echoes of discrete thunder rounded the cliffs. Naroin sat down, resting hand and arm on the tiller once more. "No matter, it won't be long now," she said.

"We can't just sit here!" Tress cried. "Lullin and the others will be blown to bits!"

"They knew it'd be rough. Showin' up now would just get us killed, too."

"Should we try running away, then?" Charl asked.

"They'd spot us soon as they circuit the island. That boat's faster, an' a cannon makes any head start useless." Naroin shook her head. "Besides, I want to get even. We'll get closer, but wait till the last shot before settin' sail."

Now that they were away from the rock face, the swells were smoother. Maia and the others let the current carry them northward. More booms shook the thick air, louder and louder. Maia felt concussions in her ears and across her face. As they approached, an accompanying sound chilled her heart, the faint, shrill screaming of desperate women.

"We've *got* to—"

"Shut up!" Naroin snapped at Tress.

Then came a noise like no other. The closest thing Maia remembered was the breaking of bulkheads aboard the collier *Wotan*. It was an explosion not of water, but wood and bone. Of savagely cloven air and flesh. Echoes dissipated into a long, stunned silence, moderated by the nearby crash of surf on rock. Maia needed to swallow, but her mouth and throat were so dry, it was agony to even try.

Naroin spoke through powerfully controlled anger. "They'll stand off an' look for a while, before movin' in. Charl, get ready. The rest o' you, set sail and then duck outta sight!"

Maia and Brod stood up, together releasing the clamps holding the furled sail, and drew it to the clew outhaul. The fabric flapped like a liberated bird, suddenly catching the wind and throwing the boom hard to port, catching Brod and knocking him into Maia. Together, they fell toward the bow coaming, atop one another.

"Uh, sorry," the youth said, rolling off and blushing. "Uh, it's all right," she answered, gently mimicking his abashed tone. It might have been funny, Maia thought, if things weren't so damn serious.

Tress joined them in the bilge, below the level of the gunwales. As the skiff rounded the northern verge of their prison isle, Charl took over the tiller, letting Naroin crouch down as well. Only Charl remained in view, now attired in a white smock that was stained around the neckline. She had put on a ragged, handmade wig that made her look vaguely blonde.

"Steady," Naroin said, peering over the rail. "I see the raft, or what's left of it . . . Keep yer heads down!"

Maia and Brod ducked again, having caught sight of an expanse of floating bits and flinders, logs and loosely tethered boxes, along with one drifting, grotesquely ruined body. It had been a nauseating sight. Maia was content to let Naroin describe the rest.

"No sign o' the reaver, yet. I see one, two survivors, hidin' behind logs. Hoped there'd be more, since they knew it was comin'. . . . Eia! There's her prow. Get ready, Maia!"

They had argued long and hard over this part of the plan. Naroin had thought she should be the one taking on the most dangerous job. Maia had responded that the policewoman was just too small to make it believable. Besides, Naroin had more important tasks to perform.

You asked for this, Maia told herself. Brod squeezed her hand for luck, and she returned a quick smile before crawling aft.

From the moment the reaver vessel entered view, Charl began waving, shouting and grinning. *We're counting on certain assumptions,* Maia thought. Foremost, the reavers mustn't instantly see through the ruse.

It makes sense, though. Inanna wouldn't stay on the island after the raft was destroyed. She'd come to ferry a cleanup squad of killers through the secret passage, to finish off any survivors remaining above.

It was brutal logic, borne out by recent events. But was it true? Were the pirates expecting to see a blonde woman in a little sailboat? Maia ached to peer over the side.

Charl described events through gritted teeth. "They're maybe a hundred fifty meters out . . . sails luffed . . . still too damn far. Now someone's pointin' at me . . . waving. There's somebody else lifting binoculars. Let's do it, quick!"

With a heavy intake of breath, Maia stood up suddenly, and pretended to launch an attack on Charl, throwing an exaggerated punch the older woman evaded at the last moment. Charl shoved her back, and the boat rocked. Then they closed and began grappling, hands clasping for each other's throats. In the process, they managed so that Charl's back was to the reaver. All the enemy would be able to make out now, even through binoculars, would be a big blonde woman wrestling an adversary who must have climbed out from the wreckage of the raft.

Shouts of excited dismay carried across the water. *They'll finish us with the cannon if they suspect,* Maia knew. *Or if they're bloody-minded about the value of their spies.*

Even feign-fighting with Charl was a grunting, intense effort. Bobbing movements of the boat kept forcing them to clutch each other for real. Minutes into the contest, Charl's grip tightened on Maia's windpipe, setting off waves of authentic pain.

"Maia!" Naroin hissed from below and aft, her hand on the tiller. "Where are they?"

Maia pushed Charl back and affected to punch just past the

woman's ear. Looking over Charl's shoulder, she saw the reaver turn and
fill its jib enough to gain some headway. "Under . . ." Maia gasped for
breath as Charl shoved her against the skiff's mast. "Under a hundred
meters. They're coming. . . ."

The next thing Maia knew, Charl had picked up an oar and aimed
an awfully realistic swipe. Ducking, Maia had no chance to mention what
else she had seen. Among the crowd of rough women gathered at the bow
of the ketch, two had brandished slender objects that looked chillingly
like hunting rifles. The only thing saving Maia right now was her close
proximity to a figure the reavers thought to be their accomplice.

"Eighty meters . . ." Maia said, elbowing Charl in the ribs, knocking aside the oar and lifting her locked hands as if to deliver an over-
hand blow. Charl staved this off by ducking and grabbing Maia's midriff.

"Uh! . . . Not so hard! . . . Sixty meters . . ."

The ketch was a beautiful thing, lovely in its sleek, terrible rapac-
ity. Even with jib alone, it prowled rapidly, striking aside flotsam of its
victim, the ill-fated raft. Logs and boxes rebounded off its hull, wallowing in its wake. The sheer island face now lay behind the skiff. There
was no escape.

"Fifty meters . . ."

In their wrestling struggle, Charl's makeshift wig suddenly slipped.
Both women hurried to replace it, but one of the reavers at the bow could
be heard reacting with tones of sudden outrage. *The jig is up,* Maia
realized, looking across the narrowing gap to see a pirate lift her rifle.

There was no sound, no warning at all, only a brief shadow that
flowed down the stony cliff and a patch of sun-drenched sea. One of the
corsairs on the ketch glanced up, and started to shout. Then the sky
itself seemed to plummet onto the graceful ship. A cloud of dark, heavy
tangles splashed across the mast and sails and surrounding water, followed by a lumpy box of metal that struck the starboard gunwales,
glanced off . . . and exploded.

Flame brightness filled Maia's universe. A near-solid fist of compressed air blew Charl against her, throwing the two of them toward the
mast, sandwiching Maia in abrupt pain. *Sound* seized the flapping sail,
causing it to billow instantaneously, knocking both women to the keel
where they lay stunned. The skiff rocked amid rhythmic, heaving after-
shocks.

Still conscious, Maia felt herself being dragged out from under
Charl's groaning weight, toward the bow. Through a pounding ringing in
her ears, time seemed to stretch and snap, stretch and snap, in uneven
intervals. From some distant place, she heard Brod's reassuring voice
uttering strange words.

"You're all right, Maia. No bleeding. You'll be okay . . . Got to get ready now, though. Snap out of it, Maia! Here, take your trepp. Naroin's bringing us along the aft end. . . ."

Maia tried to focus. Unwelcome but frequent experience with situations like this told her it would take at least a few minutes for critical faculties to return. She needed more time, but there was none. Climbing to her knees, she felt a pole of smooth wood pushed into her hands, which closed by pure habit in the correct grip. *Inanna's trepp bill*, she dimly recognized, which had been among the dead spy's possessions. Now, if only she recalled how to use it.

Brod helped her face the right way, toward a looming, soot-shrouded object that had only recently been white and proud and exquisite. Now the ship lay in a tangle of fallen cables and wires. Its sails were half torn away by the makeshift bomb, which had been catapulted at the last moment by two captives who had remained high on the bluff, hoping to do this very thing.

"Get ready!"

Maia's ears were still filled with horrific reverberations. Nevertheless, she recognized Naroin's shout. Glancing right, she saw the bosun already using her bow and arrows, shooting while Tress guided the skiff across the last few meters. . . .

Wood crumped against wood. Brod shouted, leaping to seize the bigger ship's rail, a rope-end between his teeth. The youth scrambled up and quickly tied a knot, securing the skiff.

"Look out!" Maia cried. She commanded urgent action from her muscles, ordering them to strike out toward a snarling woman who ran aft toward Brod, an illegally sharpened trepp in hand. Alas, Maia's uncoordinated flail only glanced off the railing.

Brod turned barely in time to fend off the attacker's blows. One smashed flat along his left shoulder. Another met the beefy part of his forearm, slashing his shirt and cutting a bloody runnel. There was an audible crack as part of the impact carried through, striking his head.

The young man and the reaver stared at each other for an instant, both apparently surprised to find him still standing. Then, with a sigh, Brod pushed the pirate's weapon aside, took her halter straps, and flung her overboard. The reaver screamed indignant fury until she crashed into the sea, where other figures could be seen swimming amid the wreckage of the raft.

Tress and Naroin were already scrambling to join Brod, followed by a groggy Charl. Maia grabbed the rail and concentrated, trying twice before finally managing to throw one leg over, and then rolling onto the upper deck. In doing so, however, her grip on Inanna's bill loosened and it slipped from her hands, clattering back into the skiff.

Bleeders. Do I go back for it now?

Maia shook her head dizzily. *No. Go forward. Fight.*

Dimly, she was aware of other figures clambering aboard, presumably raft survivors, joining the attack while enemy reinforcements also hurried aft. There were sharp cracks as firearms went off. Feet scuffed all around her as grunting combat swayed back and forth. Looking up, Maia saw two women attack Brod while another swung a huge knife at Naroin, armed only with her bow and no arrows. The scene stunned Maia, its ferocity going far beyond the fights in Long Valley, or even the Manitou. She had never seen faces so filled with hatred and rage. During those earlier episodes, there had at least been a background of rules. Death had been a possible, but unsought, side effect. Here, it was the central goal. Matters had come down to abominations—blades and arrows, guns and fighting men.

Maia's hand fell on a piece of debris from the explosion, a split tackle block. Without contemplating what she was doing, she lifted it in both hands and swiftly brought it around with all her might, smashing one of Brod's opponents in the back of the knee. The woman screeched, dropping a crimson knife that Maia prayed was innocent of boy's blood. Without pause, she struck the other knee. The reaver collapsed, howling and writhing.

Maia was about to repeat the trick with Brod's other foe, when that enemy simply vanished! Nor was Brod himself in view anymore. In an instant, the fight must have carried him off to starboard.

Maia turned. Naroin was backed against the rail, using her bow as a makeshift staff, flailing against *two* reavers. The first kept the policewoman occupied with a flashing, darting knife-sword, while the second struggled with a bolt-action rifle, slapping at the mechanism, trying to clear a jammed cartridge. Before Maia could react, the reluctant bolt came free. An expended shell popped out and the reaver quickly slipped a new bullet inside. Slamming the bolt home again, she lifted her weapon . . .

With a scream, Maia leaped. The riflewoman had but a moment to see her coming. Eyes widening, the reaver swung the slender barrel around.

Another explosive concussion rocked by Maia's right ear as she tackled the pirate, carrying them both into the rail. The lightly framed wood splintered, giving way and spilling them overboard.

But I only just got here, Maia complained—and the ocean slapped her, swallowed her whole, squeezed her lungs and clung to her arms as she clawed through syrupy darkness, like coal.

Lamatia and Long Valley hated me, the damn ocean hates me. Maybe the world's trying to tell me something.

Maia surfaced at last with an explosive, ragged gasp, thrashing through a kick turn while peering through a salty blur in hopes of finding her foe before she was found. But no one else emerged from the sea. Perhaps the raider so loathed losing her precious weapon, she had accompanied the rifle to the bottom. Despite everything she'd been through, it was the first time Maia had ever knowingly killed anybody, and the thought was troubling.

Worry about that later. Got to get back and help now.

Maia sought and found the reaver ship, awash in smoke and debris. Fighting a strong undertow, exhausted and unable to hear much more than an awful roar, she struck out for the damaged ketch. At least her thoughts were starting to clear. Alas, that only let her realize how many places hurt.

She swam hard.

Hurry! It may already be too late!

By the time she managed to climb back aboard, however, the fight was already over.

There were strands of cable everywhere. The tangled mass, remnants of the broken winch mechanism, had been the centerpiece of their intended trap. A net wide enough to snare a large, fast-moving boat, even using an inaccurate, makeshift catapult. It had been Brod's suggestion that the booby-trapped gearbox might also make a good weapon. Naroin had said not to count on it, but in the end, that had provided the crucial bit of luck.

Well, we were due a little, Maia thought. Despite all the damage wrought by blast, collision, and battle, the ketch showed no sign of taking water. Just as fortunately, the fickle currents now swept it away from the rocky cliffs.

Still, the rigging was a mess. The masthead and forestay were gone, as well as the portside spreader. It would take hours just to clear away most of the wreckage, let alone patch together enough sail to get under way. Heaven help them if another reaver ship came along during that time.

Barring that unpleasant eventuality, a head start and favorable winds were what the surviving castaways most wanted now. Even the wounded seemed braced by the thought of imminent escape westward, and a chance to avenge the dead.

Although the reavers had been stunned and wounded by the ambuscade, it would have been madness for four women and a boy to try attacking all alone. But Maia and the rest of the skiff crew had counted on hidden reinforcements, which came from a source the pirates never suspected. Only a few of those who had been aboard the raft when the reaver ship was first spotted had remained aboard to face the brunt of the cannon's shells. The rest had by then gone overboard, taking shelter under empty crates and boxes already jettisoned—apparently to lighten the raft's load. In fact, they were tethered to float some distance behind, where the enemy would not think to shoot at them.

Only the strongest swimmers had been chosen for that dangerous role. Once the skiff crew began boarding, drawing all the reavers aft, five waterlogged Manitou sailors managed to swim around to the bow and clamber aboard, using loops of dangling cable. Shivering and mostly unarmed, they did have surprise on their side. Even so, it was a close and chancy thing.

Small-scale battles can turn on minor differences, as Maia learned when she pieced together what had happened at the end. The last two Manitou sailors, those responsible for springing the catapult trap, had been perhaps the bravest of all. With their job done, each took a running start, then leaped feetfirst off the high bluff to plunge all the way down to the deep blue water. Surviving that was an exploit to tell of. To follow it up with swimming for the crippled ketch, and joining the attack in the nick of time . . . the notion alone put Maia in awe. These were, indeed, tough women.

Before Maia made it back from her own watery excursion, that last wave of reinforcements turned the tide, converting bloody stalemate into victory. Now ten of the original band of internees, plus several well-watched prisoners, labored to prepare the captive prize for travel. Young Brod, despite bandages on his face and arms, climbed high upon the broken mast, parsing debris from useful lines and shrouds, eliminating the former with a hatchet.

Maia was hauling lengths of cable overboard when Naroin tapped her on the shoulder. The policewoman carried a rolled-up chart, which she unfurled with both hands. "You ever get a good latitude fix with that toy Pegyul gave you?" she asked.

Maia nodded. After two dips in the ocean, she hadn't yet inspected the minisextant, and feared the worst. Before yesterday, however, she had taken several good sightings from their prison pinnacle. "Let's see . . . we must've been dumped on . . ." She bent to peer at the chart, which showed a long archipelago of narrow, jagged prominences, crisscrossed by perpendicular coordinate lines. Maia saw a slanted row of cursive lettering, and rocked back. "Well I'll be damned. We're in the Dragons' Teeth!"

"Yeah. How about that." Naroin replied. These were islands of legend. "I'll tell you some interestin' things about 'em, later. But now—the latitude, Maia?"

"Oh, yes." Maia reached out and tapped with one finger. "There. They must have left us on, um, Grimké Island."

"Mm. Thought so from the outline. Then that one over there"—Naroin pointed westward at a mist-shrouded mass—"must be De Gournay. And just past it to the north, that's the best course toward deep water. Two good days and we're in shipping lanes."

Maia nodded. "Right. From there, all you need is a compass heading. I hope you make it."

Naroin looked up. "What? You're not coming along?"

"No. I'll take the skiff, if it's all right with you. I have unfinished business around here."

"Renna an' your sister." Naroin nodded. "But you don't even know where to look!"

Maia shrugged. "Brod will come. He knows where the man sanctuary is, at Halsey Beacon. From there, we may spot some clue. Find the hideout where Renna's being kept." Maia did not mention the uncomfortable fact that Leie was one of the keepers. She shifted her feet. "Actually, that chart would be more useful to us, since you'll be off the edge just a few hours after . . ."

Naroin sniffed. "There are others below, anyway. Sure, take it." She rolled the vellum sheet and slapped it gruffly into Maia's hands. Clearly she was masking feelings like the ones erupting in Maia's own breast. It was hard giving up a friend, now that she had one. Maia felt warmed that the woman sailor shared the sentiment.

"O' course, Renna might not even be in the archipelago anymore," Naroin pointed out.

"True. But if so, why would they have gone to such lengths to get rid of us? Even as witnesses, we'd not be much threat if they'd fled in some unknown direction. No, I'm convinced he and Leie are nearby. They've got to be."

There followed a long silence between the two women, punctuated only by the sounds of nearby raucous chopping, hammering and scraping. Then Naroin said, "If you ever finally reach a big town, get to a comm unit an' dial PES five-four-niner-six. Call collect. Give 'em my name."

"But what if you aren't . . . if you never . . . I mean—" Maia stopped, unable to tactfully say it. But Naroin only laughed, as if relieved to have something to make light of.

"What if I never make it? Then if you please, tell my boss where you saw me last. All the things you've done an' seen. Tell 'em I said you got a favor or two comin'. At least they might help get you a decent job."

"Mm. Thanks. So long as it has nothing to do with coal—"

"Or saltwater!" Naroin laughed again, and spread her small, strong arms for an embrace.

"Good luck, virgie. Keep outta jail. Don't get hit on the head so much. An' *stop* tryin' to drown, will ya? Do that an' I'm sure you'll be just fine."

Part Three

Peripatetic's Log:

Stratos Mission:

Arrival + 53.369 Ms

T oday I told the heirs of Lysos all about the law. A law they had no role in passing. One they cannot amend or disobey.

The assembled savants, councillors, and priestesses listened to my speech in stony silence. Though I had already informed some of them, in private, I could still sense shock and churning disbelief behind many rigid faces.

"After millennia, we of the Phylum have learned the hard lesson of speciation," I told them. "Separated by vast gulfs of space, distant cousins lose their sense of common heritage. Isolated human tribes drift apart, emerging far down the stream of time, changed beyond recognition. This is a loss of much more than memory."

The grimness of my audience was unsettling. Yet Iolanthe and others had counseled frankness, not diplomatic euphemisms, so I told the leaders accounts from the archives of my service—a litany of misadventure and horror, of catastrophic misunderstandings and tragedies provoked by narrow worldviews. Of self-righteous ethnic spasms and deadly vendettas, with each side convinced (and armed with proof) that it was right. Of exploitations worse than those we once thought jettisoned in Earth's predawn past. Worse for being perpetrated by cousins who refused to know each other anymore, or listen.

Tragedies that finally brought forth Law.

"Till now, I've described how renewed contact might prove advantageous. Arts and sciences would be shared, and vast libraries containing solutions to countless problems. Many of you looked at me, and thought, 'Well, he is but one man. To get those good things, we can endure rare visits by solitary envoys. We'll pick and choose from the cornucopia, without disrupting our ordered destiny.'

"Others of you suspected more would be involved. Much more. There is."

I called forth a holographic image to glimmer in the center of the council hall, a glistening snowflake as broad as a planet, as thin as a tree, reflecting the light of galaxies.

"Today, a second service links the Phylum worlds, more important than the one provided by peripatetics. It is a service some of you will surely loathe, like foul-tasting medicine. The great icecraft move between ten thousand suns—more slowly than messengers like me. But their way is inexorable. They carry stability. They bring change."

A Perkinite delegate leaped up. "We'll never accept them. We'll fight!"

I had expected that.

"Do what you feel you must. Blow up the first icecraft, or ten, unmindful of the countless sleeping innocents you thus consign to die. Some callous worlds have murdered hundreds of snowy hibernibarges, and yet, finally surrendered.

"Try what you will. Bloodshed will transform you. Inevitably, guilt and shame will divert your children, or grandchildren, from the path you choose for them. Even passive resistance will give way in time, as curiosity works on your descendants, tempting them to sample from the bright new moons that circle in their sky.

"No brutal war fleets will force compliance. Vow, if you must, to wait us out. Planets are patient; so are your splendid, ancient clans, more long-lived than any single human or government.

"But the Phylum and the Law are even more persistent. They will not have 'no' for an answer. More is at stake than one world's myth of mission and grand isolation."

The words felt hard, yet it was good to have them out. I sensed support from many on the council who had coached my presentation to shock matters from a standstill. How fortunate that here, unlike Watarki World or New Levant, a strong minority sees the obvious. That solitude and speciation are not human ways.

"Look at it this way," I concluded. "Lysos and the Founders sought seclusion to perfect their experiment. But have you not been tested by time, and validated, as well as any way of life can be, in its context? Isn't it time to come out and show your cousins what you've wrought?"

A lingering silence greeted my conclusion. Iolanthe led some tardy, uncomfortable applause that fluttered about the hall and fled through the skylights like an escaping bird. Amid frigid glowers from the rest, the Speaker cleared her voice, then dryly called adjournment.

Despite the tension, I left feeling stronger than I have in months. How much of that was due to the release of openness, I wondered, and how much did I owe to ministrations I've received lately thanks to Odo, under the sign of the ringing bell.

If I survive this day, this week, I must go back to that house, and celebrate while I can.

21

D ragons' Teeth. Row after row of jagged incisors, aimed fiercely
at the heavens.

I should have realized, Maia thought. *On first seeing these islands in
the distance, I should have known their name.*

The Dragons' Teeth. A legendary phrase. Yet, on contemplation,
Maia realized she knew next to nothing about the chain of seamounts,
whose massive roots of columnar crystal erupted from the ocean crust far
below, rising to pierce surface waves and bite off hearty portions of sky.
Their lustrous, fluted sides seemed all but impervious to time's erosion.
Trees clung to craggy heights where waterfalls, fed by pressure-driven
springs, cascaded hundreds of meters, forming high, arched rainbows
that mimicked aurorae, and gave Maia and Brod painful neck cricks as
they sailed by, staring in awe.

Their gunter-rigged skiff threaded the tropical archipelago like a
parasite weaving its way through the spines of some mighty half-
submerged beast. The islands grew more densely clustered the deeper
the little boat penetrated. Packed closely together, many of the needle
isles were linked by natural causeways, even narrow, vaulting bridges.
Brod always made a sign across his eyes before steering under one of
those. A gesture not of fear, but reverence.

Although Brod had lived among the Teeth for several months before
being taken hostage, he only knew the area near Halsey Beacon, the sole
official habitation. So Maia took care of navigation while he steered.

Their chart warned of shoals and reefs and deadly currents along the course she chose, making the circuitous path just right for folk like them, not wishing to be seen.

Clearly, Maia and Brod weren't the first to reach this conclusion. Several times they spied evidence of past and present occupation. Huts and coarse, stony shelters lay perched on clefts, sometimes equipped with rude winches to lower cockleshell boats even smaller than the one they sailed. Once, Brod pointed and Maia caught sight of a hermit quickly gathering her nets as the skiff entered view. Ignoring their shouts, the old woman took to her oars, vanishing into a dark series of caves and grottoes.

So much for getting advice from the locals, Maia thought. Another time, she glimpsed a furtive figure staring down at them from a row of open casements, half-collapsed with age, part of a gallery of windows carved long ago, partway up one sheer tower face. The construction reminded her of the prison sanctuary in Long Valley, only vaster, and indescribably older.

Shadows cast by innumerable stone towers combed the dark blue water, all pointing in the same transitory direction, as if the stony pinnacles were gnomons to a half-thousand igneous sundials, tracking in unison the serene march of hours, of aeons.

This was a place once filled with history, then all but emptied of a voice.

"The Kings fought their last battle here," Naroin had explained shortly before parting with the surviving castaways on their captured ketch. Maia and Brod had been about to board the resupplied skiff, in preparation to turning south. "All o' the united clans an' city-states sent forces here to finally squash the man-empire. It's not much talked about, to discourage vars ever thinkin' again about alliance with men against the great houses. But nothin' could ever really stop a legend so big." Naroin had gestured toward the sere towers. "Think about it. This is where the would-be patriarchs an' their helpers made their last stand."

Maia had paused to share her friend's contemplation. "It's like something out of a fairy tale. Unreal. I can hardly believe I'm here."

The sailor-policewoman sighed. "Me neither. These parts ain't visited much, nowadays. Way off the shippin' lanes. I never pictured anythin' like this. Kind o' makes you wonder."

Wonder, indeed. As she and Brod sailed deeper among the Dragons' Teeth, Maia considered the unreliability of official history. The farther they went, the more certain she grew that Naroin had told the truth as she'd learned it. And that truth was a lie.

Maia recalled the riddle of the pit—that awful, glassy crater back on Grimké Island, where she and the others had been marooned. Since setting course southward on their separate journey, she and Brod had seen other peaks bearing similar stigmata. Seared tracks where stone had run molten under fierce heat, sometimes tracing a glancing blow, and sometimes . . .

Neither spoke while the steady wind took them past one ruined spire, a shattered remnant that had been sundered lengthwise by some power beyond anything she could imagine.

I don't know about Kings and such. Maybe the patriarchists and their allies did make a last stand here. But I'll bet a niche and all my winter rights they never caused this . . . devastation.

There was another, more ancient story. An event also seldom spoken of. One nearly as pivotal to Stratos Colony as its founding. Maia felt certain *another* enemy had been fought here, long ago. And from the looks of things, it had been barely beaten.

The Great Defense. Funny no one in our group made the connection, telling stories round the campfire, but that battle must also have raged here in the Dragons' Teeth.

It was as if the Kings' legend served to cover up an older tale. One in which the role of men had been admirable. *As if those in power want its memory left only to hermits and pirates.* She recalled the ancient, eroded, bas-relief sculpture she'd found amid the buried ruins at the temple in Grange Head, depicting bearded and unbearded human forms grappling horned demons under the sheltering wings of an avenging Mother Stratos. Maia added it to a growing collection of evidence . . . but of what? To what conclusion? She wasn't sure, yet.

A formation of low clouds moved aside, exposing the expanse of sea and stone to a flood of brilliant light. Blinking, Maia found herself jarred from the relentless flow of her dour thoughts. She smiled. *Oh, I've changed all right, and not just by growing tougher. It's a result of everything I've seen and heard. Renna, especially, got me thinking about time.*

The clans urged single vars to leave off any useless pondering of centuries, millennia. Summerlings should concentrate on success in the here and now. The long term only becomes your affair once your house is established and you have a posterity to worry about. To consider Stratos as a world, with a past that can be fathomed and a destiny that might be changed, was not how Maia had been raised to think.

But it's not so hard, learning to picture yourself as part of a great chain. One that began long before you, and will go on long after.

Renna had used the word *continuum* meaning a bridge across generations, even death itself. A disturbing notion, for sure. But ancient women and men had faced it before there ever were clones, or else they would never have left old Earth. *And if they could do it, a humble var like me can, too.*

Such thoughts were more defiant than measuring constellations, or even playing Game of Life puzzles. Those had been mere man-stuff, after all. Now she dared to question the judgments of savant-historians. Seeing through maternalistic, conservative propaganda to a fragment of truth. *Fragments are almost as dangerous as nothing at all,* she knew. Yet, somehow, it must be possible to penetrate the veil. To figure out how everything she had seen, and been through, held together.

How will I explain this to Leie? Maia mused. *Must I first kidnap her away from her reaver friends? Haul her, bound and gagged, somewhere to have the meanness fasted out of her?*

Maia no longer meditated wistfully on the missed joy of shared experience with her sibling. The Leie of old would never have understood what Maia now thought and felt. The new Leie, even less so. Maia still missed her twin, but also felt resentment toward her harsh behavior and smug assumption of superiority, when they had last, briefly, met.

Maia longed far more to see Renna.

Does that make me a daddy's girl? The juvenile epithet held no sting. *Or am I a pervert, nurturing hearth feelings toward a man?*

Philosophical dilemmas such as "why?" and "what?" seemed less important than "how?" Somehow, she must get Renna to safety. And if Leie chose to come also, that would be fine, too.

"We had better start thinking about putting in somewhere. It's that or risk hitting rocks in the dark." Brod held the tiller, constantly adjusting their heading to maintain southward momentum. With his other hand, he rubbed his chin, a common male mannerism, though in his case another distant summer must come before he felt a beard. "Normally I'd suggest putting out to open ocean, " he continued. "We'd lay a sea anchor, keep watch on wind and tide, and rejoin the archipelago at daybreak." Brod shook his head unhappily. "Wish I didn't feel so blind without a weather report. A storm could be just over the horizon, and we'd never know in time."

Maia agreed. "At best, we'd waste hours and come back exhausted." She unrolled the map. "Look, there's one large island in this area with a charted anchorage. It's not too far off our route, near the westernmost line of Teeth."

Brod leaned forward to read aloud. "Jellicoe Beacon. . . . Must've been a lighthouse sanctuary once, like Halsey. Deactivated and deserted, it says."

Maia frowned, feeling suddenly as if she had heard that name before. Although the sun still lay some distance above the horizon, she shivered, ascribing the feeling to this creepy place. "Uh . . . so, shall we jibe to a sou'western tack, Cap'n?"

Maia had been half-teasing him with the honorific all day. Grinning, Brod responded with a grossly exaggerated accent. "Thet well bee doin', Madam Owner. If yell be so kinned as te lend a help wit'de sail."

"Aye, sir!" Maia took the taut, straining boom in one hand, setting a foot at the kick-strap. "Ready!"

"Coming about!" Brod swung the tiller, propelling the skiff's bow sharply toward the wind. The sail luffed and flapped, signaling Maia to haul the boom around from port to starboard, where the sail snapped full with an audible crack, sending them rushing on a new heading, surging up the long shadow of a tall island to the west. The late sun lit a luminous aureole of water vapor, a pinkish halo, turning the rocky prominence into a fiery spear aimed beyond the clouds.

"Assuming we find shelter in the lagoon at Jellicoe," Brod said. "We'll resume southward at dawn. Around midafternoon tomorrow, we can strike east, hitting the main channel near Halsey Beacon."

"The active sanctuary. Tell me about the place," Maia asked.

"It's the one citadel still operating in the Dragons' Teeth, sanctioned by the Reigning Council to keep order. My guild drew short lot to staff the lighthouse, so they sent two ships and crews they could most easily spare—meaning dregs like me. Still, I never expected the captain'd try picking up extra cash by hiring out to reavers." He frowned unhappily. "Not every fellow feels that way. Some like watching women fight. Gives 'em a summery hot, they say."

"Couldn't you get a transfer, or something?"

"You kidding? Middies don't question captains, even when a cap'n is breaking an unwritten guild tradition. Anyway, reaving's legal, within limits. By the time I realized Captain Corsh was selling out to *real* pirates, it was too late." Brod shook his head. "I must've shown how I felt, 'cause he was glad enough to offer me as hostage, while out loud yelling to the reavers what a great loss I was, and they'd better take good care of me!" The boy laughed harshly.

We're alike, poor fellow, Maia thought. *Is it my fault I don't have any talents right for the world of women? Or his, that he's a boy who was never meant to be a sailor?* Her bitter reflection was unalloyedly rebellious. *Maybe it's just wrong to make generalizations like that, without leaving room for exceptions. Shouldn't each of us have the right to try what we're best at?*

They were also alike in both having been abandoned by people they trusted. Yet he was more vulnerable. Boys expected to be adopted by a guild that would be their home from then on, while girl summerlings grew up knowing exactly what they were in for—a life of lonely struggle.

"We'd better be careful, then, when we reach Halsey. Your captain may not—"

"Be happy to see me?" Brod interrupted. "Hmph. I was within my rights, escaping with you and the others. Especially after Inanna and her murdering schemes. But you're right. I don't guess Corsh will see it that way. He's probably already worried how he's going to explain all this to the commodores.

"So we'll try getting there near nightfall, tomorrow. I know a channel into the harbor. One that's too shallow for ships, but just right for us. It leads to an out-of-the-way dock. From there, maybe we can sneak into the navigator's suite and look at his charts. I'm sure he's written down where the reaver hideout is. Where they're keeping your starman."

There was a slight edge to Brod's voice, as if he felt dubious about something. Their chances of success? Or the very idea of consorting with aliens?

"If only Renna were being held right there, at Halsey." She sighed.

"Doubtful. The reavers wouldn't leave a male prisoner where he could talk to other men. They have too much riding on their plans for him."

On Grimké, Brod had told Maia about the Visitor's actions, just after Manitou was seized. By Brod's account, Renna had stomped among the jubilant victors, protesting every violation of Stratoin law. He defiantly refused to move over to the *Reckless* until all of the wounded were tended. So stern had been his otherworldly countenance, his anger and clench-fisted restraint, that Baltha and the other reavers had backed down rather than be forced to hurt him. Brod never mentioned Renna paying special notice to one victim in particular, but Maia liked to imagine her alien friend's strong, gentle hands soothing her delirium, and his voice, speaking in low tones, promising her firmly that they would meet again.

Brod had little more to say about Leie. He had noticed Maia's sister among the reaver band, notable mainly for her eager eyes and intense interest in machines. The motor-room chief had been glad to have her, and hadn't given a damn what gender a soot-stained crewmate carried under shirt and loincloth, so long as he or she worked hard.

"We only spoke privately once," Brod said, shielding his eyes as they sailed toward the late afternoon sun. He adjusted the tiller to a change in the wind, and Maia reacted by tightening the sail. "I guess she chose me since no one would care if *I* laughed at her."

"What did she want to talk about?"

Brod frowned, trying to remember. "She asked if I had ever met an old commodore or captain, back at my guild's main sanctuary in Joannaborg. One named Kevin? Calvin?"

Maia sat up quickly. "Do you mean *Clevin?*"

He tapped the side of his head absentmindedly. "Yeah, that's right. I told her I'd heard the name. But they shipped me out so quickly after adoption, and so many crews were still at sea that I'd never actually met him. The shipname, Sea Lion, was one of ours, though."

Maia stared at the boy. "Your guild. It's the Pinnipeds."

She stated it as fact, and Brod shrugged. "Of course, you wouldn't know. We lowered our ensign before the fight. Pretty shameful. I knew right then things were no good."

Maia sank back down, listening through a roil of conflicting emotions—astonishment topping the list.

"Starkland Clan has known the Pinnipeds for generations. The mothers say it was once a great guild. Shipped fine cargoes, and its officers were welcome in High Town, winter and summer both. These days, the commodores take jobs like staffing Halsey Beacon, and now even hiring out to reavers." He laughed bitterly. "Not a great billet, eh? But then, I'm no prize, either."

Maia examined Brod with renewed interest. From what the boy said, he might be her distant cousin, several times removed . . . only a temple gene-scan could tell for sure. It was a concept Maia had to struggle with, along with the irony that here, after so many frantic adventures, she had finally made contact with her father-guild. The manner wasn't at all as she'd imagined.

They sailed on quietly, each of them deep in private thought. At one point, a swarm of sleek, dark shapes cruised into view, some meters below their tiny vessel, undulating silently with sinuous power and speed. The largest of the creatures would have outmassed the Manitou, and took several minutes to progress, yet its smooth passage scarcely caused a ripple above as the skiff passed at an angle. Maia barely glimpsed the monster's tail, then the mysterious underwater convoy was gone.

A few minutes later, Brod shifted forward in his seat, staring as he shaded his eyes with one hand, his body abruptly tense. "What is it?" Maia asked.

"I'm . . . not sure. I thought for a second something crossed the sun." He shook his head. "It's getting late. How close to Jellicoe?"

"We'll be in sight after that next little spire, ahead." Maia unfurled the chart. "It seems to consist of about two dozen teeth, all fused together. There are two anchorages, with some major caves noted here." She looked up and gauged the rate of sunset. "It'll be close, but we should have time to scout a channel before dark."

The young man nodded, still frowning in concern. "Get ready to come about, then."

The maneuver went smoothly, the wind snapping their rugged sail into line as it had all day. *Maybe our luck really has changed,* Maia thought, knowing full well that she was tempting fate. Once they were cruising steady on the new tack, she spoke again, bringing up another imminent concern.

"Naroin made me promise to try calling her superiors, in case we find a radio at Halsey."

It wasn't a vow she relished. Maia personally trusted Naroin, but her superiors? *So many groups want Renna for their own reasons. He has enemies on the Council. And even supposing honest cops answer a call, will the reavers let Renna be taken alive?*

One disturbing thought after another had occurred to her. *What if the Council still has weapons like those that burned Grimké?* What if they conclude a dead alien is better than one in the hands of their foes?

Brod's answer sounded as halfhearted as Maia felt. "We could try for the comm room, I suppose. It might be unwatched late at night. The idea gives me a pain in the gut, though."

"I know. It'd be awfully risky, combined with burgling the chart room—"

"That's not it," Brod cut in. "I'd just . . . rather someone else called the cops on my guild."

Maia looked at him. "Loyalty? After the way they treated you?"

"That's not it," he said, shaking his head. "I won't stay with 'em after this."

"Well, then? You're already helping me go after Renna."

"You don't understand. Another guild might respect me for helping you save a friend. But who's gonna hire a man who's squealed on his own crewmates?"

"Oh." Maia hadn't realized the added risk Brod was taking. Beyond life and freedom, he could lose all chance of a career. *Something I never had,* Maia almost murmured, but recanted. It takes courage for a person with prospects to gamble them on a hazard of honor.

The skiff began rounding the nearest headland. Beyond, just as Maia had predicted, a large, convoluted island hove gradually into view. To Maia, it looked as if a great claw had frozen in place while reaching out of the sea. Some mysterious geological process had welded the fingerlike talons, joining multiple slender spires in a mesh of stony arches.

Jellicoe Island had been even bigger, once upon a time. Stubby, fused remnants showed where a more extensive network of outlying islets had been blasted apart by an ancient power, presumably the same as excavated Grimké. Linear tracks of seared stone glistened like healed scar tissue across the jutting cliffs, adding contortions to the convoluted outlines ordained by nature. The resulting coastline had the horizontal contours of a twisted, many-pointed star, with rounded nubs instead of vertices and edges. Irregular openings broke the rhythmic outline.

A few minutes later, one of those gaps let Maia glimpse a lagoon within, as placid as glass.

"There it is!" she announced. "Perfect. We can sail right through and set anchor—"

"*Shiva an' Zeus!*" Brod cursed. "Maia, get down!"

She barely ducked in time as Brod steered hard, sending the boom flying across the little boat, whistling where Maia's head had been.

"What're you *doing*?" she cried. But the young man did not answer. Gripping the tiller, his hands were white with tension, eyes all concentration. Lifting her head to see, Maia gasped. "It's the Reckless!"

The three-masted, fore-and-aft schooner bore toward them from the southwest, almost directly out of the setting sun. The sight of its gravid sails, straining to increase a speedy clip, was breathless and dreadful to behold. While Maia and Brod had been wrestling their tiny vessel on a series of sunward, upwind tacks, the reaver ship had already crossed most of the space between two islands.

"Do you think she's seen us?" Maia felt inane for asking. Yet, Brod was clearly counting on that hope, trying to duck back behind the spire they had just passed. If only the reavers had lazy lookouts. . . .

Hope vanished with the sound of a whistle—a shriek of steam and predatory delight. Squinting against the glare, Maia saw a crowd of silhouettes gather at the bow, pointing. The image might have triggered déjà vu, bringing back how the day began, except that this was no little ketch, but a freighter, augmented for speed and deadliness. Smoke trails told of boilers firing up. Maia's nose twitched at the scent of burning coal. She did a quick calculation in her mind.

"It's no good running!" she told Brod. "They've got speed, guns, maybe radar. Even if we get away, they'll search all night, and we'll smash up in the dark!"

"I'm open to suggestions!" her partner snapped. Perspiration beaded his lip and brow.

Maia grabbed his arm. "Swing back westward! We can tack closer to the wind. Reckless will have to reef sails to follow. Her engines may still be cold. With luck, we can dodge into that maze." She pointed at the corrugated coastline of Jellicoe Island.

Brod hesitated, then nodded. "At least it'll surprise 'em. You ready?"

Maia braced herself and grabbed the boom, preparing to kick. "Ready, Captain!"

He grimaced at the standing joke. Maia quashed rebellion in her stomach, where the bilious, familiar commotion of fear and adrenaline had come back, as if to a favorite haunt.

So much for that string of luck, she thought. *I should have known better.*

"All right," Brod said with a ragged sigh, clearly sharing the thought. "Here goes."

Everything depended on nearest passage. How tight could the bigger vessel turn? What weapons would be brought to bear?

As expected, the diminutive skiff was far better at drawing a close tack. The Reckless hesitated too long after Brod changed course. When the reaver ship came about at last, it fell short and wound up abeam to the breeze. Brod and Maia gained westward momentum while seamen struggled aloft, lashing sails so the still-warming engines would not have to fight them pushing upwind. The rest of the reaver crew watched from the railings. *Do they recognize the skiff?* Maia wondered. *By now surely they know something's happened to Inanna and their friends on the ketch. Lysos, they look angry!*

Even with the big ship wallowing, there would come a moment when the two vessels passed by no more than a couple of hundred meters. What would the pirates do about it?

Working hard to help Brod maneuver as tightly as possible, Maia trimmed the sail for maximum efficiency. This meant having to throw herself from one side of the skiff to the other, leaning her weight far out, wherever balance was most needed. She had never sailed a small boat in this way, literally skating across the water. It was exhilarating, and might have been fun if her gut weren't turning somersaults. In glimpses, she sought to see if, by some chance, Renna stood upon the pirate ship. There were men on the schooner's quarterdeck, as during the taking of the Manitou, but no sign of Renna's peculiar dark features.

As the skiff swung broadside to the wallowing vessel, Maia heard furious shouts across the span of open water. Words were indiscernible, but she recognized the livid, red-faced visage of the ship's male captain, arguing with several women wearing red bandannas. The man pointed at more reavers wrestling a long black tube at the schooner's portside gunwale. Shaking his head, he made adamant forbidding motions.

Underneath his outrage, the captain seemed blithely certain of his authority. So certain, he showed no suspicion as more wiry women, armed with truncheons and knives, moved to surround him and his officers . . . until the man's tone of command cut off abruptly, smothered under a sudden flurry of violent blows.

From a horrified distance, Maia could not make out whether trepps or blades were used to cut the men down, but the attack continued many seconds longer than seemed necessary. Loudly echoing yips of pleasure showed how thoroughly the women pirates relished a comeuppance they must have long yearned for, breaking a troublesome alliance and the last restraint of law.

"We're pullin' away!" Brod shouted. He had been concentrating too hard even to glance at his former shipmates, or hear meaning in the recent spate of shouts and cries. A good thing, for the fall of the officers had been just part of the coup. When Maia next found time to scan the rigging, most of the remaining male crew members had vanished from where they were working moments before.

The Pinnipeds may be suffering hard times, Maia reflected, still in shock from what she'd seen. *But they drew the line at deliberate murder. So, they get to share our fate.*

These reavers were fanatics. She had known that, and had it reinforced during this morning's ambush. But this? To deliberately and cold-bloodedly attack and slay *men*? It was as obscene as what Perkinites constantly warned of, the oldtime male-on-female violence that once led to the Founders' Exodus, so long ago.

Renna, she thought in anguish. *What have you brought to my world?*

Maia cast a brief prayer that her sister, part of the engine crew, hadn't been involved in the spontaneous bloodletting. Perhaps Leie would help save any men belowdecks, though realistically, the pirates seemed unlikely to leave witnesses.

Right now, what mattered was that the mutiny had won Maia and Brod seconds, minutes. Time that they exchanged for badly needed meters as the shouting reavers reorganized and finished turning the ship. "Ready about!" Brod cried, warning of another jibe maneuver. "Ready!" Maia answered. As her partner steered, she slid under the boom and performed a complex set of simultaneous actions, moving with a fluid grace that would have shocked her old teachers, or even herself a few months ago. Practice, combined with need, makes for a kind of centering that can increase skill beyond all expectation.

The next time she glimpsed the Reckless, it cruised several hundred meters back but was picking up speed. The gunners kept having to reposition their recoilless rifle each time the schooner shifted angle to track the fugitives. They could be seen shouting at the new helmswoman, urging a steady course. Straight-on wouldn't do, as the larger vessel's bowsprit blocked the way. Eventually, Reckless settled on a heading that plowed thirty degrees from the wind. It reduced the closing rate, but finally allowed a clear shot.

Shall I warn Brod? Maia pondered, more coolly than she expected. *No, better to let him stay focused every possible moment.*

She watched her friend flick his gaze to the trembling sail, to the choppy water, to their destination—the rapidly nearing cluster of vast, stony monoliths. Using all this data, the boy made adjustments too subtle to be calculated, based on a type of instinct he had earlier denied possessing, seducing speed out of an unlikely combination of sailcloth, wood, and wind.

He's growing up as I watch him, Maia marveled. Brod's youthful, uncertain features were transformed by this intensely spotlit exercise of skill. His jaw and brow bore hardened lines, and he radiated something that, to Maia, distilled both the mature and immature essences of maleness—a profound narrowness of purpose combined with an ardent joy in craft. Even if the two of them died in the next few minutes, her young friend would not leave this world without becoming a man. Maia was glad for him.

A booming concussion shook the air behind them. It was a deeper, larger-caliber growl than the little cannon of this morning. "What was that?" Brod asked, almost absentmindedly, without shifting from the task at hand.

"Thunder," Maia lied with a grim smile, letting the hot glory of his concentration last a few seconds longer. "Don't worry. It won't rain for a while, yet."

Water poured down from the heavens, soaking their clothes and nearly swamping the small boat. It fell in sheets, then abruptly stopped. The cascade, blown into the sky by another exploding shell, sent Maia with a bucket to the bilge, bailing furiously.

Fountains of falling ocean weren't their only trouble. One near miss had spun the skiff like a top, causing the hull to groan with the sound of loosening boards and pegs. All Maia knew was that her bailing outflow must exceed inflow for as long as it took Brod to single-handedly find them a way out of this mess.

The gun crew on the Reckless had taken a while settling down, after their mutinous purge. They shot wide, frustrated partly by the skiff's zigzagging, before finally zeroing in amid the deepening twilight. For minutes, Maia nursed the illusion that safety lay in view—an open channel leading to the anchorage of Jellicoe Lagoon. Then she glimpsed a familiar and appalling sight—the captured freighter Manitou, anchored within that same enclosure of towering stone, its deck aswarm with more crimson bandannas. All at once, she realized the awful truth.

Jellicoe must be the reaver base! I led Brod straight into their hands!

"Turn right, Brod, hard!"

A sudden, last-minute swerve barely escaped the fatal entrance. Now they skirted along the convoluted face of Jellicoe itself, alternately drenched by near misses or the more normal ocean spume of waves crashing against obdurate rock. There were no more delicate, optimizing tack maneuvers. They were caught in a mighty current, and Brod spent all his efforts keeping them from colliding with the island's serrated face.

Darkness might have helped, if all three major moons weren't high, casting pearly luminance upon the fivers' imminent demise. It was a beautiful, clear evening. Soon, Maia's beloved stars would be out, if she lasted long enough to wish them goodbye.

Again and again she filled the bucket, spilling it seaward so as not to watch the glistening nearness of the "dragon's tooth," which towered nearly vertically like a rippling, convoluted curtain. Its rounded fabric folds seemed to hint a softness that was a lie. The adamantine, crystal-line stone was, in fact, passively quite willing to smash them at a touch.

Maia couldn't face that awful sight. She poured bucket after bucket in the opposite direction, which fact partially spared her when the reavers tried a new tactic.

A sudden detonation exploded behind Maia, bouncing the skiff in waves of compressed air and near vacuum, pummeling her downward to the bilge. To her own amazement, she retained full consciousness as concussions rolled past, fading into a low, rumbling vibration she could feel through the planks. Reflexively, she clutched at a stinging pain in the back of her neck, and pulled out a sliver of granitic stone, covered with blood. While purple spots swam before her eyes, Maia stared at the daggerlike piece of natural shrapnel. While the world wavered around her, she turned to see that Brod, too, had survived, though bloody runnels flowed down the left side of his face. Thank Lysos the rock fragments had been small. This time.

"Sail farther from the cliff!" Maia shouted. Or tried to. She couldn't even hear her own voice, only an awful tolling of temple bells. Still, Brod seemed to understand. With eyes dilated in shock, he nodded and turned the tiller. They managed to open some distance before the next shell struck, blowing more chunks off the promontory face. No chips pelted them this time, but the maneuver meant sailing closer to the Reckless and its weapon, now almost at point-blank range. Looking blearily up the rifled muzzle, Maia watched its crew load another shell and fire. She felt its searing passage through the air, not far to the left. An interval passed, too short to give a name, and then the cliff reflected yet another terrible blast, almost hurling the two fivers from the boat. When next she looked up, Maia saw their sail was ripped. Soon it would be in tatters.

At that moment, the convoluted border of the island took another turn. Suddenly, an opening appeared to port. With quaking hands, Brod steered straight for the cul-de-sac. It would have been insanely rash under any other circumstance, but Maia approved wholeheartedly. *At least the bitchies won't get to watch us die at their own hands.*

One side of the opening exploded as they passed through, sending cracks radiating through the outcrop, blowing the skiff forward amid cascades of rock. The next shell seemed to beat the cliff with bellows of frustrated rage. Cracks multiplied tenfold. A tremendous chunk of stone, half as long as the Reckless itself, began to peel away. With graceful deliberateness, its looming shadow fell toward Brod and Maia. . . .

The boulder crashed into the slim gap just behind the tiny boat, yanking them upon the driving fist of a midget tsunami, aimed at a deep black hole.

Maia knew herself to have some courage. But not nearly enough to watch their ruined boat surge toward that ancient titan, Jellicoe Beacon. *Let it be quick,* she asked. Then darkness swept over them, cutting off all sight.

Dear Iolanthe,

As you can see from this letter, I am alive . . . or was at the time of its writing . . . and in good health, excepting the effects of several days spent bound and gagged.

Well, it looks like I tumbled for the oldest trick in the book. The Lonely Traveler routine. I am in good company. Countless diplomats more talented than I have fallen victim to their own frail, human needs. . . .

My keepers command me not to ramble, so I'll try to be concise. I am supposed to tell you not to report that I am missing until two days after receiving this. Continue pretending that I took ill after my speech. Some will imagine foul play, while others will say I'm bluffing the Council. No matter. If you do not buy my captors the time they need, they threaten to bury me where I cannot be found.

They also say they have agents in the police bureaus. They will know if they are betrayed.

I am now supposed to plead with you to cooperate, so my life will be spared. The first draft of this letter was destroyed because I waxed a bit sarcastic at this point, so let me just say that, old as I am, I would not object to going on a while longer, or seeing more of the universe.

I do not know where they are taking me, now that summer is over and travel is unrestricted in any direction. Anyway, if I wrote down clues from what I see and hear around me, they would simply make me rewrite yet again. My head hurts too much for that, so we'll leave it there.

I will not claim to have no regrets. Only fools say that. Still, I am content. I've been and done and seen and served. One of the riches of my existence has been this opportunity to dwell for a time on Stratos.

My captors say they'll be in touch, soon. Meanwhile, with salutations, I remain—Renna.

22

In near-total darkness she stroked Brod's forehead, tenderly brushing his sodden hair away from coagulating gashes. The youth moaned, tossing his head, which Maia held gently with her knees. Despite a plenitude of hurts, she felt thankful for small blessings, such as this narrow patch of sand they lay upon, just above an inky expanse of chilly, turbid water. Thankful, also, that this time she wasn't fated to awaken in some dismal place, after a whack on the head. *My skull's gotten so hard, anything that'd knock me out would kill me. And that won't happen till the world's done amusing itself, pushing me around.*

"Mm . . . Mwham-m . . . ?" Brod mumbled. Maia sensed his vocalization more via her hands than with her shock-numbed hearing. Still unconscious, Brod seemed nevertheless wracked with duty pangs, as if at some level he remained anxious over urgent tasks left undone. "Sh, it's all right," she told him, though barely able to make out her own words. "Rest, Brod. I'll take care of things for a while."

Whether or not he actually heard her, the boy seemed to calm a bit. Her fingers still traced somnolent worry knots across his brow, but he did stop thrashing. Brod's sighs dropped below audible to her deafened ears.

In its last moments, their dying boat had spilled them inside this cave, while more explosions just behind them brought down the entrance in a rain of shattered rock. Amid a stygian riot of seawater and sand, her head ringing with a din of cannonade, Maia had groped frantically for Brod, seizing his hair and hauling him toward a frothy, ill-defined sur-

face. Up and down were all topsy-turvy during those violent moments
when sea and shore and atmosphere were one, but practice had taught
Maia the knack of seeking air. Rationing her straining lungs, she had
fought currents like clawing devils till at last, with poor Brod in tow, her
feet found muddy purchase on a rising slope. Maia managed to crawl out,
dragging her friend above the waterline and falling nearby to check his
breathing in utter blackness. Fortunately, Brod coughed out what water
he'd inhaled. There were no apparent broken bones. He'd live . . . until whatever came next.

All told, their wounds were modest. *If the skiff had stayed intact,
we'd have ridden that wave straight into some underground wall,* she
envisioned with a shudder. Only the boat's premature fragmentation had
saved their lives. The dunking had cushioned their final shorefall.

Maia felt cushioned half to death. Even superficial cuts hurt like
hell. Sandy grit lay buried in every laceration, with each grain apparently assigned its own cluster of nerves. To make matters worse, evapora-
tion sucked the heat out of her body, setting her teeth chattering.

But we're not dead, another voice within her pointed out defiantly. *And we won't be, if I can find a way out of here before the sea
rises.*

Not an easy proposition, she admitted, shivering. *This undercut cave
probably fills and empties twice a day, routinely washing itself clean of
jetsam like us.*

Maia guessed they had at least a few hours. More lifespan than she
had expected during those final moments, plunging toward a horrible,
black cavity in the side of a towering dragon's tooth. *I should be grateful
for even a brief reprieve,* she thought, shaking her head. *Forgive me,
though, if I fail to quite see the point.*

In retrospect, it seemed pathetically dumb to have gone charging off
to rescue Renna—and to redeem her sister—only to fail so totally and
miserably. Maia felt especially sorry for Brod, her companion and friend,
whose sole fatal error had been in following her.

*I should never have asked him. He's a man, after all. When he dies,
his story ends.*

The same could be said for her, of course. Both men and vars
lacked the end-of-life solace afforded to normal folk—to clones—who
knew they would continue through their clanmates, in all ways but direct
memory.

*I guess there's still a chance for me in that way. Leie could succeed
in her plans, become great, found a clan.* She sniffed sardonically. *Maybe
Leie'll put a statue of me in the courtyard of her hold. First in a long row
of stern effigies, all cast from the same mold.*

There were other, more modest possibilities, closer to Maia's heart.

Although the twins' minor differences had irked them, important things, like their taste in people, had always matched. So, there was a chance Leie might be drawn to Renna, as Maia had. Perhaps Leie would forsake her reaver pals and help the man from outer space, even grow close to him.

That should make me feel better, Maia pondered. *I wonder why it doesn't?*

In successive ebbs and flows, the waterline had been gradually climbing higher along the sandy bank where they lay. Soon the icy liquid sloshed her legs, as well as Brod's lower torso. *Here comes the tide,* Maia thought, knowing it was time to force her reluctant, battered body to move again. Groaning, she hauled herself upright. Taking the boy by his armpits, Maia gritted her teeth and strained to drag him upslope three, four meters . . . until her backside abruptly smacked into something hard and jagged.

"Ouch! *Damn* the smuggy . . ."

Maia laid Brod down on the sand and reached around, trying to rub a place along her spine. She turned and with her other hand began delicately exploring whatever obdurate, prickly barrier loomed out of the darkness to block *her* retreat. Carefully at first, she lightly traced what turned out to be a nearly vertical wall of randomly pointed objects . . . slim ovoids coated with slime. *Shells,* she realized. Hordes of barnacle-like creatures clung tenaciously to a stone cliff face while patiently awaiting another meal, the next tidal flood of seaborne organic matter.

I guess this is as far as we go, she noted with resignation. Depression and fatigue almost made her throw herself on the sand next to Brod, there to pass her remaining minutes in peace. Instead, with a sigh, Maia commenced feeling her way along the wall, trying not to wince each time another craggy shell pinched or scraped her hands. The thick band of algae-covered carapaces continued above her farthest reach, confirming that full tide stretched much higher than she could.

Still she moved from left to right, hoping for something to change. Shuffling sideways, her feet encountered a gentle slope . . . alas, rising no more than another meter or so. Yet it made a crucial difference. At the limit of Maia's tiptoe reach, her fingertips passed beyond the scummy crust of shells and stroked smooth stone.

High-water mark. The ceiling's above high tide! This offered possibilities. *Assume I waken him in time. Could Brod and I tread water and float up with the current, keeping our heads dry?*

Not without something strong and stable to hang on to, she realized with chagrin. More likely, the waves' flushing action would first bash them against the abrading walls, then suck their fragments outside to join other rubble left by the reavers' bombardment.

The only real hope was for a cleft or ledge, above. *If there's some way to get up there in time.*

She returned to check on Brod, and found him sleeping peacefully. Maia bent a second time to drag the boy up the little hillock she had found. Then she began exploring the cave wall in earnest, working her way further to the right, patting the layer of barnacle creatures in search of some route, some path above the killing zone. At one point she gasped, yanking her hand back from a worse-than-normal jab. Popping a finger in her mouth, Maia tasted blood and felt a ragged gash along one side. *May you live to enjoy another scar,* she thought, and resumed searching for a knob, a crack, anything offering a hint of a route upward.

A minute or two later, Maia almost tripped when something caught her ankle. She bent to disentangle it and her hands felt wood—a shattered board—snarled with scraps of canvas and sodden rope—fragments of the little skiff they had wrecked without ever giving it a name.

Shivering, she continued her monotonous task, whose chief reward consisted of unwelcome familiarity with the outline of one obnoxious, well-defended marine life-form. A while later, the sandy bank began to descend again, taking her even farther from her goal, and nearer the icy water.

Well, there's still the area leftward of where I put Brod. She held out little hope the topography would be any different.

On the verge of giving up and turning around, Maia's hand encountered . . . a hole. Trembling, she explored its outlines. It felt like a notch of sorts, about a meter up from the sandy bank. It might serve as a place to set one's foot, to start a climb, but with a definite drawback: the proposed procedure meant using the sharp, slippery barnacle shells as handholds.

Maia turned around, counted paces, and knelt to grope amid the wreckage she had found earlier. From remnants of the shredded sail, she tore canvas strips to wrap around her palms. For good measure, she looped over her shoulder the longest stretch of rope she could find. It wasn't much. *Hurry,* she thought. *The tide will be in soon.*

With difficulty, she found the notch again. Fortunately, the soles of her leather shoes were mostly intact, so Maia only winced, hissing with discomfort as she set one foot in the crevice and reached high above, tightly grasping two clusters of shells. Even through canvas, the things jabbed painfully. Tightening her lips together, she pushed off, using muscles in first one leg and then the other, drawing herself upward with both arms till she stood perched on one foot, pressed against the wall. Now sharp stabs assaulted the entire length of her body, not just the extremities.

Okay, what next?

With her free foot, she began casting for another step. It seemed chancy to ask a cluster of shells to bear her entire weight. Yet it must be tried.

To her astonishment, Maia encountered a better alternative. *Another* slim, encrusted notch in the wall—and at just the right height!

I don't believe it, she thought, pushing her left foot inside and gingerly shifting her weight. *It can't be a coincidence. This must mean . . .*

Checking her conclusion, she freed one hand and felt about until, sure enough, it met another notch. One that *had* to be exactly where it was. *The notches are woman-made . . . or man-made, since this place used to be a sanctuary. I wonder how old this "ladder" is.*

No, I don't. Shut up, Maia. Just concentrate and get on with it!

The notches made climbing easier. Still it was an agonizing ascent, even when her face lifted above the scouring layer of plankton-feeders and she had only to contend with smooth, rectangular cuts in the side of an almost-sheer wall. Maia's muscles were throbbing by the time her groping hand encountered a ring of metal, bolted to the rock. The rusty tethering collar proved useful as her final handhold before Maia was able at last to flounder one leg, then another, over a rounded lip and onto a stony shelf.

Maia lay on her back, panting, listening to a roar of her own heavy breathing. It took some moments to appreciate that all of the sound wasn't internal. *I can hear. My ears are recovering,* she realized, too tired to feel jubilant. She rested motionless, as echoes of each ragged inhalation resonated off the walls, along with a watery susurration of incoming swells.

Her pulse hadn't yet settled from a heavy pounding when she forced herself up, onto one elbow. *Got to get back to Brod,* Maia thought, wearily. The re-descent would be hard, and she had not figured out how to drag her friend up here, if it proved impossible to rouse him. As always, the future seemed daunting, yet Maia felt cheered that she had found a refuge. It drove off the sense of hopelessness that had been sapping her strength.

She sat up, letting out a groan.

More than her own echo came back to her, muffled by reverberations.

"M-Maia-aia-aia?"

It was followed by a fit of coughing. *"M-my god-od-od . . . what's happened? Where is she? Maia-aia-aia!"*

Resounding repetitions caused her to wince. "Brod!" she cried. "It's all right! I'm just above—" Her calls and his overlapped, drowning all sense in a flood of echoes. Brod's overjoyed response would have been more gratifying if he didn't stammer on so, offering thankful benedictions to both Stratos Mother and his patriarchal thunder deity.

"I'm above you," she repeated, once the rumbling resonances died down. "Can you tell how high the water is?"

There were splashing sounds. "It's already got me cornered on a spit of sand, Maia. I'll try backing up . . . Ouch!" Brod's exclamation announced his discovery of the wall of shells.

"Can you stand?" she asked. If so, it might save her having to climb down after him.

"I'm . . . a bit woozy. Can't hear so good, either. Lemme try." There were sounds of grunting effort. "Yeah, I'm up. Sort of. Can I assume . . . everything's black 'cause we're underground? Or am I blind?"

"If you're blind, so'm I. Now if you can walk, please face the wall and try working your way to the *right*. Watch your step and follow my voice till you're right below me. I'll try to rig something to help you up here. First priority is to get above the high-water line."

Maia kept talking to offer Brod a bearing, and meanwhile leaned over to tie one end of her rope around the metal grommet. It must have been put there long ago to moor boats in this tiny cave, though why, Maia could not imagine. It seemed a horrid place to use as an anchorage. Far worse than Inanna's tunnel hideaway on Grimké Island.

"Here I am," Brod announced just below her. "Frost! These bitchie barckles are sharp. I can't find your rope, Maia."

"I'll swing it back and forth. Feel it now?"

"Nope."

"It must be too short. Wait a minute." With a sigh, she pulled in the cord. Judging from Brod's ragged-sounding voice, he wouldn't be a good bet to make the same climb she had, unassisted. There was no choice, then. Fumbling at the catches with her bruised fingers, she unbuttoned her trousers and slid them off, over her deck shoes. Tying one leg to the rope with two half-hitches, she also knotted a loop at the far end of the other leg, then dropped everything over the side again. There was a gratifying muffled sound of fabric striking someone's head.

"Ow. Thanks," Brod responded.

"You're welcome. Can you slip one arm through the loop, up to your shoulder?"

He grunted. "Barely. Now what?"

"Make sure it's snug. Here goes." Carefully, step by step, Maia instructed Brod where to find the first foothold. She heard him hiss in pain, and recalled that his cord sandals had been in worse shape than her shoes, unfit for tackling knife-edge barnacles. He didn't complain, though. Maia braced herself and hauled on the rope—not so much to lift the youth as steady him. To lend stability and confidence as he moved shakily from foothold to handhold, one at a time.

It seemed to last far longer than her own laborious ascent. Maia's abused muscles quivered worse than ever by the time his huffing gasps came near. Somehow, drawing on reserves, she kept tension in the rope until Brod finally surged over the ledge in one gasping heave, landing halfway on top of her. In exhaustion they lay that way for some time, heartbeats pounding chest to chest, each breathing the other's ragged exhalations, each tasting a salty patch of the other's skin.

We must stop meeting like this, thought a distant, wry part of her. *Still, it's more than most women get out of a man, this time of year.* To Maia's surprise, his weight felt pleasant, in a strange, unanticipated way.

"Uh . . . sorry," Brod said as he rolled off. "And thanks for saving my life."

"It's no more'n you did for us on the ketch, this morning," she replied, covering embarrassment. "Though I guess by now that was yesterday."

"Yesterday." He paused to ponder, then abruptly shouted. "Hey, look at that!"

Maia sat up, puzzled. Since she couldn't see Brod well enough to make out where he pointed, she began scanning on her own, and eventually found something amid the awful gloom. Opposite their ledge, about forty degrees higher toward the zenith, she made out a delicate glitter of —she counted—five beautiful stars.

I believe it's part of the Hearth. . . .

Abruptly reminded, Maia grasped along her left arm and sighed in relief when she found her forgotten sextant, still encased within the scratched but intact leather cover. *It's probably ruined. But it's mine. The only thing that's mine.*

"So, Madam Navigator," Brod asked. "Can you tell from those stars just where we are?"

Maia shook her head seriously. "Too little data. Besides, we know where we are. If there were more to see, I might be able to tell the time—"

She cut short, tensing as Brod laughed aloud. Then, noting only affection in his gentle teasing, Maia relaxed. She laughed, too, letting go as the fact sank in that they would live awhile longer, to struggle on. The reavers hadn't won, not yet. And Renna was nearby.

Brod lay back alongside her, sharing warmth as they watched their sole, tiny window on the universe. Stratos turned slowly beneath them, and there passed a parade of brief, stellar performances. Together, they feasted on a show neither had expected ever to see again.

. . .

By day, the cave seemed less mysterious . . . and far more so.

Less, because dawn's filtered light revealed outlines that had seemed at once both limitless and stifling in pitch darkness. A mountain of rubble blocked what had been a generous cave entrance. Sunlight and ocean tides streamed through narrow, jagged gaps in the avalanche, beyond which the two escapees made out a new, foamy reef, created by the recent barrage.

There would be no escape the way they'd arrived; that much was clear.

Increased mystery came associated with both hope and frustration. Soon after awakening to the new day, Maia got up and followed the ledge to its far end, where it joined a set of stairs chiseled deep into the cave wall. At the top there was another landing, cut even deeper, which terminated in a massive door, over three meters wide.

At least she thought it was a door. It seemed the place for one. A door was desperately called for at this point.

Only it looked more like a piece of sculpture. Several score hexagonal plates lay upon a broad, smooth, vertical surface made of some obdurate, blood-colored, impervious alloy.

Impervious because others had apparently tried to break through, in the past. Wherever a crack or chink hinted at separable parts, Maia noticed burnished edges where someone must have tried prying away, probably with wedges or crowbars, and succeeded only in rubbing off a layer of tarnish. Soot-stained areas told where fire had been used, presumably in efforts to weaken the mètal, and striated patches showed signs of acid-etching—all to no avail.

"Here are your pants," Brod said, coming up from behind, startling Maia from her intense inspection. "I thought you might want them," he added nonchalantly.

"Oh, thanks," she replied, taking the trousers and moving aside to slip them on. They were ripped in too many places to count, and hardly seemed worth the effort. Still, she felt abashed without them, last night's fatigued intimacy notwithstanding.

While struggling into the pants, gingerly avoiding her worst cuts and contusions, Maia noticed that her arms were pale once more, as well as what hair she could pull into view. Without a mirror, she couldn't be sure, but recent multiple dunkings appeared to have washed out the effects of Leie's makeshift dye job.

Meanwhile Brod perused the array of six-sided plates, some clustered and touching, some standing apart, many of them embellished with symbols of animals, objects, or geometric forms. The youth seemed oblivious to his physical condition, though under his torn shirt Maia saw too many scratches and abrasions to count. He moved with a limp, favoring the heels. Looking back the way he had come, she saw specks of blood on the floor, left by wounds on his feet. Maia deliberately avoided cataloging her own injuries, though no doubt she looked much the same.

It had been quite a night, spent listening to tides surge ever closer, wondering if the assumed "high-water mark" meant anything when three moons lay in the same part of the sky. Surges of air pressure had made them yawn repeatedly to relieve their abused ears. The shelf grew slippery from spray. For what felt like hours, the two summerlings held onto each other as waves had lapped near, hunting them with fingers of spume. . . .

"I can't even figure what the thing's *made* of," Brod said, peering closely at the mysterious barrier. "You have any idea what it's for?"

"Yeah, I think. I'm afraid so."

He looked at her as she returned. Maia spread her arms before the metal wall. "I've seen this kind of thing before," she told her companion. "It's a puzzle."

"A *puzzle*?"

"Mm. One apparently so hard that lots of folks tried cheating, and failed."

"A puzzle," he repeated, mulling the concept.

"One with a big prize for solving it, I imagine."

"Oh yeah?" Brod's eyes lit. "What prize do you think?"

Maia stepped back a couple of paces, tilting her head to look at the elaborate portal from another angle. "I couldn't say what the others were after," she said in a low voice. "But *our* goal's simple. We must solve this . . . or die."

There had been another riddle wall once, a long time ago. That one hadn't been made of strange metal, but ordinary stone and wood and iron, yet it had been hard enough to stymie a pair of bright four-year-olds filled with curiosity and determination. What were the Lamai mothers hiding behind the carven cellar wall, inset with chiseled stars and twining snakes? Unlike the puzzle now before her, that one had been no massive work of unparalleled craftsmanship, but the principle was clearly the same. A combination lock. One in which the number of possible arrangements of objects far exceeded any chance of random guessing. One whose correct answer must remain unforgettable, intuitively obvious to the initiated, and forever obscure to outsiders.

Shared context. That was the key. Simple memory proved unreliable over generations. But one thing you could count on. If you established a clan—your distant great-great-granddaughters would think a lot like you, with similar upbringing and near-identical brains. What had been forgotten, they would recover by re-creating your thought processes.

That insight had opened the way, after Maia failed in her first attempts in the Lamatia Hold wine cellar, and Leie's efforts with a small hydraulic jack threatened to break the mechanism, rather than persuade it. Even Leie had agreed that curiosity wasn't worth the kind of punishment *that* would bring on. So Maia had reconsidered the problem, this time trying to think like a Lamai. It wasn't as easy as it sounded.

She had grown up surrounded by Lamai mothers, aunts, half sisters, knowing the patterns they exhibited at each phase of life. The cautious enthusiasm of late three-year-olds, for instance, which quickly took cover behind a cynical mask by the time each towheaded girl turned four. A romantic outburst in adolescence, followed by withdrawal and withering contempt for anything or anyone non-Lamai—a disdain that intensified, the more worthy any outsider seemed. And finally, in late middle-age, a mellowing, a relaxation of the armor, just enough for the ruling age-group to make alliances and deal successfully with the outer world. The first young Lamai var, the founder, must have been lucky, or very clever, to reach that age of tact all by herself. From then on, matters grew easier as each generation fine-tuned the art of being that continuous single entity, Lamatia.

Pondering the problem, Maia had realized she knew nothing of how individual Lamais felt, deep within. Mentally squinting, she pictured a Lamai sister looking in the mirror and using words like *integrity . . . honor . . . dignity.* They did not see themselves as mean, capricious, or spiteful. Rather, they viewed others as inherently unreliable, dangerous.

Fear. That was the key! Maia had not been able to speak after that flash of intuition, on realizing what drove her mother clan.

It was more than fear. A type of dread that no amount of wealth or security could wipe out, because it was so woven into the personality matrix of the type. The genetic luck of the draw, reinforced by an upbringing in which self perpetually reinforced self, compounding and augmenting over and over again.

It was no crippling terror, or else the offshoots of that one var could never have turned themselves into a nation. Rather, Lamatia rationalized it, *used* it as a motivator, as a driving force. Lamais weren't happy people. But they were successful. They even raised more than their share of successful summer progeny.

There are worse, Maia recalled thinking on the day she had had that insight, while turning a crank to lower the dumbwaiter into that crypt below the kitchens. *Who am I to judge what works?*

Her mind afroth with possibilities, Maia had approached the wall with new concepts in mind. *Lamais aren't logical, though they pretend to be. I've been trying to solve the puzzle rationally, as a series of orderly symbols, but I'll bet it's a sequence based on emotion!*

That day (it felt like ages ago), she had lifted her lantern to scan familiar patterns of stone figures. Stars and snakes, dragons and upturned bowls. The symbol for Man. The symbol for Woman. The emblem of Death.

Picture yourself standing here with an errand to perform, Maia thought. *You're a confident, busy, older Lamai. High-class daughter of a noble clan. Proud, dignified, impatient.*

Now add one more ingredient, underneath it all. A hidden layer of jibbering terror. . . .

One long year later, and a quarter of the way around the globe, Maia tried the same exercise, attempting to put herself in the shoes of *another* type of person. The kind who might have left a complex jigsaw of hexagonal plates upon a metal wall. An enigma standing between two desperate survivors and their only hope of escaping a death trap.

"This place is old," she told Brod in a soft voice.

"Old?" He laughed. "It was a different world! You've seen the ruins. This whole archipelago was filled with sanctuaries, bigger than any known today. It must've been the focus, the very center of the Great Defense. It might even have been the one place in all of Stratos history where men had any real say in goings on . . . till those King fanatics got big heads and ruined it all."

Maia nodded. "A whole region, run by men."

"Partly. Until the banishment. I know, it's hard to imagine. I guess that's how the Church and Council were able to suppress even the memory."

Brod was making sense. Even with the evidence all around her, Maia had trouble with the concept. Oh, there was no denying that males could be quite intelligent, but planning further than a single human lifespan was supposedly beyond even their brightest leaders. Yet, here in front of her lay a counterexample.

"In that case, this puzzle was designed to be solved by men, perhaps with the specific purpose of keeping women out."

Brod rubbed his jaw. "Maybe so. Anyway, standing around staring won't get us much. Let's see what happens if I push one of these hexagon slabs."

Maia had already stroked the metal surface, which was curiously cool and smooth to the touch, but she hadn't yet tried moving anything, preferring to evaluate first. She almost spoke up, then stopped. *Differences in personality . . . one providing what the other lacks. It's a weakness in the clan system, where the same type just amplifies itself.* Maia no longer felt a heretical thrill, pondering thoughts critical of Lysos, Mother of All.

Brod tried pushing one hexagonal plate with a circle design etched upon it, standing by itself on an open patch of metal wall. Direct pressure achieved nothing, but a shear force, *along* the plane of the wall, caused movement! The piece seemed to glide as if being slid edgewise through an incredibly viscous fluid. When Brod let go, Maia expected it to stop, but it kept going in the same direction for several more seconds before slowing and finally coming to rest. Then, as she watched in surprise, the hexagon began sliding *backward*, in the exact opposite direction, retracing its path unhurriedly until at last settling precisely where Brod had first found it.

"Huh!" the young man commented. "Hard to imagine accomplishing a lot *that* way." He experimented with more plates, and found that about a third of them would move, but only directly along one of six directions perpendicular to the hexagonal plate-edges. There was no sign of any sort of rail system holding the slabs in track, so the queer behavior must be due to some mechanism behind the plane of the wall itself, utilizing forces beyond anything Maia had been taught as physics.

It's not magic, she told herself while Brod pushed away, trying variations. Maia experienced a shiver, and knew that it wasn't due to awe or superstitious fear, but something akin to *jealousy.* The gliding interplay of matter and motion was achingly beautiful to behold. She hungered to grasp how and why it worked.

Renna says the savants in Caria still know about such powers, but won't release anything that might "destabilize a pastoral culture."

If this was a more benign use of the same power that had fried Grimké, and many other islands in this chain, Maia could well understand why Lysos and the Founders chose such a path. Perhaps they were right, on some grand, sociological scale. Maybe the hunger she felt within was immature, wrongheaded, a dangerous, flaming curiosity like the madness Renna had spoken of—the sort that drove what he had called a "scientific age."

Maia recalled the wistful longing in Renna's eyes as he recalled such times, which he had said were rare among human epochs. She experienced a pang deep inside, envying what she had missed and would never know.

"The plates seem to always go back where they started," Brod commented. "Come, Maia. Let's see if we can push two at once."

"All right," she sighed. "I'll try this one with a horse etched on it. Ready? Go."

At first she thought her chosen plate was one of those that wouldn't budge, then it began gliding under her hand, building up momentum in response to her constant pushing. She let go after it had crossed three of its own body lengths, but it drifted onward, now slowing with each passing second, until it collided at an angle with the hexagon Brod had pushed, carrying the image of a sailing ship. The two caromed off each other, moving in new directions for several more seconds before coming to a stop. Then each of them reversed course, and the pair went through a negative version of the same collision. Finally both of the plates drifted back to rest at their starting positions. Two minutes after starting the experiment, the wall was back as they had found it, a jumble of hexagons laid out in a pattern that made no immediate sense. Maia exhaled heavily.

There's got to be a logic to it. An objective. The Game of Life looks like a meaningless mass of hopping pieces, too, until you see the underlying beauty.

Also, like the game, the men who designed this might have thought it alien enough to keep out women. That could be an important clue, especially with Brod here to help.

Unfortunately, there was a problem inherent in her "shared context" insight. For all she and Brod knew, the puzzle might be based on some fad current a thousand years ago, and now long forgotten. Perhaps a certain drinking song had been popular at the time, featuring most of these symbols. Almost any man of that era might have known the relationship between, say, the bee rendered in one plate and the house etched on another. One clever inscription seemed to show a slice of bread dripping globs of butter or jam. Another showed an arrowhead, trailing fire.

Maia changed her mind. It had to be based on something longer lasting.

Whoever put so much care into this obviously meant it to endure, and serve a purpose long after he was gone. And men aren't known for thinking ahead?

Clearly, all rules had exceptions.

A growling sound distracted Maia, accompanied by an unpleasant churning in her stomach. Her bruised body wanted to be fed, the sooner the better. Yet, in order to have a chance of doing so, she must ignore it. Somehow, she and Brod would have to make it through what had apparently stymied countless interlopers before them. The only difference being that those others—hermits, tourists, explorers, pirates—had presumably come by boat in peace, able to leave again. For Maia and Brod, the motivation was stronger than greed or curiosity. Their only chance of surviving lay in getting beyond this wall.

.   .   .

"Sorry there's no sauce, or fire to cook it, but it's fresh. Eat up!"

Maia stared down at the creature that lay on the ground in front of her crossed legs, still flopping slightly. Emerging from a trance of concentration, she blinked at the unexpected sight of a fish, where none had been before. Turning to look at Brod, she saw new lacerations that bled fine lines across his chest and legs and arms. "You didn't climb back *down*, did you?"

The boy nodded. "Low tide. Saw some stranded critters on the bar. Anyway, we needed water. Here, tip your head back and open wide."

Maia saw that he carried in the crook of one arm a sodden ball of fabric, made of bits of canvas and his own rolled-up shirt. These he held out, dripping. With sudden eagerness arising from a thirst she hadn't recognized till now, Maia did as told. Brod wrung a stream of bitter saltwater, tanged with a faint hint of blood, into her mouth. She swallowed eagerly, overlooking the unpleasant taste. When finished drinking, she picked up the fish and bit into it ravenously, as she had seen sailors do.

"Mm . . . fank you, Broth . . . Mm delishush . . ."

Sitting beside her, Brod chewed a fish of his own. "Pure self-interest. Keep up your strength, so you can get me outta here."

His confidence in her safecracking abilities was inspiring. Maia only wished it were well-founded. Oh, there had been progress, the last ten hours or so. She now knew which plates would move and which wouldn't. Of the stationary ones, some served as simple barriers, or bumpers against which moving tokens might bounce or reflect. A few others, by a process she was never able to discern clearly, seemed to *absorb* any plate that ran into them. The moving hexagon would merge with or pass behind the stable one, and *stay* there for perhaps half a minute, then reappear to reverse its path, returning the way it came. Each time one of these temporary absorptions occurred, Maia thought she heard a distant, low sound, like a humming gong.

Unfortunately, there weren't direct shots from movable hexagons to all the rigid ones. Nor would all combinations produce the absorbtion plus gong. Maia soon realized the solution must entail getting several plates going at the same time, arranging multiple collisions so that pieces would enter certain specific slots during the brief interval allowed.

For a while, I thought there was a clue in the fact that the puzzle is reversible . . . that everything returns to the same starting condition. The variant Life game that Renna used to send his radio message was a "reversible" version. But, as I think about it, that seems less likely. It's got to be simpler, having to do with those symbols inscribed on the plates.

There she counted on Brod. He knew many of the emblems from their use as labels in shipboard life. *Box, can,* and *barrel,* were tokens for containers, written, appropriately enough, across several of the static, "target" plates. Quite a few food items were included on movable ones. Beer was portrayed by a stein with foam pouring over the sides. There were also *biscuit, hardtack,* and the bread-and-jelly symbol she had seen earlier. Other insignia Brod identified as standing for *compass, rudder,* and *cargo hook,* while some still eluded interpretation. He had no idea what the fire-arrow stood for. Nor the depictions of a bee, a spiral, or a rearing horse. Still, Maia felt reinforced in her notion. This puzzle was meant to be easy for men to understand.

Or easier. I don't imagine all men were welcome, either. You'd still need to have been told some trick. Something simple enough to pass on from master to apprentice for generations.

Refreshed by food and drink, though not fully sated, they resumed experimenting for as long as the dim light lasted. That wasn't very long, unfortunately. Outside, it might remain day for several more hours. But even with their irises slitted wide, too little illumination pierced cracks in the cave wall to allow work past late afternoon, when Maia and Brod had to stop.

In darkness, huddled together for warmth, they listened to the tide return. Lying with her head on Brod's chest, Maia worried about Renna. What were the reaver folk doing to him? What purpose did they have in mind for the man from the stars?

Baltha and her crowd definitely had reason to make common cause with Kiel's Radicals, back when Renna languished in Perkinite hands. Perkinism preached taking Stratoin life much farther along the track designed by Lysos, toward a world almost void of variation, completely dedicated to self-cloning and stability. It suited the interests of both groups of vars to fight that.

Rads wanted the opposite, a *moderation* of the Plan, in which clones no longer utterly dominated political and economic life, and where men and vars were stronger, though never as dominant as in the bad old Phylum. Their idea was to sacrifice some stability for the sake of diversity and opportunity. That made the Radical program as heretical as Perkinism, if not more so.

Ironically, Baltha's cutthroat gang of reavers had a goal far less broad in scope, more aimed at self-interest. As Baltha hinted back on the Manitou, she and her group wanted no change in the way of life Lysos had ordained, only to shake things up a little.

Maia recalled the var-trash romance novel she had read back in prison, about a world spun topsy-turvy, in which stodgy clans collapsed along with the stable conditions that had made them thrive, opening fresh niches to be filled by upstart variants. She also remembered Renna's comments on Lysian biology—how it had been inspired by certain lizards and insects, back on Old Earth. *"Cloning lets you keep perfection. But perfection for what? Take aphids. In a fixed environment, they reproduce by self-copying. But come a dry spell, or frost, or disease, and suddenly they use sex like mad, mixing genes for new combinations, to meet new challenges."*

Baltha and the reavers wanted enough chaos to knock loose some ancient clans, but solely in order that *they* might take those heights. It was a scheme more classically Lysian than either of the Perkinite or Radical dogmas. *The Founders included vars like me because you can never be sure stability will last. They must have known it would mean some vars plotting to help nature along.*

In fact, it must happen more often than she had imagined. Whenever such a scheme succeeded, it would be toned down in the histories. No sense encouraging *other* vars, downstream, to try the same thing! If Baltha managed to whelp a great house, she would not be depicted as a pirate by her heirs. It made Maia wonder about those embroidered tales told about the original Lamai. Had she, in fact, been a robber? A conniver? Perhaps Leie had it right, choosing such company. If Maia's twin had tapped a ruthless side to their joint nature, should she be cheered, rather than reproved?

How does Renna fit into all this? Maia wondered. *Do the reavers plan to provoke some sort of war among factions on the Reigning Council? Or retribution from the stars? That would shake things up, all right. Perhaps more than they realize.*

She worried. *What is Renna doing, right now?*

Earlier, while twilight settled, Maia had spoken to Brod about these quandries. He was a good listener, for a man, and seemed genuinely understanding. Maia felt grateful for his company and friendship. Nevertheless, after a while she had run out of energy. In darkness, she eventually lay quietly, letting Brod's body warmth help stave off the night chill. Breathing his male musk, Maia dozed while an odd sensation of well-being pervaded within the circle of his arm. Half-dreaming, she let images glide through her mind—of aurorae, streaming emerald and blue-gold sky curtains above the glaciers of home. And Wengel Star, brighter than the beacon of Lighthouse Sanctuary, at the harbor mouth. Those summertime themes blended with a favorite memory of autumn, when men returned from exile, singing joyously amid swirls of multicolored, freshly fallen leaves.

Seasons mixed in Maia's fantasy. Still asleep, her nostrils flared in sudden, unprovoked recollection—a distant scent of frost.

She awakened, blinking rapidly, knowing too little time had passed for it to be dawn. Yet she could see a little. Moonlight shone through cracks in the cave entrance. The whites of Brod's eyes were visible.

"You were quivering. Is something wrong?"

She sat up, embarrassed, though she knew not why. Within, Maia felt an odd stirring, an emptiness that had nothing to do with hunger for food.

"I . . . was dreaming about home."

He nodded. "Me too. All this talk about heretics and rads and Kings, it got me thinking about a family I knew, back in Joannaborg, who followed the Yeown Path."

"Yeown?" Maia frowned in puzzlement. "Oh, I've heard of them. Isn't that where . . . it's the *clone* daughters who go out to find niches, and the vars who stay behind?"

"That's right. Used to be some of the cities along the Méchant had whole quarters devoted to Yeown enclaves, surrounded by Getta walls. I've seen pictures. Most boys didn't go to sea, but stayed and studied crafts along with their summer sisters, then married into other Yeown clans. Kind of weird to imagine, but nice in a way."

Maia saw Brod's point of view. Such a way of life offered more options for a boy—and for summer girls who stayed where they were born, living with their mothers. . . .

And *fathers*, she supposed, finding it hard to conceive.

Without her recent studies, Maia might not have perceived how, unfortunately, the Yeown way ran counter to the drives of Stratoin biology. There were basic genetic reasons why time reinforced the tendency to need a winter birth first, or for mothers to feel more intense devotion to clone-daughters than their var-offspring. Humans were flexible creatures, and ideological fervor might overcome such drives for a generation, or several, but it wasn't surprising that Yeown heresies remained rare.

Brod continued. "I got to thinking about them because, well, you mentioned that book about the way people lived on Florentina World. You know, where they still had *marriage*? But I can tell you it wasn't like that in the Yeown home I knew. The husbands . . ." He spoke the word with evident embarrassment. "The husbands didn't make much noise or fuss. There was no talk among the neighbors of violence, even in summer. Of course, the men were still outnumbered by their wives and daughters, so it wasn't exactly like a Phylum world. With everyone watching, they kept real discreet, so as not to give Perkie agitators any excuse . . ."

Brod was rambling, and Maia found it hard to see what he was driving at. Did the lad have his own heretical sympathies? Did he dream of a way to live in one home year-round, in lasting contact with mates and offspring, experiencing less continuity than a mother, but far more than men normally knew on Stratos? It might sound fine in abstract, but how did the two sexes keep from getting on each other's nerves? Clearly, poor Brod was an idealist of the first water.

Maia recalled the one man she had lived near while growing up. An orthodox clan like Lamatia would never condone the sort of situation Brod described in a Yeown commune, but it did offer occasional, traditional refuge to retirees, like Old Coot Bennett.

Maia felt a shiver, recalling the last time she had looked in Bennett's rheumy eyes. Demi-leaves had swirled in autumnal cyclones, just like the image in her recent dream—as if subconsciously she had already been thinking about the coot. *I used to wonder if he was the only man I'd ever know more than in passing. But Renna, and now Brod, have got me thinking peculiar thoughts. Keep it up, and I'll be a raving heretic, too.*

This was getting much too intense. She tried returning things to an abstract plane.

"I imagine Yeownists would get along with Kiel and her Radicals."

Brod shrugged. "I don't think the few remaining Yeowns would risk trouble, making political statements. They have enough problems nowadays. With the rate of summer births going up all over Stratos, making everybody so nervous, Perkinites are always looking for var-loving scapegoats.

"But y'know, I was thinking about the people who once dwelled here in the Dragons' Teeth. Maybe *they* started out as Yeown followers, back at the time of the Defense.

"Think about it, Maia. I'll bet these sanctuaries weren't originally just for men. Imagine the technology they must've had! Men couldn't keep that up all by themselves. Nor could they have ever managed to beat the Enemy alone. I'm sure there were women living here, year-round, alongside the men. Somehow, they must've known a secret for managing that."

Maia was unconvinced. "If so, it didn't last. After the Defense, there came the Kings."

"Yeah," he admitted. "Later it corrupted into a fit of patriarchism. But everything was in chaos after the war. One brief aberration, no matter how scary, can't excuse the Council for burying the history of this place! For centuries or more, men and women must've worked together here, back when it was one of the most important sites on Stratos."

The temptation to argue was strong, but Maia refrained from pouring water on her friend's enthusiastic theory. Renna had taught her to look back through a thick glass, one or two thousand years, and she knew how tricky that lens could be. Perhaps, with access to the Great Library in Caria, Brod's speculation might lead to something. Right now, though, the poor fellow seemed obsessed with scenarios, based more on hope than on data, in which females and males somehow stayed together. Did he picture some ancient paradise amid these jagged isles, in that heady time before the Kings' conceit toppled before the Great Clans? It seemed a waste of mental energy.

Maia felt overwhelming drowsiness climb her weary arms and legs. When Brod started to speak again, she patted his hand. "That's 'nuff for now, okay? Let's talk later. See you in the mornin', friend."

The young man paused, then put his arm around her as she lowered her head once more. "Yeah. Good rest, Maia."

"Mm."

This time it proved easy to doze off, and she did sleep well, for a while.

Then more dreams encroached. A mental image of the nearby, blood-bronze metal wall shimmered in ghostly overlay, superimposing upon the much-smaller, stony puzzle under Lamatia Hold. Totally different emblems and mechanisms, yet a voice within her suggested, *True elegance is simplicity.*

Still more vivid illusions followed. From those Port Sanger catacombs, her spirit seemed to rise through rocky layers, past the Lamai kitchens, through great halls and bedrooms, all the way up to lofty battlements where, within one corner tower, the clan kept its fine old telescope. Like the wall of hexagons, it was an implement of burnished metal, whose oiled bearings seemed nearly as smooth in action as the flowing plates. Overhead in Maia's dream lay a vast universe of stars. A realm of clean physics and honest geometries. A hopeful terrain, to be learned by heart.

Bennett's large hand lay upon her little one. A warm, comforting presence, guiding her, helping Maia dial in the main guide stars, iridescent nebulae, the winking navigation satellites.

Suddenly it was a year later . . . and there it was. In the logic of dreams, it had to show. Crossing the sky like a bright planet, but no planet, it moved of volition all its own, settling into orbit after coming from afar. A new star. A *ship,* erected for traveling to stars.

Thrilled at this new sight, wishing for someone to share it with, this older Maia went to fetch her aged friend, guiding his frail steps upstairs, toward the gleaming brass instrument. Now dim and slow, the coot took some time to comprehend this anomaly in the heavens. Then, to her dismay, his grizzled head rocked back, crying into the nigh—

Maia sat bolt upright, her heart racing from hormonal alarm. Brod snored nearby, on the cold stone floor. Dawn light crept through crevices in the rubble wall. Yet she stared straight ahead for many heartbeats, unseeing, willing herself to calm without forgetting.

Finally, Maia closed her eyes.

Knowing at last why they had sounded so familiar, she breathed aloud two words.

"Jellicoe Beacon . . ."

A shared context. She had been so sure it would turn out to be simple. Something passed on from master to apprentice over generations, even given the notoriously poor continuity within the world of men. What she had never imagined was that luck would play a role in it!

Oh, surely there was a chance she and Brod would have figured it out by themselves, before they starved. But Coot Bennett had spoken those words, babbling out of some emotion-fraught store of ragged memory, the last time she heard him speak at all. And the phrases had lain in her subconscious ever since.

Had the old man been a member of some ancient conspiracy? One that was still active, so many centuries after the passing of the Kings? More likely, it had started out that way, but was by now a tattered remnant. A ritualized cult or lodge, one of countless many, with talisman phrases its members taught one another, no longer meaningful save in some vague sense of portent.

"I'm ready, Maia," Brod announced, crouching near one blank-featured hexagon. She placed her hand on another. "Good," Maia replied. "One more try, then, at the count of three. One, two, three!"

Each of them pushed off hard, setting their chosen plates accelerating along the wall on separate, carefully planned, oblique trajectories. Once the first two were well on their way, Maia and Brod shifted to another pair of hexagons. Maia's second one bore the stylized image of an insect, while Brod's depicted a slice of bread and jam. It had taken them all day to get launching times and velocities right, so that their first pair would arrive in just the right positions when these later two showed up for rendezvous. Ideally, a double carom would result—two simultaneous collisions at opposite ends of the wall—sending the inscribed hexagons gliding from different directions toward the same high, stationary target.

It seemed simple enough, but so far they had failed to get the timing close enough to test Maia's insight. Now daylight was starting to fade again. This would have to be their last attempt. Maia watched with her heart in her throat as the four moving hexagons approached their chosen intersections, collided, and separated at right angles . . . exactly as intended!

"Yes!" Brod shouted, grinning at her.

Maia was more restrained. So far, so good.

Gliding on across the bright metal expanse, the selected pair of plates converged from opposite directions toward a single static platter, whose surface bore the etched design of a simple cylinder—the symbol used on ships to denote a kind of container.

"*Bee-can!*" Old Coot had shouted, that fateful night when she showed him Renna's starship. Even then, Maia had guessed the phrase stood for "Beacon," since many sanctuaries doubled as lighthouses. The rest of his babble made no sense, however. Without context, it *could* make no sense.

But it wasn't garbled man-dialect, as she had thought. No random babble, it had been a heartfelt cry of desperate faith, of yearning. An invocation.

" . . . *Jelly can! Bee-can Jelly can!*"

There had been other prattled syllables, but this was the expression that counted. Whatever Bennett had thought he was saying that night, originally it must have meant "Jellicoe."

Jellicoe Beacon, of the Dragons' Teeth. The same reasons that had drawn Maia here with Brod, that had caused the reavers to choose its defensible anchorage, had conspired to make this isle special in ages past. One of the linchpins of the Great Defense, and of the ill-fated man-empire called "the Kings." A place whose history of pride and shame could be suppressed, but never entirely hidden.

Two moving hexagons glided before her, one bearing the image of a bee, the other the common shipboard symbol for stored jam . . . or jelly. Maia held her breath as both plates cruised toward the same target at the same time.

The most elegant codes are simplest, she thought. *All they ask here is for us to say the name of the place whose door we're knocking at!*

That is, she thought, clenching her fists, *providing we aren't fooling ourselves with our own cleverness. If this isn't just one layer of many more to solve. If it works.*

Please, let it work!

The plates converged upon the target with the *can* symbol inscribed on its face. They touched . . . and the stationary hexagon simply, cleanly absorbed them both! At once there followed a double gong sound, deep-throated and decisive, which grew ever louder until the tolling vibration forced Brod and Maia back, covering their ears. They coughed as soot and dust shook off the great door and its jamb. Then, along seams too narrow heretofore to see, a diagonal split propagated. The humming, shivering portal divided, spilling into the grimy vestibule a flood of rich and heady light.

Journal of the Peripatetic Vessel

CYDONIA–626 Stratos Mission:

Arrival + 53.605 Ms

I have not heard from Renna since his last report, over two hundred kiloseconds ago. Meanwhile, I have been picking up radio and tight-beam traffic below, which appears to indicate a police emergency of the first order. From contextual data, I must conclude that my peripatetic envoy has been kidnapped.

We had discussed the probability of precipitate action after his speech. Now it has come about. I estimate that none of this would have happened, had not the approach of iceships from Phylum Space forced his premature revelation. It is an inconvenience we did not need, to say the least. One that may have tragic consequences ranging far beyond this world.

Why were the iceships sent? Why so soon, even before our report could be evaluated? It seems clear now that they were dispatched about the time I began decelerating into this system, before Renna and I knew what kind of civilization thrived on Stratos.

I must decide what to do, and decide alone. But there is not sufficient data, even for a unit of my level to choose.

It is a quandary.

23

M aia had been in trouble before. Often more immediately life-threatening. But nothing like this.

Trouble seemed to loom all around the two young vars, from the moment they nervously forsook the known terrors of the sealed cave to walk into that blast of mysterious brilliance, hearing only the massive door shutting behind them with an echoing boom. A long hallway had stretched ahead, with walls of almost-glassy, polished stone, illuminated by panels that put out uniform, artificial light unlike any either of them had known, save coming from the sun. An even layer of fine dust soaked up bloody specks left by Brod's torn feet. To Maia, it felt as if the two of them were trespassing delinquents, tracking mud into the home of a powerful, punctilious deity. She kept half-expecting to be challenged at any moment by a resounding, disembodied woman's voice—a stern, stereotypical alto—as in some cheap cinematic fantasy.

That first stretch of hallway wasn't straight, but took several zigzag turns before arriving at another door, similar to the first one, covered with more of the same burnished hexagons. The fivers groaned aloud at the prospect of tackling yet another enigmatic combination lock. But this time, as if in response to their approach, several of the plates abruptly began moving on their own! By the time Maia and Brod arrived, the portal had already divided, opening onto another series of brightly lit twists and turns. They passed through quickly, and Brod sighed with relief.

Did a prickly corner of her mind feel just a momentary touch of cheated disappointment? As if it had actually been looking forward to another challenge? *Just shut up*, Maia told the mad puzzle-freak within. Meanwhile, her direction sense said they were plunging ever deeper into the convoluted mountain that was Jellicoe Isle.

The next barrier almost made the entire journey pointless. Upon turning a corner, the youths were bluntly disconcerted to suddenly confront a heap of broken stone and masonry filling the passageway before them. The ceiling had collapsed, spilling rubble into the hallway. Only a glimmer of artificial light showed through a gap near the top, suggesting a possible path to the other side. Brod and Maia had to scramble up a slope of rocky fragments and start pulling aside heavy chunks of debris, digging to create a passage wide enough to crawl through. It was a queer feeling, to burrow with bare hands, deep underground, your life depending on the outcome, and yet working under such pure, synthetic radiance. One conclusion was unmistakable.

If anyone else ever came this way since the tunnel collapsed, they'd have left traces here, as we're doing. All those others who tried to get past the door . . . and we're the first to make it!

Or, the first since whatever calamity had caused the avalanche. Whether that had been natural or artificial remained to be seen.

At last the two young vars broke through, sliding downslope into what seemed a rubble-strewn basement. What might have once been crushed barrels lay in rusty heaps along the walls. The only exit was a half-ruined iron staircase, missing many risers, which appeared to have slumped from an encounter with high temperatures. It was climbable . . . with great care. Helping each other to the topmost landing, Brod and Maia turned the handle of a simple metal door. Together, they pushed hard to force the warped hinges, and finally squeezed anxiously into a hallway twice as wide as the earlier one.

Terrible heat must have passed through the zone nearest the tortured cellar, once upon a time. Several more metal doorways were fused shut, while at others, Maia and Brod glanced into chambers choked with boulders. No hint remained of whatever purpose they had served, long ago. Even the sturdy tunnel walls bore stigmata where plaster had briefly gone molten and flowed before congealing in runny layers. The sight reminded the two summerlings of their awful dehydration.

Limping beyond the affected area, they soon traversed the most pristine and majestic stretch of corridor yet, which coursed beneath lofty arched ceilings, higher than any Maia had ever seen. Her shoulders tightened and her eyes wanted to dart in all directions at once. She kept expecting to hear footsteps and shouting voices . . . or at least mysterious whispers. But the place had been emptied even of ghosts.

As on Grimké, there were signs of orderly withdrawal. Most of the rooms they peered into were stripped of furnishings. *This whole corner of the island must be honeycombed,* she thought. At the same time, Maia recalled her promise to Brod—that getting through the mystery gate might offer their key to continued survival. So far, this was all very grand and imposing, but not too useful for keeping them alive.

Maybe some future explorer will find our bones, she contemplated, grimly. *And wonder what our story was.*

Then, Brod cried out, "Hurrah!" Accelerating, he hobbled ahead, leading Maia to a room he had spied. Lights flickered on as he rushed inside, limping toward a tiled basin while murmuring, "Oh, Lord, let it work!"

As if answering his prayer, a bright metal faucet began spilling forth clear liquid—fresh water, Maia scented quickly. Brod thrust his head under the stream, earnestly slurping, making Maia almost faint with sudden thirst. In ravenous haste she bumped her head against a porcelain bowl next to his, slaking her parched throat in a taste finer than plundered Lamatian wine, slurping as if the flow might cut off at any moment.

Finally, dazed, bloated, and gasping for breath, they turned to peruse this strange, imposing room.

"Do you think it's an infirmary? Or some sort of factory?" Maia asked. She cautiously approached one of several broad, tiled cubicles, each with a glass door that gaped ajar. "What are all these nozzles for?"

Leaning inside to look at a dozen ceramic orifices, she yelped when they suddenly came alive, jetting fierce sprays of scorching steam. "Ow, ow!" Maia cried, leaping back and waving a reddened arm. "It's a machine for stripping paint!"

Brod shook his head. "I know it seems absurd, Maia, but this place can only be—"

"Never!"

"It is. That really is a shower stall."

"For searing hair off lugars?" She found it doubtful. "Were the ancients giants, to need all that room? Did they have skins of leather?"

Brod chewed his lip. Experimentally, he leaned against the doorjamb and began inserting his arm. "Those little, thumb-size windows—I saw a few in the oldest building of Kanto Library, back in the city. They sense when someone's near. That's how the faucets knew to turn on for us."

More steam jetted forth, which Brod carefully avoided as he waved in front of one sensor, then another. Quickly, the stream transformed from hot to icy cold. "There you are, Maia. Just what we needed. All the comforts of home."

Maybe your home, she thought, recalling her last, tepid shower in Grange Head, carefully rationed from clay pipes and a narrow tin sprinkler head. At the time, she had thought it salaciously luxurious. Back in Port Sanger, Lamatia Hold had been proud of its modern plumbing. But *this* place, with its gleaming surfaces, bright lights, and odd smells, was downright alarming. Even Brod, who had grown up in aristocratic surroundings on Landing Continent, claimed never to have imagined such expanses of mirrored glass and ceramic, all apparently designed to service simple bodily needs.

"Laddies first," Maia told her friend, citing tradition and motioning for him to go ahead of her. "Guest-man gets first privileges."

Brod dissented. "Uh, we're in a sanctuary—or what must've been one, long ago—so strictly speaking, you're the guest. Go on, Maia. I'll see if I can find something to patch my feet."

Maia frowned at being outmaneuvered, but there was no point in further argument. They both badly needed to clean their many wounds, lest infection set in. Later, they could worry other matters, such as how to feed themselves.

"Well, stay in shouting range, will you?" she asked, tentatively moving her hand toward the controls. "Just in case I get into trouble."

Maia soon learned the knack of waving before those dark circles in the wall. She adjusted the shower to a temperature between tepid and scalding, and texture between mist and needle spray. Then, on stepping under the multiple jets, she forgot everything in a roar of bodily sensations.

Everything save one triumphant thought.

Those cheating murderers and their guns . . . they think I'm dead. Even Leie probably does. But I'm not. Brod and I are far from it.

In fact, she was sure none of her enemies had ever experienced anything remotely like what she luxuriated in now. Even when it came time to scrub and pry embedded grains of sand out of her wounds, that stinging seemed no great price to pay.

Sitting before a mirror broad enough for dozens, Maia touched her unkempt locks, which for weeks had grown out tangled, filthy, uncombed. It was, indeed, free of the dye her sister had hastily applied while Maia squirmed, helplessly bound and gagged aboard the Reckless. *I ought to hack it all off,* she decided.

Brod sang while finishing his shower. His voice seemed to be cracking less, or perhaps it was the astonishing resonance lent by that tiled compartment—no doubt a wonder of technology, designed into the cleaning chamber for some mysterious purpose lost to time. Nearby, on the countertop, Maia saw the bloody needle and thread the boy had used to stitch his worst gashes. Maia had not heard him cry out even once.

The little medical kit he had found behind one of the mirrors was woefully ill-equipped. A good thing, since that had made it small enough to overlook under wadded trash when this place was evacuated. There had been a few sealed bandages, which hissed and gave off a funny, emphatically *neutral* smell on unwrapping, plus a tiny bottle of still-pungent disinfectant, which they decided to leave alone. And finally a pair of scissors, which Maia lifted after all other matters had been attended to, taking a few tentative, uncertain swipes at her hair. There had been nothing else useful to find amid the litter.

Behind her, the clamor of water cut off, and the same nozzles could be heard pouring hot air over her companion's body. Brod whooped, as noisy in pleasure as he had been stoical in pain. "Hey, Maia! Why not use this machine to do our clothes, too! Clean and dry in five minutes. Toss me yours."

She bent to pick up her filthy tunic and breeches between a thumb and forefinger, and threw them in his direction. "All right," she said. "You've convinced me. Men are good for something, after all."

Brod laughed. "Try me out next springtime!" he shouted over the renewed roar of jetting steam. "If you wanna see what a man's good for."

"Talk, talk!" she answered. "Lysos shoulda cut all the talk-talk genes off the Y chromosome, an' put in more action!"

It was the sort of easy repartee she had envied of Naroin and the men and women sailors, devoid of real threat, but carrying a patina of stylish daring. Maia grinned, and her smile transformed her appearance in the mirror. She sat up straight, using her fingers as combs and shaking her trimmed bangs. *That's better,* she thought. *Now I wouldn't scare a three-year-old on the street.*

Not that her scars were shameful in the least, but Maia felt glad that most of the knocking around had spared her face. A face that was, nevertheless, transformed by recent months. Some adolescent roundness still hemmed the cheekbones, and her complexion was clear and flushed from scrubbing. Nevertheless, privation and struggle had sculpted a new firmness of outline. It was a different visage than she remembered back when sharing a dim table mirror with her twin, in a shabby attic room full of unrealistic dreams.

"Here they are," Brod announced, putting two folded garments on the counter next to her. Like Maia herself, the clothes looked and smelled transformed, though badly in need of mending. The same held for Brod, Maia thought, upon turning around. The young man shrugged into his own shirt and trousers, grinning as he poked fingers through long gashes. "We'll take along some thread, and maybe sew 'em later. I say we move on now, though. Who knows? We may strike it lucky and find someone's apartment, with a full wardrobe."

"Plus three bowls of porridge to swipe, and three beds to sleep on?" Maia yawned as she stood, stealing one last glance at the mirror.

I used to see Leie—whenever I looked at my reflection—as well as myself. But this person before me is unique. There is nothing else like her in the world.

Strangely, Maia found no disappointment in that notion. None at all.

Clean and partially rested, they resumed exploring and soon found themselves traversing another zone of ruin, where powerful upheavals had wracked every plastered wall. In places, damage had been rudely patched, while elsewhere, lesions exposed bare, cracked stone. Maia and Brod stepped carefully where the floor canted or faulting had riven a corridor in two. Some of this harm might have come from age—the natural action of millennia since this refuge was evacuated. But to Maia another hypothesis seemed more likely. Blows from space, the marks of which still scarred Jellicoe and other isles, must have come near to toppling even these mighty halls.

Grimké was just an outpost, she realized. *This must have been a main fortress.*

Maia and Brod soon found that not everything had been taken away when the inhabitants were banished. They came upon a region packed full of complex machinery, room after oversized room, stuffed with devices. Some clearly dealt with electricity—distant relatives of the useful little transformers and generators she knew—but on a magnitude vastly greater than anything used in today's Stratoin economy. The scale of things staggered her. There was more metal here than existed in all Port Sanger! Nor was it probable she and Brod had more than scratched the surface.

One chamber stretched a hundred meters across, and seemed to climb at least three times that height. Almost filling the entire space towered one massive block consisting of an amber, translucent material she had never seen before, braced by heavy armatures of the same adamant, blood-red metal that had made up the puzzle door. Dim flickerings within the outlandish gemstone told that its powers were quiescent, but hardly dead. It made them both want to creep away on tiptoe, lest the slightest noise waken whatever slept there.

The sanctuary-fort seemed endless. Maia wondered if their doom would be to wander forever like damned spirits, seeking a way out of a purgatory they had striven so hard to enter. Then the corridor spilled onto a broader one, with walls more heavily reinforced than ever. To their left stood another massive, crimson-metal door, this one almost a meter thick and resting on tremendous hinges. It gaped *open*. On this side, someone had set up a wooden easel, bearing a placard on which were printed bold, unfriendly letters.

YOU WERE WARNED
KEEP OUT!

So anomalous was the message, so out of the blue, that Maia could only think, in response, *Don't speak nonsense. Whoever you are, you never warned us of a thing.*

As if we care.

"Do you think the reavers left it?" Brod asked. Maia shrugged. "It's hardly like them to admonish. Scream 'n' leap, that's more their style." She bent toward the lettering, which looked professionally done.

"It must be an important room," Brod said. "Come on. Maybe we'll learn something."

Following close behind, Maia considered. *If it's so important, why do they use signs? Why didn't they just close and lock the door?*

The answer was obvious. *Whoever they are, they can't close the door. If they do, they'll never get it open again. They don't know the combination!*

The long, tubelike chamber spanned forty meters, lined all the way with adamant red-metal and triple-braced buttresses. Presumably to resist even a direct hit . . . though a hit of *what* Maia still couldn't imagine. She did recognize computer consoles, many times larger than the little comm units manufactured and distributed by Caria City, but clearly relatives. It all had the look of having been used just yesterday, instead of over a thousand years ago. In her mind's eye, she saw ghostly operators working at the stations, speaking in hushed, anxious voices, unleashing horrific forces at a button's touch.

"Maia, look at this!"

She turned around. Brod was standing before another placard.

Property of the Reigning Council
If you are here, you risk summary execution for trespass.
Your entry was noted. Your sole option is to call
Planetary Equilibrium Authority at once.
Use the comm unit below.
Remember — Confession brings mercy. Obstinacy, death!

"Your entry was noted," Brod read aloud. "Do you think they've wired all the doors? Hey, maybe they're listening to us, watching us right now!"

His eyes widened, turning and peering, as if to see in all directions at once. But Maia felt oddly detached.

So, the Council knows about this place. It was naïve to think they didn't. After all, this was the heart of the Great Defense. They wouldn't have left such power lying around, unsupervised. It might be needed again, someday.

But then, what about my idea—that old Bennett said what he did because he had inherited some mysterious secret?

Perhaps there *had* been a secret, left over from the glory days of Jellicoe. Something that survived the shame and ignominy following the brief episode of the Kings. Or perhaps it was only the stuff of legend, a yearning for lost home and stature, something carried on by a small coterie of men through the centuries of their banishment, losing meaning though gaining ritual gravity as it passed on to new men and boys, recruited from their mother-clans.

"We could follow the antenna to the entrance they normally use." Brod motioned to the comm unit mentioned in the announcement, a completely standard unit, attached to cables crudely stapled to the walls. Those cables would be severed if the great door ever sealed. "You know, I'll bet they don't even know about the route we took! Maybe they don't know we're here, after all."

Good point, Maia thought. Next to the comm unit, another item caught her interest. A thick black notebook. She picked it up, scanned several pages, and sighed.

"What is it, Maia?"

She flipped more pages. "They not only know about this place, they *train* here . . . every ten years or so, it seems. Look at the dates and signatures. I see three, no four, clan names. Must be military specialist hives, subsidized in their niches by council security funds. They come out here once a generation and hold exercises. Brod, this place is still in business!"

The young man blinked twice in thought, then exhaled heavily. Resigned resentment colored his voice. "It makes sense. After the Enemy was beaten, the tech types who lived here must've gotten uppity—both men and women—and demanded changes. The priestesses and savants and high clans got scared. Maybe they even *concocted* the Kings' Rebellion, to have an excuse to kick out all the folk who used to live here!"

Brod was doing it again, reaching beyond the evidence. Yet he spun a convincing scenario. "But it would be stupid to forget the place, or dismantle it," he went on. "So they chose women warriors suited to the job and gave them permanent sinecures, to keep trained and available in case of another visit by the Enemy."

Or by unwelcome relatives? Maia wondered. The most recent entry in the logbook was off-schedule, dated about the time Renna's ship would have been seen entering the system. That drill had lasted five times normal duration. Until, she noted, his lander departed the peripatetic vessel to alight at Caria Spaceport. Nor was there any guarantee the fighting clans would *stay* away. With the Council in an uproar over Renna's kidnapping, they could return at any time.

It might have been a cheering thought—offering a surefire way to overwhelm the reavers with a single long-distance call—if only Maia hadn't grown wary. Renna might be even worse off in the clutches of certain clans.

The comm unit lay there, presumably ready for use. The quandary was no different than it had been before, however. *Whom to call?* Only Renna knew who his friends were and who had betrayed him in Caria, a quarter of one long Stratoin year ago.

Every time it seems I've gotten myself in as deep as anyone can, don't I always seem to find a hole that goes down twice as far? Compared to this, Tizbe's blue powder is a joke, a misdemeanor!

Maia knew what she had to do.

It proved simple to trace the path used by the warrior clans. Maia did not even have to follow the antenna cable. The main entrance could be in only one place.

From the control room, she and Brod followed the main corridor as it climbed several more ramps and stairs, passing through a series of heavy, cylindrical hatches, each propped open with thick wedges to prevent accidental closure. At one point, the youths paused before a shattered wall that appeared once to have carried a map. A portion was still legible in the lower left, showing a corner of the convoluted outline of Jellicoe Island. The rest of the chart was burned so deeply that not only the plaster was gone, but the first centimeter or so of rock.

"That's okay," Maia told Brod. "Come on. This must be the way."

There followed more stairs, more wedged blast shields, before the hallway terminated at a closed set of rather-ordinary-looking steel doors. A button to one side came alight when Maia pressed it. Soon, the aperture spread open with a faint rumble, revealing a tiny room without furniture, displaying an array of indicator lights on one wall.

"Well, I'm tied down an' Wengeled," Brod exhaled. "It's a lift! Some big holds in Joannaborg had 'em. I rode one at the library. Went up thirty meters."

"I suppose they're safe," Maia said, not stating it as a question, since there was no point. She did not like there being only one entrance or exit, but the two of them must use the conveyance, safe or no. "I'll leave it to your vastly greater experience to pilot the smuggy thing."

Brod stepped inside gingerly. Maia followed, watching carefully to see how it was done. "All the way to the top?" the boy asked. She nodded, and he reached out, extending one finger till it touched the uppermost button. It glowed. After a beat, the doors rumbled shut.

"Is that all there is to it? Shouldn't we—"

Maia cut off as her stomach did a somersault. Gravity yanked her downward, as if either she or Stratos had suddenly gained mass. *There are advantages to not having eaten,* Maia thought. Yet, after the first few seconds, she found perverse pleasure in the sensation. Indicators flickered, changing an alphanumeric display that Maia couldn't read because the bottom half had gone dead. *What if another, more critical part fails while we're in motion?*

She quashed the thought. Anyway, who was she to question something that still worked after millennia? *The passenger, that's who I am!*

There came another disconcerting-exciting sensation. The pressure beneath her feet abruptly eased, and now she felt a *lessening* of weight. An experience not unlike falling or riding a pitching ship-deck down a swell. *Or,* Maia supposed, *flight.* Involuntarily, she giggled, and slapped a hand over her mouth. The other hand, she discovered, was wrapped tightly around Brod's elbow. "Ow!" he complained succinctly, as the elevator car came to a halt and they both stumbled in reaction.

The doors slid apart, making them blink and shade their eyes. "Will they stay open?" Maia asked hastily, while staring onto a stony plateau capped with a fantastic, cloud-flecked sky.

"I'll wedge my sandal in the door," Brod answered. "If you'll let go of my arm for a minute."

Maia laughed nervously and released the boy. While he secured their line of retreat, she stepped further and regarded a vista of ocean surrounding the archipelago known as the Dragons' Teeth. Sunlight on water was just one sparkling beauty among so many she had not expected to see again. Its touch upon her skin was a gift beyond words.

I knew it! The military clans from Caria wouldn't arrive by boat. They're too high-caste, too busy. Besides, they wouldn't risk someone seeing them, and noticing a pattern. So they come here only rarely to train, and only by air.

The flat surface extended several hundred meters to the south, west, and east. Here at the northern end of the plateau, the elevator shed sheltered machinery that included a substantial winch, probably for tethering and deploying dirigibles. Maia also noted huge drums of cable.

The Dragons' Teeth were even more magnificent when seen from above. Tower after narrow stony tower stretched into the distance, arrayed like staggered spikes down the back of some armored beast. Many bore forested tips or ledges, like Grimké, while others gleamed in the afternoon sunshine, bare and pristine products of extruding mantle forces that long predated woman's tenure on Stratos.

No tooth in sight reached higher than this one, at the northern edge of Jellicoe. Because of its position, she couldn't see due south, where lay other giant island clusters, such as Halsey, the sole site officially and legally inhabited. No doubt the war clans counted on this shielding effect, and timed their rare visits to minimize chances of being seen. Still, Maia wondered if the men who staffed Halsey ever suspected.

Perhaps that's why they rotate the station assignment among low-ranked guilds. Less chance of a rhythm being noticed, even if men did happen to spy a zep, now and then. Especially with visits only three times in a lifetime.

She turned and marched to the right, where more than two score monoliths could be seen clustered close at hand—some of the many peaks which, welded together, made Jellicoe the chief molar of this legendary chain of Teeth. When Maia got close enough to see how vast the collection was, she realized how even the extensive tunnel network below could easily be hidden in this maze of semicrystalline stone.

Maia had to descend a rough, eroded staircase in order to reach a lower terrace, and then crossed some distance before at last nearing the vista she wanted. Brod cried out for her to wait, but impatience drove her. *I've got to know,* she thought, and hurried faster.

At last, she stopped short of a precipice so breathtaking, it outshadowed Grimké as a gull might outsoar a beetle. Her pulse pounded in her ears. So good was it to be in open air, breathing the sweet sea wind, that Maia forgot to experience vertigo as she edged close and looked down at Jellicoe Lagoon.

The anchorage already lay in dimness, abandoned by the sun after a brief, noontime visit. Her gaze bypassed still-bright stony walls, readjusting until at last she found what she had hoped to see. Two ships, she realized with a thrill. Reckless and Manitou.

I was afraid they'd change hideouts. They should, since their ketch was captured. Maybe they're planning to, soon.

Maia realized, with not a little disbelief, that the escape from Grimké with Brod and Naroin and the others had only been three or four days ago. *That may mean we still have time.*

She felt Brod's presence as he came alongside, and heard his ragged sigh of relief. "We're not too late, after all." He turned to regard her, a glitter in his eye. "I sure hope you've got a plan, Maia. I'll help rescue your starman, and your sister. But first, there's a band of unsuspecting reavers down there with a pantry to raid. If I don't get food soon—"

"I know," Maia interrupted with a wave of one hand, and quoted,

> *"A much worse thing to see by far,*
> *Than a summer rutter,*
> *Stand between a hungry man,*
> *And his bread and butter."*

Brod grinned, showing a lot of teeth. When he spoke, it was in thick dialect.

"Aye, lass. Ye don't want me reduced to bitin' the nearest thing at hand now, do ye?"

She laughed, and so did he. Such was her trust in his nature and friendship that it never occurred to Maia, as it might have months earlier, to take him at his literal word.

.... τ⊕ fi∩∂ ωHατ iṣ HiϽϽΕ∩ ...
U∩∂Εr strα∩℘Ε ∠⊕sτ stαrs

—from the Book of Riddles

24

Maia lowered her sextant and peered at the little calibrated dials a second time. The horizon angle, where the sun had set, fixed one endpoint. The other, almost directly overhead, fell within the constellation Boadicea.

"You know, I think it may be Farsun Eve?" she commented after a quick mental calculation. "Somewhere along the way, I lost track of several days. It's midwinter and I never noticed." She sighed. "We're missing all the fun, in town."

"What town?" Brod asked, as he knotted thick ribbons of cable at the edge of the bluff. "And what fun? Free booze, so we don't notice the whispery sound of clone-mothers stuffing proxies into ballot boxes? Getting pinched on the streets by drunks who wouldn't know frost from hailfall?"

"Typical man," Maia sniffed. "You grouches never get into the spirit of the holidays."

"Sometimes we do. Throw us a party in midsummer, and we might be less grumpy half a year later." He shrugged. "Still, it could help if the reavers are celebrating tonight, wearing paper hats and going all moony. Maybe the pirates won't notice gate-crashers droppin' in while they're busy harassing male prisoners."

There's an idea, Maia thought, folding away her sextant. *Providing the men are still alive. After the massacre aboard the Reckless, the reavers' next logical step would be to eliminate all other witnesses, before moving on to a new hiding place.* That included not only the men of the Manitou, but also the rads, and perhaps even recent recruits, such as Leie. Renna was probably still too valuable, but even his fate would be uncertain if Baltha's gang were ever cornered.

Such dire thoughts lent urgency to their wait as Maia and Brod watched full darkness settle over the archipelago. With twilight's fading, the many spires of Jellicoe Island merged into a single serrated outline that cut jagged bites out of a starry sky. Below, in the inky darkness of the lagoon, tiny pale pools of color encircled lamps stationed on the narrow dock where the two ships were moored. Now and then, clusters of smaller lanterns could be seen moving quickly, accompanied by stretched, bipedal silhouettes. Faint, indecipherable shouts carried up to Maia's ears, funneled by the narrow, fluted confines of the island's cavity. "Looks like they're in a festive mood, after all," Brod commented as a company of torch-bearing shadows trooped off the larger vessel, filing down the pier and into a wide stone portal, set in the base of the cliff. "Maybe we should wait. At least till they've turned in?"

Maia also would have preferred that, but two moons were already rising in the east, and another was due soon. Within hours, they would be high enough to illuminate the lagoon and its surrounding cliffs. "No." She shook her head. "Now's the time. Let's get on with it."

Brod helped her arrange the harness he had made by using their salvaged scissors to slice the warning placards so graciously left by the Reigning Council. Maia wrapped her buttocks and thighs in strips of threatening phrases, and stepped into a double loop of cable meant for tethering and reeling transport zep'lins. The system was old, and might even predate the banishment, going back to days when men were said to have sailed the skies, as well as the seas below. Maia only hoped the warrior clans who now used the equipment kept it in good condition.

Next Brod handed her two patches of heavy cloth—the calf portions of his own trousers, which he had cut off for her to use as gauntlets. With these wrapped around her hands, Maia gripped the rough cable. "You're sure you've got the signals down?" she asked.

He nodded. "Two yanks will mean stop. Three means reel you back. Four stands for wait. And five means *I* should come on down." The boy frowned unhappily. "Listen, Maia, I still think I should be the one to go first, instead."

"We've been over this, Brod. I'm smaller and a lot less banged up than you are. Once I'm down, I might pass as one of the band in the dark. Anyway, you understand the winch machine. I'm counting on you to haul me out when I come back to the cable, after scouting around."

Ideally, that would be with Renna in tow, rescued from right under the reavers' noses. But to count on such a miracle would be like believing in lugar savants. Still a long shot, but more conceivable, was the possibility of getting close enough to whisper to Renna through the bars of his cell, or to exchange brief taps in Morse code. Given just a few minutes of surreptitious contact, Maia felt sure she could sneak back with valuable information—the names of officials on the Council whom Renna trusted, for instance. The fivers might then use the secret comm unit with some hope they weren't just inviting another band of more aristocratic thugs.

That is, providing the comm wasn't bugged, or set to call just one location. There were a dozen other malign possibilities, but what else could they do? The best reason of all to seek Renna was the near certainty he'd come up with a better plan.

"Mm," Brod grunted unhappily. "And what if you're caught?"

She grinned, shoving his shoulder playfully. "I know, you're worried about getting fed." Maia was also supposed to snatch any food she came across. But Brod looked hurt by her joke, so she spoke more gently. "Seriously, dear friend, use your own judgment. If you feel strong enough to wait, I suggest holding out till tomorrow night, before dawn. Lower yourself and try to steal the dinghy that's tethered to the Manitou's stern. Head for Halsey. At least there—"

"Abandon you?" Brod objected. "I'll not do anything of the—"

"Sure you will. I've been in jail before; I'll manage. Besides, if they catch me sneaking around the sanctuary tonight, their guard'll be up for more of the same. The only way you can help is by trying something different. Tell your guild how Corsh was murdered. Surrounded by witnesses, and with an unbugged comm, you can call the cops and every member of the Lysodamned Council. It's still risky, but any conspirators may think twice about pulling dirty stunts with the Pinnipeds around as bystanders."

"Mm. I guess it makes sense." He shook his head, scuffing gravel with his sandals. "I still wish . . . Just be careful, okay?"

Maia threw her arms around him.

"Yeah, I will." She squeezed, feeling him tense briefly in typical winter withdrawal, then relax and return her embrace with genuine intensity. Maia looked into his face, briefly glimpsing moistness in his eyes as Brod released and turned away without another word. She watched him cross the broad terrace and then disappear beyond the stone steps. It would take several minutes, as they had rehearsed, for her partner to reach the winch house. Meanwhile, she went to the edge of the plateau and pulled the line taut, bracing her feet and backing up until most of her weight hung over the precipice.

I should be terrified, but I'm not.

Maia seemed to have progressively lost her fear of heights, until all that remained was a pulse-augmenting exhilaration. *Funny, since Lamais are all acrophobes. Maybe it was growing up in that attic. Or perhaps I take after my father . . . whoever the vrilly bastard was.* Despite Brod's revelations, a name was still all she had of him. "Clevin." No image formed in her mind, though someone midway in appearance between Renna and old Bennett might do.

Always alert for possible niches, Maia wondered if this calmness at the edge of a cliff might hint a useful talent. *I must talk it over with Leie when I get a chance,* she vowed. *Maybe I'll put her in a cage, suspended from a great height, to see if it's genetic, or simply the result of environmental influences I've been through, since we parted.*

Of course, Maia would do no such thing. But the fantasy discharged some tension over the possibility of encountering her twin again. At Maia's waistband she felt the pressure of a wooden cudgel she had made from the leg of a broken placard easel. If necessary, she would use it even on her sister. The tiny scissors, bound in cloth, finished Maia's short inventory of weapons.

It had better not come to a fight, she reminded herself. Stealth was her only real chance.

A sudden vibration transmitted down the cable, starting her teeth chattering. Maia set her jaw and braced. At a count of five, cable started unreeling at a slow, steady pace. Maia overcame a momentary instinctual pang, allowing her weight to sink with the makeshift saddle. Her feet began walking backward, first over the edge, then in jouncing steps along the sheer face of the cliff. The plateau rose past her eyes, cutting off the faint, distant glimmer of the elevator shed.

All that remained of the sky was what Jellicoe chose to let within its ragged circle—a cookie-cutter outline that narrowed with each passing moment. Only a wedge of reflected moonlight colored silver the tips of the highest western monoliths. Maia dropped into starlit gloom.

Despite the darkness, she listened for any sign she'd been spotted. Her wrapped hands were ready to jerk hard at the cable, signaling Brod to throw the mechanism into reverse. Neither of them felt certain the crude signals would work, once a great length of cord had played out. Not that it made that much difference. Forward lay all their hopes. Behind lay only starvation.

As her eyes adapted during the descent, Maia surveyed her surroundings. The lagoon was larger than it first appeared, since several small bays extended past partial gaps in the first circle of soaring spires. The wharf and ships lay some distance south and east, near the harbor entrance she and Brod had glimpsed while desperately evading the pirates' shelling. The pier led to a shelf of rock that rimmed part of the island's inner circumference at sea level. Bobbing lanterns could still be seen hurrying to and fro, mostly destined for the large stone portal lit on both sides by bright sconces. Interior illumination glowed through other openings, flanking the main entrance.

That's the old residence sanctuary. The portion of Jellicoe the Council didn't seal off, she realized. As far as history is concerned, it's the only part anyone knows about. Long-abandoned ruins of a lost era, free to be used by any band of derelicts that happens along.

Neither the ships, nor the ledge, nor any windows lay conveniently beneath her. She was headed for a swim. *Not my best sport, as I've well learned.* Maia didn't look forward to it, but her confidence was bolstered by experience. *I may not swim well, or fast, but I'm hard to drown.*

Distance was difficult to gauge, since only a few warbled lamplight reflections distinguished the inky lagoon surface. As she descended, Maia fought a crawly sensation of vulnerability. If she was spotted now, she would be easy meat for reaver sharpshooters before ever climbing out of range, even if Brod read her signal at once and reversed traction. Maia consoled herself that any lookouts would be posted to watch for ships approaching from sea. Besides, reliance on lanterns only ruined a woman's dark-adaptation. Old Bennett had taught her that long ago, when she first learned to read sky charts by starlight.

I'm no more visible than a spider dropping at the end of a web. True or not, the mental image cheered Maia. To protect her eyes' sensitivity, she resisted the temptation to look at the lanterns, even as shouting voices could be distinguished, floating past like smoke up a chimney. Maia looked away, allowing her gaze to stroke the outlines of two score mighty peaks, looming like the outstretched fingers of Stratos-Mother, pointing at the sky.

Pointing specifically at a dark nebula known as the Claw, which lay overhead as Maia looked up. It was a fitting symbol, of both obscurity and mystery. Beyond that great, starless sprawl lay the Hominid Phylum. All the worlds Renna knew. All that Lysos, and Maia's own foremothers, by choice left behind.

It was their right, she thought. *But where does that leave your descendants? How far do we owe loyalty to our creators' dream? When have we earned the right to dream for ourselves?*

Time once more to check her progress toward the water's chill surface. As she lowered her eyes, however, she caught a flicker. Faint as a single star, it gleamed where no star should—amid the sable blackness of Jellicoe's inner flank, where an expanse of dark stone should block light as adamantly as the Claw. Maia blinked as the dim, reddish spark shone briefly, then went out.

Did I imagine it? she wondered afterward. It had been across the lagoon, far from either her own towering peak, which concealed the

Council's defense base, or the adjacent one containing the old public sanctuary. Peering at a now-unrelieved wall of blankness, it was easy to convince herself she had seen nothing but a mote in her own eye.

Much closer nearby, the sheer cliff was a blank enigma that occasionally reached out to brush Maia's feet or knees. Her arms were starting to hurt from holding on to the cable for so long. Diminished circulation set her legs tingling, despite Brod's improvised padding, but she could only shift gingerly, lest the makeshift, knotted harness loosen and drop her toward the inky surface below.

Seawater smells rose to greet her. Shouts that had been garbled resolved into spoken words, surging in and out of decipherability as echoes fluttered against the cliff, meeting Maia's ears at the whim of random rock reflections.

". . . *callin' for ever'body . . .*"

". . . *quit that an' come help! I tol' ya there's no . . .*"

". . . *wasn't my dam' fault! . . .*"

It didn't sound all that festive to Maia—certainly not like the normal, whooping frenzy of Farsun Eve. Maybe her calculations were wrong. Or, since there was no frost, and the only males present were presumably hostile, the reavers might be in no mood to celebrate.

In that case, all this nighttime activity worried Maia. Perhaps the pirates were packing up, getting ready to leave. A sensible move, from their point of view, but a damned nuisance—and possibly fatal—from Maia's.

Other sounds reached her. A soft rippling, the lapping of gentle waves against rock. *I must be getting close.* She peered straight down, trying to gauge the remaining distance to a vague boundary between shades of black.

Her waving feet abruptly touched frigid liquid, breaking surface tension with ripples that sounded oily and loud. Maia drew in her knees and yanked hard, perpendicular to the taut cord, repeating the motion to let Brod know to stop. There was no response; cable kept rolling off the drums, high overhead. Once more, Maia's legs met water and sank into a chill embrace, sending tremors of shock up her spine. Thighs, buttocks, and torso followed, slipping into an icy cold that sucked both heat and breath out of her with gasping speed. Frantically, Maia overcame muscle spasms to worm out of the constraining harness, awkwardly kicking free with a relieved sense of release. Only when she felt sure of not being reentangled did she flounder back, searching for the cable in order to try again signaling Brod.

She was surprised, on snagging it at last, to find it motionless. *Brod must have noticed a change once my weight was gone. We should've expected that. Anyway, it worked.*

She grabbed the cable in both hands, and yanked four times to confirm that she was all right. Her friend must have picked up the vibrations, for power flowed into the winch again in two rapid, upward jerks. Then it was still.

Maia held on for a while longer, shaking sleep out of her legs. The initial shock of contact faded. With her free hand, she pulled on the slack until her former seat reappeared. Pieces of placard came loose and she retied them to float near the surface. If all went well in the period ahead—or very poorly—she would need this marker to find the hanging cord again. Maia felt sure no casual onlookers would notice it till morning, and Brod was to retract well before that, whether or not she had returned.

In the course of turning around, memorizing landmarks, she looked up at the narrow patch of sky directly overhead, toward where Brod must be standing, peering down. Although there was no chance he could see, Maia waved. Then she cast off and started swimming as quietly as possible toward the dark shadow of the unlucky ship, Manitou.

High tide had come close to being fatal, back in the collapsed cave. Now it proved convenient, as Maia sought a way to reach dry land.

She breaststroked amid the pier's thick pilings, coated with pointy-shelled creatures up to the water's lapping edge. Plank boards formed a ceiling not far over Maia's head as she made for the dark bulk of the larger sailing vessel. There were no more excited shouts. Apparently, most of the reaver crew had entered the mountain sanctuary on some urgent errand. All was not silent, however. She could hear a low murmur of conversation—muffled voices coming from an indistinct location nearby.

Maia swam past the dinghy she had spotted from high above. It bobbed gently, tethered to the Manitou's stern, and seemed to beckon, offering an easy way out of this calamitous adventure. First a silent drift to the lagoon's exit, then step the little mast and set sail . . . All she'd have to deal with after that would be pursuit, possible starvation, and the wild sea.

The thought was alluring, and Maia dismissed it. The dinghy was Brod's, should it come to that. Anyway, she had other destinations, other plans.

Manitou's scarred flank drifted past as she swam quietly, searching for a way up. The pier was equipped with a ladder, over near the ship's gangplank. Unfortunately, one of the bright lanterns hung directly above that spot, casting a circle of dangerous illumination. So Maia tried another location. One of the lines tethering the freighter to the wharf stretched overhead amidships, far enough from the lantern to lie in darkness.

Maia trod in place underneath the hawser, where it drooped closest to the water. She let her body sink, and then kicked upward, stretching as far as possible. Despite high tide, however, she came up short by half an arm's length and fell back with an unnerving splash. Maia stroked back under the pier and waited to be sure no one had heard. A minute passed. All appeared quiet. The low voices continued undisturbed in the distance.

She undid the remaining buttons of her ragged shirt and struggled free of the sopping cloth. *When in need, use what's at hand.* It seemed she was getting more use of her clothes as tools than as coverings. Maia wrapped one sleeve around her right wrist and balled the rest into her palm, then she stretched her arm behind and, with all the force she could muster, threw the loose mass so that it draped over the rope. By flicking the end she held, Maia was able to cause the other sleeve to flop down. This time, when she surged upward, she had something to grab onto. Yanking on both sleeves, she lifted herself out of the water. The Manitou seemed to cooperate, the rope bowing a little farther under her weight while Maia tensed her stomach muscles and threw her legs around the cable.

She hung there, breathing heavily for half a minute, then began inching along the hawser toward the ship. The struggle soon became as much vertical as horizontal. Maia was working so hard, she barely noticed the fierce chill as water evaporated from her skin. She gripped the rough, scratchy rope with her feet, knees, and hands, fighting bit by bit toward the railing overhead.

The hull bumped her head. Maia turned and saw a dark vista of wood stretching in both directions. She also spied a row of portholes, each no wider than two outspread hands, running along the length of the ship, below the level of her knees. They were too small to enter, but the nearest lay open and within reach. Tightly clutching the rope with both hands, Maia let go with her legs so they swung toward the tiny opening. Second try, she hooked one foot inside and swung her center of gravity after it. Now she could rest nearly all her weight on the ledge, offering respite to the hands still clinging the rope. Waves of fatigue washed out of her arms and legs and back, until her pulse and breathing settled to a dull roar.

So far so good. You've only got another couple more meters to climb.

Something touched her foot. It settled around her ankle and squeezed. Maia very nearly screamed. Biting her lip fiercely, she forced

herself to unwrap the knot of panic in her breast and open her tightly
shut eyes. Fortunately, surprise was the only demon to overcome, since
the presence below wasn't hurting her, yet. For now, it seemed content to
rhythmically stroke the top of her foot.

Maia inhaled and released a shuddering breath. She managed to
turn her head, and saw a hand emerge through the small porthole. A
woman's hand, making beckoning motions.

What, no shouts of alarm? Maia wondered blankly.

*Wait! That's the upper cargo level. Would reavers live here? Not
likely.*

A far better place to keep prisoners.

It took an awkward contortion to pull the hanging rope so that she
could hold on with one hand while squatting closer to the porthole. As
she bent over, the wooden cudgel dug into Maia's belly. Her right foot
started to hurt from bearing all her weight.

With her free hand, she stretched down to touch the wrist of whoever was silently calling, which went rigid for an instant, then withdrew.
Near the opening, Maia saw a dim outline press close . . . the outline
of a human face. There lifted the faintest of whispered words.

"*Thought* I recognized my spare set o' shoes. How ya doin', virgie?"

The murmur lacked all tonality; still, she knew the speaker.
"Thalla!" Maia hissed. So this was where the radical var partisans were
being kept! There came a faint clanking of chains, as the prisoner
pressed closer to the porthole.

"It's me, all right. In here with Kau an' the others."

"And Kiel?"

There was a pause. "Kiel's bad off. First the fight, then from arguing
with our hosts."

Maia blinked. "Oh, I'm sorry."

"Never mind. Good to see ya, varling. What're you doin' here?"

Surprise and pleasure at this discovery were rapidly being replaced
by pain, from both her twisted posture and fear that even whispers might
carry elsewhere. She knew nothing of the conditions of Thalla's imprisonment, and did not relish finding out firsthand.

"I'm going after Renna. Then to get help."

Another long pause. "If we got broke out of here, *we* could help."

Yeah, like a lugar in a porcelain store, Maia thought. The idealistic
rads were no match for the reavers. That had already been proven, and
this time they'd be fewer and weaker still. *Besides, I don't owe you lot
anything.*

Still, Maia wondered. Did she have a better plan? If a rad breakout
accomplished nothing more than casting the two ships loose, it could

make even an abortive rebellion worthwhile. "You'd do as I say?" she asked.

If there hadn't been a moment's hesitation, Maia would have known Thalla was lying. "All right, Maia. You're the boss."

"How many guards are there?"

"Two, sometimes three, just outside the door. One of 'em snores somethin' awful."

There was more she might ask, but the quaking in Maia's right leg was getting worse. Any longer and she might land in the lagoon, right back where she started. She sighed heavily. "I'll see what I can do. No promises, though!"

There was a tremor in Thalla's grateful squeeze. Maia shifted her weight in preparation for resuming her climb. The pressure of the wooden cudgel eased and she exhaled in relief, only to wince as something else jabbed her thigh. With her free hand, Maia fished under her belt and pulled out the cloth-wrapped scissors. On impulse, she bent once more and tossed it through the small, dark opening. The touch on her ankle vanished.

Maia wasted no more time. While her right leg and back throbbed, her arms felt refreshed, so they did most of the work at first. Soon she was shinnying almost vertically, with the hull stroking her back. It was a journey she could never have imagined making as a newly fledged fiver, stepping out of her mother-hold. Now she thought no further ahead than the next straining pull, the next coordinated slither of hands and knees and ankles. When, at last, one leg floundered over the side, Maia rolled onto the ship's lower deck and quickly sought shelter behind the mainmast, panting silently with a wide-open mouth, waiting for the pain to dull. Waiting till she could listen once more to the sounds of the night.

There was a faint creaking as the ship rocked gently at anchor. The lapping of wavelets against the hull. A soft murmur of conversation. Maia lifted her head to look across the wharf toward the smaller pirate vessel, the *Reckless*. A pair of women in red bandannas crouched next to an upturned barrel with a lantern set upon it. Although they were playing dice, no coinsticks lay in sight, which explained the desultory nature of the game. The players seemed not to keep score as they alternated rolls of the ivory pieces, talking quietly.

Turning around, Maia realized with some shock that Manitou looked deserted. Of course, from Thalla's description, there would be a brace of beefy vars on duty below, just outside the cargo hold. Still, whatever had pulled the rest of the reavers away must be awfully important.

Sound and sight were vital for warning of danger. Once she felt more secure, however, Maia felt a sudden wash of other sensations, especially smell. *Food,* she realized suddenly, acutely, and hurried aft quick as she could scuttle silently. Just below the quarterdeck, she found where supper had been prepared and eaten. Stacks of grimy plates lay within a stew pot, soaking in a swill of brine. The resulting goulash was hardly appetizing, even in Maia's state, so she kept looking, and was rewarded at last in a far corner when she found a small pile of hard biscuits atop a rickety table and an open cask of fresh water nearby.

She drank thirstily, alternately moistening baked crusts into a feast. While devouring voraciously, Maia searched for a sack, a piece of cloth, anything to stuff and take back to Brod. At least she could leave a stash of food for him in the little boat.

There was nothing in sight to use as a bag, but Maia knew where else to look. With biscuits in each hand, she hurried to a row of narrow doors at the rear of the main deck. Opening one, she looked down a slanted ladder into the selfsame room where she herself had lived, up to a few weeks ago, along with a dozen other women, amid bunk beds stacked four high. Maia descended quietly, eyes darting till she verified by close inspection that no bed held sleeping reavers. It hadn't seemed likely, with everyone called off on some mysterious errand.

She had entered in search of a bag, but now Maia noticed she was shivering. *Why not swipe fresh clothes, as well?*

She started with her old bunk. But somebody several sizes larger, and much smellier, had taken over occupancy since the battle on the high seas. She moved on, sorting in near darkness until at last she found a shirt and well-mended trousers roughly her size, neatly folded at one end of a bunk. Still munching stale bread, Maia wriggled out of her own tattered pants and slipped into the stolen articles. The rope belt had to be cinched extra tight, but everything else fit. A clean, if threadbare, coat finished her accoutrement, though she left it unbuttoned, in case it became necessary to dive back into the water. The thought made her shudder. Otherwise, Maia felt better, and a little guilty about poor Brod, cold and hungry, almost half a kilometer overhead.

What next? she wondered, picking up her cudgel and sticking it in her new waistband. The rads might be imprisoned on the Manitou, but Maia doubted Renna would be kept anywhere so insecure. Probably, he was deep inside the sanctuary. Did she dare try to brazenly walk in, looking for him? The more she thought about it, the idea of springing Thalla and the others made sense. If the rads could take over Manitou, then lay doggo while Maia snuck near the sanctuary entrance, they might at a chosen moment create enough distraction to let her slip inside.

First task is eliminating their guards. Sounds simple. Only, how am I supposed to do it?

She pondered possibilities. *I could go to the cargo gangway and pretend to be a messenger . . . shout down some made-up call for help. When one emerges, I'd knock her out and then . . . try the same thing again? Or go down after the other one?*

What if there are three? Or more?

It was a lugar-brained scheme . . . and Maia felt fiercely determined to make it work. At least once that phase was over, she wouldn't be alone anymore. Maybe the rads would have an idea or two of their own to offer. Maia cast around the room one last time for weapons. She only found a small knife, embedded in the wooden post of one of the bunk beds, which she wrestled out and slipped into the coat pocket.

She was halfway up the ladder when the door suddenly swung aside, spilling light upon her face and outlining a large figure. Maia could only stare upward in dismay.

"*Thought* I heard someone down here," a gruff woman's voice said. "Come on, then. No duckin' work. I won't cover for ya, next time!"

The silhouette turned, leaving Maia blinking in surprise. Hurriedly, she followed, hoping to catch the reaver from behind while they were still out of view from the Reckless. At the doorway, however, Maia's heart sank upon spying four other women on deck. They were wrestling open a sealed box, pulling out long gleaming objects.

Rifles, Maia realized. They seemed well-supplied, this bunch. Even the Guardia at Port Sanger wasn't better armed. Maia was past being shocked, however. *It is the victors who write history,* she now knew. *If Baltha and her gang succeed amid the chaos they want to create, no one is going to quibble over a few extra crimes.*

"Well? Come on!" The first woman called to Maia, who shuffled forward unwillingly with her head averted, eyes downcast. She concealed her surprise when three of the slender, heavy weapons were thrust into her arms, and clutched them tightly, not knowing what else to do.

"Don't forget to bring enough ammo, Racila," the leader told a slight, scar-faced pirate, who pounded the crate shut again. "All right, you lot, let's get back, or Togay'll have us eatin' air for a week."

Maia tried to take up the rear, but the leader insisted that she go ahead, tromping with the others down the gangplank, onto the pier, and then along thumping, resonant wooden slats toward where bright sconces cast twin pools of brilliance on both sides of the sanctuary entrance.

Loaded rifles, shouted calls, groups of anxious women hurrying through the night. This was surely no Farsun Eve celebration. What in the name of the Founders was going on? For Maia, the worst moment came as they climbed spacious, cracked steps and passed under the fierce electric dazzle of the sconces. When she wasn't denounced on the spot, she realized it hadn't been darkness that saved her, back at the ship.

Either there are so many women in the gang that they don't all know each other—which seemed highly unlikely—*or else they think I'm Leie.*

The possibility of playing such a ruse—pretending to be her sister —had naturally occurred to Maia. Only it had seemed too obvious, too risky. All Stratoin children, whether clone or var, learned to notice subtle differences among "identical" women. Leie no doubt wore her hair differently, carried distinct scars, and would acknowledge with a thousand disparate cues that she knew these people who were utter strangers to Maia. Besides, what to do when Leie herself showed up?

Maia had finally chosen to try the subterfuge only if stealth utterly failed. Now there was no choice. She could only try brazening it out.

"This dam' hole is big as a scullin city!" One short, rough-looking var in the group told Maia *sotto voce* as they marched up the broad, splintered portico, then between tall, gaping doors. "We must've sniffed a hunnerd rooms already. Can't blame ya for duckin' out to catch a snore."

Shrugging like an unrepentant schoolgirl caught playing hooky, Maia muttered in mimicry of the other woman's sour tone. "You can say that again! I never signed up for all this runnin' around. Had any luck yet?"

"Nah. Ain't seen beard nor foreskin o' the vrilly crett since watch shift, despite the reward Togay's offered."

That confirmed Maia's dawning suspicion. *They're searching for someone. A man.* Her chest pounded. *Renna.* She suppressed her feelings. *You can't be sure of that, yet. It might be another prisoner. One of the Manitou crew, for instance.*

The entrance showed signs of that long-ago battle that had shaken Jellicoe with blasts from outer space. A rough-cut, makeshift portal of poorly dressed and buttressed stone led from the shattered steps into a vestibule that might once have been beautiful, with finely fluted pilasters, but now bore jagged cracks. Rude cement repairs had peeled under attack by salt and age.

These effects ebbed as the group passed into the sanctuary proper, where thick walls had sheltered a grand entrance foyer. From there, broad hallways stretched north, south, and east. Strings of dim electric bulbs cast islets of illumination every ten meters or so, powered by a hissing, coal-fired generator. Beyond those light pools, each passage faded into mystifying darkness, broken by brief glimpses of occasional bobbing lanterns. Distant, echoing calls told of feverish action, nearly swallowed by the chill obscurity.

At first sight, the place reminded Maia of her first imprisonment—

that smaller, newer sanctuary in Long Valley—another citadel of chiseled passages and thick, masculine pillars. Only here, the scent of ages hung in the air. Soot streaks and daubed graffiti on the walls and ceilings told of countless prior visitors, from hermits to treasure hunters, who must have come exploring over the centuries, torches in hand. By comparison, the pirates were well-equipped.

There was another difference. In this place, the walls were lined with a deeply incised frieze, running horizontally just above eye-level. As far as Maia could make out, the carved adornment ran the length of each hallway, snaking into and out of every room, and consisted entirely of sequences of letters in the eighteen-symbol liturgical alphabet.

Taking the center route, which plunged deeper into the mountain, Maia's party passed through a stately hall where flames crackled in a spacious, sculpted hearth, underneath gothic vaulting. There was no furniture, only a few rugs thrown on the ground. Bottles lay strewn about, along with mugs and gambling equipment, all abandoned in apparent haste. "Seems an awful lot o' trouble," Maia probed, choosing the nearby short var who had spoken before. "I don't s'poze anyone's suggested we just set sail, and leave the vril behind?"

A wide-eyed glance from the husky little reaver told Maia volumes. The spoken response was barely a hiss. "Go suggest it yerself! If Togay 'n' Baltha don't quick make ya swim like a lugar, I may say aye, too."

Maia hid a smile. Only loss of their chief prize would provoke such wrath. Although this would make Maia's own task of finding Renna harder, it was nevertheless great news to hear that he had given them the slip. *Now to reach him before they get really desperate.*

Abruptly, Maia recalled what she was carrying in her arms—long, finely machined articles of wood and metal and packaged death. The weapons gave off a tangy smell of bitter oil and gunpowder. Apparently, after hours of searching, someone had decided: that which cannot be recaptured must not be lost to others.

The anomalous frieze helped distract Maia from her nervous dread. As the group passed room after empty room, they were accompanied by that row of stately, engraved letters, punctuated by occasional, ill-repaired cracks. Now and then, she recognized a run-on passage from the Fourth Book of Lysos, the so-called Book of Riddles. Other stretches of text seemed to parrot nonsense syllables, as if the symbols had been chosen by an illiterate artist who cared more how they looked next to each other than what they said. The effect, nevertheless, was one of grand and timeless reverence.

Certainly males were welcome to worship in the Orthodox church, which even attributed them true souls. Still, this wasn't what you expected to find in a place built solely for men. Perhaps, long ago, males were more tightly knit into the communion of spiritual life on Stratos, before the era of glory, terror, and double-betrayal leading from the Great Defense to the toppling of the Kings.

The group continued past gaping doorways and black, empty rooms, which must have already been searched hours ago. Finally, they arrived at another vast foyer, encompassing six spacious stone staircases, three descending and three ascending, again divided among the directions north, south, and east. It was a monumental chamber, and the running frieze of enigmatic psalms expanded to glorify every bare surface, seeming all the more mysterious for the stark shadows cast by a few bare bulbs shining angularly across deeply incised letters. All this grand architecture might have impressed Maia, if she did not know of greater vaulting wonders that lay just a kilometer or two from here—secret catacombs containing power unimaginable to these ambitious reavers. The reminder of her enemies' fallibility cheered Maia a little.

Two bored-looking fighters stood watch at this nexus point, armed with cruelly sharpened trepp bills. They spoke together in low voices, and barely glanced at the passing work party. Which suited Maia just fine. She averted her face anyway.

The string of electric lights continued down only one staircase to the right, while Maia's group plunged straight across the open foyer to the dark center steps, leading upward and further into the heart of the dragon's tooth. Two lantern-bearers turned up the wicks of their oil lamps. As Maia and the others climbed, she glanced down and caught sight of several figures, two levels below, standing at the start of the illuminated hallway. Four women were exchanging heated words, pointing and shouting. Maia felt a chill traverse her back, on hearing one harsh voice. She recognized a shadowed face.

Baltha. The erstwhile mercenary stood next to one of the other Manitou traitors, a wiry var Maia had known as Riss. They were debating with two women she had never seen before. Emphasizing a point, Baltha turned and began waving toward the stairs, causing Maia to duck back and hasten after her companions. High on her list of priorities was to avoid contact with that particular var, not least because Baltha would recognize her in a shot.

Maia's group plunged deeper into the mountain. Since leaving the last electric light, stiltlike shadows seemed to flutter from their legs and bodies, fleeing the lanterns like animated caricatures of fear. To Maia, the effect seemed to mock the brief, earnest concerns of the living. Each time a black silhouette swept into one of the empty rooms, it was like some prodigal spirit returning to exchange greetings with shades of those long dead.

If experience had taught Maia to endure water, and even enjoy heights, she felt certain her habituation to deep tunnels would never grow beyond grudging tolerance. She could stand them, but would never find confines like these appealing. Of late, she had begun wondering if men did, either. Perhaps they built this way because they had no other choice.

Maia leaned toward the woman warrior she had exchanged words with, earlier. "Uh, where are they . . . er, we . . . looking for him, now?" She asked in a low voice. Her words seemed to skitter along the walls.

"Up," the short, husky pirate replied. "Five, six levels. Found some windows lookin' over both sea an' lagoon. We're to skiv anyone comin' or goin', them's the orders. We also look for any signs the vril's been that high. Footprints in the dust, and such. Cheer up, maybe we'll get th' reward, yet."

The ruddy-faced var leading the party glared briefly at the one talking to Maia, who grimaced a silent insult when the leader's back was turned once more.

"What about the room where he was kept?" Maia whispered. "Any clues there?"

A shrug. "Ask Baltha." The reaver motioned with a vague nod behind them. "She was still checkin' out the cell, after everyone else had a turn." The reaver shivered, as if unhappy to remember something weird, even frightening.

Maia pondered as they walked on silently. Clearly, this expedition was taking her farther from any useful clues. But how to get away?

At last, the group arrived at the end of the long hallway, where a narrow portal introduced a spiral staircase set inside a cylinder of stone. The women had to enter single file. Maia hung back, shifting from one leg to the other. When the boss woman looked at her, Maia acted embarrassed and pushed the rifles into the older woman's arms. "I have to . . . you know."

The squad leader sighed, holding a lantern. "I'll wait."

Maia feigned mortification. "No. Really. Climbing's simple. No way to get lost, and there's a rail. I'll catch up before you're two levels up."

"Mm. Well, hurry then. Fall too far behind th' lantern, and you'll deserve t'get lost."

The leader turned away as Maia ducked into a nearby empty room. When the footsteps receded, Maia emerged and, with only a distant glow to guide her, swiftly retraced the way they had come. *Could I have gotten away with holding onto a rifle?* she wondered, and concluded this had been the right choice. Nothing would have been more likely to elicit suspicion and alarm. Under these circumstances, the weapon would have been a hindrance.

Soon she arrived back at the great nexus hall and cautiously looked down. Two guards still kept watch where the string of light bulbs made a downstairs turn. Maia would have to get by them, and then past Baltha and Riss, in order to reach the site where Renna had been kept, and vanished. That was clearly the best place to look for clues.

Do I dare? The plan seemed rash, more than audacious. *Maybe there's another way. If all passages end in spiral stairs, there may be one at the far end of the south hall—*

Sounds of commotion reached her ears. Maia crouched next to the stone banister and watched as women converged on the guard post from two directions. Climbing from below came Baltha, Riss, and two tall vars, one carrying an air of authority to match Baltha's. At the landing, the foursome turned and looked west, toward the sanctuary entrance, where a single figure appeared, a slender shadow marching before her. Maia felt a numb frisson when she recognized the silhouette.

"You sent for me, Togay?" the newcomer asked the tallest reaver, whose strong-boned features stood out in the harsh light.

"Yes, Leie," the commanding presence said in an educated, Caria City accent. "I am afraid it's out of my hands, now. You are to be kept under confinement until the alien is found, and thereafter till we sail."

Maia's sister had her face turned away from the light. Still, her shock and upset were plain. "But Togay, I explained—"

"I know. I told them you're among our brightest, hardest working young mates. But since the events on Grimké, and especially tonight—"

"It's not my fault Maia escaped! Isn't it enough she died for it? As for the prisoner, he just disappeared! I wasn't anywhere near—"

Baltha's companion cut in. "You was seen talkin' to the Outsider, just like your sister!" Riss turned to Togay and made a chopping motion. "Like seeks as seeks like. Ain't that what they say? You may be right 'bout her bein' no clone, an' I guess she don't smell like a cop. But what if she wants revenge for her twin? Remember how she was against us tuckin' in Corsh an' his boys? I say drop her in the lagoon, just to be safe."

"Togay!" Leie cried imploringly. But the tall, strong-jawed woman looked at her sternly and shook her head. With an expression of satisfaction, Baltha motioned at the two guards, who stepped alongside the fiver and took her elbows. Leie's shoulders slumped as she was led away. All seven women descended the southward set of stairs, leaving behind a dusty, silent emptiness.

Creeping as quietly as possible, wary of the betraying reach of shadows, Maia followed.

A single electric cable continued down to the lower level, bulbs spaced far apart. Maia let the reavers and their captive get some distance ahead before hurrying after in short bursts, ducking into dark doorways whenever any of the women seemed to even hint at turning around. After they passed into a side corridor, she sped at a dead run, stopping at the edge to cautiously peer around.

The group halted at the first of several metal-bound doors, where stood another pair of guards. This time, one of them was armed with a vicious-looking firearm, the likes of which Maia had seen only once before in her life. This was no hunting rifle, being misused in pursuit of human beings. Rather, it was an automatic killing machine, built for spraying death in mass doses.

There was low conversation, a rattling of keys. As the door flung open, Maia glimpsed figures within, stirring in surprise. Her sister was shoved through. A reaver laughed. "Be nice to yer new friends, virgie. Maybe you can shuck your nickname b'fore drownin' with 'em!"

"Shut up, Riss," Baltha said, while Togay locked the door. Then, all except for the second pair of guards, they filed twenty meters or so down the hall, into the chamber next door. From an angle, Maia saw ranks of benches lining one wall of the room. Baltha and the others could be glimpsed walking around inside, frustration evident on their faces each time they reappeared in view. Shouts of anger and recrimination could be heard. One time, Baltha's voice rang out loud enough for Maia to make out clearly, "—ack in the city aren't gonna be happy about this. Not happy t'all! . . ."

Maia was concentrating so hard, she only noticed the sound of footsteps after they echoed behind her for some time. Her hackles shot up when she realized, turning around quickly, ready to run. A single form could be seen approaching, entering and leaving succeeding pools of light. It soon manifested as a heavyset woman with a pocked complexion, whose reddish hair was bound by a like-colored bandanna. She carried a bucket in each hand, and wore a broad grin along with a stained apron. The smile kept Maia stationary, frozen with indecision.

"Zooks, you don't haveta perch so close, ya little query-bird. I could hear 'em arguin' all th' way to the main hall! What're they up to now? Found their man o' smoke, yet? Or do they plan t'keep us up all night, lookin'?"

Maia forced a smile. Pretending to be her sister would work only until word of Leie's arrest spread . . . a matter of minutes, at best.

"All night it is, I'm afraid," she answered with what she hoped was the right note of blithe resignation. "What's in the buckets?"

The reaver shrugged as she drew near and set the pails down with a sigh. "Supper for th' vrils. Late 'cause of the excitement. Some say what's the point, given the luck planned for 'em. But I say, even a man oughta get fed 'fore joinin' Lysos."

Maia's nostrils flared. Time was even shorter than she had thought. As soon as the scullery drudge entered the prison cell and saw Leie, all would be lost.

"I know why yer here," the older woman confided, moving a little closer.

"Oh yes?" Maia's hand crept toward her belt.

A wink. "You're hopin' for clues. Peep on th' boss women, then off quick, after the reward!" The middle-aged var laughed. "S'okay. I was a younger, too—full o' frosty notions. Ye'll get yer clanhold yet, summer-child."

Maia nodded. "I . . . think I already found a clue. One all the others missed."

"S'truth?" The scullery wench leaned forward, eyes glittering. "What is it?"

"It'll take two of us to lift it," Maia confided. "Come, I'll show you."

She gestured toward the nearest dark doorway, motioning the bluff, eager woman ahead. As she followed, Maia's right hand slipped the cudgel from her waistband and brought it high.

Afterward, despite all her valid reasons for acting, she still felt guilty and mean.

The dim room wasn't quite empty or devoid of hints at its past life. Bare rock shelves and flinders of ancient wood planking testified that once upon a time, a substantial library might have stood here. Except for curled bits of former leather bindings, all that remained of the books was dust. After dragging the cook's unconscious body inside, and hurriedly fetching the buckets, Maia swapped coats and borrowed her victim's bandanna, which she tied low, almost over her eyes. She finished in time to hear muttering voices and footsteps approach. From the shadows, Maia counted figures moving past, back toward the foyer of stairs. Six women, still arguing. From close range, Maia glimpsed seething anger in Baltha's eyes.

". . . won't be happy to get nothin' out o' this but a little box full of alien shit. Some bugs taken from an outsider's vrilly gut may help knock down a clan or two, but we needed a political deal too, for protection! Without his tech-stuff, it won't matter how many smuggy clones die . . ."

Their voices faded. Still, Maia forced herself to wait, though she knew there was little time left. Soon, the first group—that had found her aboard the Manitou—would report "Leie" missing. That would set folk wondering how a fiver could manage to be two places at the same time.

With a pounding heart, Maia pulled the bandanna down further, picked up the food pails, and stepped out of the dim room. She approached the corner, turned, and made herself shuffle at a droopy, desultory pace toward the two burly vars guarding the sealed door. Trying to calm her frantic pulse, Maia reminded herself that she had one advantage. The wardens had no reason to expect danger in the form of a woman. Moreover, her arrival so soon after the leaders' departure implied she must have passed them on the way here. That, too, should reduce vigilance.

Nevertheless, she heard a wary click, and glimpsed the warrior with the automatic weapon lift it in the sort of tender but firm embrace women usually reserved for their own babes. Maia had only heard rumors of such mass-killing machines, until she was four, when she had first learned how much lay hidden in the world.

Unbeckoned—a brief, recollected image of a stone portal, grinding open at long last to reveal what the Lamai mothers and sisters wanted no one else to see. In light of so many things Maia had witnessed since, what had seemed so awful on that day had been, in fact, dreary, mundane. The irony was enough to make one laugh. Or cry.

Maia had no time or concentration to spare for either. She trudged forward, keeping her head down, and in a low voice muttered, "Grubbstuff for th' vrils."

Laughter from the one cradling the gun. "Why're we still botherin'?"

Maia shrugged, rocking from side to side, as if in fatigue. "Why ask me? Just lemme get rid o' the stink."

The second guard laid her trepp bill across one shoulder, and with her free hand took up jingling keys. "I dunno," she commented. "Seems a shame to waste all these boys. There oughta be frost, sometime soon. We can pass it 'round, then make a big, pretty fire . . ."

"Oh, shut up, Glinn," the guard with the assault rifle said, as she positioned herself behind and to Maia's left, ready to spread fire at anyone who tried breaking out. "You'll just get yourself all worked up and—"

Maia had been rocking in anticipation. As the door pushed open, she took a step, then swung the righthand pail in an arc, passing in front of her and then toward the guard with the gun. The riflewoman's eyes barely registered surprise before it drove into her gut, doubling her over without a sound. *One down!* Maia thought elatedly.

And prematurely. The tough reaver, stunned and unable to breathe, nonetheless steadied on one knee and fought to bring her weapon toward Maia . . . only to topple when the second pail clipped the back of her head with a deep clunking sound.

Maia accelerated her return swing, releasing the bucket to fly toward the second guard. The second warrior was already swiveling, lifting her trepp bill. With the agile grace of a trained soldier, she dodged Maia's hurled pail, which struck the door, spewing brown glop like a fountain. Maia charged, taking a glancing blow to her shoulder before plowing into the pirate's midriff and driving both of them into the room.

Second by stretched second, the fight was a blur of continuous buffets in which her own blows seemed ineffective, while her opponent was expert. Desperately, Maia grappled close but was soon thrown back, giving the reaver room to swing her trepp. Dazzles of exquisite pain swept Maia's left side. Another lancing coup ripped just below her knee.

Dimly, Maia was aware of figures nearby. Haggard men clutched outward, reaching to help, but were bound by chains to rows of benches lining the sloping walls. Meanwhile, the pirate's hot breath seared Maia's face with onion pungency, spraying her with spittle as they wrestled over the trepp. *I can't hold on,* she realized despairingly.

Suddenly, another set of hands appeared out of nowhere, wrapping around the reaver's throat. With a howl, Maia's foe flung her away. The sharp bill barely missed in a frenzied swing, then flew off as the bandit let go to claw at her new assailant, a much smaller woman who clung to her back like a wild cat. Though her drained body tried to refuse, Maia forced one final effort. Sobbing with fatigue, she launched herself forward, and in a series of fierce yanks, she and her ally finally brought the thrashing, heaving guard within reach of Captain Poulandres and his men.

When it was over, they lay together on the ground, wheezing. Finally, Maia's sister took her hand and squeezed.

"Okay . . ." Leie said between gasps, the expression on her face more contrite than Maia had seen in all their years growing up together. ". . . I guess my plan didn't . . . work so good. Let's hear yours."

The nearby corner from which Maia had spied on Baltha and Togay would prove a handy enfilade looking the other way. Still, at first Poulandres was reluctant. He and his men were brave, angry, and fully aware of their fate should they be recaptured. Yet not one of them wanted to touch the automatic rifle.

"Look, it's simple enough. I've seen the type before. You just slide this lever—"

"I can see how it operates," Poulandres snapped. Then he shook his head and lifted a hand placatingly. "Look, I'm grateful. . . . We'll help any way we can. But can't one of you two operate the thing?" Revolted, he looked away from the metal machine.

Before she had met Renna, Maia might have reacted differently to this display—with incomprehension, or contempt. Now she knew how patterns established by Lysos had been reinforced over thousands of years, partly through myth and conditioning, as well as deep within their genes and viscera, all so that men would tend to loathe violence against women.

Still, humans are flexible beings. The warrior essence wasn't excised, only suppressed, patterned, controlled. It would take strong motivation to persuade a decent man like Poulandres to kill, but Maia had no doubt it could be done.

Nearby, the rest of the male crew rubbed their ankles, where chains had bound them to rank after rank of stone benches, arrayed in a bowl-shaped, enclosed arena. Three groggy, half-conscious women now languished in their place, mouths gagged. A few of the men were picking distastefully at one of the spilled buckets. Someone ought to get to work conserving the stuff, Maia thought. They might be in for a long seige.

Other matters came first. "I haven't time for this," she told Leie. "You explain it to him. And don't forget to look for other stairs leading to this level! We don't want to be flanked."

"All right, Maia," Leie answered, acquiescent. There hadn't been time for more than a moment of reunion, while recovering from the fight. Nor was Maia ready for complete reconciliation. Too much had happened since that long-ago storm separated a pair of dreamy-eyed summer kids. In time, she might consider trusting Leie again, providing her sister earned it.

Gingerly toting the horrible firearm, Leie escorted Poulandres and several crewmen down the hall. Maia, too, had an errand. But as she started to go, she was halted by a curt tug at her leg.

"Just a minim!" the ship's physician commanded as he finished tying strips of torn cloth around her gashed knee. "There, that's the worst of it. As for the rest o' your dings . . ."

"They'll have to wait," Maia peremptorily finished the sentence, shaking her head in a way that cut short protest. "Thanks, Doc," she finished, and hurried, limping, out of the arena-prison. At the doorway, she turned left toward the second large room, where she had earlier glimpsed Baltha and the other reaver commanders, arguing. One male accompanied her—the cabin boy who had been part of the opposing Game of Life team, back on the Manitou. It was his self-chosen job to bring Maia up to date on what had happened since she was marooned with Naroin and the women crew, on Grimké Island.

"At first the starman was kept with us," the boy explained. "We was all put together in a different part o' the sanctuary, nearer the gate. But he kept makin' a fuss about needin' the *game*. Always the game! S'prised the scutum outta us, 'specially as he still had that 'lectric game board o' his! Claimed it wasn't good enough, tho. He needed more. Wouldn't eat nor talk to the reavers less'n they moved us all down here, where the old tournament courts were."

Maia stopped at the entrance to the second room. She had expected another chamber like the first—a large oval amphitheater surrounding an expanse of crisscrossing lines. But this volume was different. There were benches all right, descending in ever-smaller, semicircular arcs from where she stood. Only this time their ranks faced one huge bare wall with a platform and dais in front of it. The chamber reminded her of a lecture or concert hall, like in the Civic Building, in Port Sanger.

"We all thought he was crazy," the cabin boy continued with his story about Renna. "But we played along, on account of his act vexed the guards. So the cap'n told 'em we also needed the game, for religious reasons." The boy giggled. "So they fetched our books an' game pieces off the ship, an' brought us all down to the arena where you found us."

"But then Renna was taken over here," Maia prompted.

"Yeah. After a couple days, he started complainin' again—about our snorin', about our company. Actin' like a real wissy-boy whiner. So he got put next door. Heard no trouble after that, so we figured he must be happy."

"I see."

Inwardly, Maia cursed. Upon hearing that Renna had vanished in a fashion none of the reavers could fathom or duplicate, her first thought was that he must have found another of the red-metal sculptures, covered with arcane, hexagon symbols. Such a puzzle door would fit the bill —just the sort of thing to stump pirates, yet allow Renna to escape. And, naturally, her own experience would give *her* an edge, as well.

But there was no red-metal. No riddle of movable symbols. Just row after row of benches. The only other noticeable feature was more of the carved phrases, covering every wall save the one behind the dais, carrying mysterious epigrams in the liturgical dialect of the Fourth Book of Lysos. Otherwise, it was just a damn, deserted lecture hall. Maia looked around as she descended the aisle between the benches, wondering why Renna went to so much effort to get himself transferred here.

"What is this place?" the cabin boy asked, somewhat awestruck. "Ain't no Life arena. No playin' field. Did they pray here?"

Maia shook her head, puzzled. "Maybe, with all this scripture on the walls . . . though not all of these lines are holy text, I'm sure."

"Then what—?"

"Hush now, please. Let me think."

The boy lapsed into silence, while Maia's brow knotted in concentration.

Renna escaped from here. That's the key piece of data. We can as-

sume the reavers searched high and low for hidden doors and secret passages, so don't bother duplicating that effort. Instead, try to follow Renna's reasoning.

First, how did he know to get himself moved here? He went to great lengths to manage it.

Although Renna, like Maia, had been imprisoned in a sanctuary before, nothing in that earlier experience could have led him to anticipate a place like this. Maia herself would have found it hard to credit, had she not already seen the nearby, separate defense catacomb.

I've got to figure this out, and quicker than it took him. The reavers will be crazed when they find out what we've done.

Another pang increased her anxiety.

With every hand on war alert, they're sure to spot Brod when he tries coming down. They'll drop him like a helpless wing-hare.

Concentrating, Maia tried to view this room with unbiased eyes, to see what Renna must have seen. She spent a few minutes poking through the blankets and piled straw where he must have made his bed, long since torn apart by others searching for clues. Maia moved on, finding nothing else of interest until her gaze once more stroked the chiseled epigrams, running the length and breadth of each side and rear wall. Some she knew well, having learned them by heart during long, tedious hours spent in Lamatia Chapel, singing heavy paeans to Stratos Mother.

.... τ⊕ fin∂ ωHατ iς Hi⊐⊐∈n ...
Un∂∈r ςτrαn℘∈ ∠⊕ςτ ςταrς

Which, transforming into normal letters, translated to

. . . find what is hidden . . . under strange, lost stars

Maia grimaced at the thought. It was an appropriate-enough image, as she might not live to ever again see stars. *I wonder what time of day it is,* she pondered idly while turning, scanning the walls. Then she stopped, resting her gaze on one anomalous patch. Despite her throbbing wounds, Maia hurried downstairs, then edged past the raised semicircular center stage. Where lines of incised symbols neared the unadorned forward wall, she had spotted what looked like orderly arrangements of brown smudges. They weren't writing. To Maia's eye they connoted something much more interesting.

"What does that look like to you?" she asked the cabin boy, pointing at a cluster of stains, just below one of the arcane symbols in the liturgical alphabet. The youth squinted, and Maia wished fervently that Brod were here, instead.

"Dunno, ma'am. Looks like a feller tossed his food. Same guk we been gettin', I reckon."

"Look closer," Maia urged. "Not tossed. *Dabbed.* See? Carefully painted dots—a cluster of them, under one syllabary letter. And here's another grouping." Maia counted. There were a total of eighteen little clusters of spots, none of them alike. "See? No letter is repeated. Each symbol in the alphabet has its own, unique associated cluster! Interesting?"

"Uh . . . if you say so, ma'am."

Maia shook her head. "I wonder how long it took him to figure it out."

She considered Renna's situation. Imprisoned for a second time on an alien world, bored half to death, despairing and exhausted, he must have stared at the riddle phrases till they blurred with the floating speckles underneath his drooping eyelids. Only then might it have occurred to him to play out a *game,* using the incised words as starting points. But first, they must be transformed from written letters into—

Sudden shouts floated in from the hallway. Maia turned, and seconds later a man appeared at the back of the arena, waving vigorously.

"Three o' the bitchies just strolled round the corner, right into our hands! The bad news is, they yelled 'fore we could get 'em gagged. There's a ruckus brewin' back at the stairs. Cap'n says there'll be trouble soon."

Maia acknowledged with a curt nod, and returned to contemplating the primitive markings on the wall. *Renna must have used them as a reference cipher, while working in this room.*

But working on what? He still had his electronic game board with him—which the reavers would have seen as no more than a toy—so he could have experimented with countless combinations of point-clusters and rules for manipulating them. *All right, picture him fiddling around with the symbols in the room where he and the prisoners were first kept. Let's assume that from the wall writing he learned something. He learned that, somewhere else within the sanctuary, there was a better place to be . . . and he managed to wheedle himself into being taken to that place. Okay, then what?*

That still left the question of modality. An intellectual game was one thing. Moving through walls was another matter, entirely. Even the red-metal puzzle door, looming adamantly before Maia and Brod back in the sea-cave, had been an enigma with a clear purpose, a combination lock to open a gate. Scanning this room, she saw nothing like a gate. No way to leave, other than the one she had entered through. Nothing at all.

"Agh!" Maia cried, clenching her fists. Her left side and leg hurt and her head was starting to ache. Yet, somehow she must retrace mental steps taken by a technologically advanced alien, without even having access to the same tools he had possessed.

Groaning, she sat down on one of the benches in the first row, and laid her head in her hands. Even when a savage boom of gunfire rattled the walls above, causing ancient dust to float in soft hazes, she did not lift her tired, salty eyes.

"I've got it so Poulandres understands, I think. For the time being he'll shoot to miss, one bullet at a time. That's kept 'em back so far. If it does come to a charge, I think he'll do what's needful."

Leie sat down next to Maia, about half a meter away. Her voice was hesitant, as if she felt uncertain of her welcome. Twice Leie started to speak, and Maia felt sure it would be about what had passed between them—about their long separation, and regret over the cavalier way Leie had treated their bond. No actual words emerged, yet the strangled effort alone conveyed enough to ease some of the tension. In her heart, Maia knew it was as much apology as she was likely to get. As much as she should demand.

"So," Leie resumed in a strained voice. "What'll it take to figure out what happened here?"

Maia exhaled heavily, at a loss where to start.

She began by summarizing the cipher key Renna had drawn upon the wall, how each cluster of dots probably represented an array of living figures on a Game of Life board. Or, more likely, a variant game, differing in its detailed ecology. Maia could perceive that each configuration dabbed on the wall might be self-sustaining given the right rule system, though it was hard to explain *how* she knew it.

While she told Leie about this, they were interrupted twice more by loud reports—single warning shots, fired to keep the reavers at bay. There were no cries of full-scale attack, so neither of them moved. Leie's rapt attention encouraged Maia to accelerate her story, rapidly skimming over the violence, tedium, and danger of the last few months, but revealing her astonishing discovery of a talent—one bearing on a strange, intellectual-artistic realm.

"Lysos!" Leie whispered when the essentials were out. "And I thought *my* time was strange! After I heard you were ashore at Grange Head, and had a safe job in Long Valley, I decided to stay awhile at sea with—" She stopped and shook her head. "But that can wait. Go on. Does this Life stuff help us figure how Renna got out of a sealed room with no exits?"

Maia shrugged. "I told you, it doesn't! Oh, the game can carry data, like a language transformed into another kind of symbol system. Renna must've translated something out of these phrases on the walls . . . maybe in context of stuff he learned at the Great Library, in Caria.

"But even when you have information, and know how to read it, you still need a way to *act!* To apply that data to the real world. To cause physical events to take place."

"Like breaking out of jail."

"Exactly. Like breaking out of jail."

Leie stood up and stepped before the first row of benches, onto the semicircular stage where lay a rectangular dais-podium made of polished stone. "After he vanished, most of us took turns looking over this room," she said. "Hoping to find secret panels and such. It wasn't that I was trying to be helpful, not since they killed Captain Corsh and his men . . . and especially after I thought you'd been blown up. . . ." Leie briefly closed her eyes, memory of pain written on her face. "Mostly, I was searching for a way to follow Renna, to make my own getaway. That's how I can tell you there aren't any secret panels. At least none I could recognize. Still, I did notice a thing or two."

Maia's dour mood kept her looking down at her hands. "What did you notice?" she asked, sullenly unresponsive.

"Get your butt up here and see for yourself." Leie rejoined, with a hint of the old sharpness. Maia frowned, then stood and hobbled closer. Leie waited beside the broad dais, where she stooped and pointed at a row of tiny objects embedded in the side of the giant stone block. Some of them looked like buttons. Others were little metal-rimmed holes.

"What are they for?" Maia inquired.

"I was hoping you'd tell me. Each of us tried pushing them. The buttons click as if they're supposed to do something, but nothing happens."

"Maybe they were for turning on lights. Too bad there's no power in the sanctuary."

For lack of time, Maia hadn't given any details about the military catacombs that she and Brod had explored, and which still hummed with titanic energies. Maia assumed the two networks of artificial caves were completely severed, so that hermits and treasure-hunters using this part would never stumble across the hidden defense facility, just next door.

"I said nothing happens," Leie replied. "That doesn't mean there's no power."

Maia stared at her sister. "What do you mean?"

At that moment, another gunshot pealed, echoing down the hallway to resonate within the chamber, setting Maia's teeth rattling. Both girls waited in suspense, and sighed when no more shots followed. With the tip of a finger, Leie pointed to a pair of tiny metal rings, about a centimeter apart, set into the edge of the dais near the buttons. The rings surrounded thin, deep holes. Maia pressed her finger against one, and looked up, perplexed. "I don't feel anything."

"Have you got a piece of metal?" Leie asked. "Like a coinstick? A half-credit will do."

Maia shook her head. Then she recalled. "Maybe I do have something." Her right hand went to her left forearm and unstrapped the leather cover of her portable sextant. Gingerly, she drew the tiny instrument from its padded case.

"Where'd you get that?" Leie commented, watching the brass engraving of a zep'lin pop open. Maia shrugged. "It's complicated. Let's just say I found it useful, on occasion."

She unfolded the sighting arms. One of them terminated in a pointed prong—normally used as an indicator for reading numbers against a measuring wheel—that could be rotated outward. It seemed narrow enough to use as a probe.

"Good," Leie said. "Now, I don't claim to be the only one who had the idea, inspecting for electricity. Others tried, and felt nothing. But I figured, maybe the current was too low to detect by hand. Remember how we used to check those pitiful, weak saline batteries Savant Mother Claire had us make, back in silly-ass chem class? Well, I did the same thing here. When no one was looking, I inserted a coinstick and touched the metal with my tongue."

"Yes?" Maia asked, growing more interested as she slipped the narrow prong into one of the tiny holes.

"Yes indeed! I swear you can taste a faint tickle of . . ."

Leie's voice trailed off as she stopped and stared. Maia, too, looked down in astonishment at the little sextant.

Across the center of its scratched, pitted face, a blank window had come alight, perhaps for the first time in centuries. Tiny, imperfect letters, missing corners and edges, flickered, then steadied into a constant glow.

.... τ⊕ fi∩∂ ωHατ iς Hi⊃⊃∈∩ ...

"Great Mother of life!"

The exclamation made both girls look up from the transfixing sight. Still blinking in surprise, Maia saw that Captain Poulandres and one of his officers stood in the doorway at the top of the aisle, staring with dumfounded expressions.

Maia's initial thought was pragmatic. *How are they able to see the sextant from all that way up there?*

"I . . ." Poulandres swallowed hard. ". . . came to tell you. The pirates say they want to talk. They say . . ." He shook his head, unable to concentrate on his urgent message. "By Lysos and the sea, how did you two manage to do that!"

It dawned on Maia that the captain *couldn't* see the tiny letters glowing on the sextant's face. He must be looking at something else. Something above and behind her back. Together, as if pulled by the same string, she and Leie turned around, and gasped in unison.

There, spread across the huge, formerly pale front wall of the hall, now lay an immense grid of faint, microscopic lines, upon which danced myriad, multihued particles, innumerable, smaller than specks. An orgiastic, colorful spectacle of surging, flowing patterns panoplied in whirling currents, eddies, teeming jungles of simulated structure and confusion . . . ersatz chaos and order . . . death and life.

Despite all trials and experience, some aspects of character might be too deep ever to change. Once more, it was Leie who recovered first to comment.

"Uh," she said in a dry, hoarse voice, glancing sideways at Maia. "Eureka . . . I think . . . ?"

The effect was even more spectacular when, a while later, the pirates tried to intimidate the escapees by cutting off the lights. Power no longer flowed to the string of electric bulbs. By then, however, those of the Manitou crew not on guard had already gathered in Renna's former cell, under the storm of pigmented, convoluted shapes that slowly twisted across the "Life Wall," as they called it. The men sat in huddled groups, or knelt below the dancing display, spreading open their treasured reference books, riffling pages by the soft, multispectral glow and arguing. Although they had confirmed that the eighteen simple patterns were components of this particular pseudo-world, not even the most expert player seemed able to make any more sense of the vista of swirling shapes.

"It's magic," the chief cook concluded, in awe.

"No, not magic," the ship's doctor replied. "It's much more. It's *mathematics*."

"What's the difference?" asked the young ensign Maia had met on the Manitou, speaking with an upper-clan accent, trying to be blasé. "They're both just symbol systems. Hypnotizing you with abstractions."

The elderly physician shook his head. "No, boy, that's wrong. Like art an' politics, magic consists of persuadin' others to see what you want 'em to see, by makin' incantations and wavin' your arms around. It's always based on claims that the magician's *force of will* is stronger than nature."

The colors overhead laid lambent, churning reflections across the old man's pate as he laughed aloud. "But nature doesn't give a fart about anybody's force of will! Nature's too strong to coerce, an' too fair to play favorites. She's just as cruel an' consistent to a clan mother as to the lowliest var. Her rules hold for ever'body." He shook his head, sighing. "And She has a dear-heart love of math."

They watched the awesome gyrating figures in silence. Finally, the young ensign complained angrily. "But men aren't any good at math!"

"So we're told," the doctor answered in a heavy voice. "So we're told."

Overhearing the conversation, Maia realized the crewmen would be of little help. Like her, they were untrained in the high arts on which this wonder must be based. Their beloved game was a fine thing, as far as it went. But the simple Life simulations they played on ships and in modern sanctuaries were no more than an arcana of accumulated tricks and intuition. It was like a bowl of water next to the great sea now in front of them.

She had tried peering at individual dots, in order to decipher the position-by-position rules of play. At first, she had thought she could make out a total of nine colors, which responded four times as powerfully to nearest neighbors as to next-nearest, and so on. Then she looked more closely, and realized that *every dot* consisted of a swarm of smaller specks, each interacting with those around it, the combination blending at a distance to give the illusion of one solid shade.

"Maia." It was Leie's voice, accompanied by a tap on her shoulder. She drew back and turned as her twin gestured toward the back of the hall, where a messenger could be seen hurriedly picking his way down the stair-aisle. It was a tricky task in the shifting, ever-changing illumination. The cabin boy arrived short of breath. He had only three words for Maia.

"They're comin', ma'am."

It wasn't easy to tear herself away from the dazzling wall display. She felt sure she'd be more useful here. But after several fits and starts, the reavers were apparently sending their delegation, at last. Poulandres insisted Maia join him to speak for the escapees.

"Why can't you do it yourself?" she had asked earlier, to which he replied enigmatically. "No voyage lands without a captain. No cargo sells without an owner. It is necessity."

Poulandres met her at the doorway. Slowly, allowing for her limp, they walked toward the strategic corner. The shifting colors followed and Maia kept glancing backward, as if drawn by a palpable force. It took effort to shake free of the contemplative frame of mind. Their prospects for successful negotiation did not look good, and she said as much to the officer.

"Aye. Neither side can charge the other without taking heavy losses. For now, it's a stalemate, but with us stuck at the wrong end of a one-way hole. Given enough time, they can flush us out several ways."

"So it's a death sentence. What is there to talk about?"

"Enough, lass. The pirates can tell something's happened down here. They won't rash us till after trying persuasion."

Maia and the captain found the ship's navigator prone at the corner, nursing the rifle, peering along its sights toward a faint glow that hinted the distant flight of stairs. That much light remained so that the reavers could detect any assault staged by the men. Otherwise, a surprise melee in the dark might cost them their advantages of arms, numbers, and position. The impasse held, for now.

Two faint blobs moved against that remote grayness. Even at maximum dark-adaptation, it took Maia's eyes time to clearly discern twin female silhouettes, approaching at a steady walk.

"Ready?" Poulandres asked. Maia nodded reluctantly, and they set off together with the navigator aiming carefully past them. Now that it was a matter of protecting comrades, she felt certain the officer could overcome his queasiness, if necessary. At the other end, markswomen were just as surely drawing bead past their own emissaries.

The blurry forms took shape, resolving into arms, legs, heads, faces. Maia almost stopped in her tracks when she recognized Baltha. The other delegate was the assistant to the reaver leader, Togay. Maia swallowed and managed to keep walking, half a pace to the captain's right.

The two groups stopped while still several meters apart. Baltha shook her head, a swish of short, blonde hair. "So. What d'you curly-pecs think you're accomplishin'?" she asked.

"Not much," Poulandres replied in a lazy drawl. "Stayin' alive, mostly. For a while."

"For a while's right. You're still here, so don't pretend *you've* found a secret way out. What's your pleasure, Cap'n? Want to see your men die by fire? Or water?"

Maia overcame her dry mouth. "I don't think you'll be using either right away."

"Stay outta this, snip!" Baltha snarled. "No one asked you."

Poulandres replied in a low voice, icy calm. "Be polite to our adopted factor-owner."

Maia fought her natural reaction, to swivel and stare at the man, who spoke as if this were a negotiation over some contested cargo. Clearly, his feint was meant to shake up the enemy.

"*This?*" Baltha asked, pointing at Maia, as incredulous as Poulandres might have wished. "This unik summer trash? She's even lamer than her dead prissy-sis."

"Baltha, use your eyes," Maia said evenly. "I'm not *quite* dead. Anyway, where does a shit-stealer like you get on, calling others names?"

". . . *Shit-stealer* . . . ?" Strangling on the words, Baltha abruptly stopped and stared. Moving involuntarily forward she breathed, "You?"

Pleasure overcame Maia's reticence. "Always a fast learner, Baltha. Congratulations."

"But I *saw* you blown to—"

"Shall we get back to the subject at hand?" Poulandres interjected, with graceful timing. "Each of our respective sides has certain needs that are urgent, and others it can afford to give up. I, for instance, have a personal need to see every last one of you bitchies put in chains, workin' like lugars on a temple rehab farm. But I admit that's a lower priority than, say, gettin' out of this mess with all my men alive." He grinned without humor. "Tell me, what is it you people desire most, and what'll you give up to get it?"

Baltha continued staring at Maia. So it was the other woman who answered in a prim, Méchant Coast accent.

"We seek the Outsider. Less than his recovery is unacceptable. All else is negotiable."

"Hm. There would have to be assurances, of course."

"Of course." The Méchanter seemed used to bargaining. "Perhaps an exchange of—"

Baltha visibly shook herself free of the quandaries implied by Maia's presence. The big var interrupted acidly. "This is crazy. If they knew where the alien was, they would of followed. I'm callin' your bluff Cap'n. You got nothin' to trade."

The sailor shrugged. "Take a look behind us. See the strange light? Even from here, you can tell we've accomplished more than you did in almost two days of searching."

Baltha glanced past their shoulders at the faint, shifting, multihued glows reflecting off the distant wall. Frustration wrote across her hard features. "Help us get him back, and we'll leave you livin', with the Manitou, when we sail."

Poulandres sucked his lower lip. Then, to Maia's surprise, he nodded. "That'd be all right . . . if we thought we could trust you. I'll put it to the men. Meanwhile, you'd help your case by turning the lights back on. We'll talk in a little while about food and water. Is that all right with you for now, Maia?"

The hell it is! she thought. Still, she answered with a curt nod. Surely the captain was only buying time.

Baltha started to respond with a snarl, but the other woman cut her off. "We'll talk it over among ourselves and send word in an hour." The two reavers turned and departed, Baltha glancing poison over her shoulder as Poulandres and Maia began their own walk back.

"Would you really turn Renna in?" Maia asked the man, in a low voice.

"You're a varling. You know nothing about what it's like to have many lives depending on you." Poulandres paused for several seconds. "I don't plan on making such a devil's deal, if it can be avoided. But don't take it as a promise, Maia. That's why you had to come on this palaver, so you'd know. Guard your own interests. They mayn't always be the same as ours."

Sailor's honor, Maia thought. *He's bound to warn me that he may have to turn on me, later. It's a strange code.*

"You know they can't afford to let you go," she said, pressing the point. "You've seen too much. They can't let their personal identities be known."

"That, too, depends," Poulandres said cryptically. "Right now, the important thing is that we've won a little time."

But what happens when no time remains? When the reavers run out of patience? "Fire or water," Baltha said. And if those don't work—if they can't pry us out by themselves—I wouldn't put it past them to send for help. Perhaps even calling their enemies.

It wasn't farfetched to imagine the gang striking a deal with their political opposites, the Perkinites, in exchange for whatever it might take to tear this rocky citadel apart. In the end, both extremes had more in common with each other than either did with the middle.

The navigator's dark young features relaxed in relief when they rounded the corner, and he put the weapon back on safety. Leie embraced Maia, and she felt her shoulders relax a fierce tightness that had gone unnoticed till now. "Come on," Maia told her twin. "Let's get back to work."

But it was hard concentrating at first, when Maia stood once more before the massive stone dais, looking alternately at the little sextant and the vast, ever-changing world-wall. Her task was to find a miracle, some way to follow Renna out of here. Yet, Baltha's offer and Poulandres's disturbing answer unnerved her. Suppose she did manage to solve the problem. Might that only doom Renna, and in the end prove futile for them all?

Soon, the fascinating vista of ever-changing patterns overcame her resistance, drawing her in. So much so that she hardly noticed when the string of faint bulbs came on again at the back of the room, evidence that the reavers were at least considering further discussion.

It was Leie who made the next breakthrough, when she discovered that the sextant could be used to *change* the wall scene. Fiddling with the finely graded dials, which Maia normally used to read the relative angles of stars, Leie turned one while the little tool was attached to the data plug. At once the patterns shifted, left and right! They moved *up* when she twisted the other wheel, disappearing off the top edge of the display, while new forms crowded in from below.

"Terrific!" Maia commented, trying for herself. This verified what she had suspected, that the great wall-screen was only a window onto something much vaster—a simulated realm extending far past the rectangular edges before them. Its theoretical limits might stretch hundreds of figurative meters beyond this room. Perhaps there were no limits at all.

The eye kept grasping for analogies amid the swirling patterns. One instant, they were intertwining hairy fingers. The next, they collided ecstatically like frothy waves breaking on a seashore. Rolling, convoluted configurations writhed without hindrance across the borders of the display. By turning a little wheel on the sextant, the humans might follow, but only in abstract, as observers. Only the shapes themselves knew true liberty. They appeared to have no needs, to fear no threats, to admit no physical bounds. The thought conveyed to Maia a sense of untold freedom, which she envied.

Did Renna somehow change himself? She wondered. *Did he know a secret way to join the world in there, leaving this one of rock and flesh behind?* It was a fantastic notion. But who knew what powers the Phylum had developed during the millennia since the Founders established a world of pastoral stability on Stratos, turning away from the "madness" of a scientific age.

On a hunch, Maia tried pushing the buttons they had found earlier, near the little holes in the massive podium. But they proved as useless as before. Perhaps they really had once controlled something as mundane as the room lights.

Then Leie made another discovery. By bending one of the sextant's sighting arms, another kind of simulated movement became possible. Of the men who had been watching, transfixed, several moaned aloud in awe as the shared point of view suddenly appeared to *dive forward,* plunging past billowing foreground simulacra, plowing through objects as intangible as clouds.

Maia felt it, too. A wave of vertigo, as if they were all falling together through an infinite sky. Gasping momentarily, she had to turn her eyes away and found that her hands were gripping the stone podium like vices. A glance at the others showed she wasn't alone. The earlier breakthroughs had been stunning, but not like this. Never had she heard of a Life-like simulation in *three* dimensions! The rate of "fall" appeared to accelerate. Shapes that had dominated the scene grew larger, revealing minutia of their convoluted forms. The centermost structures ballooned outward, while those at the fringes vanished over the edge.

The falling sensation was an illusion, of course, and with a little concentration, Maia was able to make it evaporate in a sudden mental readjustment. Moving "forward" seemed now to be an exercise in exploring *detail*. Any object centered before them was subject to expanding scrutiny, revealing ever-finer structures within . . . and then finer still. There seemed no limit to how minutely a formation could be parsed.

"Stop . . ." Maia worked hard to swallow. "Leie, stop. Go the other way."

Her sister turned and grinned at her. "Isn't this great? I never imagined men had such things! Did you say something?"

"I said, stop and back up!"

"Don't be afraid, Maia. As you explained to me, it's just simulated—"

"I'm not afraid! Just reverse the controls and back away. Do it now."

Leie's eyebrows raised. "As you say, Maia. Reversing course." She stopped pushing and started pulling gently at the little metal arm. The appearance of a forward plunge slowed, arrested, and began to withdraw. Now curling patterns in the middle receded, diminishing toward a central vanishing point while more and more bright, complex objects swarmed in from the periphery. The visceral sensation was one of pulling away, of rising up, so that each passing second meant they attained a larger, more godlike view.

It was a briefly glorious sensation, as Maia imagined it might be like to fly. Moreover, she felt a sense of restored contact with Renna, if only by sharing this thing he must also have delighted in.

At the same time, another part of her felt overwhelmed. Renna had explained that the Game of Life was only among the simplest of a vast family of pattern-generating systems, called cellular automata. When the big wall first came alight, Maia had hoped the sailors and their books might help solve this vastly more complex "ecosystem," despite none of them being savants. But if the men had been as baffled as she by the former intricacy, this addition of a third dimension shattered all hopes of easy analysis.

In her heart, Maia felt certain there *were* comprehensible rules. Something in the patterns—their diverging yet oddly repetitive sweeps and curls—called this intuition to her. *I could solve it,* she was sure. *If I had the computerized game board to work with, instead of this balky little sextant, and as many hours as Renna had in here, alone. And some of his knowledge of math.*

Alas, her list of deficits exceeded assets. In frustration, she pounded the table, jiggering the little tool. "Hey!" Leie shouted, and went on to complain that it wasn't easy piloting gently enough to keep it all from becoming a vast blur. The sextant's wheels and arms were old, loose, in need of simple mechanical repair. *Someone* had let the poor machine go straight to pot, Leie insinuated over her shoulder.

It's a wonder it still works at all, Maia thought.

At first, she had been awed by the coincidence, that her old, secondhand navigation tool could be used in this way. But then, many older instruments she had seen on shipboard featured diminutive blank windows. In former times, it must have been customary to hook up to the Old Network frequently . . . although Maia doubted spectacular wonder-walls were ever common, even before the Great Defense. Or the Founding, for that matter.

She leaned forward. Something had changed. Till now, the new shapes swarming in from the periphery had always appeared roughly similar to the smaller patterns vanishing into the center. But now, fingers of blackness crowded from the wings. The curling shapes seemed to roll up ever tighter, taking the form of giant balls that streamed inward as discrete units, not cloudlike swirls. Spheroids flew in from top and bottom, left and right, growing more compact, more numerous, bouncing and scattering off one another while the front wall grew blacker overall.

The last and largest swarm of balls coalesced into a new entity—a thick slab of phosphorescence. The slice of shimmering color seemed to strum like a bowstring as it crossed into sight from the lower right. As their point of view continued its apparent climb, the slab shrank in dimension. More such membranes entered the scene, linking to form a thrumming, vibrating, many-sided *cell*, like that of a quivering honeycomb. More cells thronged into view, becoming a multitude, then a foam, of iridescent color.

Leie was perspiring, tugging gently at the tiny sighting arm while Maia leaned forward to see the foam scintillate, fade, and in an instant, vanish!

The wall was a terrible, empty blankness. "Uh!" Maia's twin grunted in dismay, her features glistening by the faint light of the electric bulbs behind them. "Did I break it?"

"No." Maia assured. "The wall was pale before. The machine's still on. Keep going."

"You're sure? I can go back the other way."

"Keep going," Maia repeated, this time firmly.

"Well, I'll pull a little faster, then," Leie said. Before Maia could respond, she yanked harder at the little arm. The blackness lasted another fraction of a second, just long enough for an eyeblink swarm of pinpoint sparkles to flash. Then, all at once, the colors were back! Again, the simulated point of view fell backward, climbing imperiously as waves of convoluted rainbow brightness crowded in from the borders. All of this happened in the moment it took Maia to shout, "No! Stop!"

Motion ceased, save the slow, coiling dance of patterns and their constituent particles, merging and separating like entities of smoke. "What?" Leie inquired, turning to stare at her sister. "It's working again . . ."

"It never stopped working. Go back," Maia insisted, suppressing the impatient urge to push her sister aside and do it herself. Leie's marginally better coordination might make all the difference. "Go back to the black part."

Sighing, Leie turned around and delicately pushed the tiny lever. Once more, there was the sense of plunging forward, downward . . . of getting smaller while everything around them grew and loomed outward.

The blackness resumed in a blur, and was gone again, even faster than the first time. They were already across it and amid the foamy, lambent honeycombs before Leie could arrest the motion of her hand. "It's not easy, dammit!" Maia's sister complained. "The levers move jerkily. *I* wouldn't ever let a machine get in such disrepair."

Maia almost retorted that *Leie* never had to carry a tiny device on horseback, trains, ships, while drowning, crashing, climbing cliffs, and fighting for her life. . . . But she let it go while Leie bent over the tool, trying to pull the balky arm in microscopic units. As before, the cell structures became foam and then vanished into blackness. Blackness that was unrelieved, save for an occasional, sudden blur that crossed the scene too quickly to follow.

"Do you . . . mind tellin' me . . ." Leie grunted. ". . . what it is we're looking for?"

"Just keep going," Maia urged. All around her, she sensed the confusion of the men. Put off by the disappearance of the transfixing patterns, but awed by her intensity, they crowded forward, staring at the blank wall as if peering through dense fog for some miracle light of harbor. Their company was welcome, especially when one of them cried out "Stop!" before she could form words.

This time, Leie reacted quickly. The brush of illumination the man had noticed still lay in the upper left corner. At first glance, it was almost pure white, although there were pale dustings of blue and reddish yellow. Leie moved over to the finely knurled measuring wheels, which controlled lateral motion. Nudging them gently, she coaxed the object into view.

It was a bright, pinwheel shape. A "cyclone," one sailor identified. A hurricane, or whirlpool, suggested others.

But Maia knew better. Old Bennet would have identified its species on sight. Renna would perceive a friend and signpost.

She stared in wonder at the majesty that spread across the forward wall, a galactic wheel, its spiral splendor filled with shining stars.

... ταim αω∈its ∩⊕ ωU∩s ωHim ...

25

*C*aptain Poulandres sent word for her to come. There was to be another parley with the foe. Maia's curt message of reply, carried by the hesitant cabin boy, suggested irritably that the captain choose someone else.

"I need time!" she snapped over her shoulder, when Poulandres came in person. "I was just there for show, last time. All I ask is that you buy us more time!"

Maia barely heard his muttered promise to try. "And send your navigator down here, will you?" she added, calling after him. "We can use help from a professional!"

Relieved from guard duty with the rifle, the young, dark-complexioned officer arrived as Leie and Maia managed to pull back from the spiral nebula, revealing its membership in a cluster of gauzy galaxies. And that cluster proved to be but one glittering ripple in a sinuous arch that lay draped across the void, shimmering like a cosmic aurora. The navigator exclaimed upon seeing the wondrous display.

Maia agreed it was a sight, but what did it mean? Was this a clue to whatever path Renna had taken? She had to assume so, since nothing else in the vast game-simulation seemed to make the slightest sense. Were they supposed to find a particular destination amid this macrocosm, and "go" there? Or were the whirlpool entities meant to be guideposts in another sense?

Problems barred progress at many levels. Nudging the controls was like trying to pilot a coal barge through a narrow, twisty channel, a trial of fits and starts and overcompensations. Inertia and mechanical backlash kept jerking the image too large in scale, then too small. Moreover, Maia soon realized that nobody, not even the navigator, had any idea where in the sky they "were."

"We don't use galaxies to chart our way at sea," he started to explain. "They're too fuzzy and you need a telescope. Now, if you could show me *stars* . . ."

Unable to keep her frustration from spilling out, Maia muttered, "You want stars? I'll show you smuggy stars!" She took the controls and with a yank caused the point of view to dive straight toward one of the galactic wheels. It ballooned outward at frightful speed, causing some of the onlookers behind them to moan. Suddenly, the wall was filled with sharp, individual pinpoints, spreading out to fill the artificial sky with constellations.

But what constellations? Among the patterns sifted by her mind, no familiar friends leaped forth. No well-known markers flashed out longitude, latitude, and season to a practiced eye.

"Oh," the navigator murmured slowly. "I get it. They'd be different, dependin' on . . . which way we looked, an' from where . . ." He paused, struggling with new notions implied by the wall. "It's prob'ly not even our galaxy, is it?"

"Great insight!" Leie snorted, while Maia's own irritable mood shifted toward sympathy. These concepts were probably difficult for a man rooted in traditional arts. "We don't know that *any* of these galaxies is ours," she commented. "They may all be just artificial models, arising out of a complicated game, having nothing to do with the real universe. We better hope not, if my idea's to mean anything. Back up again, Leie. We've got to try finding something familiar."

As the island starscape receded to take its place once more among the others, Maia knew the search might prove impossible. The only intergalactic object she had much hope of recognizing was Andromeda, nearest neighbor to the Milky Way. What were the odds against catching sight of that particular spiral, from just the right angle, however long they searched?

All of this assumes my hunch is right . . . that maneuvering around inside this fancy pretend reality has something to do with how Renna escaped.

If so, it would have been much easier for him. The Visitor might have programmed his game board to search for traits specific to the Milky Way. A shape to the spiral arms, or perhaps even a color profile. Once specified, the machine would do the rest.

Whereas I don't have a game board. Nor his knowledge. Nor the slightest idea how any of this relates to escaping from pirates.

"You move around by twiddling that little sexter?" asked the navigator as he bent over to watch Leie delicately prod the tiny, recalcitrant controls. "Does it have to be this one?"

"I don't think so. There's nothing special about it, except that it has a data tap."

"Lots of old ones do. If only I'd known, I mighta sweet-talked a reaver into fetchin' mine from Manitou. It's bigger, and in a whole lot better shape."

Maia grimaced. Everyone seemed to think she was negligent of her tools.

"What's it say here in the data window?" He went on. "Some sort o' coordinates?"

"Nah," Leie replied without turning. "Puzzle phrases, mostly. Temple stuff. Riddle o' Lysos." All of her attention was devoted to nudging the controls, while Maia carefully watched the sweep of galactic clusters, flowing from left to right across the wall, seeking anything familiar. Absently, Maia corrected her sister. "That's what they appear to be. Actually, I think they're commands. Starting conditions for whatever game is being played here."

"Hm," the navigator commented. "Could fool me. I'd have sworn they were coordinates."

Maia turned and looked at him. "What?"

His chin rested on the podium top, next to the tiny display, almost brushing Leie's wrist. He pointed to the row of minuscule red letters. "Never saw anything like this written in a temple. The numbers keep changing as she touches the controls. Seems more like—"

"Let me see." Maia tried to squeeze in. "Hey!" Leie complained. Politely, the young man withdrew so Maia could see four groups of symbols, glowing across the little array.

$$A \subseteq Q \oplus \quad 41E{+}18 \quad {-}\,35E{+}14 \quad 69E{+}15$$

Apart from the first enigmatic grouping, the other three clusters of numbers quivered in a constant state of flux. As Maia watched, the "41" became "42," then briefly "41" again, before jittering further down to "40." Maia glanced at Leie. "Are you moving anything?"

"No, I swear." Leie showed both hands.

"Well, go ahead," Maia said. "Push something, slowly."

Leie bent to grasp one of the measuring wheels between two fingers. At once the second grouping began to blur. "Stop!" Maia cried. The

numbers stuttered, then settled to tiny excursions around the value
12E+18.

"Again. Keep going that way."

Maia stood up, watching the screen as Leie resumed. Galaxies
scrolled from left to right at an accelerating pace. Only one of the number groups in the tiny window seemed affected. The "E" shone steady,
but Maia watched the "+8" turn into "+7" . . . and eventually "+6."

"You're right," she told the navigator. "They are coordinates. I wonder why they replaced what was written there before." She turned the
other way. "Leie, let's try taking down to zero—"

Her words were cut off by shock waves that reverberated through
the chamber. Echoing booms spread out from the entrance. This time, it
was no single, warning shot, but a rapid series of loud reports, followed
by clamoring voices. The men who had been watching from the benches
leaped up, scrambling toward the door, rushing to aid their comrades on
duty in the corridor. The navigator dithered only a second before making
the same choice and joining the pell-mell dash.

Leie looked at Maia. "I'll go."

Maia shook her head. "No, I must. If they get past us, though . . ."

"I'll smash the sextant." Leie promised.

"Meanwhile, make all the numbers small as you can!" Maia
shouted back as she followed the men, limping. Her knee had swollen
and was hurting more than ever. Behind her, the model universe resumed its blurry race across the wall.

Sailors jammed into a tight mob near the hallway's right-angle turn.
All gunfire had ceased by the time she arrived, and the jabber of milling
males evoked consternation and fear, not impending combat. Maia had to
nudge and elbow her way through an aromatic throng of men. When she
reached the front of the crowd, she gasped. The ship's doctor knelt beside the prostrate form of the Manitou's first officer, stanching a flow of
blood from a jagged wound. A knife, dripping crimson ichor, lay on the
ground nearby. Of Captain Poulandres, there was no sign.

"What happened?" she asked the ensign she had spoken to earlier.
The youth seemed distressed, his face as white as the wounded
man's.

"It was a trap, ma'am. Or maybe the reavers just got mad. We heard
lots o' yelling. The cap'n tried to keep 'em calm, but we could tell they
were accusin' him of something. One of 'em pulled a knife while the
other kicked the cap'n, real bad." He winced in recollection. "They
dragged him off while guns shot at us from that end, keepin' us pinned
down."

Damn, Maia thought, quashing her natural impulse toward sympathy for poor Poulandres. She had been counting on him to buy time, not provoke open warfare! Now what remained, but to prepare for Baltha's threatened assault?

The first officer was mumbling to the doctor. Maia crouched lower to hear.

". . . said we must've helped the rads. . . . Cap'n tried askin' how? How an' why'd we help a buncha unniks do in our *own* ship? But they wouldn't listen . . ."

Maia rode out a lancing shock to her wounded left knee as she dropped to the ground beside the officer. "What did you say? Do you mean the Manitou is—"

"Gone. . . ." The sailor sighed. ". . . didn't say how. Just took th' cap'n, and . . ." His eyes rolled up in their sockets as he swooned.

A moment's stunned silence followed, then arguing broke out among the men, many of them shaking their heads with the hopeless passivity of despair.

"Don't see any other choice. We've *got* to surrender!"

"Cap'n blew it with somethin' he said. We should send 'nother embassy . . ."

"They'll come an' cut us to bits!"

Somebody helped Maia stand. Suddenly, it seemed that everyone was looking at her.

Just because I broke you halfway out of jail—and got you all into even worse trouble—that doesn't make me a leader, she thought caustically, seeing incipient panic in their dilated eyes. Robbed of their top officers, they fell back on old habits of childhood, looking for a woman authority figure. The time of year didn't help. "Wissy as a winter man," went one expression. Still, Maia knew that seasons alone weren't decisive. The crew might stand a chance, if someone got them busy, building momentum based on action. She saw an older bosun standing next to the corner, holding the automatic rifle. "Can you handle that thing?" she asked.

The gruff sailor nodded grimly. "Yes, ma'am. I figure. Just half o' the bullets left, but I can wait an' make 'em count."

That fierce statement helped change the mood a bit. Other males murmured tentative agreement. Maia poked her head around the corner and peered down the gloomy corridor. "There's plenty of old trash and debris in nearby rooms. The quickest of you could dash from one to another, too fast for them to draw a bead in the dark, and toss stuff into the main hall. If not a barricade, the junk might at least slow down a charge."

The ensign nodded. "We'll look for planks and stones . . . things to use as weapons."

"Good." Maia turned to the doctor. "What can we do, in case they use smoke?"

The old man shrugged. "Tear pieces of cloth, I guess. Dampen them with—"

A sharp cry interrupted from behind them. It was Leie's voice, resonating even out here.

"Maia! Come back and see this!"

Torn by conflicting duties, Maia bit her lip. If the men fell apart now, there'd be surrender or worse just as soon as the reavers chose to push. On the other hand, even tenacious resistance wouldn't do much good in the long run, unless an overall solution was found. All hope for that lay at the end of the hall.

"As senior officer, I should stay," the navigator told her, and Maia knew he was right, by normal standards. These weren't normal circumstances.

"Please," she urged. "We need you below." She turned to the young ensign. "Can your guild and shipmates rely on you?"

The young man was but a year older than Maia. Now, though, he stood up straighter, and squared his shoulders. "They can," he answered, and seemed as relieved as Maia to hear the words. "Count on it!" he finished with determination, and swiveled to face the men, snapping orders to implement Maia's suggestions.

"All right," the navigator said, reassured. "But let's hurry."

When they turned to start down the hall, Maia almost fell as her left leg threatened to give out. The young officer took her weight on one arm, and helped her limp back toward the chamber containing the miracle wall. Behind them, sounds of brisk, organized activity replaced what had verged, only moments before, on outright panic. During the brief walk, Maia fretted. *Something's happened to the Manitou. Something that made the reavers throw out their promise to Poulandres.*

Had the first officer mentioned it having to do with the rads? Did Thalla and the other prisoners break out? The possibility gladdened Maia, but in a dry and hopeless way, for anything that made the pirates upstairs more desperate only provoked more dire threat down here.

Maia suppressed her worries as she let the navigator help her toward glimpses of starlight. For a moment, it made a fine illusion. *As if the screen were just a great big opening in the wall,* she wished. *Leading straight into a winter night.*

On arriving at the doorway, she and her companion cried out at the same time, in joyful recognition. Before them, splayed across a twinkling firmament like a great blot, lay the multitendriled nebulosity known as the Claw. It grew smaller, incrementally, until familiar patterns of stars crowded in along each side.

"Took you long enough!" Leie chided as they approached. "Look, I just can't get it any closer than this."

Maia glanced at the tiny window and saw that the display was greatly changed. The numbers to the right of each letter "E" were much closer to zero.

$$A \subseteq Q \oplus \quad -94E\text{-}1 \qquad 13E\text{+}0 \qquad -69E\text{+}1$$

"It *is* a coordinate system!" the navigator cried. "And it's got to be centered on Stratos. Can't you get them any smaller?"

Leie snapped, "If you're so smart, *you* try it!"

"Good idea, Leie." Maia nodded. "He's worked with tools like this all his life. Go ahead," she told the young man, who frowned uncertainly as he took over Leie's position. Maia's sister stretched, trying to stand up straight. "Careful, vril," she said. "It's touchy as a—"

She yelped as the scene shifted abruptly. The simulated image of the dark nebula swarmed forward, engulfed the scene in blackness, and then swept aside in a blur that made both twins briefly dizzy. The numbers on the display increased. Leie laughed derisively, as the young man grimaced. "It's a little balky," he commented. Then he bent closer, concentrating. "I always find I can prevent the wheels jerkin' if I twist a little while I turn. Cuts down on the backlash."

Numbers stopped growing and reversed. The constellations, which had started to warp from altered perspective, gradually resumed forms Maia knew. The Claw nebula passed again, taking up its familiar position.

Then, from the left, an object entered the view so huge and radiant the whole room lit up. "It's our sun!" the navigator called. A moment later, he gasped as another, smaller entity merged from the right. Its sharp, biting hue of blue-tinged white stabbed Maia's eyes, triggering a tingle that flowed straight down her spine. The effect was doubtless minor next to what it did to the young lieutenant. He staggered, shading his eyes with one hand, and softly moaned. "Wengel Star!"

The light spread past them, through the open door and into the hall. There was no uproar, so perhaps no one consciously noticed. Still, Maia wondered if remnant traces of wintry male indecision washed away under that shine, to be replaced by a hormonal certitude of summer. Conceivably, the stream would energize the men for what was to come.

Maia watched the sextant's diminutive display whirl rapidly as the navigator moved back and forth among the three controls.

$$A \subseteq Q \oplus \quad -\quad 42E\text{-}0 \qquad 17E\text{-}0 \qquad -\quad 12E\text{-}0$$

"We're gettin' close to the limit of what I can manage," he grunted, concentrating on the glowing digits. Suddenly, the sextant emitted an unexpected sound, an audible click. The tiny numbers froze in place and the window winked.

$$A \subseteq Q \oplus \qquad 10E\text{-}0 \qquad 10E\text{-}0 \qquad 10E\text{-}0$$

The midget number display went blank for an instant. When it lit again, the old symbols were replaced by a new set.

$$P \angle R \oplus \quad \text{-} \quad 1103.095 \qquad \text{SIDEREAL.}$$

"What does it mean—?" Leie began, only to be cut off as the navigator shouted. "Hey! Something's changed in the controls, too!"

"What do you mean?"

"I mean the response is different. I touch 'em, and the stars barely budge now. Watch." He pushed one of the knurled wheels, and the constellations moved, but only slightly. A minute earlier, such a turn would have sent them reeling across the galaxy. Maia looked down at the sextant screen, and saw that the new reading was utterly unchanged. Realization came in a flash.

"I get it!" she cried. "It's a test!"

"A what?"

Maia spread her arms. "A test. You have to pass each phase to get to the next. First we had to figure out how to turn the machine on. Then how to find a model universe inside the huge Life game. Next step was to find our own solar system. Now we must figure out how to maneuver *within* the system." She didn't add that these were all skills currently rare on Stratos. At any point they might run into a barrier beyond their meager abilities.

The navigator was breathing hard, despite the hand he kept upraised to block the cutting light of Wengel Star. "Well . . . in that case," he said. "The next stage oughta be easy. We both know these stars. It's Farsun time right now. Midwinter. So Wengel's on the opposite side of the sun from where we want to be." He started to bend over the sextant again.

"Let me," Maia said, realizing the light had him distracted. He stepped back to give her access to the controls. Maia took her little astronomical tool in hand and made a few tentative turns. The sun's tiny blue-white companion slipped aside, vanishing over the screen boundary. The young man breathed a ragged sigh, half regretful, half relieved.

They commenced a steep dive straight toward the larger, familiar fireball, which loomed outward in a rush, its reddish surface growing in both apparent size and mottled minutia with each passing second. A thrill coursed Maia's body as a sense of swooping motion overcame her. Imagined heat flushed her cheek as the sun blazed by to the right, seemingly close enough to reach out and touch. Leie gasped.

In an instant it was gone, vanished "behind" them. At nearest passage, Maia had noticed that the level of detail seemed washed out, as if the simulation was never meant to represent every flicker in the star's chromosphere. That fit with her best guess, that the universe within the wall computer wasn't a *perfect* copy of reality.

Close enough, though. As if suddenly unleashed, constellations burst forth across the simulated heavens. *Hello, friends,* Maia greeted them. While seeking the known patterns of winter, she kept watch for the blue glitter of a planet, her homeworld. Soon all star positions were proper. She slowed, circled, and performed a spiral sweep. But however she hunted, no blue marble swam into view. "I don't get it. Stratos should be somewhere about here."

They stared together at the empty patch of sky. Maia dimly heard a messenger come and mutter to Leie that the tense status quo was holding in the hallway, but signs of bustling activity at the far end were making the men nervous and worried. Clearly, something was going to happen, soon.

Meanwhile Maia struggled with frustration and pride. Once upon a time, at least some folk on her world had felt comfortable enough with spaceflight to simulate it, use it in games and tests. Probably, now and then, they even ventured out—at least in order to remain able. It meant that Lysos never insisted that her heirs stay forever grounded. That must have been a later innovation.

The navigator, too, seemed puzzled, thwarted. Then, suddenly, he pointed. "There! A planet!" He frowned. "But that's not Stratos. It's Demeter."

Maia saw he was correct. The gas giant was a familiar sight, dominant member of the planetary system. "It's Demeter, all right. Sitting smack dab in the middle of the Fishtail. Oh, Lysos," she groaned.

"What's wrong?" Leie asked. "Can't you use Demeter to fine-tune—"

"It's in the wrong part of the sky!" Maia cut in. "As of a few days ago, Demeter was in the Trident. That must mean—"

"Time," the navigator agreed, looking at Maia. "We're displaced in time." His eyes widened, apparently sharing Maia's thought. They almost knocked heads bending to look again at the sextant's little display. "Sidereal? That's a word used by astronomers, isn't it?"

"Yeah," Maia replied. "It has to do with measuring time by the stars. Then the number must be—"

"A coordinate," he finished. "A date? But it's a negative number."

"The past, then. With a date set in decimals, instead of years and months. Let's say it's based on the same calendar. There's only a small fraction after the decimal, which implies—"

"—that the date's just after New Year, with the sun at the vernal equinox."

"So we're a quarter of an orbit and ninety degrees off! We should be looking for a springtime sky!"

This time the man took the controls, while Maia guided him. They were getting the hang of it, and things sped quickly. "Steady . . . steady . . . Port ten degrees . . . down five . . ." Stars and planets swept by, until Leie cried out in joy. The sun and Wengel Star were gone from sight, but their combined light was seen once more, reflecting off a blue-, brown-, white-, and green-hued globe that swelled rapidly into view, its continents and seas punctuated by polar caps and gauzy films of stratospheric clouds. A retinue of silvery moons swept past as the scene drove steadily toward the great azure ball.

This must be what Renna saw, when he approached in his starship, Maia realized. Envy had never flowed so strongly within her veins. *I never imagined it so beautiful. My homeworld.*

For the soul, it was a feast that satisfied hungers more yearning than the one in her belly. Despite the preachings of orthodox and heretic temples alike, the maternal deity, Stratos Mother, was but a lovely abstraction in comparison. How, Maia wondered, could anyone know or appreciate a world without looking on its face? One didn't ask such absurdity of *human* lovers.

How could we ever have abandoned this? Maia marveled, recognizing features from globes and atlases, minus all the lines and labels that made human presence seem so urgent. In fact, the vast reaches of mountain and forest and desert seemed barely touched. The view was an instant cure for vain conceit.

The approach slowed as a subjective transition took place. Formerly, they had seemed to move horizontally, heading *toward* the planet. Now, with ocean and islands covering the entire scene, all sensation of motion abruptly turned vertical. They were *falling*.

The outline of Landing Continent enlarged, sweeping to the left. The Méchant Coast gleamed. Maia briefly caught sight of checkerboard farmlands and silver rivers arched by spidery bridges, before the landmass fled at an angle and southern seas filled the scene, scintillating with profuse sunlight reflections, brushed by phalanxes of heavy clouds. To the southeast loomed a chain of narrow, pinpoint peaks which, from a distance, were detectable more by how great currents split into a thousand ruffled streamers in their wake. The combed sea changed color downstream from those jutting spires.

Maia recognized the outline of this very archipelago—the Dragons'
Teeth—from the chart she and Brod had used to sail from Grimké Isle.
"How can you control the approach so fine?" Leie asked the naviga-
tor. In reply, he stepped back from the dais, raising his hands. "I felt
another click, a few seconds ago. Since then, it's not been me at all.
Maybe we set off a homing program, or something."

Maia sought Grimké, at the northern tip of the island chain. That
monolith, where she and Naroin and others had been interned, fought,
and escaped, showed no sign of a crater. No blasted, glazed hole in its
center. Rather, she briefly glimpsed buildings, shimmering in a morning
glow just before the isle fell off the upper border of the screen. In the
center, meanwhile, a great cluster of connected stony towers loomed
toward them.

Jellicoe.

And yet, *not* Jellicoe. Not the Jellicoe of today. What surged larger
with each passing second was a thing of unmarred beauty. A hollow star-
shaped glory of both nature and artifice. Every spire was adorned with
edifices of polished stone or the metallic glitter of sleek, tethered air-
ships. Within the lagoon, she counted three great cruisers, with sails not
of dingy canvas but some black, filmy material that seemed to drink in
sunlight, reflecting none.

All three watchers quailed as one of Jellicoe's easternmost teeth
plunged toward them. There was a breathtaking rush of rock and vegetation, and instantly the scene was enveloped in a blurry stream of dark
stone, flowing past like rushing fluid. "Ack!" Leie commented. No one
exhaled. *This is some damn simulation,* Maia thought numbly.

Someone shouted terse words that were tense and excited, from the
back of the room. But she had only regard for the swarming motion,
decelerating in front of them.

Light returned and motion ceased with an abruptness that caused
them all to stagger. The youths found themselves staring, as if through a
window, into a room that was a clone to this one. A younger, better-
attired clone. Reddish-colored cushions graced the benches, and the
walls were uncracked, polished to a glistening sheen and rimmed with
cheery banners.

"Long ago," Maia said. "It's showing what this place was like,
a long time ago." She coughed behind her fist, and leaned over the
sextant.

$$P\mathbb{Z}R\oplus \quad - \quad 1103.095 \quad \textbf{SIDEREAL.}$$

"The fourth coordinate." The navigator cleared his throat. "Time must be
the next step."

Leie spoke hastily. "If we could move forward to the present, would it be possible to see what's going on outside, right now?"

"Might it show what happens in the *future*?" the man added, in a hushed tone.

Maia's thoughts whirled. Leie's question implied a machine that kept records, and was still monitoring events, as they spoke. To tap such real-time inputs would be a huge asset, in their present straits. Yet she doubted it was like that. What about all those galaxies and such? She couldn't imagine a machine capable of monitoring the *universe*, constantly, over thousands of years.

The navigator's idea was even wilder. Yet, in a weird way it made more sense. Maia still believed this was all a simulation, a vast, godlike cousin to the Game of Life. If so—if the facsimile took into account every variable—might it be able to project likely events, into the future? The implications were staggering, affecting everything from their present predicament to the temple's teachings about free will.

"Let's try to do something about that fourth coordinate," Maia suggested, rubbing her scratchy eyes.

The young navigator coughed twice and bent over. "We've already been usin' all the obvious movin' parts." Gently, delicately, he touched pieces of the sextant, until his hand stroked the eyepiece, where one normally looked to sight horizon and stars. The image ahead of them jiggered slightly, and the number in the little indicator screen shifted just a little. "Of course," he said, with another cough. "It's the depth-of-focus adjustment. Give me room, please."

Maia stepped back. Her eyes itched and she sniffed a smoky smell. Abruptly, at the exact same moment, she and Leie sneezed. They looked at each other, and for the first time in several minutes surveyed the room. The air had changed noticeably. There was a sooty, hazy quality.

Shouts came from the back. Maia turned to see the cabin boy hurry downstairs, calling and waving. Around his nose, he wore a torn strip of cloth.

"Ensign an' doctor want t'know . . . you havin' any luck?"

"That depends," Maia replied. "We're getting some exciting philosophical insights, but not many practical applications."

The boy looked puzzled by her reply, and anxious. "*We're* gettin' smoke, ma'am. Doc says it'll take a while, since we're below the pirates, but the good air's gonna get sucked out, in time. They may attack before that, when it gets hard to see."

Maia had figured as much, from the evidence stinging her nose and lungs. This time she spoke earnestly. "Please tell the doctor and the ensign . . ." She turned to point at the forward wall—and instantly forgot what she had been about to say.

The image of the room's past was changing moment by moment. What had looked like an elegant, well-appointed lecture hall began deteriorating rapidly. First the banners and cushions vanished. Then, in a single, abrupt instant, cracks propagated across the walls. The artificial light, which had bathed the chamber until now, went out, leaving the depicted room visible only by a strange, luminous glow, apparently given off by the rocks themselves. In the speeded time frame, dust could be seen settling and spreading in thin, advancing ripples, like wavelets washing ashore. Then even the dust froze in place.

"That's it," the man said, standing up. On the sextant dial, the number read,

$$P \alpha R \oplus \qquad +0000.761 \qquad \textbf{SIDEREAL.}$$

There was another click. The display went blank for two seconds, and relit.

$$.... \tau \oplus \text{ fi} \cap \partial \text{ } \omega H \alpha \tau \text{ i} \varsigma \text{ Hi} \supset \cap \equiv \cap ...$$

Maia exhaled a tense breath. She had half expected, when the simulation caught up to its "present," to come face to face with images of themselves, staring back as if from a mirror. But the room ahead of them lay dark and empty. "It won't go any farther forward, in case you're wondering," the navigator said, with a note of disappointment.

Leie coughed. "This is all very interesting. But how's it helping us get *out* of here?"

Maia's lips pressed together. "I'm thinking!"

She glanced back and saw that the messenger boy had departed. The haze, which had already lessened visibility, caused things to get even worse when scratchiness in her eyes triggered the nictitating inner lids. From the hallway, she overheard harsh coughs and frantic mutterings.

Are they planning to charge out of here? It may come to that, if the reavers are willing to wait us out.

But if the smoke and heat were bad here, they would be worse upstairs, and the pirates' wood supply was limited. So this might be just the prelude to an attack.

Maia shook her head, trying to break out of a desolate spiral. She reached for ideas, and found none. The picture wall lay static before them, showing—if not today's desolation—then what might have been the scene when the simulation was last updated.

We could find out when that was, by using the other controls to go outside and check the stars . . . or, better yet, zoom over to the nearest

*town and read the date on a newspaper! Providing the simulation parses
that finely.*

Such thoughts were a sign of oxygen deprivation, she felt sure. Maia
coughed, lowering her head. *At least Renna ought to be all right, wherever he's gone to.* Stronger still, her never-absent concern over Brod
caused her to pray briefly to the Mother of All, and also to the God of
Justice honored by men. *Let Brod get out of this. Please let him live.*

"I guess . . ." Leie wheezed behind a closed fist, "we oughta go
join the boys. Help get ready . . . for what's next."

The air was going bad faster than Maia had expected. Visibility
dropped rapidly, and breathing caused an ache in her chest. "I guess
you're right," she agreed between coughs. Still, she was reluctant to
leave. *I can't help feeling we're close. So damn close!*

Leie held out her hand. With a grim smile, Maia turned and made a
step forward to take it. When her weight came down on her left knee,
however, it gave way and she fell, striking the hard stone floor beside the
podium. The impact sent bolts of pain up her arms. Leie's hands were on
her, solicitous, helping, and Maia knew a kind of gladness. At the end,
they would be reconciled. She looked up to meet her sister's eyes, and
felt refreshed by a wash of poignant love.

Refreshed? Her body bathed in a rush of welcome coolness. It
wasn't psychological, she realized, but a strong physical sensation. "Do
you feel that?" she asked her twin. After a moment's puzzlement, Leie
nodded.

"Feel what?" the navigator said, squatting anxiously beside them.
"Come on! They're calling muster for—"

"Quiet!" Leie hissed. "Where's it coming from?" She began crawling, casting left and right, searching for the source of the soft breeze.
"It's over here!"

Helped by the man, Maia followed on eager instinct, for by now
there was no other supply of good air. It seemed to come from a crack
where the many-ton podium met the semicircular platform. A thin breeze
emanated from that narrow passage, though it would never have been
detected except under present circumstances.

Overhead, smoke billowed. The plumes shook visibly as several
rocking explosions concussed the air. The men in the hall were firing,
either to repel attack or in preparation for one of their own. "Go!" Maia
urged the navigator. "Make them hold on awhile longer!"

Without another word, he was on his feet and gone. "Help me up,"
Maia told her sister, although leaving the fresh airstream was like tearing
away from life itself. Coughing, they both managed to reach the sextant.
"Aim downward!" Maia gasped as Leie seized one of the measurement
wheels. It was increasingly difficult to see the image of the dim room,

portrayed on the magic wall. It jiggled at Leie's touch, then took a jerk upward. There was a glimpse of naked rock, some dark emptiness, a quick blaze of color, and then dark rock again.

"Don't say it!" Leie snapped, bending over to focus on one thumb and forefinger, despite her body's quivering. Maia marveled at her twin's concentrated intensity. In her own case, it was all she could do to keep from folding over and vomiting.

The picture wall jittered, shifting in fits and starts.

Must break the sextant, if reavers get through, Maia reminded herself. *Mustn't let 'em see the simulation . . . or know that the wall can come awake.*

More shattering booms echoed, and there were loud cries. Had battle been joined? If so, the scene outside was appallingly sinful even to imagine . . . men against women . . . a Perkinite propagandist's dream come true. In fact, sex had almost nothing to do with the issues in question—crime versus law, ambition against honor. Gender was incidental, but legend would say otherwise, when and if word ever spread.

The picture jogged again. A bright wedge appeared across the upper fifth of the wall, hurtful in its brilliance. Leie grunted and tried again; the bright patch shot downward so that now the lower half of the screen blazed.

Blinking through the choking haze, Maia saw something she hadn't expected. It was not a simulated image of a room, some chamber below this one, but an abstract set of nested rectangles. Against a radiant background, three squares contained distinct glowing symbols—a snowflake, a fire-arrow, and a sailing ship. As Leie gradually nudged the scene so that it filled the wall before them, the borders around each of the squares began to throb.

A red dot appeared. Responding to Leie's controls, it wandered about. Both twins reached the obvious conclusion, at the same instant.

"I'll pick the sailboat," Leie said. But Maia shouted, "No!" She coughed, a series of rasping hacks, and shook her head. "Too obvious . . . go . . . with the arrow."

Behind them, they now heard screams. More gunfire and an angry clamor of combat. Leie's brow furrowed, running with perspiration, her eyes riveted on the screen. Wheezing from the effort, she brought the red dot into the square chosen by Maia.

A deep-throated tone rose beneath their feet. A growling, deeper than the groans coming from the hallway. Those shouts grew closer as Maia and Leie fell back from the podium, which began vibrating powerfully. Rumbling from age and disuse, a hidden mechanism rolled the heavy stone aside. Light spilled from the widening gap, along with a welcome rush of cool, fresh air.

Masked figures were tumbling down the aisle behind them. The first rush of males arrived in an orderly fashion, bearing wounded comrades. After them spilled others, panicky, near-doubled-over, their makeshift smoke veils askew. There was no time for organization. "In here!" Leie cried, guiding refugees toward a set of stairs that had appeared below the podium. Sailors tumbled downward, pell-mell, although Maia now wondered.

What have I done?

A rear guard fought on, five or six men wrestling desperately with twice as many smaller figures, expertly wielding trepp bills. A gunshot bellowed, and one of the men clutched his abdomen, falling.

"Come on, Maia!" Leie screamed, shoving her into the bright aperture. Howls of angry pursuit rose as three reavers broke free to leap down rows of benches after them. One tripped and fell, then Maia was too busy negotiating the steep steps to look back. At bottom, a waiting man took her arm, preventing her from turning.

It's okay, Leie was just behind me, Maia told herself as she fled with other fugitives along a narrow hallway, under a low luminous ceiling, between cables and conduits. The constrained passage filled with sound as everyone seemed to be shouting at once. Alternate steps sent waves of pain swarming from her knee. At last, they reached a set of double doors made of sheet metal. An *ad hoc* squad of wounded men were using whatever they could find to wedge one of the doors shut. As soon as Maia was through, they started on the other. "Wait!" she cried. "My sister!"

She kept screaming while they finished, ignoring her pummeling assaults. It was the doctor who took Maia's face in his hands and repeated, over and over, "There was reavers behind ya, honey. Just reavers, a little ways behind ya!"

In confirmation, the doors shook resoundingly as they were struck from the other side, again and again. "Go on!" one dark, bloodstained man urged, leaning against the portal. "Get outta here!" Blinking, Maia recognized her recent fellow investigator—the navigator.

"But—" she complained, before being lifted into the arms of a massive sailor, who turned and ran, leaving crimson blemishes behind him on the cold stone floor.

What followed was a blur of shaking, wild turns, and sudden reverses. Yet, combined with pain and fear and loss came a strange sensation, one she had not experienced since infancy—of being carried and cared for by someone much larger. Despite knowing countless ways men were as frail as women—and sometimes, much frailer—it came as a kind of solace to feel engulfed by such gentleness and power. It coaxed a deep part of her to let go. Amid a headlong plunge through eerie corridors, chased by despair, Maia wept for her sister, for the brave sailors, and herself.

The passage seemed to stretch on and on, at times descending like a ramp, at others climbing. They mounted a steep, narrow stair where some men had to duck their heads and others lagged behind. Sounds of pursuit, which had faded a while back, now grew closer once more. At the top, the diminished band of fugitives found another metal door. Several men laid down their wounded comrades and formed one last rear guard, vowing to hold on while Maia, her bearer, the doctor, and the cabin boy hurried ahead.

What's the point? Maia thought miserably. The men seemed to believe in her ability to work miracles, but in truth, what had she accomplished? This "escape route" was intrinsically no good if the foe could follow. Most likely, all she had done was lead the reavers straight to Renna.

Her original thought was that she had found a secret path to the old defense warrens, which the Council in Caria had kept preserved for millennia. Now Maia knew they had traveled much too far, no doubt threading narrow stone bridges through one after another of the Dragon's Teeth comprising the Jellicoe cluster. Except for Renna, they might be the first humans to tread these halls since the great banishment, after the Age of Kings.

They heard no more clamor at their rear. The last detachment must still be holding out at their barricade. Upon coming to a flat stretch, Maia insisted that the panting sailor let her down. Gingerly, she put weight on her knee, which throbbed, but deigned to let her walk. The sailor expressed willingness should she need help again. "We'll see," Maia said, patting his huge forearm and hobbled ahead.

Soon they came to another set of doors. On pushing through, the group stopped, staring.

A vast chamber stretched ahead, taller than the temple in Lanargh, wide as a warehouse. She marveled that the entire spire-mountain must be hollow. Maia's eyes couldn't take it all in at once, only by stages.

To the right, a series of semicircular bays had been gouged out of the rock, ranging from ten to fifty meters across, each containing jumbled mechanisms or piles of stacked crates. But it was the wall to the left that drew them, in awe. It appeared to consist of a single machine, stretching the entire length of the chamber, consisting of a numbing combination of metals and strange substances embedded in stone, plus crystalline forms like the huge, dimly flickering entity she and Brod had glimpsed, back in the Defense Center. At intervals along its length, there were what appeared to be doors, though not shaped for the passage of people. Maia guessed they were meant for the entry or egress of materials, and speculated as much to the doctor.

The old man nodded. "It must be . . . We all thought it lost. The council had it. Or else it was destroyed."

"What?" Maia asked, drawn by the man's reverential tone. "What was lost?"

"The *Former*," he whispered, as if afraid of disturbing a dream. "Jellicoe Former."

Maia shook her head. "What's a former?"

As they walked, the doctor looked at her, struggling for words. "A former . . . *makes* things! It can make *anything!*"

"You mean like an autofactory? Where they produce radios and—"

He shrugged. "The Council keeps some lesser ones runnin', so as to not to forget how. But legends tell of another, the Great Former, run by the folk of Jellicoe."

Blinking, Maia grasped his implication. "*Men* made this?"

"Not men, as such. The Old Guardians. Men an' women. All banished after the Kings' revolt, even though the Guardians had nothin' to do with macho traitors.

"The Council an' Temple were scared, see. Scared of such power. Used the Kings as an excuse to send ever'one away from Jellicoe an' the other places. We always thought Caria kept the tools, for themselves."

"They did, some of them." And Maia spoke briefly of the Defense Center, elsewhere in this honeycombed isle, maintained by specialized clans.

"Just as we thought," the doctor said moodily. "But seems they never found this!"

Till now, Maia pondered unhappily. It might have been better if they had all died, back in the sanctuary. Over the short term, this windfall would give Baltha and her reavers more power, wealth, and influence than they needed to set up their own dynasties, enough to win high places on the social ladder of Stratos. Once established, though, they would quickly become defenders of the status quo, like any conservative clan. In the long run, it would not matter that criminals first seized this prize. Council and Temple would control it.

This must be what made the weapons Brod and I saw, that were used against the Enemy. Now Caria will be able to manufacture all it wants, to shoot down Renna's ship and any other that dares venture close.

Oh, Lysos, what have I done?

"If only we had time," the doctor went on. "We could make things. Guns to defend it. Radios to call our guild, an' some honorable clans."

As they hurried along, he turned to survey the row of storage bays to the right. "Maybe the Guardians left somethin' behind. You see anything useful?"

Maia sighed. Most of the enclaves contained machines or other items that were completely unrecognizable. Nevertheless, she learned something from what she had just seen and heard. *Lysos and the Founders didn't turn completely away from science. They felt it needful to hold onto this ability. It was a later, frightened generation that clamped down, scared of what trained, independent minds might do.*

It made her angry. The councillors in Caria didn't know about this place—not yet. But surely the savants at the university had books containing the basic wisdom all this technology was built upon. *How?* she wondered. *How could people with access to so much knowledge turn away from it?*

The question underlay so much of her pain at all the death and futile struggle. Like a trail of broken pieces, she had left in her wake first Brod, then Leie and so many others. And ahead . . . Where was Renna? Was she a judas goat, foiling his brilliant escape?

Now the bays on the right revealed frayed remnants of curtains, drooping from teetering rods. There were beds, chairs, items of clothing. "Legend says, after the banishment, a secret lodge stayed at the Former." The doctor sighed. "No one knows what for. In time, those with the secret died out."

On Stratos, continuity was reserved to clans. Commercial companies, governments, even the sailing guilds, had to recruit members from the offspring of hives, who controlled education, religion. These barracks —this sad tale of perseverance—had been doomed to futility. Perhaps the effort lasted many generations . . . still too little time to make any difference.

Maia wondered if Renna had slept in one of these alcoves. Had he combated ennui, and slaked his curiosity, by piecing together the melancholy tale of this lost refuge? Had he found anything to eat? Maia feared discovering his corpse, and thereby knowing that all of this—losing everything—had been for nothing.

They had crossed more than three-quarters of the vast chamber when the cabin boy noticed a sound. "Listen!" he urged. They paused, and Maia detected it. A bass thrumming, which came from somewhere up ahead. "Come on," she said.

The doctor looked longingly at the mammoth machine, the Former. "We might *try* . . ."

There came another sound, a faint bang of metal far behind them, accompanied by shrill, excited exclamations. "Come on," urged the big sailor. They limped forward and made it through a set of doors at the chamber's far end, just in time to look back and see a crowd of women warriors pile through the distant entrance. The reprieve won by the brave rear guard was over.

The fugitives plunged into a new corridor, this time as dark as a mine. Only a single glow ahead eased their way. As Maia and the others approached, they saw that it was a hole in the right-hand side of the passageway. She sighed at the welcome touch of sunlight and fresh air. For a moment, despite the dread of pursuit, the four of them paused to look out upon the lagoon, and each, in his or her own way, expressed astonishment.

Down below, where two sailing ships had lain moored to a narrow dock, only one stood partially intact—the smaller Reckless, whose sails were burned away, its masts singed. Of the Manitou, just the burnt prow remained, still tethered to the smoke-stained pier. The sailor and cabin boy moaned at the sight. But there was more.

The sheltered harbor now thronged with other vessels. One, Maia saw clearly, bore at its pointed bow the figurehead of a sea lion. Row-boats set forth even as they watched, carrying stern-visaged men toward the sanctuary entrance. Perhaps, she hoped, one of them was Brod, having somehow managed to escape and call his guild-mates.

"Look!" The cabin boy pointed much higher. Maia craned her head and was able to make out the tops of the sleek, stony monoliths opposite. She gasped at a vision of power and loveliness. A zep'lin, far bigger and more powerful than the mail couriers she had known, hovered above one scarred, flat-topped peak, tethered to a straining cable.

Your presence has been noted . . . She recalled the placard, within the Defense Center. It might have been wise to take the Council at its word.

Meanwhile, the thrumming sound was growing louder, causing vibrations to be felt through the soles of their feet. "We must go," intoned the big sailor. Despite fascination with the view outside, Maia nodded. "Yeah, let's hurry."

They hastened with the light now on their backs, striving to reach the far end before the desperate reavers, with their long rifles, came into sight behind them. Yet it took some will to approach the growling sounds ahead. There were now two tones, one a grumbling, urgent, bone-shaking basso, and another climbing in pitch and penetration with each passing second.

The cabin boy banged through the far set of doors and light spilled around him. More sunlight, this time pouring down from above. They stared across a vast, cylindrical volume, its stone walls lined with machinery. Overhead, the source of the rumbling grew apparent—an iris made of crimson metal was widening with each passing second.

But what had the four fugitives transfixed was an object filling the center of the room—a vertical multi-twined spiral coil of translucent crystalline material, which started high overhead and plunged downward into a central cavity. The coil throbbed with imprisoned lightning. Inside those windings, they glimpsed a slender, pointed shape, burnished gold, which had already begun descending slowly down the tube. In moments, its tip vanished from sight. "Come on!" Maia called to the others, and rushed, limping, ahead.

They reached the coil but were held back by a force they could not see, which palpably resisted all efforts to approach closer. Their hair stood on end. Maia could now see that the pit plunged vertiginously some indeterminable distance, girdled all the way by spiral coil. Within that tight embrace, the slender javelin-shape continued its descent.

"Wait!" she screamed. "Oh, wait for us!"

It was almost impossible to hear her own voice over the rising keen. Someone yanked her arm. She resisted, then blinked in surprise as a strange, tiny object entered view. A tapered cylinder of metal, no larger than her smallest toe, had arrived from her left, pushing forward into the unyielding field, decelerating rapidly. It came to rest, then reversed course, accelerating swiftly the way it came, to be expelled with a report of riven air.

The same thing happened again. This time, Maia's brief glance recognized a *bullet*, before it, too, was ejected backward toward its source. She stopped fighting the tug on her arm. Accompanied by a roar and swarming vertigo, the four of them ran tangentially to the coils and the surrounding, impenetrable field. To her left, Maia glimpsed kneeling markswomen, firing at them, while others, armed with trepps and knives, approached cautiously, their flushed faces alive with conflicting emotions —wrath versus frightened astonishment.

"Uh!" the big sailor cried, and foundered, clutching his thigh. Maia and the cabin boy took his arms and helped him stumble toward another set of doors at the far end of the chamber. While more bullets pinged around them, they could feel awesome power building nearby, intensifying toward some titanic climax.

The doors were still thirty meters distant when the big sailor collapsed again. "Gowon!" he cried hoarsely. "Get 'er outta here!" he urged the other males. But already bullets were striking the metal doors. Maia pointed. "Over there!"

They towed the wounded man toward what appeared to be a junk pile. A midden of boxes, crates, broken and discarded machines. Detritus of whatever project had created this incredible, mysterious edifice. As they were about to dive behind the nearest hulking mound of debris,

Maia cried out. A searing stroke of pain had brushed the back of her right calf, like a hot poker.

The doctor dragged her the rest of the way. A bullet had grazed her skin, plowing a long red trail. "Never mind that!" she urged the physician. "Take care of him!" The sailor was clearly much worse off.

Ignoring her own bleeding, Maia cast around for anything to use as a weapon. There were bits of metal, but none in any useful shape. For lack of an alternative, she drew from her jacket pocket the small paring knife she had found aboard the Manitou. The cabin boy helped her rise, and they both crouched behind the pile of debris. They heard shouts. Approaching footsteps.

Suddenly, the keening noise halted. The growling had stopped moments before, as the roof-iris finished opening. The abrupt silence felt pregnant with expectation. Then, as if Maia had known it all along, there came a combination of sound and sight and every other sensation that felt like the clarion of Judgment Day. The world shook, while powers akin to, but violently more potent than she had experienced near the coil, tried to fill all space. That included space she had formerly occupied alone, forcing each of her molecules to fight for right of tenancy. Air needed for breath blew out as a presence passed nearby at terrible speed, streaking toward the sky.

From her back, Maia blearily watched as a sleek object tore through the heavens, leaving a blaze of riven, flaming air in its wake.

A fire arrow . . . she thought, blankly. Then, with but a little more coherence, she cast after it a silent call.

Renna!

Air returned, accompanied by a sound like thunder clapping. The debris mound shook, and then collapsed, tumbling rough, heavy shards over her battered legs. Yet she was left able to continue staring upward. Undistracted by distant pain, Maia had a clear view of the streaking, diminishing sparkle in the sky, wishing with all her heart that she was part of it . . . that he had waited only a little while longer, and taken her with him.

But he did it! she thought, switching over to exultation. *They won't have him. He's out of their reach now. Gone back to—*

Her rejoicing cut short. Overhead, almost at the limits of vision, the sparkling pinpoint abruptly veered left, brightened, and exploded in radiance, splitting apart amid an orgy of chaos, scattering fiery, ionic embers across the dark blue firmament of the stratosphere.

Part Four

Is ambition poison? Is Phylum society's headlong rush to power and accomplishment synonymous with damnation?

Ancient cultures warned their people against hubris, that innate drive within human beings to seek God's own puissance, whatever the cost. Wisely, early tribal folk restrained such fervid quests, save via spirit and art, adventure and song. They did not endlessly bend and bully Nature to their whim.

True, those ancestors lived just above the animals, in primeval forests of Old Earth. Life was hard, especially for women, yet they reaped rewards—harmony, stability, secure knowledge of who you were, where you fit in the world's design. Those treasures were lost when we embarked on "progress."

Is there an inverse relation between knowledge and wisdom? At times it seems the more we know, the less we understand.

I am not the first to note this quandary. One scholar recently wrote, "Lysos and her followers chase the siren call of pastoralism, like countless romantics before them, idealizing a past Golden Age that never was, pursuing a serenity possible only in the imagination."

His point is well-taken. Yet, should we not try?

The paradox does not escape me—that we mean to use advanced technical tools to shape conditions for a stable world . . . one which, from then onward, should little need those tools again.

So we return to the question at hand. Are human beings truly cursed to discontent? Caught between conflicting yearnings, we strive to become gods even as we long to remain nature's beloved children.

Let the former pursuit be the chaotic doom of frantic, driven Phylum Civitas. We who depart on this quest have chosen a warmer, less adversarial relationship with the Cosmos.

—*from* My Life, *by Lysos*

26

L oss of consciousness was not the result of her injuries, or even the gassy, pungent odor of anesthesia. What made her let go this time was a morale sapped beyond exhaustion. Distant sensations told her that the world went on. There were noises—anxious shouts and booming echoes of gunfire. When these ceased, they were followed by loud cries of both triumph and despair. Sounds intruded, swarming over her, prying at windows and doors, but none succeeded in making her take notice.

Footsteps clattered. Hands touched her body, lifting objects away so that a hurt of ministration replaced that of crushing injury. Maia remained indifferent. Voices rustled around her, tense and argumentative. She could tell, without caring, that more than two factions engaged in fierce debate, each too weak or uncertain to impose its will, none of them trusting enough to let others act alone.

There was no tenor of vindictiveness in the manner she was lifted and carried away from the bright, ozone-drenched chamber within a hollow mountain-fang. Rocked on a stretcher, moaning at each jostling shock to her stretched-thin system, she knew in abstract that her bearers meant her well. They were being gentle. That ought to signify something.

She only wished they would go away and let her die.

Death did not come. Instead, she was handled, prodded, drugged, cut, and sewn. In time, it was the simplest of sensations that brought back a partial will to live.

. . .

Flapjacks.

A redolence of fresh pancakes filled her nostrils. Injury and anomie weren't enough to hold back the flood that faint aroma unleashed within her mouth. Maia opened her eyes.

The room was white. An ivory-colored ceiling met finely carved white moldings, which joined to walls the color of pale snow. Through a muzzy languor left over from chemical soporifics, Maia had difficulty fixing clearly on the plain, smooth surfaces. Without conscious choice, her mind begin toying with one blank expanse—imagining a laying thereon of grainy, abstract, rhythmic patterns. Maia groaned and closed her eyes.

She could not shut her nose. Alluring smells pursued her. So did growls from her stomach. And the sound of speech.

"Well now, ready to join the livin' at last?"

Maia turned her head to the left, and cracked an eyelid. A petite, dark-haired figure swam into focus, wearing a wry grin. "Now didn't I say to stop gettin' conked, varling? At least this time you weren't drowned."

After several tries, Maia found her voice. "Should've . . . known . . . *you'd* make it."

Naroin nodded. "Mm. That's me. Born survivor. You, too, lass. Though you love provin' it the hard way."

An involuntary sigh escaped Maia. The bosun-policewoman's presence wrested feelings that hurt, despite her body's drugged immobility. "I guess you . . . got through to your boss."

Naroin shook her head. "When we got picked up, I decided to take some initiative. Called in favors, swung deals. Too bad we couldn't arrive sooner, though."

Maia's thoughts refused to center clearly. "Yeah. Too bad."

Naroin poured a glass of water and helped Maia lift her head to drink. "In case you're wonderin', the docs say you'll be all right. Had to cut an' mend a bit. You've got an agone leech tapped into your skull, so don't thrash or bump it, now that you're awake."

". . . leech . . . ?" With leaden inertia, Maia's arm obeyed her wish to rise and bend. Fingers traced a boxy object above her forehead, smaller than her thumb. "I wouldn't touch it if I was—" Naroin started to advise, as Maia gave the box a spastic tap. For an instant, all that seemed muddy and washed out snapped into clarity and color. Along with vividness came a slamming force of pain. Maia's hand recoiled, hurling back to the coverlet.

"Did I warn ya? Hmp. Never seen a first-timer who didn't try that, once. Guess I must've, about your age."

The dulling murkiness returned, this time welcome, spreading from Maia's scalp across her body like a liquid balm. She had seen injured women with leeches before, though most hid them in their hair. *I must be hurt much worse than I feel,* she realized, no longer resenting the numbness. That fleeting break in function had briefly revealed another blocked sensation, more fearsome than physical pain. For an instant, she had been overwhelmed by waves of all-consuming grief.

"Makes ya feel like a zombie, eh?" Naroin commented. "They'll crank it down as you improve. Should already be gettin' back some of your senses."

Maia inhaled deeply. "I . . . can smell . . ."

Naroin grinned. "Ah, breakfast. Got an appetite?"

It felt odd. Her insistent stomach seemed unaware of the blunt nausea pervading the rest of her body. "Yes. I—"

"That's a good sign. They serve quite a table on the Gentilleschi. Hang on, I'll see to it."

The policewoman stood up and started to go, her movements too quick and blurry for Maia to follow clearly. Maia tracked them in a series of receding glimpses as her eyes flickered shut for longer and longer intervals. She fought to hold the lids apart as Naroin stopped, turned back, and spoke once more, her voice fading in and out.

"Oh . . . almost forgot. There's a note from . . . young boyfriend an' sister over . . . table by your bed. Thought . . . ike t'know they made it all right."

The words carried meaning. Maia felt sure of it as they crested over her, soaked in through her ears and pores, and found resonance within. Somewhere, a crushing burden of worry lapsed into gladness. That much emotion was too exhausting, however. Sleep swarmed in to claim her, so that Naroin's final words barely registered.

"Not a lot of others did, I'm afraid."

Maia's eyes stayed closed and the world remained dark for a long, quiet, unmeasured time.

She next awoke to find a middle-aged woman leaning over her, gently touching the top of her head. There were faint clicking sounds, and Maia's vision seemed to clear a bit. Swells of rising sensation caused her to tense. "That's not too bad, is it?" the woman asked. From her manner she must be a physician.

"I . . . guess not."

"Good. We'll leave it there awhile. Now let's look over our handiwork."

The doctor briskly pulled back Maia's gown, revealing an expanse of purpled skin that they both regarded with dispassionate interest. Livid stitches showed where repairs had been made, including a semicircle near her left knee. The doctor clucked earnestly, making soothing, patronizing, and ultimately uninformative noises, then departed.

When the door slid open, Maia glimpsed a tall woman of soldierly bearing standing watch in the uniform of some mainland militia. Beyond lay the jet, fluted panels of solar collectors. Maia heard the soft rush of water along a laminar-smooth hull. The vessel's rock-steady passage spoke partly of the weather, which was brilliantly fair, and also of technology. This was a craft normally devoted to transporting personages.

But the personage it was sent for did the unexpected. He made his own transportation arrangements, and nearly got away.

That wound was still too raw, too gaping to bear. What hurt most about the image seared in her mind was how *beautiful* the explosion had been. A wondrous convulsion of sparks and dazzling spirals, which scattered glowing shards across a sky so chaste and blue. It had no *right* being so beautiful! The memory triggered a welling of tears, which brimmed her lower eyelids, spilling salty, silent streamlets down her cheeks.

Her last waking episode felt no more real than an unraveling dream. Had she really met Naroin? She recalled the ex-bosun saying something about a letter. Turning to look at the side table, Maia saw a neatly folded piece of heavy paper, sealed with wax. By heavy, conscious effort, she reached over to take it in one clumsy hand, slumping back amid receding waves of pain. Lifting the letter, she recognized her own name scrawled across the front.

From Brod and Leie, Maia recalled. She was able to feel gladness, now . . . a colorless, abstract variety. Gladness that two people still lived whom she loved. It helped ease the sense of desolation and forfeiture lodged in her heart, ready to emerge as soon as the doctor turned down the agone leech some more.

Her vision was still too blurry for reading, so she lay quietly, stroking the paper until a knock came at the door. It slid open, and Naroin leaned into the room. "Ah, back with us. You missed breakfast. Ready to try again?"

She was gone again without waiting for Maia's answer. *So, I didn't imagine it,* Maia thought, starting to wonder about the implications. Why was Naroin here? Where *was* here? And why was Naroin helping look after her? The policewoman surely had more important things to do than play nursemaid to one unimportant summerling.

Unless it has to do with all the laws I've broken . . . the places I've been that I wasn't supposed to. . . . Things I've seen that the Council doesn't want widely known.

Another knock on the door. This time a young woman entered, bearing a covered tray. Maia wiped her eyes, then opened them wide, staring in surprise.

"Where do you want this, ma'am?" the girl asked. Her voice was softer, a little higher, but otherwise almost identical to the last one Maia had heard. The face was a younger version of the last one Maia had seen. Realization came in a rush.

"Clones . . ." Maia murmured. "A police clan?"

The youngster wasn't even Maia's age. A winterling fiver, then. Yet there was something in her smile. A hint of Naroin's relaxed self-confidence. She put the tray on the side of the bed, and occupied herself propping pillows, helping Maia to sit up.

"Detectives actually. Freelance. Our clan stays small on purpose. We specialize in solitary field work. Normally, you never see two of us together, outside the hold, but I was sent out when we got Naroin's urgent-blip."

It was hard to credit. The fiver spoke with a crisp, upper-clan accent. She had none of Naroin's scars. Yet, in her eyes danced the same vigorous zest, the same eagerness for challenge.

"I guess you don't think me a threat," Maia suggested, "to break your cover."

"No, ma'am. I've been instructed to be open with you."

Sure. What harm can I do? Maia trusted Naroin to some extent, enough to pull strings so that Maia's next cage would be more pleasant than any she had occupied before. That didn't mean letting her run around Stratos, blabbing what she'd seen.

The fiver placed the table-tray securely over Maia's lap and lifted the cover. There were no pancakes, but a predictable, medically appropriate bowl of thin porridge. Still, it smelled so heady Maia felt faint. Rivulets of orange juice ran over her fingers as she clutched the tumbler in both shaking hands. The reddish liquid tasted like squeezed, refined heaven.

"I'll wait outside," said the young winterling. "Call, if you need anything."

Maia only grunted. Concentrating to control her trembling grip, she pushed a spoonful of porridge into her mouth. While her body quivered with simple, beast-level pleasures of taste and satiation, a small part of her remained offset, pondering. *I wonder what their family name is. I should've known. Naroin was always too damn competent to be another unnik var.*

Sooner or later, Maia knew she must start cataloging her ream of losses, against her slim résumé of assets. Later sounded better. One thing at a time—that was how she planned living from now on. Maia had no intention of giving up, but neither was she ready yet for linear thinking.

Despite her earlier famishment, she couldn't more than half finish her meal. Feeling suddenly fatigued, Maia let Naroin's younger version carry off the tray. Not once did she look directly at the neatly folded letter, but she kept in physical contact with it, as a drowning woman might hold onto a plank from a shattered ship.

When she next awoke, it was dark outside. Shreds of a dream were evaporating, like shy ghosts fleeing the pale electric lamp by her bedside. Her body was prickly with goose bumps and beads of sweat. Her thoughts still seemed dispersed, one moment focused and coherent, and the next hurtling somewhere else, like windblown leaves.

That made her recall Old Bennett and his rake, in the courtyard of Lamatia Hold. *What would he think of where I've been . . . what I've seen?* Probably, the coot no longer lived. Which might be best, given what Maia had done—inadvertently delivering into the archreactionary hands of Church and Council the last remnants of that secret hope the old man had kept next to his heart. A dream gone blurry from being passed down generations in secret lodges—as if men could ever know the constancy of clones.

Renna, Bennett, Leie, Brod, the rads, the men of the Manitou . . . there was room enough for all on the honor roll of those she had let down.

Stop it, Maia told herself numbly. *The deck was stacked long ago. Don't blame yourself for things you couldn't prevent.*

But she might as well tell the winds and tides to stop, as shuck off that sense of fault, which seemed less refutable for being so vague.

Maia saw that she still tightly clutched the letter. Red bits of crumpled wax lay scattered across the coverlet. She tried smoothing the paper with her hands. Lifting it to the light, she peered to make out, amid wrinkles, a fine, flowing hand.

Dear Maia,

Wish I could be with you, but they say we're needed here. I've got to play tour guide, showing all sorts of vips around the defense center. (They sure act mad, so I guess it was secret from a lot of high mothers in Caria, not just the public!) Leie has a job, too—

Naroin had said they both lived, but this confirmation was stronger. Maia abruptly sobbed, her vision clouding as emotion flooded back from being dammed away.

—Leie has a job, too, demonstrating that incredible simulation wall you found. Neither of us can match you for figuring this stuff out, but we're helping each other, and look forward to talking to you, soon as you're well.

I guess by now they've filled you in, and I'm kind of rushed getting this off before the Gentilleschi takes you away. So here's what happened from my point of view.

When you didn't return by an hour before dawn, I pulled in the cable, as you made me promise to do. I hated doing it, but then something changed my mind. Just after sunrise, fighting broke out, down on the ships. I later learned it was the rads, who you'd helped escape—

Maia blinked. I what? All she had done was make a promise to Thalla, one she never got a chance to keep. Unless the big var had managed to use the *scissors*, somehow. As a lockpick, perhaps? To slip their chains, then trick the guards? Or perhaps Baltha and Togay had already pulled the sentinels away, when battle seemed imminent with the men.

The revolt went well, at first. But then reavers rushed out before the rads could set sail. There was shooting. Some rads escaped in a little boat after setting fire to both ships.

It didn't seem a good time to lower myself down. I paced like crazy, worrying about you, till I arrived at the east end of the tooth, looking to sea. That's when I saw the flotilla coming up from Halsey. Not just the creaky old Audacious, which had been on duty when I was last there, but the Walrus and the Sea Lion, too! I guess the guild finally decided it had enough of its former clients, and was coming to settle accounts.

I ran to the elevator, went downstairs to the bathroom and broke a mirror. Grabbed a piece and hurried back up. The sun in the east made it easy to signal the ships. To give them some idea what to expect. There was shooting when they tried to enter the lagoon, then Sea Lion broke through just about the time everyone else in the world arrived!

One pair of fancy ships swung around the south side of Jellicoe, waving temple banners. And up north, I saw several fast cruisers appear. Later learned these were from the Ursulaborg Commercial Police Department! A little out of jurisdiction, but who cares? Naroin had called 'em out as militia, it seems. Honest, local cops with no Council connections.

Just as this crowd was jostling into the lagoon, and smoke started pouring out of the old sanctuary, that's when a big, smuggy zep'lin showed! I didn't like the looks of the clones leaning out of the gondola. (They were mad as hell!) So I turned on the winch and lowered myself. Made it down in time to help my guildfolk settle with the temple nuns and Naroin's posse that we were all on the same side.

It took a while overcoming the reavers' rear guard—they're hellion fighters—then we ran after them while they chased after you . . .

Maia's eyes blurred. Although Brod's simple account was dramatic, she had only limited stamina and her mind felt full to bursting. Not rushing matters, she waited for vision to clear before resuming.

Things were a mess, especially outside the auditorium, where your Manitou people had fought the reavers. Fortunately, there were docs along, to care for the wounded.

That wall of lights stopped us cold for a moment, and I got scared when I saw Leie, groaning on the floor, and thought it was you. She's fine, by the way, but I already said that. Just woozy from a bump on the head. Leie wanted to chase after the ones chasing you. But I was told to help her out to where the air was better, while Naroin's pros led the pursuit from there.

We limped outside just in time to get knocked to our knees by what seemed like thunder. We looked up and saw the space launcher fire its pod into the sky . . . and what happened next.

I'm sorry Maia. I know it must hurt awful, like when they brought your poor body out, and I thought you were dying. To me, that felt like you must have, when you saw your alien friend blow up.

Again, Maia's heart yawned open. This time however, she was able to smile poignantly. *Good old Brod*, she thought. It was the most romantic thing anyone had ever said to her.

Leie and I waited outside while the nun-doctors operated on you. (That's the one group I still can't figure out where they came from, or why. Did you call them?) Meanwhile, there were so many questions. So many people insisting on hearing what everyone else

knew, even though it meant repeating everything over and over. The
story's still coming out, bit by bit, while more boats and zeps keep
arriving all the time.

Oh, hell. I'm being called again, so this'll have to be it for
now. I'll send more, later. Get better soon, Maia. We need you, as
usual, to figure out what we oughta do!

With winter warmth, your friend and shipmate—Brod.

There was an afterword in another hand—a left-handed scrawl Maia
instantly recognized.

Hey, Sis. You know me. Lousy at writin'. Just remember, we're a
team. I'll catch up, wherever they take you. Count on it. Love, L.

Maia reread the last few paragraphs, then folded the letter and slipped it
under her pillow. She rolled over, away from the soft light, and fell
asleep. This time, her dreams, while painful, seemed less desolate and
alone.

When they wheeled her on deck the next day, to get some sun, Maia
discovered she wasn't the only recuperating patient aboard. Half a dozen
other bandaged women lay in various stages of repair, under the gaze of
a pair of militia guards. Naroin's young clone—whose name was Hullin
—told her that others rested below, too ill to be moved. The injured men
were being carried separately, of course, aboard the Sea Lion, which
could be glimpsed following a parallel track, so sleek and powerful it
almost kept pace with this white-winged racer. Hullin couldn't give Maia
any information about which of the Manitou crew survived the fight at
Jellicoe Sanctuary, though she promised to inquire. There had not been
many, she knew. The doctors, inexperienced at treating gunshot wounds,
had lost several on the operating table.

That news left Maia staring across the blue water, dejected, until a
presence wheeled up alongside. "Hello, virgie. . . . S'good to see you."

The voice was a pale shadow of its former mellow, persuasive croon.
The rad leader's nearly-black skin now seemed bleached, almost pale
from illness and anemia.

"That's not my name," Maia told Kiel. "The other thing's none of
your business. Never was."

Kiel nodded, accepting the rebuke. "Hello, then . . . Maia."

"Hello." Pausing, Maia regretted her harsh response. "I'm glad to
see you made it."

"Mm. Same to you. They say survival is Nature's only form of flattery. I guess that's true, even for prisoners like us."

Maia was in no mood for wry philosophy, and made her feelings known through silence. With a heavy sigh, Kiel rolled a few feet away, leaving Maia to watch the world-ocean glide by in peace. There were questions Maia knew she should be asking. Perhaps she would, eventually. But right now, her mind remained stiff, like her body, too inflexible for rapid changes of inertia.

A little before lunch, ennui began to rob even petulance of its attraction. Maia reread the quick-scrawled letter from Brod and Leie a few more times, allowing herself to begin wondering about what lay concealed between the phrases. There were tensions and alliances, both stated and implied. Local cops and priestesses? Acting at odds from their official bosses, in Caria? Had their union with the Pinnipeds extended only to wiping out a band of pirates? Or would it go farther?

What of the special, secretive defense clans who had also arrived at Jellicoe to secure their hidden base?—which was no longer hidden, after all. Then there were Kiel's radical supporters, on the mainland. And the Perkinites, of course. All had their own agendas. All felt passionately endangered by possible change in the order of life on Stratos.

It might have been a situation fraught with even more violent peril, perhaps risk of open war, had the object of their contention not evaporated in midair before everyone's eyes. With the centerpiece of struggle removed, the frantic mood of excess may have eased. At least the killing had stopped, for now.

It was much too complicated to focus her mind on, for long. She was glad when an attendant came to wheel her back to her room, where she ate, then took a long nap. Later, when Naroin knocked and entered, Maia felt marginally better, her mind a little farther along the path toward rational thinking.

The former bosun carried a stack of thin, leather-bound volumes. "These were sent over before we sailed, for when you felt better. Gifts from the Pinniped commodore."

Maia looked at Naroin. The detective's accent had softened quite a bit. Not that it was posh now, by a long shot. But it had lost much of its rough, nautical edge. The books lay on the side of the bed. Maia stroked the spine of one, drew it closer, and opened the fine linen pages.

Life. She recognized the subject instantly and sighed. *Who needs it?*

Yet, the paper felt rich to the touch. It even *smelled* voluptuous. Brief glimpses of the illustrations, featuring countless arrays of tiny squares and dots, seemed to tease a corner of her mind in the same way that a bright, sharp light might tickle the beginnings of a sneeze.

"I always figured that for some men it was, well, addicting in a way, like a drug. Is that how it is with you?" Naroin seemed genuinely, respectfully curious.

Maia pushed the book away. After several seconds she nodded.

"It's beautiful." Her throat was too thick to say more.

"Hm. With all the time I've spent around sailors, you'd think I'd see it, too." Naroin shook her head. "Can't say as I do. I like men. Get along with 'em fine. But I guess some things go beyond like or dislike."

"I guess."

There was a moment's silence, then Naroin moved closer to sit on the edge of the bed.

"That's why I was on the ol' *Wotan,* when you first came aboard, in Port Sanger. My experience as a sea hand gave me cover for my assignment. The collier would make many stops along the coast. Let me look around all the right places for clues."

"To find a missing alien?"

"Lysos, no!" Naroin laughed. "Oh, he was already kidnapped by then, but my clan wasn't brought in. Our mothers knew somethin' fishy had happened, all right. But a field op like me sticks to her assignment . . . at least till given clear reason to switch tracks."

"The blue powder, then," Maia said, remembering Naroin's interest in events at Lanargh.

"That's it. We knew a group had started pushin' the stuff again, along the frontier coast. Happens every two or three generations. We often pick up a few coinsticks helpin' track it down."

There it was again, the change in perspective separating vars from clones. What a summerling had seen as urgent *must* appear less pressing in the patient view of Stratoin hives. "The powder's been around a long time, then. Let me guess. Each appearance is a bit less disrupting than the last time."

"Right." Naroin nodded. "After all, winter sparkings don't have any *genetic* effect. It's only during summers that new variants come about, when a man's efforts profit him in true offspring. Males who react less to the drug are just a little better at stayin' calm and passin' on that trait. Each outbreak gets a smidgen milder, easier to put down."

"Then why is the powder illegal?"

"You saw for yourself. It causes accidents, violence during quiet time. It gives rich clans unfair advantages over poor 'uns. But there's more. The powder was invented for a purpose."

Maia blinked once, twice, then realized. "Sometimes . . . it may be useful to have men . . ."

"Hot as fire, even in the dead o' frost season. You get it."

"The Enemy. We used this stuff during the Defense."

"That's my guess. Lysos respected Momma Nature. If you want to

push a trait into the background, fine, but that's not the same as throwin'
it away. Thriftier to put it on a shelf, where it might come in handy,
someday."

Maia's thoughts had already plunged ahead. *The Council rulers
must have flooded Stratos with the stuff, during the battle to fight off the
Enemy foeship.*

Imagine every male a warrior. Almost overnight, it would have multiplied the colony's strength, complementing female skill and planning
with a wrath like none other in the universe.

Only, what happened after victory?

The good men—those who might have been trustworthy on any Phylum world, even before Lysos—would have voluntarily given up the powder. Or at least kept their heads until it ran out. *But men come in all
types. It's not hard to picture a plague like the Kings' Revolt erupting
during the chaos after a war. Especially with tons of Tizbe's drug floating
around.*

Was that enough cause to betray the Guardians of Jellicoe?

Maia knew that the Council didn't do things without reasons.

"I guess your assignment changed, by the time we met again," she
prompted Naroin.

The petite brunette shrugged. "I heard some odd things. Known
mercenaries were gettin' offers, down the coast. Radical agents were
reported drifting into parts around Grange Head. Wasn't hard to figure
where I might get a billet close to things going on."

Maia frowned. "You didn't suspect Baltha . . ."

"Her treason, going over to the reavers? No! I knew there was tension, of course. Lookin' back, maybe I should have surmised. . . ."
Naroin stopped, shook her head. "Take it from an experienced hand,
child. It's no good blamin' yourself for what you couldn't prevent. Not so
long as you tried."

Maia's lips pressed together. That was exactly what she had been
telling herself. From the look in Naroin's eyes, it didn't get much more
believable as you got older.

That evening she learned who had lived, and who had died.

Thalla, Captain Poulandres, Baltha, Kau, most of the rads, most of
the reavers, nearly all of the Manitou crew, including the young navigator who had helped Maia and her twin find their way through the
dazzling complexity of the world-wall. The tally was appalling. Even
hard-crusted Naroin, who had seen many formal and informal battles,
could scarcely believe the prodigious manufacturing of bodies that had
taken place at and near Jellicoe. *Is this what war is like?* Maia thought.

For the first time she felt she understood, not just in abstract, but in her gut, what had driven the Founders to such drastic choices. Nevertheless, she felt determined not to let Perkinite propagandists seize on this episode. *If I keep any freedom of action at all, I'm going to make sure it's known. Poulandres and his men were forced to fight. This was more than a simple case of males going berserk.*

What was it, then? There would surely be those who pictured *Renna* as the culprit, a blight carrier whose mere presence, and threat to bring more of his kind, inflamed the worst in several branches of Stratoin society. To Maia, that seemed cruelly like blaming the victim. Yet, the point could be made.

After dinner, while Hullin wheeled her along the promenade deck, Maia encountered Kiel a second time. On this occasion, she saw the other woman more clearly, not through a curtain of resentment over things that were already ancient history. The rad agent had lost everything, her closest friends, her freedom, the best hope for her cause. Maia was gentler with her former cottage-mate. Commiserating, she reached out to console and forgive. In gratitude, the forceful, indomitable Kiel broke down and wept.

Later, as dusk fell, the western horizon began to glitter. Maia counted five, six . . . and finally ten slowly turning beacons whose rhythmic flashes cut across the miles of ocean with reassuring constancy. From maps studied in her youth, she recognized the tempos and colors and knew their names—Conway, Ulam, Turing, Gardner . . . famed lighthouse sanctuaries of the Méchant Coast. And, beyond far Rucker Beacon, a vast dusting of soft, glimmering diamonds covering a harbor and surrounding hills. The night spectacle of great Ursulaborg.

She was taken to a temple. Not the grand, marble-lined monument dominating the city from its northern bluffs, but a modest, one-story retreat that rambled over a fenced hectare of neatly coppiced woods, several kilometers upriver from the heart of the busy metropolis. The semirural ambience was an artifact, Maia could tell, carefully nurtured by the small but prosperous clanholds that shared the neighborhood. Clear streams flowed past gardens and mulch piles, windmills and light industrial workshops. It was a place where generations of children, and their daughters' daughters, might play, grow up, and tend family business at an unhurried pace, confident of a future in which change would, at most, arrive slowly.

The walled temple grounds were unprepossessing. The chapel bore proper symbols for venerating Stratos Mother and the Founders in the standard way, yet Maia suspected all wasn't orthodox. Vigilant guards, arrayed in leather, patrolled the palisade. Within, the expected air of cultivated serenity was overlaid by a veneer of static tension.

Except for Naroin and her younger sibling, none of the women looked alike.

After passing the chapel, the lugars bearing Maia's palanquin approached an unassuming wooden house, detached from the main compound, surrounded by a covered plank veranda. The doctor who had treated Maia aboard the Gentilleschi conferred with two women, one tall and severe-looking, dressed in priestly habits, the other rotund, wearing archdeaconess robes. Naroin, who had walked alongside during the brief journey from the riverside quay, took a quick lope around the house, satisfying herself of its security, while Hullin briskly looked inside. Upon reuniting near the porch, the pair exchanged efficient nods.

With the help of a nurse-nun, Maia stepped down, bearing stoically the profound pain spreading from her knee and side. They assisted her up a short ramp into the house, pausing at the entrance when the tall, elderly priestess bent to meet Maia's eye.

"You will be at peace here, child. Until you choose to leave, this will be your home."

The round woman wearing deacon's robes blew a sigh, as if she did not approve of promises that might prove hard to keep. Despite pain and fatigue, Maia felt she had learned more than they intended. "Thank you," she said hoarsely, and let the nurses guide her down a veranda of polished wood into a room featuring sliding doors made of paper-thin wood panels, overlooking a garden and a small pond. The mat bed featured sheets that looked whiter than a cloud. Maia never remembered being helped to slip between them. The sounds of plinking water, and wind rustling boughs, lulled her to sleep.

She awoke to find, next to her bed, the slim volumes given her by the Pinnipeds, plus a small box and a folded slip of paper. Maia opened the note.

I'll be gone a while, varling, it read. *I'm leaving Hullin to keep an eye open. These folk are all right, tho maybe a bit nutty. See you soon. Naroin.*

The detective's departure came as no surprise. Maia had wondered why Naroin stuck around this long. Surely she had work to do?

Maia opened the box. Inside a tissue wrapping she found a case made of aromatic leather, attached to a soft strap. She opened it and found therein a gleaming instrument of brass and gleaming glass. The sextant was beautiful, perfect, and so well-made she found it impossible to tell how old it was, save by the fact that it possessed no readout window, no obvious way to access the Old Net. Still, it was on sight far more valuable than the one she had left behind, at Jellicoe. Maia unfolded the sighting arms and ran her hands over the apparatus. Still, she hoped Leie would manage to recover the old one. Cranky and half-broken as it was, she felt it was hers.

She pulled the blanket over her head and lay in a ball, wishing her sister were here. Wishing for Brod. Wishing her mind were not full of visions of smoke spirals and glittering sparks, spreading sooty ashes amid stratospheric clouds.

A week passed slowly. The physician dropped by every morning to examine Maia, gradually notching downward the anesthetic effects of the agone leech, and insisting that the patient take gentle walks around the temple grounds. In the afternoons, after lunch and a nap, Maia was carried by lugar-litter for a promenade through the suburban village and up to a city park overlooking the heart of Ursulaborg. Accompanying her went several tough-looking nuns, each flourishing an iron-shod "walking stick" with a dragon-headed grip. Maia wondered why the precautions. Surely nobody was interested in her, now that Renna was gone. Then she noticed her attendants glancing backward, keeping a wary eye on a four-some of identical, formidable-looking women trailing ten meters behind, dressed as civilians but walking with the calm precision of soldiers. It marred the sense of normality that otherwise flowed over her while passing through bustling market streets.

For the first time since she and Leie had explored Lanargh, Maia felt immersed back in ordinary Stratoin life. Trade and traffic and conversation flowed in all directions. Countless unfamiliar faces came in trios, quintets, or even mixed-age octets. No doubt it would have seemed terribly exotic, had two innocent twins from the far northeast come ashore here on their first voyage from home. Now, myriad subtle differences from Port Sanger only seemed trivial and irrelevant. What she noticed were *similarities*, witnessed with new eyes.

Within a brick-lined workshop, open to the street, a family of artisans could be seen making a delicately specialized assortment of dinner ware. An elderly matriarch supervised ledger books, haggling over a wagonload of clay delivered by three identical teamsters. Meanwhile behind her, middle-aged clonelings labored at firing kilns, and agile youths learned the art of applying their long fingers to spinning wet mud on belt-driven wheels, molding shapeless lumps into the sturdy, fine shapes for which their clan was, no doubt, locally well-known.

Maia had only to shift her mental lens a little to imagine another scene. The walls withdrew, receding in the distance. Simple handmade benches and pottery wheels were replaced by the clean lines of pre-molded machinery, accurately tuned to squeeze clay into computer-drawn templates, which then passed under a glazing spray, then heat lamps, to emerge in great stacks, perfect, untouched by human hands.

The joy of craft. The quiet, serene assumption that each worker in a clan had a place—one that their daughters might also call theirs. All that would be lost.

Then, as her litter bearers threaded the market throng, Maia saw the stall where the potter clan sold their wares. She glimpsed prices . . . for a single dish, more than a var laborer earned in four days. So much that a modest clan would patch a chipped plate many times before thinking of buying a replacement. Maia knew. Even in wealthy Lamatia Hold, summer kids seldom dined off intact crockery.

Now magnify that by a thousand products and services, any of which might be enhanced, multiplied, made immeasurably cheaper and more widely available with applied technology. *How much would be gained?*

Moreover, she wondered, *What if one of those clone daughters someday wanted to do something different, for a change?*

She spied a group of boys running raucous circles around the patient lugars, then onward toward the park. They were the only males she had seen, even now, in midwinter. All others would be nearer the water, though no one barred their way this time of year. Maia found it odd, after so long in the company of men, not to have any around. Nor were vars like her common, either. Except within the temple grounds, they, too, were a tiny minority.

On arrival at the park, Maia gingerly got off the litter and walked a short distance to a walled ledge overlooking Ursulaborg. Here was one of the world's great cities, which she and Leie had dreamed of visiting, someday. Certainly it far exceeded anything she had seen, yet now it looked parochial. She knew the place would fit into the vest pocket of any metropolis, on almost any Phylum world . . . save only those others which had also chosen pastoralism over the frantic genius of *Homo technologicus.*

Renna had earnestly respected the accomplishments of Lysos and the Founders, while clearly believing they were wrong.

What do I believe? Maia wondered. *There are tradeoffs.* That much, she knew. *But are there any solutions?*

It was still terribly hard, thinking of Renna. Within a corner of her mind, a persistent little voice kept refusing to let go. *The dead have come back before,* it insisted, bringing up the miraculous return of Leie. Others had thought Maia herself finished, only to find out reports of her demise were premature.

Hope was a desperate, painful little ember . . . and in this case absurd. Hundreds had witnessed the Visitor's vaporization.

Let go. She told herself to be glad simply to have been his friend for a while. Perhaps, someday, there might come a chance to honor him, by shining a light here or there.

All else was fantasy. All else was dust.

As she gradually improved, Maia started getting visitors.

First came a covey of erect, gracile clones with wide-set eyes and narrow noses, dressed in fine fabrics, modestly dyed. The priestess introduced them as mother-elders of Starkland Clan, from nearby Joannaborg, a name that sounded only vaguely familiar until the women sat down opposite Maia, and began speaking of Brod. Instantly, she recognized the family resemblance. His nose, his wide-open, honest eyes.

Her friend had not been exaggerating. The clan of librarians did, indeed, keep caring about its sons, and even, apparently, its summer daughters, after they left home. The elders had learned of Brod's misadventures, and wanted Maia's reassurance, firsthand. She was moved by their gentleness, their earnest expressions of concern. Midway through an abbreviated account of her travels with their son, she showed them the letter proving he was all right.

"Poor grammar," one of them clucked. "And look at that penmanship."

Another, a little older, chided. "Lizbeth! You heard the young lady speak of what the poor boy's been through." She turned to Maia. "Please excuse our sister. She true-birthed our Brod, and is overcompensating. Do go on."

It was all Maia could manage, not to smile in amusement. A prim, slightly scattershot sweetness seemed a core, heritable trait in this line. She could see where Brod got some of the qualities she admired. When they got up to leave, the women urged Maia to call, if she ever needed anything. Maia thanked them, and replied that she doubted she would be in town for very long.

The night before, she had heard the priestess and the archdeaconess arguing as they passed near her window, no doubt thinking she was asleep.

"You don't have to wade through the thick of it as I do," the rotund lay worker said. "While you var idealists sit here in a rustic stronghold, taking moral stands, there's heaps of pressure coming down. The Teppins and the Prosts—"

"Teppins cause me no unsleep," the priestess had answered.

"They should. Caria Temple spins at the whim of—"

"Ecclesiastic clans." The tall one snorted. "Country priests and nuns are another matter. Can the hierarchs call anathema on so many?

They risk heretics outnumbering orthodox in half the towns along the coast."

"Wish *I* felt as sure. Seems a lot to risk over one poor, battered girl."

"You know it's not about her."

"Not overall. But in our little corner of things, she'll do as a symbol. Symbols matter. Look at what's happening with the men. . . ."

Men? Maia had wondered, as the voices receded. *What do they mean by that? What's happening? With* what *men?*

She got a partial answer later, after the matrons of Starkland Hold departed, when an altercation broke out at the temple gates. Maia was by now well enough to hobble onto the porch of her guest cottage and witness a fierce argument taking place near the road. The var dedicants who doubled as watchwomen warily observed a band of clones like those Maia had seen before, following her litter through town. These, in turn, were trying to bar entry to a third group, a deputation of males wearing formal uniforms of one of the seafaring guilds. The men appeared meek, at first sight. Unlike either group of women, they carried no weapons, not even walking sticks. Eyes lowered, hands clasped, they nodded politely to whatever was shouted at them. Meanwhile they edged forward, shuffling ahead by slow, steady increments until the clones found themselves squeezed back, without room to maneuver. It was a comically effective tactic for males, Maia thought, compensating for winter docility with sheer bulk and obstinacy. Soon, they were through the gate, leaving the exasperated clone-soldiers puffing in frustration. The amused temple priestess made the men welcome, gesturing for them to follow Naroin's younger sister. Shaking her head, Hullin led the small company to Maia's bungalow.

The leader of the company wore twin crescent emblems of a full commodore on the armlets of a tidy, if somewhat threadbare, uniform. His bearing was erect, although he walked with a limp. Under a shock of dark gray hair, and dense eyebrows, his pupils reminded Maia of the northern seas of home. She shivered, and wondered why.

Inside, the officers seated themselves on mats while nuns arrived with cool drinks. Maia struggled to recall lessons about the courtly art of hosting men during this time of year. It had all seemed terribly abstract, back in summerling school. In the wildest dreams she and Leie had shared in their attic room, none had pictured facing an assembly as lofty as this.

Small talk was the rule, starting with the weather, followed by dry remarks about how lovely the men found her veranda and garden. She confessed ignorance of the exotic plants, so two officers explained the names and origins of several that had been transplanted from far valleys, to preserve threatened species. Meanwhile, her heart raced with tension.

What do they want from me? she wondered, at once excited and appalled.

The commodore asked how Maia liked the sextant she had received as a replacement for the one abandoned on Jellicoe. She thanked him, and the art of navigation proved an absorbing topic for several more minutes. Next, they discussed the Game of Life books—more as fine exemplars of the art of printing and binding than for the information they contained.

Maia tried hard to relax. She had witnessed this sort of conversation countless times, while serving drinks in the Lamatia guesthouse. The prime commandment was patience. Nevertheless, she sighed in relief when the commodore finally got to the point.

"We've had reports," he began with a low rumble, stroking the tendons of one hand with the other. "From members of our guild who participated in the . . . incidents at Jellicoe Beacon. We Pinnipeds have also shared observations with our brethren of the Flying Tern Guild—"

"Who?" Maia shook her head, confused.

"Those to whom loss of Manitou . . . Poulandres and his crew . . . come as blows to the heart."

Maia winced. She hadn't known the guild name. At sea, with Renna, it hadn't seemed important. On meeting the Manitou crew again, deep underground, there hadn't been time to ask.

"I see. Go on."

His head briefly bowed. "Among the many guilds and lodges, there is much confusion over what was, what is, and what must be done. We were astonished to learn the true existence of Jellicoe Former. Now, however, we are told its discovery is unimportant. That its significance is solely to archaeologists. Legends mean nothing, it is said. *Real* men do not seek to build what they cannot shape with their two hands."

He lifted his own, scarred and callused from many years at sea, as lined as the eyes which had spent a lifetime squinting past sun and wind and spray. They were sad eyes, Maia noticed. Loneliness seemed to color their depths.

"*Who's* been telling you this?"

A shrug. "Those whom our mothers taught us to accept as spiritual guides."

"Oh." Maia thought she understood. Few boys were born to single vars or microclans. For most, the conservative upbringing Maia shared with Leie and Albert at Lamatia was the norm. It was as important to the Founders' Plan as any vaunted genetic manipulation of masculine nature, and explained why flamboyant exploits such as the Kings' Revolt were doomed from the start.

"There is more," the commodore went on. "Although there will be compensation for our losses, and those of the Terns, we are told that no blood debt was incurred with the ruin of the so-called Wissy-Man. He was part of no guild, nor ship, nor sanctuary. We do not owe him any bond of memory or honor. So it is said."

He means Renna, Maia realized. Her friend had spoken of the cruel nickname back on the Manitou. While admiring the hearty, self-reliant craftsmanship of the sailors, Renna had implied that it trapped men in a ritualistic obsession, forever limiting the scope of their ambitions.

After Jellicoe was forcibly evacuated, how many generations did it take for the high clans to accomplish this? It can't have been easy. The legend must have fought back, clung to life, despite suppression at nearly every mother's knee.

Whether or not she ever learned the whole story, Maia was already certain of some things. There had once been a great conspiracy. One that had come close to succeeding, long ago. One that might have altered life on Stratos, forever.

The Council in those days had not been without reason, when it used the pretext of the Kings' Revolt to seize Jellicoe Beacon and oust the old "Guardians," as the Manitou's physician had called them. Those ancient wardens of science had been up to something more subversive, more threatening to the status quo, than the Kings' dim-witted putsch. The existence of the orbital launching gun used by Renna made it all clear.

A plot to reclaim outer space. And with it a radically different way of living in the universe.

More remarkably still, the Guardians managed to keep secret the location of their great factory—their "Former." The Council swiftly confiscated the great engines of defense without ever guessing how close nearby a secret remnant continued working to complete the plan. For generations it must have gone on. Men and women, sneaking in and out of Jellicoe Former, carefully recruiting their own replacements, losing expertise and skill with each passing of the torch until, at long last, the inexorable logic of Stratoin society ground their brave, forlorn cabal to extinction. A thousand or more years later it was but a threadbare fable, no more.

Renna must have found the ship and launcher almost completed. He used the Former, programming it with his own experience and knowledge to make the last needed parts.

It was a staggering accomplishment, to have achieved so much in but a few days. Perhaps he would have made it, if not forced to launch early by the premature discovery of his hiding place.

Guilt was a more potent voice than reason. But now Maia felt something stronger than either—a desire to strike back. It would be futile, of course, especially over the long run. In the short term, however, here was a chance to lay a small blow in revenge.

"I . . . don't know the whole story," she began hesitantly. Maia paused, inhaled deeply, and resumed with more firmness in her voice. "But what you've been told is unjust. A lie. I knew the sailor you speak of, who came to our shores as a guest . . . with open hands . . . after crossing a sea far greater and lonelier than any man of Stratos has known. . . ."

It was late afternoon when the men finally stood to take their leave. Hullin helped Maia hobble with them to the porch, where the commodore took her hand. His officers stood nearby, their expressions thoughtful and stormy. "I thank you for your time and wisdom, Lady," the guildmaster said, causing Maia to blink. "In leasing one of our ships to wild reavers, we unintentionally did your house harm. Yet you have been generous with us."

"I . . ." Maia was speechless at being addressed in this fashion.

The commodore went on. "Should a winter come when your house seeks diligent men, prepared to do their duty with pride and pleasure, any of these"—he gestured at his younger comrades, who nodded earnestly—"will cheerfully come, without thought of summer reward." He paused. "I, alone, must decline, by the Rule of Lysos."

While Maia watched in stunned silence, he bowed once more. With a tone of flustered, confounded decorum, he added, "I hope we meet again, Maia. My name . . . is Clevin."

There was glory frost that night, floating slowly downward from the stratosphere in a haze of soft, threadlike drifts that touched the wooden railings, the flagstones, the lilies in the pond, with glittering, luminous dust. Most of it evaporated on contact, filling the air with a faint, enticing perfume. Maia watched the gossamer tendrils waft past, and felt as if she were *rising* through a mist of microscopic stars. For a long time after, she would not go to sleep, afraid of what might happen. Lying in bed, her skin tingled with strange sensations and she wondered what would happen if she dreamed. Whose face would come to her? Brod's? Bennett's? The men of Pinniped Guild?

Would womanly hormones set off renewed, painful longing for Renna, her first, though chaste, male love?

The shock of meeting her natural father had not ebbed. Her thoughts roiled and she tossed in confusion. When Maia finally did dream, it was a strangely intangible fantasy—of falling, floating, amid the startling, abstract, ever-changing figures of the Jellicoe wonder wall.

Soon after dawn, the doctor arrived and announced in satisfaction that it would be her next-to-last visit. When she removed the agone leech, it was a chance for Maia to look closely at the box that had suppressed full vividness from both her body's ache and her heart's grief. It seemed a modest item, mass-produced and plentiful enough to furnish even the humblest medic, anywhere on Stratos. Now Maia also knew it as another product of a lesser Former, one of those automatic factories still operated under close watch by the Reigning Council. Clearly, some manufactured items were too important to be left to pastoral puritanism. If Perkinism prevailed, however, even these merciful boxes might go away.

"You'll still be needin' a bit more rest an' recoop here in Ursulaborg," Naroin explained later that morning, on returning from her urgent errand. "Then it's off to Caria for a command performance before as posh a gaggle o' savants as you've ever seen. What d'you think o' that?"

Maia unfolded the arms of her replacement sextant and sighted on a grimlip flower. "I think you're a cop, and I shouldn't say anything more till I see a legalist."

"A legalist?" The small woman's brow knotted. "Why would you be needin' one?"

Why, indeed? Naroin might be her friend, but a clone was never entirely her own person. Once Maia was brought to Caria, Maia could think of a dozen excuses the powers that ruled Church and Council might use to lock her away. In a *real* prison, this time. One without secret byways, patrolled by clone guardians tested over centuries, genetically primed for vigilance.

Maia had decided not to let it come to that. This time, she would act first. Before she was taken from Ursulaborg, there should come a chance to slip away. Perhaps during her daily ride. Once away through the city crowds, she would seek shelter in an out-of-the-way place where important people might never trace her. *Some quiet, dead-end seaside town. I'll find a way to get word to Leie, Brod. We'll open a chandler's shop. Repair sextants damaged by lazy sailors.*

Perhaps Naroin could be persuaded to look the other way at the right moment. Best not to count on it, though.

"Never mind," she told the short brunette. "Had a nightmare. Can't shake the feeling I'm still living in it."

"Who could blame you, after all you've been through." Naroin grinned. When Maia failed to respond, she leaned forward. "You think you're under arrest or somethin'? Is that it?"

"Could I walk out the front gate, if I so chose?"

The wiry ex-bosun frowned. "Wouldn't be wise, right now."

"I thought not."

"It's not what you think. There's folk who don't hold your health as dear as we do."

"Sure." Maia nodded. "I know you're lots nicer than some would be. Forget I asked."

Naroin chewed her lower lip unhappily. "You want to know what's goin' on. It's all changing so fast, though. . . . Look, I'm not supposed to say anythin' till she arrives, but there's someone comin' tomorrow to talk to you, and then escort you to the capital. I know it's fishy sounding, but it's needful. Can you trust me till then? I promise it'll all make sense."

A petulant part of Maia wanted to cling to resentment. But it was hard to stay wary of Naroin. They had been through so much together. *I'd rather be dead than so suspicious I can't trust anybody.*

"All right," she said. "Till tomorrow."

Naroin left again. Later, Maia and her escorts were about to depart on the afternoon litter ride when Hullin reached up to hand Maia a second folded sheet of heavy paper, sealed with red wax. Maia's heart lifted when she saw Brod's handwriting. She waited until the palanquin was jostling through the suburban market square, then tore it open.

> Dear Maia,
>   Leie's fine and sends her love. We both miss you, and are glad to hear you're in good care. Here's hoping life is nice and boring for you, for a while.

Maia smiled. Just wait till they get her next letter! Leie would julp with jealousy that she hadn't met Clevin first! There were other, more serious matters to discuss, but it would be good to report that *one* of their childhood fantasies had actually come true.

Lysos, how she missed Brod and Leie! Maia desperately wished they would come soon.

> We've been less busy lately. Spending most of our time just stand-ing around while high-class mothers point and wave their arms and yell a lot. In fact, I'm surprised Leie and I are still here, since a bunch of savants arrived from the University with big consoles, which they proceeded to attach to your picture wall. They've been making it do amazing things. Stopped asking Leie questions about it, so I guess they think they've figured it out.

Maia wondered, *Why does that make me feel jealous?* Now that the secret was out, it only made sense to have scholars investigate the wonders of another age. Perhaps they'd learn a thing or two . . . even change their minds about some stereotypes.

> All the men are gone now, except those serving the ships which bring supplies. So are the vars and local cops who helped retake Jellicoe from the reavers. We've been told not to talk to any of the sailors, who aren't allowed into the Sanctuary or Former. The men spend whatever time they have, between loading and unloading sealed crates, just rowing around the lagoon, checking out caves, sightseeing. I don't think I'll have any trouble slipping this letter to—

The litter jerked, breaking Maia's concentration. The market was unusually crowded today. Peering over the throng, Maia saw a disturbance a few dozen meters ahead. A trio of shoppers were arguing vehemently with a storekeeper. Suddenly, one of them picked up a bolt of cloth and turned to leave, causing the merchant to screech in dismay. Maia picked up the word "Thief!" shouted over the general hubbub. Ripples of agitation spread outward as clone sisters of the sales clerk spilled out of the building behind her. Others converged to aid the shoppers. Shoving and yelling escalated with startling rapidity into unseemly grabbing, and then blows, spreading in Maia's direction.

The temple wardens moved to interpose themselves while Hullin tugged at the upset lugars, urging them to turn around. They managed to swing off the main thoroughfare into a side alley, the only avenue of escape, ducking awkwardly under a jungle of clotheslines. "Uh," Maia started to suggest. "Maybe I should get down—"

Hullin gave a startled cry. The fiver's head vanished under a blanket thrown from a nearby shadowed doorway, drawn tight with cord. The lugars grunted in panic, dropping one pole of the litter, teetering Maia vertigously outward as she grabbed futilely after Brod's fluttering letter.

Suddenly, she found herself staring straight into the blonde-fringed face of—Tizbe Beller!

Maia had only an instant to gasp before black cloth surrounded her as well, accompanied by the rough clasping of many pairs of hands. A jarring tumult followed as she sucked for breath while being lugged, pell-mell, along some twisty, abruptly shifting path. It was a hurtful, bone-shaking ordeal, surpassed only by her frustrated helplessness to fight back.

At last, the black cover came off. Maia raggedly inhaled, blinking disorientation from the searing return of sunshine. Hands yanked and pushed, but this time Maia lashed out, managing to elbow one of her

captors and catch another in the stomach with her right foot, before
someone cuffed her on the side of the head, bringing the stars out early.
Through it all, Maia caught brief glimpses of where they were taking her,
toward a set of stairs leading upward, into the belly of a gleaming, bird-
shaped contraption of polished wood and steel.

An aircraft.

"Relax, virgie," Tizbe Beller told Maia as they trussed her into a
padded seat. "Might as well enjoy the view. Not many varlings like you
ever get to fly."

Journal of the Peripatetic Vessel

CYDONIA – 626 Stratos Mission:

Arrival + 53.755 Ms

I have watched and listened ever since the explosion. Ever since receiving warning of Renna's desperate gamble. Official Stratoin agencies say different, often contradictory things, and all appears in chaos, down below. Yet, at least one thing has been achieved. The fighting has stopped. With the irritant removed, warlike preparations among the factions have subsided, for now.

Was Renna right? Was a sacrifice necessary?

Will it suffice?

It was urgent not to disrupt Stratos any more than we already have. Yet, sometimes duty requires of us more than we can bear.

I, too, must do my duty. Soon.

27

A fter the initial tussle, it proved Maia's most comfortable abduction, by far. Tied down, with no option for resistance, she made the best of things by gazing through a double-paned window at the vastness of Landing Continent. Soon, even her headache went away.

Luminous yellow and pale green farmlands stretched as far as the eye could see. These were combed by long fingers of darker forest, interlaced to leave migration corridors for native creatures, from the coast all the way to mist-shrouded mountains that began to loom in the north. Small towns and castlelike clanhold manors appeared at periodic intervals, squatting like spiders amid spoked roads and surrounding hamlets. Strings of lakes were punctuated by regularly spaced fish farms that shone glancing sunlight into Maia's eyes.

Stubby barges with gray sails leisurely plied the rivers and canals, while throngs of quick, flittering *mere-dragons* flapped in formations of two hundred or more, warily skirting farms and habitations on their way to fallow rooting grounds. Lumbering heptoids wallowed through the fens and shallows, their broad back-fans turned to radiate the heat of the day. And then there were the floaters—zoors and their lesser cousins—bobbing in the breeze, tethered like gay balloons to the treetops where they grazed.

Maia had traveled far in recent months, but now she realized that one can only gain true perspective from above. Stratos was bigger than she had ever imagined. In all directions were signs of humanity in rustic codominion with nature. *Renna said humans often turn whole worlds into deserts, through shortsightedness. That's one trap we avoided. No one could accuse Lysos, or Stratoin clans, of thinking short-term.*

But Renna also hinted there are other ways to do it, without giving up so much.

Maia watched the pilot touch switches and check small indicator screens as the plane entered a gentle bank and turned west well short of the mountains. The aircraft interior was a finely wrought mix of hand-crafted wood panels and furnishings, accoutered with a compact array of instruments. If she had been in friendly company, Maia might have frothed with questions. Her bound hands were adequate reminder, however. So she kept silent, mildly ignoring Tizbe and yawning when the young Beller tried for the fourth time to initiate conversation. The implication couldn't be missed. She had escaped Tizbe twice before, bringing ruin to her plans, and thought nothing of doing so again. Maia sensed the attitude upset the Beller clone.

I'm learning, Maia thought. *They keep making mistakes and I keep getting stronger.*

At this rate, someday I may actually gain control over my life.

The pilot warned her passengers of turbulent air. Soon the plane was bouncing, pitching, and yawing in abrupt jerks. Tizbe and her ruffians blanched, turning discolored shades, which Maia enjoyed watching. She helped worsen the symptoms by staring at the Beller courier like a specimen of unpleasant, lower-order life. Tizbe cursed with flecked lips, and Maia laughed, unsparing in her scorn. Curiously, the tossing didn't seem to affect her like the others. Even the pilot looked a bit ragged, by the time they finally regained settled air. *The storm aboard the Wotan was much worse,* Maia recalled.

Then a golden light seized her attention, causing her to squint in wonder at what lay beyond the forward windscreen. A shimmering reflection, coming from a spacious, dimpled territory surrounding and covering a cluster of hills at the intersection of three broad ribbons of river.

Caria, she realized. Maia watched the capital city glide nearer, its skirts yellow with the tiles of countless roofs, its tiara of white stone girdling the famed acropolis plateau. Atop that eminence, twin basilicas swam into view, stately beyond measure. Any schoolgirl knew the pillared shapes at sight, the Universal Library on one side and on the other, the Great Temple dedicated to guiding worldwide reverence of Stratos Mother. All of her life, Maia had heard women speak of pilgrimages to Caria, of venerating in solemn awe the planetary spirit—and her apostles, the Founders—under that vast iridescent cupola on the right, with its giant dragon icon cast in silver and gold. The other palace, built to the same glorious scale, was unadorned and hardly ever mentioned. Yet it became Maia's focus as the aircraft circled toward a field, south of the city.

Lysos never would have built the Library co-equal to the Temple if she intended a seedy clubhouse for a few smug, savant clans.

She contemplated the grand edifice until descent removed it behind a nearby hill covered with middle-class clansteads. From that point until final landing, Maia concentrated on watching the pilot, if only to keep from helplessly worrying over her fate.

Her kidnappers installed her in a room with floral wallpaper and its own bath, unpretentiously elegant. A narrow balcony stepped down to an enclosed garden. A pair of stolid, servant-guards smiled at Maia, keeping her discreetly in sight at all times. They wore livery with fine piping on the shoulders and a gold-chased letter *P*, for the name of their employer-clan, she supposed.

Maia had expected to be taken to one of the pleasure houses operated by the Bellers, perhaps the very one where Renna had been abducted. From there, perhaps she would be sold to Tizbe's Perkinite clients, in revenge for what she'd done in Long Valley, months ago. This didn't look like a business establishment, however, nor did the hills near the rolling compound seem the kind of precinct where one found bordellos. Colorful silk banners flew from fairy turrets, and crenelated battlements rose above the tall, elderly groves of truly ancient estates. It was a neighborhood of noble clanholds, as far above Tizbe's hardworking family on the social ladder as the Bellers towered over Maia. Beyond the garden wall on one side, she often heard the strains of a string quartet, along with shouts of playing children, all laughing the same, syncopated trill. In the opposite direction, coming from a tower room whose lights remained on late into the night, there were recurrent sounds of anxious adult argument, the same voice taking on multiple roles.

After the landing, and Maia's first-ever ride in a motor car, she saw no more of Tizbe, or any other Beller. Nor did she particularly care. By now Maia realized she had become a pawn in power games played at the loftiest heights of Stratoin society. *I ought to be flattered,* she thought sardonically. *That is, if I survive till equinox.*

At her request, she was brought books to read. There was a treatise on the Game of Life, written three hundred years ago by an elderly savant who had spent several years with men, both at sea and as a special summertime guest in sanctuary, studying anthropological aspects of their endless tournaments. Maia found the account fascinating, though some of the author's pat conclusions about ritualistic sublimation seemed farfetched. More difficult to plow through was a detailed logical analysis of the game itself, written a century earlier by another scholar. The math was hard to follow, but it proved more orderly and satisfying than the books provided in Ursulaborg, by the Pinnipeds. Those had emphasized rules of thumb and winning technique over basic theory. It was a mental meal that left her hungry for more.

The books helped pass time while Maia's body finished mending. Gradually she resumed a regimen of exercise, building her strength while keeping eyes peeled for any chance of escape.

A week passed. Maia read and studied, paced her garden, tested the relentless vigilance of her guards, and worried ceaselessly over what was happening to Leie and Brod. She couldn't even ask if there were any more letters, since Brod had apparently been forced to smuggle out the last one. The inquiry itself might only give her friend away.

She refused to show frustration, lest her captors gain the slightest satisfaction, but at night the image of Renna's fatal explosion haunted her sleep. Several times, she awoke to find herself sitting bolt upright, both hands over her racing heart, gasping as if trapped in an airless space, deep underground.

One day the guards announced she had a visitor. "Your gracious host, Odo, of Clan Persim," the servants proclaimed, then obsequiously bowed aside for a tall elderly woman with a wide face and aristocratic bearing.

"I know who you are," Maia said. "Renna said you set him up to be kidnapped."

The patrician sat down on a chair and sighed. "It was a good plan, which you helped snarl, in several ways."

"Thank you."

The noblewoman nodded, a genteel gesture. "You're welcome. Would you like to know why we went to so much risk and trouble?"

A pause. "Talk if you want. I'm not goin' anywhere."

Odo spread her hands. "There were countless individuals and groups who wanted the Outsider put away. Most for visceral, thoughtless reasons, as if his deletion might turn back the clock, erasing *de facto* rediscovery of Stratos by the Hominid Phylum.

"Some fantasized his removal might stop the iceships from coming." Odo shook her head with aristocratic derision. "Those huge liners full of peaceful invaders will arrive long after we now living are dead. Time enough to worry out a solution. Taking revenge on a poor courier would only weaken our position, when and if full contact is restored."

"So much for the motives of others. Of course, *you* had more mature reasons for grabbing Renna. Like squeezing information out of him?"

The old woman nodded. "There were elements of inquiry, certainly. Our Perkinite allies were interested in new gene-splicing methods, which might lead to self-cloning without males. Others sought improved defense technology, or to learn iceship weaknesses, so we might destroy them at long range, far from Stratos."

"Too far for the public to observe, you mean. So most would never know we're murdering tens of thousands."

"I was told you catch on quickly for a mouse," Odo replied. "Nor were those the sole ideas for using your alien friend and his knowledge."

Maia recalled Kiel's Radicals, who had hoped to alter Stratoin biology and culture at least as much as the Perkinites, though in opposing directions. Maia knew Renna would have disapproved of being used by either party.

"Let me guess about the Bellers. Their motive was strictly cash, right? But you Persims, you blue-bloods, had reasons all your own."

Odo nodded. "His presence in Caria was becoming . . . disruptive. The Council and curia had vital matters to discuss, yet were growing unpredictable whenever he was around. His calm restraint during summer had defied our expectations, winning him allies, and we realized it would only get worse with winter and first frost. Imagine how persuasive a fully functioning, articulate, old-style male might be then, to those with weak wills and minds! That describes many so-called 'moderates,' who were fast slipping out of our faction's control.

"For reasons of political convenience, it was deemed necessary to remove him."

"*What?*" Maia stood up. "Why, you smug bitchie. Are you sayin' *that's* why—"

Odo lifted a hand, waiting until Maia reseated herself before resuming in a lower voice. "You're right. There's more. You see, we'd made a promise . . . one we were unable to keep."

Maia blinked. "What promise?"

"To send him back to his ship, of course. And replenish his supplies when his mission was done. It's why he came down in a simple lander, in the first place, instead of making other arrangements." The old woman exhaled heavily. "For months, those believing in him had been working to fix the launching facility, not far from here. The machinery functioned when last used, a few centuries ago. Our records are intact.

"But too many parts have failed. Too much skill is lost. We couldn't send him home, after all."

Odo hurried on before Maia could interrupt. "To make matters worse, he was in constant contact with his ship. Some already wanted him put away to prevent relaying information useful to future invaders. Those demands grew urgent when he started politely asking to inspect our launch preparations. Soon, he was bound to report that Stratos no longer had access to space."

"But Renna—"

"One night, in a confiding mood, he told me that peripatetics—interstellar couriers—are considered expendable. With numberless lives already sacrificed in the new crusade sweeping Phylum space, that of recontacting lost hominid worlds, what does another matter? Ironic, isn't it? His own words finally convinced my clan and others to ally with the Perkinites."

Yes, that was Renna, all right, Maia thought miserably. Her late friend's odd mixture of sophistication and naïveté had been one of his most charming traits, and most alien.

"I take it the new launcher at Jellicoe has changed a few minds?" she asked.

The aged clone tilted her head. "You'd expect so, wouldn't you? In fact, it is complex. Political tides are at work. The Great Former and its consort facilities are causing much dispute."

No kidding. I can tell you're scared spitless.

"Why are you telling me all this?" Maia asked. "What do you care what a var like me thinks?"

Odo shrugged. "Normally, not much. As it happens, we have need of your cooperation. Certain things will be required of you—"

Maia laughed. "What in Lysos's name makes you think I'd do anything for you?"

A reply was ready. From her capacious sleeve, Odo drew forth a small glossy photograph. Maia's fingers trembled as she took it and regarded Brod and Leie, standing together beside a vast, crystalline, spiral-shaped tube—the muzzle of the great launching gun on Jellicoe Island. Maia's sister seemed engrossed, drawing a closeup sketch of one of the machine's many parts, while Brod ran his finger alongside a chart, covered with figures, leaning over to say something to Leie. Only their hunched shoulders betrayed the tension Maia felt emanating from the picture. Nearby, at least a dozen women conversed or lounged casually for the photographer. Almost a third of them were clones of the matriarch sitting across from Maia now.

"I think you care about the health and safety of your sister and her present vril companion. That persuades me to assume that you will do us a favor, or two."

The noblewoman seemed impervious to Maia's stare of unadulterated hatred. "For your first task," Odo resumed. "I want you to accompany me tonight. We are going to the opera."

The elegance of it all did not take Maia completely by surprise. She had been to the Capital Theater many times, vicariously, via tele broadcasts

and scenes in drama-clips. As a little girl, she had fantasized dressing in
the sort of fancy gowns worn by rich clonelings, gliding in to watch
magnificent productions while, all around her, the whispered intrigues of
great houses went on behind demure smiles and shielding fans.

Fantasies were one thing; it was quite another matter to struggle
with unfamiliar fasteners and stays, coping with billowing, impractical
acres of drapery that could have no function other than to advertise the
wealth and status of the wearer and the wearer's house. Finally, a pair of
young women from Odo's hive came to help Maia prepare for her first
evening of make-believe. They managed to arrange the puffy sleeves and
pleated trousers to conceal most of her recent scars, but Maia drew the
line at makeup, which she found repulsive. When Odo arrived, the old
woman concurred for her own reasons.

"We want the child to be recognized," she ruled. "A small bruise or
two will cause notice. Besides, doesn't she cut a superb figure, as is?"

Maia turned before a precious, full-length mirror, amazed by what
she saw. The outfit emphasized what she had barely noticed till now, that
she had a woman's body. She was four centimeters taller and much fuller
than the scrawny, gawky chicken who had shyly stepped out of Port
Sanger, months before. Yet it was her own face she found most surprising: from one thin, healing scar under her right ear; to her cheekbones,
now entirely free of baby fat; to the sweep of her brown hair, brushed to a
fine gloss by one of Odo's attentive servants. Most astonishing were her
eyes. They remained unlined, apparently youthful and innocent, until
you took them full on. Slightly narrowed, they seemed at once both skeptical and serene, and from an angle she recognized the brow of her
father, master of ships and storms.

It was an image of herself she had never envisioned.

Damn right! Maia thought, nodding. *Take things as they come. And
let 'em watch out, if they leave me a single opening.*

That didn't seem likely, unfortunately. Leie and Brod relied on her
good behavior for their lives. Still, Maia turned away from the mirror
with a smile for Odo. *You made an error, letting me see that. Let's find out
how many more mistakes you make.*

The Great Theater sprawled gaudily a short distance down the
acropolis esplanade from the Temple and Library. Horse-drawn carriages, lugar-litters, and more than a few motor-limousines coursed up to
the steps, depositing the topmost layer of Caria society for tonight's revival opening of a classic opera, *Wendy and Faustus*. High priestesses,
councillors, judges, and savants climbed the broad steps. In many cases,
the matrons of great clans were accompanied by younger cloneling
daughters and nieces, too callow for real power, but the right age for

procreation. These youthful ones, in turn, escorted small groups of men, tall and erectly impressive in their formal guild uniforms. The winter cream of Stratoin maledom, here to be wooed and entertained.

Maia watched from the carriage she shared with Odo and a half-dozen older women from various aristocratic clans. It had been a chilly ride. Some of the old trepidation returned under their withering disdain. That enmity was based on a wide range of fanaticisms, but what made these women powerful went far deeper, to the core of the society established by Lysos long ago.

From the moment she stepped down from the carriage, Maia felt eyes turn her way. Whispered comment followed her up the steps, through the ornate portico, and along a sweeping, ceremonial stairway to the box where Odo arranged for her to sit prominently forward, on public display. To Maia's relief, the house lights soon went down. The conductor raised her baton, and the overture began.

The opera had its points. The musical score was beautiful. Maia hardly paid attention to the libretto, however, which followed a hackneyed theme about the ancient struggle between womanly pragmatism and the spasmodic, dangerous enthusiasms of old-fashioned males. No doubt the drama had been revived at the behest of certain political parties, as part of a propaganda campaign against restored Phylum contact. Her presence was meant to signify approval.

During intermission, Maia's escorts took her to the sparkling elegance of the lobby, where var waiters circulated with trays of drinks and sweetmeats. Here it would be simple to elude her escorts . . . if only Leie and Brod weren't counting on her. Maia choked down her frustration and tried to do as she'd been told. Smiling, she accepted a fizzy beverage from a bowing attendant, a var like her, with eyes lowered deferentially.

Maia's smile widened in sudden sincerity when she saw, coming toward her, a tight group of figures, two of whom she knew. Shortest, but most intense, strode the detective, Naroin, looking out of place in a simple, dark evening suit. Next to her, and half again as tall, walked Clevin, the frowning, earnest commodore of Pinniped Guild. *My father,* Maia contemplated. The reality seemed so detached from her dreams of childhood, it was hard to sort true emotions, except to relish the proud light when his gray eyes saw her.

Two women accompanied Naroin and Clevin, one of them tall, silver-haired, and elegant. The other was darkly beautiful, with mysterious green eyes. Maia did not know their faces.

Odo slid alongside Maia as the group approached. "Iolanthe, how good to see you back in society. It seemed so dull without you."

The tall woman nodded her simply-coiffed gray head. Her face was delicately boned, with an air of quiet intelligence. "Nitocris Hold has been mourning its friend, who came so far across the galaxy, only to meet betrayal and untimely death."

"A death drenched in irony, and by his own hand," Odo pointed out. "With rescue just meters away, if only he knew it."

Maia would have gladly, unrepentantly, killed Odo on the spot. She remained rigidly still, save to give one quick nod to Naroin, another to her father.

"So you feel delivered of your crime?" the woman named Iolanthe asked, her voice prim, like that of a savant. "We'll find other witnesses, other testimony. Such a grand cabal of tensely diverse interests cannot hold. You play dangerous games, Odo."

Odo shrugged. "I may be sacrificed at some point. In Macro Chess, a side may lose many queens, yet still win the game. Such is life."

It was Clevin who spoke next, to the surprise of both disputing women. "Bad metaphor," he remarked in a terse, gravelly baritone. "Your game isn't life."

Odo stared at the man, as if unable to credit his effrontery. Finally, she broke into derisive laughter. Behind Maia, others of the conspiracy joined in. The Pinniped commodore didn't blanch. In his stern silence, Maia felt greater weight of argument than all their ridicule. She knew what he meant, and said so with her eyes.

Naroin stepped toward Maia. "Missed ya, varling. Sorry, I didn't figure on a snatch like that. Underestimated your importance once again."

That was the part Maia still couldn't figure out. *What's so important about me?*

"You all right?" Naroin finished.

"All right," Maia answered, almost a whisper. "How about yourself?"

"Fine. Catchin' hell for lettin' you get taken. How was *I* to know you'd get t'be a livin' legend?"

Around them on every side, people were watching. Maia sensed attention not only from stately matrons, but quite a few male onlookers, as well.

Iolanthe spoke again. "It won't do, Odo. She cannot remain your prisoner." The savant turned to Maia. "Come with us now, child. They cannot prevent it. We'll protect you as our own, with powers you cannot imagine."

Maia somehow doubted that. She had, of late, seen forces beyond anything this pale intellectual could have known. Moreover, like the sword of Lysos breaking symbolic chains on the Lanargh City statuary clock, events had shattered all fetters on Maia's imagination.

On another level, she felt the offer was doubtless sincere. Though Iolanthe's side in the political conflict was probably doomed, she could almost certainly shield Maia's person. All Maia had to do was start walking.

There are many kinds of prisons, she thought acidly.

"That's kind of you," she replied. "Some other time, perhaps."

The elderly savant winced at the rejection, but Naroin looked unsurprised. "I see. You like it in Persim Hold? They're your friends now?"

Maia first thought Naroin was expressing bitterness. Then she read something in the ex-bosun's eyes. A feral, conspiratorial gleam. Her sarcasm had another objective.

Maia nodded. She took a deep breath. "Oh—yes. Odo—is—my—friend . . . as—much—as—she—was—Renna's."

It was the general message she had been ordered to convey, delivered so woodenly, no one with sensitivity would believe a word. Maia heard Odo hiss sharply restrained anger.

Leie, Brod, have I just murdered you? On the other hand, maybe Naroin would now add two and two, and realize how Maia was being coerced. Perhaps there were still honest layers in government, who could be called on to rescue two innocent fivers from captivity. To get that message across was worth stretching the Persim's patience. Once.

Clevin growled. Maia watched his gnarled hands clench and unclench. In the dead of winter, she felt a kind of blazing heat from the man. His trouble wasn't remembering how to make a fist, but controlling his wrath. Naroin took his elbow, applying urgent pressure to his arm.

"This won't stop the strike," he rumbled.

Strike? Maia wondered.

Odo laughed. "Your so-called strike is a mere irritant, already unraveling. In days, perhaps weeks, it will be over. All women will unite to reject the participants. They'll get no more summer passes. No more sons. Isn't that *right*, Maia?"

Maia made no further efforts to send messages, only to obey. "Yes," she assented, completely ignorant of what she was agreeing to. Naroin and Clevin understood her predicament. All that mattered were her sister and her friend.

"Our past differences evaporated with the unfortunate Visitor," continued Odo. "Now Maia wants to join the cause of restoring peace and order to the Founders' Plan."

For the first time, the fourth member of Naroin's party spoke up.

The dark-haired woman was of medium height and poised bearing, with a distinctive oval face and intense eyes. "In that case, you won't mind if I pay a call on you, at Persim Hold?" she said to Maia.

Before Maia could answer, Odo demanded, "Which are you? *Which* Upsala?"

It was a decidedly strange query to Maia's ears, as if a clone's individuality ever mattered.

"I am *Brill*, of the Upsala." The graceful brunette inclined her head. "I perform tests for the Civil Service."

Maia sensed Odo's tense reaction, as if she had encountered something more worrisome than any gambit by Naroin, or Clevin, or even the aristocratic Iolanthe. "I'd be honored, Brill, of Upsala," Maia blurted impulsively, feeling sticky from anxious perspiration under her heavy gown. "Come at your convenience."

The atrium lights dimmed to the sound of a gentle chime, signaling intermission's end. Odo pointedly took her hand, giving it a brief, painful squeeze. "Time we took our seats," she said to Iolanthe and the others. "Enjoy the show. Come, Maia."

There was chill silence during the long, exposed climb back to the theater box. As they resumed their seats and the lights went down, Maia felt Odo lean near. "If you try another stunt like that, my dear young scattered seed, you'll live to regret it. More than your own life rides on doing a better job of acting."

Maia had even less taste for watching the second act. The music sounded like clashing engines; the colorful costumes seemed foppish, ridiculous. Only one thing caught her eye, to distract momentarily from her misery. While listlessly scanning the sea of extravagance below, her lethargic gaze picked out a pair of faces, each of them identical to the woman, Brill, she had just met in the lobby.

The first belonged to the conductor of the orchestra. The second was the tenor, her chin covered with an artificial beard, leaping and crooning with ersatz masculine abandon, playing the archetype operatic role of Nature's conceited challenger, the epitome of hubris, Faust.

Another week passed. Each morning, Odo arranged for Maia to be dressed in a stunning new outfit before taking her for an open carriage ride down the esplanade. It showed her off to strollers and pedestrians without risking further close personal contact.

At first, Maia was captivated by the sights of Caria—Council Hall, the University, the Great Temple—almost as much as any tourist. The fascination didn't last, however. Each time she returned to her room in Persim Hold, Maia quickly stripped off the grotesque finery and threw herself into an orgy of exercise, to vent her frustration. The guards were gone now, yet she felt more securely imprisoned than ever in Long Valley, or on Grimké Isle.

On Fridinsday, during the morning ride, Maia witnessed a scene of commotion taking place before one of the majestic, many-pillared public buildings. Uniformed soldiers and proctors strove to keep back several groups of demonstrators. One, consisting of men in varicolored guild tunics, appeared listless, demoralized. Maia could only partly read one of their drooping banners. JELL . . . RMER said the portion visible between folds.

Suddenly, Maia's heart sped. Just ahead, standing at the curb where the carriage was about to pass, she saw Clevin, her father, talking earnestly with Iolanthe. Odo spoke to the driver, who flicked her reins. The horses sped to a canter as Clevin looked up, met Maia's eyes, and started to raise a hand.

The moment passed too quickly. Odo let out a short, satisfied grunt as Maia sank back into the plush upholstery.

The men need help, she thought, miserably. *If I were free, maybe I could buck up their spirits. If only . . .*

She shook her head. Nothing was worth spending her sister's life or Brod's. Certainly not in a cause that was lost from the start. No effort on her part would change destiny.

They rode back to Persim Hold without another word. Maia tossed off her stiff clothes, exercised, ate, and crawled into bed.

The next day, on her breakfast tray next to the orange juice, Maia found a newspaper. A simple, four-page tabloid, printed on fine, slick paper. From the price and circulation, both written on the masthead, it was clearly meant only for subscribers at the pinnacle of Caria's many-tiered social strata. Several portions had been razored out. The lead article was riveting, nonetheless.

Strike Outlook Positive

While seaborne traffic remains snarled in most ports along the Méchant Coast, analysts now predict a quick conclusion to the work-stoppage by seventeen shipping guilds and their affiliates. Already, defections have weakened the resolve of the ringleaders, whose objective, to pressure the Planetary Reigning Council into reopening the infamous Jellicoe Sanctuary, appears no longer to have any realistic chance of success. . . .

So, Maia thought. It was her first partial accounting of events since her capture. Also her first clue to her status as a pawn in big-time struggles.

The reavers were crushed. Kiel's rads are broken. Loose alliances of liberals, like those backcountry temple vars, might lean toward change, but they lack cohesiveness. The high clans have long experience coping with such grumblings.

But there's another group giving them a scare. The sailing guilds.

In Ursulaborg, the Pinnipeds had spoken of propaganda. *The Great Former means nothing,* they had been told. *The Wissy-Man was not your kind. . . .*

Maia didn't overrate her own contribution. The sailors might have rejected the official line anyway. But her narrative must have helped when she told what she had learned about the ancient Guardians—about a forlorn struggle by ancient men and women to devise another way. A way of including more than one round patch of earth and sea and sky, in the Stratoin tale. A way to amend, without rejecting, what the Founders had once willed their heirs.

And she had spoken of Renna, the brave sailor whose sea was the galaxy. The man who flew, as no man of this world had since the banishment. When they departed on that day, she had felt certain the seamen knew her friend from the stars. That he was one of them. That he was owed a debt of honor.

The Persim brought me here to help undermine the strike. That's why they flaunt me around town. The men at the opera must have reported back to their guilds. If I was in Odo's company, how serious could I ever have been, about being the starman's comrade?

Reading between the lines, it grew apparent why the high clans were concerned. The sailor's job action was hurting.

> . . . Half of the sparking season was over before
> the walkout was declared. Still, it is clear that lack
> of male cooperation will depress this winter's breed-
> ing program.

That caused Maia to smile, proud that Clevin and the others hadn't missed a trick.

> Perkinite priestess-advocate Jeminalte Cever today
> demanded that "those responsible for this flagrant
> neglect of duty must be made to pay."
> Fortunately, this radicalization took place after

Farsun Day, so politicians needn't fear a rush to
polling booths by disgruntled males. Their irate minority vote might have swung several tight races in
recent elections.

Will it remain a factor by next winter? Estimates based on recent episodes of male unrest, six,
ten, and thirteen decades ago, lead savants at the
Institute for Sociological Trends to suggest that this
somewhat more severe interlude may not pass in
time to prevent short-term economic loss to many of
our subscribers. However, they predict that, by next
autumn, only residual ferment should remain, at a
level corresponding to . . .

It went on, describing how the guilds would predictably fall away from
each other, accepting generous deals and compromises, unable to maintain righteous ire in a season when the blood ran cool. Maia sighed,
finding the scenario believable, even predictable. The dead hand of
Lysos always won.

No wonder they let me see this. She allowed for the fact that the
reporting was biased and incomplete. Nevertheless, the newspaper left
her depressed.

Odo arrived as Maia finished dressing. She expected the Persim
matriarch to gloat over the article, but apparently Odo had other matters
on her mind. Clearly agitated, the old woman dismissed the maids and
bid Maia sit down.

"There will be no excursion today," she said. "You have a visitor."

Maia lifted an eyebrow, but said nothing.

"Shortly, you will meet Brill Upsala in the east conservatory. You'll
be supplied pencils, paper, other equipment. Brill has been informed
that you are willing to be examined, under the terms of ancient law, but
that you do not wish to discuss matters having to do with the alien."

Odo met Maia's eyes. "We will be listening. Should you make liars
of us, or imply distress of any sort, you might as well accompany the
Upsala when she goes . . . and live forever with guilt of your sister's
fate. Let it be on your head."

Maia knew she had stretched Odo's patience once, almost to the
limit. Odo and her cohorts were busy pulling a thousand threads, political, social, and economic. Open and furtive. If they felt Maia and Leie
and Brod were more trouble than useful as pawns in their game, she
could expect ruthlessness. Maia nodded agreement, and followed Odo
out the door.

By now, she knew the Persim household well. There were Yuquinn

maids and Venn cooks and Bujul handywomen, all of whom seemed
nimble and content in their inherited niches, needing no command or
incentive to anticipate every Persim whim. Why not? Each was descended from a var woman who had served peerlessly, and been rewarded with a type of immortality. An immortality that could end any
time the Persims withdrew patronage. No violence would be required. No
one need even be fired. The Persims had only to stop sponsoring expensive winter matings for their clients, then wait the brief interval of a
generation or two.

Was the relationship predatory? Unfair? Maia doubted the Yuquinn
or Venn would think so. If they were prone to such thoughts, their lines
would have ended with the natural passing of their first var ancestress.
Of late, though, Maia had come to adopt Renna's attitude. All of this was
well-designed, as natural as could be, and from another point of view,
appalling.

I am no longer a daughter of Lysos, she realized. *I'll never adjust to
a world whose basic premise I can't bear.*

"In there," Odo said, pointing through a set of double doors. "Behave."

The threat, implicit, sufficed. Odo turned and walked away. Maia
entered the conservatory, where the striking, dark-haired woman she had
met at the opera was laying papers on a fabulously expensive table made
of metal frames supporting nearly flawless panes of glass. While one of
Odo's younger clone-sisters observed from the corner, Brill indicated a
chair. "Thank you for seeing me. Shall we begin?"

Maia sat down. "Begin what?"

"Your examination, of course. We'll start with a simple survey of
preferences. Take these forms. Each question features five activities—"

"Um, pardon me . . . what *kind* of examination?"

Brill straightened, regarding her enigmatically. Maia experienced a
fey sensation of depth. As if the woman already saw clear through her,
and had no real need for exams.

"An occupational-aptitude test. I've accessed your school records
from Port Sanger, which show adequate preparatory work. Is there a
problem?"

Maia almost laughed out loud. Then she wondered. *Is this a pose?
Might she have been sent here by Iolanthe Nitocris and her allies?*

But then, Odo would have checked Brill's bona fides. The small
civil service of Stratos was supposedly outside politics, and its testers
could go anywhere. If this was a pose, Brill made it believable. Maia
decided to play along.

"Uh, no problem." She looked left and right. "Where are your calipers? Will you be measuring bumps on my head?"

The Upsala clone smiled. "Phrenology has its adherents. For start-ers, however, why don't we begin with this?"

There followed a relentless confrontation with paper. Rapidfire questions, covering her interests, tastes, knowledge of grammar, knowl-edge of science and weather, knowledge of . . .

After two hours, Maia was allowed a short break. She went to the toilet, ate a small snack from a silver tray, walked in the garden to stretch her back. Ever businesslike, the Upsala clone spent the time processing results. If she had been sent to convey a message from Naroin or Clevin, she was good at concealing the fact.

"I saw two of your sisters after we spoke at the opera," Maia com-mented, aware of the watching Persim clone. "One of them played Faust . . ."

"Yes, yes. Cousin Gloria. And Surah, at the baton. Bloody show-offs."

Maia blinked in surprise. "I thought they were very good at what they did."

"Of course they were good!" Brill glanced sharply. "The issue is what one chooses to be good at. The arts are fine, for hobbies. I play six instruments, myself. But they pose no great challenge to a mature mind."

Maia stared. It was passing strange to hear a clone disparage her own kin. Stranger was the implication of her words.

"Did you say *choose*? Then your clan doesn't—"

"Specialize?" Brill finished the word with a disdainful buzz. "No, Maia. We do not *specialize*. Shall we resume work now?"

The return to neutral professionalism cut short Maia's line of in-quiry. Brill next presented a wooden box, and asked Maia to grip two levers while peering down a leather-lined tube. Within, a horizontal line rocked back and forth, reminding her of an instrument she had seen in the aircraft carrying her from Ursulaborg. "This is an artificial horizon," Brill began. "Your task, as I add difficulty, will be to correct devia-tions . . ."

An hour later, Maia's finery was damp with perspiration, her neck hurt from concentration, and she moaned when Brill called time for a halt.

"O-oh-h," she commented in surprise. "That . . . was *fun*."

The Upsala clone answered with a brief, thin smile. "I can tell."

After more physical tests, there came another break, for supper in the nearest of Persim Hold's many dining rooms. To Odo's clear irrita-tion, Brill seemed blithely to assume she was invited to table, obliging the Persim matriarch to attend as well, keeping an eye on things.

She needn't have bothered. The conversation was less than en-thralling across an expanse of fine-grained Yarri wood, embroidered linen, and fine porcelain, lit by sparkling chandeliers. For most of the time, Brill shuffled papers, except when meticulously thanking the servants for each dish that was served. Maia enjoyed the effect on Odo. Clearly, the matron thought the test-taker's visit a chess move by her faction's opponents, and was writhing to figure it out. Also clearly, it frustrated Odo to spend so much time worrying over a mere pawn.

Was that all it was? A gambit to waste the enemy's time? If so, Maia was pleased to help. The exams were exhausting, but a pleasant diversion. She only wished Brill seemed more sensitive to her own efforts hinting at messages to be relayed to Naroin and her father.

"The Upsalas are a funny lot," Odo commented while the main course was cleared away, and she finished her third glass of wine. "Do you know of them, summer child?"

Maia shook her head.

"Then let me enlighten you. They are a successful clan by normal standards, numbering about a hundred—"

"Eighty-eight adults," Brill corrected, regarding Odo with relaxed, green eyes.

"And my sources say their fortune is secure. Not first rank, but secure. There are two Upsalas on the Reigning Council, and forty-nine with savant chairs at various institutions. Nineteen at Caria University itself, in diverse departments. And yet, do you know what's most peculiar about them?" A servant refilled Odo's glass as she leaned forward. "They have no clanhold! No house, grounds, servants. Nothing!"

Maia frowned. "I don't follow."

"They all live on their own! In houses or apartments they purchase *as individuals*. Each makes her own living. Each makes her own sparking arrangements with individual men! And do you know why?" Odo giggled. "They hate each other's guts."

When Maia turned to regard Brill, the examiner shrugged. "The typical Stratoin success story demands not only talent, upbringing, and luck to find a niche. Gregarity is another customary requisite . . . self-sacrifice for the good of the hive. Sisterly solidarity helps a clan to thrive.

"But humans aren't ants," she went on. "Not everyone is born predisposed to get along with others identical to herself."

Nerves and alcohol had transformed the normally-aloof Odo, who laughed harshly. "Well put! Many's the time a bright young var gets something going, only to see it spoilt by her own pretty, bickering daughters. Only those at peace with themselves can truly use the Founders' Gift."

Maia recalled countless times she and Leie had been less than selfless with each other while growing up. They had attributed it to the rough passage of a summer background, but was that it? Might the tense affection between them *worsen* with prosperity, rather than growing into perfect teamwork? Maia sensed an evolutionary imperative at work. Over generations, selection would favor the trait of getting along with different versions of *yourself.* If so, perhaps the twins' plans had always been moot, as likely as frost in summer.

"There are exceptions," Maia prompted hopefully. "Your clan manages, somehow."

Brill sighed, as if bored with the topic. "Eventually, we Upsala learned how to maintain the needful functions of a clan, without all the trappings or constraints."

"She means they have grand meetings, about once an old Earth year. Half of 'em don't attend, they send their lawyers!" Odo seemed to find it hilarious. "They don't even like their own clone daughters. That's why their numbers grow so slow—"

"It's not true!" Brill snapped, showing the first strong emotion Maia had seen. The woman paused to regain her composure. "Everything's fine until adolescence, when . . ." She lapsed a second time, and finished in a low voice. "I get along fine with my other kids."

"Your *vars*, you mean. That's another thing. Upsala prefer summer breeding! Makes 'em popular with the boys, it does," Odo slurred as she sloshed more wine.

"Your way would never work in the countryside," Maia told Brill, fascinated.

"True, Maia. City life offers public services, a wealth of career choices. . . ."

"Tell her about career choices! Don't you all pick different professions 'cause you hate to even run into each other?"

While Odo chuckled, Maia stared. Apparently, the Upsala excelled at anything they tried, starting from scratch with each cloned lifetime. Maia wondered if Renna, her late friend, ever encountered this marvel during his stay in Caria. If not handicapped by one defective trait, the Upsala might own all of Stratos someday. No wonder this one's presence had Odo nervous, despite Brill's innocuous chosen profession.

In their case, genius overcame a crippling lack of harmony. Leie and I aren't geniuses, but we don't exactly hate each other, either. Maybe something in between is possible. If we both get out of this mess alive, perhaps we can learn from the Upsalas.

Brill took out a pocketwatch and cleared her throat. "That was awfully pleasant, yes? Now might we get back to work? I'd like to finish soon. My babysitter charges extra after ten."

·   ·   ·

The next series dealt with Maia's "cryptomathematical talent," or her unforeseen affinity for games like Life. For an hour, Maia waged midget battles on a computerized board like Renna's, trying—usually in vain— to prevent the gadget from wreaking havoc on her patterns. Brill kept demanding that Maia use new "recursion rules," meaning ways to make things progressively, then impossibly, harder. It was a tense, sweaty exercise of guesswork and raw skill. Maia loved it . . . until the patterns started blurring and her endurance ran out.

"Why are you doing this to me?" she moaned at the end.

"It is suspected that you may qualify for a niche," Brill answered dryly, turning off the machine. Maia rubbed her eyes. "What niche?"

Brill paused. "I can tell you what *not* to expect. Do not hope for entry to the university based on your talent with patterns and symbol systems. If it carries across generations, a winter child of yours might apply on its basis, but for you it is already too late to be a mathematician."

Thanks, Maia thought, with bitterness that surprised her. *Who asked, anyway?*

"Moreover, you appear to have too high an action potential for the contemplative life," Brill went on, scanning a chart. "That isn't a drawback to my client, although other factors—"

Maia sat up quickly. "Client? You mean this isn't for the civil service?" She sensed the Persim clone edge forward, suddenly alert. Brill shrugged, as if it didn't matter. "I've been commissioned by a member of my own family, to seek workers for a new venture. Frankly, it's a long shot, not a safe niche, by any means."

"But . . ." Maia sensed anger in the tense silence of the Persim cloneling. "Odo assumed this was for—"

"I'm not responsible for Odo's assumptions. Any potential employer may contract with the examination service. This isn't relevant to Persim Clan's present political struggles, so Odo has no cause for concern. Now, shall we get back to work? Our last item will be—"

"I'm a good navigator!" Maia blurted. "And I'm pretty good with machines. My twin's better. We're mirror twins, you know. So maybe . . . between us . . ." Maia's voice trailed off, weighed down by embarrassment over her outburst. Some lurking, childish remnant had leaped out, pleading a case she no longer even cared to make.

"Those factors may be relevant," Brill commented after a beat. There was a brief light of kindness in the examiner's eyes. "Now, the last item is an essay question. I want you to describe three episodes in which you solved puzzle locks to enter hidden chambers. You know the events I speak of. Succinctly note what factors, logical and intuitive, led you to

surmise correct answers. Limit each answer to a hundred words. Pick up
your pencil. Begin."

Maia sighed and started writing. Apparently, everyone knew of her
adventures under Jellicoe Isle. By now, the place was back in the hands
of those same conservative forces that had, for centuries, maintained the
Defense Center. But the secret was out for good.

. . . *so our success at the red-metal door was partly luck* . . . she
wrote. *I once overheard some words which made me realize the symbols in
the hexagons could mean* . . .

Maia knew she was doing poorly, failing to organize her thoughts in
coherent order. Pondering Jellicoe also reminded Maia of problems more
real than these stupid tests. If only Leie and Brod had noticed the gradual transition of power there, and snuck out with Naroin's friends while it
was still possible! Now, apparently, it was too late.

Maia finished describing the crimson door she and Brod had found
in the sea cave, and moved on to summarize her logic in the sanctuary
auditorium. She started by giving full credit to Leie and the ill-fated
navigator, for their parts in solving the riddle that led to discovering the
Great Former. Except that also meant sharing blame for what followed—
the violent invasion of those cryptic precincts, forcing Renna to cut short
his preparations and attempt that deadly, premature launch into a terrible blue sky.

It's my doing. Mine alone. She had to close her eyes and inhale
deeply. *I can't think about that right now. Save it. Save it for later.*

Maia finished that summary, putting the second piece of paper atop
the first. She stared at the third blank sheet, then looked up in baffle-
ment. "*What* third puzzle lock? I don't recall—"

"The earliest. When you were four. Breaking into your mothers'
storeroom."

Maia stared in surprise. "How did you—"

"Never mind that. Please finish. This test measures spontaneous
response under pressure, not skill or completeness of recollection."

Maia suspected the jargon hid something, some meaning hidden in
the words, but it escaped her. Sighing, she bent over to write down what
she could remember of that long-ago day, when the creaking dumbwaiter
carried two young twins for the last time into those catacombs beneath
the Lamai kitchens.

In her hand, Maia had clutched a scrawled solution, her final effort
to defeat the stubborn lock. With Leie holding a lantern, she pressed
stony figures—twining snakes, stars, and other symbols—which *clicked*
into place, one by one. Neither twin breathed as the defiant, iron-bound
door at long last slid aside to reveal—

Bones. Row after row of neat stacks of bones. Femurs. Tibia. Fibia. Grinning skulls. Maia had leapt back, and Leie's surprised cry had rattled the wine racks behind them, her eyes showing white clear around as they tremulously entered the secret chamber, gaping at generation after generation of ancestresses . . . each of whom had been genetically their own mother. There were a lot of mothers down there. The ossuary had been chill, silently eerie. Maia gratefully saw no whole skeletons. Lamai neatness—sorting and stacking the bones primly by type—made it harder to envision them twitching to vengeful life.

Other things had lain hidden in the chamber. Icy cabinets held dusty records. Then, toward the back, they encountered more menacing items. Weapons. Vicious death machines, outlawed to family militias, but stored in keeping with the motto of Lamatia Clan—"Better Safe Than Sorry."

Afterward, both twins had had lurid dreams, but soon they replaced qualms with jesting scorn for that great chain of individuals leading back to a mythical, lost set of genetic grandparents. The intermediary—the Lamai *person*—had conquered time, but apparently would never overcome her deep insecurity. In the end, what Maia recalled best were the months spent tantalized by a puzzle. Once solved, she realized, a riddle that had seemed compelling all too often turns out to be nothing but insipid.

After Brill went home, Maia crawled between the bec-silk sheets, exhausted, but unable to stop thinking. *Renna, too, was immortal in a way. Lysos would've thought his method silly, as he probably thought hers.*

Perhaps they both were right.

Sleep came eventually. She did not dream, but her hands twitched, as if sensing a vague but powerful need to reach for tools.

The next day dawned eerie as Maia watched frost evaporate from flowers in the garden, perfuming the air with scents of roses and loneliness. When Odo collected her for their daily ride, neither woman spoke. Maia kept mulling over Brill Upsala's parting remarks the night before.

"I can't say much about the venture," the examiner had said, referring to the enterprise her clan was funding. "Except that it involves transport and communications, using improved traditional techniques." Brill's smile was thin, wry. "Our clan likes anything that lets us spread ourselves out thinner."

"So it doesn't have to do with the Former, or the space launcher?"

Brill's green eyes had flashed. "What gave you that idea? Oh. Because I was with Iolanthe and the Pinniped, that night. No, I only came along to be introduced. As for the Jellicoe finds, those are sealed by

Council orders." Brill lifted her satchel. "You must have known there was no other prospect. A dragon's inertia is not shifted by yanking its tail."

Aware of the Persim clone trailing nearby, Maia had asked one final question at the door. "I still can't figure how you knew about our visit to the Lamatia bone room. The Lamai never found out, did they?"

"Not to my knowledge."

"Then you must've spoken to Le—"

"Don't make assumptions," the older woman had cut in. Then, after a beat, she held out her hand. "Good luck, Maia. I hope we meet again."

It wasn't hard to interpret Brill's meaning. *I hope we meet again . . . if you survive.*

Those words came to mind as the carriage bore Maia and Odo by the marble portico of Council House. Fewer demonstrators held banners, which hung limper than ever. There was no sign of Naroin or her father.

The strike is failing, Maia sensed. Even if it were still active on the coast, how could loosely organized men overcome great clans and win back things lost ages before living memory? What did ancient Guardians, or the Great Former, mean to the average seaman, anyway? How long can passion be maintained over an abstract grievance, nearly a thousand years old?

Something unsettling occurred to Maia. Brill's examination had covered many of the skills needed by the pilot or navigator of a ship. Might it be part of a scheme to recruit *strike breakers*? There were enough women sailors to staff some freighters, after all. Without officers, those ships would soon founder, but what if women were found as replacements on the quarterdeck, as well?

I'd refuse, Maia vowed. *Even if it turned out to be the one thing I was born to do, I could never help deprive men of their one niche, their one place of pride in the world. The Perkinite solution would be more merciful.*

She knew she was leaping to conclusions. The situation was making her paranoid and depressed.

Watching the faltering demonstration, she saw Odo smile.

The next day, the heavens opened and there was no ride in the park. Maia tried to read, but the rain turned her thoughts to Renna. Strangely, she found it hard to picture his face. *Eventually, he would have gone away, anyway,* she told herself. *You never would have had anything lasting together.*

Was her heart hardening? No, she still mourned her friend, and would always. But she owed duty to the living. To Leie. And she missed Brod terribly.

That night, Maia woke to words in the hallway. She heard passing footsteps, and shadows briefly occulted the line of light under her door.

". . . I *knew* it couldn't last!"

"It's not over, yet," commented a more-cautious voice.

"You saw the reports! The vrilly lugs'll accept the token offer and be happy about it. We'll be moving cargo well before spring!"

The words and footsteps receded. Maia threw off the covers and hurried to the door in her nightgown, in time to see three figures round a far corner—all Persims, ranging from early to late middle age. After a moment's temptation to follow, Maia turned and headed the way they had come, her bare feet silent on the hand-woven carpet. No guards were stationed to keep her prisoner anymore. Either they felt sure of their hold over her, or cared less what she did.

Her way lay past the main foyer of this wing and into the next, where a staircase led up to an ancient tower. Voices drew near, descending. Maia ducked into shadows as another pair of Persim entered view.

". . . not sure I like sacrificing so many to the courts, dammit."

"Ten is the least the Reeces say'll pass. Sometimes you must trust your lawyer clan."

"I suppose. What a farce, though. Especially when we've won!"

"Mm. Hard on those going down. Glad it won't be me."

The pair turned past Maia, the second voice continuing with a sigh. "Clan and cause, that's what matters. Let the law have its . . ."

When the way was clear, Maia hurried up the stairs the two had just vacated. The first landing was dim, and she felt sure her goal lay higher. From her room, she had watched a light burn many times, accompanied by reverberations of tense argument. Tonight there had been jubilation.

Three levels up, an open set of doors faced the landing. An electric bulb burned under a parchment lampshade, casting shadows across towering bookshelves. An ornate wooden table lay strewn with papers, surrounded by brass-studded leather chairs in unseemly disorder. Presumably, the mess would be cleaned up in the morning.

Maia entered hesitantly. It was a more impressive room, by her prejudices, than the ornate opera house. She yearned for the volumes lining the walls, but headed first for the detritus of the adjourned meeting, uncrumpling bits of scrap paper, poking through sheets apparently torn out of ledgers and covered with scribbled accounts . . . until she found something more easily interpreted. Another newspaper, complete this time.

Indictments Filed in Visitor Kidnapping

The tragic events which took place in the Dragons' Teeth, during Farsun Week, reached a climax to-

day when the Planetary Prosecutor presented
charges against fourteen individuals allegedly responsible for the abduction of Renna Aarons, Peripatetic Emissary from the Hominid Phylum. This
event, which led to the alien's unfortunate, accidental demise, aggravated an unpleasant year of
turmoil which began when his ship . . .

Maia skimmed ahead.

. . . rogue individuals from the Hutu, Savani, Persim, Wayne, Beller, and Jopland clans are now expected to file guilty pleas, so the case will likely
never go to trial. "Justice will be served," announced prosecutor Pudu Lang. "If the Phylum ever
does come nosing around, they will have no cause
for complaint. An uninvited guest provoked some of
our citizens into unfortunate actions, but this will
have been dealt with, according to the traditions of
our ancestors."

To demands for an open public trial, officials of
the High Court reply that they see no need to in-
flame today's atmosphere of near-hysteria. So long as
the guilty are punished, added sensationalism will
not serve the civic interest. . . .

This explained some of what she had overheard. The good news was that
even the winners in the political struggle, Odo's side, could not completely co-opt the courts. Public servants were enforcing the law, by
narrow Stratoin standards.

Yet ironies abounded. The law emphasized deeds by *individuals*.
That might have made sense back in the Phylum, but here, actions were
often dictated by groups of clans. As in elections, the law pretended
universal rights, while securing the interests of powerful houses.

There was another article.

Twelve Guilds Accept Compromise

Agreement appears to have been reached in the
labor dispute now disrupting commerce along the
Méchant. In giving up their more absurd demands,
such as shared governance of the newly created
Jellicoe Technical Reserve, the sailing guilds have

at last acceded to logic. In return, the Council
promises to erect a monument in honor of the Visitor, Renna Aarons, and to pass regulations allowing male crew to help staff certain types of
auxiliary vessels which heretofore . . .

So Brill was right. The men and their allies couldn't fight inertia, the
tendency of all things Stratoin to swing back toward equilibrium. The
guilds had won a token concession or two—Maia felt especially glad that
Renna would be honored—and Odo's side in the struggle might have to
sacrifice a few members. Nevertheless, Jellicoe was restored to its old
wardens, who would now quietly resume their deadly exercises, practicing to blow up great, unarmed ships of snow.

Maia glanced at a photograph accompanying the article.

Commodores and Investors Discuss New Venture, the caption read.

Pictured were several sailors dressed in officers' braid, looking on
as three women showed them a model ship. Maia bent to look closer, and
stared. "Well I'll be . . ."

One of the women in the photo was a younger version of Brill Upsala, eagerness lighting her eyes like fire. The sleek ship was of no
design Maia knew, lacking sails or smokestacks. Then she inhaled
sharply.

It was, in fact, a zep'lin.

*Is that the "auxiliary vessel" they're talking about? But that would
mean—*

A voice came out of nowhere.

"So. Always one to show initiative, I see."

Maia swiveled catlike, arms spread wide. Behind the door, in a dim
corner of the room, a solitary figure lay slumped in a plush chair, clutching a cigar. A long ash drooped from the smoldering end.

"Too bad that initiative won't take you anywhere but the grave."

"*You're* the one that's going to feed the dragon, Odo," Maia said
with satisfaction. "Your clan's dumping you to buy off the law."

The elderly Persim glared, then nodded. "We're taught to consider
ourselves cells in a greater body. . . ." She paused. "I never considered, till now . . . what if a cell doesn't *want* to be sacrificed for the
smuggy whole?"

"Big news, Odo. You're human. Deep down, you're just like a var.
Unique."

Odo shrugged aside the insult. "Another time, I might have *hired*
you, bright summer child. And left a diary warning our great-grand-
daughters to betray your heirs. Now I'll settle for warmer revenge—
taking you with me to the dragon."

Maia fell back a step. "You . . . don't need me anymore. Or Leie or Brod."

"True. In fact, they have already been released to the Nitocris. Their vessel docks in less than a week."

Maia's heart leaped at the news. But Odo went on before she could react.

"Normally, I'd let you go as well, and watch with pleasure as your fancy friends all fall away, hedging their promises, leaving you with a tiny apartment and job, and vague tales to tell one winter child—about when you rubbed elbows with the mighty.

"But I won't be around for that bliss, so I'll have another. The Persim owe me a favor!"

Maia whispered. "You hate me. Why?"

"Truth?" Odo answered in a low, harsh voice. "Jealousy of the hearth, varling. For what you had, but I could not."

Maia stared silently.

"I knew him," Odo went on. "Virile, summer-rampant in frost season, yet with the self-control of a priestess. I thought vicarious joy would suffice, by setting him up at Beller House, with both Bellers and my younger siblings. Yet my soul stayed empty! The alien wakened in me a sick envy of my own sisters!" Odo leaned forward, her eyes loathing, "He never touched you, yet he was and remains yours. That, my rutty little virgin, is why I'll have a price from my Lysos-cursed clan, which I served all my wasted life. Your company in hell."

The words were meant to be chilling. But in trying to terrify, Odo had instead given Maia a gift more precious than she knew.

. . . he was and remains yours . . .

Maia's shoulders squared and her head lifted as she gave Odo a final look of pity that clearly seared. Then she simply turned away.

"Don't try to leave!" Odo called after her. "The guards have been told. . . ."

Odo's voice trailed off as Maia left the muted room and its bitter occupant. She descended the drafty stairway, but instead of turning toward her room, she continued down one more level to the ground floor, and then crossed a wide, dimly lit atrium beneath statues depicting several dozen identical, joyless visages. She pulled the handle of an enormous door, which opened slowly, massively.

Cool garden air washed her face, cleansing foul odors of smoke and wrath. Maia stepped onto a wide gravel drive and looked up at the sky. Winter constellations glittered, save where the luminous dome of the Great Temple cast a bright halo, just over the next rise. City lights sprawled below the acropolis, along both banks of a black ribbon of river crisscrossed by many bridges.

The driveway dropped gently through an open park, then past a grove of ancient, Earth-stock trees, ending at last with a wrought-iron gate set in a high wall. Maia approached without stealth. A liveried sentry stepped out of the guard booth, offering a slight, quizzical bow.

"Can I help you, miss?" the stocky, well-muscled woman asked.

"I'm leaving."

The guard shook her head. "Dunno, miss. It's awfully—"

"Do you have orders to stop me?"

"Uh . . . not since a few days ago. But—"

"Then kindly do not stand between another daughter of Stratos and her rights."

It was an invocation she recalled from a var-trash novel, which seemed ironically apropos. The keeper shifted uncertainly from foot to foot, and finally shuffled to the gate. As it swung open, Maia thanked the attendant and stepped through, arriving on a strange street, in a strange city, barefoot in the dead of night.

Of course Persim Clan wanted it this way. She was no longer needed, an embarrassment, in fact. But murder was risky. What if it restoked the waning sailors' strike? What if her disappearance prodded the lazy machinery of the law past some genteel threshold of tolerance? This way, the Persims might even solve their predicament in Odo, who had outlived her usefulness to the clan. Maia's escape might provoke that broken piece of the hive to end things neatly, skirting a degrading ritual of sentencing and punishment.

I'm still being used, Maia knew. *But I'm learning, choosing those uses with open eyes.*

And now . . . what *will I choose?*

Not to be the founder of some immortal dynasty, that much she knew. A home and children were still fond hopes, as was warmth of the heart and hearth. But not that way. Not by the cool, passionless rhythms of Stratos. If Leie chose that route, good luck to her. Maia's twin was smart enough to start a clan, with or without her. But Maia's own goals went beyond all that now.

Earlier, she had declared herself free of duty to the legacy of Lysos. That assertion had nothing to do with returning to ancient sexual patterns, or preferring the bad old terrors of patriarchy. Those were separate issues, in her mind already settled.

What she had decided was that, if she could not live in a time of openness, of ideas and daring, then she could at least *behave* as if she did. As if she were a citizen of a scientific age.

She wasn't alone. Others surely had the same thing in mind. Brill had hinted as much. The "token" concession won by the guilds—regaining for men the right to fly—would change Stratos over time, and there were doubtless other moves afoot to nudge society in subtle ways. Gradually diverting the ponderous momentum of a dragon.

Renna set things in motion. And I had a role, as well. For both his sake and mine, I'll keep on having one.

Still, the Upsala and the Nitocris might be surprised by her reaction, when they made her an offer. She would listen, politely. But, on the other hand . . .

Why not do what I want, for a change?

It was the final irony. She faced the challenges of independence willingly, equipped to stand on her own, while at the same time ready to share her heart. It seemed a natural stage in her personal renaissance, cresting from adolescence to true adulthood.

Stratos might take a while longer, but worlds, too, must waken from dreamy illusions of constancy. The cradle built by Lysos no longer protected, but constrained.

Reaching a turn in the road, Maia came upon an overlook facing west. There, slowly setting beyond the mountains, was the great nebula that Stratoins called the Claw—known in Phylum space as God's Brow. Somewhere in the cold, empty reaches between, vast crystalline ships were bearing down to finish an isolation that Lysos must have known would end, in time. Only then would it become clear if humans had achieved a kind of wisdom here, a new pattern of life worthy of adding to a greater whole.

Suddenly, the surroundings were illuminated by a sharp glow from above. Maia turned to look upward, where a single, starlike glimmer pulsed, throbbing rhythmically as it brightened, until it shone more radiant than any moon, or even summer's beacon, Wengel Star. Wavelike patterns of color stabbed her eye, causing her to squint in wonder.

At first, Maia felt she had this marvel to herself, amid a city of a hundred thousand souls. Then came sounds—doors banging open, people flooding out of houses and holds, murmuring as they faced skyward and stared. Women, children, and the occasional man, spilled into the streets, pointing at the heavens, some fearfully, others in growing awe.

It took hours before anyone was certain, but by dawn all could tell. The spark was moving away. Leaving the folk of Stratos alone again.

For a time.

Afterword

T his book began with a contemplation of lizards. Specifically, several species from the American Southwest that reproduce parthenogenetically—mothers giving birth to daughter clones. Perfect copies of themselves.

From there, I discovered aphids, tiny insects blessed with *two* modes of reproduction. During periods of plenty and stability, they self-clone, churning out multiple duplicates like little xerox machines. But when the good times end, they quickly swing back to old-fashioned sexual mating, creating daughters and sons whose imperfect variety is nature's mortar of survival.

These miracles of diversity prompted me to wonder, "What if humans could do the same?"

The idea of cloning has been explored widely in fiction, but always in terms of medical technology involving complex machinery, a dilettante obsession for the very rich. This may serve a pampered, self-obsessed class for a while, but it's hardly a process any species could rely on over the long haul, through bad times as well as good. Not a way of life, machine-assisted cloning is the biosocial counterpart of a hobby.

What if, instead, self-cloning were just another of the many startling capabilities of the human womb? An interesting premise. But then, only female humans have wombs, so a contemplation of cloning became a novel about drastically altered relations between the sexes. Most aspects to the society of planet Stratos arose out of this one idea.

These days, nothing is politically neutral. The lizards I referred to earlier have recently been cited in a thought-provoking, if inflammatory, radical feminist tract posing the question "Who needs males, anyway?" Many times, over the ages, insurgent female philosophers have proposed independence through separation. Given the plight of countless women and children in the world, they can hardly be blamed. In fact, the name "Perkinite" was taken from Charlotte Perkins Gilman, whose novel *Herland* is one of the best and pithiest separationist utopias ever penned. Her brand of sexual isolationism is far gentler than the extremist doctrine I depict, which shamefully misuses her name on planet Stratos.

Unfortunately for gender segregationists—though not, perhaps, for men—biology appears to thwart simplistic secession. Mammals seem to require a male component at a deeper level than do insects, fish, or reptiles. Recent studies indicate that "male-processed genes" initiate important fetal-development processes. So even if self-cloning without machines became possible, conception might still require at least cursory involvement by a man.

Anyway, stories excluding men altogether seem almost as bombastic as those that crudely turn the tables, in naïve role-reversal fantasies. (Amazon warriors, dueling over harems of huge but meek bimbo-males? The subgenre is a dandy source of giggles, but bears no relation to the way biology works in *this* universe.)

On the other hand, there are no scientific reasons not to show males relegated to the sidelines of history, a peripheral social class, as has all too often been the lot of women in our own civilization. Men are still men on Stratos, give or take some alterations. Their society isn't designed purposely to oppress them, only to end the age-old domineering and strife that accompanied patriarchy. In consequence, the folk of Stratos miss some of the joys we seek (and sometimes find) in monogamous family life. They also avoid much familiar pain.

Would self-cloning lead kinship lineages to imitate the social life of ants or bees, dwelling in "hives" with like-gened sisters? This notion, too, has been explored before, often by cramming antlike behavior into bipedal bodies. On Stratos, the daughters of an ancient clan would exhibit solidarity and self-knowledge unimaginable to vars like ourselves, but that wouldn't necessarily make them automatons, or stop them being human.

Try to look at it from their point of view. Our world of nearly infinite sexual-genetic variation might seem too chaotic to be civilized. A society of vars would be inherently incapable of planning beyond a single generation—which is exactly our problem today, according to many contemporary critics. Too much sameness may be stifling on fictional Stratos, but too little sense of continuity may be killing the real Earth of here and now.

Some may accuse me of preaching that genes are destiny. Far from it. Men and women are ingenious, marvelously self-trainable creatures. Stratoin society is as much a matter of social evolution as it is of bioengineering. One of the lessons of Maia's adventure is that no plan, no system or stereotype, can suppress an individual who is boldly determined to be different.

At the opposite extreme, some early readers said, "Women are inherently cooperative. They would never compete the way you depict." I reply by referring to the works of animal behavioralist Sarah Blaffer Hrdy (author of *The Woman That Never Evolved*) and other researchers who show that competitiveness is just as common in the female as the male. Women have good reason to differ from men in *style*, but one would have to be blind to say their world is free of struggle. The intent of Stratos Colony was to craft a society in which natural feedback mechanisms *temper* inevitable outbursts of egotism. Its founders sought to maximize happiness and minimize violent disruption. Maia's exploits are exceptions, occurring in a time of unusual stress, but they do illustrate that a culture based on pastoral changelessness has drawbacks all its own.

In other words, I penned Stratos Colony as neither utopia nor dystopia. Many Westerners would find the place boring, but no more unjust than our world. While I hope my descendants live in a nicer place, few male-led cultures on Earth have done as well.

That sentiment notwithstanding, it is dangerous these days for a male to write even glancingly on feminist themes. Did anyone attack Margaret Atwood's right to extrapolate religio-machismo in *The Handmaid's Tale*? Women writers appear vouchsafed insight into the souls of men—credit that seldom flows the other way. It is a sexist and offensive assumption, which does not advance understanding.

This author claims only to present a *gedankenexperiment*—a thought experiment about one conceivable world of "What If." I hope it provokes argument.

On a different track, the game of cellular automata, which its inventors named "Life," is a fascinating topic which I chose to graft into Stratoin society for various reasons. I took liberties with the rules, as originally designed by Conway & co. back in the sixties, and described in the excellent books of Martin Gardner. (Plot and story take precedence over lectury accuracy.) Nevertheless, I am grateful for the advice of Dr. Rudy Rucker and others, in helping correct the worst errors.

Beyond obvious allegories to reproduction, creativity, and ecology, the game allowed discussion of *talent,* and the essential difference between individuals and averages. It is senseless to proclaim that it's evil to make generalizations about groups. Generalization is a natural human mental process, and many generalizations are true—in *average.* What often does promote evil behavior is the lazy, nasty habit of believing that generalizations have anything at all to do with individuals. We have no right to pre-judge that a specific man can't nurture, or a particular woman cannot fight. Or that a girl cannot master a game that for generations was the dominion of men.

While I have the floor, here's a question that's been bothering me for some time. Why do so few writers of heroic or epic fantasy ever deal with the fundamental quandary of their novels . . . that so many of them take place in cultures that are rigid, hierarchical, stratified, and in essence oppressive? What is so appealing about feudalism, that so many free citizens of an educated commonwealth like ours love reading about and picturing life under hereditary lords?

Why *should* the deposed prince or princess in every clichéd tale be chosen to lead the quest against the Dark Lord? Why not elect a new leader by merit, instead of clinging to the inbred scions of a failed royal line? Why not ask the pompous, patronizing, "good" wizard for something *useful,* such as flush toilets, movable type, or electricity for every home in the kingdom? Given half a chance, the sons and daughters of peasants would rather not grow up to be servants. It seems bizarre for modern folk to pine for a way of life our ancestors rightfully fought desperately to escape.

Only Aldous Huxley ever wrote a scenario for social stratification that was completely, if chillingly, self-consistent and stable. You get no sense of oppression, or any chance of rebellion, in a society where people truly *are* born for their tasks, as in *Brave New World.*

It may be a possible result on Stratos, as well.

Finally, the issue of *pastoralism* deserves comment. Countless bad books —and a few very good ones—have extolled the virtues of a slower pace, emphasizing farming life over urban, predictability over chaos, intuition over science. Often, this is couched in terms of feminine wisdom over the type of greedy knowledge pursued by rapacious Western (read "male") society. One unfortunate upshot has been a tendency to associate feminism with opposition to technology.

This novel depicts a society that is conservative by design, not because of something intrinsic to a world led by women. (Many fine tales have been woven of high-tech matriarchal cultures.) On Stratos, the founders' objective was a pastoral solution to the problem of human nature—a solution that has many intelligent and forceful adherents today.

They have a point. Anyone who loves nature, as I do, cries out at the havoc being spread by humans, all over the globe. The pressures of city life can be appalling, as are the moral ambiguities that plague us, both at home and via yammering media. The temptation to seek uncomplicated certainty sends some rushing off to ashrams and crystal therapy, while many dive into the shelter of fundamentalism, and other folk yearn for better, "simpler" times. Certain popular writers urgently prescribe returning to *ancient, nobler* ways.

Ancient, nobler ways. It is a lovely image . . . and pretty much a lie. John Perlin, in his book *A Forest Journey,* tells how each prior culture, from tribal to pastoral to urban, wreaked calamities upon its own people and environment. I have been to Easter Island and seen the desert its native peoples wrought there. The greater harm we do today is due to our vast power and numbers, not something intrinsically vile about modern humankind.

Technology produces more food and comfort and lets fewer babies die. "Returning to older ways" would restore some balance all right, but entail a holocaust of untold proportion, followed by resumption of a kind of grinding misery never experienced by those who now wistfully toss off medieval fantasies and neolithic romances. A way of life that was nasty, brutish, and nearly always catastrophic for women.

That is not to say the pastoral *image* doesn't offer hope. By extolling nature and a lifestyle closer to the Earth, some writers may be helping to create the very sort of wisdom they imagine to have existed in the past. Someday, truly idyllic pastoral cultures may be deliberately designed with the goal of providing placid and just happiness for all, while retaining enough technology to keep existence decent.

But to get there the path lies *forward,* not by diving into a dark, dank, miserable past. There is but one path to the gracious, ecologically sound, serene pastoralism sought by so many. That route passes, ironically, through successful consummation of this, our first and last chance, our scientific age.

.   .   .

Comments and criticism by many individuals helped eliminate even worse blunders than the purchaser finds in this published version. Among my insightful helpers: Bettyann Kevles, Carol Shetler, Jean Lee, Steven Mendel, Brian Kjerulf, Trevor Placker, Dave Clements, Amanda Baker, Brian Stableford, Eric Nilsson, Dr. Peter Markiewicz, Dr. Christine Carmichael, Jonathan Post, Deanna Brigham, Joy Crisp, and Diane Clark were helpful during this phase.

Thanks also go out to members of Caltech Spectre, who surveyed an uncompleted draft and mailed many comments while my wife and I lived in France. Participating members included Marti DeMore, Kay Van Lepp, Ann Farny, Teresa Moore, Dustin Laurence, Eric C. Johnson, Gorm Nykreim, Erik de Schutter, M.D., Steve Bard, Greg Cardell, Steinn Sigurdsson, Alex Rosser, Gil Rivlis, Michael Coward, Michael Smith, David Coufal, Dustin Laurence, David Palmer, Andrew Volk, Mark Adler, Gregory Harry, D. J. Byrne, Gail Rohrbach, and Vena Pontiac.

For technical advice on biology, as well as general criticism, I am grateful to Karen Anderson; Jack Cohen, D.Sc.; Professor William H. Calvin; Janice Willard, D.V.M.; Mickey Zucker, M.D.; and professors Jim Moore, Carole Sussman, and Gregory Benford.

Deserving special thanks, as always, are Ralph Vicinanza and Lou Aronica, as well as Jennifer Hershey, Betsy Mitchell, and Amy Stout, for their patience, Gavin Claypool for invaluable assistance, and, especially, Dr. Cheryl A. Brigham, without whom none of the good parts would have been possible. Blame me for the bad stuff.